Triple Threat

Books by Helen MacInnes

NOVELS

Above Suspicion

Assignment in Brittany

While Still We Live

Horizon

Friends and Lovers

Rest and Be Thankful

Neither Five nor Three

I and My True Love

Pray for a Brave Heart

North from Rome

Decision at Delphi

The Venetian Affair

The Double Image

The Salzburg Connection

Message from Málaga

PLAY

Home Is the Hunter

Helen MacInnes

Triple Threat

Three Novels

Above Suspicion
North from Rome
Double Image

Harcourt Brace Jovanovich, Inc., New York

First edition

ISBN *0-15-191155-X*

Library of Congress Catalog Card Number: 72-79921

Printed in the United States of America

Above Suspicion

The Song Which Frances Sang

Lully, lulla, thou little tiny child,
By by, lully lullay.

O sisters too,
How may we do
For to preserve this day
This poor youngling,
For whom we do sing,
By by, lully lullay?

Herod, the king,
In his raging,
Chargèd he hath this day
His men of might,
In his own sight,
All young children to slay.

That woe is me,
Poor child, for thee!
And ever morn and day,
For thy parting
Neither say nor sing
By by, lully lullay!

Coventry Carol: Pageant of the Shearmen and Tailors, Fifteenth Century

THIS SONG IS SUNG BY THE WOMEN OF BETHLEHEM IN THE PLAY, JUST BEFORE HEROD'S SOLDIERS COME IN TO SLAUGHTER THEIR CHILDREN

1

This June day seemed, to Frances Myles, very much like any other summer day in Oxford. She walked slowly along Jowett Walk, watching the gentle five-o'clock sun bring out the bronze in the leaves overhead. This was her favorite part of the road leading to her husband's College. On her left, the gray walls which hid the gardens of the Holywell houses were crowned with rambler roses. To her right were the playing fields with their stretches of soft green grass, and beyond them were the straightness of poplar, the roundness of chestnut and elm. Today, there were only a few men practising at the nets: most of them were packing, or going to end-of-term parties. Like herself, she thought, and quickened her pace. She was probably late again. She hoped guiltily that Richard would have enough work to occupy him, while he waited for her at College. He generally had. . . . But it was difficult to hurry on a summer day like this: there were so many things to enjoy, like the twenty shades of green all around her, or the patterns of unevenly cut stones in the high walls, or the way in which a young man would catch a cricket ball and lazily throw it back. Little things, but then the last few months had made the little things important.

She entered Holywell, and hurried along its curve of old houses until she reached the Broad. There her pace slackened again, and she halted at a bookseller's window. Richard's new book on English lyric poetry was well displayed. It was selling, too, which had been a pleasant surprise. (The bookseller had explained that away rather harshly: people were buying strange books now, it sort of soothed their minds.) She smiled to herself in the window at her totally unpoetic thoughts. A selling book would be a help towards another summer among the mountains. Another summer, or a last summer, she wondered, and turned away from the window. Once, all you had to do was to decide what mountains you'd like to climb, and then spend the winter writing reviews and articles to cover the train fares, and there you were. But each year it was becoming more difficult. She thought of past summers in the Tyrol, in the Dolomites. Once you could walk over mountain paths and spend the evenings round a table in the village inn. There had been singing and dancing, and lighthearted talk and friendly laughter. But now there were uniforms and regulations. Self-consciousness and uncertainty controlled even the jokes. Now you might only laugh at certain things. Now conversations with foreigners were apt to end in arguments.

Richard had discussed all this with her last night before they fell asleep. He had voted for one last look at Europe in peacetime, such as it was. There were still countries where one could breathe as one liked. Perhaps the premonition that this day was far from being much like any other summer day for Frances Myles had laid its cold finger on her heart . . . Or it could have been the thought of Oxford as it might well be next term. At any rate, the lightness had gone out of her step.

The young college porter was standing at the lodge gate. She tried to make her smile brighter than she felt.

"How is the new baby?" she asked.

He beamed with pride. "Just splendid, ma'am, thank you. Mr. Myles is waiting in his room. He has just phoned down to ask if you had arrived. I'll tell him you're here." He moved back into the lodge. Frances remembered he had joined the Territorial Army in March, just after the seizure of Prague. Nowadays she kept remembering details like that. She hurried through the quadrangle, and began the climb to Richard's room.

The oak was sported. She thumped on its massive panels, and drew back as she heard Richard open the room door first before he could let the heavy oak door swing out. He was smiling, with that guess-what look.

"Hello, darling," she said. "Quite like old times to sport your oak. Why all the precautions?" He wiped her lipstick off his chin as he drew her into the room, fastening the two doors behind them.

"We've a visitor, Fran."

It was Peter, Peter Galt.

He grinned and held out both his hands. "Hello, Frances, you look quite startled."

"Peter! But we thought you were in Bucharest. When did you get back?"

"Two or three weeks ago. I would have written you if I could. I've just been explaining to Richard. I've purposely not written you. And I am not staying with you, either. I am putting up at the Mitre."

Frances turned to her husband in dismay. "Richard, what's the matter with him?"

Richard handed her a glass of sherry. He refilled Peter's glass and then his own, with maddening concentration, before he spoke.

"Peter got into a jam."

"A jam? Peter?" She sat down on the nearest chair. She looked so charmingly anxious under her ridiculous hat that Peter hastened to reassure her.

"Don't worry, Frances. It all turned out rather well in the end. But it did make it necessary for me to be recalled." He grinned, and added, "Ill-health, of course."

"Of course. . . ." Frances was less alarmed, but she was still curious. She waited for an explanation. It was Richard who said in a noncommittal way, as he placed an ashtray beside her, "He got entangled with a spy."

"Well, I only hope she was beautiful," Frances said. "I mean, if you *will* do things like that, you may as well make the most of it." She smiled as she looked up at the correctly dressed young man balancing against the fireplace. She had always hoped that Peter would never get entangled with anyone who wasn't beautiful. She watched his calm face and the shy smile, and wondered. To a stranger, he would seem just another elegant minor secretary to a British Embassy.

"Unfortunately, it was a he," said Peter. "And to be quite truthful, I didn't get entangled with him. He got entangled with me."

"You look such easy meat, really, Peter."

"That was an asset, anyway."

"And so you had to come back to England . . ." Frances was still unable to take Peter quite seriously. "He isn't after your blood, is he?"

"He can't do that. Bucharest dealt with him. But his friends might think I learned too much before that happened."

"But, Peter, you don't mix that kind of—politics with diplomacy, do you?"

"He did the mixing. Now I am waiting for all the commotion to die down."

Peter gave a good imitation of his old smile, but Frances, watching his eyes, was already revising her opinion about this visit. Something serious was behind it all. When she spoke, her voice had dropped all hint of teasing.

"Is that all?"

Richard, sitting on the edge of his desk, gave a laugh.

"Out with it, Peter, whatever it is. It's no good being diplomatic with Frances. She can see through a brick wall as quickly as anyone."

Peter finished his sherry. As he looked from Frances to Richard, he seemed to be making up his mind about something. . . . Or perhaps he was deciding how to begin. They both suddenly realized the change in him. He was an older, a more businesslike Peter. And he was worried. His fingers played nervously with the stem of the sherry glass. He was choosing his next words with care.

"Frances is quite right. I am not in the F.O. any longer: I've been put onto other work. And that's why I am here." He glanced at his watch, and his next words were spoken more quickly. "I'm afraid this visit combines business with pleasure, and we haven't very much time for everything I want to tell you. So you'll understand if I begin abruptly. . . . We haven't the time for any build-up which would enlist your sympathy, and make things easier for me. I'll just have to start with the story, and hope for the best.

"First of all, I didn't want to give anyone the idea that I have been in touch with you. So I didn't let you know I was coming to Oxford, and I can't stay with you. Even the porter at the lodge doesn't know I'm with you: he thinks I am visiting old Meyrick. The reason is—I have a job for you to do, and I hope you'll agree to do it. It shouldn't be dangerous: tiresome, perhaps, and certainly a blasted nuisance, but not actually dangerous if you stick to the directions." He shot a quick glance at Richard, and added with emphasis: "You are just the people we need for it. You are both above any suspicion, and you've a good chance of getting through."

Richard looked at Peter speculatively. "What on earth is it?" he asked. "And why?"

"I'd better tell you about the job, first," Peter answered. "The whys and wherefores can wait until the end. I am sorry if it develops into a kind of lecture, but I'd like you to get all the details quite straight. One of the reasons why I thought of you for this job, Richard, is your memory. If you'd take a mental note of things as I explain them, that would save a lot of time."

Richard nodded.

"The job is simply this. I've been hoping that you would go abroad as usual this summer, and that you'd travel by Paris, meet a man there, and then continue the journey as he directs. At the end of it, you should be able to send us some information which we need very badly. That's the general outline. Now here are the particulars. I'll give you no trimmings—just the facts.

"When you get to Paris, just do as you always do. Stay at your usual hotel, eat at your favorite places, visit the usual mixture of museums and night clubs. Keep on doing that, for some days: long enough, anyway, to establish your innocent-tourist reputation. And then, on Saturday night, visit the Café de la Paix. Sit at an outside table towards the left. Order Cointreau with your coffee. Frances will be wearing a red rose. Don't notice anyone or anything in particular. About eleven o'clock, Richard will upset his Cointreau. He will be glad of an excuse not to drink it anyway, if I know Richard. Your waiter will come and mop up. That and the red rose are the signal. A man will approach your table, and that's the moment for one of you to speak. The sentence should begin: 'Mrs. *Rose* told me we must see . . .' and add the name of some place you've decided on. Pretend to talk, keep it all natural, but be on guard for the number which the man will give you, somehow. That's the key of this whole business. For if you go next day, to the place which you mentioned, at exactly *one hour later* than the number which he gives you, you will get into real touch with him. And he has a message for you.

"It's all very much easier than it sounds. He identifies you by the position of the table and the red rose and the upset glass of Cointreau; reaches your table at the time you expect him; hears the name of the place you've chosen along with the right sentence; and gives you a clue to the time for a meeting on the next day. Have you got all that, Richard?"

"Yes. But before we go any further, why choose us? I mean, we shall be such amateurs for that job: we'll probably mess it all up. There must be something fairly important at stake, and it seems to me as if you needed someone with quick wits. I don't know if mine have been sharpened well enough—in that way. As for Fran . . ." Richard shrugged his shoulders.

Frances only looked amused. "Darling, I love you," she said. "Do go on, Peter."

Peter took her advice.

"When you get the message, it will probably be in some code. And that's another reason why I want Richard to tackle this job. I can rely on him to get a meaning out of that message. His brain has had just the right training and discipline for that sort of work. Well, the message will direct you to another agent, and he will direct you farther still, and you will find yourself passed on from agent to agent until you reach the chief of them. He's the last one on the line, and he's the chap we are worried about. That is the information we need."

He paused, and watched Richard pour some sherry into his glass. Again Frances had the feeling that he was once more weighing his words very carefully before he spoke. His trouble was to tell them enough in the right order, without telling them too much.

"I think you'll find the rest of this travelogue more interesting. We are now reaching the whys and the wherefores." Peter allowed himself the suspicion of a smile. "You've heard of what is called the underground railway in Germany, haven't you? It's a version of the old *Scarlet Pimpernel* technique. It helps anti-Nazis to escape, and covers up their tracks. One of the brains behind it is the chief of this group of agents. On the side, of course, he collects information which has been very useful, indeed. Until about five weeks ago, we had the normal reports from him: accurate and regular. But since then, we have had no really informative messages. Two of them, in fact, were dangerously misleading. Fortunately, we had other sources of information about these facts which made us suspicious, and we didn't act on his advice. These suspicions were increased when two men, escaping from Germany by his route, disappeared completely. They have simply vanished into thin air."

Frances put aside her glass, and leaned forward, cupping her face in her hands. Richard held a cigarette unlighted. The eyes of both were fixed on Peter.

"What we want to know is this—before the harvests are gathered in, to put it quite bluntly—: does the man still exist, or has he been sending us false messages to warn us that things aren't just right, or has he been liquidated? So your job is to follow the route directed by various agents, always keeping in mind that you are just the simple traveler, until you find him. The one clue I do know is that he will be an Englishman, the only Englishman in that chain of agents. I can't help with his name or appearance, because he has too many of both. In any case, the less you know, the easier it will be for you to play your role, and the better it will be for all of us. He probably won't seem at all English when you meet him, but if you give him the correct high-signs, which the previous agent will pass on to you, you will find out that he's an Englishman all right."

"But why all this agent-to-agent business?" Richard asked. "Why doesn't the Paris man direct us to him straight away?"

"The plan is his: he invented it to suit his own particular work. And it has been very successful. It's been fool-proof for a longer time than most systems. It's simple enough. The Paris agent is the only stationary one, and that's the reason why he takes so many precautions, just to safeguard himself. The others move about as their chief directs. It is just as well to keep moving, for they often work in Nazi-dominated territory. Each agent knows only the name and address of the man next to him, and any information they collect can be posted along the chain of agents until it reaches the chief. Anyone who wants to get in touch with him must begin at the Paris end, and no one can begin at Paris unless he knows how to make the difficult contact with the agent there. There are only two sources which can direct anyone to manage that contact. We are one of them; the other is just as careful as we are. So you see, there is some method in his madness."

"And what about the information which he sends to you? He must have another line?"

Peter nodded. "Yes, and it's a much more direct way, naturally. I knew you'd cotton on, Richard. Anything else which strikes you?"

Richard hesitated, and then, as Peter waited for an answer, he said, "The system is obviously pretty safe, except for one drawback. If the chief man himself is caught, then all information traveling out to him will get into the wrong hands. His agents might even be picked off one by one, if he were—persuaded into any confession. *Not* to mention the fate of the poor devils who thought they were escaping from Germany."

"Exactly. That's why the job has got to be done."

"Your man must have been pretty sure of himself to think up that system, I must say."

Peter said, "I suppose it looks that way, but you've got to take risks in his profession. It has been very much worth our while to take a chance on him. And, strangely enough, it is just this kind of system which gets the best results. Until now, he has always been agile enough not to be caught; he has been doing this kind of thing, you know, since we were being pushed round the park in our prams. You may depend on one thing, Richard: he won't talk. Anyway, you see how vital it is to know whether he is still functioning, before the volcano in Europe blows sky-high. We've got to be sure of him, before then."

"Yes, I can quite see that," Richard said gloomily. "But I still think you need a professional man on the job." It was a good sign, anyway, thought Peter, that Richard was still arguing about it. He was clearly not very much in love with the idea, but he was still at the stage of objections rather than that of a downright refusal. Peter wondered if he should tell them anything more. He thought wearily, "I'm devoted to both of them, but can't they see, in God's name, that I was counting on them to accept, or I wouldn't have let them in on all this?" Yet people changed, and being a don at Oxford might very well make you too contented, too unwilling to act against your own security. Richard was waiting for his answer.

"We sent one," Peter said briefly. "We should have heard from him by this time. When we didn't I suggested to my Chief that we should try an amateur; that line served me well enough in Bucharest. A couple of innocents abroad might be able to get through all suspicion. The thing to remember is that you are *not* agents; don't let yourself get mixed up in any sideline snooping. All we want to know is whether an Englishman is there, or not. If things get too hot, then just pull out, using your own good sense. If there's any questioning, then stick to your story. You are just two holiday-makers having your annual trip abroad. There is one other point: your job will be finished when either you find the man, or you've reached the sixth agent without finding him. He never worked with more in a line. You will have a margin of safety all through, because the contacting clues will be vague enough to let you have an out and your amateur status will be an additional help. That really is your strongest safeguard."

Richard said nothing, but Galt, watching him closely, was satisfied.

It wasn't a comfortable, peaceful way of life which had held Richard back: it was the fact that Frances would be in this too.

"When you've finished, wire to this address in Geneva," Peter said. He wrote some words quickly on a piece of paper, and handed it to Richard, still looking undecided, worried . . . But Galt knew he had won.

"Better memorize the address, and then destroy it," he advised. "If you find your man, then wire ARRIVING MONDAY, or TUESDAY, or whatever day you actually saw him. If you don't find him, wire CANCEL RESERVATIONS." He drew a deep breath. "Thank God that's over," he said. "Is it all clear, Richard?"

"I've got it memorized, if that's what you mean. But look here, Peter, if you have really decided that I ought to do this job, don't you think I'd better go alone? I'm not running Frances into any risks." His tone was grim. Frances looked at him suddenly. So that was what had made him hesitate.

When she spoke her voice was low, but equally determined. "Richard, I am *not* going to be left behind."

Peter said, "Unfortunately I agree with Frances. Since you've been married, you've never separated on your holidays. It really would be better if you were just to do what you always do. And you'll be safer with Frances, because you won't take risks if she is with you." He looked anxiously at Richard. "I know it's going to ruin your summer," he began, and then stopped. He had said enough as it was.

Richard was staring at the red geraniums in the window box.

"It isn't the ruining of it," he said slowly. "Everyone's holidays are ruined this year. But I don't think we'd really be of any use."

Peter was picking up his gloves and umbrella and his black hat. He was still watching Richard intently. Something seemed to decide him. He moved over to Frances to say good-by.

"I would never have asked you if I didn't think you could pull it off," he said. "And I would never have asked you if the whole thing wasn't so urgent, Richard. I'd have done it myself, except that the people we are working against have got me docketed since Bucharest. I'll be on the files, by this time. I thought of someone else, but your qualifications for this job are just what we need. I didn't enjoy asking you, I may as well say . . . Time I was leaving, now. I see I've kept you late for Frame's party. I met him this morning in front of the Mitre, and he asked me to come along too." He waved his hat towards the invitation card propped up on the mantelpiece.

"How long," said Richard, "should this job take?"

"We allowed two weeks to our man, but he knew the ropes. We'd better say about a month. It will be safer if you don't hurry things. You will have to spend a few days in each place to make it look convincing. Remember, I want you to steer clear of any suspicion, or danger. . . . For God's sake, take care of yourselves."

His voice was normal again by the time he had reached the door.

"Good-by, Frances; good-by, Richard. See you when you get back."

The door closed softly, and left a silent room.

Frances was the first to move. She pulled out her compact and powdered her nose. She readjusted her hat to the correct angle.

"You'll do," she said to her reflection in the mirror. "Come on, my love, we are three quarters of an hour later than I had meant to be late. . . . You've got it all memorized?"

Richard nodded. "That's the least of it. Frances, this is the time to back out. Now."

Frances rose, and looked at the seams of her stockings. She altered a suspender. "When do we start?" she asked. "As soon as you have finished all your teaching?"

Richard looked at his wife's pretty legs.

"Blast Peter," he said, and took her arm as they left the room.

They talked of other things as they went downstairs.

The party in Frame's rooms had just reached the right temperature when Frances and Richard Myles arrived. They stood for a moment at the doorway rather like two bathers about to plunge off a springboard. Their host, armed with sherry bottles, pushed his way through to meet them.

"I'm *so* glad," he breathed. "Sorry about this *awful* crowd: such a mob." He turned to welcome some other new arrivals. Actually, thought Frances, he was just delighted that the room was jammed with people talking their heads off. She smiled good-by to Richard. This wasn't one of those ghastly affairs where you knew only the host. They wouldn't have to put on their special act today, when they would meet each other with surprise in the middle of the room, greet each other warmly and start the vivacious conversation of two friends who rarely met. They always found that others, with an ear for preposterous remarks, would drift towards them. As Richard had said, splendid isolation didn't mix with sherry.

But tonight, Richard had already seen two men he wanted to talk to, and Frances waited in the corner she had chosen for herself as three young men gravitated towards her. They had, in their typical manner, only smiled politely when they caught her eye, and had then, without another glance in her direction, started a quiet but determined progress towards where she stood. She noticed Richard was looking round him in that particularly ingenuous way he had when he was most on guard . . . But Peter Galt had not arrived yet.

The three young men arrived from their various directions, and began one of the usual adroit conversations which sherry parties inspire. They all avoided talking present-day politics with an understanding as complete as it was tacit. This was perhaps the last conversation they would have together for a long time, and they wanted to keep it gay. They discussed the Picasso exhibition in London, and his Guernica, and that led to Catalonian art and Dali. Frances wanted to know if the pineapple Cathedral at Barcelona was still more unfinished. (Michael had been there with the International Brigade—it was a bad show about his arm; Frances had heard that the shrapnel still imbedded there might end in amputation.) But Michael steered the conversation to Gaudi and his architectural fantasies. Frances remembered a chapter somewhere by Evelyn Waugh on Gaudi's telephone kiosks. It was an amusing description and they laughed.

"Eternal Oxford: how delightful it is to return and be so far removed from the rigors of life." The voice had a very pronounced, almost too careful Oxford accent. The speaker was tall, and remarkably good-looking. A dueling scar marked his chin, another his cheek; they gave his blondness a certain formidable quality. His smile was very self-possessed. "Mrs. Myles, as lovely as ever." He bowed low over Frances' hand.

Frances collected herself. "Oh, hello. How are you?" She made hasty introductions. "Freiherr Sigurd von Aschenhausen—John Clark, Sir Michael Hampton, George Sanderson. Herr von Aschenhausen was an undergraduate along with Richard."

There was a pause.

"Charming to return and find Evelyn Waugh and Oxford still inseparable." Von Aschenhausen's voice was friendly. The three undergraduates kept a polite smile in place. Frances knew they were placing his date of residence at the University very accurately. She thought of explaining that it wasn't black-satin sheets but Catalonian architecture which they had been discussing, and then gave up the idea as being more trouble than it was probably worth. Even allowing for the foreigner's favorite indoor sport of underestimating the English, surely von Aschenhausen couldn't be serious. After all he had been to three universities, one in Germany, one in England and one in America. One thing he must know about undergraduates by this time, and that was they were always in revolt. They were never static. The only way they could form their minds was by opposing accepted opinion. Frances herself had seen the swing of the pendulum away from the esthete to the politically conscious young man who Studied Conditions. The esthete himself had been in rebellion against the realism of the postwar group.

George made some polite remark to cover up their embarrassment. Michael was lighting a cigarette. John was gazing into the middle distance. Frances remembered he was allergic to Germany, since that kick four years ago when he hadn't saluted a procession in Leipzig. The conversation limped along, the undergraduates hoping that von Aschenhausen would go; but he didn't. Frances did her best: she talked about summer holidays. The undergraduates were going to France; von Aschenhausen was returning to Berlin. She explained that Richard and she would like to have their usual view of mountains.

"Where exactly were you thinking of going?" asked von Aschenhausen.

"We were in the South Tyrol last year. I'd like to get back there just once more—" Frances' voice was honey-sweet—"just before the volcano erupts." The Englishmen smiled grimly. The German protested politely.

"What! With this peaceful England? There will be no war, no general war. Just look at everyone in this room. . . ." Unconsciously he straightened his back as he looked around the room. *And there's not a soldier among you* was the implication. He might just as well have said it. Michael flicked a piece of cigarette ash off his wounded arm. He spoke for the first time.

"There's a limit to everything, you know. Good-by, Frances. I must go now. Have a good time this summer."

The others had to go now, too, it seemed.

Von Aschenhausen remained. Frances shook herself free from her embarrassment. After all, he used to be amusing and gay. He had made many friends when he was up at Oxford; he had been invited around a good deal. She wondered how he was getting along in the new Germany; he used to laugh off any political discussions by protesting he wasn't interested in politics. She racked her brains for something tactful to say. It was difficult in this summer of 1939. You were so conscious of nationality now. She was relieved when von Aschenhausen spoke.

"I am afraid that young man did not like me particularly," he said.

"Is it because I am a German, or is it his usual manner? I have noticed that a cripple is usually more bitter than the ordinary man."

"Cripple?" Frances' eyes widened; she was at a loss for words.

"Of course, there *is* a change in the attitude here towards me," he continued. "Six years ago I had many friends. Today—well—" he smiled sadly—"it would be better if I came as an exile."

"I wondered at first if you were, and then I thought not."

"How did you know?" He looked at her amusedly.

"By your clothes." She looked pointedly at his Savile Row suit. He hadn't liked that; his smile was still there but it was less amused. Good. Cripple, indeed!

"It is really very sad for a German to find how misjudged and abused his country is. Of course, our enemies control the press in foreign countries, and they have been very busy. They have clever tongues."

"Have they? It is strange, isn't it, how criticism of Germany has grown even in countries which were once really very close to her. I wonder how it could have happened." He looked as if he didn't know quite how he should take that. She gazed at him steadily with wide blue eyes.

He smiled sadly. "You see, even you have changed. It is depressing to return to Oxford, which I loved, and to find myself surrounded by glaciers." Was the man being really sincere, wondered Frances, or was it just another of those poor-mouth stories?

"Perhaps it is the change in you which has changed us."

He looked surprised. "Oh, come now, Mrs. Myles. I haven't changed so very much. I am still interested in literature and music. I haven't become a barbarian, you know. Politically—well, I have progressed. Everyone does, unless he is a cow. I am more realistic than I once was, less sentimental. I've seen the stupidities committed in the name of idealism and abstract thinking. People are made to be led. They need leadership, and with strong leadership they can achieve anything. At first they must take the bad with the good; in the end they will forget the bad, because the ultimate good will be so great for them." He spoke with mounting enthusiasm.

"You believe you have not changed. And yet, under the leadership which you praise so much, you may only read certain books, listen to certain music, look at certain pictures, make friends with certain people. Isn't that limiting yourself?"

"Oh, well, limiting oneself to the good, eliminating the bad—all that is better in the end."

"But *who* is to say what is good for you, or bad for you? Is it to be your own judgment, educated at Heidelberg, Oxford and Harvard, or is it to be some self-appointed leader who can't even speak grammatical German?" Von Aschenhausen didn't like that either. He obviously had no answer ready for that one.

Frances kept her voice gentle. "You see, you have changed. Do you remember the Rhodes scholar who preceded you here? Intelligent man, quiet, and very kind. What's his name? Rotha, wasn't it? You liked him then. But where is he now? Oranienburg, I heard."

Von Aschenhausen made an impatient gesture. "That is all very sentimental, Mrs. Myles. It is time that the British really saw the things which matter. Discipline and strong measures are needed in today's Europe. It is a more dangerous and forbidding place than it was six or seven years ago."

"That is just our point," said Frances. "What made Europe more dangerous and forbidding?"

He laughed, but it didn't sound jovial.

"You are a very prejudiced person, I can see. I suppose you will now lecture me gravely on the wickedness of Germany's claims to natural *Lebensraum*. It is easy to talk when you have a large Empire."

"On the contrary, Herr von Aschenhausen, I like to think of all people having their *Lebensraum*, whether they are Germans or Jews or Czechs or Poles."

His voice grated. He was really angry. "It is just such thoughts as these which have weakened Britain. In the last twenty-five years, she could have established herself as ruler of the world. Instead, she makes a Commonwealth out of an Empire, and they won't even fight to help her when she has to fight. She leaves the riches of India untapped; she urges a representative government on Indians who were about to refuse it. She alienates Italy with sanctions. She weakens herself all the time, and she thinks it is an improvement."

"Hello, you are being very serious in this corner." It was Richard.

"I've been having lessons in statecraft," said Frances, conscious of Richard's eyes on the two pink spots on her cheeks. I shouldn't let myself get angry, she thought, and listened to von Aschenhausen, once more smiling and plausible. She had the feeling that he was trying to cover up, as if he were annoyed with the impression he had given her. He was very polite as they said good-by. He bowed low, his composure completely regained.

"I hope we meet again," he said. "And don't worry, Mrs. Myles. You will see that England will not be at war. You are all good pacifists, here. Enjoy yourselves abroad."

Richard said, "I hope so," and smiled. He took his wife's arm and piloted her skillfully to the door. Frame waved a sherry bottle from two groups away.

"Lovely party," Frances called over to him, but the noise of voices around her drowned her words. Frame's answer was also unheard. They exchanged smiles of understanding, a wave of the hand, and then Frances and Richard were outside the room into quietness and fresh air.

Richard lowered his voice. "I got to you as quickly as I could when I saw an argument had developed. I thought you had sense enough by this time not to waste your breath arguing with a Nazi. He is, isn't he?"

"Yes. I think he didn't mean to show it, but I made him angry."

"What interests me is what he said to anger *you.*"

"Was it obvious?" Frances was dismayed.

"To me, yes. No one else would notice. What was it anyway?"

"Britain."

"Anything else?"

Frances shook her head.

"All right; let's drop it. I hope you weren't too intelligent, though. Peter wants us to be the unworldly don with his dim wife."

Frances stared. "But we needn't start that business until we are on the boat train."

"Probably not: still, you didn't notice Peter taking any chances, did you?"

"I must say I thought he was a little—theatrical. He was very unlike himself."

Richard shook his head slowly. "No to both of these. He was too worried to be theatrical. By the way, he didn't turn up at the party."

"Perhaps he changed his mind," said Frances.

"Perhaps. Or perhaps he was just being very sure that he wouldn't meet us again. That's probably nearer it." Richard's voice was gloomy.

Frances pressed his arm to her side. "Cheer up, Richard, or you'll have me worried in case I spoil your fun. It's one of the troubles of having a wife, you know. You just can't get rid of her." She was rewarded with almost a smile.

But the sun had gone, and with it the bronze in the leaves overhead. The playing fields were empty. Over the gray walls and the sharply pointed rooftops the sound of bells followed them as they walked slowly home.

The rest of the week passed quickly. Frances was busy with the closing of their house. She also made a hectic dash to London for some clothes she "simply must have." Richard finished the odds and ends of work which face a tutor towards the end of term—but from Peter Galt they heard nothing.

"Which means we are to go ahead," said Richard at breakfast on Wednesday.

That morning, he bought their tickets to Paris and interviewed the bank about a supply of travelers' cheques and some French money. The expense of their unknown journeys had worried him, but his bank manager, who had always been tactful about overdrafts, met him with a discreet smile. The bank had been authorized to give Mr. Myles a letter of credit. Richard did not ask who had authorized it. The bank manager treated it all as something merely routine.

In the evening, Richard hunted through his bookshelves and picked out the Baedekers and maps. He had a fair collection of these, for since his first year at Oxford he had spent part of each summer walking and scrambling his way across mountains into villages. He spread them out around him as he sat on the floor of the study, and lit his pipe. He wondered which he could omit: surely the Pyrenees and Majorca would be unnecessary. Peter had hinted in the direction of Central Europe. Still, it was better to be safe; he knew his way around these maps, and they ought to go along, all of them. He would take less clothes, if his suitcase got too crowded.

Frances came in, her hair brushed loosely to her shoulders.

"Don't overwork, darling," she said with mock concern. "I begin to feel exhausted. I came in to ask you to sharpen my pencil." She held out a miserable stub.

"What on earth do you do with your pencils?" asked Richard. "Gnaw them?"

Frances disregarded this with the adroitness of four years' marriage. She looked at the notebook in her hand, and checked off the items she had written there. Richard watched her as she bit her lip and counted. He felt that wave of emotion which came to him when he looked at Frances in her unguarded moments; and he had the bleak horror which always attacked him then when he thought how easy it might have been never to have met her.

Frances straightened her legs. "That's that," she said.

"Just my own things to pack tomorrow after Anni departs. Richard, that is going to be a difficult moment. Other summers, it was different. She always knew she would be coming back in time for October. She seems to feel she will never be back here. I found her packing in floods of tears this evening. I've sent her out now to say good-by to her friends. So there goes the best cook we shall ever have. It was really rather painful this evening. I've got just as much attached to her as she has to us. She wants her father's farm to have the honor of a visit from the *gnädige Frau* and the *Herr Professor,* if they should visit Innsbruck this summer."

Richard finished sharpening the pencil. "Her people were pro-Dolfuss, weren't they?"

"They were. . . . I have a feeling that they have changed. Anni has been very silent about them since she returned last year. One thing she did tell me. Her sister told her that if she came back to England and a war broke out, she would be stoned to death. That is what they said we did in 1914. Isn't it appalling?"

"Well, I suppose if a nation allows concentration camps, it will find it hard to believe that other people don't use similar methods. Cheer up, old girl, who cares what a lot of uncivilized people think anyway? It's only the opinion of the civilized that really matters."

"Yes, but it looks as if a lot of the civilized will be killed because they ignored the thoughts of the uncivilized. Ignoring doesn't abolish them, you know, Richard." She traced a pattern on the carpet with her pencil. "Sorry, darling. I'm tired, and depressed. We've all gone so political these days. I worry and worry inside me, and I think everyone else is doing the same; it is difficult to forget what we all went through last September."

Richard tapped the stem of his pipe against his teeth. "Yes, it's difficult," he said slowly. "I shan't forget helping to dig trenches in the parks, or the paper tape on all the windows, or the towels we were told to keep beside a bucket of water. All the time I was digging I kept wondering whether the trenches would be any good at all, and I knew they wouldn't be. I didn't think much of the towel idea either. But what else was there? And then bastards like von Aschenhausen come along all smiles and bows. And wonder why people are not enthusiastic about them. They blackmail us with bombers one year, and go back on the agreement they had extorted out of us, and then expect to be welcomed as friends. All within nine months. All that, Frances, makes one of the reasons why I listened to Peter. If I could put a spoke of even the most microscopic size in the smallest Nazi wheel, I'd think it a pretty good effort." He had risen, and was pacing up and down the study.

"I think this interruption is due. I see that proposition-look dawning in your eye. Don't try, don't you try to leave me at home. I'm coming."

"I was afraid you were."

"Richard, my dear, you know that whenever you imagine exciting things they always turn out duller than a wet day in Wigan. It's the parties you don't get excited about which turn out to be fun. Now here we are, both thinking of ourselves in terms of Sard Harker. What will happen? We'll go to Paris, and then find that the man does not turn up. I'll wear a red rose for three nights, and you'll spill Cointreau for three nights, until the whole café is gaping at us. And then we'll go on our holiday, wondering if Peter's sense of humor has become overdeveloped since Bucharest."

Richard laughed. "You sound almost convincing, Frances. But I know that you know what I know. This is no bloody picnic."

She rose from the floor, and went over to the window. It was wide open. She leaned forward to breathe in the dewy smell of the earth. The lilac trees at the end of the garden had silver leaves. Richard came to her, and slipped an arm round her waist. They stood there in silence watching a garden moonlit. Frances glanced at him. He was lost in thought.

"If you want to know," he said at last, reading her thoughts in the uncanny way two people living together learn to do, "I am thinking we should photograph this in our memory. We may need to remember it often for the next few years."

Frances nodded. Around them were the other gardens, the mixed perfume of flowers. The walls hung heavy with roses and honeysuckle, their colors whitened in the strong moonlight. The deep shadows of trees, blurring the outline of the other houses, were pierced here and there with the lights from uncurtained windows. The giant elms in the Magdalen deer park stood sentinels of peace.

She said suddenly, "Richard, let's go up the river; just for half an hour."

"The dew is heavy. You had better wrap up well."

"I shall. It won't take five minutes." She kissed him suddenly, and left him. He heard her running upstairs, the banging of the wardrobe door in their bedroom. So Frances had this feeling too, this feeling of wanting to say good-by.

She came downstairs in less than her five minutes, dressed in a sweater and trousers, and with one of his silk handkerchiefs round her neck. They walked the short distance to the boathouse in silence. They got out the canoe in a matter-of-fact way, as if they were defying the moonlight to weaken them. They paddled swiftly up the narrow river. White mists were rising from the fields on either side of them, encircling the roots of the willows which edged the banks.

"When I used to read my Virgil, this is what I thought the Styx might be like," said Frances. Then suddenly, "Richard, what are you planning to do in Paris?"

"Water carries sound," he reminded her. To prove his words, they heard low voices and the laugh of a girl, before they saw two punts drifting to meet them.

"You have your moments, don't you, Richard? By the way, I think you will like the hat I bought yesterday in London. A little white sailor with no crown to speak of, yards of black cloud floating down the back, and a saucy red rose perched over one eye." She heard Richard laugh behind her. "Practical, isn't it?"

"Very," he said, and laughed again. "Good Lord—trust a woman to think up something like that."

Frances was serious again. "Richard, do you think there will really be war this summer?"

"It's anyone's guess. The President was lunching yesterday with Halifax. He said—"

"Halifax?"

"Yes. He said no one in the Cabinet knew. It all depended on one man."

Frances was silent for a space. When she spoke, her voice trembled with its intensity.

"I resent this man. Why should the happiness of the whole civilized world depend on him? Why should I, an Englishwoman, have to look at my countryside, for instance, and even as I look have to remember that last September I had planned to help to take the Symons children in this canoe up this river, to hide them under the willows until the air raids had passed? I had blankets and towels and tinned food and chocolate all packed in a basket. A Hitler picnic indeed. There was not one of us who hasn't had fear and horror creep into all his associations. As I pass these willows I keep wondering just which one of them might have been sheltering the Symons children, and whether it would have done its job. And all because of one man. Think of it, Richard, there wasn't a farmer who didn't look at his land and the farmhouse his great-great-grandfather had built and wonder. There wasn't a townsman who didn't look at his business or his home and everything he had earned for himself and wonder. There wasn't a man or woman who did not look at the children and wonder. Richard, I resent this man and his kind of people."

"You aren't the only one." Richard pointed the nose of the canoe back down the river. "You aren't the only one. We have all had a year of brooding. And we have all come to the same decision. If anything does start, the man who starts will be sorry he ever thought of himself as a kind of god. But take it easy, Frances. Promise me you will stop worrying while we are on this holiday. It may be the last—" he paused—"for a long time, anyway. There is nothing more that rational beings can do, anyway, except wait and watch. And when it comes, the Symons children will have better protection than the willows this September. And that's something."

"Yes, that's something." Frances' voice was quieter. "But when I meet some of those armchair critics who sit beside their radio in a part of the world which can't be bombed from Germany, and hear them tell me how England should have fought, I am liable to be very very rude. *And* I bet, if war does come, these same people will suddenly start talking about the greatness and glories of peace. Britain will then be just another of those belligerent countries. That is how we will be dismissed, as if neutrality implied a special sanctity. There now, Richard, I've got it all out of my system. I shan't mention it again."

"That's the girl. Remember this part of the river?"

Frances gave a shaky laugh. "Yes, darling. I was a sweet girl undergraduate, and you were in all the importance of your final year. Good bathes we had, too, in just this kind of moonlight. Look, there's some more of us." Some punts were moored under a bank, and the wet figures as they balanced to dive gave a moment's illusion of silver statues.

"I've found the difference between twenty and thirty," said Richard. "At twenty you never think of rheumatics or a chill in the bladder."

They guided the canoe back to the boathouse. They stood together on the landing place in silence, looking at the river and the white mist rising.

They walked slowly home. At the gate, they met Anni.

"Guten Abend, gnädige Frau, Herr Professor." She was a tall girl, with a pleasant open face, and fair hair braided round her head.

"Good evening, Anni. Did you see your friends all right?"

Anni nodded. Her arms were full of small parcels. "We had cake, and tea, and then we sang. It was very *gemütlich.*" She looked down at the parcels. "They gave me these presents," she added. She spoke the careful English which Frances had taught her. "I've had so much pleasure."

"I'm glad, Anni. You should go to bed soon: you have a long journey tomorrow."

Anni nodded again. "I wish you good night, *gnädige Frau, Herr Professor. Angenehme Ruh'.*"

They walked round the garden after she had left them.

"It's funny, Richard. I really am tired, and there is a nice large bed waiting for me upstairs, and yet I keep staying out here looking at the stars."

"I hate to be unromantic, but I do think it is time we got some sleep. Tomorrow's a bad day. It always is: you have a genius for finding last-minute things to do." Frances smiled, and felt Richard's arm round her waist guide her to the house. On the steps, he stopped to kiss her.

"That's to break the enchantment," he said. His lips were smiling, but his eyes were the way Frances loved them most.

There was always a feeling of excitement after the unpleasantness of a Channel crossing, while the train waited patiently on the Dieppe siding for the last passengers. They emerged, in straggling groups, from the customs and passport sheds. Frances, already comfortably settled in her corner, watched them with interest. She glanced at Richard opposite her, leaning back with his eyes closed. He was a bad sailor, but he managed things like customs officials very well indeed. Thank heaven for Richard, she thought, watching other wives followed by harassed husbands whose tempers didn't improve under commiserating looks from unhurried bachelors. It was the stage in the journey when most people began to wonder if it all wasn't more trouble than it was worth.

The last nervous lady was helped into the train. The confusion along the corridors was subsiding. They were moving, very slowly, very carefully. Two young men had halted at their compartment.

"This will do," said one, after hardly seeming to glance in their direction. They swung their rucksacks on to the rack, and threw their Burberries after them. Undergraduates, thought Frances, as she looked at a magazine. Like Richard, they wore dark gray pin-stripe flannel suits, brown suède shoes well-worn, collars which pointed carelessly, and the hieroglyphic tie of a college society.

The train traveled gently along the street, like a glorified tramcar. The children with thin legs and cropped hair and faded blue overalls halted in their games to watch the engine. Their older sisters, leaning on their elbows at the tall narrow windows, looked critically at the people traveling to Paris. The women, standing in the doorways or in front of the small shops, hardly bothered to interrupt their gossip. It was only a trainload, and a full one too. All the better for their men, who worked on the piers: the arriving tourist tipped well. The old men, who sat reading the café newspapers at the marble-topped tables, looked peacefully bored. One of them pulled out a watch, looked at it, looked at the train, and shook his head. Frances smiled to herself. Things had been different when he worked in the sheds, no doubt.

She discarded her magazines. It was almost impossible to read on a foreign train. The differences in houses and people, in fields and gardens, fascinated her. She looked at Richard. He was staring gloomily at the fields, making up his mind to move. As he caught her glance, he roused himself.

"Come on, Frances, tea or something. You've eaten nothing since breakfast and I haven't even that now." He rose, and steadied himself. "There's nothing like being back on solid ground, even if it does lurch at the moment."

They negotiated the two pairs of long legs, with the usual "Not at all" following them. In the corridor, Richard gave a grin and squeezed her arm.

"Excited?" he teased. "I believe you are."

"I have two excitements inside me," said Frances, and smiled back. It was like being a child again, when a deep secret *(cross your lips and heart)* churned in your stomach and the intoxication of knowing you were important, even if no one else thought you were, made your eyes shine. Frances controlled her exhilaration and tried to look bored. She remembered Richard's words last night. "Keep cool, don't worry. Don't talk about anything important, even when you think it's safe. Don't speak on impulse. Don't show any alarm even when you've just had an attack of woman's intuition. I can tell from your eyes when you are really worried. We can talk things over at night when we get to bed. We won't lose by being careful." *We won't lose!* She had chased away the exhilaration, and now she knew it had been guarding her against fear. *We won't lose.* The certainty of the words panicked her. She heard Richard order tea. *Won't lose, won't lose, won't lose,* mocked the wheels of the train. She suddenly knew that Richard and she had never been so alone before, in all their lives.

"That's better," said Richard as he lit a cigarette. "The compartment was much too crowded. Now what do you want to see in Paris?"

It was strange, she thought, how people seemed to change in a foreign train. More than half in this coach were English, but already they seemed so different. She became aware that Richard was watching her carefully. She smiled to him and calmed her imagination. Nice beginning, indeed, when every stout Swiss commercial traveler seemed to be a member of the Ogpu, or that pinched little governess looked like a German agent. I've seen too much Hitchcock lately, she thought; at this rate I'll be worse than useless.

Richard was talking continuously as if he had sensed her stage fright. She concentrated on listening to him; he had helped her this way before. Like the time she had climbed her first mountain, and had got badly stuck, so badly that she accepted the fact that she was going to be killed, actually accepted it with a peculiar kind of resignation—but Richard had talked so calmly, had compelled her attention so thoroughly, that she forgot she was already dead at the bottom of a precipice, and her feet followed his to safety. He was talking now about the French peasants. A French peasant, he was proving, would not be able to understand *The Grapes of Wrath.*

Frances, watching the farmhouses which seemed to grow from the earth as much as the little orchards which guarded them or the fields so carefully planned to the last inch, was inclined to agree. She thought of the despair of peasants similar to these during the last war, when they saw their fields shell-racked, torn with barbed wire, poisoned with gas, evil-smelling with death. . . . And yet, a few years later and these fields were again persuaded back into neat rows of earth, new trees were planted, new houses built.

"It is strange how little credit we give to the courage of quiet people," she said. "We sympathize most with those who find someone to champion their woes. We take all this for granted." She pointed to the farms. "We never think that this could be a wilderness. We look at it and think 'How pleasant to live here,' and yet to live here would mean back-breaking work and a continual struggle, if we wanted it to stay this way."

"There's nothing like self-pity for thoroughly dissipating a man. And when a nation indulges in that luxury it finds itself with a dictator. Wrongs and injustices come in at the door, and reason flies out the window. It's a solution which does not flatter the human race." He paused. "But what on earth brought this up?"

Frances nodded to the fields. "The earth itself."

People were now crowding into the restaurant car, looking reproachfully at their empty plates.

"Feeding time at the Zoo," said Richard. "Let's move." As he concentrated on the problem of francs and centimes, she caught sight of the gray-suited man and girl in a mirror. This was how we look to strangers, she thought. Richard had noticed the direction of her glance. His eyes were laughing.

"Beauty and the beast?" he suggested.

In their compartment, the two young men uncrossed their legs to let Frances and Richard pass. Frances had the feeling that they were interrupting a discussion. The dark-haired undergraduate seemed depressed and worried. She didn't look at the other, because she knew he was observing her in his detached way. She tried to concentrate on her magazines. She resisted the feeling of sleep which the train rhythm invited. . . . She never slept in the afternoon, but four hours' sleep last night could be an excuse. She looked at the field, she looked at the magazines, she looked at three pairs of brown suède shoes. When she awoke, they were in Paris. Richard was handing his rucksack and her handcase with voluble instructions to a blue-overalled porter.

He smiled down at her. "Time to powder your nose, my pet." Frances, in confusion, grabbed her handbag. She hated to arrive so disorganized.

The undergraduates were leaving. Frances' eyes were startled into looking at them over her compact mirror as she heard them say good-by to Richard, and then, more shyly, to her. She hid her surprise enough to smile, and bow, and say good-by to them in turn, before they disappeared.

Richard was still smiling. "Had a good sleep?"

"Marvelous. I've really got to admit I feel better. Did I make any peculiar noises?"

"No, you slept like a child. It quite won all our hearts."

A bulky shadow fell across the doorway. It belonged to a man with a neat black beard and a neat black suit, making his way slowly down the corridor. He was decidedly large, and he carried a suitcase in each hand, so that he had to walk crabwise. He gazed benevolently into their compartment over his pince-nez. Richard didn't seem aware of him.

He chose this moment to ask, "What about dinner at the Café Voltaire tonight?" Frances was enthusiastic. Her clear voice carried well down the corridor.

"Oh, yes; do. And we'll have decent Vouvray."

Their porter waited patiently. The platform was remarkably crowded, thought Richard, for this year of grace. His eyes searched for the two Englishmen. He saw them striding towards the main entrance, their felt hats in their hands. Behind them, at some distance, was a fat black figure, carrying two bags. . . . And then the crowd closed in again. He felt a sudden wave of relief. In the taxi, he avoided discussing anything except the streets and buildings.

Their hotel was one of the small ones on the Left Bank. They had stayed there on their first visit to Paris together, when they had little money to spend, and they always returned to it.

Inside their bedroom, Frances paused and said, as she always did, "It's just the same, even the wallpaper." Unconsciously, she always got the same note of surprise into her voice each year. Richard had come to the conclusion that she was surprised over anyone continuing to endure such wallpaper; she was probably right about that. It was hideously artistic. Frances was already in the bathroom, unpacking toothbrushes. He leaned against the door and watched her disapprovingly.

"Help me, darling," she said, throwing a sponge and talcum-powder tin at him.

"I'm damned if I am going to unpack now. I'm hungry."

"Richard, you know we'll be late tonight before we get back—we always are—and it will be too late to unpack then, and I hate going to sleep without washing or teeth brushing. I'll shake out my Paris clothes now, if you'll run my bath, like a darling." She went back into the bedroom, and he heard her moving about with her light step.

"It's just the thin edge of the wedge, if you ask me," he said. "First it is only a toothbrush, and then it's Paris clothes, and I bet you are starting on the whole suitcase by this time. You've too much damned energy, Frances. After last night, I thought you would never want to look at another piece of tissue paper for days."

"That sleep on the train made me all right." She slipped off her gray flannel suit. "Talking about the train, who were your young friends? The blond was just too beautiful for words, wasn't he? I felt sorry somehow for the dark ugly one: he was feeling grim about something."

Richard came back into the room, and stretched himself along the chaise longue which stood in front of the tall windows. He propped the rose-embroidered cushion under his head, and watched Frances unfasten her suspenders.

"If you want to know, you can come here. The bath can wait five minutes. It's too hot anyway. You'd only come out a rich lobster color."

Frances looked across the room at him, and smiled as she slipped the smooth silk of her dressing gown round her. She knew Richard, by this time. The bath would have to wait.

From the chaise longue they could watch the green leaves in the small courtyard outside the windows. The fears and uncertainty which had suddenly attacked Frances that afternoon seemed so remote now that they were almost silly. She lay feeling safe and warm and comfortable. Dangers and cruelty didn't exist; nor did lies and treachery, nor hatred and jealousy. It was fine just to lie like this, just to feel safe and warm and comfortable.

Richard watched the smile on her lips. "How do you feel, darling?" So he had been worried too about that attack of nerves this afternoon.

"Wonderful, Richard. Like a contented cow." He laughed. He knew now that everything was all right. When he got round to telling his story, there wasn't much to tell. The men had been undergraduates—Cambridge men. They had been vague about their holiday. The fair-haired man had said something about Czechoslovakia, but the dark one had shut him up rather abruptly, Richard had thought. What had actually started them talking was the man in the black suit. He had passed the compartment door twice, each time looking benevolently at Frances asleep in her corner seat.

"And that," said Richard, "aroused all our protective instincts. The dark-haired undergraduate muttered something about being haunted by black beards since Victoria. The other suggested it might only be a touch of Blackbeard's old bladder trouble again. That sort of broke the ice. I capped that suggestion, and then we just talked. Mostly the fair-haired glamour boy and myself. It turned out he was the brother of Thornley who was up at Oxford in my time. A friend of Peter's. As a matter of fact Peter visited them for a couple of days this week."

At the mention of Peter's name, Frances had stiffened. She didn't like it somehow, and for all Richard's calm voice, she knew he didn't either. She kept her voice low like his. "Complications?" she asked.

"You can't tell. I've been thinking about that. The dark-haired chap was certainly jumpy, but that doesn't prove anything. Probably they really are quite oblivious of anything except their own holiday, and our meeting them was just another of these coincidences. On the other hand, Peter might have roped them in just like us, or used them as decoys, and perhaps Blackbeard was trailing them. If so, then we had downright bad luck meeting them. All we can do is to disinterest anyone who might have become interested in us through them." Richard smiled wryly. "You see, young Thornley didn't mention his brother or Peter until we had reached the station. So there we were, talking for most of the journey, and anyone who passed the door of the compartment might have thought we were all together. The joke was on me."

Frances kissed him. "It probably is only a harmless incident. What about throwing off suspicion with dinner?"

Half an hour later, they left the hotel. The streets were quiet, the restaurants and cafés crowded. A worried Frenchman, hurrying past them, caught sight of a girl's laughing face under a pert white hat with a red rose, and turned to watch. English, he guessed, as he marked the cut of the man's suit and that peculiar stride which goes with such a suit. And without a care in the world, he thought. He hurried on, speculating on that peculiar people.

At that moment he was right. Frances and Richard had abandoned care. Their holiday had begun.

June ended with their first week in Paris. They were very much on holiday. They rose late and breakfasted at their open window in the warm sunlight which then invaded the small courtyard. The insignificant little man who had watched them from the shadows of his room since their first morning at the hotel still sat far back from his window, but his interest was waning. He wasn't a romantic, and the appearance each morning of a pretty blonde girl in a dressing gown pouring coffee for a tall young man who lazily stretched himself on a couch at the open window was beginning to bore him. The leisurely manner in which they breakfasted and dressed annoyed him as much as the sound of their laughter and their English voices. He was wasting his time, he thought angrily, as he watched them leave their room after midday as they always did. The chambermaid could take care of them.

The second insignificant man who took over at this point was equally bored. His feet hurt, and he had never been interested in history anyway. He followed Frances and Richard from one church to another, from exhibition to exhibition, from palaces to slums. Towards the end of the week, he was beginning to wait for them in a café and let them visit the inside of the buildings themselves. For he too had become convinced he was wasting his time.

The third insignificant man, who joined Richard and Frances while they were having dinner, had slightly better luck. He liked theaters and night clubs. Even the two evenings which they spent more soberly, just sitting at a table in the Café de la Paix, were pleasant, because by that time he was convinced that the Englishman and his wife weren't going to complicate life for him. So he relaxed and enjoyed the thought that his expenses were paid. He was the only one of the insignificant men who was sorry to receive instructions at the end of the week to switch over to a newly arrived American. He had become so accustomed to their obvious approval of drinking their coffee and liqueur on the pavement in the French manner that he would not have been surprised to see them approach the Café de la Paix again, on Saturday night. He would have approved the fair-haired girl's black dress and the small white hat with its gay red rose perched over her right eye.

Frances was nervous, so she talked constantly as they walked up the Avenue de l'Opéra. "I've enjoyed this week, even if my feet feel two sizes bigger," was how she summed it up.

Richard nodded. "It hasn't been so bad. Life has been simpler than I thought it would be. I begin to feel I was oversuspicious of Blackbeard."

Frances stared. "I haven't seen him again; have you?"

"No, nor any possible relatives, either." Which would have pleased the insignificant men; no tribute to their ingenuities could have been handsomer. Richard piloted Frances carefully across the Boulevard des Capucines, and gave her an encouraging smile. "Cheer up, old girl. The first bathe is always the coldest."

They had arrived between the dinner and the after-theater crowds. There were a few vacant tables. Richard led the way to one on the left-hand side. As they sat down, a waiter appeared like the traditional white rabbit out of a hat.

"Coffee," said Richard, "and Cointreau for you as usual, Frances? I think I'll have one too. Yes, coffee and two Cointreaus."

Frances repressed a wifely smile. He always enjoyed ordering in French, even in moments like these. Poor old Richard, how he hated Cointreau.

They settled comfortably in their chairs, lit cigarettes, and looked at the traffic with the right amount of interest. The people at the other tables were the usual mixture of foreigners and Frenchmen. Two nights ago, the same kind of crowd had seemed gay and harmless. Tonight they seemed gay. Frances shook herself out of her imagination to admire the way in which the waiter poured the Cointreau.

"Penny for them," said Richard.

"I was thinking how people with guilty consciences develop persecution mania."

"Yes, they could, couldn't they? I felt the same." But what worried them most was how long they had to wait. Frances sipped her Cointreau. She noticed with amusement that Richard was restricting himself to coffee. As she listened to him, making conversation with one eye on his watch, she repeated to herself just what she had to say when the time came. She was the amateur actress taking one last look at her script as she waits in the wings. Her cue came sooner than she had expected.

A large, expensively draped woman was making her way with difficulty past their table. It seemed to Frances that it might have been the large lady who had brushed against the table, and sent the coffee swilling into the saucer. Yet Richard's Cointreau glass lay carefully pointed away from them, so that the liqueur trickled slowly over the other side of the table. Richard looked at it with some annoyance and resignation. The large lady continued oblivious on her way, trailing clouds of Matchabelli. The waiter staged his arrival from nowhere. He wiped and apologized with equal vigor.

Frances sat very still. She was conscious of the smile on her lips which had settled there and wouldn't come off, as if she were having her photograph taken. Richard's back was turned towards the man, and he hadn't noticed him yet. She let her eyes travel slowly back to their own table; she sensed, rather than saw, him making his way out of the restaurant. He was walking unhurriedly, and he would pass their table. Now he was almost behind the waiter, whose broad back blocked the narrow passage effectively as he bent to pick up the coffee cups. Richard was watching her. He was waiting.

"I was telling you about Mrs. Rose." As she spoke she flipped her cigarette case open. "Mrs. Rose told me we must see Le Lapin Agile. She said we would like it."

"Why?" Richard seemed more interested in ordering another drink.

That's just my sweet husband, she thought a trifle bitterly, and lighted her cigarette. She noticed the rug vendor with the turban who was silently offering his wares to another table.

"She was born in India," she said. Now let's see what Richard can make of that.

The waiter became aware of the man who was trying to edge impatiently past him. He stepped aside, but not in time. He must have knocked the man's elbow, for the cigarette fell from his hand onto their table. The man caught it as it rolled, and picked it up. There was just time for them to notice the peculiar way he wore the watch on his wrist, and the peculiar time it showed on its clearly marked face.

"India?" Richard was asking with a display of interest. "Oh, yes, she was a great rope climber in her day, wasn't she?"

The man had already reached the pavement; he paused for a moment as he lit his cigarette. He might be making up his mind how to spend the rest of his evening, and by the time Frances had replied gently but forcibly he had merged into the crowd.

"Did I ever tell you about my life among the Eskimos?" asked Richard, and shook his head in reply to the rug seller. He sipped the cognac which the waiter had brought, and added with approval, "Much more like it. Where were we? Oh, yes, with the Eskimos. . . ." He talked on. Frances was glad of the opportunity just to relax. She listened to Richard's inventions with a smile, and waited for him to finish the liqueur. Then they could get back to the hotel.

The dark-haired, sallow-faced chambermaid had just come out of their room. The towels over her arm were the obvious excuse. She smiled in her tired way.

"Good evening, Madame, Monsieur. You are back early tonight. Perhaps Madame is tired."

Frances agreed to that: she had just caught a glimpse of herself in the gilt-edged mirror on the wall. Perhaps it was the very large, very pink flowers on the wallpaper that made her feel so wilted. Richard said good night rather brusquely, and opened their door. The woman wasn't usually conversational, he thought, but she must have been surprised to see them. People generally talked too much when they were embarrassed. He locked the door behind them, and stood there, listening. Frances watched his face as she took off her hat. She liked him when he was worried: she liked the frown on his brow, the intent look in the thoughtful eyes. It had been his eyes which she had noticed when they had first met. She couldn't guess what lay behind their calm grayness; there was a hint of so many things. If that had been one of the reasons why she had married him, then she hadn't been disappointed.

Richard seemed satisfied. He had left the door, and started to undress.

"Bed," he said, and his eyes were smiling, now. "And don't, my love, clean each tooth for five minutes, tonight."

Frances laughed, and started to brush her hair, and then stopped with the hairbrush poised in midair. Her eyes were puzzled as they rested on her make-up box lying on the dressing table.

"I could *swear* that . . ." she began.

"I shouldn't," said Richard, his lips smiling, his eyes warning.

Frances bit her top lip. "I shan't be long now," she ended. Richard nodded approvingly. Good girl, he thought; she could take a hint without having it underlined.

Frances always lay on Richard's right side. It was hot and stuffy in the room, but Richard would open the windows before they went to sleep. He held her close to him. They could feel each other's breath coming in little warm waves as they talked, their low voices smothered in the pillow.

"What was wrong, Fran?"

"Someone has been meddling with my things. The cream jars were in the wrong order; you know how I always have them arranged in a certain way. They stand on a little tray, which you've got to lift up to get at the space underneath. Someone probably wanted to know what I kept there."

"What do you keep?"

"Just face tissues and cotton wool and odds and ends."

"Was anything missing?"

"My address book. You know the one, the little one I keep for addresses of hairdressers or hotels or cleaners in any place we have stayed abroad."

"That won't be much help to them."

"But who are they?"

"God knows. It might be friends of Blackbeard, or it might be someone who followed Peter more successfully than he thought. The maid is the obvious agent, anyway. I just couldn't place her when we met her in the corridor. And how did she know what time we usually returned to the hotel? She may have just been interested in how you get that complexion, or she may be yawning in that empty room next door, this very minute." He gripped Frances more tightly, and she let out a sudden squeal. Richard was nearer the truth than he would have cared to be. The dark-haired sallow woman, standing motionless in the empty room, her ear close to the wall, shrugged her shoulders: only murmurs and squeals in bed. A simple-minded race, the English. She moved silently to the door. She could go off duty now and report . . . Nothing, as usual.

Frances had asked, "You think we have been watched?"

"Only remotely. Our room has been searched, obviously, but there is nothing incriminating to find. And if they did follow us about Paris, then our movements have been innocent enough. The important thing will be whether anyone realized the meaning of tonight's incident, or whether we shall be watched tomorrow. They can follow us about, otherwise, until they are blue in the face."

"You sound confident." In the darkness, Richard smiled to himself. Confident? He had seldom felt worse in his life.

"The chap we met tonight seemed pretty calm and collected. He made everything look quite simple. Damned clever too. You got it, didn't you? One cigarette, and then, as neat emphasis, the watch which he wore the wrong way round so that we could see that it had stopped at one o'clock. I rather liked that touch."

"To be perfectly frank, I could hardly believe it was the clue. It was so easy."

"Well, it's all we've got to go on. Add one to one . . . and what do you get?"

Frances laughed. "It's too simple, really. And if at first you don't succeed . . ."

"Darling, why mention that when I'd like to get some sleep?"

"Sorry, Richard." She moved to kiss him and bumped her nose against his chin. "I'll pack tomorrow afternoon, and then we can leave anytime," she added sleepily. She stifled a yawn against his shoulder. "It's all this whispering," she said. "It makes me sleepy."

She was asleep by the time Richard had opened the windows and let the night air surge in with its welcome coolness. He looked at his wife's fair hair on the pillow, the curve of her cheek and the dark lashes. She slept like a child, with her hands resting above her head.

He remembered her voice, blurred with sleep. *We can leave anytime.* Leave, perhaps—but for where, and for what? He cursed Peter and himself. First instincts were often the right ones, when it was a matter of self-preservation. And keeping Frances safe was a matter of self-preservation for him. He should have stuck to his dislike of involving Frances. He ought to have come alone. But it had been easy to be persuaded, for the selfish reason, quite apart from the more practical one that this mission must seem a holiday as usual, that he would have been miserable without her. He lay and thought of the way in which two people, each with their own definite personality, could build up a third personality, a greater and more exciting one, to share between them. When two people succeeded in that, then they were complete. Without Frances, however definite his own personality might be, he was incomplete.

Sleep was impossible. He lay and watched the blackness of the courtyard bleach to gray, and felt the coldness of early morning strike his bare shoulders.

A sudden coolness had come to the city. Frances shivered as she stepped out of the taxi. Above the roofs of the twisting narrow streets, she could see the illuminated dome of the Sacré Cœur. Behind her, withdrawing modestly into its shadows, was Le Lapin Agile. The doorman, like a nimble gnome in his red cap and tunic, darted down to meet them, and guided them through the narrow gate to the dark doorway.

Nothing had changed since they had last been here. It never did. The old grandfather, who had founded it, had died, but the rest of the family carried on in the way he had established. In the small entrance hall, Madame sat behind the counter with its shaded light gleaming on the trays of cherry brandy. The girl who sang so well to the guitar was leaning on the counter, talking to a young man in his shirt sleeves. She was dressed as usual in a skirt and blouse. There was a sound of a piano and of laughter from the narrow doorway at the end of the counter.

Frances and Richard waited until the applause told them that the Rabelaisian improvisor had finished. The girl nodded approvingly.

"I'll find you a place," she said, and led the way up the few stairs into the room. The long benches on either side of the monastery tables were well-filled, but the girl's eyes, accustomed to the dimness of the lighting, had found a bench where two more could sit. The shirt-sleeved man followed them, carrying two glasses of cherry brandy. You drank either cherry brandy or not at all.

The others at the table made room for Frances and Richard good-naturedly. They joked with the girl.

"Why don't you bring your guitar over here and sing to us?" asked one of the men. "It's only Marius here who is going to do a little recitation next. He is with poem, again. But we don't need to listen to it, we have been hearing it all evening." His round face creased with laughter. Everyone laughed, including Marius, a little self-consciously.

The girl smiled to Marius. "What is it tonight—a new one? Go on, do it now. I have time to listen, too."

Marius rose and hesitated. His thin, rather hard face relaxed. He might be a student, or an apprentice, thought Frances. He looked apologetically round the table and saw that Frances was watching him.

"I am not sure about the last couplet," he explained shyly to her. They were all looking at her, waiting for her to reply. She gulped, felt her cheeks afire, and decided to risk it.

"*Poète, prends ton luth!*" she declaimed with her best Alexandrine accent. Everyone laughed again. The fat jovial man was enjoying himself.

"The trouble with women," he said with mock seriousness, "is that they never finish quotations." He looked at his wife. "One of the troubles," he finished. Frances blushed again, and joined in the new chorus of laughter.

Richard was pleased. We couldn't have arranged it better, he thought, and looked sympathetically across the shadows of the room at a table where other foreigners had been grouped together. He leaned back against the stone wall, and filled his pipe. Marius had reached the ancient piano. He cleared his throat, and the conversations and arguments at the other tables politely diminished. He cleared his throat again, and, sweeping back the hair which fell over his eyes, began. Everyone was listening. Richard took the opportunity to look carefully round the room; his seat gave him a good view. He could observe without appearing to.

There was the usual crowd there. At first he couldn't see anyone remotely like their friend of the Café de la Paix. There might be the possibility of disguise of course. He looked at his watch. It was just after one o'clock: time enough. He looked at the large figure of Buddha at one end of the room, and his eye naturally traveled to the large figure of Christ on the Cross on the opposite wall . . . And then he saw the man. He couldn't be sure, but something about one of the men at the table at that end of the room seemed familiar. It might be . . . He gave all his attention to Marius, who was gathering himself to deliver the uncertain couplet. It was effective, judging by the applause. Marius, flushed with success, was returning.

The girl in the blouse and skirt rose to go.

"I have something new for you tonight," she explained.

"Sing, sing," they chanted.

"She has," explained the fat man, "a most charming voice, and she chooses her songs well. Or perhaps you know?"

"Yes, I know," said Frances.

"Aristide has set some of Villon's songs to music for her voice," the Frenchman continued. He nodded towards the man in shirt sleeves, who was now sitting down at the piano. He played softly to himself, as he waited for the girl to appear.

Marius and Richard had begun a discussion for two about the symbolist poets. Frances turned to the others. They were on to politics, now: one of the women had begun the argument.

"Don't spoil my evening," said the large man, almost savagely. "Politics, politics. There is no living, nowadays." He addressed himself suddenly to Frances. "I am sorry, but you will understand." Frances could think of several reasons. She wondered which of them was responsible. The Frenchman looked at her gloomily; the laugh-lines round his mouth straightened, giving it an unexpected bitterness. His brown eyes had become hard. He leaned over the table on his elbows and his hands marked each point as he spoke.

"Twice within seven months, I have had to look out my old uniform, close my business—I am a contractor—and make my good-bys. Twice. September 1938, April 1939." His wife beside him looked away quickly. His eyes, under the heavy brows, held Frances motionless. She could not even smile in sympathy. "There may be a third time. It will be too much. The third time will be just *two* too much."

Everyone sat silent for a minute, and then all began to talk at once.

"One war is enough for one lifetime," said his wife without lifting her eyes.

The girl in the blouse and skirt had entered again, carrying her guitar. The many voices of the crowded room faded into silence. Even the foreign visitors sat politely curious. The girl raised the guitar, its red ribbons falling over her arm. She smiled to the man at the piano.

"Aristide here has found music for the words of our François Villon. I shall sing two of his ballads."

Frances looked at the silent faces; she wondered how many of them hid the thoughts of uniforms waiting for the third time. It may have been the low sweet voice of the singer, or the simplicity of the music, or the poetry of the words. She felt her heart stifle. In it there were tears for the courage of ordinary people, hot rage against the disturbers of their lives. The Frenchman was right: it was too much. The singer's voice dimmed, sweetly lingering:—

Que ce refrain ne vous remaine:
Mais où sont les neiges d'antan!

Richard's hand lay on her arm. "Steady," he said, "steady." There was something as well as gentleness in his voice. So he had seen the man, or hadn't he? She had no idea of the time. Perhaps they had failed. A moment of panic seized her. But Richard appeared calm. His eyes told her nothing was wrong, only to be prepared.

"I am afraid we must leave soon," he explained to the others. A chorus of genial protests rose.

"Then you must come back often. To this table," said the large Frenchman. "Let us drink to this." They lifted their glasses.

Frances suddenly said, "To all men of good will, who live and let live. And perdition to their enemies, breeders of hate and destruction." She was going to weep after all. Oh hell! . . . They drank. The good-bys were over. Richard led the way. The man from the Café de la Paix had just three minutes' start.

Others had begun to go too. A few late-comers were just entering. The little entrance hall was jammed. They made their way through with difficulty. Richard had got his hat, with the help of the man in shirt sleeves. He spoke for a moment to Madame. Still no one came. They left, as slowly as would seem natural, but the man had completely disappeared. They went down the steep steps. It had begun to rain, and the doorkeeper put up his enormous umbrella for them as they waited for a taxi. Richard swore softly. Frances knew then that something had gone wrong. He fished in his pocket for a tip for the doorkeeper, who was showing them his poems which he had printed on single sheets for sale.

And then the door behind them opened, and there was a path of light over the wet pavement. It was the man in shirt sleeves.

"Monsieur has left behind his book." He handed something to Richard.

"Oh, yes," said Richard. He thought quickly. "Careless of me. Where did I drop it?" It was a small book and fitted into his pocket neatly.

"In the hall when you spoke to Madame, and bought some cigarettes. The gentleman behind you saw it fall."

"Well, thank you very much," began Richard, but the man had given an easy wave of his hand and was already back in the shelter of the doorway. Again the street was in darkness; a taxicab had halted on the slope of cobblestones, and the red gnome was shutting the door. Richard leaned forward to give the taxi-driver their address. He noticed that more guests were leaving Le Lapin Agile. They stood grouped round the lighted doorway, and hesitated before the wet pavement. The man from the Café de la Paix was there among them. He might have been with the others, or he might have been alone. But one thing, anyway, thought Richard as the taxi skidded on the greasy streets: no one could say that he had been with the Myles'.

When they reached their room, Richard threw the book on the bed and went into the bathroom. Frances began to undress. She was determined she would wait for her cue. Inwardly, she was annoyed with herself. She had missed everything. She had been so interested in the people at their table that she had almost forgotten about the man, and she hadn't even seen him. She guessed that Richard was satisfied anyway, or he wouldn't be whistling. He undressed quickly, and sat on the edge of the bed as he set the small traveling clock's alarm for half-past six.

"We can always sleep in the train," he said philosophically, and picked up the book curiously. He hadn't even noticed that she had done his packing for him this afternoon when he made a tour of the chief Paris stations. (There were only three ways by which they would probably leave Paris: either by the north or by the south or by the east; and Richard had said it was just as well to know the early-morning express trains which left these stations.) But Frances had been mistaken. . . .

"Did you have a nice afternoon?" He nodded to the suitcases and grinned.

"Thank you, darling. Did you have a nice walk?" There was almost too much sweet solicitude in her voice.

Richard looked up quickly. "Come off it, Frances. You know I told you to leave my stuff."

"Someone had to . . ."

"My poor put-upon wife." He drew her down onto the bed and rolled her between the sheets. Frances began to laugh. It was no good harboring righteous indignation: not with Richard.

He picked up the book again. "Do you mind if I read in bed?"

"Not if you talk first; I'm too sleepy to wait until you've finished reading. I'm almost bursting with curiosity."

Richard was looking at the book in a puzzled way. "Yes, I may take quite a time to get through this." He held it out so that the title was towards her. Frances looked at it with a mixture of amazement and excitement. It was a guide to Southern Germany.

Richard kicked off his slippers and slid in beside Frances. His voice dropped naturally. "You didn't see him? He was there all right. Sorry to hurry you away, but if he didn't mean to get in touch with us inside the room, the only other alternative was for us to follow him out. He left on the dot of two. Then I lost him, or I thought I did. I had been expecting something unusual to happen. This book was the only thing that did. It's it—or nothing."

"And if you don't find any information there?"

"We are completely and beautifully stuck."

Frances adjusted herself comfortably for sleep. "Darling, you had better begin. It looks an all-night job." She yawned heartlessly and closed her eyes.

Richard settled the lamp beside the bed to suit him, and opened the book. It seemed a new edition. He began at the first blank pages, and examined each successive page carefully for any markings. His care was rewarded.

There was a small lightly penciled star opposite one of the sections in the contents list following the large map, title page and two introductions. It was the section on Nürnberg. There were still two other pencil markings on the list of contents; one was a small horizontal stroke, the other a vertical one. Star first, obviously, thought Richard and turned to the pages on Nürnberg.

The description of Nürnberg followed the usual thorough pattern. It led off with stations and hotels and other helps to tourists. Richard examined the small print carefully. There were so many helpful hints to tired travelers after each entry, so many abbreviations of map references and prices enclosed in neat brackets. It made finicky reading. A careful glance at a page wasn't enough. Richard groaned and started at the beginning of the page again. His eye-straining concentration was rewarded by the time he got to the section on tramways. Route 2 seemed interesting: from Gustav-Adolf-Strasse *via* Plärrer, Lorenzkirche, Marientor, Marienstrasse to Dutzendteich. A small horizontal line was neatly penciled before Marienstrasse. With so many brackets and hyphens and commas and colons mixed into the text, the line was scarcely noticeable. The marking connected with the pencil line in the list of contents. Nürnberg, Marienstrasse, horizontal line. He turned back to the contents page. The horizontal mark there lay beside Augsburg.

He studied Augsburg as he had done Nürnberg. Hotels, restaurants . . . He read on carefully, but it wasn't until he came to the historical details about the city that he made any further advance. There, among the early benefactors, was the name of one Anton Fugger (1495-1560). He liked the name of Anton Fugger, especially with that neat vertical line just in front of the A.—Nürnberg, Marienstrasse, Anton Fugger, vertical line. He turned quickly back to the contents list. It was difficult to keep his excitement down. He forced himself not to be too confident. The vertical line marked Heidelberg.

This time, the information began with the air service and railway station. His eyes might have begun to tire with the strain, or perhaps he was too excited, or perhaps it was sleep. He knew he was jumping words. Frances slept comfortably beside him. He looked at the alarm, and checked it unbelievingly with his watch. It was nearly half-past five. There was no time to waste. He groaned again, and began to read, with his fist pressed hard against his chin. The discomfort checked that seductive idea of sleep.

He read on. Suddenly he sat up. It fitted in. God, it fitted in. He looked again: *Archæological Institute, free on*—yes, that was the penciled star all right—*free on Wednesday and Saturday,* 11 A.M.–1 P.M. So there it was, in its neat circle: Nürnberg, Marienstrasse, Anton Fugger, free on Wednesday and Saturday from eleven until one o'clock. A telephone book in Nürnberg would probably give the number of Fugger's house in Marienstrasse. But how to identify themselves when they met Herr Fugger? There must be some other clue. There had been no writing on the title page. What about a colophon? Failing anything there, he would have to examine the book right through perhaps in Nürnberg itself. But among the last blank pages he found two things. One was a red-rose petal, neatly pressed and pasted onto the paper. On the back of the page there were some music-notes, roughly jotted down in pencil after a treble clef. He whistled the notes to himself. The simple tune was vaguely familiar. All the notes were of the same value; it was this which had made the song seem vague at first. But it now was clearly recognizable. He relaxed back on his pillow and smiled amiably at the ceiling. He had forgotten about sleep. In any case, Frances would have to be wakened in less than fifteen minutes. What he needed now was a tub and a shave.

The sound of the running water drew Frances gradually out of sleep. Slowly and then suddenly she realized she was alone. She awoke fully with a panic of fear.

"Richard," she began, "Richard . . ." and then connected the sound of running water with a bath. She was calm again as Richard came out of the bathroom, the towel draped round him with one end slung over his shoulder. He had a crisp, curling beard of shaving soap.

"The elder Cato," he announced, "come to reprimand a slothful wife."

Frances looked at him sadly.

"No response? Is it as bad as that?"

"Go away, darling. I love you, but not at this hour." She settled drowsily on her pillow.

"Not on this morning, you don't, my love." He heartlessly pulled the sheet off the bed. Frances looked resigned. She lowered her voice.

"Where are we going?"

Richard sat down beside her. "Nürnberg."

"You've been there."

"Yes. Wake up, Frances."

"I haven't."

"No."

Frances roused herself. "What else did you find out?"

"You are like a red red rose."

"Oh. . . . I'm *what?*"

"My love. So the notes say."

"Richard, there is something peculiarly horrible about you this morning. God, how I hate men when they are secretly elated." She looked sadly at her husband, and then she began to laugh.

"Good. So you like Cato at last?"

"It's your beard, my sweet." She giggled weakly. "It pops."

"What?"

"The soap bubbles," she began, "listen . . ." She smothered her laughter.

"Anything to cheer a girl up. Are you really awake now? Well, listen, Frances. Get dressed. Get everything collected. Then we pay the bill and depart at once for the station. I got the train information yesterday, so everything is simple."

Frances sobered up. Richard was in earnest now. "All right. What actually did you find out last night?"

Richard was noncommittal. "A name and address in a town and the time we might visit it. Also that your hat will still be worn, and the first seven notes of a song."

"My love is like a red, red rose?"

Richard nodded. "Come on; rise and shine."

He obviously did not want to tell her any more than that, decided Frances as she bathed and dressed quickly, and packed away the final odds and ends. Richard was ready before she had put on her hat. He had finished writing the labels on the suitcases. Frances saw their name followed by the words *Passenger to Nice.* The room, stripped of their belongings, looked colorless in spite of the wallpaper. It was just another hotel bedroom.

The dark-haired, sallow chambermaid came in at half-past twelve. They were generally out by that time. The room looked empty. She had a sudden suspicion. Yes, she was right, they were not only out but gone. The boy who brought up the breakfast trays was whistling in the corridor. She ran to the door.

"Well, I see they have left. It is a bit sudden, isn't it? They must have been early."

"Yes. They didn't have breakfast. Pierre was downstairs on duty when they left."

"They are lucky, wandering about like that with no work to do. Did they go back to England?"

"Pierre said the labels were for Nice, and Michel drove them to the station."

"Nice? Well, some people have all the luck."

She waited for the boy to leave the corridor, and then she want downstairs. She searched for Michel before she slipped into the phone box. It was risky, if Madame saw her—but she couldn't wait until she was off duty. Fortunately this corner of the hall was dark, and she kept her voice low.

"Gone this morning. Gare de Lyon. For Nice. Nothing out of usual last night." Well, that was that nice little fee earned.

When they arrived at Gare de Lyon, Richard paid the taxi-driver, Michel, as he directed the porter to the train for Nice. They were very early, the porter said. In that case, they would leave their bags at the left-luggage office while they had breakfast. Richard had the satisfaction of seeing the naïvely inquisitive Michel—it was part of his friendly interest—drive away. The porter was glad enough to have such a short trip. He departed with his tip, well-pleased. In ten minutes, Frances and Richard returned for their luggage with another porter. This time they drove to the Gare du Nord. Frances looked at Richard in the taxi, as he changed the labels on the suitcases. He was smiling broadly.

"I do believe you enjoy this," she said in amazement.

He laughed. "What about you?"

"I'm hungry."

"Well, we can have breakfast on the train. We'll travel luxuriously and get some sleep before Strasbourg."

As Richard had predicted, they breakfasted well. Frances watched him in the dining car with amusement.

"Every moment you look more and more like a cat before a dish of cream." Richard gave a laugh which degenerated into a yawn.

He said, "Well, I feel something is making sense. I'll tell you all about it as soon as we have finished our visit. Let's go back to the compartment."

"And sleep."

"I'll have a pipe, first."

Frances thought this strange. Richard didn't usually smoke a pipe until after lunch. However, back in the empty compartment she understood. Out of certain pages in the guidebook which he had studied last night he made very efficient lighters. When all that remained of them was curled fragments of charred paper, he threw the expurgated book out of the window. It landed satisfactorily in a broad irrigation ditch. Richard watched it disappear, and then relaxed in his corner, stretching his legs. He gave Frances a satisfied smile.

"Everything all right with you?" he asked.

She nodded.

"Good. Everything's all right with me." His eyes closed. "Sorry," he added, his voice fading.

Frances looked at the trees and the fields and the sky. The express devoured the miles. Someone, she thought, ought to stay awake. But the journey was completely uneventful and, apart from an inner excitement at crossing the frontier, it was as dull as the scenery in the last stages of their travels. Once the minor thrills at Strasbourg had passed—when the engine had been changed for a (no doubt) superior German model, when the carriages had the last French dust swept from them efficiently and contemptuously by a squad of German cleaners, when their bags and money and passport had been thoroughly examined—there only remained the sagging feeling of relief. By the time they reached Nürnberg, Frances was cross and tired. She was resigned to a holiday in which the main excitement would merely be a succession of tensions. Richard was resigned to the fact that so far their luck had been almost too good to last.

It was very late when they did arrive in Nürnberg. Frances waited at the entrance to the Hauptbahnhof and stared across the warm darkness of the enormous square. Richard had told her that the old town lay beyond. Its lights were few. It seemed already asleep within its walls.

The porter had found them a taxi, at last. Richard gave the driver the name of the hotel. The driver looked at them. His face was large and round and expressionless.

"It isn't here, any more," he said.

The porter was listening. "The Königshof is near the same place. It is highly esteemed," he volunteered.

"All right, then," said Richard, "the Königshof."

They sat in silence during the short journey to the hotel.

"You could have walked," said the driver, as they got out of the taxi. He seemed as if he disapproved of their extravagance.

Richard made no reply.

"Did you know the Goldner Hahn well?" the driver asked suddenly.

"I stayed there in '32. What happened to it?"

The man was silent.

"What happened to it?" Richard asked again.

The man hesitated. "Oh—they went away." His voice was as expressionless as his face. Richard noted Frances' speculative interest. He knew what she was thinking.

She was still silent when they reached their room. It was warm inside; the massive furniture made it feel still warmer. She opened a window and looked out into the Königstrasse. The houses had high steep roofs, some of them pitted with attic windows, while others turned their gable ends to the street. This was better, this was more like what she had imagined. She remained standing at the window, watching the moonlight on the roofs. When she moved at last, she found that Richard had unpacked some things for her. She smiled her thanks.

"Cheer up, old girl. You'll feel better in the morning," he said.

I hope, she added to herself.

But when Tuesday morning came and the constant hum of traffic outside their window awoke Frances, she did feel better. Richard was already dressed, and reading his Baedeker. They had breakfast in their room, and discussed their plans as they ate. Richard advocated the minimum of unpacking. No one noticed what you wore here, anyway.

While Frances had slept, he had decided to work in an opposite direction from their Paris experience. Instead of waiting a few days until Saturday came, they would call on Fugger tomorrow, and then they could spend three or four days playing the tourist in Nürnberg. But to Frances, he only remarked that today they could explore the old town, and leave the Castle and the Museum and the churches for the rest of the week.

"Unless I fry to death," Frances said. She looked out at the bright sunlight in the street, promising heat even at this early hour. Resignedly, she chose the thinnest town dress she had. Richard approved of the effect when she was at last ready, but he also looked at his wrist watch just slightly more pointedly than was necessary.

"Brute," said Frances, with her sweetest smile, and led the way out of the room.

There was that feeling of continual coming and going in the entrance hall which characterizes a busy town hotel. Just as well for us, thought Richard. Frances and he were only two more in the constant stream. The other guests were mostly German. They were serious-looking men and women, who walked quickly, as if they had important business to attend to. Perhaps they had. He noted the number of uniforms of one kind or another, and even—astounding thing—quick precise salutes and the violent two-worded greeting. It was astounding because it was so theatrical, so incongruous in a peaceful hotel lobby. He caught Frances' eye, and they both smiled gently. He imagined himself coming into a lecture hall at Oxford, surveying the rows of young faces before him, making a rigid salute and barking out "God save the King" in a parade-ground voice, before turning to his lecture on the metaphysical poets. He knew what his undergraduates would do. They would telephone anxiously for a doctor, two male nurses and a strait-jacket—and they would be right.

As they reached the front door, Frances paused to look at the roughly paved street and then at her shoes.

"I thought the heels were a mistake," said Richard.

Frances looked stubborn. "Well, if I change into my hiking shoes, I'll have to change my whole outfit. I'll manage."

A young man had come out of the hotel door; he halted as he heard Frances' voice, and looked at her, giving what Hollywood has perfected as the "double take." Then the pavement was crowded with the stamp of heavy boots. Frances was separated from Richard by a wall of brown shirts. She stepped backwards to the safety of the doorway, lost her balance and felt her heel sink cruelly into something soft. The young man winced, but stood his ground.

"I'm so sorry," Frances said and removed her heel. "*Verzeihung. . .*" That must have been a sore one, she thought.

"Pardon me," the young man said, lifting his hat and trying to walk away without limping.

Frances' handbag seemed to be infected with her embarrassment: it slipped from under her arm, and opened as it reached the pavement. The last uniform had passed, and in the temporary lull Richard bent down for the bag, and jammed the odds and ends back into place. The powder case rolled towards the man, who had turned as Frances had said "Damn." He picked it up, and handed it silently with a twist of a smile to Richard.

"Thank you," said Richard, and he meant it.

"You're welcome." He raised his hat again and walked quickly away, as if afraid of what Frances would do next. Richard looked down at her and shook his head.

"You surpassed yourself there, my sweet Dora. Now if you would really like to go somewhere, we can start on the old town. This way." He caught her arm as she moved off in the wrong direction.

"He was rather nice-looking. American, wasn't he? I liked his voice."

"Yes; yes; and rich baritone," Richard answered absent-mindedly. He was looking for a place to cross the street.

The exploration of the old town took care of the morning. Two o'clock found them exhausted in a beer restaurant, Richard having decided that the heat of the day called for a liquid lunch. Frances, atoning for the slow progress caused by her shoes—she *had* managed, but at a price—sat in sweet martyrdom as she talked and laughed. It was strange how the smell of beer clung to the room. The coffee did not taste very much like coffee, but she sipped it and kept her eyes off the beer mugs. She had never liked the stuff; from now on she would hate it. Even the table smelled of beer. Richard was asking her a question. How would she like a tram ride? Heavens, there was nothing she wanted less.

"Must we?" she asked as pathetically as possible.

Richard nodded. "I'm afraid so."

She lowered her voice. "Telephone book?"

"No good. I had a look at it when you were powdering your nose."

"Nothing there at all?"

"Nothing."

Frances resigned herself to the inevitable. "Well, let's go now, and get it over."

Richard finished his beer slowly. It was a good thing that one of them was having fun, thought Frances. Then she began to wonder. She had been in such a constant depression ever since they had arrived in Nürnberg. It was as if Gibbon's idea of the Middle Ages had interpreted itself here in the tortuous streets, the thick walls, the narrow crowding houses. A triumph of religion and barbarism.

"Well?" said Richard.

"I thought I liked Gothic."

"You like it spiritual and aspiring, my sweet."

"Perhaps it is that. Tell me, Richard, was Gibbon ever in Nürnberg?"

Richard laughed suddenly. Curious faces turned to look at them. They waited until the interest had subsided, and then they left.

"We must take a No. 2 tram, but God knows in which direction," said Richard.

"Going east or west?"

"Roughly east."

"Then it's this side."

A tramcar was approaching; there was no time for any argument. He followed Frances aboard with some misgivings, and then watched her trying to appear oblivious as the conductor agreed that they would be driven along the Marienstrasse.

"On a moor, or a hill or some place like that," said Richard, "but in a strange muddled-up town . . . It's quite beyond me how you know these things."

Frances relented. "I cannot tell a lie, darling. You saw the Lorenz Church?"

"Well, yes. We were just beside it."

"Well what way does a church point?"

"East, of course. . . . Upon my Sam." He grinned. "You know, Frances, just at the stage when a man thinks women have no brains, they confound him by some low cunning like that. Go on, have your laugh. You deserve it."

As they approached the Marientor, he pressed her hand.

"Keep your eyes open," was all he said. Frances remembered the name he had told her last night. They sat in silence, watching the shops and business houses, as the lumbering tramcar clanked its slow way along the Marienstrasse. They were now in the newer part of the town—the street was broader, and the names on the shops were less easy to see. Frances guessed that Richard had the idea that Fugger might be the name of some business; it was the one chance. For if there had been no Fugger of Marienstrasse in the telephone directory, then the only other way to find Mr. Fugger was either to make enquiries at the post office, which would be dangerously stupid, or to explore the Marienstrasse themselves. There must be a name to see, somewhere, or else no one could possibly get in touch with the retiring Mr. Fugger.

The tram had come to the end of the Marienstrasse. They had seen nothing which could help them.

"We'll have to walk. Sorry, Fran; you must be tired." They got off the car at the next stop, and started back towards their street.

"We'll try this side again," said Richard, and took Frances' arm. They walked slowly along, and covered two thirds of the street. Then Frances suddenly felt Richard's hand tighten. They stopped, as they had done at half a dozen other points in the street. It was a small bookseller's shop with a narrow window space and doorway, completely overshadowed by the larger, more prosperous buildings on either side. They looked at the books displayed in the window. They were mostly curiosities, with the title pages open to show the brown spots of age. There were also some music books. One, a collection of songs, was lying open.

"Very interesting," Richard said, and they walked on. He hoped Frances wouldn't look at the sign above the window. She didn't. It was of no help, anyway. It merely said BUCHHANDLUNG in faded letters; but above the door had been small, neat, white lettering: A. FUGGER.

Next morning they left their hotel at half-past nine, and began their search through the bookshops of Nürnberg. Richard wanted a certain collection of early German lyrics. The two bookshops which they first tried were very modern; they specialized in books with streamlined printing and magnificent photographs, or in imposing editions of carefully selected authors. In the second shop, the assistant shook his head decisively. The only place they would be likely to find such a book might be in the smaller, second-hand dealers'. They thanked him, and walked towards the Marienstrasse. It was just eleven o'clock as they reached the small bookshop with the brown-spotted title pages displayed in the window. Richard noted that the books had been changed since yesterday, except for the collection of old songs, and that it had been moved to another corner of the window.

Inside the shop, there was the sleepy, dusty feeling which its outside had promised. The bookshelves ran ceiling height around the walls, and there were books overflowing onto the two large tables which crowded the narrow room.

At a corner of one table, a girl with glasses was working with scissors and paste. She had a white face, and dull blue eyes, and her hair was tightened back so ruthlessly that it hurt Frances to look at it. She looked up expectantly as the door creaked shut behind them. Frances had the feeling that the girl was disappointed. She left her work reluctantly, and came forward with no smile on her pale lips. No, she didn't think they had any such edition. She had never heard of it. As she made out that they were foreigners, she asserted her knowledge still more: she was sure, absolutely sure that such an edition did not exist. She neither offered to verify it from any catalogue, nor moved over to the poetry section to find anything else which might interest Richard. He exchanged glances with Frances, and then he searched in one of his pockets and brought out a small clipping. He handed it to the girl.

"The edition does exist," he said, as politely as he could. "Teubner printed it in Leipzig in 1836."

The girl took the sheet of paper, and held it without looking at it. The truth is, thought Frances, she doesn't want us here at all.

Richard raised his voice. "Is there anyone here, then, who *does* know about German lyric poetry?" The girl's face was still expressionless, but her eyes shifted for one moment to a door in the back wall of the shop.

"We haven't got it," she said.

"I'm sorry," said Richard. Frances knew by the cold edge in his voice that he was angry. She moved over to the pile of books on the nearest table, and lifted a volume. If it came to a test of endurance, she was determined to outlast the girl.

"Music, here," she said with charming surprise. She kept her voice as lighthearted as she could, and gave the silent girl a dazzling smile.

"You don't mind if I look through these? Thank you so much." Without waiting for an answer, Frances proceeded to blacken her white gloves on the dusty covers.

The door at the back of the shop opened. A short, stout man entered. He was in his shirt sleeves, and mopped his brow with a handkerchief. He had shut the door behind him, but not before Richard had smelled something singeing, something burning. Paper, could it be?

The small man looked at the girl in some irritation as he said, "I thought I heard customers." He turned his back on her abruptly and listened to Richard's question. The girl picked up her scissors again, and went on with her work, but Frances noticed that she made only a pretense of being busy.

The bookseller was interested. "That was a very fine collection," he said. "I had a copy at one time, but I believe it was bought. Over here I have some of the older editions of lyrics; I've so many books I sometimes forget what I have." He pointed to the farthest bookshelves. His eyes were fixed for a few moments on the red rose of Frances' hat.

She said, "I am very interested in some of these old song collections."

She waved her hand towards the music table. The bookseller looked at her gloves in dismay.

"But the books are filthy," he cried. "Ottilie, where is the duster?" Ottilie mumbled something about the next room.

"Get it then," he said sharply. Ottilie went reluctantly towards the back door.

"Helpful creature," said Richard, more to himself than to the others. Frances had already picked up a large green volume, which she had noted particularly. SONGS OF ALL NATIONS read the fading gold letters. She turned quickly to the page which the index had numbered. She smiled to the bookseller.

"You are very kind," she said, and smoothed down the page with the back of her hand. She held the book flat on the table so that both men could see the song title clearly. The bookseller's eyes flickered as they read "My love is like a red, red rose" *(translated from the English).* And then he smiled gently, his round fat face creasing with genial puckers. He mopped his brow again, and Frances closed the book carefully. She had just replaced it exactly when Ottilie was with them again. She had come back quickly indeed, for such a slow-moving person. She shook her head disapprovingly over the soiled gloves.

She actually spoke. "It would have been better to take off your gloves," she said.

"But my hands would have become dirty."

"It is easier to wash hands than gloves."

"But I couldn't put my gloves on again, over dirty hands," explained Frances gently. Ottilie shrugged her shoulders, and then suddenly became aware of the fact that the two men had gone to the far corner of the room. Frances hardheartedly pointed out a book to dust. It was a curiosity on early Church music.

"Do you like to sing?"

The girl said, "Sometimes." She looked as if she were going to follow the men.

"Do you like Mozart or do you prefer Wagner?" Frances continued relentlessly.

"Wagner." If eyes could poison, I am already writhing on the ground, thought Frances.

At that moment, the bookseller was shaking his head sadly. His voice was clearer. "No, I am afraid it's gone. Ottilie, do you remember a small book bound in red calf which I bought from Professor Wirt?" Ottilie shook her head too; she made a movement as if to go over to where the men stood.

"Have you got any editions of *Lieder* for a soprano voice?" cut in Frances with her disarming smile. Ottilie threw one last glance at the bookseller. The words "edition," "Leipzig," "difficulty" reached them. It sounded the usual business talk. Ottilie searched for the songs. Despite the foreigner's smile, there was a certain firmness in her tone of voice. Ottilie knew that type of customer. The quickest way to get rid of them was to find what they asked for; they knew what they wanted. If only she had recognized the type when they entered the shop, they would have been away by this time. But they had seemed easy to deal with, judging from their appearances. She found two editions, and watched Frances look through the contents with interest. Her last suspicion melted as the men came back to the table.

Richard addressed Frances. He spoke in English, carefully, noting the sudden gleam of concentration in Ottilie's eyes. He chose simple words, which would be understood by anyone who had had English at school.

"He cannot find the book. He must order it from Leipzig. Perhaps it may not be there. It may take time to find it elsewhere. It is a pity."

Frances recovered herself, and said gravely and just as clearly, "I am sorry. Perhaps we should go to another bookshop." She was enjoying herself immensely.

Richard returned to German. "My wife suggests another shop. Would you be so good as to advise us?" The bookseller smiled benignly. He dictated two addresses to Ottilie, who wrote them down, and Richard put the slip of paper in his pocket.

"If you cannot find it," the bookseller said, "then come and see us again. If I am not here, then Ottilie will take the order." He was looking speculatively over Frances' shoulder, out into the street. "Good day," he added suddenly, and walked with quick short steps to the back room.

The abrupt ending startled Richard. He saw a look of warning in his wife's eye. She had either noticed or felt something. As Ottilie wrapped one of the songbooks for Frances, they made their way to a bookcase near the door. Richard observed that the girl was glancing at her wrist watch, that she was taking little interest in tying up the parcel. As Richard handed her the money, she seemed as if she were not even counting it. . . . And then the front door swung open. It opened with such terrific violence that the hinges shrieked a protest which made Frances jump.

Three large men strode in, nearly upsetting Ottilie. Richard could have sworn that there was almost an approach to a smile on her face. She gestured quietly towards the back door. The three men strode on. Their boots hypnotized Frances. They moved as if they belonged to the same body. They drew their revolvers. The leader turned the handle of the door, and then kicked it open. But there were no shots, no voices. Frances found herself breathing again.

She looked with just sufficient amazement at the girl. "What's wrong?" she asked. "Burglars?" The girl gave her first real smile. Frances watched its contempt and was satisfied.

The men filed out of the back room. Their self-assurance was replaced by bad temper.

"Where is he?" the leader snapped. The girl's smile faded. Contempt gave way to fear.

"He went in there." She pointed to the back room. "There is no way out."

"There is a window, fool. Who are these?" He nodded towards Frances and Richard.

"Customers." The girl was sullen in her disappointment.

"What is your name? What do you want here?" He fired questions at Richard.

Richard looked surprised, and then let the right tone of slight annoyance creep into his voice as he answered. Frances registered appropriate amazement but she left everything to Richard. This was his show, and he was doing remarkably well as the innocent bystander. He was explaining at some length that they had tried two other bookshops and had failed in their search for this book; that they had been directed to the smaller secondhand dealers; that the book was still unfound; that the assistant in this shop had been good enough to write down the names of two other shops where . . . He at last found the slip of paper with Ottilie's sharply pointed script, and handed it to the leader of the men. Ottilie, on the verge of tears, verified the statement. It suddenly dawned on Frances that A. Fugger was gaining some very valuable minutes. It seemed to dawn on the leader too, or perhaps his first suspicions were fading. He impatiently interrupted Richard's description of the book.

"I shall leave this man with you to get further particulars. I have work to do." He stepped back, brought his heels sharply together, and raised his arm. He barked out his war cry. Now we're sunk, thought Frances. She saw Richard stiffen slightly, and then relax again as he gave an inclination of his head and said, "Good day."

The German trooper raised his voice. "I gave you our German greeting!"

"And I gave you our English one." Richard's voice was very quiet. "That is only politeness."

At the word *politeness,* the German looked searchingly at Richard, and then at Frances. They held their expression, and returned look for look. There was a moment's tension, and then the two uniforms had marched away, leaving the third to produce a notebook and pencil. It was a good sign that they hadn't been taken to some kind of police station, thought Frances, and touched the wooden table.

It was all over in ten minutes. The Nazi snapped his book shut. They all made such businesslike gestures, thought Richard irritably. Did it really prove greater efficiency to walk with a resounding tread, to open doors by practically throwing them off their hinges, to shut an insignificant notebook with an imitation thunder clap? Probably not at all, but —and here was the value of it—it made you look, and therefore feel, more efficient. The appearance of efficiency could terrify others into thinking you were dynamic and powerful. But strip you of all the melodrama of uniforms and gestures, of detailed régime worked out to the *n*th degree, of supervision and parrot phrases and party clichés, and then real efficiency could be properly judged. It would be judged by your self-discipline, your individual intelligence, your mental and emotional balance, your grasp of the true essentials based on your breadth of mind and depth of thought. Richard studied the young man opposite him. Viewed dispassionately, he was tall and thin; he was already going bald; his chin was weak despite the poised pout of the lips; but whatever strength his chin lacked, his eyes with their intense stare sought to gain. It was a pity the effect was so like that of a goldfish.

"That is all," the Nazi said. "We shall find you at the hotel if there is anything else we need to know."

Frances leaned over the table and fixed him with wide-open, innocent eyes. "Why?" she asked gently.

"Why?"

"Yes. Why? We are English visitors, we visit your bookshops, we buy a book, and then you ask us questions and questions because the man who owned this shop was a burglar."

"A burglar?"

"Well, don't tell me he was a *murderer!*" Frances was shocked. The trooper looked perplexed.

"I mean," explained Frances as if to a child, "in England the police come to arrest a man if he is suspected of a crime like theft or murder."

The man exchanged a look of amusement with Ottilie. Then he said stiffly, "This is not England, thank God."

"Quite," said Richard.

Frances was keeping her jaw clenched; keep me from laughing out loud, she prayed, especially when it comes. It came. The arm shot out, the heels clicked, the magic words were invoked. The Myles' bowed and said "Good day," gravely.

When they left A. Fugger's bookshop, Ottilie had again picked up her scissors and was bending over the table.

"Charming wench," said Richard. "One of the higher types, I suppose, of Nordic womanhood."

Frances had her own private joke. "No one told her to stop her work and so she goes on. How long will it take before she realizes that she is already out of a job? Richard, if ever a sailor needed grog, that sailor's me."

They walked back to the old town at a medium pace. They didn't see anyone following them, but probably someone would. Richard, continuing his role of the wandering scholar, discovered another small bookshop with much secondhand material. The assistant, a pleasant young man with really gentle manners—Frances sat on a chair and watched him with a mixture of pleasure and relief—promised to make enquiries for the book, after Richard had spent half an hour in the poetry section. He bade them good morning like a human being. In fact, thought Frances, he is the first really obviously human being I've met since I arrived here.

When they got to their hotel, Frances went upstairs to change her gloves. Richard sat in the entrance hall and looked through a Nürnberg paper. It seemed as if the inhuman Poles and the wicked Jews were behaving with abominable, not-to-be-tolerated cruelty to the Germans who were living in Poland. The editorial worked itself up into a fine lather. It made crude reading. By the time Frances came downstairs, he was very bored. It was not only crude, it was an insult to intelligence.

He looked at Frances, and was instantly aware that something had happened. The look she gave him was too intense. She surprised him by suddenly standing on her toes and kissing him; but it brought her close enough to him so that he could hear the word "Searched," spoken with motionless lips. So they had taken advantage of their slow return to the hotel, as he had hoped they might. He returned her kiss and said, "Good."

Frances saw the American, whose foot she had mutilated yesterday morning, halt in amazement. On an impulse, she smiled to him. He reddened as he raised his hat and turned hastily away. Perhaps he didn't like to be found looking quite so amazed.

"Let's eat," she suggested. "I'm ravenous. Only, not a sausage place." She shuddered. Last night's dinner had been at one of the sausage showplaces, small and amusing, except that the whole menu was devoted to sausage. It was strange how her mind, as well as her stomach, rebelled when the choice was sausage or sausage or sausage.

"I'd like an omelet, and not one with apricot jam in it either, and fruit, and some hock, and coffee such as it is," she decided.

"I must say that for someone who comes from England you are pretty snooty about coffee."

"Well, it is even worse than ours, and that's something."

They found a restaurant near at hand, where they had their late lunch. They ate it leisurely, and sat smoking their cigarettes long after Richard had paid the bill. The room had emptied, much to the annoyance of two uniformed men who were seated in one corner. As Richard said, it made things look a bit too obvious. The men may have come to the same conclusion. At any rate, they rose at last with bad grace, and on their way out clumped past the table where Frances and Richard sat. Richard had a Baedeker opened in front of him—lying between his elbows as he leaned forward to light his fifth cigarette. As the men passed, he looked up and spoke. Would they be so good as to help him? He and his wife were strangers, and wondered if it were possible to explore the charms of Dutzendteich this afternoon, or would it be better to make a day's excursion? The men were obviously at a loss for words. One said yes, the other said no, and then they both left the table.

"Well, it might be better to see the Burg this afternoon, after all," said Richard. Even if the men couldn't understand any English, at least the clearly spoken *Burg* would stick.

Frances watched their progress to the door. "They are phoning," she reported.

"Time to leave," said Richard, and tucked the Baedeker prominently under his arm. They walked quickly to the door, past the man at the public telephone and his worried companion. Frances gave him a sweet smile. She felt suddenly generous.

They entered a tramcar, at the Königstor, which carried them westwards and then northwards round the whole town. The heat was intense. Frances was glad of the open windows of the tram, which, as it moved, gave at least the impression of a breeze. They skirted the thick walls and their broad dry moat, and at last reached the Castle. There were a number of visitors to the Burg. Frances and Richard mixed casually with them and made a leisurely tour of the grounds. They didn't look back once. Richard said it would make whoever was following them in whatever uniform happier. It would have been discouraging for them really if Frances had insisted on carrying out her idea of looking back every hundred yards, smiling broadly and waving a cheery hand. . . . And Richard didn't really mind being followed in this way. They had nothing to hide . . . now. He added to himself, if A. Fugger made it, that is.

Richard had left the Five-Cornered Tower to the last. He had a feeling that Frances might discover another allergy there. It was full of frightfulness, he remembered.

"Are you sure you really want to see this— It is rather monotonous, you know—" he asked as they reached the doorway. "There's no law compelling us to go in."

Frances looked surprised. "Why not? It's only an old prison tower with a torture chamber. I've been to the Tower of London, and the Conciergerie . . ."

Richard shook his head doubtfully. "This one could teach those places a thing or two." But he had only piqued her interest. Frances had already entered. Richard bought the tickets, and followed, with a shrug of his shoulders.

He had been right, after all, but Frances wouldn't admit it at first. Halfway through the tour of the long rooms, she began to move more quickly as the exhibits became more diabolic. Her eyes viewed unbelievingly the directions for extracting the greatest amount of pain which were hung on the wall above each instrument of torture. They were printed in black-letter for the most part, and were complete with diagrams, in case the minute detail of text wasn't sufficiently clear to ensure the fullest effects.

She suddenly spoke. "The cold-blooded beasts." Her voice was a mixture of incredulity and disgust. A tall young man, standing morosely before an intricate object of spiked iron, whose function had been to pierce and tear and burn all at the same time, turned as he heard her voice. There was an expression of fellow-feeling on his face, followed by a look of recognition. Frances, whose remarks had been for home consumption, stopped in embarrassment. The man looked as if he would speak, and then didn't. Frances felt he was leaving it to her.

"How's your foot?" she asked. "I'm really sorry, and I assure you it isn't a habit of mine."

"That's all right." His face relaxed, but he still didn't smile with any enthusiasm. "Enjoying this?" he added, with just the right note in his voice.

Richard grinned; he liked this man. "They made it quite an art, didn't they? The pages from the *Torturer's Handbook* are peculiarly thorough," he said, and won a smile from the American. Something caught the man's eye at the other end of the room, and a slight frown appeared; but it was gone so suddenly that Frances wondered if she was beginning to imagine things. She looked carelessly in the same direction. There were two uniformed men, who seemed to be interested in them rather than in the exhibits. She let her eyes pass through them, then over them, and then on to a German family who were arguing over one of the printed directions with naïve interest.

"Is there much more of this?" she asked.

The man said, "Piles of the stuff. I've just taken a look into the tower place and gotten a cold welcome from the Iron Maiden. There are several models of her."

"She would seem mild after these. At least she would kill you, and not turn you into a piece of gibbering flesh," said Frances. She turned to Richard. "You win. I thought I could manage historical objectivity. After all, I was brought up on Foxe's *Book of Martyrs* . . . But where's the way out?"

The American smiled. "It's past the tower dungeons. You can't escape them."

Frances looked at him. "You are in league with my husband. Our name is Myles, by the way. Would you come and have something to drink? I'm parched."

The American gravely acknowledged that he was parched too, and he knew of a good beer place just down the hill. They left the Five-Cornered

Tower, to the amazement of the man on duty at the exit door, who pointed out to them that they had only seen half of the display. Outside, it was pleasant to feel the warm sunshine, and see the green trees and ordinary people looking neither efficient nor thorough. And then a detachment of troopers marched past them; actually, they were only a group of men going to some meeting, but they had chosen to march in military formation. Their faces were expressionless under their uniform caps. Frances felt her depression return. Men who marched like that, who dressed like that, whose faces held the blankness of concentration and dedication, were a menace, a menace all the more desperate because of the hidden threat.

"You are looking very solemn," said the American.

"I was thinking of icebergs. You know, one tenth above to impress you, and the rest beneath to terrify you."

"*If* you know the peculiarity of icebergs," said the American, with a quick glance at Frances. "There are still plenty of people who think there's very little of them under the water. But why did you come to Germany this year? I haven't met any English here so far. At first I thought you might be here to worship at the shrine, but you seem to have the wrong reactions for that."

Richard answered that. "Oh, the usual inquisitiveness. We wanted to see for ourselves. We haven't been in Germany proper since the new era got well under way. We thought this might be our last chance."

They had reached the Rathaus-Keller, and the American hadn't any opportunity for further questions until they were settled at a table, and beer was ordered for the men—Frances insisted on tea. She noted that her order gave the American some delight, although he really was very polite about trying to hide his amusement. I suppose I ought to play true to form, she thought, to keep up the national character. She had begun well with the big-footed note when she had trampled on him yesterday, and tea in the afternoon was another authentic touch; tonight, she really ought to ask him to dine with them, and wear a dinner dress. Only, Richard and she never traveled with dinner clothes; it would be such a pity to disappoint him. However, the American seemed less amused, and more convinced, when two hot cups of tea had produced more visible coolness than his two steins of beer. Frances caught his eye.

"There's method in our madness," she suggested, and noticed he looked a little disturbed, as if he had been found impolite. It was difficult talking to someone who didn't know you, especially when you both had a common language and thought that that made everything easy. There was always the chance that your words would be taken to mean too little, or too much. That was what made all the English-speaking peoples so damned touchy with each other. Someone who spoke a foreign language had more allowances made for him.

"By the way, we don't know your name, yet," Frances said. "We can't go on just calling you 'the American.' " The man smiled. Thank goodness, thought Frances, he gave up the idea that I was trying to reprimand him. He was searching in his pocketbook for a card.

"This makes it easier," he said. He was, they read, HENRY M. VAN CORTLANDT from High Tor, New York. He was, he said, a newspaperman, originally working in New York City, but now on an assignment in Europe looking for symptoms.

"War?" asked Richard.

"Well, perhaps that. What do you think?"

Frances looked at the well-cut features opposite her, and the well-brushed fair hair. The jaw was determined; the slightly drawn eyebrows gave a certain intensity. You would hardly notice the color of his eyes; it was as if the other features of his face overshadowed them. His skin was tanned—if it hadn't been tanned it might have seemed pale, even sallow. He had gone on talking without waiting for Richard's reply, and he talked well, with a fluency which showed he had either thought about his subject a lot or had already argued it into a neat pattern. As he talked, he smiled a good deal, showing very white, even teeth; but in repose, his mouth looked firm, even tight-lipped. Frances watched him as she listened to the well-tailored phrases. A very direct, a very controlled and a very impulsive young man.

"But surely you never took Munich seriously?" he was asking Richard.

And a rather disbelieving one, too, it seemed.

Frances spoke. "We were still at the stage of taking anything seriously or at the least hoping we could take it seriously, as long as the magic word of peace could be spoken. Until this spring. The march into Prague ended that coma."

Van Cortlandt shook his head. "Well, we never thought that in America."

"You mean you think we have been playing a kind of game? That we shall go on playing it, as long as we can keep ourselves out of war?"

"Well, if you put it so frankly, yes."

Frances leaned forward on her elbows. "Your President doesn't think so. I hear you've been calling him a warmonger because he really knows what's going on in Europe."

"Nice weather we've been having," suggested Richard. "Warm, though."

The American went on: "But Britain's policy for the last years . . ."

"I know," said Frances. "In America it is called isolationism, freedom from foreign entanglements, unwillingness to die on foreign fields. We've been trying all that. It hasn't worked. We admit it . . . we've come out of the ether . . ."

"And you're telling me that Britain is going to take off its nice clean coat and get its nose all bloodied up in defending Poland? What would you get out of it anyway?"

"A country fights for two main things, either for loot or for survival. We'll fight along with our friends for survival. The Axis is after loot. If Poland, or any other country, is attacked, then it is the signal for any nation who doesn't want to become a part of Germany to rouse itself. It may be the last chance."

Van Cortlandt smiled comfortingly. "Don't worry. I don't think you'll find your country at war. Your politicians will always see plenty of other chances."

"That's my main point. The politicians won't dare. The people are aroused now."

Van Cortlandt still looked unconvinced. "Well, that's a new one to me. We have some pretty swell news-hounds, and they nearly all scent out more appeasement."

"Their sense of smell has led them to the wrong lamp post this time. They will look very funny there, when the trouble starts."

"I tried the weather," said Richard, "and that wasn't much good. I think we'd be better talking about something else, for neither of you is convincing the other in the slightest, and we'll know soon enough which of you was nearer the truth. As Count Smorltork said to Mr. Pickwick, 'The word poltic surprises by himself.' Anyway, I have the unpleasant but increasing conviction that all of us who argue so much would be wiser if we learned to make aeroplanes or shoot a machine gun. That's only my academic point of view, of course. But that seems the only answer for certain people."

He nodded to a group of men in brown shirts at another table. "Now what about dinner?" he added.

Van Cortlandt rose. "Sorry, I've got to see a man."

Richard rose too. "We are sorry too. We shall see you again soon, sometime, I hope."

"Yes." The American's voice didn't seem overjoyed at the prospect. "Thanks for the beer. Good-by."

Frances looked after him sadly. "He really was so nice, you know, before he got caught up in his theories. I suppose if your country is three thousand or whatever it is miles away you can afford the luxury of pros and cons. I think you punctured him, someplace, Richard. He's probably saying we are one of the 'bloody English' at this moment."

"Nonsense. He handed criticism out. If you do that, you have also got to expect to take it. Anyway, hairsplittings are really becoming so very out of date. The time for theories is really past. But keep off politics, after this, Frances, even if you feel you have got something approaching an answer. What do you say about something to eat, and then a movie, and then bed?"

Frances nodded her approval. There was much she wanted to know about A. Fugger. She stopped worrying about van Cortlandt and began thinking of the little man who had walked with quick short steps into that back room. Had he got away? Could it be that the Nazis were already picking out each agent in the chain, or was A. Fugger wanted on another charge? They would find out, one way or another, but it would be unpleasant waiting.

Richard had looked round the large room. At a discreet distance, the two men who had visited the Five-Cornered Tower that afternoon were sitting at a table. They had become hungry, it seemed, and had just ordered food. Richard waited until the steaming plates were put in front of them, until they had taken their first mouthful.

"Now's the time, Frances." She abandoned A. Fugger, and followed her husband quickly to the door. He seemed amused about something. As they left the room, he turned back to see the two men rising angrily to their feet.

"Would you mind, Frances, if we went to the flicks first of all, and then ate when we came out? I think that would be an idea." Frances saw the gleam in his eye. There was a joke somewhere.

So they went to a picture house. After fifteen minutes, Richard decided he couldn't see through the large woman in front of them, so they moved quietly to different seats, behind their original places. Richard's joke seemed to be getting better and better.

As he explained to Frances in bed that night, "They were hungry and when we landed in the cinema, they might have gone out in relays for their dinner. Then we moved our seats, and they didn't notice it at first. It was pretty dark, you know. We were just sitting down behind them when they noticed we were no longer in our first seats. That was really funny. It was easy for them to find us again, as the place was almost empty, but for five minutes they had quite a bad time of it. That probably decided them to stay together, standing at the back of the theater in case we changed our minds again. I could feel them getting hungrier."

"Why didn't we lose them when we had the chance?"

"And make them realize that we disliked being followed? They'd interpret that as a guilty conscience. Better pretend that it seems very harmless and amusing, the kind of silly adventure which you like to tell your friends about when you get home."

But about A. Fugger he wouldn't say anything.

"The less you know from now on, the better for you, my sweet." And that was that.

It was Frances who lay awake tonight. She thought of the bookseller; of the tall American who had either been offended, or bored; of the constant rhythm of marching boots. When she fell asleep her thoughts were still with her, and chased her through the Five-Cornered Tower. Richard was beside her, for she spoke to him and heard him answer, but she couldn't see him. A. Fugger was there trying to show her the way out, but he spoke in a strange language and she kept straining to understand it. The American was there too, observing everything, but contenting himself with a sad smile when she took the wrong turning. It must have been the wrong turning although it had seemed the only right one, because then there was no way out, and she was looking at the Iron Maiden, and the face was that of the girl Ottilie, and the hands were real. The fingernails were long and pointed, and they were colored blood-red.

Richard watched Frances closely, next morning. She had drunk several cups of tea and smoked three cigarettes. He kept silent about last night. Whatever had disturbed her sleep would gradually lose its detail and, if he didn't emphasize it by referring to it, it might lose its importance and merge into the vagueness of dreams that are past. He thought of something to do which would be interesting without being exciting. They would have to spend at least one more day in this place, perhaps even two or three if it seemed a good thing to do.

He made his voice as normal as possible. "What about the Germanic Museum today? It should be innocuous, and you'll like the costume section. If you ever do more designing in Oxford, you may find some good ideas there. Better take your notebook and pencil."

Frances nodded absently; she was wondering when they might leave Nürnberg and where they would have to go. . . . And there was always the thought whether A. Fugger had escaped. If he had been caught, there would be, no doubt, some ingenious way of trying to make him talk. And yet, did any trusted agent, such as he must have been, ever talk? Weren't they chosen for their capacity to keep silent even under the greatest persuasion? But then, they were human beings too. Somehow, her notebook and designs for Oxford dramatics seemed very remote this morning. Richard's voice had been light, but the slight emphasis with which he clipped his words proved that he was not as carefree as he would have her believe. She decided wisely not to pester him with questions about their plans. He was probably completing them now.

The silence in which they traveled to the Museum bolstered up this idea in Frances' mind. Their two watchdogs attached themselves at a reasonable distance. It seemed as if it didn't matter if they were noticeable. Frances thought this over. They had been so very obviously under watchful eyes, and their room had been so very obviously searched. She came to the conclusion that this might be especially subtle technique. Perhaps Richard and she were to feel persecuted, intimidated, very much in the power of a mighty secret police. The very cold-bloodedness of this cat-and-mouse game was to make them leave Germany if they really were only harmless tourists. If they were less innocent than they seemed, then they might be trapped into making a mistake. As for the mistake which they might make . . . Frances couldn't think of any agent trying to get in touch with one of his men at this stage. He would be liable to lie low, and he would most certainly try to lose the men who were trailing him. That might be it: if they were guilty, they might make clever efforts to free themselves from their two shadows. It was the natural reaction of any secret agent to outwit the other fellow. That indeed could be their mistake. She began to understand just how intelligent Richard had been last night, when he hadn't left the picture house.

But one thing still needed explaining. If the Nazis thought they were worth terrifying or trapping, they would surely not let them wander about for the next few days without some real shadow trailing them—someone, Frances began to believe, who would do his job very efficiently and secretly, someone who would keep on the job after the two men had been eluded. The more she thought of this, the more convincing she found it. It never paid to underestimate your opponents. Better credit them with too much than too little.

She looked at Richard. She became surer that he had guessed this too: yesterday he had taken such care not to lose the uniformed men. As they crossed the broad Sterntor, and found themselves momentarily isolated from people, Frances spoke for the first time.

She said, "They aren't the only ones." It was half a question.

Richard squeezed her arm affectionately. "Right you are. Too obvious." That confirmed her guess why they hadn't slipped out of the cinema last night, instead of innocently changing seats. One thing gave her some amusement: it looked as if the two stooges didn't know of a third man themselves. Otherwise they wouldn't have swollen their ankles, standing hungrily at the back of the picture house. They could have relaxed, depending on their accomplice, if they had known about him.

They were in the Museum until it closed at four o'clock. After that, all Frances asked was to be allowed to sit somewhere for a long long time, with something cool and liquid on the table before her—in the open air, if it could be managed. Richard arranged it, by taking her to a near-by restaurant where there was both a garden for Frances and beer for himself.

He looked thoughtfully at her as they sat in the coolness of the trees.

"I think the city heat is too much for you, Frances," he said at last. "It might be better for us to leave Nürnberg and go nearer the mountains. There's a nice little resort south of Munich on the Starnberger See. There's good bathing there. Or if you wanted some climbing, we could go farther south into the Bavarian Alps." He hadn't taken the trouble to lower his voice. Frances wondered which person at the surrounding tables would be interested in all this. No doubt their bodyguard were draping themselves behind some concealing tree, but she had ceased to worry about them.

"I've quite enjoyed it here." *Like hell I have,* she added under her breath. "But I should like to see some real country views for a change. I find the pavements very hot. And yet, you have simply got to walk if you want to see any of these too too lovely buildings." The saccharine dripped over her words. Richard was leaning back in his chair, smiling pleasantly at his wife. His eyes were applauding her; his mind was keenly aware that the handsome woman, who sat two tables away from them, was watching the foam in her beer glass with great intentness. Or perhaps she always studied beer in that way. If the woman had been interested in their conversation, he had at least this comfort: she could have heard every word of it.

They both thought it a good idea to return to the hotel and rest before dinner. Frances thought she would lie down for half an hour, and read. Richard thought he'd like a bath. He left the bathroom door open and, as he cooled off in the tepid water, he could hear a page being turned. Once she laughed. He was happier about Frances. The Museum had been a good idea; there was nothing like a Museum for calming one's emotions. This game was simple enough, he thought, and cursed the latherless soap. This game was simple enough if you could convince yourself that you really were on holiday; that as long as you carried no unexplainable documents and neither received nor sent any, as long as you were an apparently harmless tourist, nothing could really touch you. You could give yourself away, of course. If you became flustered or lost your nerve because of the continual feeling of threat which hung over you, you might do something which was either stupid or too clever. Either of these actions would be a dangerous weakness. It was no good trying to pretend that a threat didn't exist. It did, all the time. What you must do was to ignore it: acknowledge it and ignore it. The only real danger points were those of the actual contact with an agent. If you were discovered at that moment, nothing on earth could help you. Well, the danger point in Nürnberg was past. It had passed when Fugger had spoken so softly that he had had to strain to hear him. He had been looking down at the title page of a book, and the bookseller was searching through some other volumes.

"It is better in Innsbruck at this time of year. The Gasthof Bozen, Herzog-Friedrich-Strasse 37, is recommended. The owner is called Hans, and will help you. He likes music and red roses as we all do."

That had been neatly sandwiched in between their discussion on editions and editors. He had the satisfactory feeling that A. Fugger had escaped. He was too wily a bird not to have had all his preparations made for just such a day as yesterday. It wouldn't have taken him long to get through a window and lose himself in the labyrinth of passages and small streets which lay behind the shop. There were plenty of rooms there to have rented as a hide-out, or as a place to change your identity. Or perhaps A. Fugger already had another neatly established identity practically next door to his bookshop. There was no limit to the ingenuity of a foresighted man with sufficient time to arrange things.

Suddenly, there was a firm, businesslike knock on the bedroom door. He heard Frances say "Come in."

It *might* be a maid: some excuse, any old excuse. From the bathroom, he could only see the windows of the bedroom and the heavy green brocade curtains. But in his mind's eye he could see Frances, dressed in that pink frilly thing of hers and lying on their bed, raise an enquiring eyebrow from the novel she had been reading.

He heard her say, "Yes, it is warm, isn't it? Please leave the towels on that chair. My husband is having a bath. Thank you. Good day." It was only when he heard the bedroom door close sharply that he realized he was sitting bolt upright in the bath, his muscles tensed. Frances had remained where she was on the bed; nor did she call through to him.

Thank heavens for that. She must have had a fright when that knock came; it hadn't sounded like a maid. He got out of the bath quickly and made some pretense of whistling as he dried himself.

When he entered the bedroom, Frances was lying on the bed with her eyes fixed on the bathroom door, waiting for him. The novel lay as it must have dropped when the maid had left the room. He felt her force her voice to say naturally, "Hello, darling. Cooler now?"

He lay down beside her, and with his head close to hers on the pillow, she whispered, "The knock . . . I thought he had been caught."

"Don't worry, Frances. I don't think he was. Please don't worry."

She was laughing softly, but it was a poor imitation of her laugh. It was becoming louder; her hands were cold.

"Snap out of it, Fran," he whispered. He slapped her jaw sharply. That helped. At least the laughing had stopped. He lay with his arm round her shoulders, quietening her with his firm grip.

"We'll leave here tomorrow," he said at last. "I'll get you to the mountains for some days."

Frances had recovered, and was looking rather ashamed of herself.

"Yes," she said, "I can always push someone over a precipice if there's any monkey business there."

Richard grinned. He was so unworried, so confident, thought Frances. It made her feel better just to look at him.

"That's the idea," he said.

After they had dressed, they went downstairs for dinner in the hotel. Frances had recovered completely. She had worn her smartest dress as a tonic, and the results were good. She was amusing and gay, even over a not particularly good dinner—German cooking was not at its best this summer. Many of the people in the restaurant turned their heads to watch the slender, fair-haired girl. She was easily the loveliest woman in the place, thought Richard with justifiable pride.

"That rest did you good, Frances," was what he said.

Frances only referred once to that afternoon. "You mustn't worry about me, Richard," she said. "I'll be all right now. I am like that, you know. At college I used to get quite panicky three weeks before the examinations were due. But once I had got my worry over, I was always perfectly cool when the examinations came. In fact, I used to enjoy them. Sort of legitimate showing-off, you know, with no one to reprimand you for being an exhibitionist. Well, I think it will be the same when whatever is going to happen happens. I was thinking about the war, particularly, Richard. The more I see of Germany, the more I know that a showdown *must* come, some day; and perhaps the sooner the better, before they are all turned into robots. When I think of the children leaving school each year, all of them carefully educated in the Nazi way, I honestly shudder to think what the rest of the world faces in ten years' time, if it waits. So don't worry about me, or start regretting that you brought me. I'm just in the process of adjusting myself between two very different ways of life, between peace and war. Coming here was a good idea after all: it reconciles you to the adjustment."

Richard knew Frances was right in her self-analysis—she was like that—but his job right now was to see that her nerve didn't crack before she had reached the cool, calm and collected stage. That would probably come before the end of this journey; at least, he hoped so. Her handicap was imagination. It was more difficult to face unpleasantness when you had imagination. But, as she had said, coming here helped to reconcile the adjustment. It also hastened it, thank heaven.

"I know," he said, and began some amusing suggestions about what they could possibly be drinking.

"It's really only habit which makes me order coffee. A few more days and I'll probably lose it," Frances said.

"It's extraordinary what people can swallow for the sake of their beliefs. I heard of a practising surrealist who spent many months eating his wardrobe."

"That sounds a good story," said a man's voice. Both Richard and Frances looked up in surprise.

"Hello, van Cortlandt. Glad to see you."

"May I come over here, for a while? I wanted to tell your wife . . ."

"I know," said Frances quickly. "I'm sorry I got so hot and bothered yesterday in that discussion. You know, it isn't easy for us to look at these things disinterestedly."

"And I came over here because I began to feel I might have seemed too darned callous. You see, I'm trying to look at things disinterestedly, and I'm finding that isn't easy, either."

"Well," said Richard, "now that we have all kissed and made friends, what will you have?" They all laughed, and van Cortlandt said he would have beer. Frances had a feeling that he disapproved of them somehow because they were English, and yet was surprised into liking them when they caught him off his guard.

"As a matter of fact," he was explaining, "I watched you being the only real human beings in a roomful of stuffed dummies, and I thought we were fools if we didn't get together. We may be a lot different, but we aren't just like—" He nodded over his shoulder in the direction of those concentrating on the mastication of specially chosen vitamins to build a specially chosen race.

"Zombies is, I believe, the technical term," suggested Richard. "Now would you really like to hear the story about the wardrobe?"

They talked for an hour, and then decided to have a moonlight walk. The bodyguard joined them outside the hotel, Richard noted. As Frances explained that they were probably leaving tomorrow for the mountains, he wondered just who had been watching them inside the hotel dining room. Not that it mattered, not now.

They didn't choose any particular way, but just followed any twisting street which would lead them to the banks of the Pegnitz. Away from the bigger streets, the lights were economically dim, but it seemed safe enough—even with the two men marching behind them at a discreet distance. In the narrower streets where there were so few people, the men were ludicrously obvious. Richard wondered if they never felt the ridiculousness of the whole thing. The American, after his first glance back at them, had ignored the two pairs of feet keeping time with such perfect precision. Later, Richard wondered why he never then questioned the American's lack of interest. Perhaps he was relieved that van Cortlandt appeared to think that this was only normal; it would have been difficult to pretend that they hadn't noticed a thing. At the time, he only felt grateful for van Cortlandt's tact. It was a little surprising in such a forthright, I'm-just-a-plain-man type of individual. Perhaps the American found that frankness could be a very useful front, just as many a Britisher found understatement a safe enough refuge.

Both van Cortlandt and Richard were in good form. They talked with a good deal of the fervour and conversational abandon which have an unexplained way of suddenly appearing between two strangers, as much to their own surprise and enjoyment as to that of their audience. They had just cruelly dissected Gothic art, and were proceeding to rhapsodize over Baroque, when Frances clutched their arms, and they moved closer to her.

From the quiet blackness of the little alley to the left of them came a bitter cry, the high, self-strangling cry of fear or pain, or both. They looked at each other.

"And just what is that?" asked Richard quietly. He made as if to move into the alley. There was another cry. Frances felt her stomach turn, sickeningly. Van Cortlandt and Richard looked grimly at each other.

"You stay with your wife. I'll investigate." The American had taken a step along with Richard into the alley.

"Halt!"

The abrupt command came from behind them. The two men had increased their pace to a run, as they had seen the foreigners become curious.

"Halt!"

Van Cortlandt and Richard stopped; they looked belligerently at the men. Frances came to the rescue.

"Something's wrong—a murder or something—down there."

The brown-shirted men exchanged looks.

"We advise you to take a walk," the older one said.

"But something is wrong," the American protested.

The trooper who was doing the speaking said, "We advise you to take a walk. It is only a Jews' Alley."

So that was it. Frances thought for one moment that van Cortlandt was going to jab his large, clenched fist right in the middle of that mock-pleasant smile. There was a minute's silence, broken only by a faint moaning. Frances turned abruptly and walked quickly away. The others followed, and they heard the Germans laugh at something one of them said. They were silent until they were almost at the hotel, and then van Cortlandt spoke.

"That's it," he said savagely. "Just as you are enjoying yourself and are thinking that life isn't so bad after all, you meet that. Blast them to hell."

"It's our last night here, thank heavens," Frances said.

"I've got to stay for two or three days more, and then I'll get the hell out of here. Austria's next. I'm working towards Vienna. I have enough material as it is, already, but I can't print half of it. The nice kind people in the other world would think I was a liar, or another sensationalist; and my boss would say I was sent out to report and not to do propaganda which would harm his organization."

"Is that considered at this date?" asked Frances.

"From the strictly business point of view, yes." Frances began to understand why newspapermen were cynics.

They were silent again. All the charm of the night had been broken. Hans Sachs had given way to the Iron Maiden. As they said good-by in the hotel lounge, van Cortlandt gave them his card, and wrote his New York business address on the back of it.

"That will always be able to tell you where I am supposed to be, anyway," he added, with the attractive smile which had quite won Frances yesterday. Yesterday, or was it weeks ago? They gave him their address in Oxford, and watched him write it down in his diary. Oxford, thought Frances, where the only scream in the dark came from the little Athenian screech owls. Firm handclasps—*they* were something friendly and honest, anyway.

"Tomorrow," Richard said firmly, as they went upstairs to their room, "tomorrow we leave."

10

Early next morning they left for Munich. It was a town they had both known well in the old days. Richard expected that they might still be under some kind of supervision, although their uniformed bodyguard had been left behind the walls of Nürnberg. So he chose the simplest things to do. In the afternoon they walked through the central streets, and for once he had no objections to window-shopping. In the evening they visited the Hofbräuhaus.

Frances was pathetically eager to watch the people, the same people she had seen each day when she had been an art student here in 1932. She seemed as if she were trying to read a riddle. Eventually, she gave it up.

She shook her head sadly. "I don't understand it, quite truthfully. There is something in the German soul or mind which baffles other races; there must be. On the surface, all they have got out of it is a new grandiose building here or there where they can listen to more speeches, and I can't think of anything more boring. And they have also got a lot of uniforms, and high-signs, and a firm military tread. But to all appearances, the shops aren't any better, the restaurants aren't any better, the food is worse, so are the theaters and the books. The clothes of the people do not look any more prosperous; and the trains always ran on time here, anyway."

"They have also got Austria and Czechoslovakia and lots of promises," suggested Richard.

"And concentration camps, and universities which are travesties, not to mention the hatred of three quarters of the world at least."

Richard began to wish it had not been necessary to enter Germany. He thought of the pleasant holiday they might have been having in Switzerland or in the French Alps, or in Ragusa. Some place where the things you saw didn't immediately start grim speculations . . . anywhere except this doomed country. That was what had depressed Frances so much, this feeling of doom which was apparent to the outside observer when he saw how blindly these people accepted their grand illusion. Richard felt as if he were watching passengers in a train whose engine crew were increasing speed, disregarding brakes, while the tracks in front were steep and twisting. Either the train would make the journey in record time, or they would end in horrible disaster. The strange thing, the terrifying thing, was to see the passengers accept the ominous swaying of the train along with the conductor's glib assurances; to watch them disregard the fate of the passengers who did raise some objections, even although they had once praised the intelligence of those they now abandoned so heartlessly. And the strangest thing about it all was the fact that all of these passengers—except the children, who were encouraged to stand at the window and cheer violently—all of them had been in a previous train wreck. No wonder Frances was depressed. She had always believed that men were intelligent animals.

If only the methods of hate and force had been resisted at the very beginning: not by other countries (for *that* would have been called the unwarranted interference of those who wanted to keep Germany weak), but by the people of Germany, themselves. But, of course, it had been more comfortable to concentrate on their own private lives instead of dying on barricades, if in the last extreme they had had to pit force against force. It was easier to turn a deaf ear to the cries from the concentration camps, to harden their hearts to the despair of the exiles, to soothe their conscience with praise of the Fatherland. And now, it had come to the stage where other peoples would have to do the dying, on barricades of shattered cities, to stop what should have been stopped seven years ago.

Frances spoke again. "I wonder where it will all end . . ."

"In the hall of the Gibichungs," Richard said bitterly, and with that he discarded the problem of the German mind.

On Sunday, the ninth of July, they arrived in Mittenwald. If Richard had been alone, he would have risked going straight on to Innsbruck, but with Frances beside him it was quite another matter. It was probably just as well that there was Frances, to keep him from taking chances which might lead to disaster. Some days in Mittenwald would help to smooth out any complications which might have begun in Nürnberg—and Frances needed the mountains. That was important to remember, with Innsbruck and whatever else lay ahead of them.

At first, Richard would only take her for a short ten-mile walk. "Your legs are out of training, and your feet need hardening," he insisted. The following day, they did fifteen miles. On the next, they included some climbing. By Thursday Frances could manage the Karwendel Peak without any trouble. It was on that day that Richard had begun to feel at ease again. The sense of being shadowed had gone, and Frances seemed as if she had successfully reached her past-worrying stage.

They had climbed steadily since eight o'clock, resting almost on top of the mountain to eat the sandwiches the hotel had provided that morning. They sat on the path, their legs hanging down over its edge as it dropped steeply away. Richard watched Frances open the thick hunks of bread, and extract the little grains of caraway from the slabs of soaplike cheese. She dropped them gravely one by one over the cliff, on whose edge she swung her tanned bare legs. Above the heavy-wool socks and the flat-heeled shoes, they looked like a schoolgirl's, thought Richard, with that attractive mixture of slenderness and strength. The light breeze ruffled her hair, which had curled round her brow with perspiration, and flapped her loose silk shirt. She had tied her cardigan round her neck by its sleeves. Her excavations for caraway over, she slapped the sandwich together, and took a lusty bite. Richard found himself smiling. There was something touchingly intent in her face as she looked at the Isar rolling rapidly far below them.

"It is lovely," she said quietly, "quite lovely. Look!" She pointed up the valley, with its green fields and winding ice-blue river. " 'God made the country, man made the town.' Pity man couldn't learn better."

"He is a messy imitator. He thinks complexity is a proof of progress."

They were silent, with their own reactions to the simplicity of the scene.

At last, when they had finished their lunch, Richard rose.

"Time to move," he said, and helped Frances to stand up on the narrow path. "Fifteen minutes to the top and then we shall see Austria."

"We have plenty of time," Frances said, looking at the sun. "It won't take long to come down."

Richard shook his head reproachfully. That was one thing he couldn't teach Frances; she couldn't resist coming down a mountain quickly. She would never make a real mountain climber. She was plucky enough, though. She was following him up the last difficult stretch to the top with no outward trouble, although inwardly she was probably cursing in despair. She hated going up a mountain just as much as she loved coming down.

As they regained their breath on the top of the peak, they faced the Austrian Alps, rising in rugged waves of gray stone, snow-streaked.

Richard pointed. "Over there lies Innsbruck. We'll go there tomorrow. We have been recommended by one of your school friends—Mary What-d'you-call-her—to stay at the Gasthof Bozen in Herzog-Friedrich-Strasse."

Frances nodded. "Mary Easton will do. She's now married to a man in Central Africa."

"That's remote enough," said Richard, and then changed the subject. Frances took her cue from him, and they began the descent in high spirits which lasted until they came into the little hotel in Mittenwald.

They had put up at the hotel where Richard had once stayed as an undergraduate on a reading party. In those peaceful days, there had been crowds of foreigners, mostly American or English. Tonight, as they sat in the half-empty restaurant, it was all so very different. The owner of the hotel, Frau Köppler, still sat in earnest conversation over a little table with her special friends. She still wore the long-skirted black day-dress which seemed to be part of her. On Richard's first visit there, that table had always been the subject of jokes by the people of Mittenwald who came in for their beer, or their game of *Skat,* or to dance and sing if there were an accordion or fiddle to accompany them. Richard looked towards the part of the restaurant which had been partitioned off for the local people. He remembered how shocked Frau Köppler had been when the undergraduates had preferred to drink their beer there, instead of in the room she had arranged for her guests. Then one of the jokes had been that she was pro-Nazi, and that she was plotting with her special friends at her exclusive table. The joke was increased for the laughing Bavarians because Frau Köppler was a Northerner and they said she was going to

Prussianize them; and the word *verpreussen* had also come to have a coarser meaning in the South. Now it seemed as if the joke had become fact.

Richard wondered, as he watched Frances arrange the pieces on the chessboard, whether Frau Köppler was as happy as she thought she would be. The hotel certainly was less flourishing: the only other foreigners in the room were an Italian family who talked volubly and excitedly and tightened Frau Köppler's disapproving mouth. The prices for German guests were much lower, and those tourists who arrived in the middle of the day brought their own food with them. It was an extraordinary sight to watch them open their parcels of bread and sausages at the restaurant tables, ordering one glass of beer, clean plates and knives. Frances was particularly shocked when she found that not even a tip was left for the overworked waitresses.

Richard saw Frau Köppler look over to their table. He pretended to be absorbed in the game of chess. They were no longer shadowed, he felt, but it was noticeable that Frau Köppler had taken quite a lot of interest in their movements. It could very well be possible that such a strong Nazi as herself might be asked to mark anything suspicious about them. It was the kind of little job which she might enjoy doing; it would add to her feeling of authority. As he waited for Frances to attack with her knight, he wondered whether that look predicted anything, protected his bishop with a pawn, and waited. The music from the wireless set ceased. It was a pity, thought Richard, that the sounds of frying could not be eliminated instead of music with foreign or non-Aryan influences. A man's voice began to speak, peremptory as on a parade ground. As Frances ignored the pawn, and daringly took his bishop, Frau Köppler rose to her feet, and walked over to them.

Richard had risen to his feet too, taking the opportunity of offering Frau Köppler a chair to warn Frances with his eyes—and then the unseen voice ended its exhortations and the music of a very rich band filled the room. Even as the preliminary cymbals clashed they all knew what was coming. Frances remained as she had been, and lit a cigarette. Frau Köppler stood rigid beside the chair, looking straight ahead of her into the wall of the room. Poor old Richard, thought Frances, and watched him redden slightly. He couldn't sit down as long as Frau Pushface was standing, and she knew he wouldn't stand for that song. A hymn in glorification of a well-known pimp, he had called it. Frances smoked unconcernedly and watched the chessman fall from Richard's hand. It rolled under another table, and by the time he had retrieved it, the chorus of the Horst Wessel song had ended and the Munich time-signal tune was being played. Frau Köppler sat down, bowing as she did so. Richard sat down too, looking very polite and innocent.

"I hope I am not interrupting you," Frau Köppler began. "Are you enjoying your holiday?"

They said yes, they were, Mittenwald was a most delightful place. Frances let Richard handle the greater part of the conversation. She wasn't quite sure, to begin with, why they were being honored with a visit. It wasn't very much like Frau Köppler to unbend to any of her guests, particularly foreigners. She was a tall woman, but she held herself so erectly that she seemed taller than she was. Once she must have had some beauty. Her features were still excellent, but the yellow hair and blue eyes had faded, not in the soft and kindly way which gives a certain charm to age, but bleakly. Perhaps Frau Köppler would have thought such charm only a sign of weakness; she probably preferred the appearance of strength even to the point of hardness. She was, thought Frances, a grim-looking creature. She had the foundation for beauty, but the spirit was lacking. Even as she talked, she did not relax. She gave a funny twist to the phrase *Behave naturally.* Because Frau Pushface was behaving naturally, although she could never be natural.

She turned to Frances. "I am glad you are enjoying yourself. It is good for people to travel in the new Germany. There are many things we want to show them."

Frances looked quickly at Richard, and then back at Frau Köppler. She couldn't think of an answer that wasn't impolite. She smiled, which was always a solution, even if a weak one.

Frau Köppler hadn't expected an answer, for she went on, "You speak German very well, very well indeed. No doubt you have visited our country before? Did you come to Mittenwald by chance, or were you recommended to come here? I am always interested in what brings people here."

The question was out. What a bore it must have been for her to bother to make conversation in the hope of disguising her curiosity, thought Frances. It was a pity, after all her trouble, that she did not know Richard, and so couldn't interpret his smile. He always looked like that when the game was being played his way. He was ready with his answer.

"The mountains," he said. "I enjoyed them so much when I stayed here some years ago that I wanted my wife to see them."

"You stayed here before?"

"Yes; at this hotel. It must have been almost eight years ago. It was in the off-season, at the very end of September. We stayed until we returned to England to our University."

"Ah, yes. I remember now. There were nine students and two very young professors." She must have known all the time and verified his name from the visitors' record. It would have been better if she hadn't mentioned it at all. It only angered Richard. He had given her the benefit of the doubt, and had thought she was a simple-minded woman doing what she thought was her duty. Now she was a simple-minded woman who enjoyed setting traps and catching people in them. It shed a new light on her position as uncrowned queen of the village. She would wield her political power in rather a mean way.

"Yes," he said. "It was what we call a reading party."

Frau Köppler's voice was just slightly less assured.

"Well," she said, her tone on the defensive, "you see for yourselves that we are just the same, only so much happier." Her voice was polite; it would have been friendly if the smile on the lips had been less fixed. Richard looked straight into the faded blue eyes which didn't smile at all. He said nothing. She looked at the large picture of the unhappy-looking man with the ridiculous mustache, which hung prominently on the wall.

She tried again. "Thanks be to our Leader. Do you not admire all he has done for us?"

There was a difficult moment.

"The military roads are the best I've seen, and the buildings for speeches and political gatherings are very handsome," said Frances quietly.

Frau Köppler turned to her with some annoyance. "And a hundred other things. Look at our unemployment. We haven't any. Look at yours in England. It is so large."

"Yes, unfortunately it is," broke in Richard. He was damned if he was going to let this pass. "But we are very frank about our unemployment figures."

"What do you mean?"

"We count people as unemployed if they are being trained under

Government schemes for new trades, or if they are casual or seasonal workers and just don't happen to be working on the day when the census is taken. So when you talk about England you ought to remember that."

"But that's madness . . . People trained by the Government unemployed?"

"Or facing facts. They can't plan to become settled members of the State unless they have a steady job, can they? Turning them into an army is not a solution, unless waging war is one of their country's plans."

Frau Köppler dismissed the point as negligible. . . . Her patience was wearing thin.

"How long will you stay here?" The directness of her question interested Frances. The velvet glove was off.

Richard was unperturbed. "I think we'll leave quite soon, now. We've done most of the walks and climbs which we intended to do . . . Actually, we have been just discussing tonight where we should go next. Perhaps you could advise us. We had thought of the Dolomites, but I believe it is difficult to visit there, this year."

Frau Köppler was silent; she didn't want to discuss the South Tyrol.

"I think it would be too tragic to go there this year," said Frances. "Last time we were there, only two years ago, in fact, the people were so sure that the end of Italian domination was in sight. They had a second Andreas Hofer, working secretly in Bozen, and they really believed that the heart of the Tyrol would bleed no more. And now they have been forced to leave their land or to remain and become Italians. I often wonder what they think about it all."

A faint pink color surged under Frau Köppler's pale skin.

"Then there's Bohemia," said Richard. "But I think it would be equally difficult to visit there, today."

"And of course there's Salzburg. But then the singers and conductors whom I used to admire so much aren't there any longer." Frances' voice had just the proper note of regret.

Frau Köppler looked first at her, and then at Richard. They were watching her politely, waiting for her to suggest something.

"You are very near Austria, here," she said.

"Yes, Austria is lovely," said Frances. "I remember the wonderful time I had in Vienna, three years ago. Everyone was so gay and charming. You think we should go to Vienna?" Richard watched Frau Köppler's rising embarrassment. Her theory that nothing was changed, unless for the better, was not standing up very well. She shrugged her shoulders.

"Vienna has no mountains, of course. I forgot you liked them. Perhaps the Austrian Tyrol . . . it always was popular with the English."

"Do you know of any particularly good place?"

Frau Köppler gave the advice they had wanted.

"The train from here goes direct to Innsbruck. It is the center of hundreds of excursions."

"That sounds a very good idea," said Richard. "We can go there tomorrow and then make our choice from that point. Thank you, Frau Köppler, you have been the greatest help." He rose as Frau Köppler stood up.

"You seem to travel a good deal." It was almost a question.

Frances smiled. "It is a necessary part of one's education, we think."

Frau Köppler stood with her lips and arms folded. "Perhaps. But it is strange that so many English travel about, as if they were rushing away from their own country."

Frances looked at her for a moment. "But the explanation is simple. It is only when the English travel in foreign lands that they learn to appreciate many things about their own country. Good night, Frau Köppler."

They turned again to the chessboard. Frances lit a cigarette with some enjoyment. When she came to think of it, the conversation had been rather like a game of chess, itself. From their point of view, it had been really quite satisfactory.

As Richard took her queen, she thought of A. Fugger, and his neat, businesslike exit. It was just possible that the police or Gestapo or whatever they called themselves—there seemed to be so many organizations in this country, all with uniforms and high-sounding titles—it was just possible that they wanted to capture him for another matter altogether. He might have sold banned literature, or helped people to escape, or he could have distributed secret pamphlets. She remembered his first belated appearance, and the smell of burning paper which had come from the back room in the shop.

She felt a sudden rise in confidence; it seemed as if these few days of wind and sun had benefited her mind as well as her body. The mental paralysis which had gripped her last week was gone. She knew now that no matter what happened, she must keep hold of this courage and hope.

If she lost these, then all was lost. Tonight she could face a hundred Köpplers, even Nürnberg itself. It was such a relief to be nearing the last stages of this strange journey that even danger seemed welcome.

"Check," said Richard, "*and* mate, I think." He grinned self-consciously as he saw Frances smile. He could conceal his disappointment at losing a game better than his delight at winning. He bent down to pick up her handkerchief where it had fallen under the table. He tickled her under the knee.

"Sorry," he apologized with mock seriousness. Frances saw that Frau Köppler was looking at them.

As they rose, all conversation at Frau Köppler's table ended. The four men there were watching them intently, while Frau Köppler gave a queenly bow. There was the little white-bearded astrologer who was Herr Köppler, who typed all day in his room and came downstairs in the evening to sit by his wife. There was a fat, genial man; another fat man, not at all genial, who always wore uniform and his hair cut so short that it bristled; and the young schoolteacher, very conscious of his discipline and learning, acquired at a Party college. Baldur, the Almost Human, Richard had named him when he had first seen him. The group of men stared openly at Frances as she crossed the room. Richard returned Frau Köppler's bow, and Frances said good night, looking serenely oblivious of the gazes in her direction. She felt suddenly glad that she didn't live in this village. There were other reasons, apart from the fact that she was English and obviously stupid, why Frau Köppler disliked her. I'm too effeminate, she thought, and giggled as she took Richard's arm to go upstairs.

11

On Friday they arrived in Innsbruck, and succumbed, as they always did, to its outward charm. They left their luggage at the station, and walked towards the Maria-Theresien-Strasse through busy streets bathed in the soft yellow light of the late afternoon sun. As Frances said to Richard, it was always difficult to tell who was on holiday or who was at work in Innsbruck. There were as many short leather trousers, green-feathered hats, and peasant-pinafored dresses among the young men and women at work as there were among the groups of holiday-makers; but two changes became more and more evident. The holiday-makers had the hard German accent of the North, and there was the Uniform.

The cafés were busy at this hour. The tourist shops, with their colorful peasant clothes, little wood carvings, flower charms and vermilion-tinted postcards looked gay to the passing glance. Frances knew from experience not to stop and look at them. Most of the articles were less imposing, were even crude, close at hand. They had a sort of Present-from-Brighton touch. It was pathetic, she thought, that "Tyrolean" clothes, bought in the smart shops of large cities far away from the Tyrol, should be better-looking than the originals they copied. It was the tragedy of city hands being more skillful in cutting better material, of colors more carefully blended with the sophisticated designer's eye.

And now they were approaching the Herzog-Friedrich-Strasse. Frances was looking at the people, at the way in which the towers and steeples around them were superimposed on the background of jagged mountains. One of the chief attractions of this country was its White-

Horse-Inn quality. It could be felt even in a town with tramcars and tourist buses. If this region were to lose that, it would lose much. Frances wondered whether the people prized the asset of charm which lay in their countryside, or would they ever be persuaded into thinking it was effete or sentimental or valueless, persuaded into an ill-fitting imitation of the hard Northerner?

Richard's thoughts were already at the Gasthof Bozen. The best thing to do on this job, he decided, was to have a general idea of what he was going to do while he still kept his eyes open for any possible short-cuts. A girl, carrying a basket filled with flowers, had paused before them to rest for a moment. She was almost a child, and the flowers were simple garden flowers, arranged into rough bunches. Richard stopped Frances. He returned the girl's smile.

"From our garden," she said, holding out a bunch.

"They are lovely," said Richard. "But I think I like this bunch better. How much?" He lifted a bunch with some roses in it: two were red. They paid the girl, and crossed over into the narrow Herzog-Friedrich-Strasse with its arcades and balconies. As they approached No. 37, Richard took Frances' arm. They entered the insignificant doorway with its worn sign. On either side of the doorway were busy little shops with overcrowded windows, as if everything they had for sale must be displayed. Still, they had been comforting, thought Frances, as the heavy door swung behind them shutting them off from the cheery babel of the busy arcade, and left her gripping Richard with one hand and the bunch of flowers with the other.

For it was dark in the entrance hall, dark and silent. It was narrow and unfurnished; it contained only the staircase which lay in front of them. The faint light which broke the darkness came from above, possibly from a landing. It reminded Frances of some of the older houses in Oxford, except for the stuffy, sickly smell of stale beer and tobacco. She noticed that Richard brightened. His dislike was the cafés with cream-cakes. As he moved towards the stairs, she broke off a red rose, and fastened it through the lapel buttonhole of her flannel suit.

She wished she felt as confident as her heels sounded on the wooden staircase. It twisted in an uneven curve to the left and they had reached the landing, fairly broad and square in shape. This was where the light came from. It hung over a desk which faced the staircase. There was a man at the desk, watching them through his small half-closed eyes. Or it might have been the largeness of his face which gave his eyes the appearance of smallness. Like two bullet holes in a lump of dough, thought Frances. He was middle-aged, his figure had spread with his years, his square-shaped head bristled with cropped gray hair.

At either end of the landing, which seemed to be the real entrance hall to the hotel, were swing doors. They led to two rooms, one which must be at the back, the other at the front, of the house. From the front room came the surge of men's voices, whenever a waitress pushed open the swing doors. The back room seemed to be the kitchen or the taproom, or perhaps both. The two waitresses hurried towards it with empty beer mugs, and returned to the restaurant with them filled again. The two women were so busy that they hardly glanced at Frances, as she waited for Richard to finish his arrangements with the square-headed man. As the swing doors were pushed open, she could see some of the nearest tables. The men round them were middle-aged, bulky, with faces red from arguing or laughing or drinking beer or all three. Blue tobacco haze coiled over bald heads. There were uniforms everywhere. Once a waitress swung the door wide open, and held it that way with her shoulder and hip, so that another woman could pass through with carefully held tankards of beer. Then Frances saw the flags and the outsize photograph. She looked at the desk where Richard was signing all the usual papers. It had a photograph, too, scowling benevolently down on a row of keys hanging on numbered hooks. They seemed to have landed in one of the Party's own particular haunts.

Richard had finished writing. He beckoned to Frances. Perhaps the man had looked for a moment at her buttonhole, but Frances couldn't be sure of that. His eyes had a way of wandering vaguely, as if he were ill or very tired . . . And then a green-aproned boy appeared, and she concentrated on filling in the details in the printed form. Now the signing was all finished, the man handed Richard a key, and abandoned them to the boy in his slow-moving, disinterested way. As they were led up the wooden stairs, irregular and creaking, he sank heavily back into his seat, and resumed his occupation of staring into the middle distance.

Frances glanced at Richard. He gave no sign of disappointment. He was talking to the boy, and was giving him the checks for their luggage at the station. The boy would collect it, Innsbruck fashion. Clever of Richard, she thought, to remember that. An arrival by taxi in this narrow street, with its mixture of medieval houses and small shops, would have been pretentious and stupidly conspicuous.

The way to their room led them up two flights of wooden stairs. Frances had the sudden alarming feeling of being suspended in midair. The only support of the stairs seemed to be the wall on her left. On her right was a large well sinking into the hall landing below. There were banisters of course, but they were thinly spaced and quivered to her touch. After that, she climbed the rest of the stairs well towards the wall side, and tried to ignore the way in which the steps sagged gently towards the well of the staircase. She wished she wouldn't imagine at such moments what a fire would be like. Probably one could make a spectacular, if undignified exit by scrambling down the front of the house from balcony to oriel window . . . Probably.

The boy replied eagerly to Richard's questions. He seemed a friendly kind of person. Frances suddenly realized this was the first really friendly smile and voice they had met in two weeks. Except, of course, for the American. She thought of a London bus conductor or policeman, and felt a wave of homesickness strike her. This was the first time she had ever felt like this, abroad. Perhaps she was noticing too much this year, but then this year you couldn't be blamed for being coldly analytical. It would have been more comfortable to have visited Germany as a guest, to have been taken out and around by friends. Then you might not have the time to notice or compare policemen and bus conductors. Then you wouldn't take a late evening stroll past a Jews' Alley. But somehow, in spite of the grimness, Frances preferred this way; there was less chloroform, this way.

Their room faced the street and was pleasant in its simplicity. No massive furniture here, thank heavens, to smother you in bad taste. Clean poverty had its virtues. Frances went over to one of the windows. Along the street, the varied house fronts rose tall and narrow over the arcades where the shops hid. At the open windows, she could see women in their dirndl dresses looking down on the street. It was as if she were in a theater, one of those little opera theaters where white patches of faces look out of the boxes rising in tiers like those of a wedding cake. Guardi would have enjoyed detailing this scene.

Someone was standing behind her. She turned quickly. Richard was gone. It was the thin dark boy in the green apron. He held out a vase of water to her, and pointed to the flowers which she still carried in her arms.

"Thank you. That is very thoughtful."

He relaxed with a smile as he heard she could speak German.

"The gentleman has gone to the lavatory," he explained carefully.

"Oh . . ." said Frances, suddenly stymied.

"Where would the lady like the flowers?"

"Could we move that small table near that mirror and place them there?" He approved of the decision, and watched her arrange the flowers.

"I think that is pretty," she said, to break the silence.

"Very pretty, gracious lady." His brown eyes were friendly. "I shall go for the luggage now, and I shall come back with it as quickly as possible." His smile was infectious. He might have been going to play a game of tennis instead of pushing a cart with luggage through busy streets.

"Thank you." Frances paused. "What is your name?"

"Johann, gracious lady."

"Thank you, Johann."

He paused at the door. "Is there anything the lady needs? The maid is having her supper. She will be here soon." Frances shook her head, but he still stood at the door, his eyes watching the corridor. Suddenly he turned with a smile.

"Here is the gentleman," he said. "Good evening, *gnädige Frau.*"

"Good evening, Johann." So he had been staying with her until Richard came back, as a sort of watchdog. Was the hotel as peculiar as all that? She heard Richard's voice, and there was a smile on his face as he entered the room.

"Thank God for a friendly face and a kind word," he said.

"Yes, I like Johann."

"His name is Johann?" Richard's voice had changed: it was tighter, quicker. Frances raised her eyebrows, and watched Richard sit down on the bed, his eyes fixed on the scrap of rug at his feet. Johann—Hans—Johann. No; it probably wasn't . . . probably. He looked up to see Frances standing beside him, looking puzzled. He caught her arm, and pulled her down beside him.

"Anything wrong?"

"I don't think so." He lowered his voice, although the walls in this old house must have been thick enough for safety. "I was just thinking . . . What was Johann like? Chatty? I noticed he hovered about here, until I got back."

"Politeness, and really good manners. That's all. What people used to call a well-brought-up boy. You know, I had the funniest feeling that he didn't approve of this hotel, and wanted to . . . oh, it's silly. I am going all romantic."

Richard remained serious. He was still half-lost in his own thoughts.

"Frances, it's the rummiest place. I went to see where the bathroom was, and I took the chance of having a look round, in general. Most of the rooms on this floor seem empty, but I was almost run over by three expansive uniforms on their way downstairs to join the party. You noticed it, by the way?"

"Yes; it looked like an old boys' club."

"It probably is. All I've seen so far are middle-aged men, looking rather pleased with themselves. It may be one of those pubs where Nazi meetings were held secretly when Austria was still banning them. Either we've arrived in the middle of a reunion of some kind or they always are reuniting."

"That's cheery, I must say."

"I don't know if it is as bad as it looks for us. Our friends wouldn't quite expect us to come here if we had a guilty conscience, right into the spider's parlor, as it were. And then Johann told me that they used to have a lot of English and American tourists here, students who were having an inexpensive holiday; that some Americans turned up earlier this summer, but that so far we are the first Britishers. He noticed I had written Oxford University on that form at the desk downstairs, so we fit in, in a kind of a way. University people are generally thought to be odd."

Frances noted that he looked strained and tired.

"What about a spot of food, and some beer?" She smiled as she saw him brighten at the idea. She stood up and smoothed her skirt. "I'll wash first. Where's the bathroom?"

Richard grinned. "It's absolutely unique, Frances. You'll love it." She knew from his tone that she wouldn't.

"Where?" she asked philosophically.

"Straight along the corridor, past the staircase, to the back of the building. You'll find it on the balcony there. It's a square box to one side. You can wave to all the people sitting out on their balconies round the back courtyard. It's really very matey."

Frances said very slowly, "Richard, you are pulling my leg. I'll see for myself."

She walked quickly along the corridor. Apart from the additional local color of two pairs of large black boots outside one quiet room—Richard had been surprisingly discreet about that—everything was exactly as he had described it.

As they went downstairs, Richard was whistling softly to himself in a preoccupied way. Frances paid little attention; he often did that—but as they reached the desk, she suddenly realized that the last few bars had taken shape into something she knew. *My love indeed my love is like a red red red red rose.* Richard was laying their key on the desk, in front of the large, shapeless man. Without rising from his chair, he nodded his square head with its bristling hair, and grunted in reply to their good evening. He only looked for a moment at Frances' hat.

When they came in, he was still sitting there. He rose slowly and grudgingly to hand them their key. All his movements were those of a lethargic and not particularly amiable man.

This was all that happened for two days as they left or entered the hotel. The room which served as the restaurant was empty in the morning. The swing doors were propped open to air the place, the chairs were piled on the tables, and the two waitresses in old dresses were washing the floors. The tobacco smoke was gone, but the smell of beer still hung in the air. In the evening, the swing doors were closed, shutting in the dull hum of voices, except when the hurrying waitresses, now dressed in their bright dirndls, elbowed them open. Then the wave of voices rose and fell. They were always men's voices, thick and heavy. Frances wondered about the grass widows, deserted for the excitements of politics.

On Sunday morning, the silent man startled them by asking if they were comfortable in their room. They said they were, and waited. But he only hooked their key onto the board behind him, moving so slowly, with his back turned to them, that they knew the conversation was over. They didn't need to look back at the desk, as they took the first steps downstairs. He would be lowering himself slowly into his chair, folding his hands across his massive paunch, and settling his eyes on his favorite spot on the wall above their heads.

As they returned that evening, climbing slowly up the stairs to the rhythm of Frances' high heels, they braced themselves to face the desk, but no one was there. Just as Richard was wondering if he should risk getting their room key without arousing the owner's displeasure, Johann appeared. Herr Kronsteiner had just gone to have his supper, he explained, and moved round behind the desk. He had taken off his apron, and had become a very dignified Johann. Well, anyway, thought Frances, that disposed of Richard's theory that Herr Bristleneck did all his eating and sleeping at the desk. But Richard seemed in no way dismayed at having his theories confounded: on the contrary, he was in remarkably good humor as they climbed the rest of the stairs. He was whistling to himself again, softly, and absent-mindedly it seemed. But the wink he gave Frances as they walked down the corridor to their room was not at all absent-minded. Just as they reached the door, the whistling had slid into a recognizable tune. Richard opened the door quickly. He was not disappointed. Inside, standing at the window, looking at the street, was Herr Kronsteiner.

He stood just far enough behind the white curtain to see without being seen. He turned slowly round to face them as the door closed. Richard's whistling only stopped then.

Richard said quietly, "Good evening." Frances noticed that Herr Kronsteiner also kept his voice low as he answered. He was smiling politely, his eyes fixed vaguely on the wall behind them.

"I came to leave your account in your room, and then I thought I heard you coming upstairs. So I took the opportunity of waiting, so that I could explain any details which might seem doubtful. Many of our foreign visitors find German figures puzzling. I shall be away tomorrow on a short journey, and I may not return before you leave." For a man of Herr Kronsteiner's loquacity, it was quite a speech.

Richard's expression was unchanged. "Of course. It is just as well to be quite sure and to have all the details perfectly clear."

Frances glanced at him. There was just a shade of emphasis, a slowness in the phrasing of the words, which gave them a double meaning to anyone who looked for it; but if Herr Kronsteiner perceived it, he gave no sign. He held two envelopes in his hand; he chose one of them carefully and handed it to Richard. He waited. Richard ripped the envelope open, and extracted a sheet of paper. Frances, still watching him, saw a shade of disappointment pass over his face. The envelope had contained a bill, just an ordinary hotel bill. The name of the hotel headed the piece of paper, followed by the name of the proprietor. It was RUDOLF KRONSTEINER. He saw Fugger's head against the row of dusty books, saw the scarcely moving lips . . . "The owner is called Hans . . . He will help you . . ."

"Thank you. I think everything is quite clear." Richard spoke abstractedly. Would he risk it? It was now or never, he felt. On what he said or did depended everything, everything, including Frances' safety. At least the man had come to their room, with a very elaborate excuse. That had been the first step, either for or against them. The next step was his. He was amazed at the calmness of his own voice. "Except, of course, one silly idea I had. I thought you were the proprietor."

"I am," the man answered gravely, but his interest seemed aroused for the first time.

"Really? Then it's my mistake completely. I thought the owner's name was Hans, not Rudolf."

Herr Kronsteiner smiled. "Everyone knows that it is Rudolf." He looked at the envelope which he still held in his hand.

"God in heaven, how could I have made such a mistake? I gave you the wrong bill. My apologies, Herr Professor." His calm smile belied the amazement of his words.

To Frances, sitting on the edge of the bed, her hat with its red rose lying beside her, it seemed as if here were not only a maddening man, but also one who either enjoyed his own mystery, or—and that was a disturbing thought—believed in precaution even within those thick walls. Thank heavens, Richard and she had made only general conversation here, except when they had lain close together in bed. Could their low voices, deadened by the soft feather pillow, have possibly been heard, even if this room was wired for sound? Richard's precaution, which from the very beginning she had been inclined to deplore secretly, now lost all its theatrical appearance and began to look like wisdom.

Richard was smiling too, as he read the second bill very carefully. He was memorizing something.

"Everything is quite clear now," he said. "Would you like the bill paid this evening, or will tomorrow do?"

"That does not matter very much, but we have a rule in this hotel that all accounts must be paid each Monday. Tonight or tomorrow, it does not matter. One more thing I must trouble you about. All the rooms in the hotel have been reserved for a political conference this week. It begins on Wednesday."

"Oh, we intended in any case to leave Innsbruck either tomorrow or Tuesday." Did we indeed? thought Frances. The reply had pleased

Kronsteiner. He had given his warning, and Richard had taken it. He positively beamed, although his voice was as impersonal as ever.

"In that case, I am glad I saw you this evening, for I may be away when you leave. I hope you have enjoyed your visit here."

"Very much indeed." It was Frances now who spoke. It seemed to her that it was time she said something. Herr Kronsteiner bowed, and moved with unexpected quickness to the door. He paused before he opened it, slowly, cautiously. Without looking back, he suddenly slipped out. They couldn't hear his footsteps in the corridor. For a large, heavy man he could walk with surprising lightness.

Frances felt that someone ought to say something. "Was the bill high?"

"No, it was rather reasonable. Now what shoes did you want to wear?"

Frances looked at the bed . . . But if Richard wanted to go out again, there would be a reason. Any suggestion he made had its purpose. She knew that by this time. She changed her shoes and washed her hands and face in cold water. She felt the better for fresh powder and lipstick. She wound a white chiffon scarf as a turban round her head: she was beginning to hate the sight of the red rose, anyway. As she finished tucking the ends of the scarf in place, she saw Richard watching her in the mirror. He was smoking his pipe, and in the ashtray beside him were the crumbled ashes of the paper which he had used as a lighter. His Baedeker was open on his knees.

"Ready?"

Frances nodded. She picked up a clean pair of white gloves and a fresh handkerchief. Richard had risen and replaced the guidebook in its drawer. He emptied his pipe into the ashtray, and stirred the ashes with his penknife until he was satisfied that no piece of charred gray paper could be seen. The bill which had been handed to him first by Kronsteiner he left lying on the little table beside the flowers.

Downstairs, Johann was still at the desk. He interrupted his conversation with two men, whom Richard recognized as belonging to the uniforms which had practically marched over him on the evening of their arrival, to wish them much enjoyment. He could recommend the film at the cinema in the Maria-Theresien-Strasse. His friendly brown eyes followed Frances downstairs, along with the open, noncommittal stare of his companion. One of them said something, the other laughed. Frances took Richard's arm, and pressed it. Her quietening touch, she called it. They heard Johann's voice raised in their defense.

"But the English are a truly German race."

"Which is probably the highest praise one could have from a German," said Richard bitterly, as they closed the heavy front door. "I wish," he added, "that we could afford the luxury of a scene. Just once."

Perhaps Richard had been infected by Herr Kronsteiner's supercaution. Anyway, he had varied his technique tonight. As they crossed the square towards the Maria-Theresien-Strasse, he chose the moments of isolation to tell Frances they would leave tomorrow for Pertisau am Achensee.

"It looks a decent sort of place on the map," he said with some pleasure.

"Are we near the end?"

"We'll know when we meet him."

"Then what?"

"We'll go to Ragusa, and post back the letter of credit."

"And if we don't find him this time? We haven't many days left, have we?"

"We'll have to try again, and perhaps again. After that, if there are no results, I'll wire Geneva, and we'll get back to London. We were given a month. It's now the sixteenth of July. I think we'll manage it in time."

"Then you have a suspicion this may be the last stop?"

Richard only smiled as an answer. They had reached the pavement and, surrounded once more by Sunday-evening crowds, they walked in silence towards the cinema. Outside its doors, Frances paused to look at the stills.

"I think I'd rather have a drink," she said.

"You've got sense," an American voice said behind them. They both turned in amazement. Yes it was, it was Henry van Cortlandt, sardonic grin and all. He shook their hands as if he really were pleased to see them.

"It was your wife's hat sort of thing which caught my eye. It's pretty smooth; not the kind of headgear a good *Hausfrau* wears. I've just been in there, and I came out halfway through. I've been wondering what to do until it's time to go to bed. And now you are here in answer to my prayers. The drinks are on me. We'll catch up on local color. I know a place where we'll get plenty."

As they walked towards the restaurant, there were explanations. Van Cortlandt had finished his assignment in Germany, and was now heading through the Tyrol to Vienna. He tactfully did not ask them where they had been, or where they were going. Frances filled in the gaps with what she always called girlish gossip. Tonight it served its purpose well enough.

As they sat at a table in the beerhouse, they all relaxed and prepared to enjoy themselves. Both Richard and van Cortlandt had stories to tell, and there was no need to worry about the conversation. It was pleasant, thought Frances, to lean on a table, to watch the curling cigarette smoke, to listen to laughter and voices raised in friendly argument. There was one thing about living under this kind of government—every moment of enjoyment was treasured. You appreciated any moments without fear or restrictions, and when they came your way, you made the most of them. There was a pathetic kind of determination to have a good time in the faces around her. It had touched even her. When they had sat down at this table tonight, she had made up her mind that she was going to enjoy herself. She was going to forget everything except that they were on holiday.

The men ordered their second large steins of beer. Frances left the conversation to watch the people around them. She noticed a young man, sitting alone at a small table, making the best of his splendid isolation. He was vaguely familiar. He looked suddenly towards them, and his eyes met hers. He hesitated. Frances felt that he knew her, that he was waiting for her to smile. When she didn't, he looked away quickly, and became absorbed in a large family party in front of him. Richard became aware of her look of concentration. He stopped what he was saying to van Cortlandt to ask, "Anything wrong, Frances?"

"I'm just thinking, darling."

"It looks rather painful." Both men regarded her with some amusement.

"I've got it . . . the young man in the train."

Richard didn't look any the wiser.

"The *beautiful* young man in the train to Paris. Your friend's brother, Richard, you know the one. He's here."

"Young Thornley. Good Lord. Where?"

"Over there."

Richard looked. "You're quite right, Frances. It is."

"He looks rather lonely."

"Well, we're not nursemaids." Richard was annoyed.

Van Cortlandt laughed at Richard's expression.

"Why do the English abroad avoid the English abroad?" he asked.

"Well, you know what we call a holiday . . . a change. But actually, he may not want to join us, and might only do it out of politeness."

Van Cortlandt looked surprised. He wasn't convinced. "Now who would think up that reason?" They all laughed.

"He might be waiting for someone, but I think he looks too bored for that. He is not annoyed; he is just bored." It was Frances again.

The young man decided everything by looking towards their table, and smiling wholeheartedly in his embarrassment at finding three pairs of eyes focused on him. Richard gave a wave of his hand, and the young man rose and came towards them.

"I hope you don't mind my butting in," he said, "but I have got very tired of laughing by myself." The American looked at Thornley just the same way he had looked at Richard and Frances when he had met them in the Five-Cornered Tower. It was a quiet summing-up, disconcerting in its frankness, but Thornley, like the Myles', pretended to be unaware of it. He sat down beside them, and started to talk. He was amusing, and seemingly lighthearted. Frances watched van Cortlandt make up his mind; after he had had half an hour of Thornley, she felt the judgment was mainly favorable. She sighed with relief; she felt responsible for Thornley. Van Cortlandt had decided, she could guess, that Thornley was a nice, amusing individual with a lot of charm—and not much else. It would depend on how much he got to know Thornley before he could revise that estimate. Frances guessed also that van Cortlandt hadn't thought any revision would be necessary.

"Where's your friend?" asked Richard, when the rush of conversation offered its first pause.

"Tony? Oh, he should be here any day, I hope. That's why I'm hanging about Innsbruck. We went to Prague, you know, and didn't find ourselves made welcome by the—authorities. Things were a little difficult, really. It seemed easier if we split up, and if I came here to let him get his job done."

The mention of Prague had interested van Cortlandt.

"Did you run into trouble?" he asked.

Thornley nodded. "A little." He saw that they were all waiting for him to explain. He could hardly ignore the interest in all their eyes.

"Is Tony in danger?" asked Frances. At least, that would give him the chance to say no, and to turn the conversation.

"Actually, he is looking for a girl."

Van Cortlandt and Richard exchanged glances.

"What's wrong with that?" asked the American with a smile.

"Nice healthy pursuit," agreed Richard.

"Usually," said Thornley. "But in this case she is the daughter of a professor who wasn't exactly popular with the new régime."

"Don't tell us, unless you want to," said Frances suddenly.

"Probably I'd be better confiding in someone. You've no idea how miserable you begin to feel inside when you can't talk to anyone. I've been waiting here just like that for two weeks. . . . The story is simple and innocent enough, Heaven knows. Tony began worrying about this girl when he heard her father had been removed. He had met her in England last summer, and since May he has become determined to get to Prague to see if she were all right. He had the idea of marrying her and getting her out of the country as a British citizen. Well, we got to Prague. It wasn't particularly pleasant for us, being English." He paused reflectively. "It became obvious that I was inclined to get involved in things, and there was no sign of Tony's girl. In the end, he thought it was better for him to do the job alone. He can control his temper better than I can. So I came on here, and I'm waiting for Tony and his girl to arrive. I said I would wait until the end of July."

"What happens if he doesn't turn up before the end of the month?" asked van Cortlandt.

"That would be a nuisance. I'd have to go back to Prague."

"I'd like to join you."

"Would you?" Thornley was pleased. "It's mostly strain, I warn you. Not very pleasant, really. The Czechs are suspicious, the Germans are intolerable. I can't say I blame the Czechs, at all. It is just like that all the time, you see, and then you start to be haunted by the girl, too. Tony's infected me."

"Did you know her?"

"I've seen photographs. And Tony would say something, now and again. She seemed a winner."

"Perhaps she is in hiding with her father," suggested Frances.

Thornley looked at her. His gray eyes were colder, brighter. "He is definitely dead," he said gently. It was the kind of gentleness which shocked them all into silence. Frances noted, as she lit another cigarette, that van Cortlandt was looking at Thornley in a different way. The revision process had no doubt begun.

Richard ordered more beer and coffee for Frances.

"We are leaving tomorrow," he intimated, "for Pertisau."

Frances blinked her eyes, and tried to look unconcerned. It was hardly the change in conversation which she had expected.

"I envy you," said Thornley. "Good place. Mountains and lake, and plenty of atmosphere. At least, it was, four years ago. I suppose it is still: the small villages keep to their own ways longer than the towns, and mountains and forests don't change."

"I envy you, too," agreed van Cortlandt. "Sidewalks in summer become just one café table after another for me. Climbing isn't up my alley, though. I've never understood why people go up, when all they can do is come down again. But I'd like some real swimming. I haven't had much chance of it, this summer."

"Then why don't you both take a few days off, and come along?"

Both van Cortlandt and Thornley looked surprised.

"You both look as if you could do with some time off," said Richard, and left it at that.

Thornley and van Cortlandt eyed each other speculatively. Each was probably wondering if the idea would be as attractive tomorrow as it seemed tonight.

"It sounds all right to me," said the American.

"It certainly seems a good idea," said Thornley.

"I've some business to do here. It depends on that," qualified van Cortlandt.

"And I'd hate to butt in," finished Thornley.

They both looked at Frances. She sipped her coffee, and regained her composure.

"Richard never makes a suggestion out of mere politeness," she said. "If he actually invited anyone, then that means he really would like them to accept." She smiled to the two men, and added, "I think it would be fun."

"Yes," agreed Thornley.

"Well, I've had a grand evening," said van Cortlandt. "It would be a pity to miss any others we could have. If I can arrange the business on hand, I'll take you up on that suggestion."

Richard finished the debate. "We'll be there for about a week, and if we leave before you arrive, we shall phone you and let you know. If you can make it, then turn up anytime you feel like it. We'll leave it at that.

I don't know where we shall stay, yet. Let's say the Hotel Post; there's always a Post in Austria. If you can't manage it, then we'll see you in London, we hope."

They rose, and straggled to the door. The restaurant was nearly empty; it must have been later than any of them had imagined. They parted with a good deal of warmth. Frances, who had been drinking coffee, wondered how much the beer had to do with it all. She watched the American and the Englishman walk away together, still talking their heads off.

"I'd like to see them again," she said and took Richard's arm. "I wonder if they'll come. You know, Richard, you did give me a shock when you suggested it. Won't it complicate matters?"

Richard shook his head. "Beer or no beer, I liked them. It's strange, how you can meet some people, and you might as well have been spending the evening looking at a fishmonger's window. And then again, you meet others, and a small flag waves, and you are a fool if you ignore it."

"Especially nowadays," said Frances. "I'm all for gathering the rosebuds while we may."

The street was almost empty. The light tap of Frances' heels alone broke the silence. She waited until they had reached a part of it where they were sure of being quite safe. She lowered her voice.

"Did the second bill tell you whom we are to see?"

"He's a chess collector, this one. Welcomes any fellow-enthusiast to view his collection. It should be easy getting in touch with him."

That was all Richard would tell, then. When Frances spoke again, it was about van Cortlandt and Thornley; she was still worrying about endangering them.

"They can take very good care of themselves, these two. If they come. What's more, we were told to behave completely normally. So I did."

Frances added nothing to that. For one thing, they were approaching the hotel. For another, she had the dawning suspicion that Richard was going to leave her under the young men's protection while he was being a fellow-enthusiast. She would see about that.

12

Johann was charmingly regretful in his mild way, next morning, when he found them completing their packing. He advised Richard about the trains, and arranged to take their suitcases to the station. As he spoke, he watched Frances pack bottle and hairbrushes into her fitted hand case.

"How beautiful," he said involuntarily, and then reddened as Frances looked up in surprise. "That leather, how is it made? I have admired your shoes each day. The material is so good." He looked at their flannel suits. "I don't quite understand it," he went on. "Are English sheep and cattle and horses so very much better than other countries'?"

Frances kept her face serious. "No, Johann, I don't think they are. Perhaps it is because the English are a slow and careful sort of people. Sometimes slowness has results." She would like to have added that even if his country hadn't got materials like these, they had always plenty of tanks and aeroplanes, but she didn't. Johann's sense of humor didn't stretch to the irony of that.

"Yes, they are slow people, I have heard. Their thoroughness is different from ours; sometimes it seems strange that they should ever get results." He hesitated. "May I ask the *Herr Professor* a question? Do you think there will be war?"

Richard paused in locking his suitcase. He chose his words carefully.

"Well, that depends, Johann. It depends on Germany. If she makes war against Poland, then there will be war."

"But why should England go to war for Poland? The Poles are not worth it."

"They do not deserve to be obliterated."

"But you did not go to war for the Czechs."

"You agreed that the British are slow. It has taken time to change them from hopes of peace to a determination to fight, if it is necessary. If Poland is attacked, the British will see *that* as a sign that fighting is necessary. It is quite simple, Johann. If Germany does not want war, then she must not attack Poland."

"Another war would be a dreadful thing," said Johann.

"Do many of your friends feel that way?" asked Frances.

"Of course, *gnädige Frau.* We are human beings."

"It seems so strange then that Germany should have twice built up the most powerful army in the world, within thirty years. Armies cost a lot of money, Johann. And the money is wasted unless the armies are used, and pay for themselves by winning. It is a very dangerous thing to build up a huge army when the rest of the world is at peace."

Johann was searching for a reply; what was it he had heard so often? "But," he said at last, "we have to prepare against attack."

"From whom?" asked Frances gently.

"From all our enemies. France for instance."

"Johann, do you really think that if France was prepared for attack she would ever have had to sign at Munich? Tell me, when you lived in what was called Austria, were you all afraid of being attacked by France? Did you feel then that you must have the biggest air force in the world?"

Richard signed to Frances to ease up. As he explained afterwards, it would only land the boy in trouble if he really started to think for himself.

Johann was indeed looking worried. "If only you could live in our country for some years, you would understand, *gnädige Frau.*" Frances, in obedience to Richard's signal, contented herself with smiling.

Richard spoke. "The cases are ready, Johann; you can take them away whenever you like. Leave the checks for them downstairs at the desk, and we shall get them there."

"Yes, *Herr Professor.*" Johann looked unhappy about something. Perhaps it was that he hadn't made any converts to his cause. Or perhaps, thought Frances, he had found a question which the answers he had learned did not fit.

"You have made our stay very comfortable," said Frances, and was glad to see him cheer up. "And when you have that hotel of your own in the Tyrol, you must let us know, and we shall come and stay there one summer." Johann flushed with pleasure; he saw that she meant what she said.

"It would give me the greatest pleasure to have you at my hotel, *gnädige Frau,*" Johann said with unexpected dignity.

"Good-by, Johann," said Richard. It was always he, it seemed, who had to close Frances' conversations. Johann bowed deeply, smiled for Frances again, and left them at last.

Frances walked over to a window, and looked silently down on the street.

"You would have made a good father confessor," said Richard, and lit the cigarette which she held between her lips. It was really extraordinary how people would talk to Frances; more extraordinary how she would listen.

"Don't let the tragedy of the human race get you down at this time of the morning. Come and have some breakfast, first." He drew her gently from the window. "An empty stomach only turns thought into worry."

Frances smiled and kissed him. "You keep worrying about me, Richard."

"Well, whenever you start a train of thought these days, it runs non-stop to the sorrows of the world."

"I'm sorry, Richard. I'll give up the habit."

"Do. It would be frightful if you ever began to enjoy it."

Frances laughed. "A kind of mental pervert, working herself into depths of depression to enjoy her secret thrills of pity? No, thank you, Richard. Instead, I'll become accustomed to the idea that man is born in pain, lives in struggle, dies in suffering."

"Well, that's a better defense against the new Middle Ages than the nice ideas you got from your liberal education."

Over a café table, they made their plans. Frances was suddenly demanding action. She wanted to get to Pertisau as soon as possible. By the time they had finished their late breakfast and had walked back to the hotel, the baggage checks awaited them, along with a final bill. Herr Kronsteiner had already left, it seemed, and Richard paid the grim woman who sat behind the desk. He left more than the usual tip for Johann, placing it inside an envelope along with his card on which he had written *Good luck with your hotel,* and a tip for their invisible chambermaid. Perhaps she had been this grim-faced, silent woman.

At the station, their luck still held. The train for Jenbach would leave in less than half an hour. From Jenbach they could hire a car to take them to Pertisau. . . . But it wasn't until they were in the train, with their suitcases settled safely above their heads in their compartment, and they were watching the pleasant valley of the Inn spreading out before them, that Richard really relaxed. He admitted to himself for the first time that he was surprised that they had got away so simply, that his distrust of Herr Kronsteiner had been unfounded. He had looked like a man who would sell his own sister to the highest bidder. He must be a pretty useful kind of agent to have; crooked men would trust him, because they thought they could use him. Richard was still speculating about Herr Kronsteiner when their short journey ended, and the train stopped briefly at Jenbach to leave them and some other tourists on the sunlit platform. Richard lifted the two suitcases and joined the largest group which had jammed round the exit. Frances kept very close to him, slightly behind and slightly to one side, so that the man who was taking the tickets would only notice her, and no more. And then they were out into a broad roadway of hot white dust. There were two decrepit buses and some cars. The tourists, once the first burst of activity of leaving the station was over, had begun to straggle as they made up their minds. That gave them the chance to hire one of the cars. They had already left the station road, and were turning into the outskirts of the little town, before the others had found seats which suited them and places for their luggage.

Their car finished the steep twisting climb from Jenbach, and regained its speed on the road leading round the western side of the long narrow Achensee. Halfway up the lake, the road ended. And there was Pertisau, smiling with the sun on its green meadows to welcome them.

It wasn't the usual village. It gave the appearance, as the road curved into the bay in which it lay and they could see it for the first time, of being a landscape architect's dream. At the edge of the shore, divided from it by the last of the road, were the hotels and chalets. Behind these, in the large sweep of meadows stretching back to the wooded mountains, lay the peasant houses like a scattered flock of sheep. A very small, neat pleasure boat was taking on passengers at the small neat pier. Everything was neat, even the arrangement of flags fluttering from the bathing houses on their own part of the shore, or the pattern of striped umbrellas shadowing the tables in front of the hotels. It was, self-admittedly, an artificial tourist center, but its smallness and neatness gave it much charm, and some dignity. The forests and mountains were very real, anyway. The valleys between the mountains converged on Pertisau like the lines of a sundial. There would be good walking and pleasant climbing, thought Richard with some satisfaction.

Frances was frankly delighted. She had watched some of the dull collections of houses as they had skirted the south end of the lake, and had wondered dejectedly if any of them could be Pertisau. In her relief, she was enthusiastic. Even the fact that the Hotel Post had no accommodation to suit them could not dampen her high spirits. The manager of the hotel was sorry, but there were no double rooms vacant. If the lady and gentleman would consider separate single rooms, or a room in one of the villas . . . There were some which catered to visitors when the hotels were full . . . Most comfortable . . . Highly recommended. And of course they would have their meals at the hotel.

So they left their luggage at the hotel, and followed the manager's assistant across the road and over a field to a house. It was called "Waldesruhe," although the woods were at least half a mile away. But it seemed both clean and comfortable. Frances liked the petunias in the window boxes and the balcony in front of their bedroom with its magnificent view of the lake. Richard liked the impersonal owner, who took everything for granted in her calm, disinterested way. This sad-faced woman would not add to their complications. But he hadn't counted on Frances.

When he returned from the hotel again, after making "arrangements" as the manager euphemistically said, and leaving notes for van Cortlandt and Thornley, he found the quiet landlady talking to Frances on their balcony.

"It really wasn't my fault," said Frances. "It was simply that she was delighted to see someone who didn't come from Germany. They are having a rather bad year, here. Most of the visitors are Germans. With special rates, of course; and they spend next to nothing. They crowd into the hotels, and all the other visitors are chased away. I expect it's the way they eat their soup. Remember?"

"I believe you, darling."

"Really, Richard, all I said was, as she stood and looked at me on the balcony, 'How lovely it all is.' It was said to myself. And then she began to talk."

"Darling, don't explain. You're too kind; you just won't hurt people's feelings. You'll let yourself in for a lot of boredom, some day."

"I rather liked her, Richard. And she kept looking at me, not rudely, not inquisitively, but just as if she wanted to. All the time she talked, she was looking at me, and the strange thing was that I didn't feel embarrassed. There was a sort of pathetic expression in her eyes. I just couldn't ignore it."

Richard laughed, and kissed his wife. "Darling," he said for the third time, "I love you. Now come and see Pertisau."

They went down the light-pine staircase into the square-shaped room with its small windows and fluttering starched curtains. Like their bedroom, the furniture was simple in comfortable peasant style. Frances noted the number of hand-embroidered or crocheted mats on every available surface in the room. Frau Schichtl must have a lot of spare time, she thought, and followed Richard through the doorway onto the coarse green grass which surrounded the house. They chose a narrow road which led them through flowering meadows away from the lakeside and its holiday loungers. Richard was thinking about something.

At last he said, "Where does Frau What's-her-name sleep? Do you know?"

"Not near us, my pet, if that is what has been worrying you. There is an empty room next us. It separates us from a Leipzig honeymoon couple, and these are all the rooms upstairs. And a bathroom of course. The name is Schichtl, anyway."

Richard looked admiringly at her. "Now don't tell me that you found all that information popping out of Frau Schichtl's cash register. . . . I must say, my Frances, you have a knack."

"Now," said Frances, "it's your turn to tell me something."

"What?"

"Don't be a brute, Richard. No one can possibly hear us." She looked at the houses across the fields, their wide overhanging roofs anchored with roped stones, their window boxes gay with rich-colored petunias. Under the broad eaves sheltered neat piles of logs.

"You take a long time to think up an answer, Richard."

"Well, darling, there's no need, is there, for you to know more than you do already?"

"Richard, will you stop doing a Pimpernel? I don't talk in my sleep and, anyway, I sleep only with you."

Richard watched two distant figures cutting the grass. Their scythes flashed rhythmically. "All right," he said. "This is all I know. We were to come to Pertisau. There is a Dr. Mespelbrunn who has a house here. He collects chessmen. We have to see him, and tell him we heard about his collection in Innsbruck. That is what makes me think that he may be the man we are looking for. None of the others knew where we came from. But here we have Dr. Mespelbrunn who knows about Innsbruck. He is also a musician, it seems, and likes to talk music as well as chess. His love is again a red rose. If he doesn't think we stink, he will unburden himself. And then we can have our holiday, and send old Peter his Geneva telegram ARRIVING FRIDAY. That's all."

"So that's all. . . . Now, Richard, just tell me what was written in Herr Kronsteiner's second bill."

"More or less as I've said."

"Well, what was that?"

"You're an exasperating creature, aren't you?"

Frances only smiled and waited.

Richard looked at her, and then recited: "*Innsbruck recommends you to Pertisau am Achensee. Dr. Mespelbrunn. Collector of chessmen, songs, flowers.*"

"Thank you, my sweet. I just wanted to be quite sure you weren't trying to do me out of some fun."

Richard was all injured innocence. "Now, really, Frances—"

"I mean, could you have possibly thought of Henry van Cortlandt and Robert Thornley as such nice bathing companions for Frances while you went—mountain climbing, for instance?"

Richard began to laugh. "Some day," he said, "I'll have to believe in woman's intuition, or is it just woman's suspicion?"

"Now that's all settled," said Frances, "let's look at the view."

Their road had led them clear of all the houses. The fields now lay behind them; in front lay scattered twisted trees on a stretch of green grass. It was here that the paths into the converging valleys began. They found a rough wooden seat under one of the small twisted trees beside a small stream. Only the gentle murmur of the running water broke the silence of the valleys. The mountains circled round the meadows, and the sky had arranged its high summer clouds in appropriate clusters to balance the juttings of the peaks into its clear blue.

"It's a neat job," said Richard, at last, "almost too neat to be natural."

"Yes, as if a stage designer had advised nature how to make a really Tyrolean set. I expect a chorus of villagers to enter at any moment."

"I've been wondering at that. It's not exactly a hive of activity, is it? There were a few men over there working with the hay, or long grass, or whatever it is. We've seen one woman scrubbing a table at her door, and another woman gathering in some washing. Now and again I heard the sounds of trees being felled in the forest. Perhaps they find tourists more profitable than the land."

"Found," emended Frances. "Here are some children anyway."

Three large-haunched cows ambled slowly towards them, the bells at their throat sounding a gentle melancholy with each lazy step. Behind them were the children, four of them, their straight hair sun-bleached and their bare feet and legs stained nut-brown. The cows wandered past them, flicking the flies from their dun hides carelessly. Frances, looking at them, thought of some people she knew.

"Bored is the word, not contented. They have been bored so long that they don't know what to do about it. Numbed into contentment."

The children had halted. They were staring at Frances, at her suit and her silk stockings and her high-heeled shoes. When she spoke, they retreated, still staring stolidly, and then when they were at a safe distance they turned and ran, whooping with laughter, after the cows.

Richard was grinning with amusement.

"Nice to be young," said Frances. "Then you can laugh at the other fellow, and leave it at that. You never think that the things which make you laugh can also strike you cold with horror."

"Stop thinking about goose steps and a property mustache," advised Richard.

"Don't worry. I'm out of the dangerous stage of being mesmerized with fear. If I'm cold now, it's with anger."

"That's safer, anyway, when you are dealing with those birds," Richard said, and rose. He took her arm affectionately. "Nice little avenging fury you'd make."

They chose another road back to the shore of the lake. It led them towards a group of trees, sheltering houses more closely grouped together. As they approached this small center, they noticed two or three little shops, and even some women and children, in the road which had almost become a village street. There was an inn and a beer garden, which looked as if the inhabitants of Pertisau might be able to enjoy themselves after all without any help from tourists in imitation dress.

"Signs of civilization," said Richard, but he surprised Frances by not entering the beer garden. A small shop which was part of a house seemed to attract him. They crossed the narrow street, and looked at its window filled with wood carvings. Most of them were of the Present-from-the-lovely-Tyrol variety, but on the back shelf were a few carvings of really good design and careful workmanship. The finest of these were two chessmen. Frances knew Richard was pleased.

"This may be as good a way as any," he said, and led Frances into the shop.

It had been the living room of the house. Now there was a table facing the door, on which more carvings were displayed. Behind this, under a window at the side of the room, was another table covered indiscriminately with shavings, chips, blocks of wood and instruments to cut and mold them. On the bench beside the table was a man. He rose slowly, coming towards them with a half-carved piece of wood still in his hand. He looked at them keenly, and then smiled.

"*Grüss Gott!*" he said.

"*Grüss Gott!* May we look at your carvings?"

"Of course. The lady and gentleman are welcome." He went back to his bench and started his work again. Now and again, he would look up to see what held their interest. He nodded as Frances admired some figures of the Three Kings. His best, most careful work was given to Biblical themes; to them and to the chessmen which Richard was now examining with interest.

"How much are these?" asked Richard. The man watched his face as he told the price. It was reasonable for the amount of work in the carvings.

"It takes much time," the man said, as if trying to excuse the charge. Frances wondered how often it had been rudely beaten down by people who had ignored the time, the skill and the love which had gone into such work.

"The price is not high for such craftsmanship," said Richard. "I'd like a set of these to take back to England."

"The gentleman collects chessmen?" The woodcarver was delighted.

"Then you will see something. I have still better ones; some which I do not sell." He rose, quickly this time, and went to a heavy chest at the back of the room. He opened a drawer and took out a large box which he carried carefully to his work table.

"If the lady and gentleman would come over here . . ."

They went, and as they looked at the contents of the box, they found it not difficult to express their admiration.

"I do not sell these; they gave me too much pleasure when I made them," the man explained. Frances noted the large clumsy hands, knotted and gnarled with age, and wondered at their expertness, at the delicacy of their creations.

"Do you ever make copies of them, for anyone who wants to buy them?"

"Sometimes. But it takes a long time. A gentleman who lives here in the summer months has asked me to copy them for him during the winters. I have made him one set, and here is another which I am now carving for him."

They were suitably impressed.

"He must know a lot about chessmen," said Richard, hoping for the best. It came.

"Herr Doktor Mespelbrunn? Yes, indeed. He has a large collection. He lived in the South Tyrol before he came here, and he has some Grödnertal pieces."

"Really?" Richard hoped his admiration of the Grödnertal woodcarvers was emphatic enough.

"But why do the lady and gentleman not go to see Herr Doktor Mespelbrunn's collection? He shows them to people who really admire and understand."

Richard looked doubtful. "I should like to see them very much, but after all we are complete strangers to Dr. Mespelbrunn. I shouldn't like to disturb him, especially as I am only an amateur . . ." Richard's words were cut short by the old man's laughter.

"The lady and gentleman would not disturb the Herr Doktor. He doesn't work; he writes music." The woodcarver's joke lasted him quite a long time.

"Perhaps," said Richard, when he could, "perhaps I may have the honor of being introduced to the Doctor some day when I visit you again."

The woodcarver pursed his lips and shook his head.

"He doesn't come down into Pertisau much during July and August. He doesn't like tourists. But if you pass his house—it is the large house with the red shutters on the Pletzach—you should visit him. You can say that Anton advised you to go. It is a very beautiful collection."

"Perhaps we shall," said Richard, and dismissed Mespelbrunn from the conversation by placing an order. He insisted on paying Anton half the price in advance, the rest to be paid when the pieces arrived in Oxford.

"That seems fair enough," Richard said to Frances as they walked back to the lakeside. "By the time he can start work on them, summer will be over, and then he will know whether it is any use starting them at all. I've no doubt that he will be worried about the deposit, but he earned it."

They met groups of men returning from the woods, with their axes slung over their shoulders. They were lean, weather-tanned men, slow-moving and silent. They might have been a group of Scots shepherds, with the same strong bones and rugged faces. There was even the same upward lilt in their voices, as they gravely answered "*Grüss Gott.*" Some of the older men smiled in surprise as if they hadn't expected the old greeting from a present-day visitor. Children had finished their task of herding cows, and were playing outside the open doors of the houses. Their clothes made them look like miniature adults. Smoke was beginning to curl up from the stone-anchored roofs. There was the smell of cooking food in the air, and the high tight voices of women when they are hurried and tired.

Down at the lakeside, there were also preparations for supper. Here the women were changing one undistinguished dress for another, and no doubt fixing their hair as unbecomingly as possible. Those of them who had already succeeded in looking grim enough to satisfy the requirements of a superior race sat at the tables in front of the hotels, contemplating their husbands with housewifely virtue. The men talked and looked at each other. The women looked at the men. Behind them, the shadows of the mountains were mirrored in the still waters.

A gramophone played in the little café where the younger men were. There were not so many young men, Frances noticed, nor were there many young girls. Perhaps the new Germany had other plans for the holidays of its youth.

"A few more years of this, supposing that there was no war," said Frances, "and no one, who wasn't a German, could bear to come to the Tyrol."

"I always know you mean what you say when your sentences run away with themselves," teased Richard. And then he was serious again. "We had better not rush things at this stage. The ice gets thinner as we get farther out, you know, and the shore is less easy to reach. I've a feeling we ought to play doubly safe. Peter's man, the one he sent out before us, must have managed Nürnberg and Innsbruck; although to tell you the truth, I had begun to think when we were in Innsbruck that we had reached the snag. So we are going to be very innocent for a couple of days. We'll relax. What about climbing that blighter tomorrow? It's an easy one to begin with." He nodded to the Bärenjoch, black with the sun behind it.

Frances smothered a smile over her husband's idea of relaxation.

"All right, darling," she said.

They left the quiet road, and turned towards the Villa Waldesruhe. It was as peaceful as its name. There was no sign of the honeymoon couple or of Frau Schichtl. As Frances unpacked, she sang. Richard dropped his book on the balcony, and listened as he looked at the steep drop of the mountains on the other side of the darkening lake. He didn't know when Frances had stopped singing, or how long she had been watching him from the door. He rose hurriedly.

"One of those adequate five minutes," he said awkwardly. He looked at Frances' hair and lips. "Darling, you are going to be thought most awfully decadent. The master race will disapprove."

"Too busy eating soup," said Frances. "Nothing, not even their principles, could ruin their appetites." She was right.

13

They did climb the Bärenjoch next day. As Richard had said, it was easy, and it was also useful. Richard spent a lot of time on the peak, studying with his map and pencil the lie of the valleys which met in the green plain of Pertisau. They could see the Pletzach, flowing at the base of the mountain opposite them like a very narrow, very loosely-tied white ribbon. If they were to follow the stream up round that jut of mountain into the valley which it sheltered, they should find Dr. Mespelbrunn with his chessmen and music books. Frances watched Richard. He was interested in the mountains, unsuspected from the lakeside, which stretched into the distance in rough-tongued waves. Two of the valleys led to paths which would take them over that sea of jagged stone.

"Looking for a quick way out?" asked Frances.

"It wouldn't do us much good in that direction," said Richard. "That's Germany. I wish to heaven that Pertisau had tucked itself near the border of a nice healthy place like Switzerland. Still, even if we have to make a dash for it, it is just as well to have a choice of directions. Yesterday I was worried because Pertisau was such a bottleneck."

"You seem to expect fireworks. It's difficult to think of any danger or evil lurking in this kind of place." Frances settled down on Richard's Burberry, and fished for a cigarette in one of its pockets. She lit it, and lay back to look at the sky.

"How are we going to do it?" she added.

Richard folded up his map carefully and put it into his pocket. He stretched down beside her and watched the clouds.

"I think Anton is our best bet. We'll just walk in, one of these days, and ask if we dare have the great honor and pleasure of seeing the chess collection. Anton's name will get us past any servant who's about the place. All other excuses are pretty obvious."

"Such as?"

"Well, you could need a drink of water, but unfortunately there's a nice mountain stream running down that valley. Or you could sprain your weak ankle, and need help to get back to the village. But that's rather a poor effort."

"I'm glad it is."

"So we shall just blow in, probably on Thursday or Friday, when Pertisau has looked us over and accepted us. There's no use risking everything by an enthusiastic dash. For if this Mespelbrunn is Peter's man, then an explanation for his silence would be the fact that he was under observation. And if he is under observation, then his visitors had better be very natural indeed."

"He must be able to speak German pretty well, if Anton and the others in the village accepted him."

"It's his job. The accent hereabouts, anyway, is so peculiar that he could easily pass himself off as a real Berliner. When he is in Berlin, he has a Viennese accent, no doubt."

"Well, I am looking forward to meeting him."

"Are you definite about that?"

"Quite. You aren't going to leave me out at this stage. You know, Richard, the man in Paris was very efficient. So were the others, but they seemed simpler, somehow."

"I should think the Paris man is second in importance to Mr. Smith himself. The beginning and the end, as it were. Fugger and Kronsteiner are just moveable pawns in the game."

"I keep worrying about poor old Fugger," said Frances. "I wonder if he did get away."

"If he hadn't, we wouldn't be here. Or, we would have been continuously followed until they could catch us with another agent. Don't worry about A. Fugger. He's a wily bird." Richard suddenly sat up and watched the mountainside.

"I thought I heard voices," he explained. He was right. Below them were two men.

Frances rose to her feet. The two figures paused and then waved their arms and shouted.

"It's Henry M. and Robert Thornley," Frances announced. "You know," she added in amazement, "I never thought they'd come."

Richard got up. He waved and halloed back. Van Cortlandt yelled something which they couldn't make out; but Thornley was laughing, and they laughed too. The American seemed to be in good spirits. He kept calling remarks to them which sounded funny although they couldn't hear them.

At last the two men came over the last piece of rock, and dropped on the ground beside Frances. The American regained his breath, and pointed to his face. It was crimson.

"Well," said Frances, "if you will climb at twice the normal pace and make wisecracks to go with it—"

"This," said van Cortlandt with as much pride as if he had been fishing for marlin, "is my first mountain."

"We are overcome," said Frances gravely, and handed him some sliced orange. "It was a most spectacular appearance."

Robert Thornley explained. "We motored from Innsbruck this morning, at the most ghastly speed you ever saw. We found the hotel, and then your house. A nice old thing—"

"Frau Schichtl," suggested Frances.

"—told us you were up here. It looked easy, so we came."

"All lies. Perfidious British lies," said van Cortlandt. "I drove Bob as gently as if he were in a wheelchair on the Boardwalk at Atlantic City. When we found you weren't there with flags of welcome, he dragged me away from a very nice little table beside a lot of water. And then he told me it was no climb at all. Just kid's play." He looked sadly at his shoes. "They'll never be the same again."

Frances laughed. "Remember to borrow some of our first-aid kit tonight."

"Do you mean to tell me I'll feel worse tonight than when I climbed this mountain?"

"Your feet will, in these shoes. Cheer up; it wasn't a bad climb for your first."

"Wasn't bad? It's darned fine if you ask me."

"Well, have a sandwich," said Richard. "We're glad to see you."

As they ate, they explained further. The pavements of Innsbruck had become hotter and harder after the idea of Pertisau had been put before them. Last night they had met and celebrated together, and had suddenly decided to get away from cafés and conducted tours for three days. Van

Cortlandt felt he was due a vacation, anyway, and Thornley was becoming bored with being bored.

"It's the first real holiday I've had in two years," said van Cortlandt. "I'm always either going someplace or coming away from it, and I've always got an eye open and an ear listening. I'm going to forget all that for three days. I'll have to be back on Friday. Until then I am going to have some peace for a change."

Frances caught Richard's eye. "How do you like the view we arranged for you?" she said quickly.

Richard pointed out the different peaks. Over there was Germany. Down there were the Dolomites, and then Italy. Here the Danube would be flowing to Vienna. Back there would be the Alps of Switzerland.

"So this is what makes some people want to rush up to the top of every mountain they see," said van Cortlandt. He looked at Thornley pointedly, so that they all laughed, but in the end he was the last to leave the summit.

That night the promise of Innsbruck was kept. They enjoyed themselves. By the time they had finished dinner, and had gone into the hotel lounge for coffee, most of the other guests had disappeared.

"They must get their beauty sleep," suggested Frances, and giggled. She was in rather good form tonight. She had been worrying during the last two days that if the two of them did come to Pertisau, perhaps the party would be a failure. But everything was going well. She looked at van Cortlandt, leaning forward to catch Thornley's words with a smile on his lips, a smile ready to break into a laugh when the point of the long story was reached. Richard was lighting his pipe contentedly, his eyes on Thornley who had now risen to his feet to give full justice to the climax. It was when they were all laughing that Frances noticed the man. He was watching them. He sat alone at a small table, a dark-haired man with bold black eyes, heavy eyebrows and a prominent jaw. He was probably about thirty, guessed Frances; and already his muscles were running to fat, but he was powerful enough. She noticed the tightness of his shirt over the expanse of his chest, and the collar which, already tight from the thickness of his neck, seemed all the tighter because of a black tie firmly knotted. It was a strange way of dressing for a summer evening. The jacket slung over a chair was a drab green, his only concession to the Tyrol, for he wore black breeches and boots. Just as a retired

Navy man can be spotted by his taste in neat navy blue, so it was easy to guess how this man had spent much of his time. Take away the Tyrolese jacket, and add a black one, and a heavy black cap, and a holster at his belt, and a rubber club, and he was typed as accurately as in a Hollywood casting office.

His eyes had been fixed on Thornley. They suddenly swung round to Frances and became aware of her scrutiny. Frances let her eyes pass through and over him, fixing them on the deer's horns just above his head. She held them there until he had stopped looking at her, and had risen from his table. He threw some coins down with a careless gesture, ignoring two which fell on the floor. She was very busy lighting a cigarette, as he walked loudly out of the room. Van Cortlandt had noticed the last few moments, and was watching Frances with a smile of approval.

"You got out of that nicely," he said. "That's one of the boys in the back room. I'll lay you five to one."

"Big odds," said Thornley. "Don't tell me that the Gestapo finds its way to a place like this."

"They'll find their way to any place, even into countries which aren't under Germany—yet," van Cortlandt replied sourly. "They give me a bad taste in my mouth," he added. He began a story about them. Frances listened, but she watched Richard. Apart from a tightening of his lips, he did not seem disturbed by anything.

"Not one of the pleasanter types of humanity," summed up Thornley. They all agreed on that, and rose. An evening walk before they went to bed seemed a good idea. Van Cortlandt looked at his wrist watch, and raised his eyebrows.

"It's only a quarter of ten," he protested. "I haven't been to bed at this hour since I was in kindergarten."

"Don't you feel you'd like to be a dog, and just risk it once?" Frances asked gravely. He looked at her quickly, and then laughed.

"I'm learning something by living among the English. I now know when to risk a laugh."

Richard and Thornley had gone ahead. Frances slowed her pace. Van Cortlandt was trying to disguise a limp.

"Let's sit here, until the others come back," suggested Frances, as they passed some chairs tilted drunkenly against a table.

"Thanks . . . this foot is a nuisance."

"I'll give you some stuff to doctor it, tonight. Everyone has foot trouble on their first day in the hills."

He looked at her, and hesitated. He said suddenly, "You know, you're all right. I have to admit that I didn't think so much of you when we first met. Apart from being easy on the eyes, of course. I thought you were a hidebound Tory."

"You must have thought me rather suppurating." She smiled, and added, "Perhaps I am. But I'm no Tory."

"So I found out this afternoon. That was quite a talk we had, coming down that hill. I've been thinking it over since, and although I still stick to my own opinion, I begin to see why my remarks in Nürnberg made you so mad. You must have thought me—" he paused for the word.

"Smug?" suggested Frances gently.

"Now, that's pretty steep. Or did you?"

"Well, I must say I thought you inclined that way."

Van Cortlandt looked glum. "Well, that's a fine impression to hand out."

"I didn't do so well myself, did I?"

They both laughed, and then Frances was serious again. There was a sadness in her voice which she no longer tried to disguise.

"You see, if it comes to a showdown, it's the much criticized Britisher who'll have to foot a good part of a pretty bloody bill. We'll need words of encouragement from the sidelines, not jeers. And I wish you could believe me about appeasement. After all, you wouldn't call America a prohibition country today, although you lived with it for years."

"I see your viewpoint," said van Cortlandt. "It's another angle, certainly. But . . ." He shrugged his shoulders.

Frances was silent. The moon was on the water of the lake, and she could see van Cortlandt's face, white in the blue light. He looked even less convinced than his words. A thwarted idealist he had said, this afternoon. Cynic would have been the same thing. She shrugged her shoulders too and tried to smile. Van Cortlandt was watching her.

"Do you know you were being followed in Nürnberg?" he asked suddenly.

"Yes."

"In a jam?"

"Not so far."

"Sorry if I seem inquisitive, but I just wondered when I saw that bird circling us tonight."

"I don't think that meant much. Sort of incidental music."

The American looked embarrassed. "Look, I know you would have told me about it, if you had wanted to. But all I'm trying to get at is this: if you are in a jam, you can always let me know."

"I can't tell you about it, Henry. Not because I don't want you to know, but because there's no use complicating things for you. I'll tell you all about everything later—in England, if you'll come and visit us there."

"You needn't worry about me. Mrs. van Cortlandt's little boy can take care of himself."

"But you are not so sure about us?"

"Oh well. I mean, you're not the kind of people to handle trouble; you're not tough enough. I wish I could put it better. I mean—"

Frances nodded and laid her hand on his arm.

"You're all right, too," she said.

There were footsteps on the road, and they could hear Thornley's voice, and then Richard's in a fluting falsetto.

"What the . . ." began van Cortlandt.

" 'Merchant of Venice.' Last act, I think, at the beginning." She began to laugh. "We can manage the midday sun, but not moonlight. Meet it is you set it down in your tables, Henry. You know, that chapter on the peculiarities of the British."

"Now when did I tell you I was doing that?"

"All books on European travel or politics have one. Why, no foreigner would believe he was looking at an Englishman unless he was funny-peculiar or funny-ha-ha."

"And what does the Englishman think about that?"

"He doesn't really care what people think about him, as long as he knows himself."

Richard and Thornley had timed their duet well. Richard managed to get the last line in, just as they reached Frances and van Cortlandt. He grasped Thornley's arm in a fair imitation of maidenly flurry.

"But, hark, I hear the footing of a man," he ended, and looked wildly round.

"You'd be safe enough if you looked like that," said Frances.

"Limping, anyway," added van Cortlandt, "so you're safe twice over."

"That role doesn't really do my powers justice," said Richard. "You should see me as the second witch in 'Macbeth.' Now that's something."

"Not tonight," said Frances hastily. "Let's all limp home to bed."

The four of them linked arms, and limped in unison towards the hotel.

As Frances and Richard said good night, van Cortlandt looked as if he wanted to say something, but he didn't. He seemed worried again.

They crossed the road to the Villa Waldesruhe. Frances was silent as they went upstairs, and silent as she removed her earrings and brushed her hair. And then she remembered about van Cortlandt's limp. She searched quickly for the methylated spirits and boracic and lint. Richard made a good-humored grimace, and started putting on his shoes again. She heard his footsteps echo on the empty road outside, and began to undress. When he returned, she was already in bed.

"That fellow was back again, talking to the manager."

She blinked sleepily. That fellow—"Oh, Beetlebrows?"

"Yes. He must think we are lunatics, chasing about at this hour with first-aid."

"All the better," said Frances, "or isn't it?"

"Does no harm. Only next time, my sweet wife, do remember such things before I get my shoes off."

"Yes, darling." She yawned prodigiously. ". . . doing tomorrow?"

Richard folded his trousers before replying. When he did, Frances gave no answer; she was, like the rest of Pertisau, asleep.

14

Friday came quickly for Thornley and van Cortlandt, slowly for Frances and Richard. They had enjoyed the bathing and climbing, the strange conversations which had a habit of cropping up, as much as the other two, but, as Frances said, Friday was like taking medicine: she wanted to get it over as quickly as possible.

On Friday, the mists were on the mountains, and the waters of the lake looked gray and uninviting. It takes salt water to make a bathe, when the sun isn't shining. Van Cortlandt was disappointed, for this was his last day. On Saturday he had to meet a radio man in Innsbruck, who wanted some impressions from him for a broadcast to America next week. Thornley thought it would be better if he motored into Innsbruck with van Cortlandt. He had begun to worry again about Tony and his Czechoslovakian girl. He wanted to make sure that his Innsbruck hotel hadn't mixed up his Pertisau address.

Over their eleven-o'clock beer, the arrangements were made. And then came the suggestion from Thornley that once the Innsbruck business was finished, he and van Cortlandt should return to Pertisau for a couple of days. At this, Richard looked slightly taken aback. By Sunday, God knows what would have happened. The two men noticed his slight hesitation, the vagueness of his reply. There was what Frances called a pregnant pause. She felt miserable, trying to explain to them with her eyes and her smile that it was no lack of enthusiasm for them which had caused Richard's embarrassment. Van Cortlandt suddenly saw daylight.

"Of course, your movements are indefinite, we know," he said and looked hard at Thornley. Frances had the feeling that he had told Thornley about their being followed in Nürnberg. The feeling was confirmed when she heard Thornley make a good follow-up.

"We can phone from Innsbruck, and find if you are still here. That is, if you don't mind."

"That would be fine," said Richard, obviously sincere, and the difficult moment had passed.

"It's a pity you must leave today," said Frances. "There's a dance this evening." The men looked bored at the idea.

"No, not in one of the hotels," she went on, reading their thoughts. "It's the real thing, held in one of the inns back near the woods. They build a platform outside the inn, and everyone comes from miles around to dance in their best clothes. Some of the costumes are really perfect, and it's fun to see people really enjoying themselves."

"When does it begin?" asked van Cortlandt.

"Nineish."

He shook his head. "Too late for me; we'll have to leave about six. But say, if you go, tell me about it, will you?"

"How on earth did you find out about the dance? There's no notice up anywhere that I could see," Thornley said in amazement.

"Oh, I have my agents," said Frances, and then blushed as Richard looked amused. "Actually, it was Frau Schichtl. She told me about it this morning, and said very pointedly that we would be welcomed."

"That's rather strange, don't you think, considering their German cousins are all over the place? You would think that they would be the ones who were welcome, and that we outsiders would be avoided like the plague."

"Lower voice," suggested Richard quietly.

Frances followed the suggestion. "No, it was quite the opposite. Frau Schichtl was eager for us to go and meet the real Austrians. She offered me the Sunday dirndl dress her daughter used to wear. Very lovely it was too."

"She really is awfully decent, you know," Thornley said. "She waylaid us yesterday when we came round to beat you up."

Van Cortlandt stared. "Bob, what the—"

"To beat you up or to hound you out or to collect you," Thornley explained as an aside. "Anyway, while we waited in that downstairs room, Frau Schichtl was baking in the kitchen. It was a damned good smell, too. So we looked in and made some jokes in terrible German, and we had to taste the cake just out of the oven. Haven't done that for years."

"I seem rather left out of all this," said Richard.

Frances laughed. "No, you aren't. Frau Schichtl said you were very well brought up and *so* polite. And she loves your imitations of the Bavarian accent."

Richard reddened. "Oh, come!" he said, and the others laughed.

But van Cortlandt had sensed a story.

"Where's the daughter?" he asked Frances. She studied her hands and said nothing.

"I won't use it for copy, if that is what you are thinking," he added with a wry smile.

Frances hesitated, but the others' curiosity had been wakened.

"She is dead. Some years ago, she went to Vienna to study singing. Frau Schichtl had saved a little money, and the girl was eager. She must have had some talent to get her way like that. But instead of becoming a great singer, she fell in love and got married. He was an active Social Democrat. They were planning to come here to visit Frau Schichtl; they hadn't much money, so they had to plan it carefully. And then the Nazis arrived. The husband's name must have been on their blacklist. They said he committed suicide. Nothing more has been heard of the girl." She paused. "Frau Schichtl says that I look very much like her, when she left for Vienna."

Van Cortlandt said, "She may not be dead."

"Frau Schichtl hopes she is."

There was a silence.

Then van Cortlandt said again, "Just another. That's what gets me down. It isn't just an isolated case. Wherever you go beneath the surface in this damned Nazi setup, there's tragedy, or something twisted. Nothing but complications, and fears, and threats. Even those who think they've jumped on the bandwagon are still standing on one leg. Only the dumbest of them can forget they are on the edge of a volcano. A nice crop of neurotics they'll be after whatever is going to happen has happened."

"Or corpses," said Thornley unexpectedly. "They'd make a fine row of corpses." He looked speculatively at the froth rims in his beer glass. The story of Frau Schichtl's daughter had started him thinking again about Czechoslovakia, thought Frances. She watched them finish their beer, each man with his own thoughts. The truth was that there was no peace of mind left for anyone—for anyone with a heart.

Richard had risen, and changed the subject. "Now about this afternoon. Frances and I thought we'd take a walk, and let you pack and make your arrangements. We'll be back to give you a send-off about six. That's the time you thought of, isn't it?" It was more of an intimation than a suggestion. Thornley caught van Cortlandt's eye, and the two men exchanged smiles.

"That suits us," the American said, and then added almost too casually, "and if you can't be good, you know what."

Frances and Richard left Waldesruhe at three o'clock. Richard had calculated that the distance from Pertisau to the red-shuttered house was about two miles. Yesterday, as they had climbed a hill with a view of the Pletzach, Thornley had pointed the house out to them—standing isolated in a high meadow above the little river. It was a good sort of place to have for the summer, he had observed. He was one of those who got a simple kind of pleasure in choosing sites for houses which he would never be able to own. There were already three places on the surrounding hillsides which he had selected as admirable for a summer chalet.

As they passed the Hotel Post, Thornley waved to them from the doorway, but he made no move to talk to them. As they entered the road which would lead them up the Pletzach, Frances glanced involuntarily over her shoulder. He was still standing at the hotel door, his hands in his pockets, and she had the feeling that he was making a very good pretense of not watching them. So his appearance at the door had been no accident. That gave her a comforting feeling. At least someone who knew them could vouch that they had left Pertisau quite normally. The deceased when last seen appeared to be in good health and normal spirits.

"He's a good person to have around in a crisis."

"Who is?" asked Richard.

"Bob Thornley. He tries to avoid discussing anything he feels very deeply about. It's as if he were afraid to let himself get emotional. He covers up with a funny story or one of these jokes against himself. And yet he notices quite a lot that is going on around him."

"He's no fool. Neither is Henry, but in another way. Did you know that Bob was an amateur golf champion of Belgium and Germany?

Henry unearthed that. He would, of course. Now there's another who is afraid of his emotions, but he takes refuge in being so damned critical that he becomes a sort of perpetual Doubting Thomas. Yet underneath, he has plenty of the right reactions. His heart is in the right place even if he has trained his mind to respond with a firstly, secondly, thirdly. When he forgets about that, then you feel he's made of very real flesh and blood. I bet his life is a conflict between what he thinks is the clever thing to do, and what he wants to do."

"And which wins?"

"I said he had the right reactions."

"He certainly had them this morning. I liked him when he lost his temper. He summed up everything I feel very neatly. It's strange how well Bob and Henry seem to hit it off; they have so many differences. I suppose it is a case of accepting them, and resisting the urge to reform the other fellow."

"They've both got sense," said Richard, and taking advantage of the fact that they had passed the houses at this side of the village, and that they were the only people on the quiet, narrow road, began to discuss their plans for the last time. He had chosen to approach the house quite openly and directly, so that if it were being watched, their reason for the visit would be believed. If they were to approach it in any roundabout way, it would be difficult to explain such caution. Frances could see the sense in that, although it seemed almost too simple to her just to walk up to the house and ask for Dr. Mespelbrunn. In spite of her determination to keep cool, there was already a feeling of excitement prickling her spine.

It was just half-past three when the road, now scarcely broader or more definite than a cart track, curved round the foot of the hill which buttressed the mountain range on their right. Only then could anyone from the road see the house. It was planted neatly in the middle of a broad green meadow on the sheltered side of the hill, the side which had been hidden from them as they approached from Pertisau. It lay peacefully isolated. There was no sign of any life in the wooded valley which it commanded, or on the mountains which walled in the valley.

Behind them, the jutting arm of the hill had so completely cut off the road by which they had come that Pertisau seemed blotted from the map. The mists had risen from the mountains, and the wind had dropped; the branches of the trees were motionless, the leaves were still. There wasn't even the sound of a woodman's ax. Even the Pletzach had subdued its chatter; it slipped, smooth and shallow, over its gravel bed.

"This is where we branch off," said Richard, as they reached a low wooden bridge over the stream. Across it was a path leading up to the fringe of trees which grouped themselves round the meadow. Behind the house, they thickened into a small forest which covered the slope of the hill like a neatly clipped beard, and spread onto the mountainside, which lay behind. When they reached the first of the trees, they saw that a track separated from the path to take them across to the front entrance of the house.

Richard looked at Frances. "Smile for the dicky bird," he said, and forced one out of her. They left the shelter of the trees to climb up the gently sloping grass. Frances wished she felt as cool as Richard looked. His small talk on the beauties of nature was faultless. For once, she could not think of a thing to say.

It was a small house, sturdily built, with the usual overhanging eaves, a balcony encircling the upper story, and shutters with the conventional heart-shaped decorations. The large window boxes at the edge of the balcony were filled with petunias. Perhaps there were more windows than a peasant would have thought necessary, but otherwise it was the kind of house which someone who had lived in, and loved, the Tyrol might build as a summer escape from his town life. Someone who had indulged his taste for an additional romantic touch in the red of the shutters. They made a convincing and yet inconspicuous landmark.

The heavy front door was closed. Richard knocked, and as they waited, they looked at the stretching valley below them. Thornley had been right; it was a perfect place to build a house. The rain clouds of the morning had disappeared, and the sun warmed the stillness all around them. They heard the door open behind them, and they turned to face a woman. She was past middle age, large-boned, with the impassive face of a peasant. Her graying hair was tightly knotted at the back of her head; her large-knuckled hands kept smoothing her apron.

"Good day," Richard said.

The woman nodded, but did not speak.

"Is Dr. Mespelbrunn at home?" At the name Mespelbrunn her eyes moved quickly from Richard to Frances, and then back again.

Richard tried again. "I am interested in chess collections, and I have been advised by Anton in the village to visit Dr. Mespelbrunn, who has some very fine pieces, I believe. If Dr. Mespelbrunn were at home, perhaps he would have the great kindness to let me see his collection."

The woman was still silent. She was not altogether stupid, thought Richard, remembering the quickness of her glance. Could it be that she was afraid? Then the woman suddenly looked behind her, and drew quickly away from the door. Yes, it was fear, all right. A man came out of the shadows. He must have been listening quite quietly all this time.

"Dr. Mespelbrunn?" he asked. His voice had a hoarseness which coarsened his accent. He had pushed the gray-haired woman to one side, and stood in the sunlight with a smile on his dark face. It was the man who had watched them in the Hotel Post three nights ago.

He was as swaggering as ever as he held the door wide open and bowed them politely into the house. Frances felt her legs prepare to run back down the hill as she looked at that welcoming smile; but Richard was waiting for her to enter. They found themselves in the large room, a mixture of a sitting room, a lounge, and a study.

"She's just a dumb peasant," said the man with a still broader smile. Richard ignored the remark. He repeated the sentences he had addressed to the woman.

"But of course." The hoarse voice was being genial, but the effect was far from pleasant. "If you wait here, I'll get Dr. Mespelbrunn. He is reading in the summerhouse."

The man left them abruptly, his heavy heels sounding on the hardwood floor with a precision which grated on Frances' nerves. She exchanged looks with Richard, but neither spoke. She had hated this man at first sight. Still, they must see Mespelbrunn before they passed any judgments. The man might be only a very clever touch of realistic color. She remembered the grim Kronsteiner and his hotel. There was no doubt that Peter's friend had a peculiar sense of humor. This might only be another example.

She drew her cardigan more closely round her shoulders, and lit a cigarette. She walked slowly round the room, feeling it like a cat. It was a pleasant room, a man's room, smelling of pine logs and tobacco. She noted the walls of natural wood, the leather armchairs, more comfortable than elegant, the functional disorder of books on every table and music on the piano. A low table stood in front of the deep couch before the open fireplace. An open fireplace—perhaps an Englishman lived here after all. Yes, in the interior of the room there was a certain touch. An Englishman lived here. She turned to Richard. He was standing before the piano, his hands deep in his pockets, his lips pursed. He nodded silently to a piece of music displayed prominently on the stand. It was their old friend. He shook his head disapprovingly. Rather obvious, was what he thought. He moved away from the piano towards the fireplace and lit another cigarette. They heard footsteps outside; a man's voice spoke as if to a dog. It was only a short command, but the words were English. She sat down in the nearest chair and tried to look as calm as she didn't feel. Richard's calm gray eyes held her own for a moment, and then she started to count the steps in the staircase at the end of the room. She had reached the ninth stair when the front door opened.

They both stared in amazement. The tall man who had entered was equally taken aback. He recovered himself before they did.

"Well, really," he said in perfect English, "this is a pleasure."

Richard smiled; his eyes were calm again. "How extraordinary to meet you here," was all he said.

The Freiherr Sigurd von Aschenhausen moved quickly over to Frances and bowed low over her hand. She smiled, but inside she was angry. An Englishman, indeed, with that acute Oxford accent so carefully cultivated in his years of free scholarship. Would Mr. Rhodes have enjoyed this joke as little as she did? Probably less . . .

"We came to see a Dr. Mespelbrunn, or rather his chess collection. We were told in the village that it was the thing to do." Richard looked at von Aschenhausen blandly.

The German smiled. "Well, you've found him, you know."

"Are you—But why on earth—" began Frances, and hoped that the laugh she gave was sufficiently amused. "How really very funny. But why take such a wretched name as that and give up your own perfectly good one?" Help me to talk gaily, dear Heaven, she prayed, to talk nonsense like a sweet little fool.

"It's perfectly simple," said von Aschenhausen. "When I live here I have to be very careful; it would be impossible to use my own name." He paused but the Myles' only looked at him with polite surprise.

"It would be too dangerous for me," he added, lowering his voice. But they still looked at him politely, as if they expected him to go on.

"Cigarette?" he asked Frances, and flicked open his gold cigarette case. As he lit her cigarette, she noticed the bracelet on his left wrist. The bracelet was of fine gold, too.

She pretended she thought he had meant to change the subject. "You are looking very well," she said. One up, she thought, as she noticed the flicker of disappointment in his eyes. "You have a charming place here," she rushed on, before he could reply. "I think all of Pertisau is delightful."

"Yes; it is beautiful," von Aschenhausen said, emphasizing the stronger adjective. Someone ought to tell him, thought Frances, that he ought to have said "Do you think so? I'm so glad" and left it to his guests to do the praising, if he really wanted to perfect his imitation.

"You look very thoughtful," he remarked.

Frances came back to the room with a jolt. "Oh, I was thinking about forms of politeness."

"Now you have made me feel I must be very careful. I wasn't very polite according to your standards, I am afraid, when we met at that Oxford party. Why didn't you tell me then that you were coming here?"

Richard entered the conversation. "Well, first of all, we thought you were in Berlin. And, secondly, it was pure chance that we did come here. We were at Mittenwald, you know, and then one evening someone or other started to talk about the beauties of the Tyrol. You know the sort of thing: you discuss some place, and then you feel you'd like to go there, and then you go."

"Charmingly quixotic," said von Aschenhausen.

"And the most quixotic thing of all is that you should be Dr. Mespelbrunn," Frances said. She felt his interest quicken. "I had imagined someone quite different, you know." The tension was growing. "You see, I once read a book about Pertisau. It was called *The Constant Nymph.* So when we were buying some things in Anton's shop, and he said that *the* chess connoisseur of the district was a Dr. Mespelbrunn, who just adored visiting chessmen, as it were, I suddenly thought 'Another Pertisau eccentric; how amusing.' He gave you a terrific build-up, you know, until I became quite intrigued. It was really I who am responsible for the visit, because Richard went all sort of diffident. Didn't want to trouble you, and all that sort of thing. But I expected to find a house filled with a remarkable family of chess experts and unrecognized geniuses, and here you are, a very comfortable bachelor. You've really let me down, rather. I shan't be able to romanticize again without Richard . . . well, just look at him. He is enjoying his joke, isn't he?"

Richard was indeed looking amused.

"I'd still like to see the collection, if I may," he said.

"I'm afraid it isn't here at the moment. It's being exhibited at Innsbruck." Von Aschenhausen looked as if he really were disappointed too. Or perhaps it was genuine: at the beginning of Frances' little speech, he had hoped for something, something more than he had got by the end of it. He tried again.

"I think you have been mistaken about me. I've already apologized for our Oxford conversation. Can't you see there's no other course for me? Some types of work—" he paused effectively on that word—"need strong aliases."

His meaning, accompanied by that shrug of the shoulder, that pained eyebrow, that so straight, so direct look into Frances' eyes, couldn't have been plainer. In another minute, thought Frances, he will start telling us anti-Nazi jokes, just to show us how mistaken we have been about him. She looked as if she believed him; Richard nodded sympathetically; but neither of them spoke.

Von Aschenhausen waited. And then he began to ask about Oxford. His visit this summer had lasted only for a day; he had had little time to find out all about his old friends. Frances could see where this line would lead him. So he was interested in Peter Galt, was he? She left it to Richard to handle the conversation this time. She suddenly wanted to leave, but they couldn't do that until von Aschenhausen was satisfied. She looked out of the window. Her thoughts turned to Mespelbrunn. Where was he? Probably dead. Perhaps dead and buried on the mountainside opposite her. She watched the sunlight strike on the dark rich green of the fir trees, and the shadows lengthening on the hill. The afternoon was ending. She turned impatiently to the two men.

Richard, by some feat, had switched the conversation over to the women's colleges in Oxford, and there it had stuck, imbedded in the higher education of women. He refused to abandon his advantage; he had got the conversation to a nice impersonal subject, and he was going to keep it there. He was politely defending the new freedom of women. Women had learned to compromise successfully between developing their mental powers and retaining their charm. The aggressive unfemininity of the original blue-stocking was already disappearing. It was only a matter of time and adjustment to a freer aspect of life.

Von Aschenhausen smiled his disbelief. "They are too emotional. They are limited in reasoning power. They are weaker, both physically and mentally. They can never be equal to men. Compromise, adjustment, matter of time. . . . You couldn't be more English, Richard." The use of Richard's first name carried all three of them back, back to a time when suspicion and hatred had only brooded in the hearts of a few vengeful men. In the silence that followed, they looked at each other. There was no need to translate their thoughts into words; they were clear in their eyes.

The German spoke first. "You need not reproach me. What Mrs. Myles said at that sherry party was true. Our countries have gone different ways. And I have my work to do. But I think, as I said already, that you have been mistaken about me. It is a compliment, I suppose, to my powers of acting. I never knew they were so good as that." He shrugged his shoulders again and gave a rueful smile. You are not making a bad job of it, right now, thought Richard. Von Aschenhausen had been well cast for the part he had to play. To anyone who did not know that he was German, he would appear to be the authentic Mespelbrunn. Now, he was making the best of a very bad piece of luck: here were two people who could know that he was no Englishman. His hints at anti-Nazi feeling were just enough to win their sympathy, disarm their suspicions. He didn't protest too much, either; he had to pretend that their visit was innocent, in case it really was. He couldn't make any declarations; he had to give them confidence, and perhaps they would show their hand once that was established. His difficulty was that they might very well be only interested in chessmen. Considering everything which was at stake, he was not making a bad job of it at all, thought Richard again.

Von Aschenhausen suddenly rose, and walked over to the small table which was used as a bar. His voice was charmingly ingenuous.

"You used to play well. Why don't you now, while I mix some drinks?" As he measured out the whisky, Frances was aware that he was watching Richard move to the piano with more than friendly interest.

"Hello," Richard said casually, "what's this you've got? Do you sing?"

"Only for myself. You go ahead."

Richard noted the soprano setting of the song, and smiled gently.

"It's a good song, but not my cup of tea. What about 'The Two Grenadiers' or something with hair on its chest? I'll need the music, though. I'm very bad at playing things by ear." He turned to a pile of music and started to look through it.

Frances rose and went over to the piano.

"You are both so modest. I'll sing for you instead." She saw Richard stiffen slightly, and give her a blank look. Von Aschenhausen was watching her now. She returned his smile sweetly and sat down on the piano stool. Richard cursed silently to himself; surely Frances had not been duped by an earnest pair of blue eyes. Surely she couldn't . . . He cursed to himself. If he could only reach that little table and upset it by accident before she started to sing . . . But as he moved, the first notes sounded through the room, and the words of the song gathered strength as her voice grew more confident. Richard looked at von Aschenhausen. His politeness had vanished. The dueling scars on his face were very noticeable.

Frances finished the last melancholy chords. She stood up and faced von Aschenhausen. She spoke directly to him.

"It is called 'The Slaughter of the Innocents'—one of the old Coventry Carols. Do you know it?" Her voice still held the sadness of the song, but there was a challenge in her eyes.

"Sentimentalizing history, isn't it?" His accent was less English.

"Maybe. But it's only when you think of history as blood and tears that you can ever learn from it." She saw he understood the meaning underlying her words just as he had understood the application of the song. The cap fitted. Let it, she thought savagely.

There was a sudden crash upstairs, and then the thuds of hollow blows. The noises ceased as startlingly as they had begun. Von Aschenhausen saw the surprise on their faces. He was suddenly casual and polite again; he smiled easily.

"Don't worry," he said. "That's the dog. We keep him out of the way when we have visitors. He's very savage with strangers. He is just about due for his exercise, and he always lets me know very forcibly when it's time to take him out for a walk."

"Oh, we mustn't keep you, then," Frances said. "I am sure we have stayed too long, in any case."

"I am sorry I had to disappoint you about the chessmen. They may be back by Sunday. Come and see them, then."

Richard, still listening for further sounds, said they would be delighted to come, perhaps at the beginning of next week. He was thinking about the dog. It was strange to keep an animal locked up inside a room upstairs; that would hardly improve its temper. But of one thing he was certain: von Aschenhausen was determined to get them out of the house, as quickly as possible.

Frances had already reached the door. As von Aschenhausen opened it for them, they heard two other sounds from upstairs. Weaker sounds, much weaker. But they ignored them, and said their good-bys as if nothing had happened. And they equally ignored the dark man with the hoarse voice, who stood astride outside the front door, his thumbs tucked inside his belt. At a nod directed upstairs from von Aschenhausen, he sprang quickly past them, mounting the steps three at a time. Von Aschenhausen had regained his usual composure, but his smile was too fixed. He stood at the door and watched them until they had reached the trees. Frances hated the feeling of his eyes on her back; she forced herself to walk naturally, as if she were strolling down Holywell. Only now would she admit to herself what she had first known at a sherry party in Oxford. The man who had once been numbered among their friends had long since become an enemy. It was a painful admission.

When they gained the road, Frances took a deep breath.

"Well, I've made another step in my education," she said. Richard did not answer. He was lost in thought.

"What's wrong? You haven't forgotten the Geneva address, have you? Or what?"

Richard shook his head. He seemed to be paying little attention; rather, he was watching the road as if he were trying to remember something.

"It's just about here, I think," he said as if to himself. He saw Frances looking at him curiously. "Just about here, that the shoulder of the hill stopped hiding the house. We'll give it another twenty yards."

The road twisted farther behind the jutting hill; and as it passed through a fringe of trees, Richard suddenly pulled Frances up the short steep bank into the shelter of the branches. It was all so quick that Frances did not have time to say anything; her surprise held her silent. Richard looked back over his shoulder, and then relaxed his grip on her arm.

"The shoulder hid us, and they couldn't follow us yet. Not with the road so open as it is."

"What's wrong?" Frances asked again.

"Something. Haven't quite made up my mind."

He advanced into the small wood, and Frances followed; the feeling of confidence which had come to her as they left the path and reached the road quickly evaporated. Von Aschenhausen had discovered nothing, except that they didn't like the politics of his country—and that couldn't have surprised him, even if it angered him. What worried Richard? He had reached a large tree, which had sheltered the ground from the morning rain. There they regained their breath. It had only taken them two minutes to reach here from the road.

The wood had grown over a large mound, and from this elevation they had a clear view of one part of the road, neatly focused for them by the way in which the trees grew. They could see without being seen. Richard moved slightly to the left to get a better sight of the one visible patch of road. From this point, it could be seen even if they sat down. He seemed satisfied—but not with Frances' dress. He pulled off the red silk handkerchief which she wore tucked into the neckline of her white shirt.

"Put on your cardigan properly," he advised, "and button it right up to cover that white collar. I don't like the red socks: they shine up miles away. Here—" He reached for a handful of earth mold, and covered the red wool with an efficient layer of clinging brown earth.

"Here yourself," said Frances with a good touch of annoyance.

"My pet, you aren't in this for the benefit of your color schemes." He kept his voice low, but there was enough sharpness in it to tell her he was worried.

"Well, I'm glad that the cardigan is green, or I'd be rolling in the mud at this moment, I suppose . . . What's *wrong?*"

Richard put one arm round her shoulders, and kept his eyes fixed on the road.

"Frances, what did you think when you heard the noises upstairs?"

So that was the trouble. She looked at him in surprise.

"Well, it could have been a dog," she said.

"Forget about that dog. What were the noises like? As you heard them, and not as they were explained away?"

Frances studied her muddied socks for some moments. She had been standing beside the piano; the drinks they hadn't touched had gleamed amber in a ray of sunlight.

"Well, candidly, the first sound seemed a crash, as if something heavy, like a piece of furniture, something solid, had fallen. And then came some thumps."

"Well?"

"They might have been a fist, but I don't think any fist could have hammered loudly enough for us to hear, even allowing for wooden floors and ceilings. No, I don't think those thumping sounds came from a fist. They were too powerful for that. I thought afterwards that it *could* have been a dog leaping against a heavy door. A big dog."

"But those thuds were clear-cut. They were sharply defined. There were no scrabbling noises, which generally end a dog's jump against a door. Even when we were leaving, and we were standing at the foot of the staircase, there were no whines, no pawing sounds. Peculiar kind of dog it must have been."

Frances looked at Richard, who kept his eyes fixed on the road. She was beginning to see the reason for his worry.

"Yes," she agreed. "There were only clear-cut thuds. Sort of staccato thuds."

"And the last two, which we heard at the bottom of the stairs, and which should have sounded clearer to us if anything, were actually weaker."

"Yes." Something haunted her memory. "Wait," she added. If only she could think what it was that had that kind of sound. Something she had heard that afternoon . . . in that room.

"Richard—" her voice was excited now, and Richard laid a finger on his lips warningly—"Richard, if a dog jumped at the door as we are supposed to believe, the thud on the door would have a different sound from a thud on the floor, wouldn't it? Well, do you remember when that bull-necked man left us to go and tell Mespelbrunn that we had arrived? He swaggered across the floor and his heels made that same flat sound. The thumping was not against a door, it was on the ground. And I don't believe it was made by anything so soft as a hand or a dog's paw. You were perfectly right, Richard."

"You are more right, still. Good for you, Fran. Now for a spot of reconstruction. We heard a crash, as if a piece of furniture or something solid had hit the ground. What about a chair? And what about someone tied to the chair? That would make the crash quite as heavy as we heard it. Then there were the thumpings, harder and stronger than the blows from a fist. What about two legs tied together? Then they would have to be brought slowly up and allowed to fall on the floor. That would give the kind of noise we heard, all right; for with the legs or ankles tied the heels would strike the ground together. It also accounts for the fact that the blows got weaker. It's pretty difficult and tiring to attract anyone's attention that way."

"But everything was so quiet in that house until those last five minutes."

"Yes, until after you had finished your song."

"Whoever it was recognized it?"

Richard nodded. "Yes. . . . He couldn't have made out our voices when we were talking. And there would have been no hope for him if he had heard a German song sung by a German voice. But there was hope enough to try to attract our attention when he heard an English voice and a song which practically only an Englishman would recognize."

"So he may be our man? What on earth can we do, Richard? We've found him and we haven't found him." This was something which Peter Galt had not thought of; they should have either met an Englishman, or found he was dead. Something nice and straightforward, and not a hopeless complication like this.

"What's our next step?" she asked dismally.

Richard drew a slab of chocolate from his pocket. "Eat some of this," he suggested. He looked at his watch. "It's well after five now. We had better wait a bit. If any chance comes, we'll seize it. If no chance comes, I'll take you back to Frau Schichtl's, and come back here myself tonight. I'd like to look around."

"You've no gun," said Frances in a very low voice; her fears stifled her. "Perhaps he isn't our man after all," she added persuadingly.

"It's some man, anyway. I'd still like to look around. Henry may carry a gun. If so, I'll borrow it. If not, then I've always got my stick." He patted the *makhila* which lay beside them. Frances looked at the Basque stick of rough wood, with its round leather handle and its sharply pointed ferrule. It didn't look much protection; the iron point on the end was only good for helping you up a steep hill. Richard noticed her expression. He unscrewed the handle with a suspicion of a smile.

"I never showed you this. It's rather gruesome." The head of the stick and part of the top of it slipped off, and a wicked eight inches of pointed steel emerged. It was firmly fixed to the rest of the stick, and transformed it into an ominous weapon.

"I'm not really bloodthirsty," he added. "I bought it on that Pyrenees trip, when I was an undergraduate, because I liked the way the Basques swung these sticks with the leather thong of the handle fixed round their wrists, when they were returning from market. Going to the town, they kept the cattle in order with the steel point. Coming from the town, they screwed the handle back in place and slipped the thong over their wrist, and swung it jauntily—with their jacket over one shoulder, and money in their pocket, and a smile for all the girls. I liked the contrast."

Frances looked at him incredulously. "And I've looked at that stick for years, and I never . . . When you told me it was used for goading cattle, I thought it was the ferrule at the end of the stick which you meant." She began to giggle; any joke seemed doubly good at this moment.

Richard's smile broadened. "Really, Frances, you're wonderful. Have you ever seen Basque oxen?" He laughed quietly, and then kissed her. "I wouldn't part with you for all the gold in America," he said.

Frances recovered her seriousness. "Now that I've supplied the comic relief, how long are we going to stay here, and what shall we do, if and when and where?"

"First of all, I was curious to see if we would be followed. We weren't, it seems. Von Aschenhausen perhaps was quite convinced that we were harmless fools. I shouldn't be surprised, though, if he checks up on our travels. You know the Teutonic thoroughness. That may have been the reason why he had that afterthought of inviting us to come back and see the chess collection: just so that he can know more about our movements when he meets us again. Probably, too, someone will be sent to keep a watchful eye on us until we leave Pertisau. That's very probable. That leads to my second idea. I've been hoping that Beetlebrows might make one of his evening calls on Pertisau. If he does, then we'll improvise."

"And I'll be quite useless," said Frances bitterly. "What you need is another man with you. And then we might be able to do something."

Richard didn't answer that.

"If we could get to the house in a roundabout way, or something—" Frances went on—"but then we'd have to face two men, armed, as well as the dog—if there is one. It would be madness. What you need is darkness, and someone like Henry or Bob, or both. And at least one gun. It's hopeless."

"Let me do the worrying, Frances. I'll try nothing unless one of them leaves. I can manage one of them alone, easily, if I can get to the house unseen. There is no telephone, and that will be useful for us: I'm depending on Beetlebrows, and his visits to Pertisau." He looked at his watch again. "It's getting near his usual time."

Frances wondered why Richard was so confident that there were only two men to worry about . . . But his eyes were fixed on the road. She sat beside him and waited in silence. She felt she had made enough wifely objections to last for the next few hours. After all, she had insisted on coming. Richard had been against it. Wifely objections would only be doubly irritating. So she sat and finished the job of converting her red socks into a rich chestnut-brown.

15

It could only have been about ten minutes later when Richard's arm tightened round Frances, and pushed her quickly flat on the ground. She felt a stone dig into the small of her back, but Richard's grasp was firm. She lay still and watched him. He was lying flat on his stomach, his head only raised enough to let him see that free patch of road. It was the black-haired man, cycling towards Pertisau, with a wolf-hound at his heels . . . And then he was out of sight: the other trees hid him from Richard's straining eye.

Richard relaxed his grip, and Frances sat up and rubbed her back. The stone had become a boulder.

"So that leaves only von Aschenhausen," said Richard with some satisfaction.

Frances forgot her good resolutions. "How are you so sure?" she asked.

"If there were others, then the noises upstairs would have been silenced more quickly. And von Aschenhausen had to signal to that man to stop guarding the front door. It was only then that he was free to go upstairs and attend to the noises. If there had been others to stop us from getting away—supposing it had come to that—then he would not have stuck outside until he got the signal."

"But why only two of them?"

"It's a small house, and if a group of men had arrived to live there, the villagers would have started to talk. Then any prospective visitors might have had suspicions aroused. I expect that black-haired fellow poses as Mespelbrunn's new servant." Richard looked at his watch, and then added, "We had better let him get halfway to Pertisau, and then he can look round as much as he likes and it won't trouble us."

"They haven't anything definite against us, have they?" asked Frances.

"Nothing except the fact that we were found in a suspected shop in Nürnberg, and that we presented ourselves to an obviously suspected Dr. Mespelbrunn with a highly suspect form of introduction. They may dislike the coincidence. Perhaps von Aschenhausen has started to check up on us already. There isn't any phone, but he has some kind of radio transmitter and receiver, I'm sure. Perhaps Beetlebrows is going down to Pertisau to keep an eye on us. Perhaps all that. And again, von Aschenhausen may be congratulating himself on getting rid of a pair of unwelcome visitors, and Beetlebrows is cycling down to Pertisau to see a girl, or have his beer, or to keep his figure. I think myself that it's safer to overestimate your enemies than underestimate them, so I'm prepared to believe that they don't like us one bit."

"Von Aschenhausen certainly didn't like me," Frances said, and laughed gently.

"I could have strangled you, myself, when you played that trick at the piano. You had me as jittery as he was. For a moment I thought you were going to play that damned music."

"Was it as good as that? Darling, you've made me very happy."

"It was too dangerous, Frances. Never give in to your impulse for the artistic, not in a situation like that."

"Oh, it was safe enough. He thinks women have no brains. Even at the very end, he only thought I was parroting some phrases I had heard you say."

Richard smiled in spite of himself. . . . And then he looked at his watch impatiently, and then he looked at the warm glow of the evening sun.

"I wish it were darker, but we can't wait. Come on, Frances."

They made their way back to the road, and paused at the edge of the trees. There was no one in sight. They crossed quickly into the rough field which stretched towards the stream, skirting the foot of the hill. They covered the uneven ground quickly but carefully.

"No twisted ankles at this point," said Richard. Frances nodded. She was concentrating on the varying firmness of the treacherous clumps underneath her feet. The stream was shallow, fortunately. They crossed by choosing stones either jutting up or only lightly covered by the racing water. Frances congratulated herself on having her shoes only wet, and not swamped entirely. And now they began to climb the hill itself, aiming for a point in its shoulder which would bring them just above and behind the house. This side of the hill was dangerously open; there were no trees, only grass and shrubs which ultimately gave way to the rocky spine. Again Frances had the feeling that the hill which they were climbing was the buttress, and the mountain behind it was the cathedral. It was like a finger pointing out of the mountain's clenched hand. The climb was more difficult than it looked from the road, for there was no path to lead them over the easiest ground.

Two thirds of the climb found the undergrowth thinning out quickly. They paused for breath, while Richard scanned the ground above them. He shook his head as he noticed the increasing number of small screes. It was madness to try to scramble over their treacherous surface; the stones now under their feet were as knife-sharp as when they had been splintered from smashing boulders. The ridge of the hill was of rock, and, at this distance, there was a dangerous look to the last fifty feet. It would be slow work getting over that. He looked along its side to the place where the hill joined the mountain. Just at that point there seemed to be a slight hollow. It was the bed of a mountain stream, now dry, but no doubt forming a gleaming cascade of water in the spring.

"Our best bet is to strike for the stream," he said. "It will take us farther away from the house, but the dry bed of a torrent is easier than a miniature precipice." He pointed to the crest of the hill. Frances needed no convincing. They began to climb obliquely up towards the bed of the stream, avoiding any falls of loose gravel, and choosing ground where some persistent green still showed. That at least gave them some guarantee of safety.

It was slow work, until they suddenly met, to Frances' joy, a small track which had the same idea as Richard. It must have begun at the road, near the place where the shoulder of the hill had formed a jutting curve, and had traced its modest way parallel to the shoulder's crest.

"We could have followed this all the way," said Frances, with some exasperation, following their own course up the hill with a bitter eye.

"No, it began too close to the house. The road at that point might have been watched by Herr Von-und-zu strolling in his nice soft meadow."

Frances was standing very still. "Well, we only postponed it," she said so quietly that Richard stopped and turned to see her face.

"Down there," she added. Richard followed the direction of her eyes. The valley beneath them was no longer empty. Along the road which led from Pertisau a man was riding a bicycle.

"Like the hammers of hell," Richard said, and swore gently but wholeheartedly. "Don't move. Keep just the way you are."

"He looks like an ant," said Frances.

"Louse, you mean." Richard was worried. "I wonder now . . . what did he learn at Pertisau to send him back at this rate? No one there knew when we were returning, except Henry or Bob; and he can't have been talking to them."

"I wonder if he saw us. Do you think he would take me for another piece of greenery? There are at least two pieces of scrub near me." She looked fearfully at her socks, but the loam had been reinforced by some mud which she had blundered into on the soft bank of the stream. Richard watched the cyclist as he reached the curve in the road.

"He hasn't slackened pace yet; it looks as if he might not have noticed us. If he had, I should think he would have slowed up, just to make sure. God, that dog can keep up a terrific clip."

"What shall we do?"

"There's still daylight for some time," Richard said thoughtfully. "Once we are up there, we ought to have a wonderful view of the back of the house. Damn it all, if only I had left you in Pertisau, and come by myself."

"Then you wouldn't have had either an old English song or these noises. Let's go on, Richard. I don't like the idea of going down the way we came up. And once we get up—we are very nearly there anyway—we might find a decent path on the mountain itself to lead us back to Pertisau. There's no law against us trying to climb our way back towards the village and if anyone wants to know why we took so long, well then, we got lost. That's all." But the truth was, she added to herself, that Richard would have gone on if he had been alone or with another man—and that settled it.

Richard still looked doubtful, but he was wavering.

"Well, we can watch from the top for half an hour, and if it all seems hopeless, then I'll get you back to the road before it's dark."

"All right. Let's move, Richard."

They started to climb the last stretch of hill.

The path was apologetic. At best, it was little more than a foot broad;

at its worst, it effaced itself altogether under slides of stones. As they crossed these slowly, Frances held her breath. One slip here, and she would go rumplin' tumplin' down the Tankersha' brae. She kept her eyes fixed on the next step ahead, and avoided looking down to her right. For there the hill now fell steeply away, carved out by erosion into an adequate quarry. If this path had lain across a field, you could run along it, she argued. So there was no reason why she couldn't walk along it here, provided she didn't know how far she had to fall. And then the green scrub was again growing thickly, and they had reached the bushes and dwarf trees which edged the bed of the stream. The sides of the dry torrent, and even the bed itself, were piled with large rocks. They formed a staircase. A giant's staircase, thought Frances, but at least if she slipped here she would always have a boulder behind her, to block her fall.

They were both breathing heavily with the effort of hoisting themselves over the rocks which would form the bank of the torrent when the snows melted in the spring. But the worst of the climb was already past. The boulders in the bleached bed of the stream were thinning out, and the ground was leveling. They were approaching the saddle between the hill and the mountain. As it opened out before them they saw that it was broad and gently sloping. They left the stream which was turning towards the mountan itself, and walked quickly over the grass towards some scattered rocks on the saddle's crest. From there they could see the valley with the red-shuttered house. When they reached the rocks only half of their expectations was realized. All they could see of the house was some blue smoke which curled up lazily over the tops of the farthest trees.

Richard smiled wryly. "Anticlimax department, I'm afraid. It seems I dragged you up here to admire the view, Frances. I'm sorry."

Frances let her muscles relax. She pushed her damp hair away from her brow to feel the full coolness of the evening breeze.

"You can always study the paths," she said.

Richard was already doing that. The saddle seemed the meeting place of the paths on the hill and the mountain. If he could get Frances back to Pertisau as quickly as possible, and if the moon was as clear as it had been last night, then he could use the mountain paths to bring him right up behind the house. He could see both of them clearly from here; neither was difficult. Eastwards towards Pertisau stretched the first path he would use, which would bring him easily onto this saddle; and then, from here, there was a westward path, cutting across the mountain where it formed a background for the house. He could see at least one track descending from it into the trees which encircled the back of the house. Then he might try some stalking right up to the outskirts of the house itself. Thornley would be a good man to have along; he knew his way about a mountain. It was just as well that he had come up here after all. He looked at the mountain paths, and photographed what he saw in his memory.

Frances, lying beside him, her chin cupped in her hands, had been staring at the forest beneath them. Her eyes followed the well-marked path, which led from the saddle down through the trees towards the house. This was probably the path which began at the bridge in the valley. She looked at the trees, as if by sheer will-power she might see through them, through the walls of the house itself into that room upstairs. She was comparing her reactions as she had left that house to those of Richard, and the result did not flatter her. She had taken it for granted that their job was over, that there was nothing left to do except send a telegram and then go away and enjoy themselves. She had believed the story about the dog because she had wanted to believe it; it was a subconscious desire to be rid of complications, to avoid any further trouble. Now she knew that she wouldn't have been able to enjoy any holiday. She would have had to face the fact ultimately that it hadn't been a dog, and she would have remembered it just as long as she would remember the cry in a Jews' Alley in Nürnberg.

She suddenly stiffened.

"What was that? Richard, I saw something down there."

"Where?" He turned to look down the hill towards the house. The path, beginning near where they lay, twisted its way towards the forest. Beyond the last trees, the smoke curled from the chimney.

"Down there. Look. The twist in the path hid it . . . near the trees. Richard, it's a dog."

Richard grasped her wrist and the strength of his hand calmed her.

"So he did see us," he said.

The dog, bounding up the path towards them, had stopped and was looking backwards. When the two men came in sight, he again bounded on.

It was von Aschenhausen and the black-haired man. The path was broad enough to let them walk abreast. They carried no sticks, but their hands were deep in their jacket pockets. Their eyes searched the hill around them. Once they stopped, while the man looked towards the westward path on the mountain, but it had only been some animal which had attracted his attention. He had quick eyes all right, thought Richard.

"Keep cool, Frances. They haven't seen us yet."

Again the men stopped, and this time they separated. Von Aschenhausen left the path, and began to climb directly up the shoulder. His pace had slowed down, but even from that distance it was evident that he could climb. When von Aschenhausen reached the top, he would be just about the place which they had first attempted to reach. Richard reflected with some pleasure that the east side of the shoulder, which the German would then have to descend, would cramp his style a little. His plan was to encircle them, obviously. The black-haired man was plodding steadily up the path to the saddle where they lay; the dog bounded ahead.

As they backed cautiously from the sheltering rocks, and raced back over the gently sloping ground, Richard was thinking quickly but nonetheless clearly. Von Aschenhausen had taken the much more difficult way because his companion was probably a less expert climber. So much the better for Frances and himself. He would rather face brawn than brain, any day. You could outwit the former. They must make for the bed of the stream; that was their only hope for cover. Once they were hidden by the boulders and the bushes which twisted round them on the torrent's banks, they could follow the bed until they had reached the fields and the woods round the Pletzach—and then they would be safe enough. The incriminating thing for them would be to stay on the shoulder overlooking the house. If von Aschenhausen didn't find them on the hill, they could find an explanation for their late return to Pertisau. And he would have to accept it because he wouldn't be able to disprove it. But it all made tonight's plans almost impossible. They would be closely watched from now on.

If Frances had been thankful for grass under her feet when she had first reached the saddle on the way up, she now almost wept with relief. She could run swiftly on this surface and, what was just as important, run silently. She had the feeling of desperate effort which she used to have as a child when she played Cowboys-and-Indians and she was one of the chased. It was no longer a game, but the old terrifying feeling of strained muscles bogging her down, of feet sticking to the ground, was still there.

She must go faster and faster, but her body refused even as her mind urged her on. She sagged, her heart pounding and a strange thundering in her ears so that she couldn't swallow. But Richard's hand, which had not loosened its grasp on her wrist from the moment when they had first seen the dog, pulled her up and on. They had reached the stream.

Their run had slowed down to a scramble, but the first large rocks were near them. Richard had let go of her wrist now; they needed the use of their hands to steady themselves through the boulders. It would have been quicker work if they hadn't had to avoid any clatter of stones. Richard was thankful for what he had been cursing only half an hour ago, for the fact that they had worn rubber-soled shoes today to go visiting, rather than their nail-studded climbing boots.

The man could not have reached the top of the path yet; nor could von Aschenhausen have reached the crest of the shoulder. As the stream bed plunged deeply in between the crags, Richard looked over his shoulder. They were hidden now, thank God, from both the shoulder and the saddle of the hill. There was no man in sight. But there was the dog. It had marked them from the saddle, and instead of waiting there for the dark-haired man, had followed them. It hadn't barked. There was something uncanny in the silent way it calculated its powerful leaps over the rough stones, to alight on smooth rock. Its speed was checked by its twists and turns, by the way in which its thick haunches would brake suddenly on the steep side of a boulder. But its direction was unerring.

Richard hurried Frances on. They had passed the point where the track on the side of the hill had met the stream, and they were on strange ground now. The bed plunged still deeper, the banks were rockier, and more thickly screened by small wiry mountain trees. Their speed increased again, for the bed was less cluttered with boulders. The stones under their feet were sharp and uneven; those stones would hold up the dog, anyway. And then the stream curved round a mass of rock, and they saw that the narrow gorge before them suddenly ended. In front of them was nothing but space, and the precipice over which the torrents would pour in the spring, falling in a series of cataracts to the valley beneath.

They looked at each other, trying to hide the dismay in their hearts. To their left was the open mountain rising steeply; to their right, over the high bank with its crags and bushes, lay the landslide which Frances had called a quarry. They were neatly trapped.

Frances backed away from the edge of the precipice instinctively.

Richard stood, his eyes turned towards the mountain, looking for some short-cut up to that eastward-bound path which would lead them to Pertisau. The ground was open, and there was little cover, but if the man had followed the dog into the bed of the stream, his view of the mountainside would be blocked by the height of the banks long enough to let them reach that point in the path where there were some trees and scrub. Anyway, there was no other choice.

And then, behind them, they heard the panting of the dog. It had followed the boulders on the banks of the stream, and now it was poised above them, eyes gleaming, teeth showing wickedly. Even as they had turned, it gathered its muscles to spring. Frances was the nearer. She heard Richard's voice behind her, low, urgent.

"Down! On your face!"

She was hypnotized as the animal, now more wolf than dog, hurled its huge weight down at her. She heard the snarl, saw the teeth ready to tear. Her eyes closed involuntarily as the slavering jaws aimed at the level of her throat, and she dropped on the ground. She felt it pass above her body, striking something beyond. Richard . . . Richard . . . That sound, what was that sound? She raised herself on an elbow, afraid to turn her head, afraid to see. Just behind her, so that she could have touched it with her foot, lay the dog. Its throat was spitted on the steel goad of Richard's stick. Richard rose, his face white, his hands still braced on the stick's shaft. The force of the dog's leap had knocked him backwards. He tried to shake the animal's body free from the stick, but the eight inches of steel were firmly embedded. With a grimace of disgust, he put his foot on the dog's chest, and pulled the stick as if it were a bayonet. It came out slowly.

From farther up the bed of the stream had come the rattle of stones, as if a heavy man had slipped badly. Richard pointed to the bank on the mountain side of the gorge. Frances rose, and moved with difficulty towards the protection of its rocks. The man would not see them until he had got well round the bend, and then he would see the dog first. There was no time to hide it, even if they could have brought themselves to touch its dead body. Richard followed her, the stick still blood-covered. He should have wiped it on the dog's coat, he knew; but he couldn't. He felt sicker than he liked to admit.

"Through there," he whispered, pointing between two boulders. Frances obeyed, keeping her head and shoulders low. By using the uneven rocks and the thick bushes for cover, they managed to clear the stream's high bank. The man in the stream bed would not see them, because of the twist in its course. Von Aschenhausen, now probably over the shoulder, might be on the difficult track which had led them to the stream. It had taken them a good fifteen minutes. It would take him as long; there was no easy way.

They paused for a moment. Behind them lay the bank; in front of them was the mountainside, its slope covered with scrub which would hardly reach their knees. They heard the man's steps now, in the bed of the stream. He would just be coming round the bend now. The footsteps paused, and then quickened. So he had seen the dog. They heard his oaths. Richard still hesitated, wondering if they should stay quietly where they were, hidden by the boulders. . . . And then he remembered. The bloodstains. They had laid a pretty track.

"Go on," he whispered to Frances.

She looked at him despairingly. "I can't lead. You must. I'll go over the side." She pointed to the steep drop down to her right. The landslide which had created the quarry and the cataract behind them had done its work here too. The shoulder met the mountain with a spectacular precipice. Their only hope was to keep away from the treacherous edge and work up towards the mountain path as quickly as possible.

Richard had already moved ahead. There were no more blood drops from the stick. If they reached the shelter of that boulder ahead before the man could follow their trail through the rocks on the bank, they could take cover there. If he didn't see them, it was possible that he wouldn't start to search this nasty piece of mountainside by himself. He might even think this was impassable and that they had doubled on their tracks upstream again. Judging from the noise the man had made as he had come down the bed, he was not much accustomed to climbing. That was something to be thankful for.

Richard moved quickly and carefully, conscious that the ground sloped on his right towards the precipice. The boulder he had picked out as a refuge lay farther up the hill, farther away from the edge. That would cheer up Frances. And then it was that he became aware that her footsteps were not following; or was it possible that anyone could walk so quietly as that? He turned slowly, carefully balancing his weight. Frances stood almost where he had left her. She had moved up the hill slightly, back towards the rocks. She was standing quite still, her body pressed against one of them. That damned precipice, he thought, and started despairingly back towards her. But she shook her head and waved him towards the shelter of the boulder. She had heard the man climbing laboriously, the leather soles of his boots slipping on the stony surface. She moved slowly up behind the rock to which she had been clinging, avoiding the large stones which were loose to her touch. The fear, which had paralyzed her legs so that she couldn't follow Richard, suddenly left her. All she felt now was anxiety for him. She pointed frantically towards the boulder; but he didn't or wouldn't understand. He was coming back to her.

The man was almost over the bank. Like them, he had chosen to keep in cover. Perhaps he thought they were armed, and was taking no chance of silhouetting himself against the sky. He would come out down there, just where they had emerged from the bank, for it was the easiest way through, but although she had followed his progress with her ears, it was a shock suddenly to see him there, only ten feet away. He hadn't looked up towards where she remained motionless behind the rock. If he had seen her, he ignored her; his eyes were fixed on Richard. He pulled out his revolver. It was a large, efficient-looking black one. Then, as he saw clearly that Richard was unarmed, he stepped forward out of cover. If he had expected Richard to throw himself on the ground, or to run, he was disappointed. The two men stood scarcely twenty yards apart, looking at each other. There was a smile on the man's face. He was like a cat playing with a mouse. He lifted the revolver slowly, slowly. Frances raised the heavy stone which she had gathered in her two hands and threw it with all her strength from above her head.

It caught him between the shoulder blades, and sent him staggering forward. Frances saw him make a frenzied effort to regain his balance, half-turning towards her as he fell. Even then, he would have been safe if he had braked with his elbows and dug in his feet. But he had only one idea; he twisted quickly round to shoot. The sudden movement cost him his one chance. She saw the rock splinter beside her, and then heard the crash of the revolver. It was then that he realized his own danger. Frances, crouching at the side of the rock, saw the expression of hate on the man's face give way to fear. She saw him drop the Luger, his hands claw the ground, too late. There was nothing on the sloping edge to grasp except loose stones. He was clutching one in each hand as he slipped over the precipice. His scream fell with his body.

It was Richard who stood beside her, trying to loosen her grip on the rock. He put his arm round her waist and helped her up the sloping ground, back towards the stream. They had followed the sheltering bank almost to the flat ground of the saddle before Frances realized they had retraced their path.

"Richard," she said, "I'm going to be awfully sick."

"Darling, try not to. Not now. There's von Aschenhausen still. He should be almost at the stream by this time. He must have heard the shot and the scream."

She passed a hand wearily over her white face. Her voice was flat. "I forgot about him. Do you think he has seen us?"

"I hope not. We've kept under the shelter of the bank all the way up, and we are on the mountain side of the stream, while he is, or was, on the shoulder side. Anyway, he will have plenty to occupy his attention down there. It will be quite a job looking for his boy friend. He will probably think we headed for the path on the mountain. It isn't likely that he would guess we are going to use his own path down to his house."

"Richard!"

"Yes, we are. It's quite the safest way down. I don't like the idea of the mountain path now that the sun is almost gone." It was true: the mountain was hazier, and the light had turned a cold-gray. Ahead of them was the only glow in the sky, where the setting sun colored the clouds.

"Keep low," Richard warned, "as we go across the saddle. And watch the sky line." They broke into a crouching run as they crossed the grass, and when they approached the top of the saddle, they used the boulders to black-out their outlines to any watcher beneath them. They crossed the top by lying flat on the ground and edging their bodies carefully over. When they had reached the western side of the rocks, behind which they had lain this afternoon and looked down into the valley, Richard stood up and helped Frances to her feet. Normally, he thought, she would have giggled at the ludicrous figures they must have made in the last ten minutes. She would have had some joke to make about the rips on her clothes, the bruises and scratches on her legs. But she said nothing, only faced him with her large eyes still larger. He felt her hands; they were cold, like marble. He pulled out his flask of brandy.

"It's safe enough on this path," he said. "Take a good swig, Frances."

She took it obediently, and handed the flask back in surprise.

"Not even a cough or a splutter," she said in amazement. Richard's anxiety lessened. It was a good thing if she had started noticing her reactions.

"Got your wind?"

She nodded. "I'm all right." The brandy had warmed her, and the sickness was gone.

"Well, I'll let you do what you've always wanted to do. I'll let you run down a hill."

She was almost smiling. He caught her in his arms and hugged her.

And then they were running, carefully but steadily, down the broad path. Richard kept to the outside, holding her right hand as they ran. Their speed increased when they reached the darkening wood, for the path had broadened and was softened with pine needles. It twisted through the trees in zigzag curves, and these they shortened by slipping and sliding down the dry earth of the banks. The wood was already asleep. There were no sounds except the muffled pad of their feet, the occasional snap of a dry twig, the heaviness of their breathing. The trees were thinning, there was a little more light, and they were passing the edge of the meadow and the track which led to the house. Down there, in front of them, were the bridge and the road itself.

Then Richard caught Frances tightly. Through the quickly falling dusk they could see a car on the roadway, and the men talking beside it.

"O God," said Richard.

Frances looked at him in surprise.

"What's wrong, Richard? Don't you see who they are? It's an American car."

She was right. They started forward again. The two men looked as if they were getting into the car.

"Hoy!" Richard called softly. The men halted, and turned round in amazement. And then they ran over the bridge to meet them.

"Well, I'll be—" began van Cortlandt, and then stopped as he looked at them. Richard pushed Frances into his arms.

"Get her into the car, and look after her. Park off the road, and not where it can be seen from the house. Keep the lights off. Be ready to start at a moment's notice. Need your help, Bob. Are you game?"

Thornley took his eyes off Frances' face and the cut on her shoulder where her ripped cardigan and blouse showed blood.

He nodded. "I'm ready," he said, and moved off after Richard.

Van Cortlandt watched them go towards the dark house.

"Now just what's this all about?" he said. Frances tried to smile.

"I sang and we heard noises and they said it was a dog." Her voice was low and tired. He caught her as she stumbled forward, and carried her to the car.

He moved the car as Richard had said, and then turned to look at the girl beside him. She hadn't fainted; she had just collapsed . . . Pretty thoroughly, too. There were tears running down her cheeks.

"I haven't got a hankie. I lost it," she said in a muffled voice.

He looked at her torn clothes. "I'm not surprised," he said, and handed her the neatly folded one he kept in his breast pocket. "Try this."

Frances saw his concern. "I'm all right, really. All I need is a good cry."

"Well, go ahead," he said. "I've another handkerchief in my hip pocket. They are all yours." He was rewarded with a weak smile.

"I can talk, now," she said at last. "I don't suppose you have anything I could eat? I'm sort of empty inside."

"Only candy. I could give you a drink, though."

"I've had one. Candy will do, beautifully."

He watched her curiously as she ate the bar of chocolate.

"You can tell me as much or as little as you like," van Cortlandt said. "I'll not use it."

Frances looked at his firm mouth and worried eyebrows.

"I know, Henry. I suppose it's only fair to let you know what's happening, seeing that you are partly mixed up with it now, anyway. Do you mind if I eat while I talk?" Van Cortlandt restrained his grin. These people, really . . . There, he was catching it from them. *Lost it,* she had said apologetically, when she looked as if she had almost lost everything else, including her life. *Eat while I talk, do you mind?*

"Remember, not a word of this to anyone. Not until we are all safely out of this country. It's—" She hesitated for the right word.

"Dynamite?"

She gave her first real smile. "Yes, dynamite."

She tried to get the things she would say into the right order. Her story was slow and halting. She began with the visit that afternoon to the Englishman who was no Englishman. Van Cortlandt listened attentively and patiently, his eyes trying to see her face in the darkness. He didn't miss the pauses, when she would struggle for words and the story would leap forward. She was near the end of it now. There was a note in her voice which held him silent through the long hesitations between the phrases.

". . . and missed . . . and fell . . . over a precipice. We climbed back on our tracks and crawled and ran and then we saw you."

"And what about the German whom you knew?"

"I suppose he would try to trace the other. He must have heard the shot, and the scream." She stopped suddenly, and there was another pause. "There were signs of the fall, you know, where the stones slipped."

Van Cortlandt whistled. "Well," he said, "that was quite an afternoon you had yourselves."

Frances said nothing to that. She tried to see out of the car, but it was almost dark. "I wonder why they are so long?" she said.

"Don't worry; they can take care of themselves," but his face was less confident than his words.

"I could kick myself," he added. "I'm the big mouth who gave you away."

Frances looked at him in amazement. "You know, I haven't asked you how on earth you got here. You should be in Innsbruck, and Bob, too. I was so glad to see you, I forgot to ask."

"Well, it was like this. Bob saw you start off, and when you didn't get back before six as you had promised, he got worried. My guess was that you had forgotten: you were sort of vague about it. But he just shook his head and said he was going to wait. So we hung about, and then that black-haired guy arrived on his bicycle. I was standing at the hotel door —Bob was somewhere inside—and he had a look at our suitcases and the car. Just then the hotel man came out, and stopped to speak to me. He said we were late. I said yes. He said was there anything wrong? And *I* said you hadn't got back yet. At that, the black-haired chap got onto his bicycle and went over to Frau Schichtl's. I didn't like that. And I liked it less when he must have found out you weren't there, because he shot past us and went right back in the direction he had come from, with the dog just behind him.

"I had the sense to ask who he was. The hotel man shrugged his shoulders and said something about the house with the red shutters. And then Bob came out, and he and I had some beer, and we talked it over. And the later it became, the worse we liked it. We went to see Frau

Schichtl, and we worried her too. But anyway she could tell us the quickest way to get to the house. That worried Bob still more, because it was the road you had taken that afternoon. Then we thought we would go see for ourselves. Bob said you hadn't been prepared for a long walk or a climb when you left the village; he had noticed you weren't wearing your boots, and that clinched the argument. We thought we would ask at the house and find out if anyone had seen you; we were both hoping that perhaps you had tried a short-cut home and had sprained an ankle or something.

"Well, we got to the house, and we knocked loudly enough, but we got no answer. Silent as the tomb. We were talking about what we should do next, and we were just about to leave, when we heard Richard."

"Thank Heaven for that," said Frances quietly.

They were both silent.

"I'm tired," said Frances suddenly, and he saw her eyes close. He reached for the rug and wrapped it round her, and pillowed her head more comfortably against the back of the seat. She was already asleep.

He strained his eyes through the darkness, but he could only see the outlines of the bushes and trees. He could hear nothing except the gentle breathing of the girl beside him. Poor kid, he thought. What was that Gilbert and Sullivan thing? "Here's a how d'you do . . ." It was all that, and more. Expect the worst, and you won't be disappointed, he told himself. He slipped some gum into his mouth, and settled down to wait, with his gloomy speculations for company. What interested him most in Frances' story was the omissions.

As Richard and Bob Thornley moved towards the house, Richard gave a concise and abbreviated version of what had happened. Like Frances, he was careful to be vague about Mespelbrunn, but his account of the way she had saved him on the mountainside was included.

Thornley listened in silence, and then as Richard finished speaking in the low voice which was almost a whisper, said, "Pity you didn't get the other blighter, too."

The house was just as van Cortlandt had described it to Frances. Silent as the tomb. They tried the front door and windows. As they expected, they were locked. The back door was locked, too.

"Goes to bed early," whispered Richard.

"Who?"

"The maid. Or else she was packed off home."

"Can't risk breaking a window, then?"

"No, she may be asleep in her room," Richard said. He pointed to a window. "That may be our room. Can you climb?"

Thornley looked at the balcony at the side of the house. He grinned.

"Easy meat," he said softly. He swung himself up easily from a windowsill. He had a professional way of feeling for a hold and using his feet. Richard wondered if he were one of the Cambridge roof climbers. In that case, it *was* easy meat. Thornley had hold of the balcony now; he pulled the rest of his body up slowly until he could swing a leg over the railing. The whole thing looked so simple that one would hardly have guessed the strain on his arms and shoulders. He disappeared silently over the edge of the balcony.

Richard kept close to the shadow of the house. Above him, he heard a shutter being tried. Then there was a shadow on the balcony, and a whisper. "Barred and bolted. Hopeless. I'll try another room." The shadow vanished.

Richard waited. The minutes seemed like hours. He thought he had heard a shutter being forced open. . . . And that sound might be a window. He began to blame himself for not having tried to climb up himself, even with his stiff shoulder and torn knees. What the devil was keeping Bob? Just as he was trying to think of the easiest way to get up, he heard Thornley's voice in a whisper above him.

"Here. Lend us a hand." He was supporting another man. Richard watched Thornley help the man over the railing and then lower him, holding on to the man's wrists. Richard braced himself to take the man's weight as he dropped.

"Right," he whispered. Thornley, half over the railing, grunted, and let go of the man's wrists. Richard caught him by the thighs as he fell, and they rolled over together on the grass. Thornley swung himself lightly down beside them, and helped them to their feet.

"Winded?" he asked the man.

"All right, thanks. Neat job." He stood up shakily, and looked from Thornley to Richard.

"Who was here this afternoon?" he asked.

"I was," Richard said.

The man turned to Thornley. "There's a summerhouse at the edge of the wood, beside two tall trees hiding a mast." Thornley looked towards where the man pointed, and nodded. The man went on, "There's a wireless set there, and a motor bicycle. Can you put them out of action?"

"We'll start for the car," said Richard, as Thornley grinned and turned to sprint for the summerhouse. He put the man's arm round his shoulder, and held him at the waist; together they walked slowly towards the path. The man might have been thirty or fifty; he was one of those bird-faced Englishmen whose age it was difficult to guess. He was of medium height and thin. His hair was mouse-colored; his eyes were nondescript. His voice had no marked accent.

"Why were you here this afternoon?"

"We were directed to Mespelbrunn from Innsbruck."

"And you found him?"
"Not the one we were looking for."
"Who are the 'we'?"
"My wife and myself."
"You look as if you had met trouble."
"Complications. I left my wife in the car."
"You've a car? Good."
"And an American: a reporter."
"Not so good."
"He's a decent sort. We can trust him."
The man shook his head and cracked a smile. "Trust no newspaperman; they've an itch for a story. If he asks questions, I'm Smith, who helped escapes from concentration camps. That's true, anyway. Who's the other, our blond Tarzan?"
"I know his brother."
"I'll be Smith for him too."
They had reached the fringe of trees. There was no sound of running footsteps from the wood above them. There was still some safety, yet, thought Richard. He wished Thornley would come. The man's weight was tiring him.
"How are you feeling?" he asked.
"Shaky and stiff. But better every moment. Good to be free again."
"How did they get you?"
"The man who posed as Mespelbrunn was supposed to be in sympathy with the underground movement. He even helped some escapes. Got at me through them. How were Nürnberg and Innsbruck, by the way?"
"Nürnberg had to make a run for it. Innsbruck was getting suspicious about something."
They paused while Richard changed his hold on the man; the steepness of the path was a strain.
"And just what happened to my two bodyguards?"
"They chased us on the hills. Von Aschenhausen is probably coming back now. The other fell over a cliff."
"Too bad," Smith said, and looked at some burns on the palms of his hands. "And the dog?"
"Very dead."
Smith's face relaxed slightly. "You've been busy."
When they had reached the bridge, Thornley overtook them.

"There was also the bicycle itself," he reported. "I buckled its wheels. Strangely enough, it took the longest time."

Richard looked up towards the darkness which was the forest and the hill; they were both now indistinguishable. They were probably safe—probably.

"Could you run, if we both helped?" he asked Smith.

"I can try."

They linked arms round him, and half ran, half swept him along the road.

Van Cortlandt had heard them. He had the engine running, and the back door of the car open for them, by the time they reached him. They thrust Smith into the car, and stumbled after him. Richard heard the man draw his breath in sharply when his body was thrown into the corner of the car as it jerked onto the road, and began the rough journey back to Pertisau. But even if he was hurt, he was safe.

Richard leaned over to look at Frances. She was still asleep.

"How was she?" he asked. The American answered without turning his head.

"Surprising. She'll be all right when she wakens. Best thing for her."

Richard relaxed, and leaned back against the seat, taking care not to jolt against Smith.

Thornley suddenly gave a laugh. "I haven't had so much fun for a long time," he said.

"I'm glad someone enjoyed himself," Richard said. "What happened upstairs, by the way?"

"The window you pointed out was barred and bolted like nothing I ever saw in a private house. So I tried the next room, and the shutter there was only latched in the usual way. I used my knife, and got it, and then the window, open. The light was pretty bad; I just could see dimly. A sort of man's bedroom it was, with a desk at the window. There was a lot of stuff on top of it. I was hoping I might find some keys, but there weren't any. But I found this."

He held up something in the darkness of the car.

"Electric torch. Damned useful, too. It was black as pitch in the corridor outside, and in the room where I found your friend. They had tied him up again."

"And very welcome you were," said Smith. He was rubbing his wrists and ankles with his knuckles. He didn't use the palms of his hands.

"Were you always tied up?" asked Richard.

"Always when any visitor was seen approaching the house. And then, I was gagged too, like this afternoon. During the nights, I was handcuffed to the bed. In the daytime there was always one of them on guard. They also had fixed bars onto the window. On the door they had put safety chains. They used to leave it just a chink open that way through the day, so that I'd feel someone was always watching me."

"It made things quicker for us," Thornley explained. "The lock on the door was the usual type; after that there were just a couple of those chains and a heavy bolt. They didn't expect you to be reached from the outside."

"I'm glad you were still alive," Richard said.

"They just didn't want me alone. There was a lot of information they thought I could give them. I couldn't give it if I were dead."

"Judging from the time they kept you, they didn't get very much."

Smith gave a bitter smile. "Nothing of any use. Every now and again I'd pretend I was weakening; that encouraged them to keep me alive for just another few days. And then, they'd like to confront me with anyone who had come looking for me, and had been trapped. They like drama, these chaps, you know. Faked confessions and all that. They got a man from London, and two poor devils from Germany. Von Aschenhausen did the talking, and his man did the persuasion. He's good riddance."

"What about the maid?"

"Oh, old Trudi . . . She was terrified. When they took over, she just had to go on serving them as if nothing had happened. Threats against her family. You know. They locked her up in her room at night, which was quite needless of them. She was much too frightened to have done a thing for me. It is extraordinary the amount of power you can get over certain types of people if you just terrify them enough."

They were coming to the village. Smith leaned forward.

"Keep to the dark roads, and away from that inn where they are dancing. Keep well over to your left. Just grass, anyway."

They saw the lights round the platform outside the inn. Through the trees came the sound of a polkalike tune. They bumped over grass, as Smith had said, and then they were on a narrow graveled road which led towards the scattered lights at the shore. Smith directed van Cortlandt again, and the car swung south, running silently and smoothly along a track which would take them behind the string of hotels on the lakeside.

Smith had taken charge; his voice was still as cool and impersonal as when Richard had first met him.

"What were your last actions when you left here?"

"Van Cortlandt and Thornley were leaving by car; my wife and I were going for a walk."

Smith spoke to the American. "You've paid your bill, got your luggage, and actually left?"

"All here, Captain," van Cortlandt said.

"Good. You can stay out of the picture, then."

He turned to Richard. "You and your wife had better leave the car at a safe distance from your hotel. Or perhaps it would be better if *you* went alone. Can you remember the things she'll need? Don't forget her make-up box, especially the mascara. Bring something for me, too. And money. Is there more than one entrance to the hotel, so that you could slip out without being seen?"

"We are staying in a house. I think we could both go. Quicker if there were two of us."

Smith nodded. "Much. If you think you could slip away without being spotted. With ordinary luck, we have got about an hour's start. We'll take the car to the south end of the shore road. There are some trees and a good stretch of grass just off the road near the last hotel. We'll wait there. The moon won't be up for a while."

Richard had been shaking Frances gently. She sat up and looked around her in a bewildered way.

"So am I," said van Cortlandt good-humoredly. "You go with Richard. We'll wait for you. Good luck to both of you."

"Thanks," said Richard. "We'll need it." The car was slowing down. Henry was no fool, thought Richard. He had halted the car behind that chalet which hadn't been rented, standing dark and silent with its shutters tightly fastened.

He slipped out of the car into the blackness. Van Cortlandt helped Frances into his hands. He put his arm around her, and walked her over the grass. Behind them, they heard the car move smoothly away.

Waldesruhe lay just ahead. There was a light at the back of it. That would be the kitchen. The hotels around it were silent. There were lights in the bedrooms, as if most of the visitors were going to bed. Those who were going to the dance must have already set out, for the road was empty.

There was the usual weak light in the downstairs sitting room of the house. It lighted the bottom steps of the staircase. Farther up, Frances stumbled in the half darkness, and they halted, but they heard no movement from either above or below them, and they went on to their room.

It was Richard who shut the windows, drew the curtains, and lit the two candles. He didn't risk a brighter light. From the outside, this room would still seem to be in darkness. Frances looked wearily towards the bed; she had never appreciated how soft and white it was. On its counterpane was spread a very charming dirndl. Richard had seen it too, and paused at the wash basin as he poured the drinking water into a glass.

"Take a long one," he advised, when he brought the glass over to Frances. "What's that for?" He nodded to the bed.

"Frau Schichtl wanted me to wear it to the dance." Frances peeled off the mud-caked socks with a grimace. Richard brought over a damp sponge smelling of pink geranium.

"Do your face and shoulder," he commanded. He poured water into a basin and carried it over to where she was sitting. He helped her pull off the tattered cardigan and blouse. As she cleaned the cut on her shoulder, he bathed her feet and legs gently.

There was a knock at the door. Frau Schichtl's voice said, "May I come in?" They looked at each other in dismay. Again there was the same timid knock.

Richard was about to say Get to hell out of here, but he checked himself in time. That would only add to their troubles. If they kept silent, perhaps the woman would think she was mistaken and go away. Instead, the door opened. He rose to his feet.

Frau Schichtl paused in dismay. "Oh, excuse me. I am so sorry." She was just about to turn in embarrassment, when she noticed Richard's leg . . . And then she looked back again at Frances, holding the towel over her shoulder, and she saw the basin lying at her feet. Richard still held a dripping sponge.

Frau Schichtl came in, closing the door quickly and quietly behind her. Her kindly face was clouded with worry and fear. She came over to Richard and took the sponge gently out of his hand, and knelt down beside the basin.

"You must bathe your own leg, Herr Myles. It is cut very badly. I should get you some hot water."

"Please don't; there isn't any time," said Frances, and then bit her lip as she looked at Richard. It was so easy to make a slip when you were tired and miserable.

Frau Schichtl looked quickly up at her face. She compressed her lips, but she said nothing. She dried Frances' legs very gently.

"Have you iodine?" she asked.

Richard handed it to her, and she put it onto Frances' knees very lightly.

"Now some talcum powder on top of these scratches and they won't show."

Frances smiled gratefully, and then grimaced as she covered the cut on her shoulder with iodine.

"We got lost on the hills," she explained.

Frau Schichtl cleared away the towels and the basin of water, keeping her back carefully turned to Richard, who had started calmly to undress.

"I knew something must have happened," Frau Schichtl said. "Your friends were worried. They left hours ago. And now you can't go to the dance. You would have looked so pretty in that dress. It would have made me very happy to see you in it."

"I should like to wear it, all the same," said Frances, looking at Richard. That dirndl would be just what she needed. "We may go to the dance."

"But you must go to bed."

Frances shook her head. Frau Schichtl looked quickly from Richard, dressed in clean shirt and shorts, to Frances, fumbling in the chest of drawers for some underclothes.

"I think you are in trouble," she said slowly, at last.

Richard said nothing. He was distributing his money and Baedeker, letter of credit, passport, into the pockets of his tweed jacket. He was trying to think how they could leave the house . . . Unless they were to tie and gag Frau Schichtl and lock her in this room, and the idea sickened him. Still, what else?

"I thought that when I came in here, first. You were so quiet going up the stairs. So quiet in the room."

Frances had slipped into the dress; she combed her hair, and creamed and powdered the bruise on her forehead, before she turned to face Frau Schichtl. She smoothed the apron.

"It is so very pretty, Frau Schichtl. Perhaps I may spoil it . . . perhaps I shouldn't wear it?"

Frau Schichtl shook her head slowly. "It is your dress now. I have no more use for it." Her voice had a quiet sadness; she was lost in thought.

Richard smiled to himself as he watched the transparent relief in Frances' eyes. A man wouldn't have had any scruples, not at a moment like this. He folded a suit to take to Smith, along with socks and shirt and tie.

"You are going?" said Frau Schichtl.

"We are going," Frances said. Richard watched her tensely. But the sad smile on her face was honest and friendly.

"You will need food for the journey," she said. "Is it these Nazis?"

Frances nodded.

"I knew it. Ever since that rough fellow came here so rudely this evening. . . . Will there never be an end to all this hunting of people? They must not catch you . . . not as they caught my daughter. Where can you go?"

"If we hurry, we shall be safe," said Richard quietly. He hadn't rested since he had reached the room. He was now helping Frances to get her make-up things into her bag. Mascara and all. They were ready, almost.

Frau Schichtl spoke again. "When you leave, go out through the kitchen and the back door. I shall hand you bread and cheese. I wish you a good journey to a safer land."

"We cannot thank you enough," Richard said.

"It is a small thing. Perhaps I am repaying my daughter's debt to someone who helped her."

"For your own safety, Frau Schichtl, remember that you haven't seen us. You heard us come in and go out again. You thought we had gone to the dance. Can this dress be traced to you?"

"No. There are many like it, and it is a long time since my daughter was here. I have forgotten I ever had these clothes. I shall see you in two minutes, at the back door."

The bedroom door closed gently.

Frances looked as if she might cry. She tied the scarf which lay on the bed beside the hand-knitted jacket round her head, and knotted it under her chin. She buttoned on the white-wool jacket. By the time she stared at herself in the glass, she had recovered control of herself. She looked at herself critically in the mirror.

"I'll do," she said.

Richard nodded, and tucked the bundled clothes under his arm. He picked up his one decent hat. They looked round the room; Frances' eyes flickered for a moment as they rested on the fitted suitcase which Johann had admired so much in Innsbruck. Richard had given her that when they were married. As they went downstairs she wished that she did not get so much attached to certain things. She hoped Frau Schichtl would be allowed to keep it—not some little tart of a local *Gauleiter.*

The light was still on in the sitting room, but the curtains had been drawn, so that they could cross the room safely to the kitchen. It was in darkness, and the back door was open so that they could see the stars in the sky beyond. In the shadow of the opened door, Frau Schichtl handed them a large package silently. They didn't speak, but their hands caught hers and held them tightly for a long moment . . . And then they were gone.

They walked quickly over the grass, keeping as much in the shadows of trees, even houses, as was possible. The moon had risen, and the meadows of Pertisau were silvered and treacherous. From the distance came the music of a fiddle and a concertina, and an echoing "*Juchhe.*"

They had reached the last hotel. It stood far back from the road, with large gardens carefully cultivated. They skirted these, thankful for the shrubs and bushes which would make it difficult for them to be seen clearly. . . . And now they were on the road, walking as softly as they could. Smith had said something about trees, Richard remembered. There were some just beyond that patch of grass. It meant that they would have no cover at all until they reached the trees, and they might be the wrong ones. He had a strange empty feeling inside him as they covered the white stretch of road, with the silvered grass on one side of them, and the lake rippling with maddening calmness on the other. Probably hunger, he thought. He resisted the impulse to run, to cover the open ground as quickly as possible. And then he heard the car warming up. It backed out onto the road from the shadow of the trees, just as they reached them. The doors were open, and they were pulled in by eager hands. The car shot forward, and they heard Thornley say, "Good work!"

It was lighter in the car now, because of the moonlight. Smith nodded his approval to Frances.

"You've made good use of your time," he said, and began to examine the clothes they had brought him. "Mascara?" he added.

"And food," Frances said. She opened the parcel of food and shared it out.

The atmosphere in the car had changed. Van Cortlandt, without taking his eyes off the road in front of him, joked with Frances as they ate. Thornley had produced the torch again at Smith's request. He held it ready to shade it, when Smith needed it. Richard helped Smith rip off his clothes. He exchanged looks with Thornley as the shirt came away and they saw the cruel weals on Smith's back. But Smith took no notice of their stare. He was whistling to himself as he drew on the new clothes. With Richard's help he managed not at all too badly, although there was a difficult moment as he tried to pull on Richard's shirt. It was only by the stiffness of one arm that they noticed it was bruised at the shoulder into a purple jelly. The clothes were loose for him, but the effect was passable.

He began on his face, now. Thornley held the shaded torch, and Richard tried to steady the small mirror from Frances' bag. Smith creamed and powdered the ugly bruises which showed. He darkened his eyebrows skillfully, altering their shape, and with the same pencil shaded in the lines on his face. Then he found the small pair of scissors in the bag, and looked at them thoughtfully.

"We'll have to stop to get rid of these anyway," he said, kicking the rags on the floor which had been his clothes. "Better draw up for a moment; this is as good a place as any." It was the beginning of the hill down into Jenbach. On their right was a steep ravine, thickly wooded. They could only hear the water of the stream. It was impossible to see it, at this point, for the undergrowth. Thornley slipped out of the car with the old clothes, and disappeared down the steep bank. When he came back, he reported that he had found a nice thick bush, not very far down. It had been too risky to go any farther.

"Not a place for picnicking, or a roll in the hay," he said. "They should rot there peacefully."

Smith had finished emphasizing a widow's peak with the scissors.

"All right," he said, and van Cortlandt drove on.

Smith took the mascara cream and rubbed it on the back of his hands. Then he tried to smooth it on to his hair like brilliantine, but it was too difficult.

"Let me try this," suggested Richard. He remembered what he had seen of Smith's palms. "I tucked a pair of chamois gloves into that jacket pocket," he said as casually as he could. "I find them useful for traveling."

Smith shot a quick glance at him. "Thanks. I'll need them." He looked at his hair in the mirror. "That's about enough; don't need much of that stuff. Thanks. I'll comb it through now."

As Richard wiped his hands, he watched Smith carefully combing the black cream through his hair, finishing by making a neat center parting. The finishing touch was a slight dab of face powder onto the hair above the ears. The transformation was complete.

"Not bad," said Thornley with a grin. "They'll never recognize you, unless they see your back."

Smith gave his first real smile. He had cleaned the back of his hands of the mascara, and was rubbing some cream into the burns on his palms and wrists. Frances had looked round, and remained staring, so that van Cortlandt took his eyes off the road for a moment to look too. He grinned widely.

"All you need is a monocle and you'd be a natural for a Budapest café," he suggested. Smith looked pleased, but he didn't volunteer any information.

Richard suddenly remembered the label on the inside pocket of the jacket. Smith ripped it out and read it with interest.

"Nice to know your name," he said. "But it would have taken some explaining. Thanks. What about the hat?"

"It's all right. You'd better take my stick, too. But don't unscrew it until you are in a safe place and can wash it. It's rather messy. What about a passport?"

"That can be got. By the way, I think you should go right away to this address in Innsbruck. They'll see about a passport for you." He scribbled some words on a page from Thornley's diary, and handed it to Richard.

"What about some cash?" asked van Cortlandt.

Smith patted the jacket pocket. "It's already here. That's about everything, I think." He looked at Richard, and there was a kindly look in his eye.

"Richard." Frances' voice was urgent. "I've just remembered . . . what about our bill?"

The men all laughed, even Smith.

"It's all right, Fran. I've left enough to cover it inside my suitcase. It will be searched, you know."

Van Cortlandt seemed to be enjoying a rich joke.

The car was entering the village of Jenbach, running down through the steep street with its motor silent. There were few people out at this time.

Jenbach was mostly asleep, it seemed. Smith was watching the street carefully.

"Just at that corner," he said to van Cortlandt, "beside the road with the trees. The station is just to the left." He turned to Richard. "I seem to have caused you a lot of trouble. But perhaps you'll find some consolation in the fact that I really happen to have discovered something which will be extremely valuable. Quite apart from my own comfort, you really have been most useful." He leaned over to Frances. "And thank you for your song. Good-by."

The car slowed down. It paused for a moment, and they saw his shadow mix with that of the trees. He was walking, leaning heavily on Richard's stick, Richard's hat tilted over his eyes, towards the station, as the car swung to the right for the Innsbruck road.

17

They would reach Innsbruck in half an hour, or even less. Richard leaned back into the corner, and closed his eyes. It was little enough time to decide on their own plans; but at least they had done the most they could for Smith.

The road was smooth and made driving easy. On their right were continuous mountains; on their left was the broad Inn valley and the railway line. Van Cortlandt pointed out the lights of a train moving towards Jenbach.

"That takes care of your friend. We've only you to worry about now," he said. Richard nodded. He wondered if Smith would really take that train, or whether there had been some little house near the station where he might have a friend. He had better stop thinking about Smith. He roused himself to reply to the American, who had looked round at him curiously.

"I've been thinking about that, Henry. I think we should follow his example and rid you of ourselves as if nothing had happened, with the excuse if it's necessary of motor trouble and slow driving. You know the sort of thing. I think that's the only way."

Thornley said, "It's not a very good way for you."

"We'll manage, somehow—if we get that passport."

"And some money," said van Cortlandt. "You'll not go far without plenty of loose dough. Your travelers' cheques or your letter of credit will raise hell at any bank in Greater Germany. That chap just about cleaned you out, didn't he? He was a cool customer, all right."

"He has to be. I expect he has done more than that for others when they were in a jam." What was it Frau Schichtl had said in that sad slow voice of hers? Repaying a debt to someone who had helped her daughter . . . only the way she had said it was better than that.

"Help each other, or God help you?" asked van Cortlandt, half-seriously. "Have you any cash, Bob?" He threw his wallet into the back seat. Thornley caught it, and added his share. He counted it carefully.

"It will just about pay for the passport. I expect it will cost quite a lot. You'll need more than this. I can cash a cheque at the bank tomorrow, but how can I get the money to you?"

"Look," said Richard, "you dump us somewhere just outside Innsbruck. We can walk to that address Smith gave us. I think it's this side of the town. Have you that light, Bob? I'll just make sure." He studied his Baedeker. "Yes, we can reach it all right. In this costume, we'll look like any other couple returning from a moonlight walk. Your story is that we left you this afternoon to walk over the mountain towards Hinterriss. When we didn't return, you thought we must have gone right on to Hinterriss and stayed the night there. So when it reached eight o'clock, you left. You had a business appointment to keep. You were delayed in getting to Innsbruck by motor trouble. Henry, try to see your man tonight when you arrive; have a couple of drinks with him in some well-known restaurant."

"I'll need them," van Cortlandt said with a grin.

"Remember you never saw a house with red shutters. You never saw us after we set out for our walk. That's your story and stick to it."

"That's our story and we're stuck with it." Van Cortlandt was still grinning. "But what's your angle?"

"We'll get to that house, and arrange about a passport. They may take us in for the night, or send us to a safe place. And Bob will get the money, as he suggested. Tomorrow one of us will meet you some place about eleven o'clock. It may be Frances; she is better disguised than I am. The station is no good; it will be watched. A restaurant is dangerous . . . too many waitresses with an eye for their customers." He paused for a moment or two. "Try the Franciscan Church. It will have plenty of sightseers on a Saturday morning. You can potter about the Emperor Maximilian's monument; carry a catalogue, or a newspaper, and have the money in an envelope. Slip the envelope inside the catalogue. When you see Frances, go and sit down in the church itself. Choose a nice dark side. When you finish your meditations, leave the catalogue behind you. Frances will then slip into the seat you've just left. Would you mind doing that for us?"

Thornley repeated the directions rapidly. "I think I've got it all," he said.

Van Cortlandt said, "I must say for a couple of amateurs you two are showing high form."

"We go to the movies," said Frances gravely. He looked at her serious face, and then decided to risk a laugh.

"It's that dead-pan look you English have when you have your little joke which makes us think you've no sense of humor. You don't look as if you expected anyone to laugh."

Frances was smiling now. "Well, that doubles the joke for us. Our pleasures are really very simple."

"You mean that if I hadn't laughed just now, you would have been laughing because I didn't laugh because you didn't laugh."

"I would have had my giggle inside," admitted Frances. "Don't you think it's funny, too?"

Van Cortlandt just shook his head sadly. "About as funny as *punch*. And much more dangerous. It makes people underestimate you."

"But that can be funny, too."

"It's dangerous."

"What's dangerous?" Thornley asked. He was shading the torch again to let Richard study a map.

"Being underestimated," said Frances.

"Oh, *that!*" he said, and went back to the map.

Richard explained. "After we have the cash, and the passport, we'll make for the border. The nearest one is the Brenner."

"That's guarded heavily," warned van Cortlandt. "The Italians are keeping an eye on the South Tyrol."

"Well, it will depend on our disguise whether we risk the train or try the mountains. If it's guarded heavily, then the Swiss frontier will be thought to be likelier. And the Brenner is probably more strongly guarded on the Italian side than on the Austrian. That suits us."

"And after that?"

"We'll make for Paris."

"When do you think you'll be there?"

"With luck we'll leave Innsbruck by Sunday at latest. Say next weekend in Paris. We'll leave word for you there with the Consul. We'll celebrate together. The evening's on us."

"I wish I could," said van Cortlandt, "but I'm a working man. I'll see you later in England on my way home. I have your address. There's one reward I would like, and that's the whole story."

"I promise you it," Frances said. "And please come to see us. Any time." She said it so warmly and earnestly that van Cortlandt reddened, but he looked pleased.

"I hate to be the skeleton at the feast," he said, "but what if you run into difficulties in Innsbruck?"

"We'll let you know; we can phone you. If we can't phone then it's too dangerous for you to help us. You've been dragged into quite enough trouble, as it is."

"I'll have finished my business there by midday tomorrow. I can be free for the next two days, if you need me. Leave a message at the hotel for me, if I'm not there. Say that the *Times* has an assignment for me. That will pass all right, and it's phoney enough for me to know it comes from you. I'll let Bob know, unless he's mixed up with his Czechs."

"There is one very important thing, Henry. Send this message to Geneva early tomorrow. Please don't forget. RESERVATIONS UNCANCELLED. ARRIVING FRIDAY. And memorize this address." He repeated it carefully. "Got it? Good. It's really important."

The lights of the town gleamed in front of them across the Inn. Frances turned to Richard, and smiled.

Van Cortlandt said quietly, "I hate to spoil the party, but there's a couple of cars on our tail. I've seen their headlights for some time now, but they are still far enough away, if it should be your friends. I'll slow up round the first bend. Get ready."

Frances and Richard looked at each other. Frances remembered how van Cortlandt had increased his speed just when he had asked about difficulties in Innsbruck.

"We'll say our thank-yous in Paris or Oxford," said Richard. "Good-by, meanwhile. And don't forget to turn up. And remember the telegram." He was holding the door open in readiness. They were reaching a bend in the road.

The car slowed up. They slipped quickly out.

"We'll see you," Frances said quietly, and then without looking back, she raced with Richard for the cover of some bushes. Safely hidden from the road, they watched the taillights of van Cortlandt's car streak along towards the town. They waited for some minutes, and then they heard the roar of a powerful engine. A large black car, followed closely by another, flashed past them. Richard watched them disappear after van Cortlandt.

"Henry was right, I think. Two cars together look as if they had urgent business. I hope they stick to that story."

"They will," said Frances. "I can see Bob looking rather sleepy and bored, and Henry looking very righteously indignant, calling on his rights as an American citizen. They'll play it up beautifully between them. I wish I could see it."

"You're better here. How are the legs?"

"Not so bad. My arm is stiff, though." She shivered.

Richard put his arm round her shoulders, and drew her beside him. They waited in silence. One other car passed along the road; its moderate pace reassured them.

Richard watched the clouds in the sky. He chose the time when one of them, thick and white, began to cross over the face of the moon; and they were back on the road. They reached the first houses without any trouble. It seemed they were in an open residential quarter, with scattered houses and gardens, or what might be called parks, surrounding them. Richard remembered they were either in or near the district for the large garden restaurants and family excursions . . . All the better.

It was also a district for late-evening strollers, making their way slowly back to the town. Ahead of them were a young man and his girl, with their arms linked round each other. The man talked, and the girl would laugh as she looked up at him.

"Watch the technique," said Richard, and measured his step so that they kept a short distance between them and the couple. He clipped his arm round Frances' waist, and she giggled in spite of herself.

"Perfect," he said, and won another laugh.

Perfect, he repeated to himself, as they followed the man and girl towards the bridge over the River Inn. In front of the bridge was a broad, open stretch of ground, where other roads met the one they were on. From the other roads came some more men and girls, forming a slow and scattered trail back to Innsbruck. And there were some cars. These were being stopped by two efficient-looking men in uniform, as they approached the bridge.

Richard looked down at Frances, and said some words to her in German. Just in front of them were the couple they had followed. The two uniformed men gave the group of four a brief look, and then turned back to the driver they were questioning.

Once they were over the bridge, they left the man and girl. He was still talking; she still looked up into his face and laughed. They would never have noticed who had walked behind them or who had passed them. Richard had taken a street which turned away from the river. After the bright lights at the bridge, it seemed dark and safe. But the journey to the house was like a nightmare for Frances. Richard had kept their pace unhurried, so that they appeared just two more walkers going home with the usual reluctance. The slowness of their steps increased her fatigue. Shc was painfully conscious of each muscle she had to use, of the hardness of the pavement which hurt her back with each step, of the cracks in the stones which caught her dragging feet. The ill-lighted streets heightened the dark houses; their silence sharpened every sound. It was less than a mile to the address which Smith had given them, but to Frances it seemed more like five.

Richard had knocked as Smith had marked it down on the piece of paper: a spondee followed by a dactyl. In his pocket, he fingered the part of the instructions which he had kept, the part with the curious little design marked on it. The rest of the paper had been torn up and dropped piece by piece from the car. As they stood in the darkness of the doorway and looked anxiously up and down the dingy, badly-lighted street with its empty pavements and sleeping houses, he had begun to wonder if he had got mixed up with the address. They were taking a hell of a long time to answer. He visualized the piece of paper as he had seen it in the car. The name, the address, and then *Knock*– –, –vv. Then the words *Destroy at once;* and then *Keep,* and a lightly drawn arrow to the foot of the page where the design had been sketched. He remembered everything, even to the jagged line at the top where the page had been torn from Thornley's diary. He felt Frances sag against him. He knocked again.

The door opened so quickly that he knew someone had stood behind it waiting for the knock to sound again. It was only slightly open, and in any case it was too dark to see anything; but the someone waited.

Richard's voice was hardly above a whisper. "Herr Schulz?"

The door opened wider and a woman's voice answered "In!" They heard the door close behind them gently; a heavy lock was quietly turned. The hall was unlit, but light came from a room at the back of the house. The woman who had let them inside led the way towards the lighted doorway. She turned to them as she reached it, and motioned them to enter. Frances saw that she was quite young. Her face was what Richard would call just medium: it was neither pretty nor plain. It was quite expressionless.

Richard had looked past the woman into the bare, poorly furnished room. A man laid his newspaper aside, and watched them keenly from where he sat. He said nothing, just sat and looked. Richard spoke, slurring his words as he had heard the Bavarians do. The man still sat; his eyes were impassive. He picked up his newspaper again.

"But my name is not Schulz," he said, as Richard paused.

Richard's eyes met those staring down at him from the large flag-draped photograph on the wall. For a moment, doubt halted the beat of his heart. He felt the sweat break in his palms. . . . And then he was aware that he was still clutching onto the piece of paper in his jacket pocket. He pulled it out, and handed it to the man, still watching inscrutably.

The man glanced at it and threw it on the table.

"Who gave you this?"

"A man from Pertisau."

"Was his name Gerold?"

"No. Mespelbrunn."

"Where do you come from?"

So that explained Smith's aside as he had handed him the paper in the car.

"From over the mountains," Richard said.

The man looked at him again, and then at Frances who had slumped into a chair. He nodded to the woman. She closed the door, and stood there, leaning against it.

"Sit down," the man said to Richard. His voice was warm, almost friendly. His eyes were now alive, kindly. "Relax. Relax. No need to look so cold. Are you hungry?"

Richard nodded. The woman moved from the door where she had been standing and went into another room. It was probably the kitchen. Richard heard the sound of a pot being placed on a stove.

"Relax," the man said again. "And how is our friend from Pertisau?"

"He is now well."

"So, he was—ill? We thought so . . . we have not heard from him for a long time. Well, that's good news. Good news. What about you? You said you wanted a room. Is there anything else?"

"The usual."

"You are leaving our happy Fatherland?" The man's voice was filled with heavy sarcasm as he looked up at the picture on the wall. "Well, it can be arranged. How are you traveling?"

"To Italy. Probably by train. And as quickly as we can."

"Of course; that is understood," Schulz said, and smiled. "You might go as Americans or English. You look very like them. Do you know the language at all?"

Richard shook his head.

"You'll have to go as Germans, then. How would an engineer do? Or a schoolteacher? I'll get you the right clothes. That will cost you extra, of course, but you'll find it worth every pfennig. Every pfennig."

"How much will it cost?"

"How much have you?"

Richard restrained a smile. After all, Schulz had been right that his help would be worth every pfennig.

"Only three hundred marks," said Richard. "We can get extra tomorrow to cover the railway fares."

Schulz seemed pleased with the directness of the answer. "Good," he said. "Good. Three hundred marks will do."

He rose from his chair and went over to Frances. He walked with a marked limp, but he held himself erect. Richard placed his age as about forty. He was almost bald. His face and body had thickened with middle age. Frances, white and silent, looked up and saw the shrewd eyes behind the thick glasses, the kindly smile on the broad mouth.

His voice was gentler. "You look afraid of me. You must lose that afraid look. Sometimes people stay here for almost a week, until they lose it. You must look very happy and proud when you cross the frontier. You are the wife of an engineer, who is taking you for a holiday to Florence. But we must change your hair; it is too pretty. Lisa!"

The woman came back from the kitchen. She carried two bowls of steaming soup.

"Lisa, what color would you make this hair? Black?"

"Not with these blue eyes. Brown is less noticeable."

"Good. Make it brown, mouse-brown. We can begin tonight. That and the photographs. Then tomorrow we can get the clothes, and the papers.

And you will be all ready to leave tomorrow night. Is that quick enough for you? Now, eat up. Eat up."

The warm bowl of soup brought life back to Frances' hands. She held her fingers round it, and felt the warmth steal into them. It was almost as good as eating. She felt warm, warm and safe. She looked at the clock on the table. It was almost midnight. She felt warm and safe, safe for the first time in six hours.

The man was watching her curiously. "Eat up," he said gently. "That's good, isn't it?" It was the most wonderful soup she had ever tasted.

The man was speaking to Richard. "You've had a difficult time; you've come far, today?"

"Yes, we've come far."

"You will be able to travel tomorrow?" Schulz was looking doubtful.

Richard, remembering Frances' resilience, smiled. "Oh yes, we shall be all right. We recover quickly. We can keep going until we reach Italy. And then . . . well, it won't matter then anyway."

"When you first spoke of Italy, I thought I might advise you to try the mountains. They would be safer. But—" he looked at Frances doubtfully—"I think you will have to stick to your plan about the train. We shall do our best to make the train safe for you. Ready, Lisa? Good. Good."

Richard had finished eating, and the man began to cut his hair. On the table, the woman had arranged basins and some bottles and a saucer. Frances felt her eyes begin to close. Schulz waved his scissors towards her.

"If we can get her into that chair at the table before she falls asleep, Lisa can manage," he said. "We'll soon have her upstairs in bed."

Frances was helped into the other chair. I'm being very silly, she thought, but the trouble is that my eyelids are too heavy. She stretched her head back against the neck rest on the chair. It was hideously uncomfortable, but the eyelids won the struggle. She had dim sensations of the woman's fingers working with her hair, of water trickling across her face.

When she was awakened, she saw Lisa looking at her with almost a smile. It was enough to warn Frances of what she might see in the hand mirror which was held out to her. That look which only one woman can give another, that look of pity and amusement combined, roused Frances as no dash of cold water could have done. She took the mirror. Her hair was as bad as she had suspected; dull brown, lifeless, with the thickness at the back pinned tightly into a mean little knot. Frances stared in a kind of horrid fascination. Of course it would have had to be her hair, she thought, just because it had been her secret pride.

Richard was grinning at her. Then she saw that he was including himself in that grin. His hair had been clipped until it bristled. There was a funny look at the back of his neck. She began to laugh. She had the pleasure of seeing the half smile on Lisa's face give way to a look of surprise.

The man looked up from arranging a large box camera on some books on the table. He smiled encouragingly.

"That's better," he said. "Pretty ones find it harder to escape. Now, if you'll sit over here, we'll soon be finished, and you can go to a real bed."

The woman was clearing the table of its litter of basins and towels and hand dryer. She seemed to accept all this madness as a natural way of spending one's night.

Richard was being photographed now. He bulged his eyes, tilted his chin truculently, and looked on the point of uttering a loud "*Heil!*"

"Good," said Schulz, "good."

It was Frances' turn. She remembered to stare stolidly in front of her and part her lips slightly. We are all quite mad, she thought, or perhaps I am really asleep and dreaming. Sleep . . . sleep . . . it had a pleasant sound.

Schulz nodded approvingly. "That's what we want," he said. "That's what we want."

They followed the woman up a dark staircase to a room which was cold and shadowy in the meager candlelight. Frances felt Richard draw off her clothes: she awakened slightly as she heard him swear when his fingers stuck with some fastening on the strange dress. Then the cool rough sheets slid round her.

She could not have risen if six storm-troopers had come thundering up the stairs.

18

Frances awoke with a feeling of compulsion. She had something to do. She lay in the strange bed and looked round the room for the first time. Slowly she began to remember what had happened last night. Her hand went to her hair; it felt dry and coarse. So it hadn't been a dream . . . And there was Richard, with his hair cropped like that of a child who has had fever. He was still asleep; his arms were thrown above his head; his face was relaxed. She looked at the cracked ceiling, at the limp curtains drawn over the window. Why had she awakened, what was it that had to be done?

Frances felt herself slipping into sleep again, and caught herself just in time. There was something she had to do. Her eyes fell on her handbag which Richard must have brought upstairs last night and thrown onto the rickety little table under the fly-spotted mirror. That was it, of course. The money. A sudden fear that she was already too late to meet Bob Thornley urged her quickly from the warmth of her bed. After the first dizziness—she had probably moved too suddenly—she felt all right. Her body had recovered surprisingly from yesterday's punishment; even the shoulder was healing nicely.

Richard's watch told her she had ample time. She washed and dressed quietly. She searched in her handbag, and powdered her face and lips so that her natural color was hidden. Then she removed all traces of powder with her handkerchief. With the dull-brown hair and the subdued face there was quite a difference. She could do nothing about her eyes, though. They were larger and bluer than ever. However, unless she met someone who really knew her, there was little chance of her being identified with the fair-headed English girl whose description was no doubt being circulated. She combed her hair with a center parting, pinning the ends tightly into a knot at the back as the woman had done last night. Before she left the room, she found Richard's Baedeker in his jacket pocket, and verified from its Innsbruck map the best way to reach the Franciscan Church. At the door of the room, she stopped. Some small change might be useful. With a suspicion of a smile she searched Richard's pockets, and took half of what was left. It would be just enough to pay for a ride in a tramcar and the admission to the Church, if there was one. She kissed Richard lightly again. He didn't even stir. She closed the door gently and went quietly downstairs.

Lisa was in the sitting room. She seemed surprised.

"I thought you would sleep all morning."

"I must go out."

The woman shook her head disapprovingly.

"I must get money for the journey."

The woman accepted that. "You had better have some coffee, first," she said. "I've just had a cup. I'll get one for you." She went into the kitchen.

Frances waited, and looked at the little room, and the corner of the badly-kept garden at the back of the house, which she could just see from her seat at the table. Lisa was not unkind, but there was a certain businesslike attitude which paralyzed any conversation. Frances was glad of that; she was somewhat self-conscious about her Bavarian accent. She drank the coffee, and looked at the patch of garden. She felt a kind of excitement inside her. She would have liked to have given a war whoop —but Lisa was there. Her matter-of-fact kind of sanity smothered Frances' impulse, and she contented herself with looking at the garden and having another cup of coffee. She rose to leave.

"Not that way," said the woman. "Go out by this door: across the yard. Keep near the wall, under the trellis, and it will shelter you. Enter the door at the other end of the path. Walk through that house, and you'll find yourself in a shoemaker's shop. Just say as you pass that Lisa sent you. You'll be all right."

"Would you tell my husband that I'll be back about twelve?"

The woman nodded, and threw a *loden* cape lightly round Frances' shoulders. "Leave this in the shop," she said. She didn't wait for Frances to thank her. She was already carrying the coffee cups into the kitchen. As she turned to push the door open with her hip bone, she smiled—a friendly, encouraging smile. And then the kitchen door closed behind her. Frances turned toward the door in the living room which she had thought was a cupboard door. It led on to a narrow paved path beside a high wall, from which a coarse green climbing plant stretched greedily over the trellis above her head. In front of her were the backs of the houses on the next street.

Everything happened as Lisa had said it would. The cobbler in the front shop scarcely paused in his work as Frances slid the cape onto the counter. He didn't seem to hear her words. Outside in the street, there was the usual activity of a respectable working-class neighborhood. Housewives carried shopping bags made of knotted string. Children were grouped round doorways. Boys cycled wildly. Some of them wore a kind of uniform, others the usual short leather breeches and white stockings. She walked with increasing confidence to the end of the street. If she followed the tramlines from there, she would reach Museumstrasse, and then it would be easy to find the Church. It was the long, but the safe, way and she had plenty of time.

The walk was not unpleasant. In the busier streets, she felt still safer. She was just another girl dressed in another dirndl. At the corner of the narrow street which led to the square on which the Church stood, the traffic was heavy. Frances tried to avoid two women whose breadth filled the narrow pavement. She was swept against the window of a shop. Climbing boots, sports things, she noticed, and then, with her eyes still fixed on the window, she collided with a girl coming out of the shop's doorway. She was a tall, blonde girl, her arms filled with parcels.

Frances halted in amazement, and then stepped aside with an apology. The girl remained standing, her eyes on Frances' face, but Frances hurried on. It was Anni, looking just as she had looked in their garden at Oxford on her last night there.

"I looked at her too directly. She half-recognized my eyes, or perhaps she saw that I knew her," Frances thought. She glanced at her reflection in another window. She couldn't see much resemblance to herself, but she would have to watch her eyes, and her way of walking too. It was much too smooth. She would have to set her heels more firmly on the ground, in a kind of jaunty march. As she turned the corner to enter the Church, she looked back over her shoulder. Anni was still there, and, as Frances looked, she made up her mind and started towards the Church. Frances already regretted that afterlook. What a fool she was. She quickened her pace and hurried up the steps of the building.

Inside, there was the usual crowd of Saturday-morning visitors. She paid the admission to a man with heavily pouched eyes and a drooping mustache. At least that would prevent Anni from following her inside the Church: she had never spent a penny more than she could help in Oxford. Perhaps Anni was already thinking she had been mistaken.

In the nave where the Maximilian monument was she saw Thornley. He was standing, appropriately enough, in front of King Arthur's statue, with a catalogue in his hands. It was good to see him again, looking so untroubled, so completely unconscious of everything. She wandered round the statues as the other visitors did. She didn't look at him as she rudely passed in front of him to reach Theodoric the Terrific, King of the Ostrogoths. When she had admired sufficiently, she walked slowly towards the little chapel. Thornley was seated in the shadows. As she moved slowly towards him, he rose, and they passed each other without a glance.

The catalogue had been left on a chair. She sat down beside it, her wide skirt spreading over it. She waited while the other visitors came and went. Some sat down, some tiptoed about talking in penetrating whispers, others knelt. After long minutes she dared to move her fingers under cover of her skirt and feel for the small fat envelope inside the catalogue. Slowly, without any visible movement, her hand pulled it out and folded it into her palm. It was done. It was over.

She reached the street, and slipped the scarf off her head. As she tied it round her shoulders, she slipped the envelope into the bodice of her dress. Under the fringe of scarf, it wouldn't be noticed—and it felt safe. There was no sign of Bob. But there was Anni. She had got rid of her parcels, and had been sitting in the little square of trees opposite the Church. She had seen Frances; she was almost running across the street. Frances bit her lip. There were two storm-troopers standing in front of the Church steps. If she avoided Anni, their attention would be attracted. There wasn't any time, anyway. The men had already noticed Anni's haste and were watching her with casual interest.

Frances made her voice enthusiastic. "Anni! I haven't seen you for weeks! How are you?"

Anni looked at her in amazement; she was speechless. It was the accent which had dumbfounded her. It was no longer the carefully spoken German which she had heard in Oxford. Frances was glad of the silence. She began to walk along the pavement, her hand on Anni's arm warning her with some pressure. They were passing the two troopers, whose interest had become more anatomical.

"How are your Mother and Father?"

"Quite well, *gnä*—" The pressure on Anni's arm stopped her politeness.

"And your brothers?"

"Also well"

"And your sister?"

"The same."

They had passed the two men safely. Frances relaxed.

"Cheer up, Anni. You look so worried."

Anni suddenly led her across the street towards the garden in the square. In the quietness there, she faced Frances.

"*O gnädige Frau!*" She looked as if she were going to cry.

"Cheer up, Anni. It's all right. But don't call me that."

Anni said, "I knew something was wrong. I have been so worried about you."

"How?"

They were both talking in undertones, pacing slowly under the trees. Anni blinked back her tears.

"I knew you were here in Innsbruck, about a week ago. One of my brothers has a friend. He is the houseman in the hotel where you stayed. He knew I had lived in Oxford, of course, and he told me about the two English guests who came from there. That was how I found out that you were here."

"That was Johann, wasn't it?"

Anni's cheeks colored. "Yes. When he learned I had lived with you, I made him promise not to tell my family that you were here."

Frances was surprised. "Why, Anni?"

Anni looked confused.

"My sister always disbelieved me about England. When I told them about your house and clothes, she would only laugh. If she had learned you were staying in that place, she would have made fun of me to everyone."

"We stayed in *that* place because we like the old town, Anni," Frances said gently. That was true. They had chosen to live in the old town when they had last visited Innsbruck, although the hotel then had been an innocent place compared with their choice this time.

Anni looked relieved that Frau Myles was still smiling.

"Yes," she said, "that's what Johann told the police today."

Frances almost stopped walking.

"Anni, tell me all you know."

"I saw Johann this morning. We usually meet when I cycle into the town." Anni blushed again, and hesitated, but Frances waited in silence. "Early this morning, the Gestapo came to the hotel, and searched and questioned. They asked very particularly about you and the *Herr Professor.* Johann only knew that you came from Oxford and that you were on holiday."

"What about the owner of the hotel?"

"He left the hotel just after a telephone call came for him very late last night. No one has seen him since. So Johann was in charge when the police came. They seemed very angry."

Frances said nothing. Mr. Smith seemed to think of everything, she thought, even of the fact that their travels in Germany and Austria would be retraced. She would have liked to know how he had got that telephone call through to Kronsteiner without giving himself away. Possibly it had come through another agent . . . But if there had been a ghost of a chance left for their simple-traveler story, it had vanished along with Kronsteiner. His disappearance would confirm all the suspicions against them. Anni's face grew more worried as she watched Frances walk so silently beside her.

At last Frances asked, "Do the police know that you were with us in Oxford?"

Anni shook her head. "Johann never said anything about that. He didn't want to mention my name."

"I am sorry that we met today, Anni. I had better leave you now; it is too dangerous for you."

"But, *gnädige Frau,* I must help. What is wrong?"

"We must leave Austria at once."

Anni was silent. Then at last she said, "Johann could lead you over the mountains."

"Into Germany? That's worse still."

"He also knows the South Tyrol. He was born there. He escaped over the mountains when the Italians were conscripting the Austrians for the war in Abyssinia."

"That border is now heavily guarded." What was it that Schulz had said last night when she was half-asleep? . . . something about advising the mountains rather than the train, if she hadn't been exhausted . . . But she was all right now; Herr Schulz wouldn't hesitate to advise them to go by the mountains if he saw her today. She disliked the idea of the train, for in a train you were trapped in a box.

Anni was speaking again. "But there is a way, if you know the mountains. Johann knows."

Frances was tempted. But she said, "No, Anni. Besides, Johann must not risk anything for us."

"He would do it if I asked him."

"No, Anni. Better not. Don't tell anyone that you have seen me; not even Johann."

Anni was still searching for some plan. "I can't ask you to come to our house. My sister hates the English, although she has never known any. My brothers would not help. They are afraid like my parents."

"Thank you a thousand times, Anni. But you must not help."

Anni began to cry. Frances watched her tears with distress.

"Please don't, Anni . . . we shall be all right."

"Where is the *Herr Professor?*"

"He is waiting for me. I must go now, or he will be worried."

"Please tell me the address. Then when I have thought out some plan I can come to you this afternoon and tell you about it."

Frances had an idea. "You said Johann knew a way over the mountains? If he could draw a map of it would you—" no good saying *post it;* perhaps Schulz was known by another name altogether. Frances paused. How on earth were they to get hold of the map?

"I'll bring it to you," Anni said eagerly.

"Then you must come when it's dark. Can you get away this evening without making anyone suspicious?"

"On Saturday, yes. I look after my brother's shop then, and I am often late before I reach home."

"And don't tell Johann that the map is for us. Please, Anni. It would be safer for everyone. Can you think of some excuse for him?"

Anni said she could manage Johann. She repeated the address which Frances told her. Tonight she would slip the map under the door of that house; and then she would forget the address forever. She promised. She was smiling again, as Frances said good-by. She seemed happier now that she could be of some use after all.

Frances recrossed the street. She felt she had every right to be pleased with herself. Such a map would be most useful, if, for instance, the train seemed too risky. There was no doubt that the search was on. She thought of Kronsteiner. Trains would be watched, perhaps searched. As for giving Anni the address—well, Anni would keep her promise. The secret would be safe. Anni was under no suspicion. She would not be followed, as Henry or Bob would be . . . And Anni did not know the importance of the house. It would seem just a rooming house to her. There were plenty of such houses in that district.

Everything began to look easy; and that was probably her undoing. If Henry could drive them almost to the frontier, they could follow the path over the mountains, and then meet Henry somewhere on the other side. He could take along their Schulz clothes, pack them somewhere in his suitcase, and they could change in his car once they had finished the climb. It was all so simple. She imagined Richard's look of surprise and amusement when she would present him with the idea. It wasn't at all bad, she admitted with some pleasure to herself. In her excitement, it was understandable that she forgot. She forgot that if you are playing a part you must live it, and forget your own identity. She should have been Mitzi Schmidt going to meet Fritzi Müller; but at the moment she was very much enjoying being Frances Myles.

She walked quickly with her light smooth step. If she hurried she would not be late for Richard. The man in the restaurant, who had chosen a window table next to where a young American and Englishman had sat, saw the Austrian girl who walked in that familiar way. He was suddenly alert. The color of her hair and of her face were different, but there was something equally familiar in that hint of a smile and the tilt of the nose, the shape of the eyes. She passed. He recognized the set of the shoulders, the shape of her legs. Yesterday he had watched them in a green meadow, from a doorway. He didn't need to verify his guess from the table next him, where the restless Englishman and the talkative American had suddenly become still and silent.

Van Cortlandt and Thornley looked at each other.

"He's gone," said Thornley needlessly. "God, he's recognized her."

"Are you sure it's that man?"

"Richard described him. Fits in. Cheek slashes, fair hair, gold-chain bracelet."

"He thinks it important enough to leave us alone, anyway," van Cortlandt said gloomily.

Thornley rose abruptly. "I'll follow and phone you at the hotel, if I can find where he has taken her. I'll phone you anyway. You had better stick to the hotel and wait for a call from Richard. He's bound to give you a ring when Frances doesn't turn up."

Van Cortlandt began to object, but Thornley had already left. The American paid the bill gloomily. He was just to go back to the hotel and wait. He was just to wait for phone calls. That was fine; that was just fine. There were times when playing the neutral tried even a neutral's temper.

Thornley saw the tall German and the girl in the Austrian dress ahead of him. The German had made no attempt to catch up with her. He was walking at some distance behind her. That way she would lead him to Richard.

Thornley crossed the street as a precaution, but either the German had not expected to be followed, or he didn't care. Nothing these English could do at this stage would prevent the drama from drawing to its close. . . . But he had not reckoned with the inspiration of the amateur.

Thornley saw several bicycles parked outside a café. He calmly swung himself onto one of them, and raced after Frances. His improvising was more successful than he had hoped. Three angry young men rushed out of the café and mounted bicycles too. Their yells were enough to make everyone in the street look round. And Frances had looked. And she had seen, too, for her step slackened and then she turned abruptly into an alley. The German broke into a run, and a slow-moving motor car suddenly ignored all rules of traffic to cross over to him. Thornley cursed himself for ever imagining that the German would be alone. A short command had been given, and the car speeded into the next street. Thornley guessed that it probably led round to the other entrance of the alley. He hesitated, wondering desperately what his next move should be. And then the three angry young men caught up with him. They were in uniform.

"I am very sorry," he said. "I was going to bring the bicycle back. I thought I saw a girl I must speak to, and she was far away. There was no time to ask your permission." One of the boys looked amused, but the owner of the bicycle was less amenable, until he noticed the money in Thornley's hand.

"To pay for the wear on the tires," said Thornley tactfully.

"Where is she now?" asked the one who had smiled.

"She went up that small alley."

"But it has another entrance! There's a short-cut! Come on. There's still time if we hurry."

Thornley found himself cycling furiously with the three young men grouped round him. The romantic one was enjoying himself. The other two were obviously intending to find out if the story about the girl was true. They followed a very narrow side street, which brought them suddenly onto the road which the car had taken . . . And there it was just ahead of them, standing at the end of the alley, ready to drive off. The back of the car was towards them, and the only one whose face they could see was the German with the scars. He was just getting into the front seat beside the driver. Behind was Frances, wedged in between two uniforms.

Thornley screened himself behind the young men as they dismounted. They had stopped as soon as they had seen the open Mercedes. They were looking at him strangely.

"Was that your girl?" the romantic one demanded. His tone had changed completely. Thornley, his eyes fixed on the disappearing number plate of the car, shook his head. He was all disappointment.

"No. But from the distance their figures and legs were the same, though."

This proved a mild joke. The kindliest of the three relaxed again.

"Just as well she wasn't your girl," he said comfortingly. "She won't enjoy herself at Dreikir—"

"You talk too much, Fritz," interrupted the one who had taken the money. The third young man had stopped laughing. There was an uncomfortable pause.

"What about some beer?" Thornley suggested. They were stiffly sorry. There were meetings this afternoon, and processions. There was much to arrange before it began. They had all suddenly become very important. They straightened their shoulders and gave him a co-ordinated farewell. Thornley gave them a careless wave of his hand and thanked them again, solemnly. They swung onto their bicycles, but he noticed that the one he disliked looked carefully over his shoulder to watch him enter the restaurant which he had suggested. He stayed there for a few minutes, long enough to let the cyclists leave the street, long enough to write down the curious number of the black car and to find the telephone with its directory. But there was nothing under Dreikir—

He left the restaurant. Perhaps he might try the post office. He could have a letter to send, and he had forgotten the address. . . . And then he remembered Prague. No, the post office wouldn't do. It might be dangerous; too risky. It was obviously quite useless trying to trace the car. That would rouse instant suspicion. He remembered the guarded look on the young men's faces when they had first seen the car, the way in which they had dismounted so quickly at a safe distance. One thing he did know: the young man who had talked almost too much had recognized von Aschenhausen. That had been obvious.

He left the street as quickly as he could, in case the suspicious young man had changed his mind and returned, and walked quickly towards van Cortlandt's hotel. The shops were crowding round him once more. He noticed a tourist office and halted. Inside, he found a number of people booking their seats for that afternoon's excursions. They crowded round the various tables, each with its clearly-marked notice of a special tour. Beside the one labeled BRENNER, a quiet man stood. He was watching: watching and listening. It was the only advertised excursion for anywhere near a frontier. Thornley noted the size of the group round that table—the Brenner was popular, it seemed—and decided to risk it.

He approached the desk marked INFORMATION at the other end of the large room. Behind it, a girl was handing out timetables and a few kind words to two men. Thornley, with his fair hair, his shorts and light gray tweed jacket, his almost white stockings and nail-studded shoes, felt safe enough beside them. The men were satisfied, at last, and left. He purposely chose the same place they had been asking about. That would take less time for the girl; and it might muddle her, later, if she were questioned.

The girl smiled at his request. "Kitzbühel? It is very popular today. You will find all information in this." She handed him one of the brightly illustrated folders which she still held in her hand. He opened it as the others had done, and studied its pages.

He looked up with a smile. "This is excellent." The girl seemed pleased. "Now, would you be good enough to tell me where the post office is? I have just arrived in Innsbruck."

"In the Maximilianstrasse."

"Is that far from here? I am late for an engagement already."

"It is quite a little way."

"It concerns a letter I want to post at once, and I have mislaid the address. I remember it began with Drei. Dreikir—like that."

"Ah—Dreikirchen. We used to have buses which visited it. But not now." She was looking at him curiously. "Do you know someone there?"

Thornley took his cue. "I was given the address two years ago. But my friend will still be there. I never heard that he had gone."

"Did he belong to the Church?" The girl had lowered her voice.

"He was studying." That seemed to be the correct answer.

"It's all changed now."

"Well, they will redirect the letter . . . I'll post it at once. Now would you advise today or Monday for Kitzbühel?"

A man and a woman had come up behind him.

"Today will be more crowded."

"And the bus will leave outside this office?"

"Just across the street. I hope you will enjoy yourself at Kitzbühel. Everyone does." She was a nice girl, the kind who really liked to please the customers.

Thornley thanked her, and studied the folder as he made his way out of the office. The queue at the Brenner table was still large. The man beside it was listening intently to each excursionist's request.

On the pavement, Thornley drew a deep breath. He stuffed the folder into his pocket. It would make a nice little souvenir along with the electric torch. The policeman's helmet hanging above his mantelpiece at Cambridge began to seem a poor effort.

All he could do now was to go to van Cortlandt's hotel. He hoped to high heaven that Richard was already worried about Frances, and that he had phoned. At least they knew the name of the place. . . . That was something.

19

Richard woke about eleven o'clock, and his worries began with the empty bed beside him. He ought to have wakened in time to see Frances and talk to her. In fact, he ought to have gone himself, even if Frances had been more adequately disguised. He dressed quickly, cursing at his slight stiffness, his lateness, his difficulty in shaving with cold water.

When he got downstairs, the woman had reheated the coffee. It was black and bitter, but it cleared his head. Twelve o'clock, the woman had said. He drank more coffee in spite of its taste, and read the newspaper. There was no mention of the Pertisau incident. So they were keeping it quiet, meanwhile. Von Aschenhausen might be making desperate efforts to turn his failure into success, before anything was made public. If he had kept Smith on his own responsibility, in the hope of presenting his chiefs with a large and very complete haul, then he would be in a dangerous position himself, if he had failed. He had tried for too much; he had been too ambitious. That would make their own escape twice as difficult. Von Aschenhausen would have to catch them or face very unpleasant consequences. . . . And then, there was the matter of his pride, and revenge. Vindictiveness was one of the strongest German traits. Richard sat and looked at the patch of garden as Frances had done. But his feelings were very different.

Twelve o'clock had long passed. The woman was sympathetic, but calm: there was no need to worry. Innsbruck's streets were very difficult for strangers, and she assured him for the second time that his wife's appearance was safe enough.

But by one o'clock, the woman was anxious too. She was obviously afraid for Schulz and herself. Richard did not blame her.

"Can I phone safely from some place near here?" he asked. She nodded, and pointed across the back yard to a house in the next street. And then the doorbell rang. They looked at each other, with hope and fear allied in their eyes. Richard moved behind the sitting-room door, where he could see through the chink into the hall. He saw her open the front door slightly. Someone handed her an envelope, and he heard a familiar voice.

"May I see the *Herr Professor?*"

Richard was startled. It couldn't be, it couldn't . . . But the door had opened farther, and there was no doubt.

"Anni!" he almost shouted. "Come in!"

The woman was so taken aback that Anni and her broad smile were already inside the house. Richard seized her arm and pulled her into the sitting room.

"Anni," he said again. "How on earth did you get here?"

Anni was delighted with his amazement, just in the same way as when she used to produce a triumph of a cake for a birthday surprise in Oxford. For her answer, she took the envelope back from the woman and handed it proudly to him. Frances, he thought; it must be a message from Frances. What had happened? Was she waiting somewhere for him? He ripped the envelope roughly open. All it contained was a small diagram, a sheet of paper with a map and no names.

"There's the Brenner," said Anni, pointing to a small penciled circle. "I thought it was better not to write in the names; instead, you will memorize them. That is why I had to see you."

Richard looked quickly from the map to Anni. "How did you know we needed this? How did you know you would find me here?"

"The *gnädige Frau* . . . didn't she tell you?"

"When did you see her?"

"After she came out of the Church."

"At what hour was that?"

Anni looked worried. "About a quarter to twelve. I reached my brother's shop just after twelve, and that was the time Johann comes to see me on Saturdays. You see, that is the afternoon my brother goes to the mountains—he's a guide on Saturdays and Sundays—and I look after the shop for him, then. So when Johann came, I got him to draw this, and I brought it to you at once. The *gnädige Frau* said tonight, but that was only because she was afraid for me. I thought you might want it now, so that you could leave at once. I didn't tell Johann about you. I promised I would tell him later, and it will be all right because he liked both you and the *gnädige Frau.*"

Richard sat down for a moment. Anni saw the look in his face.

"The *gnädige Frau* told you nothing of our plans? What is wrong, *Herr Professor?* Is she not here?"

"No," said the woman gravely, "she has not come back yet."

"But she said she must hurry. She said you would be worried if she didn't . . . Oh, *Herr Professor!*" Anni was so upset that Richard rose and took her hand. So his fears had been real. While he had waited and worried, something had happened to Frances. Something must have happened. If he could only stop feeling so damned sick with worry. This was no damned good, standing here patting Anni's hand like a blasted idiot. Something had to be thought of, something had to be planned. They had lost an hour already.

"Tell me, Anni, how did you recognize Mrs. Myles?"

"I looked right into her eyes, and they recognized me. And then there was something in the way she walked, the shape of her legs. It was because I know her so well that I could recognize her."

"Then someone else who knew her well might have recog—" He couldn't finish. He left Anni, and walked to the window. He stood with his back to them, looking out into the garden. He thought of van Cortlandt and Thornley. He must get in touch with them, and at once . . . But what then? What then? He must stop this. He had to keep calm, had even to forget that Frances was his; he had to think of all this mess in the way he had thought of Smith, as a kind of problem. And he needed all his wits about him to find a solution. Emotion would only hinder; worry might lose her forever.

He turned back to the room. "Anni, could you go back to the shop and wait there until an American and an Englishman come to buy climbing boots?"

Anni heard his calm voice with amazement, but it lessened her fears. If the *Herr Professor* saw some hope, then there was hope. She listened to his descriptions of the two men who would come to buy climbing boots. She memorized their names carefully, and the message she had to give them. The Hungerburg at four o'clock. Anni was not enthusiastic about that message. The Hungerburg was so big that they might miss each other. It was safe enough for them there, she agreed, but they might be late before they met each other. She didn't like to take the responsibility of the message. If anything went wrong, then she would blame herself.

"It would be better to meet them in the shop, and see them yourself. It would save time," she suggested. "There is a storeroom at the back of the shop with its own entrance. You could wait there until your friends arrived. My brother has left already, and Johann must go back to the hotel as soon as I get back to the shop—I left him in charge so that I could come here. There will be no one there except me." She laughed at any danger to herself. If the worst came, he would be an unknown customer; and there was the back entrance losing itself in courtyards and alleys, so that even if everything went wrong there was at least a chance to escape. Richard agreed with her in his heart. It would be the simplest solution, and the quickest one. That was the chief thing. Now that the suggestion had come from Anni herself, he accepted it gladly.

Anni had left by the back door, with a *loden* cape thrown round her shoulders. He waited for two or three minutes until she would be safely out of the other house, hoping against hope that Frances might suddenly appear. The woman was obviously worried, but she was unexpectedly sympathetic. Herr Schulz would be home any minute now; she had the dinner table all ready for him. And he would be able to advise them. Meanwhile, she offered him a bowl of thin brown soup with dumplings submerged in it. He must eat. Richard declined as politely as his revolving stomach would permit; worry churned him up inside like a Channel crossing. He had his eyes on his watch. Three minutes, he had thought, would be time enough for Anni. In any case, he couldn't wait any longer. He suddenly left the room.

"Say Lisa sent you," the woman called after him.

The formula worked. The cobbler obligingly made the call for him, and then left him alone with the telephone. He heard van Cortlandt's voice, and such a wave of relief swept over him that he realized he had been afraid of getting no answer.

"Hello!" said van Cortlandt, and waited. "Hello, there!"

"Van Cortlandt?"

"Speaking."

It was easier to talk now; the words which had deserted him came rushing out.

Van Cortlandt said, "Oh, yes, the *Times.* I'm sorry I'm late with that article. Glad you called. I thought you would because of this delay."

"Serious?" So van Cortlandt knew already; that saved explanations.

"At the moment, yes."

"Well, there's another article to write. Beauties of the Tyrol. Have you any climbing equipment?"

"Just my own two feet."

"Well, better add something to that. If you haven't boots, get them this afternoon. This is a rush assignment. Go to any good sports dealer, and he will advise you. There's Schmidt, or Spiegelberger, or Rudi Wachter. He is particularly good. You'll find him on the Burggraben near the Museumstrasse."

"Good. I'll go there at once. Hope to see you soon."

"I'll see you soon. Get a move on with the article, won't you? No delay for this one."

"Sure; you can depend on me. Love and kisses to Geoffrey Dawson."

"And mine to Luce." Richard heard a sudden laugh at the end of the phone, and then silence.

In the sitting room, Richard found Schulz sitting at the table, his head well down to his bowl of soup. Of Lisa, there was no sign. Schulz, busy with a dumpling, motioned him to a chair and pointed to the soup pot. Richard poured himself some coffee, and gulped it down. He thought of the brandy in his flask, but they might need that later on.

"I must go at once," he said. "My wife—"

"I know." Schulz wiped his lips, and swallowed some water. "I know. Lisa told me. There are all your papers and clothes." He nodded to a large envelope and a neat brown-paper parcel on a side table. Richard rose, and brought the envelope over to the dinner table. The document looked convincing; the photographs had just the right moronic look.

"Were we quick enough for you? That's everything, I think; everything. You've paid me. Have you any money left?"

"I'll meet some friends," Richard said.

"Well, good luck."

Richard's words came haltingly. "My wife may have been arrested. They may trace her movements to this house."

Schulz swallowed some more soup noisily. "Don't worry about that. I had already decided to change my address. I saw your friend Kronsteiner early this morning, at my place of—business. He had a message last night from our friend who used to be at Pertisau. So we are on the move again. Lisa is packing now." He smiled as he saw the relief on Richard's face. Richard prepared to go. They shook hands silently.

Then Schulz suddenly spoke. "Courage!" he said. "Courage! It's the only real weapon we've got. A man can win when he still has his courage."

Richard nodded. "I'm sorry if we have upset your plans."

"They are always being upset, but we go on. And don't worry about Kronsteiner. He's all right. He's much changed since his visit to me this morning." Schulz threw back his head and laughed. Kronsteiner's change seemed to amuse him . . . And then he went back to his soup. "It would be a pity to leave it," he explained, his voice once more matter-of-fact.

Lisa met Richard at the doorway. "This was all you left upstairs," she said, and held out his small razor case, and Frances' bag. He nodded his thanks, and watched her slip them safely into the brown-paper parcel.

"We'll give you five minutes, and then we leave," called Schulz, in the middle of the last dumpling. "Good-by, young man, and courage."

Lisa gave him her first and last smile.

He closed the door softly, and walked unhurriedly down the street. The brown-paper parcel attracted no attention. It was almost two o'clock.

All Innsbruck seemed to be marching that Saturday. There had been two parades already, complete with bands, banners and uniforms. The onlookers crowded into the principal streets, through which the processions passed, and even after they had gone the people waited. Perhaps there were still other processions to come. By avoiding the main thoroughfares, Richard walked quickly through the deserted little side streets, and he arrived at the back entrance of the Wachter shop in record time. There was no one in sight, as he opened the back door and walked quietly into the small room which Anni had described as a storeroom. This was it, all right. He moved carefully and slowly between the neat stacks of boxes to a crate under the small, high window. No one would be able to look in through that window, unless he brought a step-ladder along with him. He sat down on the edge of the crate, and waited. He could hear a murmur of voices, and once Anni laughed. The sounds were distant enough to assure him that a room lay between the storeroom and the front shop itself, where Anni was serving a customer. No one had seen him, no one had heard him enter; so far, so good. If anyone were to look into the room, the rows of boxes would hide him. He began to feel better.

The two doors worried him, all the same. He rose suddenly, and examined the lock of the door by which he had entered. It worked easily, so he locked it. Better that, than to risk some unknown visitor using this street door at an awkward moment. It would be a simple matter to unlock the door and escape by the alley, if any complication arrived. There was that other door, the one which must lead into that middle room; but he couldn't do anything about it until Anni appeared.

The voices were silent now. The customer must be going, for he heard the accustomed formula, and Anni's dutiful echo. There was a sound of a bell. Of course, that would be the door closing. Anni must have brought back one of those doorbells as a present for her brother after all. She had said she would. He smiled in spite of himself. It was rather odd to hear the familiar Oxford sound right here in Innsbruck. It made him think of a dark little shop, with the smell of rich tobaccos in the air, and neat white jars on its shelves; and the polished brass scales, on which the light and dark tobaccos were weighed before they were mixed and then carefully emptied into your pouch; and the darkened oak counter, with its rubber mat for your coins, and the change which came to you from the old wooden till; and then the gentle note of the bell as you opened and shut the door.

The bell was silent again, and he heard Anni's footsteps approaching. The door into the middle room opened, and she stood straining her eyes into the dim light. He stepped out from behind the boxes.

"God be thanked," she said.

"Did you hear me at all?"

She shook her head. "No. I've been coming through here between visits from customers, just to make sure. Have you locked that door? Good. I'll lock this one too. The room next you is a dressing room, where customers try on sports clothes if they want to. If anyone should go in there, just keep quite still. But if anyone with a loud voice tries this door, and rattles it, and asks me angrily for the key, then leave at once."

The front doorbell rang.

"It has been very useful, that bell," said Anni in a whisper. She turned to go, but Richard caught her arm as he heard a cheery voice call: "Anyone here?" from the front shop. That must be Thornley. It was.

"That was a darned lucky break, if you ask me," said van Cortlandt in English. Their voices sounded as if they brought good news.

Anni looked at Richard inquiringly. He nodded, and she went through to meet them.

He heard the men ask about climbing boots, but Anni's voice was too low for him to know what she had answered. He heard them suddenly quieten, and follow her quickly towards the storeroom.

She locked the door behind them, and they were left alone in the room, standing there looking at each other.

"God, and aren't we glad to see you," said van Cortlandt.

"Frances?" Richard asked.

Thornley spoke. "They got her. Just the rottenest luck. It was the fair-haired blighter with the bracelet who saw her, and recognized something. They've taken her to Dreikirchen. That's all I could find out. That and the number and identification marks of the car." He groped in his pocket for the sheet from his diary where he had scribbled the signs down in that restaurant, just after the boys had left him.

The door was unlocked, and Anni entered the room with Tyrolese jackets over her arm. She handed them to van Cortlandt and Thornley.

"Where is Dreikirchen, Anni? Is it a village or a house? Have you ever heard of it?"

"If the doorbell rings, get back into the dressing room, and try these on, in front of the mirror," she said to the American. "Lock this door behind you, and put the key up on that high shelf, there." She turned to Richard. "Now that we've made things safe, *Herr Professor,* there is only one Dreikirchen near here. It's just two hours' walk from here—to the south of Innsbruck. If you follow the Brennerstrasse, you will reach the Berg Isel, and Dreikirchen is to the right of that. I will show you on the map; you have one?"

Richard had already taken his Baedeker out of his pocket, and was searching for the Berg Isel. Anni looked over his arm, and pointed with her finger.

"There's the road. You see that small line on its right? That is the side road which takes you to Dreikirchen. There it is—these black squares grouped together."

"Is it a village, and why isn't it named?"

"It isn't a village. It is too small—just a few small houses and the monastery and three little chapels. Monks used to live there."

"Who lives there now?"

Anni seemed embarrassed. She wasn't sure. She had heard her brothers talk, of course, but they had never explained. One of their friends had been sent there.

"Is it a concentration camp?" asked van Cortlandt.

Anni was shocked. Oh, no. Nothing like that. There were boys at Dreikirchen, who were being educated.

Specially chosen boys and young men. She admitted there were rumors. Of course, there always were rumors, but people didn't try to find out about rumors, not if they were wise.

"Has it any connection with the Gestapo?" asked van Cortlandt again.

Anni looked frightened. There were rumors, she said . . . And once Johann had made a joke about that in front of one of her brothers, and that was the only time they had quarreled. Richard thanked her; that was all she knew or wanted to know.

As she left them, Thornley stopped her. "If you were to see a large black car with these numbers on it, what would you think?" He held out the page from his diary.

"Special car," she said.

"Secret police?"

Anni nodded. "I must go back into the shop," she said, and left them.

"Were you followed?"

"We were at first," said van Cortlandt. "And then we had a break. The whole place is jammed with people. So we got mixed up with two processions, and here we are without our tail. We are probably safe for another ten minutes, until he reports to headquarters and they give him a list of our shopping places. They no doubt listened in to our talk on the phone today. So now let's get busy."

Richard said, "Thanks for all you've done. It would have been hopeless without you."

"Say, we're in on this too," said van Cortlandt. He turned to Thornley. "Imagine that . . . he thought he was going to get rid of us at this stage. It will take three of us to find Frances. And she's got to be found."

"We'll find her," Thornley said quietly.

Richard didn't waste any more time. He spread the map before them.

"We'll meet here," he said, pointing to a part of the road as it touched the Berg Isel. "Bring a car, and all your things packed. And take this parcel and pack the things in it into your case. It's our stuff for Italy."

"I've arranged about the car," said van Cortlandt. "That radio man agreed to an exchange. He'll keep his mouth shut. He's going to Vienna this afternoon, and is traveling the Jenbach road. I've already told the hotel I'm going back to Pertisau to look for my friends. It all fits in nicely."

Richard looked at the American with respect. "That's a pretty good effort, Henry. Well, that's about all. Meet me at that place any time after four o'clock. That will let me get out there safely. And bring some chocolate and cigarettes."

"Say half-past four," said van Cortlandt. They shook hands.

"We'll be seeing you," he added, and followed Thornley back into the shop.

Richard waited for Anni. She hurried into the storeroom, and unlocked the back door.

"Good-by, *Herr Professor,* and give the *gnädige Frau* my . . ." She bit her lip. "Please let me know when she is safe. Please."

"Yes, Anni."

"Please hurry, *Herr Professor.*"

"Yes, Anni." What could he say to thank her enough for what she had done? Anni seemed to sense his difficulty. She smiled sadly.

"I am only repaying your kindness in Oxford. The *gnädige Frau* was always so good to me." She opened the door and motioned him out.

"*Auf Wiedersehen,* Anni." He gripped her hand and held it.

"*Auf Wiedersehen.*" Her smile was quivering. And then the door closed behind him, and already his steps had taken him far enough away to keep Anni safe.

Here was the street corner, and the crowds. He loitered with them until he saw Thornley and van Cortlandt leave the shop. They were carrying two or three parcels. He watched them until they were lost in the crowd.

He felt suddenly hungry, but he had just enough money to take him to the Berg Isel by tramcar. That would save his legs for tonight's climb. He and Thornley could get Frances over the frontier, and van Cortlandt could take their clothes by car, and meet them in Italy. On the Berg Isel, as he waited for the others, he would memorize that map which Anni had given him, and compare it with his own. He felt safe enough, partly because of the number of people on the streets, partly because von Aschenhausen would be the only person in Innsbruck who could recognize him—and von Aschenhausen was with Frances. The German was playing a deep and subtle game. If he had taken Frances to Dreikirchen, it was because her arrest must be unofficial until he had got the information from her which would help him to retrieve his failure. Frances knew enough to compensate him for the escape of Smith, and even that might be made temporary, if Frances could be persuaded. If Frances could be persuaded.

The journey to the Berg Isel, although dull and safe enough, was one which Richard would never forget.

21

Van Cortlandt and Thornley made their way as quickly as they could through the crowd. They stopped twice: once to buy some biscuits and chocolate, and once to buy oranges. Van Cortlandt already had some brandy. In this matter-of-fact way, they quietly discussed their plans as they walked along to van Cortlandt's hotel. Thornley, with unexpected pessimism, had not unpacked his bag and in any case he always traveled lightly. Van Cortlandt, although most of his belongings always remained in his trunk or suitcases, had a lot of odds and ends to clear up in his room. So it was Thornley who would have the job of phoning van Cortlandt's broadcasting friend and of telling him the time they would meet him. He already knew the place where they were to exchange cars. Van Cortlandt had thought that out, this morning. Thornley was also to telephone Cook's agent, and have him collect van Cortlandt's heavier luggage, with the directions that it was to be sent on to Geneva.

Van Cortlandt was quite philosophic about it all.

"It was coming," he said. "I've got to the stage when I can't write at all. I've developed a sort of censorphobia. Every word I get down begins to look as if it won't get through anyway. And it's about time I changed my beat. If there are any surprises coming in the world's history, it won't be from this direction. They are all set for Poland. I'd do better to go there, myself. See it from the other angle."

"I had a letter this morning," Thornley said unexpectedly, and his tone made van Cortlandt look at him. "I'll tell you about it later. It was from Tony, on his way home."

"The girl?"

Thornley shook his head. "Alone."

Van Cortlandt was startled. He had never imagined that Thornley's face could have such an ugly look.

"Pretty bad?" he asked.

Thornley only nodded.

They finished the journey in silence. When he left van Cortlandt, Thornley's voice was normal again.

"I'll see you at four," he said.

It was four o'clock exactly when Thornley arrived at the garage. Van Cortlandt was already there, examining his car. The mechanic had lost interest, and was busy with some other work. He had overhauled the car this morning and had found nothing seriously wrong although they seemed to have had a lot of trouble last night. These Americans, if only they'd take the trouble to learn about the insides of a machine, they would save themselves a lot of money . . . But then they were all millionaires, and that ruined them. Now, it was said, they were all starving in the streets. What people had to suffer in other countries! Anyway, the car was perfect now; and he had been paid; and he had other work to do, plenty of it what with all the others at the parade. He had advised the American not to miss the processions: that was something to see. That was something to impress anyone. But the American had only smiled and nodded. Perhaps he couldn't understand German. And now the American was pottering around his car, pretending he knew all about the engine, looking for anything that had been left undone. Let him: there was plenty of more important work to be done. The money had been paid. The job was over.

Van Cortlandt motioned Thornley into the automobile, but he himself didn't enter. He kept his eyes fixed on the entrance of the garage. When a boy appeared, carrying two suitcases, van Cortlandt had the money ready in his hand. The boy was gone as suddenly as he had arrived, the suitcases were in the car, and they were driving smoothly out of the door.

"Quick work," said Thornley approvingly. "That was rather a brain wave of yours."

Van Cortlandt grinned as he guided the car expertly through the traffic.

"How did you manage?"

"It was easy enough," Thornley said. "You know what a rabbit warren my hotel was—no lift, just staircases and passages. Well, I paid the bill, said I was leaving for Pertisau roundabout five, and apparently went back to my room. I came down another staircase and took one of the back exits. I wasn't even followed."

"If I was, I lost him in the crowds. Processions have their uses. Helluva lot of uniforms today. They seem to crawl out from under every stone. Wonder what's it all about?"

"Just any old excuse. It depresses me."

"That was the Myles' reactions."

"Aren't you? It looks as if we shall all just have to learn to march too. No one can stop that spirit with arguments or good deeds."

"Well, I must say I think it *needs* stopping. But I don't think there's a democracy left with the guts to do it. We are all tied to our mothers' apronstrings—and big business keeps bleating about peace and prosperity. Between the apronstrings and the bleating, we'll all hesitate until it's too late. That is what depresses me."

Thornley said nothing to that. There were things stronger than apronstrings and bleatings, he felt. But it was no good talking about courage: you could not prove it by talking about it. It was like a pudding: the proof was in the eating. He contented himself with watching the way in which van Cortlandt drove. The timing at the corners of the streets was perfect. If any car were following them, it would be jammed by the traffic from the cross streets. Van Cortlandt had forgotten his depression, and was enjoying himself. He seemed particularly pleased when they crossed the bridge and turned west towards the Jenbach road. The two uniformed men on the bridgehead had noticed the car; this amused van Cortlandt particularly. By the time they had reached the beer garden, the traffic had thinned out and they could see clearly that no car was following them.

Van Cortlandt's eyes searched the few cars parked beyond the entrance to the garden. They widened suddenly.

"Good man," he said with some satisfaction. "Space for us, and all." He drove neatly in beside a dark-blue car. Its subdued color made it almost invisible beside van Cortlandt's. Its doors were unlocked, and Thornley slipped into the back seat. He found himself calmly handing out the suitcase he found there to van Cortlandt, who gave him their cases in exchange. The easiness of the whole business took his breath away.

A thin man in an American suit and hat was walking leisurely towards them. He threw his cigarette away as he reached his new car, and gave van Cortlandt a sardonic grin as he opened its door.

Van Cortlandt got into the blue car. "Drive like hell," he said to the steering wheel.

"Sure," the man said to himself. He backed the car smoothly in a half circle, so that it faced in the direction of Jenbach. Thornley looked after the speeding car, and watched it disappearing round the trees. Anyone who might have been watching would have difficulty in knowing just what had happened. The only way in which he could see what man had got into what car would have been to walk past them. And no one had.

Van Cortlandt watched his car until it was out of sight, and then he swung back on the road by which they had just come.

"He's all right," he said, reading Thornley's mind. "We are just two Americans who traded cars. So what? If there is anything phoney about that, then we just act dumb. He doesn't know much about our game. He was a newspaperman himself, once, and he guessed I was on to a story. And he hates the Nazis' guts. What's more, he got a bargain in cars. We're all happy."

Thornley guessed that van Cortlandt was putting a very good face on the whole business. He had been proud of that car. He was a strange mixture, thought Thornley: just as strange and unpredictable as he himself found the British. That would surprise him. Thornley smiled. Van Cortlandt saw it in the mirror.

"What's the joke?" he asked. "I could do with one myself."

"The Nazis' guts. It is funny that it should be one thing on which most Americans and Britishers can agree wholeheartedly, without any reservations. The average Frenchman hates the Nazi, too; but half, or at least part, of it is due to the fact he is a dangerous neighbor. Now you and I don't hate the Nazis because they are German. We hate the Germans because they are Nazi. And if you didn't, you wouldn't be driving a strange car to God-knows-where into God-knows-what, this afternoon. You'd be standing at a street corner shouting "*Heil!*" with the rest, and feeling all uplifted and mystic. You like the Myles', I know, but if the Nazis didn't curdle you up inside, you wouldn't be doing all this. In fact, we've got to the stage where anyone who opposes the Nazis is worth helping. Isn't that it?"

Van Cortlandt grinned. "About. I didn't tell you how I felt when I arrived here? I was going to be the complete neutral observer. My stories were going to be a model of detachment. Can you imagine that? My angle was that the Germans had had a tough time of it. If they only had gotten a square deal . . . All that hash. It only took me a few weeks to find out that every deal was square if it benefited Germany, and to hell with the rest. Now I don't mind them looking out for their own rights; we all do. But what got me down is the way no one else has any rights, unless they say so. That's the rub. They are always in the right, and the rest of us just misunderstand them. Criticism is just another stab in the back from Jews and Communists. They've kidded other people so long now that they've started kidding themselves."

"Perhaps it is because they've developed two standards," suggested Thornley, "one for Germany, one for the others. They really believe that anything which is good for them can't be evil. That is how they can lie and commit all kinds of treachery. If it is for the benefit of the Fatherland, then it doesn't seem a lie or a piece of treachery to them: it makes everything moral."

"But then, there are the exceptions."

"Yes, and they should be thanking God for the exceptions instead of driving them into exile or putting them into concentration camps. If it weren't for them, after the next war Germany might be blotted from the map."

Van Cortlandt shook his head. "You can't destroy a whole nation."

"Can't you? Just wait to see how Germany will try it with some of her neighbors. She will give the rest of us a few tips. And it worked with Carthage, too. Don't look so worried, Henry, the exceptions will get Germany her second chance. Or is it a third?"

Van Cortlandt shook his head. "God knows," he said wearily.

They had circled round Innsbruck to the west. That avoided the main streets, which were crowding up once more. They passed several formations of uniformed young men. It seemed as if they were all marching their way to some meeting place. Neither the American nor the Englishman said anything but as they passed one set of exhibitionists in goose-stepping precision their eyes met in the mirror above van Cortlandt's head.

On the road which led to the Berg Isel (the road which led to the

Brenner Pass eventually, as van Cortlandt carefully pointed out) three large black cars passed them in quick succession. They were filled with young men sitting uncomfortably erect, their faces white blurs under the uniform caps. Van Cortlandt heard a quick movement behind him, and turned to see Thornley looking through the back window of the car. He was repeating something to himself.

"Yes?" asked van Cortlandt. Thornley was clearly excited.

"One of these cars, that's it, one of them."

Van Cortlandt smiled. "Your grammar does your feelings proud," he said. "What about it, anyway?"

"One of these cars is the same one I saw this afternoon with Frances in it. Don't you see, Henry, if they have left Dreikirchen, it will be all the better for us?"

Van Cortlandt thought over this for some moments. "*If* they left Dreikirchen," he said. He was probably right, thought Thornley gloomily. And yet, pieces of luck, both good and bad, had the oddest way of turning up. Whichever way you added up your plans, you should always leave a margin on either side for luck.

"Any time now," said van Cortlandt. He had slackened the speed of the car as they approached the small railway halt; there were few passengers waiting on the toy platform. Richard had said he would be near here. Their eyes anxiously watched the road ahead and the paths which led into the surrounding woods, but it wasn't until they were round a bend in the road which hid them from the halt and its inn, and the car had stopped completely to let Thornley get out, that Richard stepped from behind some trees.

"I was beginning to think that we had missed you," van Cortlandt said, worry sharpening his voice, as the car moved on.

"Sorry," said Richard. "I forgot to ask you the color of the car, and I wasn't sure. Couldn't risk anything. Sorry. How did everything go?"

"According to plan."

"Good. Now, we've about five minutes more on this road, and then ten minutes more to the right. I did some map studying while I waited, and there seems to be a small road or track of some kind, just before we get to the Dreikirchen road. If we follow that track, then we can approach the place from the back. If it had been dark, we could have risked the Dreikirchen road itself. But we'd better not wait for darkness. We haven't time."

Thornley looked at Richard's white, set face. There was a gauntness about it which worried him.

"Had anything to eat?" he inquired casually. Richard shook his head, and then took the slab of chocolate which Thornley handed him. He ate it with his eyes fixed on his watch. He doesn't know or care what he's eating, thought Thornley; it might be linoleum for all he knows; he's all shot to pieces.

"Brandy?" he asked.

"We'll need it later," Richard said. He was still looking at his watch. Thornley began to guess the kind of time he had been having while he waited for them to arrive. Shouldn't have left him alone, thought Thornley.

"This is the track," Richard said, and the car turned from the Brenner road into a wood. Richard was still looking at his watch. He held up a hand to silence Thornley just as he was about to say something. . . . And then Thornley realized that Richard was timing the distance they had to drive.

"Now," he said, and the car swung off the track.

"I'll turn, while the going's good," van Cortlandt said, and maneuvered the car until it rested on the grass, hidden from the track by a clump of bushes, its bonnet pointed back towards the Brenner road. Van Cortlandt unscrewed his flask, and handed it to Richard.

"Bob's right," he said. "We all need it. I've plenty more."

"Rum ration," suggested Thornley.

"Any of you got a gun?" van Cortlandt asked.

They shook their heads. Thornley produced a strong-looking clasp knife and his souvenir torch. Richard had nothing. It might have been the shadow of a smile on the American's face, but his voice was serious enough.

"Well, I have, so if we get into a tight spot . . ." He didn't finish, but tapped his pocket thoughtfully. "Anything else, before we leave the car?"

They waited in the quietness of the trees, while van Cortlandt locked the car methodically. When he joined them, the three men looked at each other for some moments. Then Richard turned, and led the way up the wooded hillside.

It was a short climb. They paused on the crest, sheltered by the pines.

Below them, the hill sloped gently to Dreikirchen. They could just see three spires above the last trees.

Thornley pulled out his knife, and motioned to them to wait. He disappeared back towards the road they had left, lopping off a thin branch from every third or fourth pine, as he passed. Van Cortlandt exchanged glances with Richard. The idea was good; the cuts on the trees were white and jagged. When Thornley returned, he seemed pleased. He must have found his way back in record time. As they followed Richard down through the trees, he used his knife continuously. It slowed up their pace, but now that they were so near their objective, there was little they could do but wait, until the clear afternoon light had given way to the dusk of the evening—except for spying out the lie of the land. So they went slowly, walking carefully in order to make no noise, while Thornley worked silently and unhurriedly. The spires had disappeared as they descended through the wood. Richard, who led the way, hoped that his sense of direction was as adequate as Thornley's trail blazing. He would soon know, for at last they were reaching the edge of the wood. A steep bank and a garden were all that separated them from Dreikirchen. Behind the cover of the trees overshading the bank they lay and watched.

The Fathers who had built the community had had an eye for balance and neatness. Into a curve of the wooded hillside, which had formed both a shelter and a background, they had built their miniature castle with its large chapel. Two smaller chapels flanked the main buildings on either side, standing at a respectful distance, and round these were grouped a few cottages. The effect was that of a semicircle which paralleled the curve in the hill, so that the small castle, as the center of the crescent, dominated everything.

From where they lay they would see the road which came from the south. Straight, broad and white, it approached the center of the curve of buildings in a dramatic sweep. That was something, Richard thought, which the founding Fathers had never even imagined. He remembered the map on which this road had been marked only as roughly as the track which they had followed. Anni had been right. Dreikirchen had changed.

In front of them was the garden which lay behind the right-hand chapel. It was the kitchen garden with its rows of neatly planted vegetables protected on one side by a hedge of red-currant bushes, which stretched from the bank almost to the chapel itself. On its other side, the side which adjoined the garden of the castle and the large chapel, there was a row of fruit trees. Pear trees, Richard thought. They were obviously intended as a screen, so that anyone walking in the castle's flower garden wouldn't have his eye offended by the patchwork quilt of vegetables. They served the purpose well enough, for it was difficult for the three men to see the flower garden. It would be better to move behind the castle itself, and from there they would be able to see not only the flower garden but whatever lay behind the third chapel. For the curve of the buildings now hid that completely.

"Mark this spot," whispered Richard. The others nodded, and looked at the shapes of the trees and bushes, at the outcrop of rock behind which they lay. It wasn't easy, but it had to be remembered. If they got safely away from the castle, and were in a hurry, as they probably would be, then they would have to depend on being able to find the blazed trail quickly. Without the trail they might miss the car. It was unpleasant to imagine what it would be like to be searching desperately for the car on an unknown road with pursuers behind them. The best thing to remember, thought Richard grimly, was the outcrop of rock which lay about twenty feet away from the red-currant bushes. If they could reach the red-currant bushes, he added to that thought.

Under the cover of the trees, they worked their way carefully along to the back of the castle. It gave them the view they had hoped for. It was easy to see that an approach would be more difficult through the castle garden, planted with rose trees and small flowering shrubs, than it would be through the kitchen garden. There was much less cover here. As for the ground behind the third chapel, it was quite hopeless. It consisted of tennis courts and a stretch of grass. There was no sign of life from the cottages on this side of the castle, either . . . no movement, no sounds of men's voices. If it hadn't been for the curl of smoke which came from the back of the castle, where a low, narrow building had been added as an afterthought, they might have been looking at a picture in a German calendar.

Richard motioned the others to go farther back into the wood. They reached some bushes, and sat down behind them. They talked in whispers.

"I can do the scouting," said Thornley. "I've done some deer-stalking. This should be easy." He drew his diary from a pocket, and began making a rough diagram of the buildings and gardens. Richard and Thornley exchanged glances. Thornley was obviously the best man for the job. Richard remembered the way he had climbed the balcony of the Pertisau house.

"All right," he said. "We'll watch from the top of the bank."

"This is how I'll go," Thornley said. He traced a line on the diagram with his pencil. He would use the red-currant bushes and reach the right-hand chapel. From there he would follow the path in the kitchen garden which seemed to enter a kind of shrubbery as it reached the line of pear trees. That would bring him to the right wing of the castle, to the back of it where the smoke came from. Then he could perhaps find out who was in that part of the building, or a possible back entrance to the place, or whatever was to be seen or heard.

"All right," Richard said again.

Thornley didn't waste any time. He was already moving quietly down through the trees, in a slantwise direction which would bring him out of the wood near the red-currant hedge.

Van Cortlandt abandoned the plans he had been making while they had watched the castle. He would have liked something with more action than this—one of them to have made some kind of distraction, while the other two rushed the place. The trouble was that they had no weapons worth a nickel, not compared with the arsenal they might expect to face. Still, there seemed to be no one there; perhaps just a cook in the kitchen where the smoke came from, and Frances in a locked room upstairs with someone left to guard her, while the others held their jamboree in Innsbruck or searched for Richard. All Thornley's caution would then be a waste of good time. He had the gloomy afterthought that Frances might not be there after all; that had been worrying him ever since they left Innsbruck. In that case, they would have to imitate old Barney Finnigan. . . .

They had retraced their steps to the edge of the wood again, and had lain behind a fallen tree which would protect them from being seen. They themselves could see through its skeleton roots. As soon as Thornley reached the pear trees and followed the path towards the shrubbery at the side of the house, they could watch him. If anything went wrong before he reached the trees, then they would have to depend on their hearing. Richard raised himself to listen, but van Cortlandt shook his head. He was right; there was nothing.

They waited in the silence of the wood, and watched the tops of the trees moving gently against the background of the evening sky. The strain was beginning to tell on Richard. Again the fear came back to him that they might be on the wrong trail. Frances might be a hundred miles from here—injured, dead. He began to count the branches above him. Anything, anything to keep him from thinking.

Thornley felt a sudden wave of excitement as he neared the edge of the wood and saw the small chapel and the quiet little houses beside it. It was the kind of feeling he had when he'd stand patiently waiting for the birds to break cover; only this time he was one of the birds. It wasn't the excitement of fear or nervousness. It was the excitement of expectation. He had always lived in the country, and what might have been difficult for Richard or van Cortlandt seemed fairly simple to him.

He moved confidently and quickly, knowing that under cover of this string of bushes he could only be seen from the woods behind him. In that case, he would be seen even if he went slowly and carefully—and time was short: they could hardly wait until complete darkness, for he felt that the castle might not remain deserted so very much longer. This was what Henry called playing a hunch; well, he was going to play it as hard as he could.

He had almost reached the chapel. He flattened himself out under the last clump of bushes and waited. So far so good. He strained to hear any sound from the cottages or the chapel, but they were completely silent. What was more, the doors and windows of the cottages were shut. It would be strange for anyone inside them to sit that way on a warm summer's evening. He measured the short dash to the chapel with his eye, and timed it neatly. He stood flat against the wall, hidden from the main buildings. In two or three moments, he would slip round the corner of the chapel and reach the path. The fruit trees would shelter him from the castle gardens, the large shrubs growing along the path would shelter him from the castle's windows; the only danger lay in being seen from the other end of the path. As he waited, motionless, he became aware that the windows beside him were not the usual high, narrow windows of a church. They were square and broad, with ordinary glass. He edged to one and looked cautiously inside over his shoulder. The interior was very strange for a chapel indeed—it was a very complete gymnasium. He gained confidence; only now would he admit to himself that the responsibility of discovering Dreikirchen's existence had worried him. Now he was pretty sure of its purpose. It would be the natural place for Frances to be taken if von Aschenhausen hadn't turned her over to the regular police, and it wasn't likely that he had done that. This was more a case for secret police, with abduction, not arrest, as their weapon.

He left the security of the east wall of the chapel, and entered the kitchen garden. Fortunately, the path curved to suit the arc which the buildings formed. He was hidden from the end of the path where it probably skirted the castle. If he could reach the pear trees, then at least the path would be safer because of the shrubbery. At this point, it was rather unpleasant. There wasn't much shelter in a row of cabbages, or in the long north side of the chapel.

He had reached the pear trees. As he did so, he side-stepped into the shrubbery. The path itself was now too open. It curved straight to a door in the castle itself, a side door just where the low wing was joined to the main building. The smoke from the wing was curling up steadily. Kitchen, almost certainly, thought Thornley, and regained his breath in the shelter of the bushes. The door had been unexpected. In fact, it had given him a jolt, as he had come round the path and suddenly met it staring at him from the end of the path. It meant he would have to push his way carefully and slowly between the thick shrubs, sometimes almost through them. Not the pleasantest way of travel, he thought savagely. The earth here hadn't the clean wholesomeness of the earth in a wood. It seemed dank and stale, and a fine dust from the branches and leaves blackened his hands.

He had almost reached the castle wall. . . . And then he heard voices; at first distant, and then gradually getting louder. But they were far enough away to be indistinguishable. He must get almost to the end of the bushes before he would be near enough to hear them. The voices were clearer; two men were talking. Only two, he was sure of that. But he still couldn't hear any words. He knelt down on the moldering earth. He pushed down gently the branch in front of him. It let him see the side of the castle right up to the front corner. He saw that there was a broad path along this wall of the castle, which must meet the path from the kitchen garden in front of the side door.

Thornley moved his head to get a clearer view of the front corner of the castle. He dared not push the sheltering branch any more to the side. He judged that the men were walking in front of the castle, that any moment they would appear at the corner. The voices were coming nearer, and he could hear the heavy footsteps of men aware of their own authority. . . . And then there was a laugh, the belly laugh a man gives when he has just heard an unexpected end to a good story. The trooper who had laughed was still enjoying the joke when they reached the corner of the path. They were in their shirt sleeves, and capless, but they still wore revolvers at their side and the one who had laughed carried a loaded cane. He beheaded the large yellow daisies growing at the side of the path as he listened to his companion. They paused as they turned in their walk, and both looked up at the same window as if they had heard something. They were silent for a moment, listening. Then the one who had laughed said something to the other which made them both snicker, and they began their walk back along the front of the castle, and the corner of the building hid them.

Thornley wondered they had not heard his heartbeats. The man who had laughed and chopped off the flower heads was the one who had questioned him last night when he had returned to Innsbruck with van Cortlandt. Anyway, he had found out that there were two of them in front of the castle. They weren't on guard; they had lounged too much for that. But they were armed. It looked as if no one at the castle expected any uninvited guests. And why should they? This was one of their own strongholds, and once their prisoners disappeared from their homes the shock or the fear which petrified their friends ended all help for them. It took weeks, even months, for anyone who was mad enough to ask, to discover what had happened to those who had disappeared. So why worry about a foreign agent who had walked into an alley and had "vanished" at the other end? Her friends couldn't even make inquiries about her; they couldn't afford to. Thornley smiled grimly as he moved back towards the path from the kitchen garden. That was how these blighters worked it. Bribe enough men with a sense of power, reward them with luxury and grandeur, and they'd be loyal terrorizers. It was

Faust all over again. Body and soul for sale to the man who could give them the things they had always wanted. And the greater the sale, the greater the rewards.

Thornley had reached the path. There, at the edge of the shrubbery, he could see clearly across the rose beds to the bank of the wooded hill. Would he go back now, or would he try to find out who was in the place he thought was the kitchen? The smoke was rising in greater volume. When he had first seen it, it had only been a trickle. He looked at the door. Could he risk stepping onto the path to reach the wall, and perhaps a window? The two men pacing in front of the castle would have nearly reached the other end of it. Then they would probably turn and come back. Now was the time to move. . . . And then the door opened, and as Thornley automatically drew back into the bushes, he heard a thin voice raised in its anger as high as a woman's.

The voice followed a man out into the path.

"Don't waste any time, either," it screeched. "I've had enough of you. Everyone else does the work while you stuff your belly. Go on, now."

The young man paused, his mouth stuffed with a large piece of cake.

"Shut your gub. If you're late, then get on with your work. What do you think you are anyway?" He came slowly down the path, grumbling to himself. "It's Hermann this and Hermann that. As if I hadn't my own job to do. As if I were a . . ." He didn't finish, but pitched forward suddenly on his face. Thornley pocketed the torch again, and dragged the man into the bushes. Quite a neat rabbit punch, he thought. Pity if it had broken the torch. He reached for one of the heavy stones which edged the pathway, and cracked the man over the head with it for good measure. He used his own handkerchief as a gag, and the man's belt and necktie to truss him neatly. The only place from which his attack could have been seen was from the woods. He hoped to God that Myles and van Cortlandt had been watching.

They had. They had seen him clearly as he had come out of the kitchen garden, had seen him hesitate as he left the cover of the pear trees, had seen him slip into the shrubbery. They waited for some minutes, wondering what on earth he had found interesting there. They hadn't heard the voices, but they began to understand when they heard a man's laugh. They strained their eyes, but they could see no one, not until a trooper walked slowly down the path, past the bushes, to drop suddenly like a stone. Then they saw Thornley again as he had pulled the body into the shrubbery. Van Cortlandt grinned: this was more like it. They waited impatiently. . . . But there was no further movement, no signal which they were hoping for.

Thornley waited. He was listening for the voices: the men should have reached this side of the castle again by this time. What was detaining them? Or was he misjudging the length of the minutes in his anxiety? And then he heard them. Almost there; pause; turn. They were walking away again. He relaxed, and looked at the man beside him. He was out cold—for a long, long time. He stepped back onto the path, and waved.

The others had seen him, thank heaven. He watched them scramble down the bank near the pear trees, and then it was difficult to see them. If they hurried, they would manage it. His anxious eyes saw them again for a moment. They were moving quickly and silently. They had reached the end of the trees, and like him they had noticed the door at the end of the path. Like him, they shied from it, and worked their way along towards him by way of the shrubbery.

They found him examining the man's revolver. He gave a satisfied nod, and slipped it into his pocket.

"Complications," Thornley whispered quietly. "Two thugs in front; one overworked cook in the kitchen; and this." He pointed with his foot.

"Cook next on the list?" Richard whispered back. Van Cortlandt was testing the knots; he seemed satisfied.

Thornley nodded. "Thugs due back any minute. Quietly . . ." He motioned them to follow him, and led them to the point where he had watched the two men. Their feet made no noise in the moldering soil, and the green branches could bend without breaking. And then they heard the voices, and were motionless. Richard and van Cortlandt looked carefully through the branches as Thornley had done. Van Cortlandt pursed his lips in a silent whistle as he saw one of the men. That was the guy all right, the one who had questioned him last night when they got back from Pertisau. So Thornley might have found the right track after all. He looked at the Englishman thoughtfully. Bob was looking at the watch on his wrist. Pause; turn; walk back—he would soon have this timed to a nicety.

They suddenly stiffened, and looked at each other. They had heard a voice, excited, hurried. The heavy measured tread of the Nazis' boots broke into a run. The voice was giving directions; they could hear the tone, but not the exact words. Van Cortlandt looked inquiringly at

Richard, who shook his head. No, that wasn't von Aschenhausen. So there was still another on the list. They waited, their bodies tense, their minds alert. The commands had been given. There was a loud "*Zu Befehl!*" That at least they could hear, that and the sound of running feet, clashing on the stones of a courtyard. And then the noise of motor bicycles ripped the silence.

"Two, I think," murmured van Cortlandt. They edged to the front of the bushes, and saw the roadway which approached the entrance of the castle. The two motor bicycles had already passed through the large gates, and were sweeping down the broad road. There was something peculiarly ominous in their speed.

"I don't like it," said van Cortlandt. "It's only a hunch, but I think we should get going."

The failing light helped them. They moved silently, one by one, from the shrubbery over to the castle wall and, keeping close to its shadow, edged towards the kitchen door. They heard a sound of movement inside, as Thornley's nail-studded shoe slipped on a stone at the side of the path. They stretched themselves more closely against the roughness of the wall. Thornley slid the gun out of his pocket and held it by the barrel. The kitchen door opened, and a broad beam of light streamed down the path to the kitchen garden. They could see the edge of a white apron, as the cook halted on the threshold.

"I heard you. You can come in. Where did you find the parsley? In the red-currant bushes, I bet." He stepped out of the doorway, peering towards the darkness of the garden. "Hermann. God in Heaven, I've always to do everything myself." His thin, high voice rose. "Hermann!" He sprawled forward as the revolver butt thudded dully against his square head.

He was a heavy man. It took the three of them to lift him back into the kitchen. Thornley locked the door, and then stood guard at the only other entrance—a door which led into a passage—while van Cortlandt helped Richard to gag the man, and tie his hands and feet. Then they thrust him unceremoniously into his own storeroom, and locked its heavy door. Richard pocketed the key, and nodded; they moved silently into the passage.

Thornley whispered, "There was a room which seemed to be interesting."

Richard looked sharply at him. Had he heard something while he had waited? A cry? His speed increased.

The passage led to the main entrance hall, a large, square, imposing place, with a broad stairway curving up the paneled walls. Richard had stopped, and looked again at Thornley. Where was the room? Thornley pointed above their heads to the first floor.

They mounted the staircase slowly, carefully, because of the nails in Thornley's shoes. Richard was thankful for the second time in two days that his shoes were soled with rubber. At any moment, he expected the door above them to open, and a volley of shots to pin them against the staircase wall . . . But the door didn't open. Its double panels remained shut. It was only when they had reached them that they could hear the voices from within. A man's voice, and then another man's voice. Again the first voice. Richard looked at the two men beside him and nodded. This time the voice was von Aschenhausen's.

He was speaking in German, his voice as angry as the other man's had been. They were not arguing with each other. They were talking to a third person; talking savagely. Von Aschenhausen had raised his pitch. Richard closed his eyes: he could see the two scars ridging the cheek. The words reached them in waves.

". . . regret your stupidity . . . advantage of my humanity. In two hours my young barbarians, as you called them, will return. I shall turn you over . . . If that fails . . . Gestapo . . . murderess and dangerous spy." The voice was clearer now, as if the man's anger were becoming cold and cruelly calculating.

"Your remaining days will not be pleasant. We shall catch Myles just as surely as we caught you. And your stupidity will be quite in vain." The voice altered again. This time it was speaking in English, rapidly, persuasively.

"You know how I have always regarded you. Otherwise I should not have brought you here: you would have been at the official Gestapo headquarters as soon as I had found you. Instead I bring you here, but do not mistake my feelings. I *will* find out. If you accept my offer, you will only remember these days as a bad dream. Otherwise any unpleasantness which you have suffered will be nothing, nothing to what is to come, and I am not being melodramatic." There was a pause. Von Aschenhausen spoke again. "You fool, you stupid little fool. Don't you see I *must,* I *will* find out? My patience is limited. Kurt, try some more of your persuasion. This is really tedious. You have only one . . ."

They had heard enough . . . two men in there. Richard saw the others were watching him, waiting. Van Cortlandt's mouth had an ugly look.

Thornley was fingering the revolver thoughtfully, his eyes narrowing. Richard nodded his head towards the door. Van Cortlandt put his hand gently on the handle. He was feeling it; it was unlocked. He shoved both panels violently open. He and Richard entered as one man, with Thornley just behind them.

The surprise was complete.

In the flickering candlelight of the room, they saw von Aschenhausen sitting on the edge of a large desk. His eyes were fixed on the other man standing over the girl roped to a chair, as he himself paused in the lighting of a cigarette. The match was still burning as Richard's full weight knocked him backwards, pinning him against the desk. As he tried to throw Richard off, the grip on his throat tightened. He struggled but the increased pressure warned him. He lay still, choking. It was his only chance.

Frances felt the hand of iron release her aching shoulder. She tried to get her face away from the glare of the powerful lamp in front of her as she heard the rush of feet, but the light still pierced her eyelids with a dull-red burning. She heard the flat sound of a hard fist meeting solid flesh. She heard someone cursing loudly and exultantly with each blow. She knew the voice. . . . Van Cortlandt. Henry. She struggled weakly against the rope which held her. And then there was Bob's voice, too. Beside her. She heard the lamp fall, and the glaring circle of light had gone. The ropes had suddenly stopped cutting into her breast and thigh. Her body was falling forward, but an arm caught it before it slipped off the chair. The arm held her there gently. Bob's voice was telling her to move slowly, to get the blood in circulation again. She was not to worry; everything was all right. Everything was all right. So Richard must be safe too. Richard must be safe.

In front of her she could hear the heavy breathing of the two men as they fought, the half groan, half gasp from the man Kurt as van Cortlandt landed his blows. She forced her eyes half-open. She could see Thornley's face as a white blur, gradually steadying, slowly shaping into lines she could recognize. He was watching the punishment which van Cortlandt was dealing with a look of admiration mixed with pleasure, watching the man as he staggered under the hard punches. The man was trying to gain a moment. A gun, thought Thornley, but before he could yell his warning the man had side-stepped a blow successfully and his hand reached into his hip pocket.

Van Cortlandt had seen the movement in time: his hand gripped the man's wrist and twisted. The bullet dug into the paneled wall, and then the revolver was wrung out of the man's hand. It fell at their feet. Thornley, watching the man's bleeding face, contorted with rage, slipped his free hand into his pocket; that type knew all the tricks, he thought grimly. It came as he expected. As van Cortlandt tried to knock the gun out of reach, the man kicked suddenly, viciously. Van Cortlandt doubled up with a groan, and the man's hand was over the gun. Thornley's revolver flashed first. There was no doubt about that bullet. The man lay as he had fallen.

Frances heard Thornley say something, but his voice was so low that the words eluded her. Then he was speaking to her, his voice once more calm and clear.

"Can you hold on now, Frances? I'll come back."

She nodded, and watched him as he helped van Cortlandt to sit up against the wall where he had fallen. She could see more clearly now; she could see van Cortlandt's face twisted with pain as he doubled over.

"Trusting fellow you are," Thornley said gently, and was glad to see the attempted smile on van Cortlandt's lips.

The American spoke, his words coming in spasms. "How's that son of a bitch over there?"

"Passed out a minute ago." It was Richard's voice. "Frances . . . all right?"

"Richard." She tried to rise from the chair.

"Easy now, Frances," said Thornley, and moved quickly back to her. She was glad of his firm grip. He had picked up the rope which had bound her and, coiling it loosely round his right hand, he threw it towards the desk.

"You'll need this," he said to Richard. "I'll be with you in a minute." He helped Frances back towards the chair. He looked over his shoulder at van Cortlandt. The American was all right. He had slowly and painfully stretched out his legs, and was leaning against the wall with his hands in his jacket pockets.

Richard looked at von Aschenhausen lying limply across the desk. He was unconscious, and his arms, with which he had tried to grip Richard, sprawled inert over the dark wood. One hand fell over the edge of the desk; the other pointed helplessly towards the glimmering candles in their heavy-silver base. Richard picked up the rope with one hand, still keeping a firm grip with the other on von Aschenhausen's throat, but one hand was not enough; he sensed his mistake even as he caught hold of the rope. The split-second warning was too short. Before he could use both hands again, von Aschenhausen had swept the branched candlestick in his face. As he stumbled back under the weight of the blow, rubbing the burning wax from his left eyelid and cheek, he saw von Aschenhausen's hand come up from the drawer with a gun, and he heard the shots.

Frances saw the long barrel point towards Thornley and herself. She was pushed violently aside even as the gun crashed twice. The echo of the shots stabbed her head. Or was it the echo? Von Aschenhausen stiffened and slid grotesquely from the desk. His revolver thudded dully on the thick carpet. Richard had risen from the floor beside the burning candles. Thornley was on his knees where he had dropped as he had thrust her aside. Van Cortlandt alone was smiling, and with a grim satisfaction, as he held his still smoking revolver pointed at the crumpled figure.

For a moment they looked at each other . . . All safe.

Frances heard van Cortlandt's voice saying "I'm a quick learner, Bob," and Thornley's not very successful laugh.

Richard had picked up the fallen gun, and was coming towards her, his hand to his face. She raised her arms, and then she felt the burning pain. The men saw the expression on her face change to one of amazement, like that of a child who has fallen and only realizes it is hurt when the blood begins to flow. So Frances looked as the searing pain showed her a neat groove in her left arm. Unbelievingly she watched the blood as it welled up and overflowed the wound in a slow-moving stream. And then she felt the real pain; with each heartbeat it seemed to throb farther down her arm and claw her shoulder.

Richard was beside her. She wondered if she looked as white as he did. He was looking at her arm, but he didn't speak.

It was Thornley who said, "On the inside, by God." Van Cortlandt rose slowly, and limped painfully over to them.

"*And* a Luger," he added quietly. "How close was your arm to your body?"

Frances remembered how close. That must have been the hot wind on her left breast just before she had heard the crash of the gun.

"I'd like a . . ." she began, but the word *drink* evaded her. The men were going away from her, moving back towards the desk, down the lengthening room. It was like looking through the wrong end of binoculars, she thought, and felt the black darkness smooth round her with its velvet touch. Then it was light again, and the men were beside her, and Richard's flask was at her lips, forcing her to drink more than she could swallow.

Someone said, "She'll be all right. Better look at the arm."

Richard was kneeling beside her, fumbling for his handkerchief. Van Cortlandt produced a very white one, and folded it methodically into a wad. Thornley went over to a table and came back with a decanter of whisky. She didn't need that, she thought; not now. The clammy sickness had gone, leaving her tired, tired. But she must tell them . . . she must tell them, now. If only she could remember things in the right order, the important things first. She gripped Richard's hands as Thornley poured whisky on the wound. She struggled to control her voice as she looked at van Cortlandt.

"They stopped your car at Jenbach, and found your friend in it. They brought him back to Innsbruck. They phoned about it, and . . . that man —" she looked at Kurt's body—"was told to go down and order the two troopers into Innsbruck. They were to trace your movements . . ."

Van Cortlandt nodded thoughtfully. "Yes, they knew me well by this time. That means the car we've got is dangerous." He dug his hands into his pockets, and walked slowly across the room to the desk.

"We'll have to find another car, that's all, or travel by train, or if the worst comes to the worst we'll have to climb over the pass together." He stopped suddenly, and ran a hand through his hair.

"Say, Richard, what's the thing these boys use when they want to sneak into a country without having their baggage examined?" He prodded von Aschenhausen's body with his foot contemptuously. Frances tried to remember desperately: there had been something which fitted into all this. Richard was saying that there wasn't much chance for them that way, but van Cortlandt could take a look in the desk and see what was there. Henry was already searching von Aschenhausen's pockets. He had found some keys.

"Do you smell burning, any of you?" van Cortlandt asked as he tried the drawers in the desk. One was locked; it needed two different keys to open it. Inside the drawer lay a folder containing papers, a neatly bound notebook, a seal and a rubber stamp.

Thornley, holding Frances' arm while Richard bandaged it, looked up and said, "Probably the candles on the rug." Van Cortlandt was too engrossed as he examined the documents in the folder. He whistled to himself, and then looked towards Thornley.

"As a newspaperman, I find this all very interesting." He waved a sheet of paper in the air. He was almost excited. He looked at the rug. "Yes," he replied to Thornley, "and a nice little fire is just about to start in the wastebasket. Just like the Reichstag. . . . Such ideas these boys put into your head . . ."

Frances heard the amusement in his voice, and opened her eyes. It was true. The wastepaper basket was smoldering, and even as she looked she saw the first sign of flame. It was fantastic. There was Henry, reading the papers he had found in the desk as calmly as if he had just made a remark about the weather. Then, on the desk, she saw the crumpled envelope, still lying where von Aschenhausen had thrown it contemptuously. Money wouldn't help them, he had said.

Richard was looking at her intently.

"The money," she said, "is on the desk. That's it. They—searched me," she finished lamely. Richard said nothing, but his mouth tightened. Frances thought again of the moment when the money had been discovered. Money wouldn't help them. Oh, if only she could think straight. Money wouldn't help them. What was it he had said then? He had twisted the envelope and thrown it on the desk.

"He said," she began slowly, her eyes closed—he had said so much, but there *was* something which could help van Cortlandt—"he said money wouldn't help, that it was no use trying to hide where you had gone." Her eyes opened, and the words were now faster as she remembered. "Even if you had got over the frontier, any frontier, you would be followed at once and brought back. It wasn't the first time that escapers had been caught in Italy or Switzerland. He had all the powers, and you had none. He held up some papers with one hand and hit them with his other hand, the back of his other hand, and all the time he was looking at me." Her voice altered again. "These were some of his reasons to persuade me to be reasonable. He said that Kronsteiner had been caught, that Henry and Bob had admitted everything in order to save themselves, that our movements had been traced completely."

Thornley wondered what other kinds of persuasion had been used, as he noticed Frances' wrists, the torn blouse showing the ugly marks on her shoulder, her right cheek which was swollen and red, the angry stripes already turning purple on her legs, her eyes. Again he thought of Tony's letter, of Maria. At least Frances was alive and her body would heal, at least they had saved her from becoming a second Maria. Tony's words ate into his heart like vitriol into flesh. He moved to the door. Better begin to leave, he thought.

"I'll scout round, and find the garage," he suggested. "Don't wait too long in here: there's the makings of a good going blaze."

Van Cortlandt looked up as the door closed. "Frances, did you see where he put those papers he was waving at your face?"

"He was at the desk. They must be there." Unless, she thought, they were a lie, like the other things he had said. He had mixed lie with truth so cunningly. She watched van Cortlandt search once more, and then relaxed as he suddenly smiled.

"Well, this might be twisted to suit us," he said. Frances had never heard his voice so optimistic . . . And then the telephone rang.

The three of them looked at it as if it were a cobra.

"I might have known," van Cortlandt said, and the optimistic voice was gone.

Richard left Frances, and walked quickly over to the phone. He lifted the receiver. Frances and van Cortlandt, motionless, scarcely breathing, watched him tensely. But the German which he spoke was that of von Aschenhausen. Van Cortlandt caught Frances' eye, and nodded slowly, approvingly, before he went on with his careful writing. The wastepaper basket was flaming nicely; the thick wool carpet smoldered where the fallen candles had burned three round black holes.

Again Frances had the same awareness of unreality which would sometimes grip her for a timeless moment in the middle of a dream, which would drag her back to waking and the hotness of a crumpled pillow. But this was no dream. The high, paneled room was now filled with a stronger light from the leaping flames in the basket beside the desk. The smoldering rug and the guttering candles, the two bodies lying so quietly on the floor, the rich draperies and carefully arranged flowers, were all as real as the burns on her wrists and the blood which had flowed down her arm like a stream of warm red lava. She looked at the American, working at the other end of the desk; at Richard as he spoke in that excellent, rather hard German. So far, he had said little: he was listening to some story.

And then he cut short the long explanation impatiently. He was giving his own instructions. The American was quite useless. The girl had talked, and he knew nothing at all. He was to be released after he had given them a description of his own car. They would be able to trace that to St. Anton, where the other American van Cortlandt and the Englishman Thornley had gone. That was the meeting place; Myles would reach it tomorrow. They then intended to cross into Switzerland. That frontier was to be carefully watched.

The man at the other end of the wire spoke again. Richard listened impatiently. The flames from the wicker basket lit up his face as he concentrated on the man's words.

"Yes," he said, "I'll allow them to stay longer. I shall remain here with Kurt until the investigation is completed. I shall arrive in St. Anton tomorrow morning. Get all three of them, alive if possible. I rely on you."

Richard replaced the receiver thoughtfully.

"That takes care of your friend, Henry," he said, "and gives us a breathing space. The apprentices have had a successful parade, and are now eating heartily before they attend a meeting. I very generously allowed them to stay for that. They will return here by ten o'clock. It's getting rather warm in here, don't you think?"

Van Cortlandt rose, and handed him the sheet of paper on which he had just finished applying von Aschenhausen's seal.

"Not warm enough, yet, but it should be satisfactory by ten o'clock —with a little help."

He moved to the other end of the desk, and kicked the flaming basket over the smoldering carpet. The desk itself was beginning to glow just where the basket had stood, and a small streak of flame rushed up its side as he heaped the papers from the drawer beside it.

Richard folded the document and put it carefully into his breast pocket.

"Good piece of work, Henry," he said. The American, placing the other branched candlesticks under the long curtains as he opened the windows, only smiled. It had been easy enough: all he had had to do was to alter a very little to suit their purpose. That was the advantage of dealing with a very systematic and thorough enemy. They made the arrangements and you borrowed them. It had been almost as easy as this. He threw the last candle lightly onto the couch with its pile of cushions.

"Keep moving, fellas," he said, and picked up the two caps and the jackets from a chair.

They left the doors wide open. Richard, his arm round Frances, turned for one last look. The current of air between the windows and the wide door was serving its purpose.

"Regular Viking's funeral," van Cortlandt said. "Too damn good for them."

They walked in silence down the cool staircase. Behind them they heard the indrawn breath of the flames.

Thornley was waiting for them in the darkness beside a large official-looking car.

"There was another in the garage, and some motor bikes. I've taken care of them," he reported.

Richard was putting Frances into the car.

"Darling, we've got to get the other car and the stuff inside it. I'll see you soon." He turned to Thornley. "We'll meet you five miles south of this road. Wait for us there." Thornley nodded, and handed him something. It was the electric torch.

Van Cortlandt threw the caps and jackets into the car. "Better wear those. We'll only keep you about twenty minutes."

The large car moved off, and the two men started towards the gardens. As they passed the kitchen door, they suddenly remembered the cook. Richard cursed and tried to enter the kitchen. But they had locked the door from the inside, and it was too heavy to break open. Richard swore again.

"If you must; but we're God-damned fools," van Cortlandt said, and raced back towards the front entrance of the castle. "God-damned fools," he repeated when he opened the door into the kitchen. Together they carried the unconscious man into the shrubbery.

"Not too near the other blighter," the American said. "Hell and damnation, that's at least five minutes gone."

They broke into a run across the garden and fields. The woods were dark and silent; it was too early for any moonlight. Richard shaded the torch with his hand, as they searched for the path, scrambling along the edge of the trees.

Van Cortlandt said, "Just about here, I think. There was a mound. Rock."

Richard nodded. He tried to measure the distance to the long dark shape which must be the red-currant bushes. . . . And then the torch showed them the outcrop of stone. The path should be here.

They looked at each other with undisguised relief when they found it. The white slashes on the branches were picked out by the light which Richard held. Their feet stumbled and slipped in the darkness of the ground, but they pressed on hurriedly. They had passed over the crest of the small hill, and they were running and sliding down towards the road, following the trail which Thornley had blazed. They reached the cart track, and the bushes. The car was still there.

"Ten minutes late, already," van Cortlandt said, but his voice was good-humored again. He gave a laugh. "And there I was, having a fine joke all to myself about Thornley being the good boy scout."

Richard found himself relaxing calmly as the car jerked dangerously over the rough track and then gathered speed on the smoothness of the Brenner road. What would have seemed suicidal only forty-eight hours ago now only appeared all in the day's work. Van Cortlandt's driving had results; it was only a matter of minutes before they sighted the large dark car tactfully drawn up at the side of the road.

The first stars were beginning to appear over the Brenner. The man lounging at the doorway of the customhouse was watching the other side of the white barrier with interest. He wondered what it was this time. All day, the Germans had been giving themselves double work. They had stopped the cars coming out of Germany as well as those going in. It was a nuisance, waiting here with your eyes on the headlights, not knowing how long they would be before they came up to you. Sometimes it would be only a matter of minutes. Sometimes, a car would be held up for half an hour. Again he wondered what it could be. These Germans never told you much unless it was unimportant. He shifted his weight onto his other leg, and glanced back into the brightly lighted office. The man at the desk looked up.

"Anything happening, Corradi?"

"Two still held over there."

The tall thin Italian at his desk gave a sardonic smile and went back to his writing. The other heaved a loud sigh, and walked slowly towards the barrier. The tension, on a day like this, always unsettled him. He heard the voices of the others as they came out of the café down the street. About time too, he thought moodily. He could do with some coffee himself.

At the doorway of the café, the two officials halted. They stood looking out into the empty village street with its meager lights. Only the doorway of the customhouse was bright. The younger man shivered, and looked bitterly at the scattered houses, the long wind-swept station, the towering dark shapes on either side of them.

"Godforsaken place," he said.

"Wait until you have been here for a winter," advised the other. "You can't grumble at overwork today, at least. Not with our good friends over the way doing all our work for us."

He looked at the younger man's smart uniform, and buttoned his own crumpled jacket. It was just like the young, he thought. They never knew when they were lucky. A few more pretty girls to admire the way he wore his cap, and his young friend would have no doubt found the place tolerable.

"We could have had another coffee," he suggested, but the young man had already stepped into the street and was waiting impatiently for him.

"When you've been here as long as I have," the older man grumbled, "you will know it is hardly worth our while, on a day like this. Our German cousins don't leave much to be confiscated."

The other tilted his hat contemptuously. Here as long as this fat fool, he thought in amusement, who would now be in a comfortable office in a decent town if he had had any brains at all. Even the way he would speak of the Germans, with that sly note in his voice which he thought was funny, showed he had no brains . . . But curiosity overcame the young man's contempt.

"Is this usual?" he asked, as they reached the customhouse.

"Whenever someone who shouldn't be leaving the beloved Fatherland is being ungrateful enough to try to leave."

"They are fools to try to pass this way."

"There is only this way, or the mountains, or the railway. The border patrols have been increased, and there is pandemonium on the trains. Have you seen *them* on the trains, today?"

"It is efficient organization," the young man said sharply. The fat fool had no brains, but he was crafty enough. He always chose his words so carefully that you couldn't even report him. The tall thin Italian, who had come out from the office, exchanged amused looks with the older man and ignored the remark. They were both getting a bit tired of the new broom.

They saw the headlights of the two small cars begin to move at last. Behind them a large car advanced authoritatively in the middle of the road. Corradi seemed excited about something.

"They didn't stop this one. Salutes for this one," he called across to them. "Better not keep this one waiting. They never like it."

The tall thin man nodded, and turned to the young one.

"You deal with it, and see some of the efficient organizers of efficient organization. Probably diplomatic pass. You know."

The young man nodded as casually as he could, and moved over to the large car. He didn't feel as casual inside. Corradi had been right. The Germans didn't like being kept waiting. An officer's sleeve waved a paper peremptorily to him. He heard a request for urgency, which was a command.

The Italian took the document. His German was not so adequate as he pretended, but he knew his salute had been just right. He looked as efficient as possible as he glanced quickly at the paper. The signature on it made him hold his breath. . . . Four people in the car. That was right. He felt the cold impassive stare of the German. Further curiosity would be an impertinence. He folded the paper with a businesslike gesture. Speed and courtesy: that would show them efficiency could be found here, too. He held his salute as the officer acknowledged it, and the large black car swept past the raised barrier.

He turned back to the others. Corradi, he noticed, had saluted too. But the other fools were too busy examining and stamping passports, were even wasting good breath making polite replies to three middle-aged Englishmen.

When the two insignificant cars crawled slowly away through the village street, the others joined him.

"Well, who was it? The Archduke von Ribbentrop himself?"

He ignored their smiles. He made his voice as casual as possible.

"Freiherr von Aschenhausen, and three others, authorized by . . ." But the others had lost interest and gone back to the office.

The young man stood outside, and looked at the stars. He forgot the cold wind. There was a warm, comfortable feeling inside him.

The swift journey down the Brenner road was a nightmare to Frances. She was conscious of a stiffening arm, of the burns on her wrist nipped by the cool air. She was so tired that the muscles of her body refused to relax. Thornley, unexpectedly gentle, tried to protect her from the twists and turns of the mountain road. In front of them were Richard and van Cortlandt, both of them silent and grim under the peaked hats. Van Cortlandt's eyes never left the road. Richard had a map spread over his knees. Although the Brenner was safely passed, there was no relaxing of the strain. Thornley persuaded her to eat something. He was so obviously worried about her that to please him she tried. She was surprised to find that the sick feeling was no worse, that the coldness which had first gripped her as they waited for Richard and van Cortlandt on the Innsbruck–Brenner road began to disappear.

That had been the worst moment for her, she decided. Worse even than the frontier and the silly boy with the exaggerated cap and salute. She remembered again when she had waited tensely with Thornley at the side of the road, when she had begun to think that Richard and Henry had been caught. She remembered the sense of haste which had almost choked her as the suitcases were lifted into the Mercedes and they had waited again while Thornley had set the American car crashing down into a ravine. Each minute, each passing car, were full of danger. Already, behind them, there had been a tell-tale glow of fire. Bob had said simply, "Garage, too, by this time, I'd think." After that they had driven in silence towards the frontier, and she had felt sick and cold. When the

Brenner was passed (if it were passed) she had told herself she could sleep. That would heal the throbbing of her eyes. But the Brenner lay behind them, and the sleep which she had resisted refused to return.

It was not until they had driven through Bolzano and all the villages in between that she felt the tension lessen. Bob even made some mild jokes about all these places called Believe Obey Fight, like the English stations called Ladies and Gentlemen. He got her to sip some more brandy, as she ate the dry biscuits. They tasted wonderfully. The others were eating, too. She watched them drowsily; she was warm at last, and her body relaxed. *Ladies and gentlemen, ladies and gentlemen lend me your ears I come to Dreikirchen with rings on her fingers and bells where who, where who, where . . .*

At first she thought it was von Aschenhausen holding her shoulder, bending over her, but the grip did not tighten and hurt. It was Richard. Richard trying to smile and making a failure of it.

"Fran," he said, and kissed her.

The car had stopped in the shadow of trees. The trees were a different shape, the night air seemed milder, the ink-blue sky was more beautiful. And Richard's arms were round her. She suddenly remembered Bob and Henry.

"Where are they?"

"Freshening up. There's a stream over there. We'll go when they've finished. We can change, too: Henry has brought our things along with him in his case."

Frances looked at the trees again, dark islands in a sea of moonlight.

"We are farther south," she said.

"Almost at Verona, darling. It's one o'clock and all's well."

"All's well," answered an American voice. "Well, Frances, how's everything?"

She gave him her right hand.

"That's the ticket," he said. "I'll get your clothes, and Bob will guide you to the stream. Here's your towel." He handed her one of his white shirts. "And your purse." He handed Richard her bag.

They reached the stream, and they bathed their faces in the cool water. The bullet graze had bled a lot; it looked unsafe to disturb the bandage, so Richard hacked a piece off the shirt and bandaged on top of the bloodstained handkerchiefs. The clothes for her consisted of a nondescript belted gray coat, a gray beret, a shapeless dress and shoes and stockings. Richard had an *ersatz* tweed suit, a rough green-felt hat, and a tie of indescribable hideousness. Frances dressed her hair and disguised the bruises on her cheek as well as she could with her one hand. It would be almost impossible to get the dress on without starting more bleeding. Richard helped her into the coat, and even that was difficult enough. The shoes were too big, but fortunately they had straps. Richard and Frances looked at each other, and she actually smiled; and then they went back to the car, carrying the discarded clothes and the rejected dress.

"Go on, laugh," said Richard good-humoredly.

Thornley and van Cortlandt grinned.

"It's not bad, you know," Bob said tactfully. "I've seen hundreds like you traveling in Germany. Have a cigarette? How long is it since we could risk one?"

"One thing I must say for these blasted Nazis," said Henry, and paused to enjoy his effect. "They make you damned well appreciate the simple pleasures of a peaceful life."

Thornley drove them, this time. In the swaying car, they made their last plans. They were brief. They were to travel on their German passports, complete with Italian entry stamps (Schulz had earned his money), towards Grenoble. If the station would accept their marks, they could catch an early morning train. If not, they would have to wait until the banks opened. Van Cortlandt and Thornley, cutting back on their tracks, would drive through Lombardy until daylight made the car too dangerous. They would then get rid of it, and make for the Swiss border, if they hadn't reached it by that time. Van Cortlandt was confident that they would. They divided the marks they had, and van Cortlandt emptied the smaller of his suitcases to carry the dress and two extra shirts and socks for Richard. They could think of no other main points; the details would depend on quick wits and luck. They would meet in Paris. Van Cortlandt gave them the address of a hotel he knew.

"It's run by an American, who stayed over from the last war. You'll feel safe enough there. Just lie low until we get there. And then we'll celebrate. Better catch up on your sleep before we arrive."

His confidence and high spirits were infectious. Frances found herself laughing. And then the tears were running down her cheeks; even the pain they caused in her eyes couldn't check them.

"Well," said van Cortlandt, "well, now."

Thornley switched on the wireless tactfully. The overture of "Aida," badly recorded, swelled scratchingly into the car. Thornley tuned it down.

"Goes well with the writing on the wall," he suggested, and nodded towards the house they were passing. The lights from the car pointed the lettering on its wall. "WHO TOUCHES THE DUCE TOUCHES DEATH. Dear me!"

"One up on the Victorians," said Richard. "They only hung banalities round the house. Now we get totalitarian mottoes in two-feet-high letters all over the gable ends."

Van Cortlandt, keeping his eyes away from Frances, tried to think of something to add to that, but he could only think of the silent way in which she wept. He peered out into the darkness.

"Houses are getting closer now," he said at last. "Better waste no time."

Frances had regained her control. She made a pretense of powdering her face.

"I'm ready," she said, "any time. We'll see you in Paris." She managed a smile. "I'm sorry. It was all my fault. I've ruined all your plans."

The American shook his head. "My plans were going to be ruined anyway, although I kept persuading myself that they wouldn't be. We all have our wishful thinking, but it's just as well to come out of it."

Thornley switched off the motor carefully, and turned to face Frances.

"I have no plans either, Frances. Don't worry about that. I had a letter from Tony this morning."

"Tony?"

"Yes. He's on his way home to enlist."

"And the girl in Czechoslovakia?" Frances could have bitten her tongue. Thornley examined the back of his hand.

"Suicide," he said, too coldly.

Frances saw the three men exchange glances. So they knew. Bob must have told them as she had slept. It must have been something which they thought would have sickened her, unnerved her. As if the man Kurt, when he had tried to break her silence, had not described in detail her possible future. As if she couldn't guess. . . . But knowing evil could be worse than guessing. When you guessed, you could always hope that evil things might not be so bad as your worst fears. But when you knew, then there was no hope left. Then you knew this and this, and the evil of it drove away all hope.

She said nothing, only remembering the look on Thornley's face when he had looked down at the man Kurt. He had spoken as if to himself, and the words had made no sense then. Now they took shape. One for Maria . . . the first one for Maria. Frances leaned forward and touched Thornley's shoulder with her right hand, and then van Cortlandt's.

Richard helped her to step out of the car. The savageness of his voice did not startle them.

"Yes. I'm all for international understanding: *real* understanding." He looked at the other two men, and voiced their thoughts. "This isn't the end for any of us. It's just the beginning."

They were all silent for some moments, and then Thornley switched on the engine, and the car moved into the night.

Richard picked up the suitcase, and gripped Frances' right arm. They walked softly through dark streets, guided by scattered lights. At last, they saw the station. Frances pressed his hand to her breast, and held it there.

North from Rome

To my traveling companion

1

At last, the city was quiet.

Quiet enough for sleep, William Lammiter thought as he finished his cigarette on the small balcony outside of his hotel bedroom. It was three o'clock in the morning—no, almost half-past three by his watch—and Rome was at peace. Practically. Only an occasional car now passed through the old Roman wall by the broad Pincian Gate, only a solitary Vespa roared its way up the wide sweep of the Via Vittorio Veneto. The café-table sitters, the coffee-drinkers and Cinzano-sippers had gone back to their rooms, leaving the broad sidewalks free at last. And, on the other side of the Roman wall, over the vast stretch of the Borghese Gardens, with its tall pine trees, pleasant pavilions, careful flower beds, sweet-smelling shrubs, there was now a cloak of darkness, darkness and silence, for even the night club which lay incongruously just within this entrance to the Borghese Gardens had stopped blowing its trumpets and banging its drums in steady four beats to the bar.

Time for sleep, Lammiter told himself again, but he still stayed on the balcony, a little narrow ledge of balustraded stone jutting over a street of parked cars, with a clear view over the Roman wall into the Borghese Gardens. He still watched the tall pines, with their straight trunks and massive crowns silhouetted against the city's night sky. They seemed as grateful for this hour of rest as he was. They sighed gently, as if they felt the same cool breath of air that had touched his cheek.

He ignored the group of young men who were walking smartly home, the two white-uniformed policemen who were pacing slowly from the

Via Veneto through the Pincian Gate, the woman clacking lightly along on high heels in the darkened street below his balcony. He wanted to concentrate on the pine trees, on the feeling that this had once been the limits of ancient Rome, that wild and unknown country had once stretched outside there, northward, away from the old city. Then, that red brick wall, built to keep the barbarians out, had been manned by troops; and at a gateway such as this one, there would be soldiers on guard duty. On a warm summer evening in late July, such as this, nearly seventeen hundred years ago, a sentry must have stared northward, into the darkness, and wondered what lurked out there.

What was it like, Bill Lammiter wondered, to have been a Roman sentry standing guard duty at the Pincian Gate? Would the soldier, looking northward from his post on top of the high wall—there was a path there, broad enough for two men to march abreast—have felt loneliness, fear? Would he have stared out at the vast night, and felt a premonition stir uneasily in his mind? Or was he just bored, waiting for his relief to come marching along with the squad leader, hoping no trouble would break out tonight or any other night before he got out of the service and began farming that strip of land up near Perugia? Perugia in the Umbrian hills . . . That's where I ought to be right now, Lammiter thought. There's nothing to keep me in Rome any longer. I've been here a month. I haven't done a stroke of work. And I've lost my girl.

He stubbed out his cigarette angrily, straightened his shoulders, and turned to go indoors. From the now quiet street, beneath his balcony, he heard a woman's cry.

It was quick, startled, strangled into silence. He leaned over the stone balustrade. Under the shadow of the Aurelian Wall were spaced trees and street lights, a line of parked cars and two huge empty tourist buses. For a moment, that was all he saw, patches of bright light, patches of deep shadows, the small neat cars sheltering under thick tents of green leaves. Then, by one car, already pointing its nose out from the curb, ready to leave, waiting with its door open, he saw a woman and a man. They were standing rigid, it seemed, and then he realized it was the rigidity of force and resistance equally matched. The woman—a girl it was—drew back with desperate strength. The man, one hand on her wrist, another clamped over her mouth, was trying to draw her into the car.

Lammiter let out a yell, a loud call for help blotted out by the unmuffled roar of a solitary motor scooter, its rider oblivious of everything except the fine angle he cut as he swept through the Pincian Gate from the Borghese Gardens to curve down the Via Vittorio Veneto. But the two police officers, now pacing together so quietly on the other side of the wall, had stopped their earnest conversation and were looking searchingly in his direction. In a quick moment, Lammiter waved, shouted, pointed beneath him. "Here!—On this side!" He wondered if his English were understood, tried to think of the word for "Help!" in Italian, looked down once more at the startled man (who had heard the yell, all right), and shouted again. The girl broke loose as the man stared up at the balcony. She began to run, toward the brighter lights of the Pincian Gate.

Lammiter turned from the balcony and raced through his room into the red-carpeted hall. Behind him he left half-querulous, half-asleep voices, matching the dusty shoes standing outside their doors. He didn't wait for the elevator, a stately and shaky descent in a gilded cage, but ran down the three flights of steps that encircled its open shaft. He sprinted across the dimly lit hall, half sliding on the marble floor, giving the night porter scarcely time to look up from his desk, and was out on the wide sidewalk. He was breathless but pleased with himself. Not bad, not bad at all for a man of almost thirty, he decided. (Since his twenty-ninth birthday, he had become conscious of age.) He couldn't have taken more than two minutes to reach the street. Then he was amused by himself for being so pleased. He slackened his pace abruptly, and felt a stitch in his side just to keep him in his proper place. Ahead of him, in front of the Pincian Gate, the running girl had been stopped by the two policemen. The car, and the man with it, had vanished.

The policemen looked at him speculatively. For a moment he had the impulse to walk on, to pretend he was out for an early-morning stroll. Now that the girl was safe, there was no need to get mixed up in any complication. But he had been running, he was still breathing faster than normal with that proud burst of speed, and he was dressed exactly in the clothes he had worn on the balcony—a white shirt, sleeves rolled up, tie off, neck open, thin gabardine trousers. He glanced over his shoulder, to see how clearly the balcony was visible from the street. It had been extremely visible. He wasn't surprised when the grave-faced policemen identified him.

They were puzzled. The girl, even after she had regained her breath, was too frightened to speak sensibly. So now they turned on the stranger from the balcony.

An American, obviously. One could always tell most Americans; they had a young look to their faces, a peculiar expression of trust, a confidence in their eyes, a strange mixture of diffidence and decision in their movements. This one was no exception. They had to look up at him as they asked him their polite but puzzled questions, for he was tall, and thinner than they considered appropriate. (Strange that an American with money—his clothes were well-cut, his wrist watch expensive, he stayed at a good conservative hotel—should spend so little on food. But no stranger than the fact that he wore no tie, no jacket, and stood nonchalantly on the street, in this fashionable quarter of the city, without even being aware of how he was dressed.) His face was lean, strong-boned, with a good forehead and well-shaped chin and nose. His mouth was pleasant when he smiled. His teeth were excellent. Gray eyes under well-marked eyebrows, with a tendency to frown in concentration. His hair was brown, and—another peculiar American custom—cut short. His voice was agreeable to listen to, but his words were difficult to follow. A polite man, the policemen decided, for he was now trying to answer them in Italian. His words were still difficult to follow: his Italian was too careful, there was no natural flow to it. And he kept looking at the girl.

Why not? She might be stupid, or shy, or both, but she was extremely pretty, with shining black hair cut short, large dark eyes, an excellent figure, slender ankles, small feet in pointed-toe shoes with high Italian heels. "Thank you," she said huskily in English to the American.

"Excuse me, signore," one of the policemen said brusquely but tactfully, as he turned to the American. "You are staying at the Hotel Pinciana?"

"Yes. My name is Lammiter, William Lammiter." He added that he was an American, but no one seemed surprised. And then, as he tried to explain what he had seen from the balcony of his room, first in Italian, then in French, and then—defeated—in English, the two policemen tried to help him.

"No, no!" he had to insist. "The car wasn't passing by. It had been parked under my balcony. Over there! See? It must have been waiting. When I noticed it, it had its engine running, its nose pointed out, ready to leave. So there must have been two men, one driving, one trying to snatch the girl. No, I don't think there could have been three men. Why? —Well, there would have been two men on the sidewalk, one keeping her from screaming, one pulling her into the car. But why don't you ask her, herself?"

He turned to the girl standing back so quietly in the shadow of the wall. It was time she did a little explaining.

But she wasn't there.

The two policemen had turned, too. They stared at him. Then, quickly, they all moved through the broad archway of the Pincian Gate to the other side of the Roman wall. There she was, running across the wide empty street toward the entrance of the Borghese Gardens. And stopping near her, braking suddenly beside one of the islands formed by the circular wall guarding the roots of a giant pine tree, was a gray Fiat.

Lammiter had just time to say, "No, that isn't the same car. The other was smaller." Its door opened, the girl jumped in, and it streaked down the tree-shaded road that led through the gardens to the outskirts of Rome. The policemen looked at each other, and then at the American. One of them said a couple of lines in Italian, quick, low, tense. The other laughed and shrugged his shoulders. He said, "The price must have suited her that time."

"But—" Lammiter said, and then he, too, shrugged his shoulders and raised an eyebrow in his best Italian accent. There was really nothing else to do.

Briskly, the two policemen saluted him. They were no longer annoyed by the girl, but amused by him. It had become merely a slightly comic interlude to break the monotony of their night patrol. Now, hands clasped behind their backs, they began walking in step and grave talk of more serious matters, along the Aurelian Wall.

Lammiter went back to the hotel. The night porter in front of his honeycomb of keys looked at him without much curiosity—Americans were a nation of eccentrics, he had decided years ago, and nothing they did surprised any hotel desk. The elevator wasn't working, anyway, so Lammiter climbed the three flights to his corridor. The shoes formed a jeering honor guard, right to his room. The voices had subsided into measured breathing and choking snores.

He went out onto the balcony. Beyond the Roman wall, the pine trees in the Borghese Gardens waited quietly for the dawn. And there it was, the first pale streak of gray, washed along the east rim of distant hills.

A house swallow sounded its unmusical notes. Soon, others would form a vague chorus: they would start skimming over the mushroom-shaped trees, filling the air with the sound of their twittering and the swoop of their wings. And soon, too, the automobiles and the motor bicycles and the scooters and the horns and the unmuffled exhausts and the screeching brakes . . .

He closed both shutters, the windows, the heavy velvet curtains. Perhaps that would give him a chance to sleep. But long after he had had a quick shower and lay stretched on top of the heavy linen bedspread, he kept thinking of the girl who had said "Thank you" as if she had meant it. Eventually, to save himself from suffocation, he rose and opened all the layers of protection that covered his windows. The pale gray edge on the horizon had spread and changed to a fringe of green and gold. Above the renewed traffic, the swallows, in hundreds, were diving and soaring with their loud screams of frenzied delight.

"Idiots!" he told them angrily. And yet he had to smile. Bad-tempered as he was with lack of sleep and a surfeit of noise, the swallows were a comic mixture of graceful flight and ugly sound. "See, see, see!" they screeched in their thin scratched notes as they skimmed the tall pine trees, the old Roman wall, the hotel roof. "I'll leave Rome today," he told himself wearily. "I'll go up to an Umbrian hill town, and catch myself some quiet and some coolness." He had been saying that for two weeks, but now he knew he meant it. And either the pleasantness of the idea or his rediscovered powers of decision lulled him into sleep. Daylight or swallows or traffic or not, he didn't awaken until nine.

Early, while it was still cool, he began to pack. He was traveling light: one two-suiter case and one grip besides his typewriter and camera. Yet, foot-free as he was, it was odd how he had seemed to have taken root in this hotel room—every small drawer and corner turned up another belonging, or something he had bought since he arrived four weeks ago. He was trying to fit some typing paper into the typewriter's neat case when the room waiter arrived to clear away the breakfast. It was the one Lammiter liked least, the small thin man, middle-aged, morose, who was never interested in anything except the size of the tip lying on the tray. But this morning he suddenly turned vivacious as he looked at the luggage. "The signore is leaving today?" The dull eyes were extremely clever, Lammiter noticed with some surprise.

"Yes," Lammiter said, and went on packing.

"The signore is a writer?"

Lammiter nodded. If you could call a man a writer who had written exactly one play. True, it had been successful enough, and that was something both unexpected and pleasant. But if he didn't write a second one pretty soon, and have another success, too, he would have to go back to Madison Avenue and advertising. In the last ten days or so, he had begun to wonder if he had resigned too rapidly from the steady job, the steady money, the rent and the butcher's bill and the dry Martinis all definitely paid for.

"The signore likes Rome?"

Lammiter nodded.

"The signore stayed a long time here. He has many friends in Rome?"

"The signore," Lammiter said firmly, "has no friends in Rome at all." That was accurate enough. Eleanor Halley was in Rome, but after their last disagreement two weeks ago—Disagreement? Let's face it, he told himself: Eleanor and you have had your ultimate quarrel.

What had she called him? A man too jealous to be able to accept with any kind of grace the fact that she had decided to marry someone else. A man too narrow-minded to approve of her marrying a foreigner. A man too much of a snob-in-reverse (it had taken him a few seconds to puzzle that phrase out) to like anyone who had a title. "Look," he had told her, "I don't care whether this new fellow of yours has a title or not. I don't hate him because he calls himself a count. I just want to know more about him." But this phrase (calculated, he had to admit now)—"this new fellow of yours"—had had a most final effect. Afterward, he had phoned Eleanor twice at the Embassy, twice at the apartment she shared with two other secretaries. Miss Halley was not at her desk. Miss Halley was not at home. And three days ago he had loitered round the Embassy entrance, hoping to have a few minutes' talk with her. But either she had left early or she had seen him and taken another exit.

Now he would never be given the chance to make the apology he ought to have offered in the first place, instead of letting his hurt pride sharpen his tongue. He ought to have said, "You were right. I was letting the theater swallow me up, I was turning into the re-write machine, the rehearsal haunter, the director's little helper, the willing autograph-signer, the luncheon speaker; the man who wanted to prove success hadn't gone to his head; the man who couldn't say 'No,' trying to oblige everybody, failing the only person who really mattered." For a moment he was startled by the picture he had drawn of himself. Was it just his eloquence, or had he been as neglectful of Eleanor as all that?

The waiter coughed discreetly and arranged the breakfast tray's dishes once more. Lammiter searched automatically for a tip, but he was still thinking about Eleanor. If only she had complained. . . . Why hadn't she spoken out, given him some warning? Instead, just as he was about to leave for six weeks in Hollywood last spring, she had taken off quietly for Rome. He ought to have followed her, right then; but the Hollywood assignment was important: it was his own play, wasn't it, that was being turned into a film-script? Then the job was postponed. Then it was scheduled for May. Then it was delayed again. Then arranged eventually for the end of June. By that time, he was ready to say, "The hell with all this, anyway," and join Eleanor in Rome. But by that time, too, he had got her letter about Luigi, Count Pirotta. Goddammit, he thought in sudden anger, did she think I had arranged all these postponements, these delays? Did she imagine I enjoyed waiting in New York, when she was in Italy? She knew I loved her, didn't she? My career was hers, too: didn't she know that?

"Oh, forget it," he told himself. "Forget Eleanor." But how?

The waiter had left, quickly and suddenly, as if he had decided the fifteen-per-cent tip on the tray was all that was forthcoming. Add to that the fifteen per cent that the manager charged for all services rendered, and the waiter had a thirty-per-cent tip for one small jug of coffee, one small jug of tepid milk with skin on, two rolls (one stale), two transparent slivers of butter, and one small jar of dark brown strawberry jam.

I wish, Lammiter thought bitterly, someone would reach into a pocket and add thirty per cent onto all my royalties. Then, by God, I perhaps could afford to stay a summer in Rome, and argue Eleanor out of her titled dreams. Argue? That was false hope: everything was beyond arguing now.

His annoyance with the waiter, he realized, was simply because the man had stirred up memories of his trouble with Eleanor. Wasn't it enough that his mind had gone blank of creative ideas, that the play he was about to begin when he arrived in Rome had vanished into thin air? How could he work? He could neither think nor concentrate. He could only look at ruins (for he was standing at the window again) and speculate about the past—a pleasant way of spending the present to avoid thoughts about the future.

He went back to his packing. It was then that he remembered his photographs. He had six rolls of film being developed and printed at that photography shop just off the Via Vittorio Veneto. He was to collect them just before eight o'clock this evening, when the shop closed. How could he have been so inept as to forget all about them? He'd have to stay one more night in Rome, after all.

He called down to the hotel desk, and told them that he would not be checking out that afternoon, that he'd stay one more night. The voice replying to him was genuinely perturbed. It was sorry, extremely sorry, but his room had been assigned to someone else. All rooms were occupied. This was July, the busiest month . . .

A sudden revulsion seized him, a quick reaction to cut all losses. "The hell with it," he said aloud. He called the porter's desk, with instructions to get him a seat on a plane, any plane, any flight leaving Rome tonight for New York.

The chambermaid appeared as he ended his call. Without even seeing his suitcase and grip, she said smilingly, "The signore is leaving today?"

"Yes." How quickly the news got around! It was a matter of protocol in hotel work: Room 307 is checking out, get in line for the tips, pass the word along. But he had liked this middle-aged woman with the warm smile and kindly phrases. "I'm going home," he told her.

"To America?" She looked a little startled. She came from Perugia, and had known he meant to visit there some time. Then, quickly, "The signore likes Italy?"

"Yes, yes," he told her reassuringly. It wasn't Italy that was out of joint. It wasn't the times, either. It was himself. If the whole trip had been a mistake, it was simply that he had been unwilling to admit failure. He was admitting it now. He had been overconfident, too sure of Eleanor. He had let her slip away from him months ago, in New York. At last, he was really facing the truth. He had lost the girl, and he had deserved to lose.

"Just leave everything," he told the maid. "I'll be around until this afternoon, at least." He found a thousand-lire note. She was pleased by that, and more than pleased by the careful speech of thanks he made in Italian. Then he was left in his room to wait for word about his flight space to New York.

He sat down to write some letters. The first was to the man who had produced Lammiter's play and now was eager to read a second script. Provided, of course, it was the same as the first, only different. He doesn't want a playwright, Lammiter thought bitterly; all he wants is a little Mr. Echo, who'll be a sure investment; he doesn't want a piece of creative work, he wants a piece of property. First, he decided, I shall write him the letter I'd like to write. Then I'll tear that up, smother all indignation, resentment, accurate descriptions of his mentality (I.Q. probably a high 80) and of his education (progressive to the point of being perpetually retarded). And I'll write a note saying his observations were interesting (he'll never know how) and that I'm sorry I cannot agree with him.

How did a man like that ever get into a position of power in the world of art? He had money. But so had cigarette advertisers and buttonhole manufacturers. At least, New York wasn't yet plagued by the problems of the London theater, where it was almost compulsory to belong to the esoteric clique if you wanted to be produced or recognized at all.

The telephone rang.

He glanced at his watch. Only half an hour since he had ordered his ticket. His ill temper vanished. Quick work, he thought approvingly. He picked up the phone, expecting the porter's voice. Instead, it was a woman who was speaking.

"Hello," the voice said in English. "Mr. Lammiter?"

"Yes," he said, puzzled at first.

"I wanted to say thank you again."

There was no doubt who it was. The way she said thank you made him think of last night and a pretty face turned urgently, almost pathetically, to him under the cold lights of the Pincian Gate.

"Oh, it's you—" he recovered himself. "Glad to know you got home safely."

She laughed. "I have allies as well as enemies."

"So I saw. But I thought your friends were a little late in arriving last night."

"That's why I'd like to thank you."

"Oh, forget it. Glad I was there to shout at the nasty men. Who were they, anyhow?"

"I told you. The enemy." She laughed softly. He had to admit that he had rarely heard a more attractive sound. She said "Please—could we meet?"

Startled, he blurted out, "Meet? Where? Here?"

"Oh, no! That would be dangerous."

"At your place?"

"Still more dangerous. Meet me at Doney's. At noon."

"But I can't. I've got to wait here until—"

"Please. At noon. I must see you before you leave."

That made him suddenly wary. "Who *are* you?" he asked. How could she know he was planning to leave today? Did she or her friends have some kind of intelligence service working among the hotels? What was all this, anyway? "Who are you, what are you?" he asked.

"Someone who needs help. Badly." Her voice was low, fearful, but determined. Very quietly she added, "When you see me, pretend our meeting is accidental. Completely accidental." And with that tense warning, she ended the call abruptly.

After a minute's thought, he asked the hotel switchboard to inquire where that call had just come from—was it possible to trace the number, or had the operator any idea of the district in Rome where the call was made? At first, he thought it was his Italian that created the confusion, and then—after several long outbursts of explanation ranging from the polite to the irritated (he must have sounded incredibly stupid)—he suddenly realized it was his question. Because no one had telephoned him.

He began to argue about that, and then (as he saw the futility of all this questioning) he broke it off hastily with a "Sorry, sorry. Please excuse me," disentangling himself from a conversation that was now beyond his powers to control. "And thank you, signorina. Thank you for your help," he added. Politeness in Italy, politeness was the key to everything—for the annoyance in the operator's voice vanished, and he could imagine the smile spreading over her face as she said, "Thank *you,* signore. And is it possible that another guest was calling you from his room?"

Yes, it could have been possible. Or the girl could have walked through the lobby to the row of house telephones near the elevator, and used one of them. But how had she known his room number? He might as well ask how she had known his plans for leaving Rome.

He went downstairs at a quarter to twelve. He hadn't quite decided if he were going to walk past the café called Doney's. Or not. It was just like that. He was interested, yes; and curious, definitely curious, but he was still wary. What was this girl? A confidence trickster, a prostitute as the police had suggested last night, a possible blackmailer? Somehow —perhaps he was too gullible—somehow he didn't believe any of that. He kept remembering the pleading note in her voice. "Someone who needs help. Badly."

The lobby, large, dark, and cool, shaded rigorously from the glare of the brilliant Italian sun, was filled with young people returning from their morning pilgrimages. Students clustered in groups: girls in cotton dresses with wide skirts and neatly bloused tops, flat heels, large handbags, and short white gloves; young men in seersucker jackets and crew cuts. It seemed as if half the college population of the United States was visiting Rome this summer of 1956.

He handed over his room key at the porter's desk. "Any word of a reservation?"

The senior porter shook his head. "Not yet, Signore Lammiter. We do not expect to hear anything definite until four o'clock."

Ah yes, Lammiter thought: now is the time for everyone to shut up shop for lunch. And after lunch, the siesta. Half-past four might be a more accurate prediction before any business would be done on that hot July afternoon. He turned toward the door, leaving an anxious group of schoolteachers from Ohio inquiring about seats for *Traviata* at the Baths of Caracalla. He halted at the entrance, hesitating behind the heavy curtain of white sailcloth which cut off the sunlight at the threshold. For a moment he watched the crowded hotel lobby; for a moment he listened to the babel of tongues. He could recognize at least six foreign languages being spoken in addition to occasional Italian—Spanish, Brazilian Portuguese, French, English, Swedish or Danish (he wasn't quite sure), and Austrian German. Labels on neat piles of luggage near the doorway came from practically every country in western Europe; from Egypt and Israel and Syria; from Ceylon, Hong Kong, Australia. For a moment, the noise and movement added to his indecision as if they hypnotized him. Then he noticed the large clock over the porter's desk. Five minutes to twelve.

He pushed aside the gently blowing screen and stepped through the open doorway into the brilliant blinding light. The light breeze puffed its hot breath into his face. He turned sharply left and entered the broad sweep of the Via Vittorio Veneto. He walked at an even pace on the wide sidewalk, as the other foreigners were doing. He was a man on his way to Doney's for a drink and a pleasant view of the world strolling by.

The Via Vittorio Veneto is the main promenade in Rome, a wide curve of a slowly descending hill, edged with trees, sweeping down from the old Roman wall to the more commercial streets of the modern city, covering no greater distance than half of a brief mile. But it contains much. It is the street of big hotels and sidewalk cafés, of small expensive shops for perfume and pretty shoes; of banks and imposing buildings; of lovely bareheaded girls strolling, breasts out, waistlines in, between the rows of café tables; of the Capuchin church with its coarse-gowned tonsured friars welcoming visitors to view its crypts filled with dead brothers' bones—skull and rib and pelvis laid out in patterns like a carefully arranged flower bed or a burst of fireworks. It is the street of thick trees giving dappled shade to broad sidewalks; of crowded taxis, smart cars, white-uniformed traffic policemen; of young men swerving on flatulent Vespas, foreigners on foot, young Italian soldiers on wide-eyed leave in ill-fitting uniforms; of crisp, khaki-suited tourist police with a protective air; of the United States Embassy sitting placidly among walled gardens and ornamental balustrades; of grave-faced, tall, handsome *carabinieri* with gold braid, black cavalry boots, and carefully held swords, pacing majestically in matched pairs; of the Excelsior, where Texas oil men and Hollywood stars scatter largesse and perpetuate the myth that every American is a millionaire; of neighboring Doney's, where the chic and the odd, the dramatic and the beautiful, the bad and the vicious, the known and the strange, the quiet and the flamboyant, the tragic and the farcical, the enchanted and the charming, all gather before the midday and evening meals to eye and be eyed.

The girl couldn't have chosen a meeting place more favored by foreigners, Lammiter thought as he reached Doney's. The pre-luncheon crowd had started to gather. The little round tables, which edged the wide sidewalk like a guard of honor, leaving a center path for the pedestrians (and it was surprising how many people would saunter past, not only once or twice but three times and more), were already half filled. In another fifteen minutes they would all be occupied.

He kept his pace slow, untroubled, his eyes looking for a table where a gay umbrella would provide sufficient shade. He had the sudden fear that she wouldn't arrive, that this little incident would end as a dreary hour of waiting, of false alarms, of fading hopes, and a suddenly angry retreat to a lonely meal. Everything had gone so badly for him in the last four weeks that he had begun to expect nothing but disappointment. And then he saw her. He didn't have to try very hard to look surprised.

"Hello!" he said, stopping abruptly. She was alone at one of the tables that lined the grass edge of the sidewalk. Behind her was a row of parked cars, and then a stream of steady traffic. One table, to her left, was still empty; the other, on her right, was occupied by a handsome red-haired Italian, who was too openly interested in the girl to be anything but what he seemed—someone who admired a pretty woman. Pretty? She was beautiful. Lammiter stared down at her in amazement. "Well," he added, beginning to smile, "well—"

"It can't be!" she said, startled, smiling, delighted. It all seemed a natural succession of emotions. "But in Rome, everyone meets," she added. "Sooner or later, everyone meets."

"Are you waiting for a friend? Or may I join you?"

"Please do."

So he pulled round the other wicker chair to the side of the small round table, and sat down to face her. Behind him, he heard almost a sigh of disappointment from her Italian admirer.

"Have I changed so much?" she asked as he kept looking at her. She was wearing a sleeveless white linen blouse, low-necked. Her bare arms were tanned, rounded, firm.

"In a way, yes. Last time we met, you weren't so cool-looking."

"Cool? In this temperature?"

"It's hot," he agreed. "And I hear it's going to get hotter." Behind him, a chair scraped as it was pushed back. A waiter hurried forward to lift the money that had been left to pay for the Italian's Cinzano and to take Lammiter's order.

"Beer: Danish," he told the waiter, watching the Italian walk away. "Too bad. I spoiled his plans for a pleasant luncheon." And possibly a cosy siesta, he thought. He studied the girl's face, and he was smiling again. He hadn't felt as relaxed as this, or as little unhappy, for a whole month. Was he beginning at last to get over Eleanor? If so, this girl might be the pleasantest cure he could find. Her dark eyes were wide-spaced, richly lashed under excellently marked eyebrows. The forehead was broad and intelligent. Her features were classical, as Roman as one of the pretty stone girls in the Campidoglio museum. And, most startling against the honey color of her glowing skin, she wore no make-up on her lips. They were soft, natural. It was a current fashion among the Roman girls, he had noticed. With a white face, it would have had a drab effect. With their deeply tanned faces and skillfully mascaraed eyelashes, the natural lips were startling.

"At least we can talk now," she said, "and quickly. Before someone else sits down. Or perhaps the sun will discourage them."

He realized then that only their table was shaded at this time of day by the small tree behind them. Other tables had their sheltering umbrellas or awnings. But here, the three tables usually depended on the tree. He looked at the girl speculatively. It was always difficult to remember that anyone as decorative as this could also be clever. But it was necessary to remember that. More guardedly, he said, "Why did you want to see me?"

"To thank you."

He shook his head, smiling. "Try again."

"To warn you."

"Me?"

"We must keep smiling. We are talking about America—about Harvard in 1950—just before you went off to Korea."

"Look—" he said.

"Please smile," she urged, her voice low. The waiter brought a bottle of beer, opened it, poured it, and left. Lammiter said, as if there had been no interruption, "How do you know about Harvard? Or Korea? And who is watching us now so that we've to keep this bright and breezy merriment stuck all over our faces? And why should I be warned? I'm in no danger. I'm just a peaceful guy who has been minding his own miserable business for four weeks. I'm leaving Rome today, anyway."

"Yes, we know that too. And that worries my friends."

He looked at her, startled. "Friends" had been bitterly spoken.

"They don't like your plan to visit Perugia, not after your interest in me last night."

"Perugia? Your friends aren't quite up to date on all my plans. I'm going back to America."

"Oh no!"

"You are forgetting to smile," he said. She stared at him. She looked, suddenly, so young and defenseless that he relented. "What's this all about, anyway?"

She shook her head.

"Come on, tell me," he urged gently. "You didn't come here just to advise me to avoid Perugia."

"It was my friends who didn't want you to go there."

He noticed again the bitterness with which she emphasized the word "friends." "But you wanted me to go there?" She was silent, watching him. It seemed better to concentrate on her so-called friends. "Why did your—friends not want me in Perugia?"

"They think you could very well be an agent, an American agent." He stared at her. But she was serious. "You *were* in the Army Intelligence, weren't you?"

He began to laugh. "Oh, I burned the bits of paper in the trash basket for a month or two. Then the office caught fire one day, and I was demoted. I held the door open for the big brass when they visited my colonel."

She wasn't persuaded. And she wasn't amused, either. She said slowly, "You've been in Rome for four weeks. Without any apparent purpose."

"I am a writer. At least, that's what my passport says: 'writer.' "

"That is always a very good cover."

"Not since Somerset Maugham wrote *Ashenden.*"

"You have friends in Washington. In Intelligence work." She was trying to fight down some major disappointment.

"They stayed on in the service. Why shouldn't they get promoted to Washington? You can't expect them to live in foxholes or army tents forever." He looked at her with curiosity. "Did *you* hope I was connected with Intelligence?" he asked quietly.

She nodded. "Or the FBI. Or the CIA. Something like that . . ." She looked at him quickly, as if to surprise the truth.

"No," he could assure her frankly. "I've even lost touch with most of my old friends. I never seem to meet them nowadays." He frowned, as he suddenly realized that was not quite accurate. Three days ago, right here in Rome, Bunny Camden had thumped on his shoulder blade and practically given him curvature of the spine. But Bunny was probably in Naples right now, and you didn't talk about Bunny without Bunny's permission. Bunny was the type who knew what he was doing even if no one else ever did.

"Yes?" she asked quickly, noting the frown.

He said, "I'm puzzled. How did your 'friends' do all this research on me?—Just how did they learn—"

"They have a good source of information on you."

"They have?" He was suddenly annoyed. "And who are 'they'?"

"We must keep our voices low," she said. Her eyes flickered briefly toward a table under the café awning, where two men were seated. It lay opposite theirs, divided from them by the stream of passers-by. He noticed, now, that she always seemed to speak when people passed in front of them, as if their movement would hide her expression from the opposite table.

"All right," he said. "Who are 'they,' anyway?" He studied her face. "You don't really like them very much, do you? Then why call them friends?" She looked away, as if absorbed by the three American movie stars who were walking so slowly along the aisle between the tables. "Did they tell you to meet me here?"

She nodded.

"Then, if they expected us to meet, why were we to pretend it was all accidental? Who else is watching us?"

"I can't be sure," she said. "But it is likely I am being watched by other people, too."

"By the men who tried to kidnap you last night?"

She shrugged her shoulders, but she was worried. She took the cigarette he offered her with a strained smile of thanks.

"Weren't you afraid to come here?" he asked.

"I'm well guarded at this moment. And besides, the two men of last night are—" she hesitated "—they are dead."

"What?" He was incredulous, and then frankly disbelieving.

"Please," she said, "we must keep our voices low."

"Who killed the men who attacked you? *Your* friends?" He began to smile a little. What a story, what undiluted hogwash! Either that, or she'd better change the company she keeps, he thought.

"So they told me. This morning. But perhaps it may have been a lie —to make me feel all is safe. But—" She took a deep breath. Her lips trembled for a moment. Suddenly, watching the fear she was trying to hide, he believed at least part of her story.

He said, "Do your friends know that you are working against them?"

Her face went rigid with surprise at his guess. Quickly, with a pathetic smile, she said, "Please—please pretend I'm finding out about you, instead of your finding out about me."

"And what do your friends want to learn about me?"

"Why are you in Italy? Are you dangerous to them?"

"Dangerous?" He was now amused. Her sense of the dramatic was more Italian than American, although her accent was practically regulation Miss Hewitt's Classes. She must have lived for a number of years in the United States, been to school there. Her manners were the recognizable pattern of the well-brought-up Eastern girl. "Wellesley or Smith?" he asked suddenly.

"*Please* take me seriously," she said sharply. "And my college was Radcliffe."

"Then we've got Cambridge in common." That was always a useful point of departure in any friendship. In a way, he thought, it was a pity that this one was going to be so short.

"Take me seriously," she repeated, her voice dropping. Her eyes were unhappy. Her smile was pleading.

"How can I? I don't know who you are. Or what you are really trying to tell me."

"*Don't* leave Italy," she said, turning her head to look at the traffic behind them in the busy street. If anyone had been lip reading her remarks, this little move would have defeated him neatly. "Please don't go. I need your help."

"I don't think your friends would approve of that suggestion. What's their line of business, anyway?"

She considered her answer for a long moment, and in the end she didn't give it. "The sun is moving around," she said, her voice as unhappy as her eyes. She pulled back her arm into the shade, and moved her chair a few inches into the narrowing shadows. "Soon we shall have to leave." She glanced over once more at the table with the two men. One was a middle-aged English-looking type: he still sat there, reading a book. The other, a handsome dark-haired Italian in an expensive gray suit, had left. But his drink was unfinished. He could be visiting another table. Lammiter found himself suddenly, unexpectedly, sharing the girl's tenseness. He looked at the reading Englishman—the thin haggard face and shadowed eyes seemed vaguely familiar, so did the lock of long wayward hair falling over the narrow upraised eyebrow—and then back at the girl.

"Something wrong?" he asked her quietly.

"I'll soon know," she said, watching the waiter approaching them. "Mr. Lammiter, can I say you've asked me to luncheon with you?"

"Yes, you can say that." But to whom? "And I hope you've accepted."

The waiter said, "Signorina Di Feo? Telephone for you, if you please."

"Ah yes," she said. "Thank you." She looked at Lammiter, and rose slowly.

"What comes before Di Feo?" he asked.

"Rosana," she said. She had a proud way of carrying her head, a most attractive and tantalizing way of turning to give a glancing smile over her shoulder.

"I'll wait here until you get back. Don't be long, or I'll get sunstroke."

Then, as he settled down to wait, he wondered whether she would come back. If she really needed help, she would. And yet, where did that place him? He was leaving Rome tonight. What help could he give? It would be kinder if he walked away, so that when she came back to this table—if she did come back—she would know that he couldn't give any help. Then she'd have to begin looking for some other obliging idiot. Yet he didn't start counting out money to cover the two paper tabs that the waiter had left under the ashtray on the table. He didn't make one move to leave. Instead, he leaned back in his chair, felt the warm sun play on his spine, and watched the parade of handsome Romans mixing with the eternal tourists.

As he waited for Rosana, Lammiter again noted the preponderance of young America: the college girls; and the high-school boys; and the young men just out of service, their hair still close-cut, their shoulders still squared away, and their GI savings in their pockets. There were older Americans, too, mostly family men shepherding their flocks back to their hotels: the gray-haired and baldheaded fathers, in button-down collars and the new drip-dry jackets posing as seersucker, patiently accepting a summer vacation spent in museums and churches while dissembling their worry about the low evaporation point of money; the wives, who had read the guidebooks and provided the enthusiasm, now harried and hurried but still determined on culture in spite of the problems of food and drink for the children, of nylon laundry all over the bathroom, of the chore of keeping a family neat while it lived from suitcases; the children themselves, remarkably good-natured, who must have had better ideas on spending a hot summer day than by breathing the gasoline fumes of a modern city. The English tourists were mostly middle-aged. The men wore high-waisted trousers held up by taut suspenders over transparent nylon shirts open and neatly folded back at the neck. And their choice in holiday shoes was odd: crisscrossed leather sandals displaying lots of heavy wool sock. Their women weren't what Lammiter expected, either: they didn't look like the Englishwomen he met in New York or Washington: these Roman tourists were more solidly constructed, sensible in shoes and ankles, more like Brussels sprouts than the well-advertised roses, nice and wholesome and all so very much alike. With some pepper and salt and butter, they'd probably taste alike, too. Once outside of the buses which had brought them across Europe, the English couples kept together, in tight phalanxes of four or six, as if they distrusted the friendliness of the natives. Perhaps they were new to travel, and were still worried about white-slave traffic, unmentionable diseases, and pickpockets. The thin middle-aged Englishman sitting at the table opposite Lammiter seemed both horrified and fascinated by his own countrymen: he kept looking up at them in pained disbelief. Not one tie, far less an old school tie, among them.

If the English stiffened into set molds when they traveled, the French became as shapeless as a melted candle. Not for them was the clean shirt, and the trousers at least pressed under the mattress, or the dainty afternoon frock; they dressed for a comfortable journey (which usually meant five packed into a small beetle-like car with bits and pieces of luggage strapped all around): crumpled shorts and hairy legs, wrinkled skirts and soiled blouses, bare feet in equally dusty sandals. They sauntered slowly, carelessly, dropping into a ragged single file as often as not, like a column of Bedouins cautiously straggling into rival territory. If they were impressed, it was well disguised. And the worse a French tourist was dressed, the more contemptuously he looked at others. The carefully washed, brushed, and dressed Italians—even those who could afford only one meal a day—refused to be scorned. They ignored the tourists (after all, Rome had been invaded by barbarians for centuries) and watched the pretty Roman girls with national pride. From sixteen until twenty-two or so, they were beautiful, as beautiful as any Lammiter had ever seen anywhere. But what happened after twenty-two, he wondered? Then he saw Rosana Di Feo coming toward him at last. She was an exception to the general rule, he considered. She must be twenty-three or -four, and she was still a beauty.

"I'm sorry," she said, "to have been so long." But she didn't sit down.

So he rose. "I was watching the tourists," he explained.

Her voice was very low. "I've watched them for three days, watched and watched and wondered. Did you see anyone who looked as if he'd risk danger?"

He glanced at her curiously, and counted out the money and the tip for their drinks. "Shall we lunch now?"

"I can't." Her voice dropped almost to a whisper. She stood with her back to the other tables, to the café's windows. "They've learned you are leaving Italy tonight."

"Oh?" He hoped his face was under control. "So you're under orders to leave me alone now. I'm no longer dangerous?" He had spoken half jokingly. But she faced him, her back to the crowded tables, her face unguarded for a moment, and he suddenly realized that she was both afraid and hopeless.

"Yes," she said. "Those are the orders."

"And did the orders come by telephone, or by that handsome black-haired Italian in the gray suit? The one who sat opposite us for a while with the thin Englishman?"

"How did you know?"

"Because he is standing at the café door, watching you, right now." She said nothing to that. He said, suddenly serious, "Perhaps it would have been safer for you not to come back to this table."

"I told him it would be very suspicious if I left you without saying good-by."

"Who is he?" The Italian was a tall man, about thirty-five or so, with dark hair, thick, carefully brushed. He had a superior air, as if he were accustomed to behave correctly. He was obviously well fed, but also well exercised. He was most carefully dressed. Handsome, yes. Attractive to women, definitely. Now he was going forward to another table, to spend a few minutes in conversation with an aging beauty, exquisitely dressed, her white face sheltered from the sun by an elaborate hat, her vanity bolstered by the adulation of the two young men who kept her company.

Rosana hesitated. But she didn't answer his question. "If you change your mind about leaving," she said, holding out her hand to shake his, "it would be safest to keep it a secret." She pressed a small wad of paper into his palm. "Good-by."

"Safest for whom?"

"For both of us."

He shook hands solemnly, but the amusement quickened in his eyes. He was convinced that a good deal of dramatics had gone into persuading him to stay. There was too much emotion, too much play acting around here for his taste. He'd stick to the theater for that kind of thing, keeping it safely in a world of make-believe. But the day stretched out in its lonely fashion before him till he'd get on that homebound plane, and he tried to prolong the good-by.

"Have a safe journey," she said, a little bitterly, as if she had read his thoughts, and she turned away.

Quickly, he started after her. He raised his voice to normal. "I'm sorry we can't lunch together."

She said urgently, quietly, "Don't follow me. Stay at your table!"

"Let me walk with you to the corner," he said. "Even acquaintances do that."

"There's no need."

"None. But I want to. Besides, if I didn't walk a pretty girl to the corner, it *would* look odd."

They were passing the table now where the aging beauty, her two young men, and the handsome dark-haired Italian were sitting.

"Oh, Rosana!" It was the older woman speaking, her white face cracking delicately around the lips and eyes. "You never come to see me any more," she said chidingly.

"I shall, Principessa," Rosana promised, halting unwillingly but politely as the three men at the table rose to their feet. Lammiter walked on slowly for a few paces, plunging his hands into his pockets as if he had nothing to do but wait. It was a relief to let the small wad of paper drop free from his palm into safety. Then he halted, looking at the traffic, while he lit a cigarette.

The princess's voice held Rosana. "We move soon to the hills. So come tomorrow, Rosana. The boys want to go to Ischia"—Lammiter could almost hear the flutter of their eyes and the pouting of their lips as they mimed their disappointment—"but I refuse to have anything to do with the Bay of Naples in August." And then there was a new inflection in the clear carrying voice, one of subtle sarcasm. "Luigi, do let me introduce you. Luigi Pirotta—the Signorina Di Feo." Lammiter almost swung round to face the dark-haired Italian. "But of course," the princess halted the introduction halfway, "you have met. How stupid of me! Wasn't Luigi a great friend of your brother's, my dear?" Her voice was elegiac now, hinting at disaster. Lammiter glanced casually around. The dark-haired Italian was very much at ease, sympathetic, regretful. Was it the charm of his manners that had caught Eleanor Halley so surely? Or his profile, or his shoulders? They were all good. Lammiter threw away the cigarette, which had suddenly turned bitter. "How sad it all was, my dear, how indescribably sad!" the princess told Rosana, and then the girl, with a small bow and a fixed smile, walked on to join Lammiter.

He said nothing until they had passed the last table on the sidewalk.

There was still something of shock and disbelief in his voice when he said, "Pirotta? Luigi Pirotta? . . . Or was she lying?"

"The princess may be tactless, malicious, even rude. But she never lies. Yes, that is Pirotta. He has a title, too, to impress his American fiancée." Rosana glanced at him swiftly. "I'm sorry," she added.

He didn't speak. He was still trying to accustom himself to the idea that the dark-haired Italian was Eleanor Halley's choice for a husband.

She said, "All right, I'll be honest. I'm not sorry. Except that the princess played my trump card. I was going to tell you his name, before we parted. So that you would stay."

"Why?"

"I am offering you revenge."

He began to smile, without much humor. He shook his head.

"You won't call it revenge, of course. That's too elemental. But Pirotta did steal your girl, didn't he? And now you begin to find out that, although he has a title and a distinguished family, and totally innocent friends with some kind of name or fame attached, and everything seemingly blameless, he still is not quite right, is he? He is not what Eleanor Halley thinks he is. Or what you thought he was."

"Would you tell me *what* he is?" he asked angrily.

"Only three people have known that. One was my brother Mario, and he is dead: a suicide, it was supposed." (How sad, the princess had said, how indescribably sad.) "One is Tony, my friend—" she glanced at him quickly "—my only true friend, and he is in hiding. And the third is I, Rosana Di Feo. Do you expect me to tell you the truth about Pirotta unless you stay here and help Tony and me? We don't want to be 'suicides' like my brother."

Lammiter caught her arm and prevented her from walking in front of a large American car feeling its way slowly out from the Hotel Excelsior's porte-cochère. He looked at the piles of luggage on the sidewalk, at the usual crowd waiting in front of the hotel, their cars edging in and out of the driveway. It was all so normal, so routine, that he told himself, This is fantastic. Here's the Excelsior, and women with diamond clips and tight silk suits; and that's the garden wall of the American Embassy down the street; and over there is the bookstall where I get the *Tribune* and *Time* and the *Rome Daily American* and anything else in English. I know this quarter backwards. The people look the same, the voices sound the same; the street is filled with sunshine and noise, with warmed spines and easy smiles, with pretty barelegged girls in low-necked dresses. And beside me is the prettiest of them all, talking earnestly about suicide, glancing over her shoulder at that moment as if she expected we were being followed. Fantastic, the whole thing's fantastic. It just can't be happening. Not to me.

And yet, it was.

She hadn't even noticed the near-accident. Or perhaps she brushed it away as quickly as she freed her arm. "You pretend to be shocked when I offer you revenge," she said, intent on her own emotions, and her voice trembled as if she were on the verge of tears. "What else can I appeal to? Your patriotism? Don't you want to help your country? Or will you do less for it than I am willing to do?"

He said gently, trying to calm her down, "Now, Rosie—ease up, old girl, or you'll be bursting into sobs. Wouldn't Pirotta find that interesting?" And as she took a deep breath, he went on, his eyes watchful, "Tell me—what kind of business is Pirotta caught up in? What is it?"

The moment of weakness was over. Her bitterness returned. Again she ignored his question. "What else must I say? Shall I fall back on the appeal to Sir Galahad? If you aren't a patriot, aren't you at least a romantic? You may not consider me much of a lady any more, but I assure you—I am in distress."

He persisted with his own questions. "What is Pirotta's racket? He *is* mixed up with something unpleasant, not honest, secret. Isn't he?"

She bit her lip.

"What is it?"

"Not here. They are still watching us probably."

"Must I stay in Rome—" he began angrily.

"But quietly, don't advertise it," she warned him quickly.

"—to hear what kind of a man Pirotta is?"

She halted at the corner of the street, her eyes on the red light which was about to change to green. She put her hand out to say good-by. He caught it and held it. "Rosana—look, if I stay in Rome, will you answer my questions?"

She looked up at him then. "Yes. All of them." Her voice softened. "So gladly, so very gladly."

Around them he heard the beginning of complaints. "What is wrong with those traffic lights?" someone asked angrily. Then Rosana laughed, and glanced toward the white-uniformed policeman who was in charge of the lights. Lammiter looked, too. The policeman was watching them both with a broad smile.

"Is he giving us time to say good-by?" Lammiter asked.

"He's a romantic. That's what Tony would call him," Rosana said, and took her hand away from Lammiter's grasp. "I want you to meet Tony. And he wants to meet you." The policeman pressed the switch, the lights changed, and Rosana stepped off the sidewalk. Lammiter watched her cross the street. Then he turned and walked slowly back to the café. He needed another drink.

She's got you, Bill, he told himself. She's got what she wanted. She wanted you to stay in Rome. And you agreed. Then he called himself a fool, an idiot, a moron, and larded the descriptions with imaginative adjectives. He might plead that he hadn't actually committed himself, yet he had been near enough to a promise to be irritated by a sense of guilt if he were to retreat from it. Then he swung away from his own emotions to take another look at Miss Di Feo. At this distance, away from those large dark eyes which could look so appealing and afraid at one and the same time, away from the best collection of physical attributes he had ever noticed gathered together around one spine, away from the soft voice and its gentle inflections (had a man ever fallen in love with a voice?), he could think of her more rationally. Miss Di Feo was a very smart little girl.

What facts had she given him?

None.

Nothing but a sense of danger threatening Eleanor—as if he hadn't been too ready to believe the worst about her God-damned count. Why should he go on worrying about Eleanor, anyway? She was just about as smart a little girl as Miss Di Feo, and as pretty, too, but don't let him start remembering that. Anyone who could get engaged to a determined bachelor on the night of his first play's success was not in need of much worry. And anyone who could manage to use her father's name (he was a magazine editor when he wasn't busy worrying about Eleanor) to find herself in Rome for Easter (just when a fiancé was deciding he had to settle down to work and no more parties and good-by to all the publicity and let's hie me to a monastery—preferably Trappist) was not in need of any worry at all. So there it was: Easter in Rome, important friends of her father's who took her around, a nice job as mixture of linguist and coffee-brewer and decorative asset in the Embassy, and Eleanor could write charming letters back to New York. Until the last one. That was on the thirtieth day of June. . . . "Dear Bill, I am sorry, but—" His name was Luigi Pirotta. A title, too. A very, very old family. Handsome and charming. "In ways, so very like you, Bill. I know you'd approve of him. And this decision I've made, however painful for both of us, is wise. You have your work and all the people connected with it. There isn't much room for me—and I was never quite able to fit into the picture. So I shouldn't be surprised if this letter was something of a relief to you. I know you'll understand." Understand? After the first angry shock, he broke all engagements, including that visit to Hollywood, and took the first plane that had a canceled reservation, the new ideas for his next play already sifting away from his mind like grains of sand scattering before a wind. The weakness of determined bachelors was that they took an engagement seriously. Once committed to the idea of marriage, they expected it to stay with them for a lifetime. But take Eleanor—she was the kind who'd have at least one broken engagement, three upset marriages, and come out thriving on all the wasted emotions and bitter recriminations. If he wanted to be sorry for anyone at all, he ought to be pitying this fellow Pirotta.

Just as he had persuaded himself—using every unfair argument, he would admit later—that he had no more interest in Eleanor, he saw her. She was sitting with the princess who was so afraid of loneliness, the two simpering boys, Pirotta, and—back with him once more—the thin, vaguely familiar Englishman. And Eleanor had seen him, too. It was too late to change course. All he could do was to walk on. He'd drink his beer somewhere else.

But he didn't. For the old princess suddenly called out as he approached their table, "There's Rosana's young man! Eleanor, didn't you say you knew him? I'd like to meet him! Stop him, somebody!"

If only to save Eleanor embarrassment, he halted and smiled. "Hello, Eleanor, how are you?" Besides, it might be time to meet Pirotta. The Italian had risen to his feet. Yes, we're just about the same height, Lammiter thought: perhaps I could give him half an inch and he could give me seven pounds. He drew himself erect. Pirotta was holding his head pretty high, too. Over Eleanor's smooth crown of pale blond hair, their eyes met.

The princess laughed. "Isn't this delicious?" she asked, watching them carefully. "I adore Americans."

There are some remarks at the beginning of an encounter that sound a warning bell: the wise man listens, takes heed, and makes off in the direction that will lead him most quickly out of firing range. So Bill Lammiter almost continued on his way, leaving the princess with her own special store of irony into which she would dip her well-sharpened darts. But Eleanor, quite unwittingly, changed his mind for him. "How *funny* to meet you here!" She smiled nervously at Pirotta. "Why, we were talking about you only this morning!" Then the smile trembled, and she bit her lip nervously, as if Pirotta's response had not been encouraging.

"I'm flattered," Lammiter said. And he remembered Rosana's words: *They have a good source of information on you.* Indeed they have, he thought as he smiled down at Eleanor. He hadn't really believed Rosana, not altogether. But at this moment, he began to believe a good deal more of what she had said. And now Eleanor, her thin delicate face turning to each of them anxiously, her blue-gray eyes looking darker gray (as they always did when she was nervous), her long slender body tense, had begun making the introductions. She gave the appearance of doing this very expertly, but Lammiter never managed to catch the princess's name. It sounded something like Zabaglione, which was most unlikely unless an ancestor had spent his life whipping up Marsala and hot egg yolks. But the thin middle-aged Englishman turned out to be Bertrand Whitelaw, a journalist who spent much of the year in Italy, visited America for lecture tours, wrote weekly columns for a London paper and seasonal articles for a New York literary magazine, and produced an occasional book on whither are we drifting, alack, alas. A slightly younger version of his tired and troubled face had occasionally peeked out from the glossy pages of high-fashion magazines, where American women were now having their minds as well as their chin lines lifted. For Mr. Whitelaw was an Authority. (Lammiter had never been quite sure on what Whitelaw was an authority, but then writers have a healthy disrespect for one another.)

The two boys embarrassed Lammiter by studying him with open approval. He wasn't quite sure what nationality they were, didn't even listen to their names. They now posed for him with heads cocked to one side, their brown eyes so liquid that they threatened to pour out of the large sockets and cascade over the beardless cheeks. But no one paid any attention to them, and they gradually grew disconsolate as the princess didn't even twitch their leash. They became silent and motionless, as unnoticed as the ashtrays on the table.

The princess had her sharp eyes on more entrancing sport. In her white face, their strange amber color glowed with anticipation. Her small red tongue ran its little point across her thin scarlet lips, gathering distilled malice. The dry ends of her russet-dyed hair seemed to spring loose with the electricity of her emotions, as she peered at Lammiter and then at Pirotta. She smiled. "How nice this is! Luigi, isn't there a chair for Mr. Lammiter? Find a waiter!" She turned to Bill Lammiter. "He's my nephew," she said. "My only brother's only son. He's a dear boy. Aren't you, Luigi?"

Pirotta refused to be baited. He smiled, and found a chair for Bill Lammiter. "What will you have to drink?" he asked amiably. The princess looked disappointed, but Eleanor relaxed for the first time, and all her old charm suddenly uncurled from its tight bud of worry, and blossomed. Yes, Lammiter decided, as conversation became general and harmless around him, Eleanor would make a very good countess. He could imagine her standing at the head of a marble staircase, extending a tight white kid glove to stiff white shirt fronts. She'd make a most attractive countess, he had to admit. And she was in love with Pirotta. She kept watching the Italian, silently, wide-eyed. Truly, as Eleanor herself would say, she was in love with her man, and not just with a marble staircase. What about Pirotta? He was in love, too. There was no doubt about that.

"But you aren't going? So soon?" the princess said as he rose. She stopped arranging her large gray straw hat (with its pink and blue flowers so carefully matched to the printed roses on her gray silk suit) and looked at him with amazement. "Why, you've been so polite listening to all our chatter that you haven't even told me what you've done with Rosana." She flashed a glance at his startled face. "What *have* you done?"

Bertrand Whitelaw said, "He has kidnaped her and is holding her for ransom. That is, after all, one of America's favorite indoor sports. Isn't it, Mr. Lammiter?"

Bill Lammiter studied Whitelaw silently.

"Now, Bertrand!" the princess chided, absolutely delighted. "After all, the Americans pay you enough for six lectures—or is it one lecture given six times?—to keep you living in Italy for the other forty-six weeks of the year. One shouldn't snap at the hand that feeds one. At least, not too obviously."

"Indeed I am not anti-American," Whitelaw insisted earnestly. "On the contrary, I'm the greatest admirer of America's contribution to civilization. A dry Martini, Principessa, is not to be sneezed at."

"Aren't you forgetting bubble gum?" Lammiter asked, too quietly.

The princess said quickly, "Ah, you must read Bertrand's column each week, Mr. Lammiter. Or don't you read?—I mean, the London papers?"

"*Not* column. Heaven forbid," Whitelaw said reprovingly.

"No, indeed. It's a sermon," Pirotta said and gave a genial laugh. Somehow, the tensions relaxed. Lammiter, sitting very still, had to give Pirotta credit for his expert diplomacy. The light laugh, applied at the right moment, was always a solution. There were others. But then, Lammiter decided, I am obviously no diplomat. He looked at Pirotta thoughtfully. It was disconcerting to find Pirotta's handsome eyes quietly measuring him.

"The odd thing about Bertrand," the princess said, "is that he lives so little in England and yet he is always so clever about what England ought to do. Why, he might be an American after all, mightn't he, Mr. Lammiter? By the way, I *am* curious. What *have* you done with Rosana?"

Lammiter said stiffly, and he hoped he sounded a little embarrassed and rueful and just a touch disappointed, "Miss Di Feo had another engagement."

"She ran out on you, old boy? Too bad, too bad," Whitelaw said. Then, most unexpectedly, he added, "What about lunch with me?"

"Splendid," Pirotta said quickly, and smiled over at Eleanor. "We are just about to leave, too."

"Not yet, not yet!" the princess said sharply, seeing her company suddenly dissolving. Her two young men came to life at the anxiety in her voice. They cocked their heads worriedly, like two very faithful and alert French poodles. "First, we must decide what to do with Rosana."

"Must we?" murmured Whitelaw. "'And before luncheon?" He sighed.

The princess looked at him silkily. Heaven help him, Lammiter thought. She went on talking. "Rosana runs away from all attractive young men. She never comes to see me, or any of her mother's old friends. She avoids us, I think. Of course, her brother— Do you think she is avoiding us all because of Mario?"

Lammiter, watching, suddenly saw anger in Pirotta's eyes. But the Italian's voice was noncommittal. "Let us not talk about Mario."

"Of course, you knew him. And liked him. We all did. Poor Mario," the princess sighed.

"Poor Mario?" Whitelaw asked. "Now I am interested."

"Do you remember the scandal last year? Mario was found dead, naked, in his bedroom. Odd, wasn't it, to commit suicide without one's clothes on? People are usually so careful about appearances when they are dead."

"Oh!" Whitelaw remembered now. "Drugs. Am I right?"

"Yes . . . Drugs. So vulgar . . . And it concerned the sons and daughters of several well-known families. Horrid, wasn't it, Luigi?"

Pirotta was watching her. His face was controlled. He nodded. "We were all *so* upset. One was afraid to look in the newspapers in case one knew the names. And of course, Bertrand"—and now the bright amber eyes were turned on the Englishman—"the Communists tried to make a festival of denunciation out of the whole sordid business. They began holding meetings, wrote editorials, organized parades. You know how they behave! And then—but don't you remember?"

Whitelaw said, "I was away lecturing at the time." He and Pirotta exchanged one look. To Lammiter, it seemed as if everyone had forgotten about him, as if there were a secret battle in progress. And then, suddenly, he began to feel that the princess was staging all this scene with a purpose. For his benefit? The little glance she flashed him now seemed to draw him into the center of it all.

"Then you missed *so* much fun," she told Whitelaw. "For some really clever journalist discovered that there were Communists, too, who were mixed up with all the scandal. So, of course, a great silence descended. But everyone knows that there are still some hidden drug rings. And with Communists running them, I hear."

"Oh, really!" Whitelaw exclaimed. He tried to hide his growing amusement. He smiled at the two other men. "Come, come—one doesn't believe everything one hears. Especially in Rome." He turned to Lammiter. "The Romans are so nimble-witted that they supply the most delicious gossip to suit any situation."

Pirotta laughed. "If we didn't have the situations, we'd invent them."

"Besides," Whitelaw said consolingly, "you can't be afraid of your Communists in Italy. Now really, Principessa! They're such delightful people."

The princess said, disarmingly sweet, "I did *not* mean our *nice* Communists, who want to *help* the workers. I meant the real Communists —who *shoot* the workers. As in Poznan last month."

There was a little silence.

Eleanor ended it. "I just can't forget that photograph. You know—the one with the girl walking in front holding a flag all covered with blood. And the students and workers behind her." Her gray eyes widened, her lips trembled, her face flushed. She looked very beautiful, very touching, as Joan of Arc. Pirotta took her hand gently. Lammiter was glad to see that that comforted her.

"I think you must write my next article," Whitelaw suggested with a gentle smile for the princess.

"Would it be printed?"

"Why shouldn't it?"

"But would your newspaper trust me as much as it *trusts* you, Bertrand?" Again there was that little flicker of the amber eyes toward Lammiter as she lingered on the word "trust." Then she waved her soft white hands, the pink quartz and blue sapphires glancing with the sunlight on her long thin fingers. "Now we've all worked up a pretty appetite for luncheon." She began drawing on her silver-gray gloves. "And we have quite forgotten poor Rosana. Tell me, Luigi, did you ever hear the truth about Mario Di Feo? Did he *take* drugs? Or did he *sell* them?"

There was again a brief silence. "Poor Rosana—she came home from America and found her brother a suicide, and nothing ever explained."

"How awful!" Eleanor said, all sympathy. "What is she like?"

"Young. Younger than you are, I'd imagine. And very beautiful."

"Oh!" Eleanor retreated.

"Wouldn't you say so, Mr. Lammiter?"

Bill Lammiter nodded. Eleanor was, strangely enough, watching him.

"No comment? Or did you find my story too moving? How splendid! Then I'll ask you to dinner tomorrow night along with Rosana. You and I shall cheer her up. Luigi, you must come, too, and bring your Eleanor. And you, Bertrand? We shall be six. How nice. I hate large parties."

"I'm sorry," Lammiter said, "but I'm leaving Rome tonight. So you see—"

"No, I don't," the princess said fretfully. "You can't leave Rome right now." She took a deep breath. "I want you to come to dinner tomorrow."

"I'm afraid I'll be in New York by tomorrow night."

"Really, Bill?" Eleanor asked. "Why, I thought you were going to spend the summer here, writing." She looked upset, as if she blamed herself for this change.

"I don't seem to get much work done in Rome."

"Does one *want* to work in Rome?" Whitelaw asked, with his amused smile.

"New York," the princess said, "will be as hot as Rome. Perhaps hotter. You won't work there, either. What are you writing? Another play? I know just the place for you in the Umbrian hills. I'll lend you a house. You may stay as long as you like."

Lammiter might have disliked trying to write in hotel rooms, but he distrusted borrowed houses even more. And then, just as he was about to refuse firmly, the look of disquiet that momentarily glanced over Pirotta's face made him hesitate. He looked vague, polite, uncertain.

Eleanor tried to help him. "Must you really go back to New York so soon, Bill?"

He made the mistake of not having a good excuse ready. The moment to make it came, and was gone.

"Then why don't you stay? You haven't seen a hundredth part of Italy. And there's so much to see, so much material for you to use in your next play. Don't you agree, Luigi?"

Pirotta made a polite murmur, quite unguessable but apparently friendly.

The princess suddenly tried a frontal attack. "Mr. Lammiter, what is making you *run* away?"

"Run?" Lammiter hoped he looked both startled and stupid. Then he laughed, looking at the others for support. "I guess I just got set on the idea of leaving, that's all. I only decided on it last night." He was speaking slowly in a forthright manner, trying to give the appearance of someone who was completely simple-minded. It was the kind of character they would all readily accept, because they believed in it. Except Eleanor: she had once or twice looked at him in surprise when he had sat silent and let the conversational ball slip past him; and now, when he was at last talking, she watched him with a small frown as he kept strictly to basic English. "I was standing on my balcony, having my last cigarette. I kind of like looking over that old wall. Makes a fellow think. Gives him a new viewpoint about a lot of things. I wasn't feeling too good, kind of down about everything. The weather, I guess; and not being able to get any work done, and all. Then this idea hit me. Just like that." He laughed again. He was holding the Englishman enthralled, at least. Whitelaw no doubt prided himself on imitations. "And then, a funny thing happened. Last night, or rather early this morning—you won't believe it, but it happened, all right—" He dropped his voice, and he noticed that Pirotta's interest in him had died away entirely. Pirotta would have been interested in him only if he hadn't mentioned the strange happening of last night. "I was standing—"

"I hate standing," the princess said, rising, "and there's my car. Mr. Lammiter, your arm, please." She put out a hand and let it rest on his forearm. They started walking toward the well-polished Lancia which had cruised slowly up the hill and was now stopping near the curb in front of them. He suddenly realized how slight and frail her bones were.

Very quietly she said, "I hope you understand what I was trying to tell you, Mr. Lammiter."

He nodded, noncommittally. He had reached the phase of trusting nobody. Only one thing had been decided about an hour ago. He was staying in Rome.

She went on, "At least I gave you a good excuse to change your mind about leaving. But you don't have to come to see me. I'm much too old. If only I had not been so tactful with Mussolini, I might have died while I was still attractive." She sighed. He looked at her in utter amazement, and now he wasn't acting any more. "It was thirty years ago, of course. I had gone to ask Mussolini a favor—my son and all his family had been arrested, ridiculous nonsense! Mussolini was standing behind the enormous desk in that gigantic room of his. He came round to where I was standing. He caught me and threw me down on the carpet. I slapped his face with the back of my hand—rings are so useful at times—and said 'Get up, you peasant!' And so he rolled off me, and I got up and smoothed my dress and walked out."

Lammiter burst into laughter. "You got away with that?" He helped her into the car, the anxious chauffeur watching each movement most critically, the two young men ballet-stepping around.

"But I had called him a *peasant.* That was what he liked to call himself. It won votes. Now, if I had called him what I *really* felt he was—a pig in the gutter—I shouldn't be here today." She sighed, settled herself on the car's white leather seat, and gave him her hand in good-by. "So I lived on. I don't really know who had the last word, though, the pig or I."

He closed the car's polished blue door carefully. Very small, quietly conspicuous was its minuscule coat of arms. He watched the car ease its way carefully into the busy traffic, before he turned back to the café. He was still smiling. Perhaps now he'd enjoy that drink he'd promised himself half an hour ago. But the little group at the table was not yet dispersed.

"My aunt amuses you?" Pirotta asked.

"She tells a good story." He began to laugh again. "I was hearing about her meeting with Mussolini."

Pirotta groaned humorously. "You really thought it was funny?"

"Don't you?"

"The first time, perhaps." He made a comical face, and yet lost none of his dignity.

Eleanor looked at them both with relief. This was the way she liked life: no jealousy, no dislikes, no animosities. "You *are* going to stay here and enjoy Italy, aren't you, Bill?" Perhaps she wanted to rid herself of all feeling that she had ruined his visit here.

"If one is offered a house," Whitelaw said, "one generally accepts." He was amused, interested, but not unkind. "You made quite a hit with the old girl, didn't you?"

"But surely," Lammiter said, "the princess didn't mean it."

They all stared at him.

"Now," he said, "don't tell me anyone can believe a word she says."

Pirotta's handsome eyes smiled suddenly with relief. "I'm afraid not," he said with regret.

"No dinner party tomorrow night?" Eleanor asked, in a strange tight little voice, the kind she used when she didn't quite believe what was said.

"If we went," Pirotta answered gently, "we might find that my aunt had forgotten to tell her housekeeper that she had suddenly invented a dinner party, here, at Doney's. She is getting old. Good-by, Lammiter."

They didn't shake hands.

"Good-by," Lammiter said, equally crisp.

Whitelaw's good-by was regretful. Perhaps, now that Lammiter seemed about to leave Rome, luncheon would be rather a waste of time and energy. "I hadn't noticed how late it was," he said, consulting his watch, "and I have an engagement this afternoon. It might be wiser to postpone our luncheon? One hates to rush coffee. Some other day?" He turned aside, then halted to exchange a few last words with Pirotta.

Eleanor took the opportunity to say, "I'll feel awful if you take the first plane home! Truly, Bill, I don't want to spoil everything." She looked at him pleadingly. "I wish you would stop thinking the worst of me. I'm sorry. I'm truly sorry." Perhaps she had seen Garbo in that recent revival of *Camille,* for now she was neither standing at the head of a marble staircase nor marching on the barricade of machine guns, but she was making the great renunciation.

"I know," he said, "it hurt you more than it hurt me." But he ought to have denied himself the pleasures of sarcasm.

She looked sharply at him, and her voice altered. "So it was all a little act."

"Eleanor!" he said reproachfully. He wondered if Pirotta's quick ears had been listening.

"I wondered—I never saw you so silent and wide-eyed."

"But I was so impressed. A princess, and a count! My, my, my . . . "

"Bill Lammiter! And I almost believed you had changed."

"Just the same old Bill," he said reassuringly. "I'm stuck with me. You know something?"

"No," she said quickly. "I don't want to know it."

"Then we'll make it a real good-by." He put out his hand. Quietly, he said, "I hope you'll be very happy."

She looked at him uncertainly, and then—as Pirotta came over to take her by the arm—she decided to accept that at its full value. "Thank you," she said, bowing a little.

"Madame la Comtesse receiving the good wishes of the local peasantry," Lammiter said with a little grin.

"Oh, Bill!" She was angry.

And suddenly, unexpectedly, he was sorry. But she was already leaving with her noble count. She was talking with vivacity and charm to emphasize how much Lammiter had lost. Oh, stop that! he told himself: it doesn't even make you feel any better.

At least, he thought wearily as he sat down for a delightfully solitary drink, she will not see me again, she won't invite me to her parties and try to find another girl for me and tell me how intelligent we are to remain such good dear friends. I'll be spared all that, thank God.

And then a most depressing thought struck him, suddenly, vehemently. At this moment, Eleanor might be angry with him, but she still liked him. She was still fond of him. But what would she feel when he discovered more about Pirotta? Hate, possibly. She's going to hate you, he told himself morosely. By God, and how! No one liked the man who unveiled the illusion. It would be easier if he cabled her father, got him to come over and save his darling daughter (and himself) from scandal. But that was too easy: ditching responsibility, escaping hate, was too easy a way out. Besides, the girl Rosana could be lying. Pirotta could be an honest son of a bitch after all. I'll have to find that out for myself, he thought. I'll have to stay in Rome, and find out the truth; and, if it's ugly, then calculate how it affects Eleanor, and then— And then?

His depression grew. He put the question away from him. He hoped he would never have to answer it.

Lammiter had another glass of beer, to let Eleanor and Pirotta put several blocks between them and Doney's. He resisted all temptation to pull out Rosana's crumpled wad of paper which had been burning a hole in his pocket for almost an hour: for now he was in a mood to listen to the need for caution. At last, and leisurely, he left the emptying tables and set off for a small restaurant he liked near the Via Ludovisi. To reach it, he crossed the Via Vittorio Veneto, its traffic now noticeably sparse, and he stopped at the paper stall at the corner of the two streets and bought himself *Time* and *Oggi*. So armed for a lonely meal, he walked on under the shady trees. And he wondered about several people.

He wondered about the princess, who must have postponed her escape to the hills this summer, for the weather was now hot and sticky and promised worse. Why? She hadn't run out of houses, obviously. The old Roman families (who never called themselves Italian) didn't usually spend the tourist months in the city. Nor did they make a habit of frequenting restaurants or cafés very much, and then usually in the late afternoon, when they'd quiz the foreigners' parade and store up some witticisms for dinner.

("Mr. Lammiter, to what do you attribute your percipient knowledge of the Roman way of life?"

"Talk with the waiters, son. Nice long conversations with waiters and barmen, the trusted friends of the lonely traveler."

"Waiters, Mr. Lammiter?"

"Sure. They are just waiting to tell you. Start them talking, son, and you cain't stop 'em. . . . They'll give you more to brood over than a carload of guidebooks. They're all strangers here, too. Did you know that people in the Abruzzi believe in werewolves? Let me tell you about the old waiter from the Abruzzi who once slept beside a werewolf.")

Werewolf . . . And I never did puzzle that story out, he thought. The man had believed what he had seen with his own eyes. In the waiters' dormitory, the young boy who had just come from the Abruzzi used to start up with a howl when the summer moon was full, while the other waiters buried their heads in the sheets to smother their breathing, and he would leap from his bed and out through the door, to return with the dawn, calm, quiet, unseeing, unhearing, already half asleep on his feet. "A werewolf," the older waiter had repeated. "Such things happen in my country." It's possible, Lammiter reflected, that the boy was simply so homesick for the mountains and forests of the Abruzzi that he'd lie awake on a hot summer night crying to himself. Italians were a regional people, their loyalty to the childhood places deep and passionate. And then there would come a moment when the memories became unbearable, the strangled sob broke loose into a howl of despair, and he'd rush from the room where the older men (their memories now blurred by city life) were lying awake, listening to him, watching.

Now, what made me start thinking about werewolves? Surely not the princess. Nor Bertrand Whitelaw, even if he was a tortured man. What troubled him, anyway? He had the best of all his possible worlds: he was published regularly; he had acclaim—and money, too, that nice expendable stuff; he enjoyed all the prestige of a free-born Englishman and suffered none of the tribulations of the British climate. Presumably he was one of those types who didn't need a wife, for he kept himself free from all female entanglements. So what had he to worry about? And then, Lammiter wondered, was Whitelaw's meeting with Pirotta this morning something that had happened quite naturally: Pirotta had been here to keep an eye on Rosana as he waited for Eleanor, and Whitelaw had come strolling along and joined him? Or had it been contrived? If so, who had contrived it? Not Pirotta, Lammiter decided: Pirotta had many things on his mind, but a quiet talk with the Englishman hadn't been one of them. In fact, Pirotta had evaded any chance of a tête-à-tête with considerable skill. Pirotta, Lammiter thought now, was the kind of man who usually got what he wanted.

Then why, if he were innocent of all Rosana's innuendos, why had he sat at that table with Lammiter? The American imagined himself in Pirotta's place: a difficult moment with the princess heaving her variety of monkey wrench into the works. But I, Lammiter thought now, I'd have risen, taken Eleanor's arm, made a firm excuse (and no one was going to refuse any lovers' excuses) and left everyone to gossip to their tongues' content. Instead, Pirotta had sat on, had listened and watched. He had been extremely polite. Almost friendly. Disarming, was the better word. Why?

Lammiter's lips tightened and he quickened his pace. He knew one thing. He would like to spend half an hour with Bunny Camden. Bunny, now one of the naval attachés at the Embassy—liaison work with visiting NATO specialists, Bunny had explained vaguely when they had met, by accident, outside the Embassy gates three days ago—had thc kind of mind that had been trained to add up the facts and subtract the fiction from a puzzling situation. And Bunny Camden was a friend, a word that Lammiter didn't bestow lightly. Even if they only met at the oddest intervals and in the strangest ways—and that, to Lammiter, was part of the amusing aspect of their friendship which kept it alive through all the gaps between their meetings—Camden was someone dependable.

He remembered Bunny's face when they had met outside the Embassy. His own had been just as delighted and amazed—for the last time he had seen Bunny had been in Korea, six years ago. Bunny was one of those Intelligence officers who had decided to stay in the service (in Bunny's case, it was the Marine Corps), and now—a little to his surprise and not altogether to his fancy—he had been promoted to a quasi-diplomatic but completely straightforward job in the Mediterranean area. "Strictly legitimate, now," Bunny had said, talking hard to cover Lammiter's embarrassment at the meeting, for once the delight and amazement were over, Lammiter was too conscious of the fact that he had been caught hovering around the Embassy gates, hoping to intercept Eleanor on her way out to lunch. Not that either Bunny or the friend with him (quite definitely a friend, a classics professor called Ferris from Pennsylvania, who was working at the American Academy in Rome for the summer) could have had any idea why they had found Lammiter waiting at the entrance to the Embassy's driveway; but those who loitered were always sensitive about being discovered. Especially when the discoverer was someone like Bunny Camden. "Hi there!" he had said, catching Lammiter by the arm. "And dammit if it isn't. Thought I knew that old bullet head and standout ears. What are you plotting now? If it's arsenic poisoning, we've already had it." And so Bunny could introduce and squash the current sensation about the Ambassadress and her bedroom ceiling, before he branched onto NATO, a prospective trip to Naples, and then suggested a party when he returned. "We must all get together," he said, including Professor Ferris in his smile, and Lammiter had agreed. Then they parted, and Lammiter hadn't thought much about Bunny Camden's old job or qualifications until Rosana had questioned him this morning. Now that he thought about it, Bunny Camden was just the type that Rosana needed.

Lammiter had reached the restaurant's entrance. He happened to glance back as he was about to enter its doorway. The heat was stifling now. The street was empty: the siesta hour had begun. Except for one man, who had halted near a tree on the opposite side of the street and was busily lighting a cigarette. Lammiter entered, paused, glanced back again over his shoulder. Yes, the man was looking in this direction. Lammiter went into the cool dark room. I saw that man at Doney's, he suddenly thought; just as I was leaving, I noticed him—a man of medium height and construction, thick-haired, dark, bareheaded like most younger Italians, wearing a blue cotton suit and white shirt such as a thousand bank clerks and office workers wore. Except that this one did not carry the usual thin black brief case, which seemed to be a necessary part of a white-collar worker's dress, the badge of his education.

The restaurant was almost empty. He chose a small table under the large ceiling fan. He agreed with the waiter that he was late, tactfully rejected a variety of pasta and hot bean soup, chose chicken *cacciatore,* to be followed by Bel Paese and fresh fruit. "Nothing to begin with, signore, nothing?" The waiter was desolated: like all Italians he enjoyed seeing people eat. But he brought a nicely chilled bottle of Soave Verona, and as he uncorked it, they talked about the vineyard from which it came: Romeo and Juliet territory, east of Verona. The waiter, Lammiter guessed, came from that part of the country, too. (If he had been a Tuscan, Lammiter would have now been drinking Chianti.)

It was a pleasant little exchange, darkened by the shadow of another possible customer, silhouetted briefly against the sunlight outside as he pulled at the door's beaded screen to peer indoors for a moment. The screen fell together again with a shimmer of sweet sound, as the man turned away. The restaurant's owner, a stout motherly woman whose quick business sense missed nothing, called sharply to the waiter to take the new customer's order. "Outside, outside!" she indicated impatiently, so the man in the blue suit must have chosen one of the little tables on the sidewalk. He obviously preferred a table under the hot awning to the emptiness of a room. The waiter halted his graphic description of the two small pointed hills, lying like a maiden's breasts among the vineyards, where the Capulets and the Montagues had built their country castles.

Lammiter sipped the cool white wine, slowly. I wish I had never noticed that man outside, or the brief case he didn't carry, or the cigarette he lit across the street but had thrown away before he looked into this room. I wish I had been left to enjoy my chicken *cacciatore* without the unpleasant thought that I'm being followed.

He took up *Oggi* and pretended to concentrate on his Italian lesson for today. He smoothed out the small wad of paper which Rosana had given him and held it closely against the magazine's printed page. All it contained was a telephone number, followed by a brief phrase: *Before half-past four?* The question mark was a politeness: he wasn't being told, he was being asked. He could almost hear Rosana's voice adding, "Please listen to me, please . . . ."

He slipped the piece of paper quietly back into his pocket. He kept his eyes fixed on *Oggi*'s front page, but his mind was trying to decide on the most discreet way of telephoning. He wished he had had more training in this kind of work. Back in the army, he had taken a course on jujitsu and eye-gouging, like everyone else in his branch of the service. He had also learned to treat elementary ciphers with respect, and deal with maps. But that was all. His friends would never believe that, and they'd be amazed at the predicament in which he now found himself. For although he had always told them the truth—his actual experience in Intelligence work had been boringly limited to routine security measures, nothing remarkable—everyone thought he was being modest about his work in G2. The more he insisted that he was on the lowest rung of the ladder, if he could be said even to have one foot halfway toward it, the more they nodded and fell into a discreet but respectful silence.

It was funny, though, to have this misinterpretation of his army service catch up with him in Rome, of all places. He could probably thank Eleanor for that: when Pirotta had questioned her about him, she had instinctively made him out to be a pretty important type. That's the way women were: anyone they had known well must be exceptional, brilliant. It depressed him now to think how Eleanor might have talked about him. He had rarely felt more depressed. It could have been partly hunger, though, for he began to feel more cheerful when a steaming dish of chicken and vegetables was uncovered before him.

By the time he had reached the stage of peeling a peach, he had decided to telephone Bunny Camden and arrange a quick meeting. There was a telephone at Madam's little desk, but that was too near the doorway and any attentive ears. Besides, it might not be wise to call Bunny at the Embassy; better to get in touch with him indirectly, better to play all this in an overcautious way, better to look ignorant, ineffective, and undangerous. The men who frightened Rosana, her so-called "friends," were just a little too quick in their suspicions. Better, much better, if he gave them no cause to speculate about him, to worry over his actions. And so, no direct telephone call to Bunny Camden. What was the name of the classics professor—the one who had been visiting Bunny at the Embassy three days ago? Ferris, Carl Ferris, now at the American Academy. That was a possibility, in fact the only one he could think of. A visit to the American Academy on the Janiculum Hill was an innocent way to spend the next hour. Quickly, he drank the small cup of bitter coffee, paid his bill, made the correct good-by with its necessary compliments, and braced himself to see the blue suit sweltering outside. But the man had gone. Perhaps Lammiter had eaten too slowly, or the sidewalk table had been too hot, or the man had simply resigned his job in disgust. Anyway, Lammiter enjoyed his walk to the corner of the Via Vittorio Veneto, where he'd find the bus that would take him across the Tiber to the Janiculum. It was only on the bus itself, almost empty at this time of day, that he realized that the man in the blue suit had probably only given way to another. He looked carefully at the three passengers who had got on board along with him. Then he began to smile. "This has gone far enough," he told himself, thankful that he still had enough perspective left to see the ridiculous. "Half of Rome is *not* following you. Stop worrying, stop imagining. Just go to the Academy, find out from the porter where Carl Ferris is staying, and then move on to the next item on your little list."

Ferris received him with some wonder on his thin tanned face. But he was both cordial and pleased to see Lammiter, even at this odd calling-hour. "Come in," he said. He was hastily dressed in shirt and trousers. "Sorry, we were just finishing a siesta." He looked a little embarrassed. He raised his voice, to keep his wife safely wherever she was. "Okay, honey. Just a friend. We'll be in the living room."

"I shan't keep you long," Lammiter said, following Ferris from the little hallway into a high-ceilinged room. "And I'm the one who should be sorry. I didn't realize what time it was." His watch told him it was half-past three.

"We've been here long enough to adopt the Roman habits," Ferris explained with a grin.

"All of them?"

They both laughed. Lammiter was looking round the room with interest. It was furnished in the usual Italian way, but Ferris had added a lot of his own things: books, as you'd expect, plenty of books, on archaeology, Etruscan art, history; large photographs of columned temples, a sculptured torso, a typewriter, and a desk piled with notebooks and manuscript.

"We like the view," Ferris said, pointing to the window, and quickly picking up a black lace brassière lying over the arm of a chair, he retreated toward the bedroom. He came back, fastening his cuffs, and trying to assume control of the interview. "Writing a new play?" he asked.

Lammiter said, "I keep trying to settle down to work. But I've had a bad attack of distraction. Today—well, I've decided to clear up the current batch of problems, and then, perhaps, I'll have some peace to settle down to a hard job of work."

Ferris lit a cigarette and dropped the match carefully into a pot of flowers. "What's on your mind?"

"I want to get in touch with Bunny."

"Well—go ahead!" Ferris pointed. "The telephone is in the hall."

"Would you call for me? I'll wait here. I don't want to call and then find he isn't there."

Ferris glanced at him with a slight look of surprise, followed by amusement. "And then have someone insist that you leave your name? It is odd, isn't it, how a reasonably honest man feels impelled to answer truthfully on the telephone?"

Lammiter grinned. It was pleasant to be judged an honest man, even reasonably so. "You were in OSS?" Ferris looked as if he might have been World War II vintage.

"No. Navy. But I enjoy a good Hitchcock."

"Oh—I'm not on any hush-hush job. Nothing like that."

"Of course not." Ferris smiled broadly. "You sound like a real pal of Bunny's. He's always engaged in some quip or merry prank."

Lammiter liked Professor Ferris's flexible use of language. He also liked the prompt way Ferris moved into the little hall and put the call through. He had to make two calls: one to the Embassy, one to a private address. In both cases he left his own name, a sure sign of failure.

"Bunny's said to be in Naples," he reported when he returned, "but he's expected back some time today. I left word for him to phone me fastest. Where can I have him reach you when he does get back?"

"I don't know. I've practically checked out of my hotel. There's just the luggage to collect and the last bill to pay."

"You're leaving Rome?"

"Well—no. Not actually." He hesitated. "I just want to keep some people guessing."

"Oh?" Ferris would make a good dean of students. Lammiter found he was clearing his throat nervously, almost ready to tell the whole story.

"Oh, just some people. Some people who seem pretty eager to have me leave." He grinned suddenly. "Don't ask me why. I'm staying to find out the answer for myself. But I'd like it to appear that I really was going back home—and when I do stay, I'll make it look like a sudden impulse."

Ferris nodded. He was bewildered but polite.

"So—" Lammiter rushed on, "I'd like to keep telephoning you here, to see if Bunny has been run to earth. I'd like his advice on something. What's your number?"

Ferris scribbled it down on a piece of paper. "I'll be here most of the day," he said, pointing to the books opened on his desk. "I'm finishing a paper to deliver this weekend at the opening of the summer school in Perugia." Then he noticed Lammiter's gradual edging toward the door. He smiled, "Well, I shan't keep you now."

"Good-by," Lammiter said, restraining his eagerness. "And many thanks. In fact, many many thanks." He added truthfully, "Hope we get together some day."

"I'll give you a ring when we come up to New York for Christmas shopping. Perhaps Bunny will be on leave then, and we can make it a party. You knew him in Korea, didn't you? He makes a good story of the time you met."

They shook hands. A clatter of high heels on a marble floor suddenly made Ferris snatch the cigarette from his lips, nick its burning end with his fingers, and then jam the broken stub into the cuff of his trousers. "Gave up smoking months ago," he said cheerfully as he opened the door. "Doctor's orders. Sure you won't stay for coffee? That's one thing our small gas ring can cook around here."

"Some other time. Oh, by the way, you are a historian, aren't you? How long did that Roman wall—the Aurelian Wall—how long did it keep out the barbarians?"

"More than a hundred years."

"Then they might have managed it?"

"The Romans? Yes. If only they had invented gunpowder." Ferris was delighted by the effect this produced. "Or a United Nations. Or both." He smiled. "Yes, they might have been here yet. Frankly, I don't know whether it's better that they aren't still around. They'd be too clever for the rest of us, by this time." He smiled again. "Good-by."

"See you in New York." Lammiter ran lightly down the flights of shallow stairs, his hand sliding down the smooth stone banisters. Once this house had been a villa standing in its own grounds; now, the various floors were broken into small apartments. Someone moved on the landing above; a small hard object, a pebble, a nail, grated under a cautious shoe. The little sound was silenced so quickly that Lammiter knew that someone regretted it and was now standing motionless, not even daring to breathe. For a moment, he wondered if he should retrace his steps just to spread more alarm and confusion. But he continued on his way, whistling cheerfully. Nothing that had been said either near or actually at the door of Ferris's apartment could possibly be interesting to anyone else.

In the hall, he stopped to look at the eighteenth-century ceiling, now peeling here and there, fading in patches, a little scabby. But there was still plenty of opulent draperies, pearly arms, pink chins, sofalike clouds, and a sunburst over all. A young man came out of the ground-floor apartment, leaving the sound of a piano, *fortissimo brillante,* behind him, and caught Lammiter craning back his neck to admire the painting.

"Hits you with a splash, doesn't it? You'll get a better view from the top floor," he suggested.

"I've had my quota of stairs for today."

"You at the school?"

"No. Just visiting an old friend before I leave for home." From above, there came no sound of movement.

"Thought I hadn't seen you around much. Like a lift into town?"

"Thanks, I would."

"Most people do. There's a long wait between buses."

They left the villa with its curlicued trim around the front door, stepped onto the half-acre of sparse gravel which formed the garden along with clusters of rhododendron bushes, and passed through the elaborate gate, broad enough to take a coach and four. The young man started his motor bicycle. "Hold my books, will you?" He thrust a small pile of learned-looking objects into Lammiter's arms. "All set?" Lammiter, perched behind, could only nod and grip with his knees.

They roared down the Janiculum Hill toward the river. Lammiter laughed. His driver half turned his head, and the bike swerved sharply.

"Nothing, nothing!" Lammiter yelled. And then he thought he ought to offer a plausible explanation. "I just thought of the people waking up from a siesta and cursing our noise."

"Noise?" The young man looked perplexed, listened for engine trouble, and then took the bridge over the Tiber at full throttle.

But even after Lammiter, temporarily bowlegged, had dismounted and said good-by to his benefactor (nameless and asking no name, just one of the friendly souls who offered a lift in the same spirit they'd accept it), he was still amused by the vision that had suddenly burst upon him as they roared down the twisting Janiculum road toward Father Tiber. It was a vision of someone most serious, who had indeed followed him into the villa, who must have come hurrying out too late, only to see Lammiter, complete with schoolbooks, perched on the rear of a motor bicycle, careering down between the Janiculum trees. He would very much like to see the written report on the Afternoon of Signore William Lammiter.

At the hotel, the porter's desk announced with quiet triumph that there was space available on the midnight plane. Lammiter paid his last bill, told the porter he'd collect the ticket himself, and found his luggage in the entrance hall, where it had already been deposited. No doubt there was some new American in his room, standing on his balcony, smoking a cigarette, wondering about the Aurelian Wall which he overlooked, admiring the giant crowns of the huge pine tree beyond in the Gardens. He wished he could have had just one minute to say good-by to that view. It had cheered him up on many a night in these last few weeks. He hadn't been happy. But he had liked that balcony, the sunset, the moonrise, the flight of the swallows. It would have been pleasant just to have had one last look around from the balcony. But life wasn't a playwright, drawing everything neatly into a final scene and last act. Life had a way of surprising and not explaining and turning you out into the street without one moment for sentiment.

Perhaps just as well, he thought: he hadn't much time to waste now. It was just after four o'clock. And what would be the safest way to telephone Rosana? He was taking not the smallest chance that his movements weren't of interest to Pirotta and his organization—Rosana's hated "friends." As for his own role in this strange fantasy, he'd find out when he saw her. He'd find out a lot of things. That was the end purpose of the telephone call as far as he was concerned. Then he decided how he could both telephone and evade anyone following him. He made his way through the crowded lobby, and signaled to the doorman for a taxi from the cab rank across the street. "To the airport," he told the doorman. He was conscious of a man who, circling vaguely around, now stood within earshot.

He had come prepared for a touching farewell. His pocket was bulging with hundreds of lire notes (he'd be glad when it was empty of the tattered scraps of paper sticky with age: handling them, he began to understand the Wyoming cowboys who wouldn't touch dollar bills; they weren't real money. Silver dollars might need leather-lined pockets but at least they felt and sounded like something) and his progress through the hall to the doorway was triumphant but embarrassing. Everyone, even the second *facchino,* who had once taken his shoes to the cobbler's, had gathered nonchalantly along his route of dispersal. A taxi was waiting—and within one minute of his last good-by, he was being driven down the Via Vittorio Veneto, past Doney's where the postsiesta crowd was already on view (all washed and perfumed and powdered, bare heads shining and carefully dressed, fresh low-necked dresses with wide skirts swirling over tanned legs and barefooted sandals), down into the business section of the city, past the fountains, the buses and jammed cars, the narrow sidewalks encrusted with human beings, to reach the American Express office near the Spanish Steps.

"The signore is going to the airport? Then I wait?" the driver asked as Lammiter prepared to climb warily out of the small green taxi—legs got trapped by the up-and-over step at the door of every Roman cab. Lammiter looked sharply at him. But then he realized it was only the Italians' magnificent communication system designed to make a traveler's life as well served as possible: it was amazing how thoughtful an Italian could be for other people's comfort. Anyway, one always had to take the first taxi in the waiting rank: this man had come to him in his right and fair turn. There was a protocol about being hired that would defeat any planted cab trying to pick up a special fare.

Lammiter relaxed. "Too long," he said tactfully. The Italian gestured that that didn't matter, he could wait. "Too much money," Lammiter added with a sad shake of the head. The Italian looked regretful, but he understood that.

"The signore speaks good Italian," he said wistfully. "*Molto bello!*"

"I know about four sentences," Lammiter said with a grin, pleased and modestly untruthful, "and you've heard two of them." They had the usual attack of conversation. The driver came from the province of

Calabria, which explained *his* accent—and then, with good wishes to the driver's wife and two *bambini* and the canary that wakened them too early every morning (better be careful, that one, Lammiter thought: the early bird in Italy was apt to end up grilled for lunch), and pleasure expressed in the success of the immigrant brother in Schenectady (*that* was something to hear pronounced) who grew his own grapes in his back yard and made his own wine, they parted. Lammiter carried his two cases, with his typewriter uncomfortably gripped under his arm, into the cheerful bedlam of the American Express offices. The noise was overwhelming: the afternoon mail was being collected and the crowd was enormous, mostly American and very young. It was odd how you instinctively raised your voice the minute you started talking to a foreigner, as if you thought that loudness would make you clearer. The Italian English-speaking clerks behind their counters listened with tolerant good humor.

Lammiter looked round for a free corner where he could unload his luggage before his arm cramped up. He found one beside a girl who was tearing open a letter she had just picked up at the mail desk. She was on the young side of twenty, a blonde, with her hair caught back at the crown of her head by a perky blue bow, smartly dressed (how did girls, traveling, keep themselves so crisp and neat?), cool, capable, confident, and—judging by the way she was opening her letter—as homesick as a six-week-old puppy dog shut up in the baggage car. "Telephones?" he asked her, as he set down his cases.

She looked up wide-eyed from the letter's first lines. "Telephones? Upstairs, I think."

"Upstairs?" He looked at his baggage and then at the crowd.

"Do you want me to look after these things for you?" she asked patiently, eager to get back to her letter.

"Would you?"

"Sure. Don't be long, though. I'm meeting some friends." And they'd all troop out with their letters to the Spanish Steps; and there they'd sit, while they read and discussed the letters from home, on the long long flight of old stone stairs, the flower stalls and the fountain at their feet, the old church raising its towers above their heads. It was the daily ritual.

"Don't worry," he promised her. She nodded, sat down on one of his suitcases, and went back to her letter. He eased his way through the tight crush. It wasn't possible that everybody knew everybody else, and yet, bumping against a quiet young man and exchanging an understanding grin for their common predicament as they made way for each other, he felt they might have all belonged to the same town. Suddenly he felt ancient, although actually he was only about ten years older than most of them.

He managed, after two false starts, to call the number Rosana had given him. "Hello there," he said. "Ready or not, here we are." Just when he began to wonder if he had been cut off, he heard Rosana's voice.

"Where are you? Not at the hotel?"

"No," he said, amused at her concern for his lack of caution. "No. Nor at any place where I'm likely to be known. And I have my luggage with me."

"Take a taxi to the station. When will you get there?"

"In twenty minutes, possibly fifteen."

"Can you delay that a little? Make it five o'clock."

"At the station? Where?"

"Just get out at the main entrance. Giuseppe will meet you. You saw him today."

"Did I?"

"He drove the princess's car."

"Oh! Well, that should be easy."

"Perhaps. I hope so. But don't be rash. Please." She sounded worried.

"Five o'clock?" he asked soothingly. He heard the telephone go dead.

Funny, he thought, all foreigners believed Americans were rash. If they only knew us properly . . . Then he smiled as he descended slowly (he had time to waste) into the crowded room. How many of the young Americans here could talk or understand Italian? How little money had they in their pockets, how few traveler's checks to last their ambitious journeys? How many thousands of miles traveled, how many still to go? Rash? Ambitious, perhaps. But not rash, if you remembered the months of planning, the budgets calculated to the last dollar, the guidebooks studied, the maps memorized in private. His thoughts halted abruptly. Near the door, he saw the man he had noticed in the hotel lobby. Coincidence? Anyway, the man was leaving.

"There you are!" the blonde girl said in relief, and rose from his suitcase. She stuffed the letter pad she had begun to use into her outsize handbag. "Are you really William Lammiter? The one who wrote *Home Is the Hunter?*"

Cursing inwardly, Lammiter glanced down at the labels on his suitcases. She had looked so childlike and unnoticing with her candid blue eyes and her pretty little bow. He smiled. "Did you like it?"

She was frank, at least. "I haven't seen it yet. I live in Burbank. That's California," she explained carefully. Californians were always so helpful. "Mr. Lammiter, would you do something for me? I'm writing to Mother and Dad. Look—here it is." She drew out the pad of paper from her handbag. "You see, I'm answering this letter I got today. Dad fusses. So I'm writing to tell him I look fine—got all my teeth and both eyes. Look—would you bear witness to that? Right here . . ." She pointed to a small asterisk in the margin of her letter.

He had given enough autographs in the last six months to have stopped hesitating at signing his name. (At first it had troubled him.) But still he glanced at what he was going to sign. He said with a grin, "I always read the small print." It was a harmless letter home, gay and affectionate. "Are you traveling alone?" he asked her. No wonder her father was worried.

"Yes."

"How long have you been here?"

"In Rome? Oh, just five days. But I've been traveling since school ended in June. I went to England first, and I saw Scotland, too—I loved that; and then I went to France, and then Spain—oh, it was wonderful in Seville. Four days there. I went out every night to hear the gypsies sing. They live in caves. Have you heard them?"

He shook his head, and began to write.

"They're the most," she said dreamily.

"You've run into no trouble?" Heavens, he thought, I'm going paternal.

She eyed him frankly. She smiled. "I've met nothing but gentlemen, except for one fat slob of a middle-aged—" She brushed that aside. "I laughed so much, I thought I'd go into a fit or something. He was furious. Funny, isn't it?—It's always the ugliest and oldest who think they are irresistible. He—" She broke off. "Hi—Tommy!" She waved to a tall young man in a shirt with a buttoned-down collar.

"Hi, Sally! See you on the Steps!" Tommy said, with a searching glance at Lammiter.

Sally confided, "I met him in London, and then again on the bus from Naples. That's the nice thing about traveling—you always keep meeting up with people. What did you write there?" She wrinkled her brow as she read the closely written lines.

All descriptions of your daughter endorsed. Wherever she has landed, the situation seems well in hand. At least half the college students in America are having their school picnic abroad this summer. Like Sally, they're healthy, still solvent, and completely cheerful. You ought to see them, though, lining up for a letter from home.

"Why, that's genius!"

"*Thank* you."

"But it is!" She gave him a wide, even white teeth gleaming, smile.

"Needs cutting," he said, rereading his composition. "I always write too much. Get carried away, I suppose. Good-by and good luck. And thank you for taking charge of my luggage."

"Thank *you,* Mr. Lammiter. I'll let you know what I think of your play."

She would, too. They shook hands solemnly.

In spite of these delaying tactics, he arrived fully five minutes early at the station. Fortunately, he had scarcely time to step out from the hot small cab onto the hot wide sidewalk before a porter arrived, which gave him something to argue about. That was better than standing alone before a modern railway station, with its vast stretches of windows and glass doors to make a man feel both observed and vulnerable.

"No, thank you," he told the porter, looking around the open square in front of the station.

"*Sì, sì, signore,*" the man insisted. "Your friend waits near the wall. His car is there." He hoisted the suitcases and led the way to the side of the station building, where an ancient wall—a collection of giant squared-off boulders—lay outcropped against the station's glass and concrete.

Here was another open space, cars, some moving, some waiting. A small gray Fiat edged toward the porter and then stopped. "*Ecco!*" the porter said, swinging a door open and the luggage inside. He didn't even count the money that Lammiter held out to him. Then all this probably *was* right, Lammiter decided, in the sense that it was arranged. But the Fiat troubled him. Not its size, not its color: he had noticed a hundred small gray Fiats since one of them had waited for Rosana beneath his hotel window last night. It was the license plate that bothered him: its three last numbers—all he had been able to see from his hotel balcony—were identical with those on the abduction car. He hesitated. Then he thought, this is interesting, this is very interesting. He moved to the car door.

"Hurry!" said the driver impatiently.

The car was so compact that Lammiter could only see the man at the wheel properly as he stooped to enter. Yes, he verified as his memory kept on stirring, it could be the same man who had driven the princess's noble and aged Lancia. A dark-eyed man, about thirty-five or so, with coarse black curling hair, combed, long and thick, back from a broad brow whose permanent wrinkles looked more like furrows, giving him a constant look of surprise. His skin, sallow and coarse, was like untanned leather. He had given up his chauffeur's dark blue uniform, and wore a white short-sleeved cotton shirt open at the neck. His arms were brown, muscular, well covered with strong black hair. His teeth were white, his smile infectious, his American strongly accented but completely fluent and assured. "I'm Joe," he said. "Giuseppe is too much to say. Call me Joe. What the hell kept you?"

Ah, we're being informal, Lammiter decided. "I thought I was early."

"Sure. That, yes. I mean when you followed the porter. You were slow. What's so funny about the car? Got a bashed fender or something?"

Lammiter made his voice as offhand as possible. "I was wondering whether I ought to buy a Fiat."

"What for?" Joe's furrows were marked.

"To take back home with me. Doesn't use much gas."

"What do you want a Fiat for?" Joe asked, shocked. "You could get a Chrysler or a Caddie."

"Or a Lancia like the princess?"

They both laughed. "That's some car!" Joe said. "Almost thirty years old. It's a—a—" he searched for the word.

"A period piece?" Lammiter suggested.

Joe's furrows deepened, trying to understand all the possible meanings, before agreeing.

"It matches the princess," Lammiter added.

"It sure does. It's period, all right. I'm nursing it through traffic and it comes to a full stop. Period. Get it?" He laughed uproariously.

"Where did you learn your American?" Lammiter asked.

"I drove for an American colonel."

"World War II?"

"Sure."

"Where are you from?"

"Sicily. Came up with the Americans, all the way."

"And you never went farther than Rome?"

Joe's face became absolutely blank. He concentrated on winding his way through traffic. At last, noncommittally, he said, "I liked Rome. It never got hurt by the war. I had enough of bombed-out buildings and ruins."

"Ruins—that reminds me. What about that wall back there?" It seemed a safer topic than Joe's life.

"Wall?"

"The huge chunks of stone, just outside the station."

"Oh, they're good and old. Older than anything else you see around this town. You like that kind of thing? What are you—a professor or something?"

"No, just curious."

Joe studied his face. "I guess you are," he said quietly, "or you wouldn't be in this car." Then he laughed and turned the conversation back to classical remains. "If you want ruins, you come to Sicily some day. We got older ruins than anybody else. Older than the princess."

"But she's better preserved?"

Joe's smile was real now. "She looks better by moonlight, too." He thought about the princess. "*She's* something, isn't she?" There was a mixture of admiration and dislike, mixed with a grudging respect, in his voice.

"She certainly is." Lammiter noticed with interest that the car had made a long detour, almost back to the Spanish Steps, before it now swerved southwest, by busy narrow streets, toward the Tiber. "How long have you worked for her?" he asked casually.

"Since Signorina Di Feo's brother died." Joe's face was blank again, but there was a new grim note in his voice.

"You worked for him?"

Joe nodded, and seemed now to be concentrating on this busy section of the city. Down here, near the river, the narrow streets crisscrossed and twisted, passing yellow walls with plaster peeling, baroque churches, small piazzas, ancient fountains, Roman pillars, posters on every wall, a ruined temple, a busy trolley-bus terminal, a hodgepodge of twenty centuries. Lammiter had the feeling that they had already doubled and then redoubled back on their tracks. It was a part of Rome that always gave you that feeling, anyway, even if you were walking as straight as the flight of a bullet. But Joe was being cautious. He had a quick way of looking into the rearview mirror, of glancing left, then right, as the car was halted at a street corner. And the only sign that he was as impatient as Lammiter to reach their destination was the way his hand, as he waited for the lights to turn green, would smack several times on the gearshift as if to say, "Let's go, let's go!"

Lammiter wasn't quite sure, but he had an idea they were approaching the Piazza Navona. (He had dined several times down there, in what had once been a Roman emperor's stadium—the Piazza was actually the long oval where the chariots had raced.) Yes, they were entering its gateway now. The three Bernini fountains were spaced down the center of the long oval where the crowds of children now played and women gossiped as they watched them. All these people lounging around, enjoying the early evening sun which turned the yellow plaster walls into a soft gold, couldn't possibly live in the houses, numerous as they were, that edged the Piazza: some did belong to these flats and rooms in the old converted eighteenth-century houses, but most must come from the dark narrow streets, cobbled lanes, which led off on all sides. It baffled Lammiter trying to think of how many families could live in the square mile around the Piazza. For once, all those pigeons looking for love and bread-crumbs would be outnumbered.

"You get out at the church," Joe said. "See that red-haired guy at the fountain opposite? That's Salvatore. Call him Sam. I always do. He'll take you from there."

"To where?" And then, "What about my luggage?"

"I'll keep it safe."

"Look—" Lammiter began. But the car had already stopped.

"Quick!" Joe said, reaching across Lammiter to open the door. There was no time to argue.

"Don't lose that typewriter!" Lammiter said sharply, and got out. The car drove on. He was left at the steps to the church, a contorted variety of baroque with just one adornment too many. Architects should beware of their afterthoughts.

"Hello!" a quiet voice said, and a friendly hand was slipped through his arm. "This way," the red-haired man said.

Lammiter glanced down at the hand on his arm. He had been told, and had believed until now, that Italians disliked and even avoided personal contact with strangers. Unless, of course, the stranger was a pretty woman with a fine pair of hips. Lammiter himself didn't particularly enjoy being arm in arm with a man whom he didn't know. He twisted round to look again at the church commanding the Piazza Navona, and the man's hand had to drop away from his arm.

"I agree that the church has a certain fascination," the amiable voice said. "A horrible sight, isn't it?"

"It isn't as bad as all that. It could have used a little restraint, perhaps."

"You must visit it some other time. But now—this way, Mr. Lammiter."

And then as Lammiter hesitated, looking at the narrow street, no more than eight feet wide, toward which his new guide had turned, the man said, "Dear me, I always forget the formalities. I'm Salvatore, although Joe insists on calling me Sam. I find it simpler not to argue with Joe. He is a Sicilian." The pleasant smile broadened. "Now, have I identified myself sufficiently? I am sorry I am such a rank amateur. I ought to have carried a broken eggshell which would fit into the one you should have in your pocket." Then the voice changed, becoming impatient and authoritative. "Come. We are not here to enjoy the view."

He led the way into the narrow street, darkened by the high buildings edging its worn cobblestones.

Salvatore was one of the red-haired Italians, a type with gray eyes, thin-cheeked face, hawk features. His head was noble, if a little out of proportion with his body, for he was short and slightly built. Yet, Lammiter remembered, the grasp on his arm had been firm and decided. But polite. As polite as the pleasant voice. The man was a superb linguist: he kept up a constant chatter in his excellent English. He never hesitated for a noun, searched for the correct tense of a verb, or failed to produce the conversational phrase.

"Yes, indeed," Salvatore was saying, now back on the subject of the church where they had met, "Bernini would have agreed with you. You know Bernini, of course? He designed the fountains in the Piazza—oh, and many more, all over Rome. Churches, too. But these fountains in the Piazza—did you notice how Bernini arranged the figures in the central one that faces the church? He made some look away and others shield their eyes with their hands from the awful sight." Salvatore laughed. "Delicious, simply delicious. And very naughty. Don't you think so, Mr. Lammiter? Or what *are* you thinking?"

"You didn't learn your English driving an American colonel around Italy." And, Lammiter thought, am I the only one around here who has a second name?

"Ah—you've been listening to Joe." He shook his head. "Those were his happiest days, driving colonels into shell holes. Actually, I was an interpreter during part of the war, with the English. Now, of course" —the gray eyes were briefly amused, and the thin mouth smiled gently —"I am a guide. The old ladies' tours love me. My historical dates are always reliable, my anecdotes pure. This way, Mr. Lammiter." Salvatore halted, looked quickly back over his shoulder, looked again ahead, and then side-stepped into a dim doorway filled with cats. "Quick!" he said, and Lammiter found himself following without argument this time. But he had plenty of thoughts as he stood in a dark stone hallway. If anything happened to him, anything unpleasant, then —well, it was too late now. He had begun walking into this hallway when Rosana Di Feo had persuaded him to meet her at Doney's. He had also the thought that Salvatore had talked in order to baffle his sense of direction. Could it be possible they had almost retraced their steps to the Piazza Navona? He had felt they had been circling around, gently but definitely.

"Where—" he began. Salvatore made a signal for caution so determined that Lammiter found himself obeying it. In any case, having come this far from a table at the Café Doney, he might as well continue without asking where he was going. He would find out, soon enough. He did allow himself to comment on Salvatore's maneuvers, "Very professional —for an amateur." Salvatore shot him a keen glance, smiled, too, and murmured, "Thank you." Then in silence they began the ascent.

The stairway was of stone, with every tread hollowed into a drooping curve by two hundred years of footsteps. Enough light filtered down from a window in the roof to let him see the cats, in the corners of the landings, scattering angrily from the crumpled sheets of newspaper which held something that looked very unappetizingly like cold pieces of spaghetti.

Salvatore stopped at the last landing, leaned over the staircase-well to check on the shadows below. Here, in the far corner of the landing, one cat was so hungry that it didn't run away. It stood looking over its shoulder, hostile, suspicious, curious, hopeful. Then, as Salvatore knocked gently on a door, the cat relaxed its taut muscles. It turned back to gulping down its cold pasta, while, in silence, they waited.

There were two people in the room: a seated man, bald-headed, who didn't rise, but turned his chin over his shoulder to look at the stranger much as the cat had done; and Rosana, standing behind the door, now closing it quickly.

It was a quiet room, shadowed at the threshold, but opposite the door —over by the wide-open window—it glowed in the warm light of a Roman evening. There was a pot of red geraniums on the broad window sill, with their clear spicy scent; some books, papers, and a small radio on the desk near the armchair where the man sat; a wardrobe highly varnished, cheap; a wooden table with wine and food—bread and cheese, a bowl of peaches; a narrow bed neatly made. Children's voices from below came soaring up along with the noise of falling water. The evening breeze, touched with unexpected coolness, flowed past the heavy shutters which were folded back to let every breath of fresh air enter and swirl round the room. The geraniums, the fruit, the scent of roses and jasmine which Rosana wore, all emphasized the freshness of the clean air, so great was the contrast between this pleasant unpretentious place and the staleness of the sour-smelling mysteries of the staircase outside.

"Here he is," Salvatore said as if he were a conjurer producing a lighted cigarette from his ear. "A little dazed, I think, but still curious. See?" For Lammiter had moved quickly over to the window and stood at its side, as he looked down.

"Thank you, Salvatore," the girl said, "I hope we didn't make you late for your own appointment. But Giuseppe is on duty at six."

"And the princess can't be kept waiting, while my flock of Swedish schoolteachers can? Now, now, Rosana, that was only a joke. I'll be in good time for the schoolteachers."

"You ought to leave now," Rosana said worriedly. She came over to the window, too.

Lammiter had been right. He was looking down at the Piazza Navona. He had been guided carefully in a wide arc, by a maze of narrow alleys, to the cobbled street that backed the buildings along this side of the Piazza. Was all the precaution to impress him? Or perhaps these people were really afraid.

"Satisfied?" the bald-headed man asked. He didn't sound either welcoming or particularly friendly. Lammiter looked at him, and saw why the man sat immobile. His right leg was out of action, its ankle bandaged, stiff, propped up on the footrest before the armchair. He was probably in some pain. That might explain his bad temper, or the fact that he had a large fiasco of Chianti too near his elbow.

Rosana said pleadingly, "Tony—please!" She tried to explain to Lammiter, "This is my friend Anthony Brewster, an Englishman who—"

"All right, all right," Brewster said. He must have been fond of the girl, for he looked as if he would have bitten off anyone else's head and chewed it into little pieces. He took a deep breath, and studied Lammiter gloomily. Lammiter was in no mood to be outstared.

The Englishman was about forty years old, with a powerful body now beginning to run to fat. His legs seemed short, so he probably was only of medium height when he stood on his feet. He wasn't completely bald. Once he had had fine reddish-fair hair to match his eyebrows and lashes; now, he had only a slight fuzz of thinned-out pinfeathers, beginning in a line over his ears and stretching back in longer strands to the nape of a weather-reddened neck. Normally, his blue eyes might have been both shrewd and merry above a shapeless clown's nose and a friendly mouth in a brick-complexioned face. He was intended to look both round and genial. But this evening he was neither. He was sharp and bitter. His general good nature had vanished. He looked angry, worried, suspicious, sullen, stubborn. "I didn't want you here," he told Lammiter abruptly.

"Then I'll leave," Lammiter said equably. He looked at the door where Salvatore still stood. On guard? Salvatore had been turning the key in the lock, slowly, carefully. For a moment he looked startled, as if he hadn't expected Lammiter to leave so suddenly. And then, it was Lammiter who was surprised: hadn't Rosana locked the door after they had entered? "If you didn't trust me, then why did you have me brought here?" He took a few steps over to the door.

"Oh, stop being so thin-skinned," Brewster said. His voice was slowing. "Come back. Over here. And stop towering over me. Sit down. Rosana insists you can be trusted." He paused. When he spoke again, his words were uttered with considerable effort. "She has a weakness for Americans, particularly when they are tall and not—not—unprepossessing." He smiled around him, as if delighted with his victory over that word. "I hear you're famous, too. And rich."

Lammiter's face had hardened. "I don't have to stay," he reminded Brewster. He didn't sit down.

Rosana said, "Please—don't leave." She looked toward the Englishman unhappily. "Tony's ill. He's had no sleep for three nights."

He's drunk, Lammiter thought. It's useless staying here. And somehow, he felt a crushing disappointment. He had expected too much from this interview. He looked at Rosana, then at Salvatore, who had come forward into the room. Brewster's eyes had closed. The hell with this, Lammiter thought, and took a step back toward the door.

Salvatore said quickly, "We never like to leave by the way we entered. Let me show you another way, Mr. Lammiter, much simpler."

Rosana was upset. "No, no—not yet."

Salvatore pointed to Brewster. "He's had no sleep for three nights. Now he wants to sleep. And you want to waken him?" He shook his head, and then he smiled gently, as he looked at the Englishman. "Let him sleep. Then he will be more himself when we have the meeting tonight. Mr. Lammiter can come back then. This way, Mr. Lammiter." He had opened another door, a small door in a side wall, which Lammiter had, until this moment, imagined as leading into a closet; now he saw it led into a small hall used as a kitchen.

Lammiter hesitated. Salvatore seemed almost too anxious to get him to leave. Perhaps Salvatore hadn't approved of his orders to conduct the strange American to Tony Brewster's rooms. He was saying now, "Come, Mr. Lammiter. I know this is all most disappointing, but I've an appointment at six. I'll have to hurry."

Rosana broke into a rush of Italian. "You brought him here. It would be better if you weren't seen with him again. I'll show Mr. Lammiter the way downstairs. I'll watch at the window until you cross the Piazza. Then he and I shall leave, too."

"Is he coming back here for the meeting tonight?" Salvatore was speaking in Italian, too.

"I suppose so."

"Then why did Tony want to see him now? Couldn't that have waited until tonight?"

"Tony wanted to brief him about our meeting."

"When is it?"

"Eleven o'clock."

"If Tony is awake," Salvatore said doubtfully. He looked down at the peacefully dozing Englishman, and his taut face relaxed into a fleeting smile of sympathy. "Better if we postponed our meeting until tomorrow morning. He needs sleep."

"But we have little time—" Rosana's voice was sharp with worry.

"Is it really so important that we meet here tonight?" he asked impatiently. "I thought our job was almost over. Is there something new?"

Rosana said firmly, "We meet tonight. Tony wants our final reports."

He shrugged his shoulders. "All right, all right." He turned toward the kitchen, and then paused. Casually, he asked, "How much does the American know?"

"Nothing at all."

"Then that's about as much as I do." He looked at Lammiter speculatively. "What is he, anyway? Our special envoy to the White House?" He laughed briefly. "You never can tell what Tony will think up next. And, Rosana—take away that bottle from him before you leave. He's had more than enough. And you'd better set the alarm clock for a quarter to eleven, or he won't be awake to let us in." Then he turned to Lammiter. "Good-by," he said in English. "I'm sorry your first visit turned out to be such a waste of time—for both of us." He made a wry grimace.

"Give me a hand to stretch Brewster on the bed," Lammiter said. "He will sleep better."

"We might only waken him again." He looked searchingly at the American. "You understand Italian?" he asked unexpectedly.

Lammiter smiled. "You mean I was listening to you and Rosana? I just liked the way she talks, that's all." It was an evasive answer, but it was all that Lammiter felt like giving, somehow.

Rosana's laugh was unexpected.

"Don't get too interested in Rosana," Salvatore said with heavy good humor. "Tony would not approve of that. *Arrivederci.*" He entered the narrow kitchen, opened the door in its end wall, listened, and then stepped quickly into the hallway outside. The door closed behind him, locking itself with a decided click.

Rosana's eyes were angry. "Salvatore makes such silly jokes—" She crossed over to the side of the window to look down on the Piazza. "He's always like that. He's too clever, too bitter."

"Perhaps he needs a bigger job than he has."

"That," Tony Brewster said, and his voice seemed brisker, "may be the explanation of Salvatore which I've been seeking for years." He opened both eyes and looked at Lammiter almost approvingly. "You see —" he said, now raising his chin, too, "I am not so drunk as you all thought me. I may need sleep, but I'll get that in its proper time." He eased his bandaged leg. "Dammit, perhaps I'll have to go to some bloody hospital after all. Rosana, get me another bottle of wine and two more glasses. Quick, we may have even less time than you think."

As she obeyed, he went on talking. Brewster was not yet drunk. But just as certainly, he was not exactly sober. Rosana brought a fresh bottle of wine unwillingly to the table. She exchanged a quick glance with Lammiter. "Tony—" she began, as Brewster poured wine for all.

"Get back to the window, Rosana," Brewster said. "You promised Salvatore. Remember? Don't worry about me. Wine increases my eloquence. You know that."

Rosana crossed to the window. Worry made her angry; she was frowning.

"I like Salvatore. We are good friends," Brewster told Lammiter, handing him a glass of wine. "But there have been developments in the last three days that go far beyond the work that Salvatore and Joe and Rosana and I have been doing for the past year—our official work, you might call it. There is no need for either Salvatore or Joe to be concerned with anything except that official work."

"I see," Lammiter said, and relaxed. "I was beginning to think you didn't trust Salvatore."

"Didn't trust him?" Brewster asked, annoyed. "We've been together, off and on, since 1944. He led a partisan group that did a very good job against the Nazis, a very good job indeed."

"What's his name?"

"Didn't he tell you?" Brewster was amused.

"I don't know him well enough to be on second-name terms with him."

Brewster's smile deepened, but he seemed to have forgotten Lammiter's question. He had one of his own. "Why did you come here?"

"Rosana—"

"Yes, yes. But why did you listen to her?"

"I want to know more about Pirotta."

"More?" Brewster was watchful now. "How much *do* you know?"

This is the moment, Lammiter suddenly felt, when Brewster either becomes interested in me or bored with me. In one case, he will talk; in the other, he will simply chitchat, and I'll learn nothing about Pirotta. He made a wild plunge. "Pirotta is connected with some narcotics ring."

"Oh?" Brewster seemed unperturbed, but he flashed a quick glance at Rosana.

"She told me nothing," Lammiter said quickly. "I've been listening to the princess, that's all."

Now Rosana and Brewster looked at each other. "And what does the princess know?" Brewster asked, very quietly.

"That Count Luigi Pirotta belongs to the same organization to which Rosana's brother belonged. There were also hints that Communists are backing this narcotics ring—certainly they're mixed up with it somehow. According to the princess, that is. There was a good deal of hinting. In fact, I'd say she was needling Pirotta, and his friend Mr. Whitelaw. That's possibly her way of being angry." He looked at Rosana for confirmation, but the girl was watching the Piazza. She waved to someone down there.

"Whitelaw? Bertrand Whitelaw?" Brewster asked.

"Yes, Whither-are-we-drifting Whitelaw. I had the feeling he was one of the princess's targets, too. Why? Where does he stand?"

Anthony Brewster's shrewd blue eyes studied Lammiter. At last he said, "Your princess is meddling with dangerous things. I wonder how she could have learned about the Communists' control of the drug ring?"

So it's true, Lammiter thought, and does knowing the truth make you feel any better? It did not.

Rosana turned quickly away from the window. "Tony—I didn't tell her. I haven't been seeing her. I've avoided her for the last three or four months."

"But no one knows about the control of the drug ring except—" Brewster's voice was worried but unaccusing. He frowned down at the table.

"Except me and you and Giuseppe and Salvatore."

"And now Mr. Lammiter," Brewster reminded her. "But who told the princess?"

"She has the quickest ears and the sharpest tongue of anyone in Rome."

"Seemingly." Brewster's brow wrinkled into red folds.

"And she also doesn't give one good God-damn for anyone on two legs," Bill Lammiter said. He looked at the Englishman. This might be a ripe moment to press his question. "What is Pirotta's connection with this drug ring?"

"He organized it. He's in control."

Lammiter felt the blood drain from his face. The truth was worse than he had imagined. Eleanor, he thought, my God, what is going to happen to Eleanor?

Brewster was watching him. "No more questions?" he asked mockingly.

Lammiter brought a chair to the table for Rosana. He pulled up one for himself. He said, "The quickest way to answer all my questions is to tell me the full story."

Rosana sat down, looked at him gravely with her large dark eyes, and then at Brewster. She smiled.

Lammiter said, smiling back, sharing her unspoken joke, "You don't see Brewster telling any complete story to anyone?"

Brewster said, "There never *is* any complete story. There are always a dozen developments, each with its own importance to different people, always a dozen possibilities for the end, and none of them conclusive. Unless someone dies. Then that *is* final—as far as he is concerned."

Rosana shivered as if she had felt a cold draft on her bare arms. The laughter had left her face. She brushed her short dark hair away from her forehead with a nervous gesture.

"Rosana doesn't like me to talk of death," Brewster said. "Don't worry, Rosana." He tapped his bandaged leg, gently but markedly. "This won't kill me. It is just one of the hazards of our game." He looked now at Lammiter. "If I tell you any part of the story, you'll have to face hazards, too. You can't just walk in here, find answers to your questions, and then walk out again, saying, 'How interesting. . . . Some day I must write a play about Rosana, the girl who was helping Brewster to find out about the Pirotta narcotics ring, the girl whom Pirotta trusted enough to make his secretary.' No, Lammiter, if I tell you anything, you are one of us."

Lammiter's grave eyes looked at Brewster steadily. He nodded, controlling his impatience. He'd have to let Brewster take his time; no doubt Brewster was still deciding whether he could be trusted.

"I just wanted to warn you of the hazards," Brewster said. "This leg of mine, for instance, is a good example. Three nights ago, I was coming back here—about eleven o'clock—walking along one of the old streets. I heard a car behind me. At first, I thought nothing about it. And then, as it almost reached me, I had a sudden odd feeling. I made a leap for a doorway and fell, twisting this leg badly. But I was lucky. The car mounted the narrow pavement and just scraped past me. It ripped my sleeve. If there hadn't been three young men walking in the street, I think the car would have reversed and tried to run me down again."

"It was aimed at you?"

"Straight for my spine."

Rosana said, "It's bad luck to talk this way. Death is quick to hear it. The wise man does not attract his attention." She tried to laugh. "That's what Giuseppe tells me."

"Yes, it was an attempt to dispose of me," Brewster said placidly. "Just as there was an attempt to kidnap Rosana last night: kidnap her, question her, and then kill."

Rosana stood up.

Brewster told her sharply, "I'm only reminding you how stupid I was three nights ago. And how stupid *you* were last night. Next time you have a message from Pirotta, to keep an appointment after midnight, you will remember to develop a high fever or a blinding headache or even an aunt's funeral."

"Pirotta didn't plan last night. I *know* he didn't. He arrived late, yes, but he didn't plan it that way. Tony, believe me: he was upset, too upset and worried, when I told him what had happened."

"And you believed him? You still can believe him?" He turned to Lammiter. "She's too much of an innocent for all this business. Are you?"

Lammiter said, just as abruptly, "I wouldn't know." He waited for another unexpected, probing question, but Brewster went on talking about Rosana as if she had left the room. "She's too intent on her own discoveries, she never thinks the enemy has *his* own discoveries: he's finding out about her just as she has found out about him. She must learn to be careful, cautious, distrustful." He looked at Lammiter shrewdly. "I still don't know if I think you are distrustful enough to keep her safe in Perugia."

Perugia? Lammiter looked sharply at Brewster. He frowned. He didn't want to go to Perugia. Pirotta wasn't in Perugia.

"A pair of bloody romantics, if ever I saw one," Brewster said bitterly, surveying them both as if they could neither see nor hear him. "But with this damned leg—what am I to do?"

Rosana said, "You'd better start trusting Mr. Lammiter. You will have to send him with me to Perugia. Because, Tony, there is no one else to send."

"What about your friend Joe, from Sicily?" Lammiter asked the girl. "You like him. He's a nimble-looking type. Why don't you take him to Perugia?"

"The less you mention Perugia, the better," Brewster advised.

"Or Salvatore," Lammiter said, turning to the Englishman. "Why don't you send him with Rosana? He's your friend, isn't he?"

"Yes." Brewster's eyes narrowed as they studied Lammiter.

"You said you trusted him."

"I do." The voice was icy.

Never question Brewster's judgment, Lammiter reminded himself.

Rosana said quickly, "Both Giuseppe and Salvatore only know about the narcotics ring, nothing beyond that."

"That's all they need to know," Brewster said. "If I had been able to walk about, Rosana wouldn't have been told any more, either. And you wouldn't be here."

"Why choose *me?*" That was the question that had puzzled Lammiter ever since he came into this room.

A slight smile hovered round Brewster's eyes. "Because you have such helpful friends."

Lammiter looked both amused and puzzled. "I'm flattered."

Brewster's voice became bitingly precise. "Such as Edward Tillinghast Camden."

"Bunny? You know him?"

"We've met."

"Surely you can do better than that for understatement," Lammiter said with a grin, remembering the kind of tangles into which Bunny could get. Anyone who had worked with Bunny was not only light-footed but sure-witted. "Why not tell Bunny about Perug—" He halted. "Sorry. Anyway, why not tell Bunny?"

"We've been unable to reach him in these last three days."

"He's been out of town." That was a mistake: to admit knowing Bunny Camden's movements was tantamount to saying he was in Bunny's confidence.

"Ah—" Brewster smiled now as he looked at Lammiter. His interest rekindled visibly.

"Look—it's just an accident that I know he isn't in Rome," Lammiter protested earnestly.

"Of course, of course. And I suppose it was just an accident that you were loitering near the Embassy three days ago and met Captain Camden so innocently?"

Lammiter said nothing.

"Rosana saw you. She was trying to get in touch with Camden, much as you did. Only, she wasn't successful. So she waited to telephone him at his apartment. But he never did go back there. Do you know where we could find him?"

Lammiter shook his head. "Let's get this straight. Bunny is no longer working in Intelligence."

"But he knows what to do, whom to contact, in an emergency," Rosana said. She looked nervously at Brewster.

Lammiter went on determinedly. "And it *was* an accident meeting Bunny. We are good friends. That's all. In fact—" he smiled, to ease the shock in Brewster's eyes—"if Bunny and his Marines hadn't adopted me on the way out from the Pujon trap, I'd have been either dead or a prisoner. There wasn't much future for me, either way, until this Marine platoon came stumbling along." He paused, sensing their complete disappointment. To fill the embarrassing silence, he rushed on. "You know the Marines: they can't bear to leave anything behind them. So they picked me up and joshed some life into me, and got me stumbling along with them." And a damn long stumble it had been, cold on the white-gray snow, over the frozen mud and the ice-glazed rocks, down that winding path to the cold white-gray sea. He could still remember the wind that cut through his shoulders, the cruel numbness in his hands, his feet weighing half a ton and every ounce packed with pain.

"I see," Brewster said. He looked at Rosana, shaking his head. She had put both her hands to her mouth. "And last night, Lammiter, you weren't keeping an eye on the car that tried to kidnap Rosana?"

Lammiter shook his head.

"Oh!" she said. "Oh!—And I thought I was so clever, so clever. . . ."

"So romantic," Brewster said. He heaved a deep sigh of weariness and reached for the bottle of wine. He had limited himself all through this conversation, so far, to one glass. Now he poured generously, drank, and poured again. "Two bloody romantics." He was neither bitter nor amused, this time. This time, he was almost philosophic; and completely depressed.

Lammiter said sharply, "The surest way to make a man useless is to keep telling him he's useless."

Brewster grunted.

"And I'd like to add that you aren't much use, right now, yourself."

Brewster looked up angrily. Then, just as quickly, his mood changed. He even laughed. "The trouble about the English," he said, "is that even when they are beggars they like to be choosers." He looked at the American carefully, and then he decided. "All right. You'll do. You'll have to."

"Thank you," Lammiter said wryly. But he also thought, this man and I could become friends. Good friends. This sudden thought, summoned by instinct, both surprised and pleased him.

"You want to know more about Pirotta. I want help. We'll exchange services, *quid pro quo.* Right?"

Lammiter nodded. "If I can be of any help to you—" He was still doubtful.

"I'm the judge of that. One thing is at least in your favor: I think, after your experiences in North Korea, you don't trust a Communist."

"That's one fact about me you have got straight."

Brewster pushed aside his glass of wine. "Thank God," he said, "that

I don't have to convince you about the miserable realities of political life before you'll even let yourself listen." He was easing his leg, hiding the pain of it, altering his hips' position in his chair. He rubbed his thigh. He gave a sudden smile that was both honest and warmhearted. "Now," he began, selecting his words with care . . .

Brewster, once he had decided to give out information, talked without pause. Either the wine had increased his eloquence or his subject was one that had haunted him so constantly that he could repeat a list of facts as calmly and impersonally as the multiplication table. Lammiter listened in shocked silence. He was quite aware he was not being told everything, just the necessary outline to establish confidence and enlist his help—but it was enough. And it was startling. Lammiter sat frozen in his chair.

It was not the fact that a powerful narcotics ring could be selling drugs from Rome, as if it were a reputable business, which was so startling. After all, the world newspapers had been reporting for months on another drug scandal in Rome. (A young girl's body had been found on a beach at Ostia, resignations had followed in high places, and several explosions had been touched off that were still reverberating around some well-known heads.) But it was the scope of this narcotics business that was news to Lammiter, news both astounding and horrifying.

The poppies for the drugs were grown in the drab fields of Asia Minor, processed by some obliging Middle Eastern countries, shipped to Italy and France, where there were even factories and well-organized salesmen and (in France) a sizable market. But the main target was America. The shipments of drugs were constantly being steered through western Europe toward the United States. There was no doubt about that. And across the Pacific, the direction of drug trafficking was still more blatant. There, in recent years, the agrarian reformers of Red China had increased production of opium, heroin, and morphine to staggering totals —all for the smugglers' trade out of Hong Kong and Thailand and Japan to San Francisco.

Lammiter looked both uncomfortable and angry, as men do when they don't quite want to believe something that they instinctively feel may be too true for comfort. "You make it seem as if western Europe were all under a constant barrage of narcotics. My God, Brewster—"

"I'm not exaggerating. I've only time to give you the barest details now. Later, if you're interested, you can trace down many more. They're all in print."

"In print?"

"Ever heard of Interpol?"

"The International Police Force? But I thought the war had killed it."

"It's been resurrected. Headquarters are now in Belgium. You must read Interpol's recent report on the narcotics business. You'll find all the facts and figures about each country's contribution to this ugly mess—who grows the stuff, who processes it, who sends it traveling, what ships have carried it, what seamen have smuggled it. They're all named. My dear Lammiter, the whole thing is a campaign against the West, planned and carefully subsidized by its enemies, aided and abetted by men whose lack of morality is amply compensated by their cupidity. Those who grow opium, or process it, or ship it, ask no questions about why it is being bought or where it is being sent. They just keep their eyes fixed on their bank accounts."

"They are monsters!" Rosana burst out.

"Yes, yes," Brewster said calmly, pulling the conversation back to cold reason. "The United Nations Narcotics Commission has also issued its reports. The facts have all been gathered and noted down. Believe me" —he was becoming a little impatient—"I am neither exaggerating nor lying. America *is* the chief target."

Rosana said, "And what is more, it is your young people who are the center of the target."

"At this point," Brewster said, "Rosana always bursts into tears with indignation and helplessness. But cheer up, my softhearted Rosana: at least one drug-exporting firm is going to be out of business within a week. Thanks to you, Rosana. And to me. I may as well admit I've had one success in my life: Luigi, Count Pirotta." He said the name with relish. He smiled benignly.

"There are a lot of people to be thanked," Rosana reminded him. "There was Bevilacqua over at the Questura." She turned to Lammiter. "Bevilacqua is the detective who has been working on the Pirotta organization ever since my brother's death. He's *very* good. He's clever, truly. He did more than anyone—" She bit her lip and smiled. "And then the two nice Americans—narcotics agents from Washington—they are now in Bari and Trieste waiting for two ships to arrive."

"They're always so interested in catching the *supplies,*" Brewster said irritably. "Opium, heroin, cocaine, marijuana. You puts in your penny and you takes your choice. But I'm interested in *people.* Such as our handsome count, who is making hay, with a nonny nonny yea." He cocked his head and looked at Lammiter. "Does my levity shock you? Good. I need something to shock you into taking me seriously."

"It's all very well for you to see Pirotta as a comic character, but it isn't your country that's getting the treatment," Lammiter reminded him grimly.

"Oh, some of the treatment blew off on us. The American bases in Britain are naturally of interest to Pirotta's friends. His salesmen found them difficult, so they couldn't resist trying to make some customers among the young and foolish in the local population. I think we caught them in time."

"It is strange," Rosana said, "how all people who take drugs try to convert others to be like them. They pretend it's nothing at all, something normal and natural. They need company, I think."

"That's how it spreads. Worse than smallpox," Brewster agreed. "Anyway, the British are definitely interested in this. Or else I shouldn't be here." He looked suddenly at Lammiter. "I'm a journalist, by the way."

"You are?" Lammiter smiled.

"Yes, indeed. The London *Echo* is hoping to get an exclusive story when it can all be told."

"When is that?"

"Next week—as soon as the two new shipments arrive and are consigned to Pirotta's warehouses."

Something in Brewster's voice caught Lammiter's attention. He said slowly, "I think it isn't the sale of narcotics that really interests you. I think it is Pirotta himself."

"You may be right."

"Why?"

"Because Pirotta is not in the narcotics business for money. He's in search of power, political power. He's a Communist."

"What?" Lammiter looked at Rosana. She was quite calm, as if she had long accepted the idea and could no longer be surprised by it.

Brewster went on quickly, "He has set up, during the last eight years, a remarkably efficient organization, international in scope, with its key men all Communists. It can be turned to political uses when necessary. Meanwhile, it adds to the Communists' secret funds, helps to corrupt their enemies, and gathers a list of future traitors—drug addicts can always be bribed by heroin, or blackmailed with threats of exposure. They'll be quislings, every one of them."

Lammiter was still thinking about Pirotta. "But he's the fellow who has everything," he said, almost to himself.

"Pirotta? Not in modern terms. What power lies in an inherited title today? What money?—Possessions now mean taxes. So what does an ambitious man do? He knows Europe is changing. He chooses the most ruthless force in the struggle for power. He sees the Communists as the wave of the future. And he is determined to stay on its crest. His family has managed to swim there for years."

"For three centuries, to be accurate," Rosana said. "They've switched sides for three centuries, always choosing the winners. Until Mussolini." She laughed softly. "His father chose wrong, there."

"So he thinks he'll regain the family's power by supporting the Communists?" Lammiter asked.

"He'll give up his title willingly, in exchange for being a leader. What's in a title? Power is the thing. And then there is another practical consideration. When the machine guns are turned against the innocents, he and his friends have determined which end of the machine guns they'll be facing. Astute characters."

"Yes," Lammiter said with marked distaste. He looked at Rosana again.

She returned his look frankly. "You are wondering why I am friendly with such people?"

"Was it your idea, or did your clever policeman suggest it, when you and he were discussing your brother's death?"

"Bevilacqua?" She laughed with relief. "See, Tony, Mr. Lammiter trusts me. He doesn't think I really belong with them."

"I see," said Brewster. "But I also think that Pirotta, too, is beginning to see. Look at last night—"

"But Pirotta said they were 'business rivals'—men from Naples who were trying to take over—"

"Did you believe him? Last night, what was the number on the car's license plate?"

Rosana looked suddenly anxious, as if she instinctively knew some bad news was about to be given to her. "I *told* you the number, Tony," she said.

"And now I shall tell you that the car that tried to run me down was a fourteen Fiat, gray, with the same number-plate you noted."

There was a moment's silence. Lammiter took a sharp breath. I wish, he thought unhappily, I wish to God I had seen the whole license plate last night. Then I'd have known whether the fourteen Fiat, gray, which brought me to the Piazza Navona tonight was the car they are talking about.

"Yes?" Brewster asked him.

Lammiter shook his head. He had nothing to add: the three last numbers on a license plate were not enough.

Brewster turned to Rosana again. "You will have to be extremely careful for the next week. I'm taking no risks with you, Rosana. Lammiter looks like a well-built young man to me. He has strength enough for the journey to Perugia by himself."

"But I could help him—there's so much I know and he doesn't—"

"I shan't ask too much of him. All I need is a pair of good eyes in Perugia, who will report back to me what I myself would like to have seen. And that—" he turned now to Lammiter, "you will do at once. At once, so that the necessary steps can be taken—"

"Look here," Lammiter said, genuinely puzzled, "if you and Bevilacqua and the two men from the Narcotics Bureau in Washington have this Pirotta organization all ready to blow apart, what need is there for anyone in Perugia? The case is practically closed, isn't it?"

"Nothing is ever closed. One thing leads to another. But I told you that before, didn't I?"

"All you have to do now is to start blocking out your special story for the London *Echo*."

"There is another story, too. And every bit as important. It could be even more so."

Lammiter said, with a sudden anger that surprised himself, "I don't think there's any business more contemptible than drug-smuggling, unless it's pimping or slave-trafficking. What's more important than catching people like that?"

"Rosana—would you hand me my file?" As she reached for the pile of books, carelessly jumbled together, and selected one ordinary-looking volume of medium size, Brewster looked at Lammiter. He had become bitterly serious. "What's more important? Not much. Unless it is catching the men who support a system of forced labor, of torture and secret police—the men whose chief business is to bring that kind of existence to your country and mine and Rosana's. I am talking about the professional Communist, Mr. Lammiter. *Not* the workman who votes Communist because he wants a better deal, a bigger share; *not* the woman who thinks that if the system were changed, men would be changed, too. I'm talking about the professional Communist. He's just another kind of narcotics smuggler, perverting minds instead of bodies. He's a liar and a cheat and a betrayer. He's the man who makes slave-labor camps possible. What's more important than catching that kind of man?" He took the book from Rosana. "To spread his empire around this world, he will plot dissension, destruction, and hate. *He* won't do the fighting or risk the dying. Oh no! He must stay alive, in order to control the peace that follows. To the professional Communist, people are always expendable." Brewster took a deep breath. "Now I step down from my soapbox."

He opened the book. It was hollowed out in its center, a bogus book, as in one of those antique leather objects that coyly display cigarettes. In the space where cigarettes usually lie, there was a small Manila envelope. Brewster opened it, searched inside, and drew out a snapshot. He studied it. He gave a strange smile, acid, contemptuous. Then he looked up, speaking casually, seemingly at random. "Pirotta was a friend of MacLean's."

"MacLean's?"

"Don't you remember two men called Burgess and MacLean?"

"Oh—them!"

"Yes, them. Now we're getting to the *real* issue," he said with sudden relish. "All that briefing on the narcotics ring was only the first slices off the roast. But now we are getting to the real meat and bone."

"You mean all that information about narcotics was only an introduction?" Lammiter's voice was both surprised and a little dismayed.

"It was both necessary and important. I hope you forget none of it. Because it all links up. If I hadn't been interested so much in Pirotta as the head of a drug syndicate, I shouldn't have tried to find out whom he was going to meet in a *trattoria* over on the unfashionable side of the Tiber. I went, expecting to find some new face to add to our rogues' gallery. Instead, I saw him meeting a man called Evans." The sharp blue eyes were watching. "You don't recognize the name?"

Lammiter searched his memory. He shook his head.

Brewster looked delighted. "I suppose not. His case was kept pretty quiet. He happened about a month later than MacLean and Burgess."

"Most unfortunate. Don't tell me he was a Foreign Office type who specialized in America, too."

Brewster glanced quickly at Lammiter. "His job didn't seem of much importance. Not until one began to study the people he met. They were all influential."

"And," Lammiter said bitingly, "they all trusted him."

"Indeed, yes. He was an expert confidence man."

"How did you get onto him?"

"You flatter me. I wasn't quite so suspicious then as I am now. Otherwise he wouldn't have left the country."

"For Moscow?"

"Of course."

"What is he doing now in Rome? Can you guess?"

"Nothing to do with drugs," Brewster said firmly. "Evans deals with power politics. He's a diplomat's diplomat. And he was always an excellent persuader." Brewster half closed his eyes as if he were trying to see the occasion for Evans's visit to Italy.

"Do you think he has brought instructions from Moscow to Pirotta?"

Brewster shook his head. "Pirotta is only the go-between."

"But he's head of the narcotics ring, isn't he?"

"That's how I know he is only the go-between. In Communist undercover work, the really important man is rarely the head of anything. Don't worry about the ambassador—look at his chauffeur; or a cipher clerk; or an undersecretary. Pirotta takes orders from someone quite outside the narcotics ring. Evans wouldn't meet the head man directly —"

"You sound pretty definite on that." Lammiter was not quite so sure.

"I ought to be. Once, I was something of an expert on people like Mr. Evans."

"That used to be your job? Before you branched into drug-smuggling?"

"Before I branched—" Brewster began to laugh. "My God—branched! I was kicked—and no pretense of upstairs, either—into a minor job, outside my own field. It was the biggest hint to resign a man ever got."

"But why?"

Brewster said impatiently, "Does that matter? What matters is that I've spotted Evans in Rome. I was given the job of uncovering a little company of spoiled brats who were playing around with heroin and opium. But—" he was laughing again, "—but I found more than anyone expected. By God, I'd like to see their faces next week when the news reaches them."

Lammiter wanted to ask, "Whose faces?" But he felt he had already asked more than his allowance of questions. Brewster talked cryptically, partly because he expected any intelligent person to grasp the full meaning of his quick allusions. He wasn't the sort of man who paid any attention to those whose wits couldn't follow his. Even drunk—for he was beginning to show the effects of this last bottle of wine—he was a formidable opponent. He must have once made a relentless enemy. Once. Lammiter watched Rosana take away the empty bottle with a shake of her head.

But Brewster had noticed it, too. "Rosana—you'll find another fiasco in the kitchen," he said angrily, as if to prove that his voice was not thickening. "Wine makes me think. You know that. It's food and drink."

Rosana went, even if slowly, toward the kitchen. Tony Brewster was a man who seemed to get his own way. It was then that Lammiter understood how fully the damaged leg must have hurt the Englishman. For once, he had become dependent.

"Yes," Brewster said, relaxing in his chair, "I'd like to see their faces when they hear about Evans. Rosana!—"

"Coming," she called back.

Lammiter was watching Brewster. Once he must have been good at his job as an Intelligence officer. Then he had gone stale, worried too much, and been transferred. And now he was drinking too much cheap Chianti, brooding about "them," who had transferred him, sobering up to get the necessary information which would damn the "spoiled brats" like Pirotta, thinking mostly of the work he had once done ("the real meat and bone"), and remembering Evans.

"So you saw Evans," Lammiter said appeasingly. "You recognized him."

"And he recognized me. Which explains *that!*" Brewster pointed to his leg, but he was watching Lammiter carefully. Suddenly, he held out the photograph. Lammiter had the feeling that until this very moment, Brewster hadn't quite made up his mind to show him the snapshot. "He still looks very much like this. Just in case you run across him in Perugia."

Lammiter, startled, looked at Brewster, and then at the snapshot. Evans was strolling along a London street with some park trees and a bus sharing the background. He was elegantly dressed, bowler hat in hand, light gloves folded, rolled umbrella, dark suit of conservative cut. He was the very perfect gentleman. He was tall, thin, with his head at a slight angle as if he were listening politely. (One could see how he had earned quiet popularity.) Fair hair; a prominent brow; a thin high-bridged nose; a tight-lipped mouth; not a particularly strong chin.

"That was taken five years ago by a street photographer. Very lucky picture. Caught his general attitude. Of course he has changed a bit. His hair is now grayish, his skin has gone sallow. He is still wearing English-cut shirts and ties, though. Just won't give them up."

"But what do I do if—"Lammiter bit off the rest of the sentence. (He had been about to say, "What do I do if I see Evans in Perugia?" But suddenly he was wary, embarrassed by the situation he had created for himself: he had started making promises that might be impossible to keep.) "I'm not the man for this job," he said frankly, holding out the photograph to Brewster. "It's an emergency, obviously. Don't waste valuable time with me. Get someone like Bunny Camden. There must be people at your own Embassy who'd like to catch up with Mr. Evans."

"I tried that," Brewster said, slowly, bitterly. "But I'm a drunk who's got persecution mania and a complex about Communists, didn't you hear? No one would see me at the Embassy—I'm an embarrassment. That's the reason I sent Rosana to find Camden." He took the photograph at last. "You'll remember this face?"

"Why don't you get the Italian police—the man with the odd name . . . Bevilacqua? He's at least friendly, isn't he?"

"I'm afraid the Italians have nothing against Evans. Except the fact that he's using a false passport. But before we can find out enough about that, Evans will have attended a most secret meeting in Perugia and be gone, as quietly as he came." Brewster considered something, and then decided to add, "Besides, some of my informants are a little nervous if you mention a policeman. No, no, Lammiter, I can't risk frightening away future sources of information."

"You trust them?"

"After I prove their stories," Brewster said with a smile. "This week I heard three very interesting pieces of news, dribbled to me in a frightened whisper. First, Pirotta was to have a quiet talk, four nights ago, with a most important man. That, as I proved, was true. Secondly, a meeting was being most secretly arranged in Perugia for this important man. That may also be true. I think it is. My informant, a very careful customer, was found knifed to death two nights ago in a back street in Tivoli. A café brawl."

"But you doubt if your man was in it?"

"It has always been a useful diversion."

"Yes," Lammiter agreed. "As poor old Christopher Marlowe found out. Which proves that playwrights should stick to writing plays."

Brewster looked at him with some surprise, and then smiled. "He made a bloody good secret-service man."

"Until he got knifed in a London tavern."

"You're nervous?" The smile was mocking.

Lammiter grinned back. "Perhaps. Or perhaps I know I'm not a bloody good agent. Frankly, I'd be of no use to you in Perugia."

"I don't expect you to do any *thinking*."

"Thank you."

"All I want you to do is to find out if Evans has actually gone to Perugia. If he turns up there, telephone me here. That's all."

"And you'll get the Embassy to listen to you then?"

"Or someone," Brewster said grimly. "At least, we'll know that second piece of information was accurate. It will no longer be in the category of rumor. It will be a fact, proven and true."

"But where will I look for Evans in Perugia? My God, Brewster, it's a sizable town."

"I'll tell you where you can look for him."

"Was that the third piece of information you received?"

"You can count, I see," Brewster said. "I'll have a map of Perugia ready for you tonight, all the details. . . . " He was tiring now. "Once Joe and Salvatore leave here, you and I will talk a little more. The final advice . . . You'll have to rent a car. No, better still, I'll persuade Joe to lend you his. Three hours, four at the most, and you'll be in Perugia."

And then, as Lammiter still looked worried, Brewster's voice broke into anger. "You're backing out! But you can't. You'll *have* to go! Just as you had to stay in Rome. When the trouble breaks, you want to try to keep as much of it away from Miss—Miss—" He looked at Rosana.

"Eleanor Halley," she said.

"From Miss Halley as possible," Brewster finished. Suddenly he was completely exhausted.

Lammiter said nothing. He rose. Brewster slowly put the Evans photograph back into the envelope, and the envelope into the hollowed-out book. His fingers, like his voice, were now overcareful and slow. Lammiter turned away, so that Brewster could not see the pity in his eyes: it was pathetic to see anyone as good as Brewster becoming a man with a mania. Evans, Perugia . . .

"What are you afraid of in Perugia?" he heard his own voice asking.

"The three-sided chess game," Brewster said abruptly. He reached slowly for the new bottle of wine. "Go and have some dinner," he added testily. "Put some sense into your thick head. Come back and listen. I'll —I'll tell you—enough to make your ears pop. And you"—he wagged a thick forefinger at the American—"can tell it some day to old Bunny. I wouldn't have to argue with him like this, damn you. He's the only one who believes me, the only one—" His voice had begun to drone into an undertone. "The only one," he said, rousing himself for a brief moment. He actually put down his half-finished glass on the table, and pushed it away. It upset.

"I'll help you to stretch out on the bed," Lammiter said. He put an arm around the thick waist and started to heave.

"I'm all right," Brewster said, pushing all assistance aside. "Where's my damned crutch? Lost again." Rosana found it where it had slipped under the table. He took it, and began moving across the room, heavily, with difficulty and considerable pain. He dropped it at the bedside, flopped down with a sigh of impatience, and eased his bandaged leg onto the mattress.

"Tomorrow," Rosana said, "Giuseppe and I shall take you to the sisters."

Brewster looked at Lammiter, as if defying him to laugh. "Nuns! That's where I have to go. Hear that, Lammiter?"

"It's safe. And quiet. And pleasant," Rosana said. She had wiped up the spilled wine and taken away the bottle. Now she was setting a small alarm clock, and putting it within reach of the bed.

"So is here," Brewster said, his eyes closing. "I think I'll sleep. At last." Brewster began to laugh, gently. "Hie me to a nunnery. . . . This old Protestant?" His eyes closed.

"But Santayana went—" Rosana began. Lammiter motioned toward the door. The girl nodded. She looked round as if checking everything. She replaced the hollowed-out book in the pile of innocent volumes. She straightened a chair, lifted the empty glasses, and then went toward the kitchen.

Lammiter looked at the man stretched out on the bed. He was already slipping into sleep. The pool of deep golden sunlight near the window had shifted on the floor, moving slowly toward the bed. The chorus of children's voices rose into a permanent happy chatter broken by loud ecstatic shrieks. On impulse, Lammiter closed the shutters, cutting out light, muffling the sounds. "No," Rosana whispered. "He likes to breathe." She opened the shutters again. The man on the bed grunted gently, and let sleep drift over him, a soft gray mist of forgetfulness.

Rosana waited for Lammiter to join her in the kitchen before she opened the back door that led onto another flight of stairs.

"When does the alarm clock go off?"

"Salvatore said a quarter to eleven, but I set it for half-past ten. I thought I'd give Tony time to awake thoroughly. He must let us in." She closed the door carefully behind them, and shook it gently to test the automatic lock.

Lammiter suddenly remembered something else. "Didn't you lock the other door after Salvatore and I arrived?"

She nodded, made a gesture for silence, and listened.

He lowered his voice. "But I saw Salvatore locking it. . . . "

She looked at him and smiled. "Testing it. He doesn't trust women." Then she motioned to him, and they began to descend the narrow staircase. In this house, the back had become the front: on this kitchen staircase, the light was warm and sun-filled; people lived behind these doors, breathed this air, flavored it generously with the meals they cooked and ate. But at this moment, these flats seemed all deserted. There were no voices, no scolding, no laughter. Two doors even stood open, showing walls needing plaster and paint, too many random pipes, a crush of wooden chairs round littered tables.

"Where is everyone?"

"Taking the air in the Piazza. It is the evening ritual." For a moment she hesitated, glanced back up the staircase, frowned. But she went on, without saying something she wanted to say.

Wasn't it safe to talk here? Lammiter wondered, as they descended the worn stairs. Safer than the Piazza. He glanced at his watch. It was after seven o'clock. Only an hour since Brewster had begun to take him into his confidence. An hour was a long time in some ways, short in others. In an hour, you could smoke half a dozen cigarettes, or read a newspaper, or write a letter, or just sit and dream. You could travel four miles on foot, sixty in a car, a hundred in a light plane. You could make a friend (or an enemy) who might last you fifty years. And in one hour, you could make decisions that would change the entire course of your life.

Rosana put her hand on his arm as they reached the last short flight of stairs, so that he halted, too. She looked up toward Brewster's door. She was still troubled.

"He will be all right," Lammiter said encouragingly. "A little sleep, and he will be biting all our heads off with his usual gusto."

She smiled. Then quickly she leaned over the worn balustrade, its eighteenth-century carvings of conch shells and triumphant Tritons partly washed away by a sea of passing hands. She decided it was indeed safe enough: the entrance, just below them, was quite empty. She faced him. She looked extremely unhappy. She said, "He *is* only a journalist."

"What?" He stared at her. "You mean Brewster wasn't sent here officially on any mission?"

She shook her head.

"He wasn't transferred to this job?" Kicked downstairs was the way Brewster had described it.

Again she shook her head.

"Was he kicked out entirely? Why? Drunk?"

"Oh no! Not then!"

"For making mistakes?" Such as letting Evans slip away from England.

"Tony says that he made only one mistake." She halted, listening. Reassured, she hurried on. "After Evans had escaped, Tony kept searching for the man who had warned Evans. The man who had helped to place him when he began his career, and promote him into the right department. For there *has* to be such a man."

"Yes," Lammiter said slowly, "there has to be such a man." It was a disquieting thought. "Did Brewster find him?"

"Tony says he must have been close, very close, to finding him. For suddenly—for no reason he or any of his friends could understand—he was given quite another problem to solve."

Lammiter couldn't see Brewster taking that lying down, not that old Protestant upstairs. "So he made several biting remarks and lost his job altogether?" Then he frowned, wondering if secret-service agents ever did get discharged. If they were of no more use, what happened to them? Given less and less important work, until they were so bored they just faded away? In more ruthless countries, they fell out of trains.

"He didn't complain, make any protests. I wish he had. I think it was then that he began to—began to drink more than he should." She looked anxiously at Lammiter. "You see how it is?"

"I see," he said gently. He was a little touched by the way she had tried to make him understand about Tony Brewster. He watched her eyes. "You believe all this?"

"But of course! Tony does not lie."

Yet it was only Brewster's word. . . . "People could say that he brooded too much over his disappointment—exaggerated the situation."

"That's what the Communists did say. It spread around. In the end, even most of his friends stopped believing him. So he threw up everything, took a journalist's job, and came to Rome. He used to be a journalist long ago—before the war."

"Tell me one thing. What did he mean by 'three-sided chess'? Wasn't that what he said?"

"It's his theory that the Middle East and the West and Russia are all playing a chess game. Russia is standing to one side, supervising the moves. Tony says 'jogging the pieces.' Making the others take certain moves that are bound to cause countermoves—and *always* trouble."

"But—no one can make nations move except the nations themselves. Governments listen to their own advisers."

"What if one of them is another Evans?" She looked at him solemnly, letting him fill out the rest for himself.

What if such a man, trusted as Evans had been, could influence opinion? Or delay an important document? Or misinterpret a piece of urgent news? One small move like that might start a whole chain of events.

"He will not be working alone," Rosana said. Anxiously she watched him. "He could begin trouble. And he will have to help to make it spread."

Yes, Lammiter thought, if someone in the foreign ministries of other western countries were working along with such a man, the trouble might well spread. Lammiter tried to muster a counterargument. This was the kind of crazy theory he might expect from Tony Brewster. "But —" he began.

Rosana seemed to guess something of his doubts. She jumped to Brewster's defense. "Tony does not say that Russia is winning this chess game. He does not even say that the Communists have men like Evans still in our governments. What he says is—the Communists have *trained* for this kind of game. They have tried to get their men in position. That, we all know." She took a deep breath. "It frightens me."

He looked down at Rosana's dark eyes, the gentle curve of cheek, the finely molded features. She pushed back the ridiculous fringe of short dark hair which had fallen onto her brow.

"Yes," he said, "they have tried. We all know that. But don't let Tony's theories worry you. Things are looking pretty peaceful just now. Why—Malenkov was even passing out boxes of chocolate in England, and patting babies' heads. What did one woman say?—'Ow, *isn't* he nice? He's just like my uncle!' "

"And four weeks later, when the workers were shot down in Poznan?" Rosana asked angrily, her eyes widening. "What did she say?"

At the entrance they heard a quick footstep. They looked at each other. Lammiter slipped his arms around Rosana, drawing her closer to him, back against the wall. He whispered, "What else would we be doing here?" She half smiled. And as the man came upstairs, Lammiter kissed her. He could feel her sudden gasp, ending in a little laugh of embarrassment as he ended the long kiss. The man, returning home from his work earlier than most (the usual hour was eight o'clock), was probably hurrying upstairs to wash and change his shirt before joining his wife and children in the Piazza. He looked at them curiously as he passed. But there was a smile on his dark face, a good-natured understanding of why two strangers should be sheltering from the world inside his doorway.

Bill Lammiter tightened his grip around Rosana's soft waist. And this time, when he bent forward to kiss her, she did not gasp. They stood in silence for a long minute, looking at each other as if they were searching for an answer to their own questions. He let his arms fall to his sides. He said, "We must go." What was wrong, he wondered? If any girl could help me forget Eleanor, here she is. And yet— Sharply, he told himself he was an idiot, a fool.

Overhead, the footsteps ceased, and a door banged shut.

"He accepted us," Lammiter said.

"Yes," she replied. She began walking down the last short flight of stairs. He followed more slowly, watching the way her graceful neck met her shoulders in a clear smooth curve. Why had that kiss been such a damned anticlimax?

Rosana said quickly, "Will you be able to find your way here at eleven o'clock? Knock three times quickly on Tony's door. And then a pause. And then a fourth knock. And then speak, when he asks you who is there, just so that he will know who it is."

"What if he is still asleep?" He had a ridiculous vision of a small line gathering outside Brewster's door.

"The alarm is the kind that keeps ringing until he does answer it."

"He'll be in a filthy temper." He hesitated. "And suppose he falls asleep again. What do I do? Wait until you and Salvatore and Joe are all there to start pounding?"

"You must be serious," she told him, horrified by such an idea.

"I'd prefer to meet you somewhere. Couldn't we have dinner together, around nine?"

She said, "If you don't want to go up by yourself, then— But why don't you?"

"I'm out of my depth here," he admitted. "Have dinner with me, and you can put me more in the picture, and we'll climb the stairs together. We've worked out a good alibi, anyway, for any stranger who comes along." He slipped his arm around her waist again. I'm a man who keeps trying, he thought. "Dinner?"

She shook her head. "Too dangerous. I'll meet you across the Piazza, at the church steps. I'll walk on, and you can follow."

"That's one thing I can always do—follow a pretty girl."

"You *must* be serious," she warned him gravely. "Eleven o'clock." She slipped away from him, and stepped out of the sharp black line of shadow, across the bright threshold, into the golden Piazza.

It's odd, he thought, as he watched Rosana disappear from sight, it's odd how I have kissed the prettiest girl in Rome, and there's so little to remember. No joy, no excitement . . . He might as well have stolen a kiss from his prettiest schoolteacher. He stopped thinking about Rosana and concentrated on his own exit.

Around the three fountains, the children swarmed, thick as ants around three sugar bowls. On this, the eastern side of the Piazza, the buildings were drenched with warm light, but the doorways were now in shadow as the sun slipped lower in the western sky. Opposite, the buildings lining that long side of the Piazza Navona were in complete shade from the hot evening sun. There, not far from the church, was the *Tre Scalini,* where he had dined before. It looked inviting, cool, and empty at this time. But it was too early to eat in Rome. He would look as conspicuous as the few hungry tourists, their stomachs geared to half-past seven, who were making their appearance by horse and cab. Tonight, he decided, it was better not to be seen hanging around this district. And there was a taxi driving into the Piazza by its northern entrance, the old gateway to the Roman circus, where the chariots had raced. He smiled suddenly at the strange quirks of memory, at the odd facts he had assimilated in this last month of wandering round the city, at the peculiar moments they would keep returning to the surface of his consciousness.

He watched the taxi curving around the Piazza toward the restaurant opposite. He timed it carefully. Now, he told himself just before it reached the restaurant, and plunged away from the dark doorway over the hot glaring sidewalk, across the cobbled street which edged the central island, among children learning to walk, children on bicycles and in baby carriages, children carried, children running, laughing, crying, children holding other children, children. This was obviously a district central enough to let the men return home for a midday dinner and a pleasant siesta.

The taxi was emptied, paid off, and about to be driven away. Bill Lammiter raised one hand and left the crowd. "Via Vittorio Veneto," he said, out of habit. But in a sense that had become his own *petit quartier.*

As the cab circled round the long island of fountains and children, he glanced out of the window. He had been reasonably certain as he had crossed the Piazza to reach the taxi that he had not been followed. And now, nothing followed him out of the Piazza. Good. And yet strange—for he had been followed this afternoon. When had it stopped? About the time he had met Giuseppe, or Joe, or whatever Rosana's Sicilian friend called himself. No, even earlier than that. About the time he had telephoned Rosana from the American Express office? It wasn't a question he liked.

One thing he did know: interest in him had faded. Or—and this thought was less comfortable—or interest in him was merely pushed aside for a certain space of time in which "they" knew what he had been going to do. One didn't need to follow a man whose movements were known in advance.

This thought, as he looked at it from all angles, became definitely ungainly. He could wish he had never conjured up this particular little monster.

He looked at his watch: it was a quarter to eight now. . . . Eight o'clock —what had he to do before eight? There had been something. Oh yes— photographs! He almost laughed aloud with relief: it was pleasant only to face such a tourist occupation as collecting photographs. By all means, let's go and collect photographs.

But he kept wondering about Rosana. Could she actually be in love with Tony Brewster as Salvatore had hinted? That was difficult to believe. Yet women were so damned unpredictable. And men, he told himself, were so damned vain: she let you kiss her, but you didn't measure up, and that's the part that really annoys you. Or perhaps, and this was less wounding but more distressing, her ideal woman was the Venus of Cyrene, classically pure, noble as marble, cold as the tomb.

The photography shop, just off the Via Vittorio Veneto, was about to close. The last customer was leaving, and two of the assistants had already gone. An elderly white-faced man in a white cotton coat looked increasingly depressed as Bill Lammiter entered. But he took Lammiter's receipt, and while he searched slowly through an immense collection of envelopes for the prints, Lammiter used the shop's telephone to call Carl Ferris over at the American Academy. It was a brief call, and a careful one. (Lammiter mentioned no names.) There was no news of Bunny Camden except that he was reported to be on his way back from Naples. Professor Ferris sounded a little glum, as though playing guardian angel over a telephone was beginning to pall. "I'll keep calling," Lammiter promised. "Sorry. But it's an emergency."

He turned to the envelope of prints, which the man had at last found. The photographs weren't particularly good. After all the fuss he had made about collecting them, they were just not any good at all. Color was, of course, the trouble. He would have to use a light meter as carefully as an amateur. But that was the kind of thing that took all the fun out of photography. To have to measure and calculate made picture-taking too serious a business.

"How much?" he asked the tired face behind the side counter. "And there's that telephone call to add to the bill." He counted out the cost in soiled and sticky lire notes that felt no longer like paper but almost like thin velvet. Behind him, a woman's high heels came clacking through the narrow door. (The tired-faced clerk had, hopefully, already pulled an iron trellis partly across the entrance, leaving only a small space for this late and slender customer.)

"Are these ready?" she asked in good Italian. She was standing at the main counter, holding out a numbered receipt. So eager was she to have her snapshots that she hadn't even looked at the other side of the shop. But Lammiter would know the sound of these heels anywhere, apart from the clear light note of her voice. He didn't have to turn around to see the supple figure in its simple dress, or to watch the way her fair head would be tilted to one side a little pleadingly, as if she could cajole the clerk into finding her photographs. It was Eleanor.

The clerk took the receipt she handed him. He searched, slowly but politely, among the bundles of envelopes. "Not here, signora." He looked at her sympathetically.

"Are you sure?" She was upset. "Please look again. They ought to be here. And I must have them."

Lammiter started toward the door quietly, quickly. You said good-by to all that, he told himself: only today, this early afternoon, you said good-by definitely. Get out of here, Lammiter—

He was at the door, about to push aside the iron gateway to let him ease his way onto the sidewalk, when he heard her say, "You see, I'm leaving Rome. For America."

He nearly said, "What?"

She was saying, "Oh, thank you. Thank you very much. I knew you'd find them."

He pushed the iron trellis a little more to one side. It scraped harshly, shivered a little, and stuck. He pulled at it impatiently.

"*Signore, signore, uno momento, uno momento!*" said the clerk, leaping into life as he rushed round to salvage his precious gate.

"Bill!"

He came back into the shop. For once, he had absolutely no idea of what he would—or even should—say. She had been crying. She had been crying a great deal.

"Oh, Bill!" She put out a hand to touch him as if to make sure he was real. "I tried to reach you by phone this evening. I didn't know—" Her voice strangled: she was crying again, quite silently. And her sudden tears distressed her still more. She bit her trembling lip and turned her head away from him and the curious clerk.

"How much?" he asked the man, pointing to the envelope Eleanor held in her hand. He paid for that, too. Quite like old times, he thought as he took her arm and steered her through the gateway. "Now where?"

"My apartment is just round the corner."

"Oh?" he said, as if he hadn't known that. How many nights he had passed by its windows and wondered— Hell, he thought as he tried to jam on some brakes: for a man who had buried his past so determinedly, he was helping it out of the grave too damn quickly.

"Please," she said, "please would you come up and have a drink? I—" She looked at him with her large blue-gray eyes. Her lips trembled again. "I—I can't trust myself in a public place. And I need—want to see you." She looked down at the envelope of photographs which she held in her hand. "I was packing, I wanted these to put in my case. The last memory . . . " She tried to laugh.

"Ah—careful!" he said, taking her arm. "Come on, Ellie, or you'll have me in tears, too. How would you like me standing on the Via Ludovisi crying my heart out?" She managed to laugh, this time.

The old name had slipped out. Ellie . . . How long do we stay vulnerable? he wondered. "All right. Let's go."

11

They were both silent, making their way for the short distance along the sidewalk, narrow here with trees, past the very small café with its three small tables outside for those who wanted a glass of wine. Round the corner, on a side street, quieter than even the quiet Ludovisi, was the house where Eleanor Halley shared an apartment with two other American girls. Like Brewster's house in the Piazza Navona, this place had once held a large private household. Now, its floors were divided into flats. Here, the ubiquitous dentist lived and worked, a designer had his carefully balanced name plate on display, a Swiss textile firm announced its Rome headquarters, and people like Eleanor paid overlarge rents. But in Rome, one had to add privacy and quiet to one's cost of living. The staircase had marble veneer, intricately worked. The elevator was venerable, limited (it held two people only), slow, quivering with its efforts.

"We'd have done better using the staircase," Bill Lammiter said.

"I'm on the top floor," she said warningly.

That was all they said during the whole journey to her apartment. He wished he had never agreed to come: conversation was going to be difficult, now that the first surprise was over. She was calmer, too. It looked as if perhaps she didn't really need him around, after all.

The apartment was rambling, with large rooms leading off a dark central hall. She led him through double glass doors screened with lace into a dimmed and elaborately furnished room, everything exactly arranged in patterns of tables and ornate chairs. There was a good deal of glass and marble and gold-tipped wood, of silk brocade and net curtains carefully draped and puckered and folded.

"We share this room for everything except sleeping," she explained. "Hideous, isn't it? And I can't move a thing—there's a maid who goes with the apartment, and she won't let us alter the position of one ashtray. The awful thing is, there's a lot of good stuff in this room, and it could look beautiful." She moved over to the two huge square-shaped windows, which began at high waist level and stretched almost to the carved and painted ceiling. She pulled them wide open, after a brief battle with yards of lace, and flung apart the outside shutters. "It's cool enough now," she said, in her peculiar way of half-explanation. Eleanor had always talked to people as if she expected them to be thinking along with her, keeping a kind of silent conversation going, so that her mental jumps needed no explanation. What she was telling him was the fact that she had adopted, along with the Italian furniture, the Italian habit of shutting windows as well as shutters while the sun was up.

She glanced at him. He had barely entered the room. He stood quite still, watching her. "Am I talking too much?" She tried to laugh. "Someone *has* to say something. The silence in the elevator nearly smashed my eardrums. Don't look at me like that! I'm all right, Bill."

"Are you?" he asked quietly, listening to the nervous edge in her voice, watching the anxiety in her wide-open eyes. Why had she brought him here? The reason had been real enough, he felt now, but she was backing away from telling it to him. "Then perhaps you don't need anyone." He turned toward the glass doors.

"But I do. I need *you*."

"Why?"

"I've never felt so—so lost in all my life. Honestly, Bill—" She gestured helplessly. "I tried to call you twice this evening."

"So you said." His voice was quite neutral. He caught a glimpse of himself in one of the several mirrors strung around the walls. He didn't look neutral, though. He looked like a man who had been strung out on a rack.

"Don't hate me, Bill. Please don't hate me—"

"I don't hate. I don't—" he took a breath and finished lamely, "—anything." He must put on a better show than this. He looked around him, thinking he would stay for five, polite, agonizing minutes; and then get the hell out. And stay out of Eleanor's life forever. He chose a chair that would be the least comfortable. "Where's everyone? All out to dinner?"

"Dorothy and Maymie are in Amalfi on their vacation. I sent the maid home this morning. I thought I had an engagement for tonight. With Luigi."

He reached in his pocket for a cigarette. "This allowed?"

She nodded, saying "sorry" as she found a cigarette box to open in front of him, and then searched for matches. Suddenly she remembered the drink she had offered him. She must indeed have been upset to have forgotten all these politenesses. Eleanor was the kind of girl who always remembered a man's little comforts: a good geisha, he used to joke. She brought him a well-mixed Scotch and soda with ice, and a large saucer to replace the Venetian glass thimble of an ashtray which he was balancing on his knee.

"And I thought," she said wryly, still following the pattern of thought that he had interrupted with the smoking ceremony, "that I was going to visit some friends of Luigi's this weekend. In Umbria. Luigi was going to join me there when he could."

He said nothing, nothing at all. Did she really enjoy hurting him like this? He even managed to look at her quite candidly. And then he saw she was not thinking of hurting him; she was too engrossed in hurting herself.

"But it's all off," she said. "All off."

"Well, you can see Umbria some other time, when you get back from America. The hill towns won't run away. They've been there for a couple of thousand years, at least."

"It's *all* off, Bill!"

"Off?" He rose.

"Luigi—I—we aren't getting married."

"What?"

"I'm going home for good." The words rushed out, ending her attempt at self-control. She turned her back on him. "I handed—I handed in my —"

He took a step toward her. But she was fighting off this attack of emotion by herself. She said, in a tight, strained voice, "I handed in my resignation at the Embassy this afternoon. They took it, too. Without one question. As if—as if they were glad I was going back to America. Suggested I leave as soon as possible."

"Thank God for that."

She swung around. "Why do you say that?" she asked sharply. "Why?"

He temporized. "What else would you expect me to say, Ellie?" he asked gently.

"You're just like the Embassy. Too quick—" Angrily, she brushed the tears from her cheeks. "They were too obliging about letting me go; no questions asked. Nothing. Bill—what's wrong? What are they trying to protect me from? What—"

"I suppose they saw your mind was made up." Not a brilliant remark, but the best he could muster at this moment.

"But it *wasn't*—not really. I could have been persuaded to stay."

"Why?" he asked. "To plead with dear Luigi?"

"Bill!"

He didn't apologize. But at least he had driven the tears away.

"The sooner you leave, the better," he said curtly.

She faced him, angry, a little frightened, but determined. She quieted her voice. "You're like the Embassy," she repeated, "pushing me off on the first plane—" She hesitated. "I think you know something," she said slowly, "something I should know. What is it? Have you heard some rumor? Some—"

"Ellie," he said very quietly, "what are you going to imagine next? I'm a stranger here. Where would I hear rumors?" He walked over to the window. The evening sky had changed from gold to apricot and orange, and now—even as he watched—the flaming colors were streaked with violet-gray. Soon it would be dark.

"You heard the princess today. . . ." She sounded worried, puzzled.

"I just don't get this." He swung round to face her. "You and Pirotta looked pretty damn well pleased with yourselves at Doney's, this lunch-time." He could have been more tactful. She flinched.

And then she said, the lines at the side of her lips suddenly drawing down so that her mouth seemed frail and miserable, "That was a pretense."

He looked at her sharply.

"Luigi didn't want his aunt to see that something was wrong—she would have been delighted: she never did think I was the right girl for Luigi; and we were hoping we could get everything straightened out. That's why I met Luigi for lunch." She took a long, deep breath. "But everything got worse instead of better."

"Look—" he began, and stopped. If ever he had seen a man in love, it had been Pirotta. "I just *can't* believe it. That guy just doesn't give up so easily."

Eleanor said, shaking her head, still hardly believing it herself, "We had some trouble two nights ago. Last night we had another quarrel—no, that isn't the right word—it wasn't a quarrel exactly. It was worse than a quarrel. Just—" She dropped her hands helplessly to her sides. "Just trouble. Which I can't understand. I just don't know what is wrong, Bill."

"Then why break off an engagement? Or is this getting to be a habit?"

She flinched again. She said quietly, "I didn't break it off. It was Luigi who—" She stopped, facing him. Abruptly, she turned away and sat down. She lit a cigarette very carefully. "He broke the engagement this afternoon," she said at last.

Involuntarily he said, "That was the only solution. I mean—it was the right thing—for your sake. But I'm sorry. It's a hard blow. Even if you sensed trouble coming, it is always hard to—"

She was staring at him. "What do you mean—'right thing'? Or 'for my sake'?" She was angry. "Look, Bill—I wanted to tell you all this just because I—well, I felt you were the only person I could trust."

"Trust with what?"

"With what?" she echoed blankly. She looked at him, utterly bewildered now. She shook her head. "Bill, what *did* you expect from me? I just wanted to tell *someone,* to have them listen, to have them understand. Someone I—I like very much. Someone who likes me, so that any advice I get will be honest."

"But why choose *me?*" he asked angrily. Why cut open healed wounds?

"I don't know, I don't know," she said, and her voice slid into tears like that of a child who is frightened. "I just wanted—I just wanted to see you."

Or perhaps, he thought savagely, the wounds had never healed. His, at least, were as raw as on the day they had been inflicted.

"Please stop teaching yourself to hate me," she said sharply, her tears changing to anger. "I watched you at Doney's today. You really had cast me for the role of villainess, hadn't you? Nothing I could have done or said would have been right. Nothing." There was a long silence. Her voice became calm, sad. "Don't, Bill! One can always sneer at people—one can always find something to laugh at. But you don't *have* to do that with me. I know how wrong I was. And how I hurt you. I'm sorry. I've said that before. And I meant it. I didn't need to lose Luigi to know how you felt when I treated you so—so badly. You don't love me any more, but you don't have to hate me."

He watched her as she spoke. It was all as painful for her to say as it was for him to listen to. But she was right about some things. He might as well admit it honestly, as she had. Today, at Doney's, he had been twisting every memory of her into a caricature, every thought about her into a bitter criticism. He had been trying to teach himself to hate her. Why? To stop loving her? Damn those big gray eyes, soft and shadowed, watching him so unhappily across the darker shadows of this room.

"I always told you I was a mean son of a bitch," he said gruffly. He finished his drink quickly, and rose.

She rose, too. "And I never believed it. Or I wouldn't have telephoned you this evening. I wouldn't have asked you to come up here." She held out her hand for his empty glass. "Let me mix you another."

"I hate Pirotta's guts," he admitted. "I'm glad you are leaving him. Glad. But I'm sorry, too. Sorry this had to be . . ." He put out a hand and touched hers. They were two shadows, facing each other in a darkened room. The deep dusk blotted out all expressions, all memories. She didn't move. He tightened his hand round hers, and took a step nearer. "Ellie—"

She came to life. Her arm and her voice were taut. "No, Bill! No—I'm selfish and vain and stupid, but I didn't ask you to come up to—oh, Bill, I'm not as cruel as that! Have you got all your memories of me so twisted?"

He dropped her hand. She didn't step away, though, not at once. She touched his arm, gently, as if to soften the sharpness of her refusal. And then she moved quietly, without haste, over to the wall and switched on the light.

"You know," he said, making his voice as natural and easy as possible, "I think we both need some dinner."

She smiled suddenly, with relief. "Do you mind if it's simple? The larder didn't expect company. Eggs, cheese—that kind of thing? And there's Valpolicella."

"Good," he said. "Hemingway characters always drink Valpolicella. Lets them get things straight." He managed a laugh. "I'll help with the omelette. Where's the kitchen?"

"As far down the hall as possible," she said, almost laughing, too. "Who wants an old kitchen near any old dining room?" She led the way into the hall, switching on lights.

He noticed a telephone. "By the way, why did you have to phone me twice? Didn't the hotel mention I had checked out, the first time?"

"Yes. But they expected you back."

"They did?"

"You had left your raincoat."

"My Burberry?" And as he stared at her incredulously, he suddenly could see it, hiding on a hook behind the opened inner door to his bedroom. His much prized, overpriced Burberry. "Darn! So that's how I found room for my camera in my suitcase."

"You should use a Minox," she said, "and carry it in your pocket. That would solve a lot of problems."

It was the old argument between two camera addicts, each trying to convert the other to his own particular love. Lammiter had always preferred the full-sized print he could get with his Rolleiflex.

He halted at a doorway, and looked at suitcases on the bed, evening dresses over the top of a trunk, clothes pulled out of a wardrobe, jars and bottles and lipsticks all pushed into a group beside a large handbag on the dressing table. "Now I begin to see why you always depended on a Minox. But have you room even for it?"

"I can always ditch my cigarette lighter. Most of this stuff will be sent after me. I'm taking just one bag."

"When do you leave?"

"Tomorrow, early." She bit her lip, looked at him uncertainly. "Bill, am I doing the right thing?—Running away like this?"

"I think it's the right thing."

"But I've nothing to be ashamed of. Why should I run?" Her gray eyes, blue when she wore green, looked obliquely at him from under the fringe of dark lashes. "Luigi is, of course, going to say that it was all my decision. Noble of him. He's telling that to his relatives, right now, at that dinner party we were going to attend tonight. Can't you see them? Horrified and angry. Shaking their heads. Saying 'I told you so, my dear boy. These Americans—' " She broke off.

"Now, Ellie," he said, and searched for a handkerchief. "Look—" he spoke sharply, to switch her mind away from the dinner party, "you didn't leave your name, did you?"

"Where?" She stopped wiping her eyes, and stared at him.

"At the hotel."

"But why not? I wanted to *reach* you, Bill. I thought you could call me when you—Bill—what's wrong with that?"

He looked at the floor, black and white marble. He looked at the walls, arsenic green fading to yellow; at the carved ceiling, the bogus Corinthian plasterwork; then back at the disarrayed bedroom.

"Look at *me,* Bill," she said gently. "What's wrong?" She looked as if she might smile.

You women, he thought, God damn it, you women, you are truly impossible.

Eleanor said, "I brought you up here to listen to my troubles—and now I think I have to listen to yours." She did begin to smile.

"No," he said sharply. "I've no troubles. But I sure as hell wish you hadn't left your name at the hotel in connection with me. I just don't want you tied up with me at all, at the moment."

That made her serious. "Why? Luigi wouldn't object."

"His friends might." He spoke jokingly.

She looked at him, startled. She said bitterly, "His friends certainly would. They object to everything I am and do." She tried to laugh. "Why don't they like me? What have they to do, anyway, with choosing Luigi's wife?"

"His friends?"

"Yes, his friends. They didn't approve of me, so he let me go. Yet, a month ago, when some of his relatives objected to an American girl who hadn't a millionaire father, Luigi laughed. Ludicrous, isn't it?"

"Who were these friends of his? Italians?"

She shook her head. "Italians are never rude—not to a woman. One had a French name, Legros. The other—well, he talked English, but he wasn't English."

"I can't see any man disliking you," he said, half smiling. "Ellie, don't hurt yourself imagining things—"

"I'm not imagining. In these last few weeks, I've had too much experience of being inspected by Luigi's family *not* to know when I am being carefully considered. Honestly, Bill— Two nights ago, Luigi took me to dinner. We drove out into the country—to a house at Tivoli, not a restaurant, a private house. I never knew who the owner was. I never met a host or a hostess. There were two middle-aged servants, men who looked as if they were made of wood: cubical faces, broad cheekbones, square-shaped bodies, and shoulders that looked like a high plateau. We had *apéritifs* on the terrace, the Frenchman, the bogus Englishman, Luigi, and I. There was a lovely view of the gorge and the waterfall and the old Greek temple up on the hill—do you know it? Thank heaven for that view: the conversation couldn't have been more boring. The men just didn't make any pretense of being sociable. They talked with Luigi and sort of watched me as I listened. They didn't like me to begin with, not even before they met me, I guess." Her voice had calmed down: she was disguising the hurt in it; she was even making a brave attempt to be amused. "Ridiculous? Yes, I know it sounds ridiculous. But it all happened just like that." She turned away. "I'll tell you the rest over dinner." She moved toward the kitchen.

"Tell me now," he said, catching her arm.

"Here, standing in the hall?"

"What happened next? You were bored. . . ." Suddenly he saw the whole picture developing in front of him. "Don't tell me you started playing around with that Minox of yours."

She looked a little startled. "How did you guess?"

"You always did play around with it."

"Yes," she said, smiling now, perhaps remembering how they had first met in New York, two strangers alone in the Romanesque garden of the Cloisters, two amateurs trying for a good camera angle, a significant view of the George Washington Bridge soaring high over the Hudson. "And you weren't always sure whether I was lighting a cigarette or taking a picture of you."

Yes, he thought a little bitterly, I almost imagined you must have liked the look of me. "So you took some pictures on the terrace of the house at Tivoli."

"Not exactly like that. I wanted to see the view from the edge of the terrace. Luigi and his friends were busy talking. So I rose and went over to the balustrade. The light was still good enough—with luck I could get some pictures. I took out the Minox. And I wandered a bit—you know how it is—the view is always better on the other side of the garden."

"No one paid any attention?"

"I suppose they didn't think I'd wander far. But I explored round some shrubbery and saw a man sitting there, all by himself. He was reading. He made a very nice composition with the Greek temple on the hill across the gorge behind him."

"So you photographed a man sitting in the garden? He didn't notice?"
"He looked up, of course. But you know how quick a Minox is. I'd already taken two photographs." She paused. "You know, he was furious. He rose and took a few steps toward me, saying, 'And what are *you* doing here, may I ask?' And I just was speechless."
"Did he see the camera?"
"I don't think so. My hands had dropped to my sides. And before I could explain or anything, he turned on his heel and walked away."
"So you went back to the terrace?"
She nodded. "Luigi was coming to meet me, and the others were standing at the balustrade. They must have heard the sound of the man's voice. Luigi saw the Minox in my hand. 'For God's sake,' he said. 'Hide that damned thing!' So I slipped it into the pocket of my skirt."
"The others heard?"
"Impossible. He spoke under his breath. It was the first time I'd ever heard him use strong language, though."
"I shall try to reform," Lammiter said gravely. "Well, that was quite a party you had."
"Oh, that wasn't all! The Frenchman wanted to know who had been talking to me. And I said, 'A very rude Englishman. He didn't even give me time to explain.' Because that really annoyed me, Bill. I hadn't been slipping through shrubbery to spy on him."
"He was English?" Lammiter asked quickly.
"I know a genuine broad A when I hear it. Besides, he *looked* English—he had that kind of thin drawn face and very neatly brushed hair—"
"What color?"
She looked at him in surprise. "Grayish."
"Tall?"
"Definitely. And thin. Almost concave." She looked at the suddenly thoughtful Lammiter. "I am *not* making this up. It's true."
"I believe you. Tell me, did he appear at dinner?"
"No. Seemingly the villa and garden had been divided into two houses. They told me he was an eccentric who rented the other one."
"And no more was said about him than that?"
"I tried to make conversation about eccentrics, but it was switched away onto Korea, of all things. And Luigi was no help at all. In fact, he excused himself for a moment, just before the dessert arrived, and he stayed away for half an hour at least."

Visiting the English eccentric? Lammiter wondered. "He was probably as bored as you were," he said.

"He came back looking worried, not bored. We left then. Very quickly. And that's when our trouble really started. Apparently I had behaved badly." She tried to smile. "That made me as mad as *he* was. And right in the middle of our quarrel, when he was absolutely white-lipped—I had never seen him like that—he snapped out, 'He is right! You're totally irresponsible, hopelessly immature.' "

Lammiter, who had been both amused and puzzled, stared at her. "He? Which he?"

"That's what I asked."

"What was the answer?"

"No answer. Luigi switched right over to my walk in the garden. Why had I explored so far, what was I doing, anyway?"

"You told him what actually had happened?"

"Why not?"

"That silenced him, I bet."

"As a matter of fact, he burst into a stream of Italian. Words that I don't even know. He only stopped when he was out of breath."

"So you said you were sorry, you must have been mistaken, let's forget everything."

"Anything for peace," she agreed.

"My, my—you did have a first-rate quarrel, didn't you? But at least you managed to keep hold of your photographs." He smiled.

"The trouble with you, Bill, is that you are not only understanding, but that you understand me too well." Then she smiled, too. "I wasn't too honest about them. I—I was so mad when he demanded the camera, I clenched my fist around it, and—well, I said I had taken the film out of it."

"Then he asked you for the film."

"No. He grabbed my purse. There were two rolls of film there. He took them both."

"Quite the commissar, isn't he?"

She looked at him searchingly. "Yes," she said slowly.

"And yesterday he had the films developed, and found—?"

She bent her head. Her voice was stifled. "People at Ostia. People at Doney's. People . . ."

"He came back for the Tivoli film?"

"Last night. But it was being developed and printed."

"Did you tell him where the film was being printed?"

"Why should I? What *right* had he to behave like that?"

"Jumping Christopher!" he said. "You must have been really angry."

"I was. That was our worst and final quarrel. Bill—what made Luigi behave like that?"

He looked at her, wondering how much she had begun to guess about Luigi Pirotta and his friends. A future commissar didn't have freedom of choice in a wife. He had two categories that were safe: he could choose a woman who was as deeply involved as he was or he could choose a placid mooing creature who turned tail to the wind like all the other cows in the field. But never could he choose anyone who asked questions and expected truthful answers. Worse still was the woman who—if she didn't get the answers—searched for them by herself. If Luigi Pirotta hadn't known all the rules of the game he was playing, he knew them now. That was the trouble about power politics: you never knew all the rules of the game until you were too far involved to be able to draw back.

"Because," she was saying slowly. "Something did make him react that way. He—he panicked." She said the word with distaste. "Most of his anger was really fear. But why?"

Lammiter said savagely, "The man's in love with you, that's why. He's afraid for you. Is that the answer you wanted?"

"Oh, Bill!—" She made a peculiarly pathetic picture, warding off this last lunge of bitterness, the frown of worry still on her brow, the dried tearstains still smearing her cheeks.

"Men are brutes," he told her cheerfully, trying to laugh away his own fears. "Perhaps you'd better feed this one. How about that omelette?"

"I never know what you'll say next," she said, completely baffled. But she turned toward the kitchen.

"May I use your telephone?"

She looked back at him, surprised again. "Of course."

"And do you mind if I look at the photographs?"

For a moment, as she hesitated, his excitement turned to worry. Suddenly, angry with everything, she said, "You can burn them if you want to!" And then she was in the kitchen, banging out her sudden temper with pans and mixing bowls, more like a volcano in brief eruption than a ministering angel.

12

Quickly, Lammiter examined the numerous prints before he went to the telephone. On Eleanor's orders, they had been enlarged almost to a two-inch square from their usual postage-stamp size and the roll of film had been cut into individual sections. Only about two-thirds of the film had been printed, indicating that the rest hadn't been worth spending the extra money on. But two-thirds wasn't a bad average for Eleanor's technique; and they were good prints, very good prints indeed. The girl could take pictures. Better than I can, he admitted to himself.

He riffled through the prints nervously. There were many studies of people. What if the Tivoli pictures hadn't come out? After all, it had been late in the day, and the light would be difficult. Then, in two photographs with darkish corners—either underexposed or taken by failing light—he saw a white circular temple on a rugged hill, and, in the foreground, a man. In one picture the man was reading, his head bent. In the other, he had looked up, but not yet turned to face the photographer. His profile was sharp and clear. It could very well be a side view of the man in Brewster's photograph, the ex-Englishman called Evans. Brewster would know, most definitely.

Lammiter laid the photograph on a table under a lamp. Then, quickly scanning the negatives against the light, he matched one with the print. He wrapped the negative and the print together in his handkerchief; the others he slipped back into the envelope. The angry clatter from the kitchen had been replaced by a pleasant smell of sizzling butter.

Brewster's humor would have appreciated the scene, Lammiter

thought as he waited by the telephone. Then he wondered, why do I keep thinking of Brewster? The man has invaded me. Do I believe him? Few people would, and I'm as wary as any New Englander. . . . Yet why else should he be standing here, in Eleanor's apartment, waiting once more for a professor of Latin to answer his call? As for his own immediate life —it had vanished into thin air: the plane reservation to New York (damn, he'd have to call the airport and cancel) might have been waiting for him in outer space; his raincoat might have been left in a hotel on Mars; and he had even stopped worrying about his typewriter and camera. The real world had become a shadow play of half-remembered dreams; and Brewster's nightmare world had become the reality. Even Professor Ferris, now speaking, was—quite unwittingly—a part of this new strange fantasy.

Ferris had a pleasant voice on the telephone. His Italian was beautiful, sonorous, spoken with care but overwhelming accuracy. You could easily tell he was a foreigner: he had learned the language abroad, away from the incredible variety of regional pronunciations and inflections. And, inexplicably, Lammiter was reminded for a brief moment of Salvatore's voice. Then he pushed that idea aside, and answered Ferris. "I bet," he said admiringly, "the cab drivers ask you to recite Dante. Have you ever discovered why they are such special connoisseurs of the first lines of the *Divine Comedy? Nel mezzo del cammin di nostra vita.* . . . Is that what makes them drive in the very middle of the road?"

"Oh, it's you!" Ferris said, in English. He sounded too annoyed to join in any fooling. "Where the hell have you been wandering?"

"Not too far. Sorry, though. Did I keep you from going out to dinner or something?"

Ferris softened a little. At least, he laughed. "Don't give that a thought. It's only half-past nine."

Lammiter glanced at his watch in surprise. Nine fifteen. When a man called that half-past nine, he was really annoyed. "I *am* sorry."

"We've been waiting here—" Ferris began, his hunger now dissipated a little by excitement.

Alert, Lammiter said, "We? Is our mutual friend around?"

"Yes. He's returned. Thank God. Now I can pass you over to him, and go back to a normal existence."

"He's *there*—with you?"

"Very much so. He's eaten all the nuts, finished the olives, and told us his stories twice over." Bunny Camden's voice cut in. "And how is my elusive friend? Carl thinks you're in need of some dinner yourself."

"I'm as sober as a Presbyterian elder. I'm just suffering from a touch of euphoria." Lammiter glanced down, approvingly, at the envelope of photographs in his hand. "I must see you."

"Where are you visible?"

"At Miss Halley's apartment."

There was a brief silence. Then Camden said, "Aren't you complicating your life unnecessarily?"

"Not unnecessarily, I hope. Where do I see you? I've an appointment later this evening. At eleven."

Behind him he heard the sound of wheels. Eleanor was pushing a trolley, arranged with food, down the hall toward the living room.

"Remember where we bumped into each other a few days ago?" Bunny was saying.

"Yes."

"Walk past there. Around—let's see—around ten. And keep on walking. I'll catch up with you."

"My feet are in good condition."

"That's fine. But don't trip over that euphoria."

They parted, as usual, with a grin on their faces. I ought to see more of Bunny Camden, Lammiter thought: he's good for my morale. But life had a peculiar way of dealing out agreeably mad companions only in little snatches. It was much more generous with the bores.

"All ready!" Eleanor's voice called from the living room. She sounded quite normally cheerful again. The room looked more cheerful, too, with all its warmly shaded lights switched on. She had cleared a round table and set out the supper, and she was studying the bottle of Valpolicella. "You'd better deal with this." She handed over a corkscrew. "Good news?" she asked, noticing the expression on his face.

"I think so. When are you leaving?"

"Tomorrow morning."

"You know—I shouldn't be surprised if I joined you." She looked a little embarrassed, as if she were nervous about that idea.

"I'll try to get a seat—damn, I've got some more phoning to do—the airport."

"Let's eat the eggs first. I'm afraid I scrambled them."

"That's the way you felt, I guess." He laid the photographs near her. She paid no attention to them.

"I imagined the eggs an English eccentric," she admitted.

"They taste better than he does, I'm sure." He put down his fork abruptly.

"What's wrong? Aren't the eggs—"

"They're fine," he told her. "But I just remembered a joke I could have made on the telephone. Dammit—why must I always be witty five minutes too late?"

"Is that why you write plays?"

"You sound as if you—" he looked at her quickly "—as if you didn't like playwriting as a profession."

"What was the joke?" she asked, dodging a straight answer.

"Oh well, I was talking to a hungry man with a beautiful wife."

"How do you know she's beautiful?"

He thought of this afternoon. "By the way she inspires him."

"Oh—he's a sensitive type?"

"Knowledgeable," he conceded. "And I ought to have quoted Max Jacob's advice to a starving lover looking at his mistress's bare shoulder. That would have silenced even a professor."

"Now," she said, "I'll just let you soar. I don't even pretend to be able to hang on to the tail end of the kite."

"Jacob was a surrealist poet—kind of 1920 vintage—before we were born, anyway."

"Just a dear old dotard," she agreed. "But what did he say?"

"Oh—" he tried to get out of this now "—wit never seems so funny when you serve it up cold."

"He was starving. He was looking at his mistress's shoulder. And what did he say?"

"*Une escalope de vous, ma divine.*"

She looked at him blankly.

"I will *not* explain," he warned her.

"You don't have to. I know my French." She shook her head. "The truth is, it isn't funny."

"Ellie—it is! It's the funniest poem—"

"If you are a man, perhaps. But it makes all women's shoulders feel nervous. Are all men cannibals at heart?"

He grinned. "How often has a man told a girl he could eat her up? Or called her honey, cookie, sugar, peach? Or even—no, I never did like tomato."

She had truly the most delightful of smiles. "Look—" she said in sudden surprise, "I'm all cheered up! I almost laughed."

"I'm glad I'm good for something."

She removed the empty plates, offered him cheese, helped herself to a peach. "Two hours ago," she admitted, "I wouldn't have dared to laugh because I'd have ended in hysterics. Two hours ago, I couldn't think straight. I couldn't even pack. I'd pick a dress up and then drop it, and lift a pair of shoes and then I'd find myself at the dressing table, looking for lipsticks and Band-Aids. I was sort of disjointed, mentally. But now I'm beginning to think, not very well, just a little. . . . Bill, won't you explain what all the trouble is about? There is something very far wrong, isn't there?"

"I think so. But I don't know very much. You probably know more than I do."

"Why should I?"

"Because Pirotta seems to be the storm center."

"Is he in danger?" She stopped peeling the peach on her plate, and pushed it aside as if all appetite had suddenly closed down, like a shop front at noon. "Is that why he picked a quarrel—to send me away?"

"Perhaps."

"But if he's in danger, I should warn him—"

"Warn? Don't look so God-damned worried about an utter, first-grade, one-hundred-and-twenty-five-per-cent heel." Perhaps he had let his own emotions carry him away a little.

She flushed. "Bill! I must say—"

"Don't!" he advised her. "You've been pressing me all evening for the truth. Well, here it is—as I see it. Think of all the decent guys walking along the streets of Rome, and you had to pick a prize like Pirotta. If he is in trouble, he's earned it. Save your sympathy for the decent guys who don't make so much money, but at least make it honestly. They're the ones Pirotta thinks he's going to boss."

"Honestly?" she repeated. She gulped and was speechless. Then, "Bill, how can you, how dare you—"

"I'll dare more than that." He was ominously quiet. "The only honest thing Pirotta has done, since he kissed Mamma and went off to school at the age of nine, was to fall in love with you."

She rose and began clearing away the last remains of supper onto the trolley. He let the silence last for at least two minutes. "How many photographs did you take out at Tivoli?" he asked.

"Five or six." The temperature was glacial, touching zero.
"Only two came out."
"Did they?"
"I took one of them along with its negative. Do you mind?"
That caught her by surprise. She shook her head, looking at him. "There *is* trouble. Isn't there?"
He nodded. "Don't take sides, Ellie, neither Pirotta's nor mine. Please just get on that plane for home. Please . . ."
"And ask no questions?" She half smiled. Perhaps his concern for her had touched her a little.
It was the moment to apologize. "I'm sorry I was so crude. But you wanted the truth from me. I gave it."
"As you saw it," she added.
"Sure. And we're all fallible, I know that."
She looked at him. "I'm sorry I was angry," she said in a low voice.
He became brisk, made a show of glancing at his watch, rising. "I'll wheel this double-decker along to the kitchen, and then I'll have to leave. Can you take care of yourself?"
She nodded.
"What is this gadget called, anyway? A super-deluxe push-me-around?"
"It's a laboratory cart. I wanted something bigger than the usual little trolley. I got this from a hospital-supply firm—one of those drug-supply houses—"
He jerked to a stop. The peeled peach rolled off its bed of Bel Paese rind and Camembert crust, and splashed like a bomb on a black square of tile. "Help!—Help!" He searched for a napkin.
Eleanor began to laugh. "Now, this *is* funny," she said.
"Very funny," he agreed glumly and set her giggling again as she mopped up the tile.
"Your face—" she tried to explain. "You had such a sudden look of horror. Now what were we talking about? Oh, yes—this laboratory cart and the drug-supply house. It's a very big medical firm, and a well-known one."
He wondered a little at all this elaborate build-up.
"Highly reputable," she said. "And honest." Her voice sharpened. "And that's how Luigi makes his money."
Fortunately, they had reached the kitchen, a dark cell lined with

wooden cupboards. The cart was safely still. He walked back into the hall.

"Well?" she asked. "Or do you think it is dishonest to be a director of a firm that supplies medicine to cure people?"

"How many directors are there?"

"I've met four. They are the most delightful men." She smiled mischievously. "*And* honest."

"I'm sure they are." And he *was* sure about that. Pirotta needed honest men and an honest firm for his support. The more reliable the firm, the less government supervision. How much opium and heroin had he diverted from the company's warehouses? He wondered if the Italian detective with the romantic name was now studying Pirotta's falsified lists of imports. All Pirotta needed was a handful of well-paid and efficient clerks in key positions to baffle any honest board of directors.

She walked along the hall with him. "Don't you believe me about Luigi?" she asked suddenly, pathetically.

"Do you want a nice comfortable answer, or the truth?"

"We had that," she said, a little bitterly. "The truth as you see it." She shook her head wearily. "I wish I'd stop asking myself questions. I wish I knew what to do."

"Pack," he told her, "and get all ready to leave. Will you do that for me?"

She nodded. But she was still trying to answer her own questions.

He said, "Keep the door locked and bolted. I'll call you around midnight, just to hear how the packing is going."

"Look, Bill," she said, "aren't you worrying about me a little too much?"

"No," he said firmly. "And don't start thinking I'm judging Pirotta badly because I don't like him." He took her hand and gave it a most formal shake. "Good night, Ellie." He hesitated. So did she. Her moment of bitterness had gone. She had banished her anger. She smiled, not too happily. Perhaps she was wishing that everyone would give up dislike and prejudice and make this a world fit for heroines to love in.

She mustered her gratitude. "Good night, Bill. And thank you for—for rallying round."

But not for giving advice, he thought. "Good night," he said again, and turned away. Behind him, the door was locked. And then bolted. She might not believe him, but at least she had listened to him. He wondered, with a stab of pain, whether good night might not mean good-by; and then, with a stab of fear, whether he might never get free of this girl even if he never saw her again.

"What's wrong with this damned elevator?" he said angrily as he heard it shivering and groaning so slowly up toward him. He glanced at his watch. Seven minutes to ten. He began to run down the staircase, lightly, easily, round and round the pivot of an elaborately carved stone column decorated with plaster acanthus leaves. You should have taken a hint from the builder of this place, Lammiter now thought; he didn't know when to leave well enough alone. Everything was fine until you had to start telling her the truth. That was the odd thing about truth: it wasn't a variable; truth was hard cold fact, and yet it varied; it could seem a prejudice, an unjustified attack, almost a slander, if the moment were wrong. Your timing was miserable, he told himself angrily.

Upstairs, Eleanor Halley didn't move away from the door. She stood there, looking along the empty hall, seeing nothing. She wished desperately that he hadn't said what he thought about Luigi Pirotta. But perhaps the fault had been hers: why had she gone on and gone on, asking Bill questions? Because she wasn't satisfied with any of her own answers?

She didn't like the thoughts that suddenly confronted her, but she didn't push them aside as she might once have done. She left the door, walking slowly down the hall, considering them from a variety of angles.

Yes, she decided, the fault is all mine: if Bill has become a jealous man, suspicious and exaggerating, I'm the one to blame. But I never thought that was the way it would turn out when I ran away from him. Ran away? Perhaps. But not from him. From Broadway and the life that would turn our own life together into something no longer ours. Rehearsals, rewrites, tryout in Baltimore, more rewrites, a chorus of darlings echoing through dressing rooms and after-theater parties, a pantomime of meaningless kisses from almost-strangers.

"Don't you see," Bill used to say worriedly, "these things mean little; it's just their way, it has nothing to do with our life."

Nothing? It took Bill away from me, using up the weeks, the months that never could be replaced. If I had been in the theater it would have been different. But I don't want to go to bed at four in the morning and rise at noon; I don't want to live in hotel rooms and furnished apartments and have mobs of people always around me. Because that's the way it was going to work out. If only his play had *not* been a success, then we could have planned— Oh well, what's the use? Even when I ran off to Rome last April, was he free to follow me and persuade me back? Oh, no! The play was a success, but Miss Whosis wanted a new speech written and Miss Whatsis objected to the cuts in her lines and Mr. Wicher needed a few more aphorisms to bring out the texture of his character, and weren't the changes made in Boston and reworked in Philadelphia perhaps a little unnecessary for New York? And on top of all that, Hollywood; six weeks dragging into months . . .

The awful thing was that if I had told Bill all this, he would have listened. He would have worried over it. He would have given up playwriting and concentrated on short stories or editing news reports. But he is a good playwright—most promising, said even the bitterest of critics. So that is that. What woman is going to spend the rest of her days remembering she has killed off a promising playwright?

And now?—Bill will recover: he was on the way to recovery until I brought him here tonight. My fault again, my fault . . . And yet he did help me; he will never know how much it helped me to hear his easy voice and his silly jokes and even his biting remarks. He made me normal again, able to face the journey home. And he will go home, too, and he will write more plays (if I keep away from him), and the only difference in them will be that they'll be less amused by life and more acid about women.The critics would like that. But every time I go to see one of his plays, I'll be hearing what he thinks about me, she thought unhappily.

And Luigi—what about him? But this will get no clothes packed, she decided abruptly. She crossed swiftly over the threshold into her room. She was folding her favorite evening dress and looking round for some tissue paper when the doorbell rang.

Could this be Bill, back again? What had he forgotten? Or perhaps—perhaps he had decided that he owed her a little explanation, a sort of half-apology for his attack on Luigi.

"Who is it?" she called through the door, her hand on the key. She was half smiling, remembering Bill's sense of humor, wondering what excuse he had concocted to disguise the apology.

A young voice, a boy's voice, replied. "The raincoat of Signore Lammiter. Here it is."

"But *he* isn't here."

"He will come to get it later."

She was a little taken aback. She would have understood an apology, even offered sideways. But this bare excuse for Bill's return later was something that angered her. "Leave it there, outside," she said sharply. How silly could Bill get?

There was a brief pause. Then the boy said, "*Sì, sì, signora.* As you say." He must have dropped the coat on the mat, for she heard his footsteps retreating. And then the elevator door closed, and the usual rattle began as the boy descended. There was only silence outside.

She let her hand drop away from the key. I suppose I am to telephone the airport for him, too, she told herself, and reserve that seat for him. Oh, really, Bill Lammiter!

Then she knew she was unjust. Bill wasn't really like that. He had left for some appointment, hadn't he? Perhaps he hadn't enough time to go back to his hotel: perhaps he had telephoned the hotel and got a bellboy to bring the coat round. And he'd collect it here, coming to say good-by (*and* to offer that explanation and half-apology, she was sure of that) on his way to the airport tonight. After what happened, he would not wait until tomorrow to catch a plane home, not unless she was going to suggest it. And she wasn't. She wasn't going to run into any more dead-end streets. But she kept thinking of the raincoat lying abandoned.

I'm the one who is being silly, she thought now. She unlocked the door, swung it open, her eyes on the mat outside. There was no coat. Only Luigi.

"Oh no!" she said, and tried to close the door. He grasped its handle, holding it ajar.

"I must see you, Eleanor—I must—" His voice was as distraught as his face. "Please, Eleanor. Please—" As she hesitated, he stepped inside, closing the door behind him, locking it.

13

Bill Lammiter slackened his pace as he reached the Via Vittorio Veneto. Now it was a curving river of brilliant lights, surging with pleasure traffic, pouring its people in a continuous current of smooth bare heads along the crowded sidewalks. Up the hill to his left, the outdoor tables on both sides of the street had multiplied and still were not enough. The chatter of voices sounded like the constant rush of a waterfall. And above all the noise and the glitter was a Roman night sky, an ink-blue silence scattered with diamonds.

He crossed the street with difficulty, for the Vespas were out in full force. The cooler air, which had blown in on the city with sunset, was almost too fresh for the sun-tanned shoulders. But for the men—and most were properly dressed in jackets—the fallen temperature was perfect. One of the joys of Rome was the pleasure of the late evening stroll. He turned to his right, following the Embassy's garden wall. Here, without benefit of cafés and crowded tables, the sidewalk was quiet and normally lit. Most people he met were on their way up the street, preparing to plunge into the endless parade. No one paid him the least attention.

Bunny Camden was standing talking to another man just outside the Embassy gates—just a couple of Americans in slim-shouldered light jackets and dark flannels of narrow cut, collars buttoned down, tie ends free, well-polished brown leather shoes, heads hatless, hair crisply cut, well-shaven faces, and a look of having stepped straight out of a shower not so very long ago.

We're developing a new type, Lammiter thought in amusement as he walked on. Gone are the Scott Fitzgeralds and the Babbitts of the twenties; gone are the horn-rimmed glasses and the conscious tweeds of the thirties; gone, too, the Hollywood shoulders and Florida shirttails of the postwar forties. The relics of these eras look odd, now, like Aunt Lavinia's marcel wave or Cousin Kitty's pompadour.

Behind him, he heard Bunny's voice saying, "Well—good to have seen you. We must get together soon." That was also the new formula of good-by—willing but not too definite, leaving a pleasant escape route for all concerned—and then Bunny's brisk heel-to-toe stride was echoing behind Lammiter.

At this point in the street, the Via Vittorio Veneto branched off on its biggest curve to the foot of the hill. It was noisy, down there. So Lammiter kept straight on as he was going, following the street that was closer to the Embassy grounds, dimly lit and quiet. He didn't want to have to shout to make himself heard when Camden caught up with him.

"And how's the euphoria?" Camden asked, falling into step. He was shorter than Lammiter, but solidly built with plenty of hard muscle and no spare fat. He had a remarkably open, ingenuous face—he looked younger than his thirty years. His neatly brushed hair was dark; his brown eyes were cheerful; his wide mouth relaxed easily into a broad smile, showing strong even teeth, very white against his deeply tanned skin. Only the decided jut of his jaw line and the marked eyebrows gave any clue to the real Camden.

"Oh!" It wasn't a beginning Lammiter had expected; but it was a cue to take things easy. "I tripped over it. By the way, was that another college professor you were talking to, back there?"

"A textile manufacturer. We did our basic training together. Why?"

"Just trying to sort out types. They're all mixed up these days."

"Very difficult for writers. How's your new play coming along?"

"It isn't," he said curtly.

"Sorry." Camden glanced curiously at him, and retreated tactfully from the danger area. "Thought you writers always had something in the works. Or perhaps you've been too occupied? I gather you've been *very* occupied." The smile in Camden's voice disappeared. The introduction was over, the mood of friendly helpfulness established. He became impersonal and businesslike. "By the way, where is your eleven o'clock appointment?"

"At the Piazza Navona."

"Then we'll walk in this direction, and circle around. All right?"

They were reaching a district of luxury offices. At night, this small quarter closed down early. It was almost empty.

"You don't think we are being followed, do you?"

"I watched you coming out of Ludovisi into the Vittorio Veneto. No one crossed the street after you. No one followed you down the street on its other side."

"I'm getting the jumps, I guess. I had the feeling in the Via Ludovisi that someone was standing under one of the trees, back in the shadows, just across the road from me. I stopped and lit a cigarette. Then a girl moved out of a dark patch into the light, and pretended she wasn't waiting, jiggled her white handbag, gave me the profile. They're so damned pathetic, they embarrass me. So I walked on and pretended I hadn't seen her—one snub less for her to count. Now I wish I had gone over and searched along that row of trees."

"And what good would it have done you? If you saw a man in the shadows, how do you know he wasn't keeping an eye on one of those girls? And what could you have done, even if he had been waiting for you? Catch him by the lapels, and say, 'Hey, you, tough guy, want me to bash your face in?' I doubt it. I very much doubt that." He touched Lammiter's arm and guided him across the street. They entered a narrower one, running obliquely away from the quiet offices. "This all right?" he asked, as he noticed Lammiter's quick glance back over his shoulder. On either side, closing them in, were silent and darkened houses.

"Sure. Just so long as we don't get a car aimed at our spines."

Camden looked at him sharply. "Say—you've been mixing with some peculiar people."

"It all began last—"

Camden said quickly, "Before you start telling me anything, you ought to know that I'm just a very minor attaché—no more, no less. I'm not an undercover type, or one of those cloak-and-dagger characters."

"Since when?"

"Since away back. I got out of the business before I got into it. I'm a bright boy, don't you know?"

"What did you do in Washington?"

"Bill, all I did was to sit at a desk and evaluate. That's the solid, unpainted truth. I sat at a desk until everything except my brain—and maybe that, too—was going flabby. I screamed, 'Let me out, let me out of here!' And I got this job eventually. Liaison mostly—NATO—Naples. At least I get some fresh air and a sun tan." He looked at Lammiter. "God damn it, you tell people the truth and they won't believe you!" He was exasperated enough to be believed. "I'll listen to your story, Bill. But, frankly, that's perhaps all I can do."

"You can always evaluate," Lammiter said with a grin. "And your liaison work nowadays may come in useful, too." Camden might know someone who would be interested in Brewster's story. "I'm only following the best advice my father ever gave me. When a picture fell off the wall or a drain clogged up, he'd yell, 'Get an expert, get an expert!' And whatever you say, Bunny, you're the expert. I'm just the man who was curious."

"And now I'm curious," Camden admitted. "Go ahead."

"Where was I, anyway?" He was flustered by Camden's casual approach.

"Expecting a car to aim straight for our spines," Camden said cheerfully, but he looked as if he were prepared to listen.

So Lammiter began. He began with Tony Brewster. That wasn't the way he had intended to start his story. But sometimes an apt cue is a better starting place than the first fact of a chronological account. And there was no doubt that the very mention of Tony Brewster's name startled Bunny Camden into complete seriousness. He listened to Lammiter's story with full attention, and—what was just as important—real interest. It was obvious that Lammiter was telling him something that was much more than he had expected.

They walked at an even pace, two men out for an evening stroll like so many others through the quieter streets of Rome, seemingly following no pattern of direction. By the time Lammiter had told of Rosana and her connection with the Pirotta narcotics ring; of the men around her —Bevilacqua the policeman, Joe the Sicilian, Salvatore the guide; of the princess and of Bertrand Whitelaw; of Eleanor Halley and her photographs, they had swung in a large arc of crisscrossed streets to the Piazza dell' Esedra. It was half-past ten. They could have walked the direct distance from Vittorio Veneto to the Esedra in an easy ten minutes.

For a few moments, Camden stood looking at the vast circle of the Piazza. Traffic swirled around the enormous central fountain, brilliantly illuminated to turn the high jets of water into golden plumes. Beyond them, on the other side of the Esedra, was the giant stretch of ruined walls and arches of the Baths of Diocletian, the enormous broken piles of bricks watching, from their withdrawn shadows, the brilliant lights of the modern arcades that curved round the other half of the Piazza.

"I like this fountain," Camden said, as if they had been discussing only the beauties of Rome. "Hear it? Falling water lighted. Helps one to think, just looking at it, listening. . . . Let's have coffee, and a seat."

"This isn't the Piazza Navona," Lammiter reminded him in a low voice.

"Plenty of taxis here," Camden said. "One will get you there in five minutes at this time of night." He led the way into the arcades and found a table that sheltered beside one of the giant pillars spaced around the half-circle of buildings to support the high curves of their arches, two stories high. Above these arches, each with its central ball of light, rose three more stories of large windows. So wide was the circle of the Piazza that the buildings didn't seem the giants that they were. Only the people, so miniature, and the cars, swirling round the fountain's pool like little water boatmen, put the scene into human proportion. The Italians, like the Romans, built for the gods.

Camden had chosen a table not too near the band that played in front of one of the cafés. For there, most people had gathered, either to sit at the crowded tables, or to stand, hundreds deep, as near the music as possible. Lammiter put away his mild protest, and settled comfortably to listen. It was his favorite aria from *Tosca,* and to judge by the silence of the crowd, oblivious to the steady hum of traffic, one of their favorites, too. Art is long, life is short. The buildings of stone looked and approved.

Camden had ordered coffee in crushed ice for them both. He drank slowly, watching the play of the fountains. Then, quietly, he said, loud enough for Lammiter, not loud enough for the nearest strangers to hear, "I had known, of course, about the narcotics trouble. Recently, I met one of our people from the Narcotics Bureau in Washington: he's only one of several top men who've come over here. That's how serious it is. And Interpol also has men on the job. And there was a man I met, just last month, from one of the United Nations committees. The Italians are worried, too. So are the French. It isn't any secret in official circles. It's one of the undersurface battles that Russia has been waging since the end of the war."

He looked casually around the tables. So did Lammiter. No one was near enough to overhear. Beside the vast pillars of the enormous arcade, the people seemed small and distant like figures in a Piranesi landscape.

Camden went back to admiring the fountains. "So I knew some of your story. But I didn't know the part Pirotta was playing. Your detective, Bevilacqua, didn't tell us all that when he visited us at the Embassy last week."

"He went to the Embassy?"

"To advise us that one of our people might find her name caught up in a mess of publicity. Nasty for everyone."

"Eleanor?"

Camden nodded. "I bet there was a sigh of relief when she asked for leave today. Solved the problem of finding an excuse that wouldn't upset Bevilacqua's investigation. Tricky."

Camden looked around again. He said, "We're out of luck. Bevilacqua usually comes here in the late evening for a quiet half hour on his way home."

Lammiter looked startled. He had forgotten that Bunny always had a reason behind his actions. Bevilacqua had been his reason for coming here.

"Oh, well," Camden said, "let's pay and go to a movie." He picked up the check and counted out the money.

"Look—"

"Now, now . . . You've still got fifteen minutes." Camden rose. And Lammiter followed. Under the arcade, side by side with shops, now closed, and the innumerable cafés and some third-class hotels, were several movie houses. Camden led the way quickly into the nearest large opening lined with the still photographs of an American gangster movie whose title and actors were complete strangers to Lammiter. "Part of our cultural exchange," Camden said with resignation. They paid, and entered a stone-floored passage, bleakly lighted, bare of furnishings or decorations, which twisted around behind the backs of the arcade's shops, with the booming sound of giant voices drawing nearer and nearer. Suddenly, Camden and Lammiter were inside a large open-air theater entirely enclosed by high buildings.

They stood for a moment, to accustom their eyes to the darkness of the sky overhead. Apart from the ghost-light from the distant screen stretched across the back of high houses, and a few shaded windows up in the buildings, and the stars above, there were no lights. The rows of collapsible wooden chairs were well filled, but most of the audience preferred the center and even the front seats. (The better to hear everything, Lammiter thought, as the booming ricocheted from wall to wall.) This left the back rows, sheltered under a pergola of vines overhead, almost empty, except for a scattering of couples.

Camden groped his way carefully to two seats at the far corner of an empty back row. Here, even the loud voices from the screen (two men fighting over a loose-haired, loose-mouthed blonde) were cut down in volume and in clarity. It was possible to talk, guardedly, and to listen. It would certainly be impossible for anyone to overhear.

Camden came straight to the point. "Now we'll discuss Mr. Evans. What does Brewster want us to do?"

"He wants to see you."

Camden let that pass. "But what can anyone do about Evans? There's no law against being a Communist. No law against a man visiting Italy from Russia."

"Unless his papers are false."

"Yes. That's why I'd like Bevilacqua to hear that part of the story. He could set something in motion."

"Brewster says there isn't enough time for that. What about the British? They'd also set something in motion, I'm willing to bet."

"Extradition? I don't think Brewster wants that—not just yet."

Lammiter felt stupid. "I guess not," he said lamely. No quick answers, he told himself: think, you lummox, think before you open your big mouth.

"It would be interesting to find out who the men are Evans is going to meet at Perugia, and what countries they've come from. That would give us the direction of Evans's mission here."

"I don't follow," Lammiter admitted frankly.

"We might learn from their identities where trouble is being planned. Supposing it is somewhere in the Far East, then the top-level agents infiltrated into that part of the world would need last-minute instructions—certainly a co-ordination of instructions—before any crisis was launched. Evans would be good at that. He has worked with both British and Americans. He knows where they are strong, and where they are weak. He's just the man to place the charges of dynamite, correctly, to start a landslide."

"But if the Far East is going to have more trouble, why did he come to Italy? I'd have thought Bombay or Karachi or Hong Kong would have been a better center for a meeting." He stopped. Camden hadn't said it was the Far East; he had only said "Supposing. . . ." Italy was a nice central meeting point for what? Western Europe and the Middle East? "If I were you, I'd contact the British Embassy right away," Lammiter said grimly.

"The trouble is, Brewster isn't exactly popular in diplomatic circles."

"So he told me. But if he has something new to say, won't someone at least listen?"

"Listen to a man who is a drunk?"

"Now—" Lammiter said quietly "—don't *you* start believing that! He likes his Chianti, but he can talk and think. He is still in control."

"I believe you, but thousands wouldn't."

Lammiter fell silent. He glared at the screen, where loud arguments had given way to gaping kisses, and the actors' faces had swelled up to the alarming size of twenty feet. He wondered what had happened to all the excellent movies he had seen last winter. Had they been torpedoed, crossing the Atlantic?

He lit a cigarette and let the match flare near his watch for a moment. "I've six minutes left," he said. "What have you decided?"

"Tell Brewster that I'd like to warn two men about Evans's appearance here. One of them is a Canadian, another is English. They are good Intelligence officers, in Rome at the moment on another job. Then, when the time comes for Evans to be picked up, England and the Commonwealth can do it together." Camden grinned. "That's diplomacy, son." Then he was serious again. "Secondly, tell Brewster I think he should let Bevilacqua in on the full story, too. He knows more experts in this kind of business than all the attachés in Rome put together. Between us all, we'll have Perugia well covered."

"Perugia— Why is Brewster so insistent on Perugia?"

"Why was Pirotta so insistent on keeping you out of Perugia?"

"That was when he thought I might be an agent—" Lammiter cut himself off. "I see," he ended.

"One last thing—ask Brewster to give you as much information for me as possible. After all, he's only given us one real fact, so far: that Evans is in Italy. That isn't much to go on."

"Why don't you come and see him yourself? I still think that makes good sense."

"I told you before—this is not my kind of business. The experts will push me out of the picture tomorrow."

"Will they indeed?"

Camden ignored that. "But meanwhile I'll start interesting them. That shouldn't be difficult. Then, after you've seen Brewster and got his go-ahead signal, they'll be ready to move. Right? Here's a number where you can leave a message for me at any hour." He slipped a card into Lammiter's pocket. "Call me as soon as you leave Brewster. Then you can relax and concentrate on your girl."

"That suits me," Lammiter said.

"Which girl?" added Camden softly, and rose.

They made their way out. The loose-mouthed blonde was now in full scream as her true love smacked her jaw. "You can see why our cultural attachés develop stomach ulcers," Camden said as the shrieks hounded them into the corridor. "They spend half their dinner parties explaining that all American children don't pull knives on their teachers because their hypodermics have been taken away from them." He stopped to search for a cigarette. "Keep your visit to Brewster short. Don't let him start making speeches." He seemed to remember something pleasing. "Or quote Shakespeare. Not tonight." He struck a match. "Keep moving, pal. Stay with it."

Lammiter recovered sufficiently to say, "Well, good to have seen you. We must get together soon," and walked away. Behind him, Camden had difficulty with the sulphur matches. He took a long, long time to light that cigarette. Lammiter was well alone as he came out into the Piazza.

The golden jets of hissing water rose into the dark sky and fell, rose and fell, bathing the nymphs and their sea monsters with spun silk spray. The music was gay and happy, a joyful rendering of *Oklahoma!* The people liked it. Their applause drifted over the sound of engines and brakes and horns. A city of contrasts, he thought: a sense of peace mingled with constant noise, the day's warm air and the night's cool breeze, stone and flowing water, shadows of giant buildings and the brilliance of delicate light. And the people, relaxing from their own troubles and worries, enjoying this moment, accepting this feeling of well-being as their due and proper right. He wondered if Bevilacqua was sitting among them now, relaxing, too, from the grim knowledge of his police work.

He had let two taxis pass him. Now he signaled. "To the entrance of the Piazza Navona," he directed. "As quickly as possible." A smile of delight answered him. He would reach there in possibly less than five minutes. But Providence protected children and drunks and Italian drivers.

He was still thinking of Bevilacqua, the man deep in the background whom he would probably never meet. And then he thought of Bunny Camden's other background friends—the Canadian and the Englishman who weren't diplomats. He'd never meet them, either. Nor the unknown men who had helped Brewster gather the small bits of information that made the whole pattern. Nor the Federal agents from Washington, now waiting at Bari. Nor the man, so deep in the background that he'd never even know all our names or nationalities, who would watch Evans's friends in Perugia and track them back to the countries where their hidden poisons were at work.

Camden had said, ". . . leave Brewster. Then you can relax and concentrate on your girl."

He had answered, "That suits me."

But now, he wasn't so sure of his answer. It wouldn't be easy to sit at a café table, even with Eleanor, enjoying the little world around you, when you kept remembering the background people. How far did they ever relax?

He looked at his watch again as they neared the Piazza Navona. Eleven o'clock. He'd be a few minutes late. Not bad, considering everything. He hoped Brewster's temper had not been too jangled by the alarm clock that kept ringing; but once he heard what had detained Lammiter, he would probably simmer down. Then Lammiter began to wonder what Brewster would tell him tonight, once the others had left and they were alone.

One thing was certain: whatever Brewster could tell would be stranger than Lammiter could ever invent.

14

The taxi jolted to a sudden halt beside the massive blocks of stone that marked the remains of the gateway to Domitian's stadium. By night, they were dark and grim.

As Lammiter walked quickly through the entrance and saw the lights and shadows of the Piazza Navona before him, he wondered how many chariots had come thundering into this enormous circus and drawn up at the starting gate, horses quivering, drivers tense. And how many men had looked up at the waiting faces and felt a moment of fear, before the mask of pride and readiness was slipped into place again? What made them risk death? Money, imperial favor, or the roar of the crowd?

The crowd . . . the crowd was strangely silent this evening. And then he noticed they were mostly clustering together, toward the east side of the Piazza, as if the wide pavement had tilted and poured them into a massed semicircle. The foreigners dining at the *trattoria* were still sitting over their coffee cups and wineglasses, but as he passed the hedge that shielded them from the Piazza, he saw that the waiters, at least, were curious. In the intervals of serving, they would group together, talking, watching the other side of the Piazza.

He was opposite the thickest bulge of the crowd, at the center point of all their interest. He looked, casually, hiding his sudden worry. He was looking at the house where Brewster lived. But everything was quiet, peaceful. Lights were in the various windows, in Brewster's, too, up there on the fifth floor. He checked his impulse to cross the Piazza and mix with the crowd. The church of St. Agnes was just ahead of him, and Rosana would be waiting.

But she wasn't there. Not yet. He thought it wiser to cross over to the central fountain in the square and admire Bernini. The church steps felt too naked. He walked slowly round the elaborate sculptures of the fountain. A few children still played, unheeding. An old woman sat slumped on a stone ledge, too old to go running to see or even to care about seeing. A few tourists were wandering around the other fountains: he didn't need to feel conspicuous here.

But his nervousness increased.

When Rosana came, she'd have to lead him round by the side street, as Salvatore had done this afternoon, and they'd enter Brewster's room from its back staircase. A pity he hadn't his pocket flashlight with him, so that they wouldn't trip over the cats. Women were always late; he should stop this worrying. She'd better come soon, though: he had spent a full ten minutes admiring Bernini's work, and the typical tourist was not as sculpture-conscious as all that. Was she over in that crowd? It was stirring now: people were moving around, talking. What had happened, anyway? Stop worrying. Thirty people or more lived in that house over there. The lights were on in Brewster's window. The curtains were open, and he could see the pot of geraniums on its window sill. Then he saw a man pause at the window for a moment, turning as if he were talking to someone behind him. The man's black silhouette retreated back into the room. There was left only the square of yellow light, and the pot of geraniums, and the strangely curious crowd far below. He felt no worry now but actual fear: Rosana had been punctual enough at noon.

He looked toward the church. Only a couple of middle-aged tourists sat on its steps and studied their tired feet. Was the church open? Was Rosana waiting inside? Perhaps she had seen the crowd and retreated, perhaps she had taken refuge inside. If so, she'd expect him to have enough sense to go in. Only, he thought as he came nearer the church doors, they look very, very closed. He turned, hesitated, and then started toward the crowd, wondering if this was the best thing to do, thankful that his Italian was good enough to find out what was wrong. Everyone in the Piazza seemed to know what was wrong, except the tourists. Rosana might be in the crowd; she *had* to be somewhere.

Now people were drifting away from the crowd, singly or in small groups. They would drift, and stop to argue, then drift again. Except one man who was cutting smartly across the center of the Piazza. Two men broke from the crowd and followed him. It was such an open maneuver that Lammiter halted in amazement. The first man, walking briskly toward the church, seemed unaware of any trouble. But his ears must have been quick, for he heard the hurrying pace behind him and he glanced briefly over his shoulder. His short stride almost became a walking run. He had reached the place where Joe had let Lammiter out of the car this afternoon and driven away with all the luggage; he looked round again. This time there was no doubt that he was being hunted. He suddenly swerved, away from the church, and headed at an open run for the cobbled pavement of the narrow *calle* near him. The two following men were running, too, lightly, easily. They were quicker.

Lammiter came to life, and set off after them. He had lost five seconds, there, staring in amazement at the man who had looked around. For it was Joe himself, Joe with his mop of black curling hair and his furrowed brow, looking more surprised than ever.

The narrow street, eight feet wide, a paved dark lane between dark houses, bleakly and scantily lit, was empty except for the three men. The two pursuers had almost caught up with Joe. He turned quickly to face them, his back safely to the wall. He held a knife in his hand. Its blade snapped open. He half crouched, waiting. His lips drawn back from his teeth, he made two sharp jabs at the air. The two men halted.

One of them had something in his hand, ready to strike. He hesitated as he heard Lammiter's running footsteps, jerking his head round for a split second. He said something. His companion was watching the waiting Sicilian, circling round as he, too, brought his gun out of his pocket. He, too, was going to use it to strike. They weren't going to shoot. Why? Lammiter wondered.

Then he understood. Noise. They didn't want noise. So he stopped running, opened his mouth, and with all the breath left in his lungs, he let out a rebel yell. A flutter of pigeons came from the roof tops. Board shutters were flung open from a window above his head, unexpectedly revealing a lighted room, and a stream of angry words in a shrill soprano voice poured down on him before the shutters were banged together again. But, more surprising, an answering rebel yell came from the Piazza behind him. And then the clatter of racing feet and laughter, girls' laughter echoing into the dark canyon of the little street.

The two men looked at each other. The one who gave orders spoke again, as the clatter of feet behind Lammiter suddenly scraped to a halt and a young man's voice called a warning. The girls' laughter changed to an excited squeal. Lammiter was too busy keeping his eyes on the gun now pointing at him to look round and welcome his unknown friends. Then another angry command was spoken, the gun was lowered, and the two men suddenly took to their heels. They disappeared round the curve of the street into the night.

They didn't want witnesses either, Lammiter thought. He walked toward Joe, whose knife had closed and vanished as quickly as it had snapped out. He glanced over his shoulder. The little group behind him —three girls and a thin young man—was clustered together as if they didn't quite know what to do now. "Thanks a lot," Lammiter called back to them. "Good night."

"I thought you were kidding," the young man said awkwardly. "That yell—I just thought you were kidding. Was that for real—the gun, I mean?"

"Why," one of the girls said, "I've never seen *anything* like that in Rome! Why, you just can walk down any old street. I've never seen anything like *that!*"

"Good night," Lammiter said.

"If I had known," the young man said angrily, "I wouldn't have brought the girls chasing in here—"

"You would, too!" said another of the girls. "Did you *ever* see *anything* like *that!* In this setting—it's medeeval, completely, utterly medeeval."

From above, the shutters banged open again. The four young faces turned upward in amazement as the stream of eloquence now emptied over them.

"Come," Joe said, his hand grasping Lammiter's wrist urgently.

"I'm looking for Rosana—"

"She had to go to the country."

"To the country? But—"

"She's all right. Come—" His impatience grew.

"I've got to see Brewster . . ."

"Later, later. Keep moving." He turned abruptly away, dropping Lammiter's wrist, and walked on. "Come on," he said impatiently.

Behind them, a girl's clear voice said, "Isn't she wonderful? Oh, *how* I *wish* I could speak Italian like *that!*"

Then the young man's voice called to Lammiter, "Everything okay?"

Lammiter looked back. He waved reassuringly. Then he caught up with Joe's short quick steps.

Joe said nothing more. He was too busy being cautious. They were, after all, following the same route that the two men had taken. At the curve in the street, he paused, keeping close to a wall, studying what lay ahead. There were no recessed doorways. And, just as important, there were witnesses available here, too. Six, in fact. A couple of elderly Italians walking slowly with their dog; four middle-aged foreigners, two husbands, two wives, looking completely frustrated. "Well, *ask* someone, Geoffrey," one of the women was saying impatiently. "We can't wander on these streets forever. Why don't you *ask* someone? There's an American, isn't it?" She quickened her pace toward Lammiter. "Can you tell us where is the Peeasa Navoena?"

"Straight ahead."

"Thank you *so* much." She looked back at the lagging Geoffrey. "See, darling, it was perfectly simple. . . . All one needs to do is use the tongue in one's head. Coming, Betty?" The women walked on, annoyance still quivering. The two men followed. They gave Lammiter a brief nod of thanks and a bitter look.

Lammiter said, "I guess I deserved that. Why hadn't I enough sense to say I was lost, too?"

Joe glanced at him sharply. He said quietly, in control of himself once more, "I parked the car about two blocks away from here. We can talk when we reach it. Now, we use our eyes and our ears." Then he fell silent. He looked like a man with several problems on his mind, all of them grim.

The two blocks stretched nearer to eight before they reached the car, parked beside others in a small square. It was Lammiter's guess that they had skirted round the Piazza Navona, almost to its other side. Or hadn't they? He was certainly as lost as poor old Geoffrey had ever been. The feeling increased as he looked at the car's license plate. "Get in! Quick!" Joe ordered in a low voice.

Lammiter hesitated. Then he got in.

"Where are we going?" he asked. He was too tense. He tried to look less worried than he felt. It was not easy. He kept his eyes ready for the slightest movement from Joe.

"Away from here," Joe answered curtly.

He headed straight for the busiest street, the Corso, with its narrow sidewalks packed with strolling people, overfilled trolley-buses, cars, the eternal Vespas and Lambrettas. They twisted west. They crossed the

Tiber briefly, and then came back again to the Via Flaminia. They drove north, then east, then south a little, climbing a hill. And at last, Joe drew up at the edge of a road, where couples in parked cars were far from conspicuous. On one side of the road were gardens, on the other a walk with seats for the view, for here the ground fell away abruptly to a lower level of streets. Lammiter could see over the roof tops, far beneath, across the whole city with its domed churches and lighted monuments.

"We'll keep the windows closed, and we'll talk," Joe said, taking out a twisted pack of cigarettes and offering one to Lammiter, "and *then* we'll know where we are going."

Lammiter said, "Keep it short." He was thinking now of the telephone call he must make to Camden. Nothing was working out the way they had expected. "What's gone wrong?"

Joe was silent.

"I saw a man at the window. Was it Salvatore?"

"That was Bevilacqua. Sam was down in the Piazza, with the crowd. We were both worried about you. Couldn't see you over by the church. Rosana told me to look for you there."

"I was staying well out of sight behind the fountain," said Lammiter, lamely. It had seemed an intelligent move, at the time. Now it seemed frankly silly. "I arrived late." He saw that Joe was watching him even more carefully than he had been watching Joe. And suddenly, too, he realized that Bevilacqua's visit was not just a friendly call, that the crowd gathered in the street was not grouped round a traffic accident. "What has happened to Brewster?" he asked tensely.

"He's dead."

"Dead?" The shocked word was jolted out of him. For several moments, he could say nothing. "How?" he asked at last. "A fake suicide?"

"Not this time. He was lying stretched out on his bed with the fiasco broken at its neck and dropped beside him. He had been struck a blow on the head."

"Was there no struggle? Didn't he shout? Did no one hear anything?" He was frankly incredulous. "A man was murdered in a room with a window wide open on a piazza crowded with people. . . ."

"Men like Brewster don't shout," Joe said abruptly. "They are trained not to shout. And there was no struggle in the room. The bed—disarranged a little." Joe was watching Lammiter very carefully now, but the

American was too troubled to notice. "It had been smoothed down again, perhaps?"

"I don't get it." Lammiter was following his own thoughts. "If there was no struggle, then he was asleep. If he was asleep, who let anyone get in? And one blow from a bottle—a fiasco padded with straw—that was enough to kill Brewster?" His face showed complete disbelief. "It must have been a hell of a blow."

Joe took a deep breath, almost of relief. "You talk like a policeman, my friend. All these questions . . ."

Lammiter stared at him. Guilty men didn't bring up the dangerous questions, guilty men didn't search for answers. Was that what the Italian was thinking?

Joe said very quietly, "You were right to have doubts. They smothered him first, with a nice soft pillow."

Lammiter rolled down the window, and threw away his half-finished cigarette. He took several deep breaths to steady his nerves. He felt sick, half stifled. A crippled man, lying helpless, perhaps asleep . . . He rolled the window up again, leaving a couple of inches open for fresh air.

"I felt that way myself," Joe agreed. "I can usually run faster than I did tonight." His eyes, watching Lammiter carefully, had lost their grim look of suspicion.

"But how—"

"Let the police find the answers. That's what they're paid to do."

"And that's another thing! How did the police get there, anyway? Who told them?"

"There was an alarm clock that kept ringing. A neighbor went to complain. She found the door unlocked, and then Brewster. She started screaming. That brought a couple of policemen up from the Piazza."

"The door had been left unlocked—and we were to walk right in?" His voice was bitter. He was beginning to understand why the unnecessary blow from the bottle had ever been struck. Rosana had handled that bottle. And there were fingerprints on the glasses, too. Fingerprints everywhere, his own included. This was much better than any faked suicide. Rosana and he would have to be questioned, perhaps held by the police. Perhaps? Most certainly. And for how long—a day, two days, three? "They made sure we weren't even going to reach Perugia," he said with rising anger.

That was a mistake. He knew it the moment it had slipped from his tongue. He remembered, too late, that Brewster had told neither Joe nor Salvatore nor Bevilacqua about Perugia, or Evans, or Pirotta's main interests.

Joe was watching him again. There was a new gleam of interest in his eyes.

Lammiter said quickly, "How did you learn all this about Brewster, anyway?"

"I reached Brewster's door just before eleven o'clock. As you said, it was open, and I walked right in. I walked right into the police."

"And did you want to meet them?" Lammiter was sarcastic.

"A Sicilian wants to meet—?" Joe laughed that off, briefly.

"The crowd could have told you there were policemen up there. But you went on upstairs." Lammiter paused. "And then the police let you go. How obliging of them, how very—"

"And thanks for helping me, after that," Joe said, branching off. "If you hadn't, I'd probably be in the Tiber right now, or dumped from a fishing boat off Ostia tomorrow. You know—it's a pity you don't trust me more."

"I trust you enough to ask you to take me to a telephone. And quickly." He touched Camden's card in his pocket to reassure himself it was still there, and brought out his cigarettes. "Have one of mine?"

"Thanks." But Joe made no move to start the car. "Why did you come running after me tonight?"

"I wanted to make sure I'd see my typewriter again."

"Save the jokes until I feel more like laughing."

"To tell you the honest truth," Lammiter said, "I just didn't think. I saw a couple of men on your heels, and I started running. It was just as simple as that."

"You just didn't think." Joe could be sarcastic, too.

"Not at first. When I started thinking, I let out a yell."

"Who were those men?"

"I don't know."

"Nor I," Joe said. He heaved one large and weary sigh. "It's a pity you don't trust me more," he repeated very gently. "I've got some questions that keep bothering me."

"Look, Joe, drive me to a telephone. You'll get your answers quickest that way."

"But I don't drive so well with questions on my mind," Joe said sadly. "Now why should those two men have been looking for me tonight? I've never seen them before in my life, and I thought I knew most of these boys. They aren't connected with any narcotics ring. Nor is Perugia."

"Who would be interested in my answers as well as you? It couldn't be Bevilacqua, could it?" And for the first time in this fencing match, Lammiter felt he had pierced through Joe's guard.

Joe started the car. "Don't guess so much," he said sharply. "That could lead you into real trouble."

"It already has." It was midnight now. Lammiter would never make that plane, even if he had wanted to. He wouldn't make any plane tomorrow, or the next day either. He glanced at Joe, who was both silent and angry. "Don't worry, Joe. My guess was all my own. I don't think any of the men you are hunting would even notice."

"Notice what?" Joe tried to be casual. But no one likes hearing his own mistakes.

"When we met, this afternoon, you were talking tough American. You were a man who had knocked around, done odd jobs, driven cars, become attached to the Di Feo family, then to the princess, part-time handyman, personal retainer, and probably black marketeer on the side. With a heart of gold, of course. But now you aren't talking that kind of language. Because you aren't thinking in that kind of language."

Joe glanced at him sharply.

"I'd say you were now a detective, an agent of some kind, one of Bevilacqua's bright boys, who's got several problems to solve. Where did you go to college in America?"

Suddenly, Joe laughed. It was a real laugh. "I like you," he said, keeping his eyes determinedly on the traffic. "You've got a sense of humor. Me, Giuseppe Rocco, one of Bevilacqua's bright boys . . ."

"Yes, that's what I'd say," Lammiter went on quietly, "except for one thing."

Joe was guarded now. "What's that?"

"The license plate on your car. Its last three numbers are the ones Rosana noticed last night when a car tried to pick her up. It's the number Brewster noticed when a car tried to run him down. Who could have borrowed your car, Joe?"

"*Mannaggia!*" Joe stared at him. For a moment, his face showed alarm; then it became blank again. "So," he said at last, "the laugh is on me, eh?" He fell silent. But Lammiter noticed that the car's speed had increased as much as the traffic would allow. Whatever Joe was, he certainly knew how to handle a car.

15

One of the greatest charms of Rome is the collection of office buildings, business headquarters, and stores which all close down at night, leaving bleak lights in their windows for cleaners and watchmen. There, the streets are not suddenly emptied after the working day ends, to let the tourists wander around like dispirited ghosts searching through a graveyard. There, the people not only work but live. Round the corner from the main streets are always the little streets and little squares, with apartments and flats and rooms and houses. There are trees, and flowers, and gardens surrounding great villas, the green touch to keep a city from turning into a suffocating blanket of stone and plaster.

Now, as Joe swung it away from the noise and light, the car turned into a street where most people had already gone to bed. They abandoned the car there, leaving it beside others equally nondescript. For a moment, Lammiter had the impulse to run, to get to a telephone. But he wasn't sure where he was, or in which direction to run, and a running man would attract attention. Besides, Joe's quick eyes were expecting a little trouble. He nodded, as if congratulating Lammiter on his wisdom, as the American waited for him while he locked the car. Then, at a brisk pace, they cut through a small square, walked across a busy intersection where a large movie house was still open, and entered a long street of high-walled gardens surrounding large villas. There was little stirring, a few pedestrians, an occasional car. The noise of the city's late pleasure traffic became a distant background to the peace of the night. It seemed warmer here, as if the trees and the flowers had trapped the hot sun and still fondled it in the moonlight. The air was heavy with the fragrance of jasmine and gardenias.

They passed two villas, standing far back from the street, dark and mysterious in their nest of trees. (They looked quite empty, as though the owners had left for their summer places among the hill towns.) As they approached the third garden, Joe pulled a ring heavy with keys from his pocket. Ahead was the entrance to this villa, an enormous double gate of elaborately wrought iron, set into high stone walls, a polished brass bell at one side and a shield with a coat of arms above. They were passing the gates. Joe glanced into the gardens. He swore softly and his pace increased. Lammiter glanced, too.

In that brief moment he saw a gatehouse, dark and empty, and then a villa, standing well back from the street, commanding a circular driveway. Its rooms were lighted, its handsome portico a blaze of hard brilliance. And he saw, too, the coat of arms over the gate, a wolf's head quartered with three beehives. Wasn't that the same coat of arms he had glimpsed in miniature today on the door of the princess's car?

Beyond the main entrance lay a small narrow gate, chained and padlocked, partly overgrown by a tangle of leaves and branches climbing along the wall. But someone had oiled the padlock and the hinges of this unused gate, for Joe unlocked it easily and swung it open soundlessly. Quickly, with a last glance along the quiet street, he pulled Lammiter inside the villa's garden. Carefully, he closed the gate and secured it once more. They were standing in a stable yard at the back of the gatehouse. The building, Lammiter now saw, was a garage, politely turning its honest utilitarian face toward the yard away from the painted elegance of the villa. (Once it had been a stable and coach house, for he passed a disused horse trough and pump as he followed Joe across the paved yard.)

Joe unlocked a panel of the garage door soundlessly, swung it open a few feet, and beckoned him in. He stood in complete darkness as the door was closed. He could hear Joe fumbling against a wall. A click, and a bare light glared down at them from a high beam. In front of him stood a venerable and highly polished Lancia.

"Quick!" Joe said, pointing to a rough flight of wooden stairs at one end of the garage. "And when you get to the top, wait. Or you'll break a leg."

Lammiter left Joe at the light switch and passed three horse stalls, a heap of tires, neatly stacked oilcans, an ancient carriage, bridles and harness hanging from hooks. Then he began climbing. At the top was a dark recess. He waited there. He had to. The light didn't penetrate as far as that. Now Joe switched it off, and the blackness was complete again.

The minute seemed interminable. And then a wooden step gave a faint groan, a more solid piece of blackness stood beside him, and Joe grasped his arm. "One moment," Joe said, edging past him, opening a narrow door. Beyond was an attic: a floor of bare boards cluttered with islands of trunks and boxes, all striped with the pale white light of stars and moon that came through the slatted shutters of the windows.

"Quiet!" warned Joe angrily. For the pale light was deceptive: Lammiter, on his way over to the nearest window, had misjudged a shadow and stumbled against a pile of harness. There was a smell of dry leather, the feeling of grit under his feet, the sound of a bat's steady whir as it circled under the low rafters. He reached the window. It was, more accurately, an oblong for ventilation, tucked into the shade of the pink-tiled roof, with only the slatted shutters for covering. But the view was excellent. He could see the driveway, with the villa far to his right; slightly to his left, almost below him, were the front gates.

"The princess goes to bed late," he said softly. Joe had no need to tell him to keep his voice almost to a whisper. From the garden the gentle splash of water in some hidden fountain came so clearly into the attic that he needed no reminder that all noise was amplified by the stillness around him or that these ventilation windows were unglazed.

Joe began talking, very quietly, in Italian. Lammiter swung round, almost falling over a couple of leather bags and a typewriter. He stood staring at Joe, who had not taken leave of his senses but was using all of them, in a long complicated conversation over a telephone. In this attic of ancient and abandoned possessions, the small black telephone was a strange intrusion. It had been installed in the wooden frame of the door itself, inside a panel cut in the jamb.

Joe had been talking about his car, probably (he spoke too quickly for Lammiter to be sure) giving its location. There was something about number plates, and a change; something about watching a garage. And then Joe began talking about Lammiter, for he looked across at the American for a quick moment and then dropped into a dialect, Sicilian possibly, which was completely unintelligible. This part was brief. Very unflattering, Lammiter thought with a smile. It was the first smile he had felt like giving for a long time. A telephone was a great help to morale.

Joe hooked back the receiver into the inside of the panel and swung it shut.

"My turn," Lammiter said.

"I must wait for a call."

"I must make one! Or shall I start heaving a few trunks around and give an Apache scream? That's worse than a rebel yell. I've all kinds of sound effects ready to use."

"I believe you would," Joe said. But he was almost smiling, and he swung the panel open again. So Lammiter at least had been declared friendly. He stepped carefully over the typewriter case, looked down and exclaimed, "Hey, that's mine!" but kept on moving as quickly as possible to the telephone. Joe might change his mind.

"I told you they'd be safe," said Joe. "You should trust me more."

"I trust as much as I'm trusted." Lammiter reached in his pocket. "I need some light," he said angrily, trying to make out Camden's writing. Was that an eight or a three? He felt for a match.

"Shield it," came Joe's quick warning.

Lammiter obeyed, put through the number, and waited. "I gather you aren't supposed to be here."

"Only when I'm working on the Lancia. I lock up, hand the key in at the house, get the gates locked behind me. There was a burglary at the villa last year, so now everything is locked and—"

"Sh!" Lammiter said. It was an American voice speaking at the other end of the line. "Camden, please. Bill Lammiter speaking." Joe had moved across to the ventilation slats. He seemed to be watching the villa, but he was listening. Lammiter was sure of that.

"Oh yes," the voice said as if that was no surprise.

"There's been trouble tonight. Can I reach Camden himself?"

"Just a moment. Here is where he can be reached meanwhile." A number, vaguely familiar, was rattled off. "Got it?" It was repeated. It was Eleanor Halley's number.

"That's enough!" Joe's urgent whisper came across the still attic. But Lammiter had already got the number. "Shut up!" he said, to silence Joe's steady stream of fine Sicilian curses. "Bunny? There's bad news."

"So I've just heard." Camden's matter-of-fact voice was a real slice of comfort. "It's breaking fast. Must be more of an emergency than we guessed." He paused. Then he said, "There's trouble here, too, Bill."

"Something has happened to—" He couldn't finish. He hadn't expected that news. And he hadn't expected the news to hit him this way, either.

"Take it easy. She isn't here."

"Isn't there?" he asked blankly. And then, savagely, "Where the hell is she?"

"*Zitti!*" Joe warned from the window. "Sh!"

"Take it easy, Bill," Camden was saying. "She left a note for the maid. She says she'll be back on Monday."

"Monday—" Today was Thursday. No—Friday now. "And where has she *gone?*"

"She didn't say."

"Did she take any clothes—any—"

"It's difficult to judge. The bedroom's in a state of eruption."

"She was packing. Going home tomorrow. Look, Bunny, stay there. I'll be right around."

"You stay *here!*" said Joe, looking angrily over his shoulder.

"No, don't come around," Camden's voice said. "That gains nothing. The case is in good hands."

"What happened? For God's sake, Bunny, tell me what's been going on?"

"I got in touch with that Englishman I mentioned. He was definitely interested. He wanted to talk to Miss Halley. We telephoned. No answer. I thought we'd better go round to her place and see her. We kept knocking at her door. No answer. So I telephoned the police, they wakened the porter downstairs, and we all got in. There was a lot of packing interrupted and dirty dishes. But no girl. No photographs, either."

"But—"

"Have you still got that snapshot?"

"Yes."

"Good. Where are you?"

"In a loft, guarded by a watchdog called Giuseppe Rocco." There was a quick rush of light footsteps behind Lammiter.

"Giuseppe Rocco?" Camden's voice repeated. Joe's hand forced its way between the receiver and Lammiter's mouth. It was not a happy gesture. Lammiter was never in a mood to be gagged, least of all now. He kicked sideways and aimed the hardest blow he could manage with his free hand at Joe's chin. "Don't do that, don't you ever do that to me!" he said in sudden fury as Joe's grip was forced off his lips.

Joe's hand was in his pocket, his balance regained, his knees slightly bent, crouched, ready. His lips were narrowed with an anger that matched Lammiter's.

"What's going on there?" Bunny's voice was suddenly alarmed. "Wait—put Rocco on the phone—here's a friend of his—Bill, put Rocco on the phone!"

"For you," Lammiter said, holding out the receiver. Joe straightened his body slowly. His right hand was still in his pocket. His eyes were wary and never left Lammiter, but he took the receiver.

Lammiter sat down on a trunk. There was sweat on his brow. He took out his handkerchief, and inside it he felt the small negative and its print. There was still one piece of identification left about Evans, still one photograph. But Eleanor could identify the man even better. Eleanor . . . Now a cold sweat broke over his brow.

Whoever was talking to Joe had authority, information, and—finally—instructions to give. Whatever he was saying had a noticeable effect: Joe's face was astonished, but it was no longer troubled. He even smiled and nodded encouragingly over to Lammiter. Now, thought Lammiter wryly, all I have to worry about is Eleanor.

He waited impatiently for the first sign of the end of Joe's instructions. But Joe gave his own brief report, in his very best Italian, before the call seemed near an end. Probably he had been on the telephone no more than five minutes all told, but to Lammiter they seemed an hour. He signaled as Joe was giving his final "*Sì, sì, capo,*" and held out his hand.

"The American wants to speak to his friend," Joe said into the phone and handed it amicably over to Lammiter. Then he walked back to the window.

Camden's voice said, "I think that's settled a lot of things."

"Where can I give you that snapshot?"

"Rocco has all the instructions."

"But, look—"

"This isn't our country, fellow," Camden said gently. "Let Bevilacqua and his boys handle this."

"And we do *nothing?*"

"Oh, we'll help when and if needed."

"Bunny—" he tried to talk calmly, "any guesses about Eleanor? Any evidence—any—"

"Not yet. But Bevilacqua is definitely interested. Brewster's murder makes all these problems very much his business."

"Where's Pirotta?"

"Seems to have left town."

"When?"

"I'm told he left his house around nine thirty, with luggage. He was driving. Just before ten o'clock his car was seen outside Rome, on the Via Flaminia, heading north. Looks as if he's the advance guard of Perugia."

Lammiter didn't speak. Just before ten o'clock he had been saying good-by to Eleanor.

"Take it easy, Bill," Camden's calm voice said once more. "We'll get all these bastards, every God-damned one of them. See you tomorrow. Follow instructions." He hung up.

Lammiter swore and tried to recall the number. Joe, at the window again, said quietly, "*Basta, basta!* Finish! Stop!" He beckoned urgently.

Lammiter took a deep breath, a slow deep breath. He hung the telephone receiver on its cradle, and closed the panel back into place. Slowly, he went over to the window. He felt suddenly tired, tired and defeated. Joe, on the contrary, was a man full of restored confidence, a man who looked as if he were sure of the road he was following. Lammiter asked bitterly, "How about that phone call you were expecting?"

"Oh, forget it," Joe said, friendly now and smiling, too. So it had been Bevilacqua whom Joe had wanted to contact. Lammiter's wishful guessing had been right, after all, but that fact gave him no comfort at the moment. "How good is Bevilacqua?" he asked. Good enough to find Eleanor long before three days were over?

"Look, will you? Look!" said Joe. Lammiter looked.

In front of the villa, slowly descending its steps, was a man dressed in a dinner jacket. Beside him, a white scarf over her shoulders, was the princess. Their voices carried over the garden in the still air, but they were still too far away to be clearly understood. They were speaking in English, the man protesting politely ". . . no need. . . ." The princess was equally polite, ". . . no trouble at all. . . ." An elderly woman, short and fat, dressed in unrelieved black, came hurrying after them with a cloak for the princess. Then they began walking toward the gate, the woman in black keeping a discreet distance behind her mistress and the departing visitor. The voices became clearer. And now, too, Lammiter could recognize Bertrand Whitelaw. The Englishman was no longer quite so amused or amusing as he had been yesterday at Doney's. He even looked uncomfortable, ill at ease. He was trying to explain his late visit, and a man who makes excuses is vulnerable.

The princess, of course, was enjoying herself. "It's *always* delightful to see you, Bertrand. Even at midnight." She had lost little of her incisive charm. "Now don't apologize again. I *like* to walk by moonlight. It's so good for one's memories. At my age, Bertrand, that is what I live on."

"Principessa—" He glanced back at the maid, and hesitated.

"Maria and I have been together for fifty-four years. Nothing surprises her. Besides, most conveniently, she knows not one word of English. You were saying—?"

"Principessa—where is Luigi? I've been trying to find him, but he has left Rome."

Lammiter, at the mention of Pirotta's name, stopped watching the scene with a casual eye. He was really listening now.

"Ah!" the princess said with drama to match the moonlit garden. "So you came to ask about Luigi, and all the time I was flattering myself that you were worried about me."

"But I was. When you didn't appear at Sylvia's dinner tonight—"

"Oh, I was suddenly tired of enormous dinner parties. And of Sylvia. She is *so* correct. How did she like my telegram?"

"She didn't read it to us."

"How very disappointing! Of course, telegrams aren't the politest forms of refusal. Don't you want to know what I said?"

"Of course," Whitelaw said patiently.

"Impossible to be with you. Lies will follow."

"It sounds much better in its original French."

"Bertrand, you know everything! Yes, I suppose it does. But I've always wanted to use it. The French have such a knack for the cynical phrase. Don't they?"

At the window above, Lammiter shook his head. The princess had such a knack for confusing an issue. Not much was left, now, of Whitelaw's simple question about Luigi Pirotta.

But Whitelaw had not given up altogether. "I heard tonight that there seems to have been some kind of—trouble between Luigi and Miss Halley."

"Trouble? Oh, he and his little American have decided not to get married. Young people are *so* changeable."

"I can't understand it."

"Who has ever understood people in love? But I'm sure our friends at dinner did their best to find an explanation for everything. What did they say—the American has had five husbands, and Luigi likes young boys?"

"No one was being malicious."

"How odd! Or perhaps they hadn't had enough warning."

"Tivoli was blamed, however. It seems the trouble started there, two or three nights ago."

"Now really, Bertrand—how completely ridiculous!"

"One of the guests at dinner was a friend of Miss Halley. She lunched with her on the day after Tivoli. She insisted that the quarrel was not at all serious. And certainly, today at Doney's, I didn't notice anything wrong. It really is so—so inexplicable. I'm a little troubled. After all—" He hesitated.

"You *are* Luigi's friend," the princess finished for him, with a touch of amusement.

Upstairs, Lammiter stood rigid. His anxiety was rising as steadily as a bead of mercury at noon. How many people had been at that dinner party? How many servants? Ears listening, tongues repeating. Tivoli . . . Tivoli. Throw one small stone into a pool, and the ripples spread out and out.

The princess had moved to the gates. In Italian, she gave Maria the command to unlock them.

"Would you tell Luigi I'd like to get in touch with him?" Whitelaw asked.

"Why do you keep thinking *I* shall see Luigi?" The princess's voice was sharp with annoyance. "He never asks my advice."

"Perhaps not. But he always takes your help."

"Why should I give it?" she demanded. "This morning, I wished he were—he were dead. That shocks you?"

"If you want me to be shocked—yes."

"Good night, Bertrand."

He still hesitated. "Principessa—I don't want to alarm you, but as I rang at the gate tonight for Maria to let me in, I noticed two men in your garden—walking around the side of the villa."

"Servants."

"They seemed to vanish so quickly when they saw me."

"Naturally. They know very well that they are not supposed to walk in the garden. Good night." She offered him her hand in a very final gesture.

He kissed it. "If you need help, do call on me. At any time. And I'm sorry I troubled you so needlessly—"

She laughed again. "I do believe you want to protect me, Bertrand! I am touched, indeed I am.—Maria, open the gate! —No car, Bertrand? Did you *walk?*"

"I prefer to walk," Whitelaw said stiffly and went into the street. Maria locked the gates behind him.

"Come, Maria," the princess said clearly in Italian. "Let us look at the gardenias, and so to bed."

Lammiter straightened his back and stretched his shoulders. What had brought Whitelaw visiting at this hour? Some talk at a dinner party? Or had the Englishman heard something more than gossip? Then Lammiter began wondering about Whitelaw himself. He ought to have asked Camden about Whitelaw, but he had forgotten. Or, rather, other questions had pushed that one to the back of his mind. "Joe—" he began, but Joe made a sign for caution. Something in the garden was holding his attention.

The princess had not gone to look at the gardenias. She was standing quite motionless in a patch of moonlight on the driveway, looking toward her house. Waiting? Suddenly the lights over the door of the villa were switched off. A man hurried from its steps, cutting across the paved garden which the driveway encircled. Lammiter's body stiffened abruptly. The running man was Luigi Pirotta. He was now reaching the princess. He said, angrily, "I thought he'd never go! What did he want?"

The princess lifted a hand in warning. "Voices carry," she reminded him.

"What did he want?" he repeated, more quietly.

She said coldly, "You cannot leave yet. Bertrand is on foot. Walking slowly. And the street is very long." She looked away from him, wrapping the cloak around her more closely. It was a gesture of separation.

"I have still some things to explain," he said gently. "Maria—"

"She will not listen."

"No? Come into the garage. She can't hear us there." He entered the courtyard. She hesitated. "Maria," she called softly to the woman still at the gate. "Keep watch!" Then she followed Pirotta.

As the garage door scraped on the cement floor, Joe moved swiftly away from the window toward the door, using the sounds below to cover his own light footsteps. Lammiter had not moved quickly enough. He was caught halfway across the wooden floor. He didn't trust either its loose boards or the treacherous light. He tested a trunk lying flat on the floor beside him. It seemed solid enough. He sat down. That way, there would be no danger of any sound from him. Joe had opened the attic door about two inches. He looked across at Lammiter and nodded; then he bent his head, listening.

The voices came up to Lammiter faintly from the dark garage. The lights had not been switched on down there. The garage door must be open. The voices were hushed, talking in Italian, sibilant and energetic, but too quick for Lammiter to understand. And somehow, he was relieved. He did not have to listen. He had had enough of the uncomfortable feeling of eavesdropping. He would be no good at this kind of business, he thought as he watched Joe. He rested his head in his hands, trying to get his own problems balanced. He had to fight hard to keep down a rising impulse to walk right downstairs, confront Pirotta, and drag him to the nearest police station. Yet it wouldn't solve anything. Joe would be doing exactly that, right now, if it was the answer. Joe was in command here. "Follow instructions," Camden had said. Yes, sir, I'm following instructions, sir, Lammiter thought. He was sitting on a battered trunk in a disused attic, sweating out instructions. Had Camden thought of that? Or of the sound of Pirotta's voice, so gentle and suave? The princess had been sharp and angry at first. No longer. Pirotta was a persuader.

Then he suddenly thought, Pirotta is here; he hadn't been leaving Rome just before ten o'clock, traveling north on the Via Flaminia. He was in Rome when Eleanor vanished. Had she gone with Pirotta?

Lammiter rose to his feet, but even as he moved to the door, the car's engine started. Joe's look of warning changed to amazement, and his signal for silence froze in the air. Caution was unnecessary, anyway, at this moment: the Lancia's drone smothered all sounds.

Lammiter stood in the recess at the top of the stairway, looking down into the empty garage. He was too late. Or Pirotta had been too quick. The car was already in the yard, swinging toward the driveway. The princess was standing very still at the door of the garage. Maria was beside her, anxious. "I opened the gate," Maria said. The princess said nothing. "The gates are open," Maria repeated, raising her voice. In the driveway, the car's engine was running smoothly, softly, then faded to nothing.

"Yes, yes," the princess said wearily. But she did not move away. "Maria, did I do right? Did I?" Her voice broke, and her head drooped. Her hands went to her face to conceal it.

Lammiter heard a light rustle of movement behind him. Joe had moved away from the door, back to the window. What had drawn his interest there? And now Lammiter heard the car once again: it was still here in the grounds. It hadn't left, not yet. As he reached the window, he saw it start from the front door of the villa to sweep down the driveway. It slowed for a brief moment at the open gates. Then it was through, turning left, traveling fast.

"No one drives that car but me." Joe's low voice was bitter. "How do you like that, eh? That's one thing I'd have sworn— Why, she's always worrying about one little scratch, and he drives like a crazy man." Then he looked at Lammiter. "Don't worry, my friend," he said gently. "I heard all their talk. It's in here." He tapped his forehead and grinned widely. "The princess said she would telephone Alberto to expect Pirotta. There's only one Alberto she would telephone. He's the caretaker of her house up in the hills. Don't worry, we know where he's taking the girl."

"Girl?"

"Sure. His girl. He picked her up at the villa. That's why the car stopped there. What's wrong? Don't—" His voice changed and his arm shot out. But Lammiter dodged.

"That's my girl, too, Joe." And he started downstairs.

Lammiter slipped into the courtyard. Maria was coming away from the front gates, heading in his direction as if she would now attend to the garage doors. She didn't catch sight of him until he had reached the corner of the building. She gave a hoarse little scream; and the princess, walking very slowly toward the house, halted and turned round.

Lammiter stepped into the driveway. "Good evening," he said to the frightened Maria. "Or good morning, perhaps."

"Oh!" the princess said. For once, she had nothing else to say. But as Maria rushed to her side (whether to defend or to be saved, Lammiter was not quite certain), the princess took command. "Quiet, Maria! Go to the house." And then, as Maria retreated unwillingly, the princess said, "Good morning it is, Mr. Lammiter." Maria, more reassured, covered another ten feet toward the villa, but there she stood, loyally disobedient, her face masked in peasant suspicion.

The princess looked at him searchingly. She was angry. "All gates are locked. Am I to believe you climbed over my wall?"

He looked down at his blackish-gray trousers liberally streaked with dust. He tried to brush it off. "I'm sorry—" he said awkwardly. "I just had to see you." He hoped he sounded like a man who had indeed climbed a wall.

"The usual way to enter is to ring the bell at the gate," she said.

"I didn't want to waken everyone at this time of night."

"Most thoughtful of you." She was still acid. "And why were you determined to wake *me?*"

"I saw your car drive off."

She hesitated. "Indeed? And so you came to warn me? How *very* kind," she said mockingly. She obviously believed that attack was the best defense.

He tried a little attack of his own. "Pirotta was driving."

"Oh?" She stood very still.

"And Eleanor was with him, wasn't she?"

"It's very late for questions, Mr. Lammiter. Come and see me tomorrow." She smiled, almost kindly, and turned away.

"You have one habit I like," he said. "If you can't tell the truth, you don't tell lies."

She halted and faced him. "Why are you here?"

He said, "Yesterday at Doney's you invited me to stay in Italy. I've decided to accept. That's all."

"I gave you more than an invitation. I gave you warning." She suddenly burst out, "*Why* didn't you talk sense into Eleanor's head and make her leave?"

"She was leaving today."

"Too late, too late," she said angrily. "Why, why did she ever come to Rome, why did Luigi have to fall in love with her? Why didn't he marry Rosana, and there would have been none of this trouble?" She halted abruptly and controlled her emotions. "Stop glaring at me like that! Do you think I'd ever have let Luigi take my car if I didn't believe we could still save Eleanor?"

"From what?"

The princess hesitated. "I only know that there is danger. She knows too much about matters that do not concern her. She must be hidden. For her own safety. Just a few days, that's all. *Please* believe me, Mr. Lammiter. Do you think that I should ever have let Luigi take her away if—"

"Was she all right?" he interrupted quickly.

She looked at him with astonishment. "But of course!"

"Did she go of her own free will?"

"Really, Mr. Lammiter! One would imagine—"

"It's too late for imagining. I want to *know.* Did she go of her own free will?"

"Yes." She watched his face. "I'm sorry," she said more gently. "She had to go. There was no other solution. She will be safe, I assure you."

"No other solution?" he asked. "You could have telephoned the American Embassy if Eleanor was in danger. You could have called the police."

"Impossible!"

"Why?"

"Because we want no publicity. There is danger in publicity. Danger for Eleanor—and for Luigi. We must keep everything discreet: no scandal, no disgrace."

"That's going to be difficult."

"Not so difficult. Luigi has resigned from his company. You see, he, at least, took my warning at Doney's."

"Do you actually believe that resigning from a company—an innocent company at that—is going to have any effect on evidence?"

"What evidence will stand up without witnesses?"

"His firm would know from its books that he has been up to mischief. What about the shipments of drugs he has sidetracked?"

"But its directors may not want such publicity, Mr. Lammiter. As you say, their firm is a good one, solid, respectable. It took too long to build up that reputation. Do you think they want it destroyed overnight? One touch of scandal . . ."

"Sure," he said bitterly. "It would empty their pockets, too." So honest men would form a solid wall of respectability around Pirotta. And the princess would cover up Pirotta's guilt for the sake of the family name. What about the crooks who had worked for him? But criminals rarely talked: they wouldn't give evidence against him. They would cover up for him, more than anyone, in order to save their own skins.

The princess was watching him with marked displeasure. She said coldly, "Must Americans always think of money?"

He looked at her, equally coldly. "But dear Luigi never thought of money, indeed not. I suppose he was only dedicated to the noble cause of spreading dope addiction?"

For a moment, her eyes blazed with anger. For a moment, he thought she was going to turn on her heel and walk away. But she did not. She dropped her eyes. Perhaps that was as near to an apology as she could ever come. "It's all over," she said in a low voice. "All that degrading and evil business is over. He has given me his word." She faced Lammiter again. "Don't think that I am excusing anything he has done," she said almost fiercely.

"Has he promised to drop all his political ambitions, too? Or at least change them to open, honest politics?"

"Politics?" She clearly did not understand what he was saying.

"If Eleanor is in danger, it doesn't come from the men who worked in narcotics."

"Do not underestimate them. They are vindictive and dangerous. Believe me, Mr. Lammiter, the danger is very great."

"We're talking at cross-purposes," he said impatiently. "What I meant —"

"Do you know what you really mean? Why, you don't even know what you've *done!* You are to blame for all this, Mr. Lammiter. And you stand there—"

"*I'm* to blamc?"

"If anything happens to Eleanor, you will be responsible. You instigated, persuaded her to—" She made a gesture of distaste. "No doubt you had the most patriotic motives for acting as one of your country's agents. But why draw Eleanor into—"

"But that's nonsense. Who told you this, anyway? Pirotta? Surely you don't believe—"

"Why was she trying to reach you this evening? Why did she want to see you before she left Rome?"

"She was trying to reach me—where?" And then suddenly he remembered Eleanor's telephone calls to his hotel. "Just let me explain," he began quietly. "It was—"

"How *could* you have drawn her into all this hideous mess?" The princess was glad to scold someone. "I hold no brief for Luigi, but he, at least, is trying to protect her."

"Does Eleanor believe that?"

The princess shrugged her shoulders. "She is a very strange girl. She kept quite silent all the time she was with Maria."

"You were not with her?"

"Luigi had a great deal to tell me. After all, he did owe me some explanation."

"And a very good job he made of it."

"That is quite enough," the princess said sharply. "Maria, let this man out at the gate."

"This man will go when he is good and ready," Lammiter said.

"I shall call the police."

"You should have called them an hour ago." He had scored a point: she must have had that impulse and then smothered it. Or been persuaded out of it. He pressed on. "Better still, you should have had an honest talk, alone, with Eleanor. Then you would have found out that she doesn't know one thing about the narcotics racket. She is in no danger from that."

"But—but she *is* in danger."

"Yes," he said very quietly.

"From what?" she asked quickly.

"I tried to tell you."

"From what?" she repeated. And now, the doubts that had troubled her and been silenced were stirring again.

It was a good time to leave, Lammiter decided. "Ask Mr. Big," he said.

"Mr. Big?"

"Mr. Big the Second. Dear Luigi. Oh, he isn't anywhere near that, yet. But that's the direction he is taking. Not fascist, of course. That's been tried. And there won't be any march on Rome, this time. His friends without faces have more subtle methods than that."

She said haltingly, "Friends—without faces?"

"Yes, his friends at Tivoli, who don't like being photographed. Good night, Principessa." He bowed. To the maid he said, "Don't trouble about the gates, Maria. I can go out the way I came in." He smiled for her. She had not understood what he said, for he had been too tired to face any Italian verbs. It had been a mistake, after all, he thought wearily, to try to talk with the princess.

He made an effort and walked smartly down the driveway. He was more than tired: he was exhausted. The gate was near, and the wall beside it looked higher than he remembered. His exit line had been good theater, but a damned silly idea. He had enough sense still left to keep well away from the garage. Would the princess watch? No, probably not. She would never be caught watching anyone. But she would have no objections to Maria's watching and telling her what the crazy foreigner did.

He refrained from looking round. And then, almost at the gates, he noticed how the bushes and flowering trees had been planted partly to screen the entrance to the yard, partly to soften the bleak stone. He plunged through this mass of shrubbery, and behind its shelter made his way slowly and carefully along the wall. It took some time. He reached the second gateway by which Joe and he had entered, and there was the path to lead him back to the courtyard. He couldn't be seen here from the driveway. He halted, and waited. If Maria didn't come round the corner of the garage in the next few minutes, he'd risk that bare and vulnerable courtyard. Everything seemed bleak and purposeless. What am I doing here, anyway? he asked himself angrily. Eleanor had gone of her own free will. That was all he needed to sink him into this cold pit of despair.

17

Maria did not appear. Perhaps she was too busy offering salts of ammonia to the princess. Anyway, the garage door was forgotten. It still gaped open. And still Bill Lammiter stood, making up his mind to cross the courtyard and climb the stairs. And then? Sleep upstairs in that attic, while each minute took Eleanor a full mile farther away? She had gone of her own free will. Had she? What was free will worth when she had not known the full truth? He could blame himself for that. He hadn't told her much tonight. And yet, he hadn't been free to talk. It always came back to the same old frustration: the eternal pull between what you wanted to do and what you had to do.

He turned and measured the wall behind him with his eye. Difficult, but not impossible. And once over? Try to find out which of the princess's villas in the country had a caretaker called Alberto. And then? Hire a car and find his way—hell, one man was useless. In trouble, one man was not enough. He heard a light step from the courtyard. Quickly he glanced over his shoulder.

But it was Joe. The garage door was left open behind him for Maria to find exactly as the princess had left it. He was carrying one of Lammiter's suitcases, and in the other hand he held his keys ready.

"What, no typewriter?" Lammiter asked as he took his bag.

Joe gave him a strange smile, looked up at the wall, and shook his head. Then, in silence, he opened the padlock of the gate and urged Lammiter through. The long street was quiet, except for a few people in the distance, where it ended in some kind of boulevard, a brightly lit *corso.* Joe set off toward the lights at a quick pace. Apparently, it was all right to talk now, for he said, "You worried me, you worried me." Suddenly he grinned. "You know, I thought you might even be climbing that damn wall. Here, let me carry that bag. You're all worn out making decisions. Just leave them to Joe, eh?"

"I'm all right," said Lammiter curtly.

"We'll get a lift."

"Not on this damned street, we won't."

"I phoned for a taxi." Joe's smile was broad. He was in bright good humor.

"Sure," Lammiter said gloomily. Joe's little jokes were even worse than his own.

Joe said, "Hope I grabbed the right suitcase. You have to look pretty when you walk down the main street of Perugia."

Lammiter looked at him.

"But first, we'll find your little American. You stay with me now, eh?" Joe was amused.

"Well, this is better than sleeping on an attic floor."

"After what happened? Look—it took me a long time getting that place fixed up. I don't want to have it discovered now."

"Sorry if I altered your plans," Lammiter said more cheerfully, "but I like them better this way."

"Yes," said Joe, "I noticed you were getting kind of restless. Come on, then. Let's keep moving. Another block, that's all." And as he quickened his pace still more, he went on, "Want to know what's happening back at the villa right now? The princess is mad. She's good and mad. She's ordered all the servants out to search the grounds, the garage, everywhere. That's my guess, but I'll bet on it. She's getting angrier every minute. With Pirotta. But she doesn't know that yet. She thinks it's you that is making her mad."

"I hope she will branch onto Pirotta, before it's too late."

"She will. She will. She's no fool. How did you know she hated Mr. Big so much?"

"Mussolini wouldn't be her idea of God's gift to Italy. He built the biggest railway stations and the biggest shell holes, too. And he divided her family: her brother on Mr. Big's side, the princess and her son against him. What happened to her son and daughter-in-law?"

"They were banished to Lipari. Died there." Joe looked at him curiously. "You've stirred a lot of memories tonight. Good! The more she is mad, the better. For then she starts thinking. And after that she acts." Joe's admiration was unbounded.

Lammiter did not share his enthusiasm. "Perhaps. I heard her at Doney's. But it must have taken her weeks to act on that gossip about Pirotta."

"Weeks?" Joe laughed. "She heard that news yesterday with her breakfast tray. Maria tells her everything. And the cook tells Maria everything. And I'm a good friend of the cook. See?"

Lammiter looked at Joe's broad grin. He had to smile, too.

"That's good," Joe said with approval. "And from now, we tell each other the truth, eh? That makes our lives much simpler, my friend. And one more thing, don't call me a policeman. And never call Bevilacqua that, either. If you meet him."

"If . . ." Lammiter said, and changed his suitcase to his other hand. He was feeling better now. In every way. It was strange how depression could slow up the body, too. "Good for you, Joe," he said as he now noticed which bag had been chosen. It was the one that had clean shirts, shaving kit, and a suit. "How did you guess? You certainly hadn't time to look."

"Not tonight," Joe admitted. "Your talk with the princess was too interesting. And then, afterward, I had to telephone."

"Next time I go traveling, I'll have special locks made."

"But you had nothing to hide, my friend," Joe said soothingly.

"I bet I disappointed you when you looked inside."

"Sometimes Rosana trusts too easily. She liked you. So—I was suspicious."

"Where is she now?"

"Pirotta sent her north."

"Pirotta?" He couldn't hide his alarm.

"He telephoned her about nine o'clock. I was with her when she got his call. He wanted her to meet his car—and drive north. We thought she was traveling with him. Now, it seems he just sent her ahead."

"You let her go?"

"Look, she's the one who gives orders. I'm only a chauffeur," Joe said angrily. "Besides, we had a chance to have someone in Pirotta's car, going to his destination. Do you think we would let that chance slip?"

"But Rosana's only a girl. My God—" He broke off as he noticed a car coming toward them.

"Girls can deal with Pirotta better than—"

"Watch out!" Lammiter interrupted. "That car is traveling too slowly." It was a gray Fiat. A Perugia license plate, he noticed. A long quiet street of sleeping houses, a few people walking, the lights and traffic nearer now but still a full block away. The car was slowing down still more.

"Take it easy," Joe said. "Don't you recognize the old bus? We've changed the plates, that's all. Now, in! Quick!"

The car barely stopped. A thin little man in a blue suit stepped out from the left-hand door as Joe slid across the front seat to take over the wheel. Lammiter was closing his door even as the car moved forward again. He leaned over to drop his bag on the rear seat. Through the window he saw the little man strolling toward the bright lights of the *corso.* "Neat!" Lammiter said with approval.

"We practice in the long winter evenings." Joe said. He pointed happily to the princess's house as they passed the gateway. The lights were still blazing, and there were two servants on the driveway. "What did I tell you? She's nobody's fool, that old girl. Nobody's." And then, as the car made a right turn and Lammiter was still silent, he added, "But what she'll do to Pirotta is one guess Joe does not make." He thought about that. "What would I do if my nephew, my only remaining relative, was a man like Pirotta?" He shook his head. "It would take courage, much courage. That worries you, my friend?"

Lammiter shook his head. He could only think about Eleanor. No good, no good to keep his mind paralyzed like this. Much better to think of other things, to fill in the gaps and learn what and why. Problems were never solved blindly. First, he must know whatever Joe could tell him, and only then would he begin to see what lay ahead. Whatever Joe could tell him . . . He glanced at the serious-faced Italian. "I'm glad I'm on your side," he said with a sudden smile.

18

The car had turned into the upper stretch of the Via Vittorio Veneto. The cafés were still bright, the tables crowded. There, just over there, was where Lammiter had sat with Eleanor and Pirotta. And here, at this table so near to the roadway, he had met Rosana.

"Tell me," he said quietly, "was Pirotta ever in love with Rosana?"

Joe shrugged his shoulders. "It would be natural. She is beautiful. She was seeing him every day. That was the job we gave her. She did it well."

"Perhaps too well."

Joe gave him a quick look.

"Is she in love with him?"

The car swerved. "That was nearly an accident," Joe said angrily. "Stop these worries. Let me drive. She hates him, doesn't she?"

They had reached the top of the Via Vittorio Veneto. Joe was intent on the streams of traffic still converging on the Pincian Gate. As they passed through, Lammiter glanced back at the long rows of hotel windows overlooking the Aurelian Wall. There was someone on his balcony: a man standing, smoking a cigarette, looking out over the wall into the Borghese Gardens, and no doubt cursing Joe's sudden blast on the horn.

"Just there last night," said Lammiter, "Rosana came to meet Pirotta. Does a girl go out at three in the morning to meet a man she hates?" He thought for a moment. "Does any girl, brought up as carefully as Rosana, go out at three o'clock in the morning unless she's in love?" People in love did fantastic things.

Joe was silent. He seemed only to be concentrating on entering the broad highway through the Borghese Gardens.

"Or perhaps she was acting on your orders, last night?"

Joe shook his head. The car, freed from cross-traffic, now sped along the avenue of trees. The dark peace of the park surrounded them.

"What are you trying to say?" Joe asked suddenly. "Rosana has betrayed us?"

"No."

"That's better, my friend." Joe relaxed a little.

"But she may have betrayed herself. At least, she has been removed. That was tried last night, and it failed. Tonight, she went of her own accord. And all because she still can't quite believe that Pirotta would ever harm a woman. What did she hope to do, anyway—convert him? My God—women!"

Joe's brow was deeply furrowed. "Did she know about your Mr. Evans?"

"Not mine," Lammiter said quickly. "I want no part of him." Then he looked at Joe carefully. "Who told you about Evans? Bevilacqua?" Was that the news Joe had heard over the telephone?

"She knew about Evans?" Joe persisted.

"Yes."

"*Mannaggia!*" Joe took a deep breath. "If I had known that, she'd never have met Pirotta tonight." Then, suddenly angry, "Why didn't Brewster tell us about Evans? Why?"

"Evans was not your business."

Joe brooded over that. At last, very quietly, he said, "I don't think they will kill her. Or the American girl. They will hold them, yes. Until the meeting in Perugia is over. Then—perhaps it does not matter what Rosana or the American knows."

"You don't believe that," Lammiter said bitterly, and fell silent. Joe said nothing. "What will happen, once the meeting is over?" That was the question that had paralyzed Lammiter for the last half hour. His mind could not, or would not, let itself think beyond it.

Joe said, "That is always the trouble with men who do violence. There is no point where it is easy to stop. The men who killed Brewster find they have to crush me out, too, just in case I knew about Evans. And Rosana must disappear so that the police will think she ran away from Rome. And you are to be held by the police for questioning. And the pretty American must not be allowed to speak."

"And Salvatore? What's happening to him?"

Joe shrugged. "So it goes on," he said softly. "Step by step the violence spreads. But not always in the form of open murder, my friend. Too many dead people make too many headlines."

"I wonder where you would have ended?"

They had left the Borghese Gardens now, and cut through a vast and imposing square. Piazza del Popolo, Lammiter noted. Joe concentrated on swinging the car into a brightly lit street, now fairly quiet but obviously a main artery of the city, before he answered. "In the Tiber. One body in the Piazza Navona is enough for one night's work. The man who planned Brewster's killing knows that. He is not a stupid man."

"*One* man?"

"He has plenty of help from people who are willing to take orders and ask no questions. And you, my friend—" Joe's voice lightened "—ask too many questions. That is how I know you are not one of them."

Was that a polite hint to stop being curious? Lammiter wondered. He didn't take it. "Evans—is he this unstupid man?"

"Violence is not his business. He has his own problems, his own mission. What his bodyguard will do to protect him is their business. The NKVD keep their own secrets. Evans will keep his."

"But he must sense that they will commit any violence to protect him."

"And he will pretend to himself that they don't. He always has. Do you think Brewster was the first to die so that Mr. Evans could complete his mission?"

No, not the first . . . There had been Brewster's informant, knifed to death at Tivoli only a few nights ago. . . . Then Lammiter looked quickly at Joe. "Did you know anything about Evans before tonight?" It had been a pity, he thought now, that Brewster and Joe had not got together for a frank exchange of bits and pieces of knowledge. Yet, in their kind of business, allies could be as difficult to identify as enemies. In their world, danger and disaster stood at each man's elbow, ready to strike. Suspicion was not something ugly or uncharitable, it was a necessity to keep them alive. Where had Brewster made his mistake?—Then Lammiter realized that Joe had never answered his last question.

Nor did he now. "Pirotta—" Joe was saying "—there's another who lives with pretense. He organizes narcotics smuggling, but does he ever let himself think of the human beings he has turned into animals? He is helping men like Evans, but does he let himself think of the people who are murdered or abducted? No, he looks the other way. The thugs and the murderers are around him, but he persuades himself he is different: he has ideals, he is a rebel, a man in advance of his time. He is a very great persuader. Like your Mr. Evans. They have persuaded so many innocent people all their lives. But most of all, they persuade themselves."

"If it is not Evans, if it is not Pirotta, who—"

"No, no. They have their own jobs. They may not even know the man who directs them to this meeting in Perugia, watches over them. His job is security." Joe frowned. "It is—how do you say?—divide the labor?"

"Division of labor."

"Division of labor," Joe repeated, memorizing, as he increased speed. They were traveling fairly fast now, although the street, stretching so straight in front of them, was still lined with apartment houses. "We're going north from Rome," Joe said with satisfaction. "No one following us, so far." Then he nodded at the blocks of modern buildings they were passing. "The Roman legions would never believe me, but this is the Via Flaminia. Yes, this is where they marched, all the way to the Adriatic."

"That's a long haul." It was two hundred miles or better, right over the spine of Italy. And the spine was all mountains, with hills on either side. Lammiter glanced at his watch. It was just after two o'clock now. "What's the driving time on that distance?"

"We only go halfway," Joe reassured him. "As far as the hills of Umbria. Perugia is the capital, and—"

"I know, I know," Lammiter said impatiently. "But where does the princess keep her country cottage?"

"In Montesecco, not far from Perugia." Joe was amused by something. "Cottage . . ." He let his amusement burst into a broad grin. "And questions, questions . . . You like them, eh?"

"Dammit all, the only information I get out of you is prised out with a question mark."

Joe said softly, "And I think you ask the little questions to keep yourself from thinking about the big one."

Lammiter was lighting a cigarette. He wasted three matches, three thin little sticks of wax that snapped too easily. The fourth attempt was successful.

"Don't worry," Joe said. "We'll find the American girl. At Montesecco." He had been constantly watching the rear window. Now he relaxed. "We're clear. Not one car behind us for the last half hour. Light me a cigarette, too." He stretched his shoulders, took a new grip on the wheel. The car leaped forward at full power.

Around them, there were vast stretches of black countryside, occasionally broken by small clusters of farmers' cottages standing together at the side of the road, in darkness and silence. The road was straight and long. And very quiet. "Now," Joe said, "we will be able to hear the march of the legions' feet and the songs they sang." Then, brusquely, "We'll stop each hour to stretch our backs. This car is too small for your legs, I know, but try to get some sleep."

"No. I'll spell you at the wheel."

Joe shook his head. "I know this road. Get some sleep."

"It's better if we talk."

"So that *I* won't fall asleep?" Joe was amused. "I like you, my friend, I like you very much. I'll even answer some questions. Or shall I tell you the story of my life?"

"Which life?"

Joe laughed. "Well," he admitted, "there's the one in Sicily. There's the one in America. There's the one in Rome. Take your choice."

"In which did you meet Salvatore?"

There was a sudden moment of stillness, only broken by the steady hum of the smooth-running engine.

Tactfully bridging the silence, Lammiter added, "Salvatore . . . What's his second name, anyway?"

"Salvatore Sabatini," Joe said slowly. "And what made you think of him?"

"He's been at the back of my mind most of this night."

"Now *I* start asking the questions. Why?"

"Oh—just a lot of little things," Lammiter said vaguely. But he was remembering more than was comfortable.

"Such as—?"

"Well—he knew Rosana and I were in Brewster's flat this evening. He knew we were to meet again at eleven."

"So did I know."

"He tried to get me to leave with him, as if he didn't want Brewster to start talking to me. In fact, he only left me behind when Brewster seemed to be falling asleep. He checked the locked door to the cat staircase, and he did that carefully. Then he looked at me as if he were afraid I had been watching him. Now I think he may have been unlocking the door."

"Sometimes a man remembers things to suit his thinking," Joe reminded him quietly.

"I'm not suiting my memory to anything. I felt uneasy at the time. But Rosana and Brewster trusted Sabatini. So I trusted him." Never play down your instincts, he told himself: listen to them, Lammiter, listen.

"And when did you start distrusting Sabatini?"

"Since I started adding up all the little things. He spoke to you in the Piazza tonight. When you told me that, I didn't think much about it. But Sabatini isn't an amateur like me. He knows the rules. When he spoke to you, he broke them. Didn't he?"

Joe made no comment.

"It was almost as if he were identifying you to the two strangers who started hunting you. How else did they know you?" He watched Joe's face.

Joe gave him a sudden smile. But his voice was quite serious, almost grim. "Yes, I thought of that. I thought of that when I thought of a man who could have used my car."

"Sabatini?"

Joe nodded.

Lammiter tried to straighten his stiff legs. "I might have guessed you—" he began. He could laugh now at his worries about Sabatini. The man was the reason Joe had been sent north. Sabatini was Joe's own particular division of labor. "You were ahead of me, Joe."

"Not me. Bevilacqua."

"No one has seen Sabatini since he spoke to you in the Piazza Navona—is that it?"

"That's just about it."

"Well," Lammiter said with some relief, "my guesses weren't so damned stupid after all, not if Bevilacqua is—"

"Bevilacqua has no guesses. But he is taking no chances."

"Then he must know something. Why else would he send you chasing north?"

"In this business," Joe said, "you do not always know. If you wait until you know, it can be too late. So you act on the greatest probability. If Sabatini is the man we want, I shall find him near Perugia. That's all in the pattern. *If* he is the man we want . . ."

"You make him sound more important than I thought he was." But Joe added nothing to that. "He isn't an Italian, is he?"

"So now *you* are telling me something? I, an Italian, don't know he isn't an Italian!" Joe was annoyed. He tried to be amused.

"Look, Joe—I make my living listening to people speak. I listen to actors up on the stage, I—"

"In America, yes. What's that to do with Italia?"

"Look, Joe—" he tried again, "I thought I could speak Italian when I came to Italy. Once—before a war in Korea—I took a degree in Romance languages—Italian and French. So when I arrived here, I thought this is a breeze, Lammiter, my boy; what's a rusty subjunctive or a forgotten pluperfect conditional between friends? But every Italian I've met—you included, so why the hell do I have to tell you all this? —has been politely amused by the way I speak his language. I'm a walking grammar book."

Joe looked somewhat mystified, but unpersuaded.

"Every city, every town in Italy, every village perhaps, has its own little tricks of language. Not only with the words and phrases, but even with the way they are spoken. Right?"

"But you hear all kinds of accents in Rome," Joe argued. He was still on the defensive.

"Sure. It's like New York. It's the meeting place for the rest of the country. But what regional accent does Sabatini have?"

"He comes from the north."

"Are you sure? Or is that what he tells you because you come from the south? Don't you see, he'd have to meet someone from his supposed home town before he could be pinned down as a liar." But no doubt Sabatini, if he ever had met such a man, would then come from a little town a hundred miles east, or west, whichever seemed safer. Then Lammiter was suddenly shocked by his own eloquence: it had led him farther than he had meant to go. "I can be wrong," he said. "I guess I was carried away. Forget it, Joe. Let's stick to what we do know."

Joe was silent for a full minute. "Now all that could be very interesting," he said at last, half lost in his own thoughts. "If it is true," he added, still a little on the defensive.

"I told you to forget it."

But something had made contact in Joe's mind. Lammiter could almost feel him thinking. "Very, very interesting," he said at last, furrowing his brows at the dark stretch of road in front of them. "If your guess is right, then Sabatini could be more important than any of us thought."

"But he's only a guide—" Lammiter began. He stopped short, remembering Brewster's warning: never look for an important agent in an important position; never look at the ambassador, look at his chauffeur.

"It would be a perfect cover," Joe conceded with grudging admiration.

Lammiter said slowly, "I don't like this, Joe. I don't like it."

"You began it."

Lammiter said nothing. For the second time that night, he forced himself to play down what women call instinct and men, more modestly if less elegantly, a hunch. Stick to the facts, Lammiter, he thought grimly.

But Joe was not going to let any deductions wither in the bud. "You still think Sabatini isn't a real Italian?"

"Yes. But what does that matter?"

"Then he's not only told one lie, he's living a hundred lies. *That* matters." He waited, but Lammiter was keeping quiet. "So I'd like to learn why you say he isn't an Italian. Sure, sure, I know we've all got our different ways of speaking. In Venice, Giorgio is always Zorzio." His voice sharpened. "But in Italy, there are people who speak as well as you do."

"Hey there!" Lammiter said quickly. "I speak bad Italian, Joe. That's my point. I speak like a God-damned book. I've no background to my voice. That's what I mean—no background. Why, even the principessa has that. She's a Roman, isn't she? She's educated and traveled, but you wouldn't say she came from Milan or Naples or Florence."

"Background . . ." Joe said thoughtfully. His feelings were less ruffled now. "You've got a quick ear, eh?"

"If I hadn't, I wouldn't try writing plays."

"Sabatini comes from around Milan. You say that's impossible?"

"I'd say you should get a Milanese to check on his voice."

"Simple, isn't it?" Joe said, sarcastic now. "But I never met any Milanese who talked with him."

"How long has he lived in Rome?"

"Eleven years. Since the war."

"He and Brewster were in the underground together. Right?"

Joe nodded. "We checked back to the day he was born. Near Milan."

"That's definite?"

"We didn't take Brewster's word for him alone. What do you think we are?" Joe still had some hackles rising. Then he calmed down. He even gave a brief laugh. "Want me to recite for you?" he asked suddenly.

Lammiter glanced at him quickly.

"Salvatore Sabatini, born 1917, Milan, father a lawyer, only child, bright boy. Won prizes at school. Did his military service in the *carabinieri,* student at Milan University. The Germans came, father was killed, mother died. He left Milan, joined some underground fighters around Como. Met Brewster. Later, joined a British battalion as interpreter. After the war, he came to Rome, worked for a travel bureau, became a guide. He did some black marketing for a while—small-scale stuff. And a little smuggling—nothing big. Just a small operator. But he got to know a lot of small operators. People on the fringe. Brewster found that useful: your best information can come from people on the fringe." Then he looked at Lammiter. "Well?"

"I was thinking his father would be kind of disappointed."

"Oh—some people drift."

"Some do."

"You are not buying?"

"Are you?"

"You heard what I told you. It all runs straight, as straight as this road."

"But it's a poor showing for such a good start." And, Lammiter thought, Sabatini hadn't given him the impression that he was content to be a man without a future.

"The war changed people. Made them—" Joe paused. He frowned again at the road ahead of them. Then he said, and his voice had altered, "The war killed some people, too. Killed them and left no trace."

For a moment, Lammiter didn't follow. "You mean, the man who took to the hills round Como could have died up there?"

"Died? He could have been killed in cold blood." Joe took a long deep breath. "Underground fighting was not always a brave story. Sometimes, for politics, a good man was murdered. Yes—that could have happened. You take a man's life, and then his name."

"But what about his friends? A murderer couldn't take them over, too."

"Often the groups of those partisans were small. Sometimes they were wiped out, killed or captured. Sometimes there was only one survivor. He would join up with another group. Who would question him if he was a fighter who hated fascists and Nazis? These were the only necessary credentials, my friend."

Grimly, Lammiter said, "We've built up a pretty picture between us. I don't like it, Joe. Less and less."

"It may be false. Perhaps Sabatini *is* the student who went into the hills. Perhaps he didn't play with the key of Brewster's door. Perhaps he was so frightened, down in the Piazza, that he spoke to me. Perhaps he wasn't the one who borrowed my car on those two special nights. You see, my friend, there's an explanation for everything. Sometimes false, sometimes true. The main thing is that we know what we are meeting if we find Sabatini walking down a street in Perugia. Because, if he's innocent, he won't be walking down a street anywhere: he was one of Brewster's little group, and it is being—eliminated."

"If he's innocent, he's dead. Is that it?"

"Or in hiding, so that he will not be dead. Certainly, he will *not* be walking around as if nothing had happened."

"What does he know about you?"

"Just what Tony Brewster or Rosana knew."

"He could have checked on your story."

Joe laughed. "Sure, he could."

"You don't sound worried."

"Giuseppe Rocco has lived a simple life. He's just a dumb Sicilian who got into trouble in Syracuse over a girl. When he got out of the prison hospital, he followed the Americans. But now he lives in Rome, and all he wants out of life is a bigger and better automobile. He went to work for Brewster, because Rosana persuaded him, and he'd do anything for Miss Rosana. Also, he hopes there will be some cash as a reward. Also, he keeps buying lottery tickets. Dumb as they come, that's our Joe."

A prison hospital, thought Lammiter, might be a good place to pick up a recently vacated identity. But it seemed indiscreet to speculate openly about that. So he gazed out at the dark fields. They had begun to slope, to rise and fall. Far-off shadows against the sky were hills. The road was beginning to meet twists and turns. They passed through a small town, with its new buildings looking square and bare among the older houses with their cracked and peeling plaster.

"A dump," said Joe, with all the scorn of an adopted Roman.

They passed other small houses, always in little groups, as if people preferred to live as close together as possible. As in the town, the new buildings replaced war damage. Brightly painted in greens and pinks, they were startlingly picked out by the car's headlights. So were the bullet holes on the older houses, pitted and pock-marked by bursts of machine guns between the cracks and strains of age. In the distance, a heavy truck changed gears. Here and there, headlights swept over the fields, and a few cars hissed past.

"Any chance of overtaking Pirotta?" Lammiter asked suddenly. Joe could drive. They were making excellent time.

Joe shook his head. "I worked too carefully over that old Lancia," he said regretfully. "She could drive from here to Geneva without a complaint."

"I still think we ought to have stopped it back at the gates."

Joe shook his head again. "We couldn't have stopped them, my friend. I had a knife, you had no weapon at all. The gates were open, the engine was running. And there were three men in the car."

"Three?" That startled him. Then amazement changed to irritation. Joe did not need to measure out his information like this.

"Pirotta, and two men who work for him. He was taking no chances."

"But—" He stopped, annoyance giving way to fear. Joe was preparing him. For what?

"I did all we could do. I telephoned. The alarm is out. The Lancia will be noticed." Then, as Lammiter said nothing, he added, "If we had tried to stop them, they'd have changed their direction. Then we wouldn't know where to follow them." Again he glanced quickly at the American. He said harshly, "Stop thinking they will kill her. That—not! I have already told you."

"Whom are you persuading? Me—or yourself?" Lammiter asked angrily. "If Sabatini is the man in control, he didn't stop at killing Brewster, his old friend, his old comrade. Did he?"

"But he has more of a problem with the American girl. She has a lot of important friends. The Embassy—what will they say? Her father and his newspaper friends—what will they keep printing? The principessa—she won't be silenced."

"The princess!" Lammiter said in deep disgust.

"She's your ally by this time. She has heard how they took the American girl from her house."

"How they took—?"

"Sure. Do you think your girl walked into the car? Take it easy, Bill, take it easy," Joe said worriedly.

"Go on," said Lammiter. "You'd better tell me it all. All."

"She came out of the villa slowly. She stood at the top of the steps and looked down at the car. Maybe she didn't like Pirotta's two men on either side of her. Maybe she had expected to stay at the villa. Maybe the car frightened her. She turned, and tried to run back into the house. But the two men were ready for that. They caught her. One had a hand over her mouth. They carried her down the steps. She was struggling. And then she didn't struggle." He hesitated. He glanced at Lammiter. "They didn't hurt her. They put her to sleep, maybe. With a needle—that's the quickest way. It would make the journey easier."

Lammiter took a deep breath and steadied himself.

"The princess saw nothing of that," Joe reminded him.

Lammiter nodded. The princess had stood in the courtyard. Maria had been walking to the gates. Neither of them had seen.

"But the princess will hear. The servants in the house would be watching. I know them. By now, she has stopped being angry with you. Now she is your ally."

And what did that matter?

"You don't think that's important?" Joe asked quickly. Then he smiled, shaking his head, and concentrated on the road. They were swinging around a large church and a group of small houses. "Past this village," Joe said, "we'll stop. Stretch our legs."

"I'm all right. Keep on going."

Joe was watching the road, now running straight again for half a mile or so. His eyes were on the far-off lights of an approaching car. The lights blinked. Joe answered with his, as he began to slow down. So did the other car. It stopped under some trees and its lights were switched off. Joe stopped and switched off his lights. "Out," he said. "Stretch your back. Get some air in your lungs." He opened his door, and crossed the road to the other car.

Bill Lammiter did as he was told. He stood looking across the fields to the east. There was a faint pencil stroke of lightened darkness along the horizon. In front of him was a little vineyard, over there a patch of corn thrusting its strong stalks toward the sky, and flowers planted wherever there was a spare corner of earth. The air was cool and sweet.

Behind him, Joe called to him softly, and he climbed back into the car. The other was already leaving.

Their car started forward. "The Lancia is keeping to the road," Joe told him. "That is one fear you can drop out of the window, my friend."

Lammiter tried to smile. Joe was doing his best to give him some encouragement. And it was true: the car that had reported to Joe made Lammiter feel better. The numbness was leaving his mind. They were not alone, two men on an endless road stretching over limitless fields.

"Next stop," Joe said, "we'll get some gas. And coffee. And more information, too. And then, the hills. And after that, Montesecco. Right?"

"Right."

"Now I tell you the story of my life," Joe said.

The dawn arrived as they turned off the Flaminian Way and branched to their left. For some time they had been traveling among spreading hills and deep woods. Now the road ran along the side of a valley so broad that it seemed more like an immense plain rimmed by steep small hills, each complete in itself, sharp-pointed, almost symmetrical, drawn by an artist with an exact eye and a sure hand. Behind the hills were more hills, their peaks peering over each other's shoulders. And every hill had its neat terraces of carefully spaced olive trees; its crest was sometimes forested, sometimes crowned by a walled miniature of a town. Down in the valley, a vast patchwork quilt of cultivated fields and trees was flung over the land, the neat squares stitched together by a very small river curving its way slowly back to Rome.

"The Tiber," Joe said, and rubbed his right shoulder and neck. They were the first words he had spoken in the last hour. Since their last stop, in fact.

That had been at a small house, solid and square, with a large number painted on its dark-red walls, standing quite alone at the side of the road. It was the house of a road-repair superintendent, numbered according to the section of the highway for which he was responsible. In the small garage built into the house, Joe had found some more gasoline, not that he needed it, but it was wise to keep the tank as full as possible. And there had been some more information, too. Pirotta's car, with Rosana presumably, had passed just before midnight, driven at a reasonable speed. The Lancia had passed two hours later; its speed had been furious.

"Crazy," the superintendent had said sadly, thinking of possible accidents to his fine road. He was a middle-aged man, thin and wiry, intelligent as good workmen are who take a pride in their jobs. At the moment, he was tired with his vigil, but he gave them a cup of hot coffee and a sandwich of sliced sausage slapped on a torn hunk of hard-crusted bread, and as he moved quietly around his little kitchen next to the garage—"The wife and kids are asleep upstairs"—he talked in a hoarse whisper with Joe, and threw Lammiter a friendly nod and a gap-toothed smile every now and again, as if to make him feel he was in this conversation, too. Then, with last instructions about heavy repairs on a bad hairpin bend of the road (a mile farther on, hard frosts last winter, the worst winter within living memory), they left the man telephoning his news of Joe's arrival back to headquarters.

That stop had only taken nine minutes—Joe and Lammiter were still finishing their sandwiches as the Fiat started from behind the shelter of the house and turned onto the road again. But instead of being reassured, Joe was worried. "Rosana can't be alone in Pirotta's car," he said. "She would have checked in at that house if she had been alone." He didn't have to add his biggest fear: that Rosana might no longer be in the car; her body, stripped of identification, might have been thrown into a ditch. But five minutes later he said, "They'll keep her as long as she can be useful to them." Then he lapsed into silence and concentrated on the road, for there were more trucks now to be passed, enormous and thundering. The road-repair superintendent would be stifling a yawn to curse their weight, as he slipped off his half-buttoned trousers and unlaced boots and climbed into bed with his wife and children.

Bill Lammiter kept himself awake, but he had not offered to drive. A strange road, climbing between broad-shouldered hills and woods, in the half-light between night and day, was better left to Joe's memory. Even when they came into the Umbrian plain, and the day was born, Lammiter did not suggest he would take the wheel. For now there were other hazards: cumbersome, slow-moving farm carts, pulled by pairs of gentle white oxen with formidable horns and amiable eyes.

"And here is the way to Montesecco," Joe said, swerving past a team of oxen, cutting ahead of them before they started blocking up the narrow dusty road, which climbed up its own neat hill. The white oxen looked after them reprovingly; their driver yelled what he thought of cars and dust. "Yes, yes," said Joe, almost to himself, "I agree. But it would take you half an hour to reach the town. We'll do it in three minutes."

The road twisted among trees up toward the walled town. Beyond the trees, on either side, the terraces of olive groves rose step by step. They seemed dead. The silver-green leaves were black and hard. Last winter's frosts must have been bitter.

Joe noticed the look on Lammiter's face. "Yes," he said, "it's tough on the people. This is the way all the hills are this year. But give the olive trees three good years, and they'll come alive again."

"Three years. It's a long time to wait." Lammiter could see the town more clearly now: a mass of roofs and towers behind an encircling wall.

"People have lived here for nearly three thousand years. That wall was first built by the Etruscans. Then the Romans came and built on top of it. What's three years to a wall like that?"

The wall, massive and high, of light-colored stone, rose abruptly before them. But they did not enter its arched gateway. Lammiter had just time to glimpse the hill inside the gate, the narrow cobbled street lined with stone houses, before Joe turned the car into a track running toward a two-storied house with yellow plastered walls and a red-tiled roof. He had not noticed it, coming up the hill. The roadside trees had obscured it. And then, almost immediately, they were in a small farmyard, scattering chickens, avoiding two men and a wooden cart, passing three giant haystacks, and coming to rest around the corner of the far side of the house, under a rough arbor of vine leaves.

"This," Joe remembered to say as he got out of the car, "is the farm where Alberto buys most of the food for the princess's house. I used to come here on my free time. Have a look at the view." Then he left, walking toward the farmer and his son, with arms outstretched and real laughter in his voice.

Well, we're among friends at least, Lammiter thought. He stood beside the car, trying to get the cramp out of his legs. American cars might be bold and brassy, but they didn't tie your muscles in knots like this. For a few minutes, he watched the farmer and his son. Like the other peasants he had seen on the Umbrian roads, they were of good height, straight-backed, decently dressed in a clean rough shirt with sleeves rolled up (and only one button open at the neck, no expanses of manly bosom advertised here), a waistcoat for warmth, work-stained trousers, and heavy boots. Their faces, turned curiously toward him for a brief glance, were tanned and high-colored. Battered felt hats were tilted over their eyes, more from habit than from sun, for the early morning light was bright but kind, and the cool night air had still no warmth in it.

Lammiter turned up the collar of his thin jacket and closed his lapels. He walked, stiffly, past a wooden yoke and a harrow, over to the haystacks. From there, the land dropped steeply downhill, and he could see all the vast sweep of valley and the neatly outlined hills. By this pale gold light, the trees down on the plain stood sharply etched, each shape clear in its long row. And over all, lay a stillness.

He turned to look at the little town enclosed in its strong wall. Over the blighted olive trees he could see the crest of the curve of wall nearest him—he was too near it to see its whole encircling arm flung round the tightly packed yellowed roofs and ancient stone towers. He heard a dog bark; somewhere a cock crew; a man was singing an endless song. Even sounds seemed as etched as the rows of trees and the folds of the hills.

The boy moved over to the car, and Lammiter joined him. He was about sixteen, with good bones in his face, blue eyes, light hair. He looked at Lammiter gravely, noting his jacket and trousers, his shoes; then he looked back at the car.

"*Molto bello,*" Lammiter said, pointing to the panorama beyond the haystacks.

The boy took his eyes away from the car. He looked now at the view he lived with. He was quite silent. Then suddenly he said, "*Bellissimo!*" A smile of happiness, of sheer joy, illuminated his face. Lammiter found he was smiling, too. "*Bellissimo!*" he agreed. The boy looked at him again, but he was no longer a stranger.

"All right," Joe said, coming back to the car, "we go inside and get us some food and sleep." He pulled out Lammiter's case. He gave a wave to the boy, who was already picking up a wooden yoke for the two white oxen his father was leading toward him. "Come on, Bill. We've made them late enough."

Lammiter left the world of golden light and followed Joe's quick steps.

"Any information?" he asked.

"Pirotta's car arrived first. Then the Lancia about an hour ago. And don't start worrying about my car. If anyone asks questions, we are just a couple of guys from Perugia, buying some extra supplies for a restaurant. You know what's happening in Perugia this weekend? The university begins its annual summer school for foreigners. Sure, for foreigners. It's packing them in. Name any nationality, and Perugia's got them. Isn't that just dandy?"

So that's why poor old Perugia was chosen for Evans's meeting place, Lammiter thought. He had a feeling that the town could have done without that honor. "Clever," he said. "Clever little bastards we're dealing with." He looked at Joe. "Can you see the princess's place from here?" he asked.

"Why?" Joe asked, suddenly suspicious.

"You're dropping back into character," Lammiter said with a grin. "That's why."

"Well, you can't climb over *that* wall, that's for sure."

They entered a dark kitchen, clean but careless, only lighted by a barred window overlying the wide door. There was a bed against one wall, three hard chairs, a table, an old chest of drawers with traces of elaborate painting, a dresser, some paper flowers on one cracked plaster wall under a woman's faded photograph.

"His wife's dead?" Lammiter asked, looking around at men's comfortable disorder. There was soup in a deep pot at the side of the low fire, cheese roughly set on the wooden table with a loaf of bread, a jug of Chianti, two earthenware plates, two wooden spoons.

"Four years ago. And three other children, too. Flu epidemic." Joe rummaged around and found two cups, and as Lammiter served up the soup, he took out his knife, picked up the loaf, held it against his chest, and cut toward himself into its hard crust. Then he tapped the thick slice of bread on the table and watched the ants fall out. "If I may step out of character again for a moment," he said with a smile, as he tapped once more to make sure that the ants had gone, "this is symbolic of our kind of work." He swept the back of his hand over the table and the ants fell to the floor. Then, as he handed the slice of bread to Lammiter, "Okay, bud. Philosophy class is over. Eat. And listen. And don't start telling me you don't need any sleep. We all do: Pirotta, his men, you, and me. Only I'm going to scout round for half an hour first; and you're staying here. Upstairs." He finished tapping his own slice of bread.

Lammiter ate. The warm soup took the chill out of his blood. And as he had time to think over his initial objections to Joe's plan, he saw they were stupid, and he was glad he had kept silent. Joe was right. A foreigner walking in the early morning through the streets of Montesecco would only rouse questions. And questions made talk. And talk carried. But Joe was known here: no one would be surprised to see him; the Lancia had arrived, hadn't it? Why not its chauffeur, too? Joe must have friends in this town. And Pirotta?

He put that question to Joe after their quick meal was over, and he stood ready to climb the stairs to the room above. "Sure," Joe said, "he's popular. Always got a smile and a kind word for everyone." He looked shrewdly at the American. "He's an attractive sort of fellow. Sweeps in here in his car, gives a wave of his hand, and everyone feels happy that a man can have some good fortune in this hard world."

"Even the local Communists feel that way?"

"You noticed the posters plastered on the walls?" Joe asked quickly.

"Couldn't miss the hammer and sickle."

"That catches the eye," Joe agreed. "But the Communists here—" he paused, shrugged his shoulders. "They're mostly anticlerical, that's all."

"There's poverty, too."

"It isn't always poverty that makes politics. Sometimes it's pride. Ever read about Umbria? The Pope's army besieged this town ninety years ago, and when the troops got inside—well, there was a lot of raping and killing. Same thing happened in Perugia. People round here remember these things. And they remember the days of their greatness, back in the fourteenth century, when each town in these hills had its commune and its captain of the people elected to govern. Then they remember how that freedom was destroyed—the big families seized it first, then the Church seized it from the big families. A real mess of power politics."

"But the Church is not a temporal power any more. Those days are over."

"Do the people in the south of your country forget the war against the north? There are people here, many of them, whose mothers saw the mercenaries break through the cannon holes in the walls of this town and what they did. It is no use pretending that such evil things did not happen. They are important in politics, even ninety years after."

"So evil lives longer than good. . . . That's depressing."

"The good is remembered, too. Garibaldi came and freed them. They remember that day, most of all." He smiled suddenly. "Don't worry so much about these posters. There are others on the wall, if you looked closer. This is still a free country. A few years ago, we gave away that freedom. Sure, Italy may be poor, but she is rich in memories. And they all teach us something."

"Yes," Lammiter said gloomily. "If we only remember all the lessons and not just the ones that suit our theories."

"Here, take this upstairs with you." Joe pulled off his crumpled blue jacket, stuffed his tie into his pocket, and handed them over. He rolled up his sleeves, unbuttoned his shirt at the neck. "The room at the left is yours. Don't leave it. I'll be back soon. Got to see some friends."

"I'm glad to hear they do exist," Lammiter said, still worried.

"Sure," Joe said cheerfully, "sure we have friends. Get some sleep and you'll feel better." He chased away some chickens which had come exploring from the yard into the kitchen, and then shut the wide door behind him.

Upstairs, Lammiter entered a small dark room. He dropped his suitcase, and Joe's jacket on top of it. Quickly, he went over to the solitary window and half opened its shutters, letting the early morning sun stream in; so this room faced east toward the wall of the town, while the kitchen downstairs had opened to the west. People around here, whatever their politics, were unanimously against windows, or perhaps solid walls gave shelter from cold winter winds and the blaze of summer. He pushed the shutters farther apart, cautiously, and looked out.

From this height, he had a good view of the road as it presented itself before the entrance to the town. From here, too, he could see a wider sweep of the wall, and the rippling tiled roofs, and even—where the hill rose inside the walls—the top-floor windows of the houses, with shutters now opened and balloons of bedding already billowing on the sills to air. To his right, there were trees, perhaps a large park, standing just within the walls where they curved round out of sight. But he couldn't see any sign of Joe.

Down at the gate, two women in light cotton dresses balanced loads of washing on their heads while they exchanged a word and a laugh with a man holding a horse by a rope halter. An old woman in black, long-skirted, came plodding up the road. But there was no sign of Joe.

His eyes searched the olive grove that stretched beneath him. It ran, to his right, along the wall for some distance and then gave way to a field and trees, trees that matched those just over the wall where the park lay. Was there some other entrance over there to the town? Or was the park a large private garden? Was that where the princess lived?

He looked back again at the main gate. The women were leaving, taking a rough trail to the left that must lead to other farms outside the walls. The horse was being led into the town, clattering over the solid paving stones. The old woman was hurrying out of sight. From one tower, a bell sounded, gentle and melancholy. And there were other sounds, too: the rattle of iron wheels over rough stone; occasional voices —distant and merging; someone calling out; someone laughing; and from the grass under the olive trees, the first chitter of insects, tuning up for their noonday concert. And then, far over to the right, in the field with the trees, he saw a man herding two goats.

In spite of himself, Lammiter laughed. It was Joe. Where did he get the goats? Lammiter wondered. Perhaps he had found them tethered among the olive trees, and had taken them along to give local color to his walk across the open field. He was herding them toward the wood which lay outside the park. So that was the direction where the princess's house lay?

Satisfied, Lammiter turned away from the window. There wasn't much in the room—a narrow bed with a mattress that looked as old as the town itself, a low carved chest, a brown-spotted piece of looking glass, and some wooden pegs on the wall. Two flies had come in from the open window, large black country flies circling slowly around the naked electric bulb hung from the ceiling.

All right, he thought, I'll play it Joe's way. I'll stay here and count those damned flies.

But first, he investigated the other room upstairs. It was innocent enough. It was used now as a storeroom. And then he stood at the top of the stairs, listening. Again he fought down the impulse to follow Joe. He went back into his room and closed the door. He took off his jacket, loosened his tie, sat down on the mattress, and lit a cigarette. Sleep? He couldn't. He had too many thoughts pounding through his brain. Play it Joe's way, he told himself again: sweat this one out. But if ever he had to learn how much he loved Eleanor, this was a hard way to do it. He ground out the cigarette under his heel. If I meet Pirotta, I'll kill him, he thought suddenly.

He stretched out on the bed and counted the flies—five now—and watched the pale sunlight deepen, and listened to the cicadas beneath his window. Sewing machines, he thought drowsily, sewing machines stitching away, stitching, stitching. . . .

20

He heard a distant voice saying, "Bill." A hand was on his shoulder. He came quickly out of sleep, sitting upright so suddenly, making such a wild grab for the hand on his shoulder, that Rosana cried out. He stared at her unbelievingly.

"Yes, it's Rosana," she said. "I did try to wake you gently."

"Eleanor?"

"No, she isn't here. She's at the Casa Grande. She's all right, Bill. So far, she's all right. She's in a locked room upstairs—one of the princess's own rooms." She looked at his face. "She's all right. She's by herself."

He suddenly noticed he still grasped her wrist. He let it go. "Sorry." He glanced at his watch. He had been asleep for almost an hour, a deep dreamless wonderful hour. "How did you get here?"

"Giuseppe sent for me."

"Joe?"

"He came in by the gate at the woods, where the gamekeeper's house stands. Jacopone—that's the gamekeeper—came up to the big house and passed the word to Anna-Maria to get me downstairs." She touched her very loose cotton dress of pink and green checks. "How do you like it? Anna-Maria lent it to me. She's Alberto's wife."

"How many servants are at the big house?"

"Just Alberto and Anna-Maria meanwhile. The princess always brings the others with her from Rome."

"And just Jacopone at the gamekeeper's cottage?"

She nodded. "Two old men and one old woman," she said as if she had guessed his thoughts. "Not much help, except in good will."

"Are you sure of that?"

"Yes. The princess telephoned and gave Alberto her orders. She woke the operator at three o'clock in the morning. It was quite a sensation. But so were the cars."

She moved to the window, looked out, and then drew the shutters closer together.

"Where's Joe? Tethering goats back into place?"

She sat down on the wooden chest. "He was going to follow me, I thought."

"Ready for rear-guard action?" Or Joe might have other friends to visit. "Well—I'm glad you're out of that place, Rosana," he said awkwardly. "What has been happening up there?"

"I'll tell you when Giuseppe arrives. He will have to hear most of it, too. I only saw him for a minute at Jacopone's cottage." She looked down at her hands. And she began to cry, very quietly, just sitting there on the chest in her shapeless dress, her head bent, the tears slowly running down her pale cheeks. She didn't want him to notice, so he sat still and looked now at the floor.

She said, "So they killed Tony Brewster." And she took a long shuddering breath. But she had stopped crying. "And Joe told me that Sabatini—" She paused. "Could it be possible? Could he have betrayed us?"

"It's possible." He remembered Joe's words last night. "If he didn't, then he is in hiding—if he's still alive. First, your brother. Then, Brewster. Who's next?"

"Not any more of us, if I can help it," she said with a sudden burst of cold anger.

Lammiter said nothing to that. He had his doubts.

"Don't look so worried, Bill," she said gently. "No one saw me come here. You see, I lived at the Casa Grande for almost two months after I came back from America. The princess was the only one of my mother's old friends who stood beside me when my brother died so—so badly. The princess knows what disgrace is—her only brother blew his brains out when he saw what his politics had done to Italy—oh well, anyway—she sent me away from Rome until the scandal died down, and I stayed up here. I know every inch of the house and the garden and the woods outside the walls; my only friends were Alberto and Anna-Maria and Jacopone. So this morning—it was easy. You see?"

She rose and went over to the window again. She turned back. She moved around, restless, not sitting down.

"It was here," she said, "in this room, that I first met Bevilacqua."

"Joe brought you here to meet him?"

"Oh no! It was I who persuaded Giuseppe to join Brewster's group. He was to be my watchdog. And he has been very good. Only—I'm difficult to watch, I think."

Indeed you are, Lammiter thought.

"It was Jacopone who brought me here," she went on. "You see, Bevilacqua had heard that the men with whom my brother had been connected were going to ask me to join them. Oh—not an important job, of course. I was just to be a sort of secretary." She was embarrassed.

These friends of her brother's had created a job for her, Lammiter thought. "Very considerate of them."

She missed the irony in his words. Earnestly she explained, "No—just very clever. I had no money, I needed a job, and then—if I ever did learn more about my brother's death, I wouldn't be free to speak out. I had become one of them. You see?"

"And Bevilacqua asked you to accept the job, if it were offered to you."

She nodded.

"That was a hard assignment," he said quietly.

She nodded again. She hesitated, and then she decided to finish her story. "The job was offered to me. And I took it. And I found that I was Luigi Pirotta's secretary."

She paused again. But Lammiter, watching her in silence and sympathy, seemed to give her courage. "That was a shock," she admitted. "I knew he was my brother's friend, but I hadn't known he was in the same horrible business. But then I persuaded myself that he had been drawn into that mess just like my brother Mario. Because—" she swung round lightly to face him, her dark eyes almost pleading with him to understand her "—if I ever admitted that Luigi Pirotta knew what he was doing, had chosen such a way to live, then I would have to condemn Mario, too. You see?"

Lammiter saw.

"I kept hoping that Luigi, like my brother, was only a—a—"

"A front man, dupe," he finished for her.

She said, "Tony was absolutely right: I trusted too easily. Because I —well, perhaps I was a snob. Our families—" She looked away. She said proudly, "Luigi and Mario never were educated to behave like that."

"Didn't Pirotta's father—the man who blew his brains out—didn't he go off the tracks?" He had spoken bluntly, purposefully. And it had its effect. She dropped her half-sad, half-excusing little piece of snobbery, and became the girl Brewster had liked.

"Yes," she flashed back at him. "But that was open politics. He chose Mussolini's side. He was wrong. But he hid nothing. He didn't deceive people, pretending one thing, doing another."

"Not like his son, dear Luigi."

She looked at him. "No," she admitted, "not like his son." She moved back to the window. "What is delaying Giuseppe?"

"You always call him Giuseppe."

"Do I? Perhaps I prefer Giuseppe to Joe."

"How did you come to choose him as your—your watchdog?"

"He drove for my brother. I couldn't afford a chauffeur, so I recommended him to the princess, who needed one. Then later, when Bevilacqua introduced me in Rome to Tony Brewster—well, Giuseppe seemed just the kind of man Tony needed. And he was devoted to my brother. Giuseppe is a Sicilian, you know. He wanted to find my brother's murderer as much as I did. So I—recruited him." She tried to smile, as if she were happy about one wise accomplishment in her life. "That's the technical word, I believe."

Poor Rosana, Lammiter thought, caught in such a web of disaster that not even those who are loyal to you have been able to tell you the whole truth. He looked at her beautiful face, strained, white, pathetic. She had changed in the last twenty-four hours: she had lost her self-confidence; something had crushed hope out of her heart. He felt a sudden cold shiver touch the nape of his neck. "Rosana," he said softly, "when all this is over—"

"Over?" she broke in. "But when? And how?"

"When it's all over," he said, with an optimism he did not feel, "then —" He stopped, listening to the footsteps entering the room below, and rose.

"It's Giuseppe," Rosana said.

Joe came upstairs whistling. Was it an act? Lammiter wondered: Joe liked to encourage people. Here were two who needed all Joe could give.

"Had a nice walk?" he asked Joe as he entered the room. Joe was more like a peasant than ever. He had borrowed a battered felt hat, and stuck a field poppy's frail stalk through its grease-stained ribbon.

"Had a nice talk?" Joe said with a grin. He took off his hat and turned to Rosana. "The signorina got here without trouble?"

"Of course," she told him severely. "We were beginning to worry about you, Giuseppe."

Lammiter looked at them in surprise. Then he remembered that Rosana believed that *she* was in authority. "Look," he said, "let's keep everything simple. Joe—Rosana—Bill. We're in this together." He gave them both a smile. There was a brief gleam of answering amusement in Joe's eyes. "Joe was on the scene last night more than either of us," he told Rosana. "So he has a better idea of how things stand. I think we'll elect him boss around here. We'll play it his way."

Rosana seemed a little startled, and then a little doubtful as she studied Joe's furrowed brow and ingenuous grin.

"He can outthink both of us put together," Lammiter answered her thought. "He's a Sicilian, isn't he?"

Rosana smiled suddenly. "He's a Saracen, you mean. He will have us storming the castle with knives out. Thumb on the hilt, and strike up. Wasn't that your father's last piece of advice to you Giusep—Joe?" But she settled herself on the wooden bench, and her smile was no longer teasing. "All right. What do we do?" She looked at Joe.

"First of all, we'll learn a few facts. Who drove you here in Pirotta's car?"

Rosana's eyes opened still more at the brisk voice. But she obeyed it. "A mechanic—one of the men at the garage—Poggioli's—where Pirotta has repairs done. He knows nothing. He was just hired to do a job. He is following instructions, though. He wouldn't let me out of the car, except at one café just beyond Terni; and then he came with me to the lavatory, and waited outside, and took me back to the car, so I couldn't telephone anyone."

"Did he talk much?"

"It's a long journey. He began to talk halfway."

"About himself?"

"His name is Giovanni. He was worried about not being able to say good-by to his girl except by a telephone call. She was angry. They were going to a party tomorrow night."

"He expects to be away from Rome, then?"

"He wouldn't answer that question. But there were three of Pirotta's suitcases in the back of the car. It looks as if he is going on a vacation."

"Did Giovanni talk about his girl?"

"Constantly. It seemed a safe subject, I think. Her name is Margherita. She works at Stefano's—that's a shop for making artificial flowers. She is seventeen. Very beautiful. Dark curls and good figure. They are getting married next month. That's about all, I think." She frowned, trying to recall anything else.

Joe took out an old envelope from one trouser pocket and a stump of pencil from another. Lammiter, sitting beside him on the bed, saw what he was jotting down. *Stefano—fiori artificiali—Margherita 17, tipo Lollobrigida—Giovanni, mecanico—Autorimessa Poggioli.* "It's good enough," Joe said. "It will be simple to track down the girl. She will know where her Giovanni is going."

Lammiter stirred restlessly.

Joe looked at him. "This is not useless," he said gently. "All we have to do is to wait for the next few hours. No one is leaving the Casa Grande until two o'clock, when the two men who forced Eleanor into the car are taking the bus. At present, they're on guard: one in front of Eleanor's room, the other at the telephone. Pirotta wants to be wakened at noon, and his car is to be ready for him at three. Signorina Halley is to be kept in her room until he returns this evening. Dinner for two." He looked at Rosana. "And one dinner on a tray in Miss Halley's room. And the mechanic eating with Alberto and Anna-Maria. Right?"

She nodded. "Anna-Maria asked how much food she must buy. The princess keeps an eye on the bills. And Pirotta said, 'Oh, enough, enough until tomorrow night. We'll be leaving then.' So it's my idea," and she glanced with a little smile at Joe, "that the important meeting at Perugia will be over by tomorrow afternoon. Is it possible?"

Joe said with a grin, "I think Tony Brewster taught you a lot of things."

"Or perhaps," she said softly, "I learned a lot of things from Joe without knowing I was being taught." She stood up. "That's about all, isn't it? I had better get back now."

"Going back?" blurted out Lammiter. "Into that place?" Dinner for two, he remembered bitterly. "Are you still hoping you can influence Pirotta?" he asked angrily.

She shook her head. "That's one idea that died last night, when I kept my appointment with his car. He was there, waiting with the mechanic. When I saw he wasn't going, I knew he had tricked us again." She turned to Joe. "*You* know he had said over the telephone that he wanted to finish some work in the country, and that I was to bring along all the papers I had on the Galante correspondence—that was an honest business deal he was arranging for his firm."

Joe said soothingly, "That's what he told you."

"But when I saw Pirotta wasn't going, I stepped out of his car. I was scared, and angry. Then he said that Eleanor was in danger, that he had to persuade her to leave Rome that night. He said that he needed me to be with her, to look after her, to keep her company. Do you know I do think he told the truth then. Perhaps," she added bitterly, "it is the only time he ever told me the truth."

"So you got back into the car?" Lammiter asked.

"I got back into the car." She looked up at him. "You helped me when I needed help. So—" she shrugged her shoulders "—I help you. I'll get into Eleanor's room when she wakens. She was still half drugged when they arrived this morning. But she has to eat. And a tray must be carried into her room."

"You won't be allowed near her! Look, Rosana, Pirotta never told you the truth once in his life, except when he said you were beautiful. Last night at his car?—The same old confidence trick. He wanted you out of Rome. Brewster's been murdered and you've run away. See what he's building up around you? Suspicion, a wall of suspicion as big and thick as that wall out there." He caught Joe's eye. "How much evidence have Pirotta's friends planted, how much fabricated? I bet, right now, that Brewster's diary is being found."

"He never kept a diary. He *wouldn't!*" she said derisively.

"Of course he wouldn't. But either a diary or a letter will be found saying he was becoming suspicious of you, that he thought you were working against him, that he had challenged you yesterday afternoon, and you had been frightened. Joe—I ask you: am I talking nonsense? Or is all that in the pattern?"

"Pattern?" Joe said and was as stupid as possible. "Well, maybe . . . You write a play about it, eh? You have a real good plot there." He said to Rosana, "Glad we've got a writer fellow with us to show how plots are made."

Rosana avoided their eyes. "Yes," she said haltingly, "that could be true. It's in their—pattern." Then her voice became bitter. "But I shall be allowed to see Eleanor if I am willing to make her listen to Pirotta's story. He needs me for that—I've already had the first hints. He will persuade me, and I have to persuade Eleanor, that right is wrong and wrong is right. His story will seem very, very good. Yes—that is also in the pattern." Suddenly, her face was emotionless, and her voice reminded Lammiter of the princess. "I'm going back to the Casa Grande. Now. At this moment. Is that agreed?"

Joe agreed.

"Bill," Rosana said, "you know someone has got to reach Eleanor. She *must* know she is not alone."

"Yes," he said. "But—"

"Oh, you Americans! But—but—but! I shall come to no harm." She began walking over to the door. She looked down at the loose pink-and-green checked cotton dress, and laughed as she pulled it in, for a moment, against her slender waist. "How thin I have grown!"

"Tell Eleanor—" Lammiter began, as he followed her to the door, and then he was silent.

"That you are here? Those will be my first words to her." Then she was looking at him, most serious with her large dark eyes. "Good-by, Bill."

He took her hand awkwardly. "Good-by, Rosana. Take care of yourself." He kissed her cheek, on an impulse he could not explain. Or perhaps hand kissing was not his line.

"I shall, I shall," she said reassuringly. She touched his arm for a moment.

"I go with you part of the way," Joe told her, picking up his hat.

"More questions? But I told you *everything!*"

"What did the princess say on the telephone?"

"I couldn't talk to her. The mechanic wouldn't let me."

"What did she say to Alberto?"

"He wouldn't tell me."

"He wouldn't?"

"It upset him too much. But one thing I do know: the princess must be against Pirotta. For Alberto wouldn't even speak to him when he arrived in the Lancia. Anna-Maria had to do all the talking." She gave a last smile to Lammiter; and a cheerful wave of her hand. Then she started downstairs. Joe was about to follow her.

"Just a minute," Lammiter said, and caught Joe by his arm. "There's a limit to everything. Do you expect me to stay up here all day?"

"I'll be back soon."

"I'd like to stretch my legs, look around, get a feel of the town."

"I can't risk you—"

"What risk? None of Pirotta's hired men know me. I'll take no chances. I won't even try to climb the Casa Grande walls."

Joe relented. "Wait until the morning bus arrives. Follow it in. Look as if you could have come that way."

"I certainly won't try to look as if I had just buried my parachute."

"Okay, okay. Keep to the narrow streets. Pirotta's car has to travel along the main one."

"When does the bus get here?" Lammiter looked at his watch. It was now a quarter to eight.

Joe shrugged. "Depends on its business at the other little towns. You'll hear it, all right."

Rosana's voice called from downstairs: "Coming?"

"Coming!" Over his shoulder, to Lammiter, he said quietly, "If it makes you feel better, I'm going to telephone. We keep in touch with the big world, eh?" He gave a cheerful salute and ran downstairs.

"You're so *slow!*" Rosana scolded him gently in Italian.

"We'll be quick now. And careful?"

"*Very* careful." You could hear the smile in her voice. "What a mess you two have left in this kitchen! Someone ought to wash these dishes, put things away—"

"Yes, yes." He closed the kitchen door firmly.

Upstairs, Bill Lammiter stood at the window and waited until he saw Rosana in her borrowed dress—it looked pink at this distance, and far too noticeable—cross the field toward the wood. Then she vanished from sight. But once more, he couldn't see Joe. Then he looked at the gate to the town. For a moment, he was startled: a girl in a pink cotton dress was standing talking to two thick-waisted women in black. Other women joined them, all with bundles of laundry on their heads. Then they scattered, shouting good-naturedly in their strong hoarse voices to each other. Some followed a path across the road, to houses that must lie outside the walls. He counted three pink dresses altogether. He relaxed then.

He took off his tie, rolled up his sleeves, opened the top button of his shirt. He studied himself for a moment in the scrap of looking glass on the wall. That buttoned-down collar was straight from Madison Avenue. He took out his penknife and with its small blade carefully cut through the threads that held the buttons. Strange how laundries could remove buttons so easily, he thought as he sawed away. But he admitted the finished effect was more in local color once he had crumpled the collar still more.

Then he remembered the jacket which he would have to leave in this room. He went through its pockets and removed the handkerchief with the Evans photograph. Cigarettes and matches, too. And his keys. But passport, traveler's checks, his wallet? The checks could be left here, in his suitcase. The passport was another matter. He hated to part with it. It could fit into his trouser pocket and probably stay there if he didn't have to run, but he couldn't always be clamping one hand to his thigh to make sure the passport was still safe. Then he found he was smiling: in a play, a character would probably make a grand exit without giving a passing thought to all the damned documents he had to stow away about him; everyone bulged when he traveled nowadays. But he wasn't writing a play. All right, he decided, and opened his suitcase and stowed away his passport, his checks, a notebook, his heavy wallet, and his jacket. Then he locked the case and carried it into the storeroom along with Joe's discarded jacket. He laid them behind an open sack of down feathers. Someone hoping for a new mattress? He closed the door and returned to the bedroom, looking around him carefully, picking up the cigarette stub. He was leaving as little noticeable sign of his stay here as Joe had. The farmer wouldn't run into trouble from any prowlers. As Joe would say, you never could tell in this game.

He pocketed the neatly folded handkerchief and some lire notes he had taken from his wallet. No bulges, at least. He looked at his watch again, and wondered when the bus would come. He was ready to go.

21

Distantly, there came the bugling of a bus horn, and then the muted drone of a powerful engine pulling up the hill to Montesecco. Bill Lammiter, lying on the bed, fallen into that strange state of waking dream when the body accepts sleep but the mind holds it a short distance away, roused himself and swung his legs onto the floor. The drone was louder. It could be a truck, but it might be the bus. He glanced at his watch once more. With a shock, he saw that it was almost noon.

He went to the window and waited there. At least he felt rested. And less depressed. Joe hadn't come back, but that didn't worry him very much: Joe had left with several purposes and he had told Lammiter only one of them. He wondered now what commands the princess had given old Alberto on the telephone at three o'clock in the morning. He could imagine the operator, roused out of bed, cross but curious, forgetting about cold feet as she listened to the princess. But the princess would imagine that, too: perhaps her directions to Alberto had been so cryptic that Alberto was still puzzling them out. What had she thought Alberto could do, anyway? Lock Pirotta in his room like a disobedient schoolboy?

Impatiently, he watched a boy cycle out of the gates, an enormous bundle of dried twigs on his back, and then veer well in to the side of the narrow road. A farmer with two yoked oxen, pulling a cart laden with barrels, looked back downhill over his shoulder and hauled the beasts off the road close to the trees, to give safe passing-room. The loud engine throbbed, changed down to an extra low gear to cope with the last hill outside the gates, and then the bus came into sight. Briefly. For behind it there was raised a cloud of dust from the loose surface of the road. The bus eased its way through the gates and gathered a spurt of speed from the rough pavement now under its wheels.

Bill Lammiter started downstairs, a little impressed by the bus. It was not so large as the CIT or Europabus giants, which he had seen so often leaving Rome for destinations as far off as Venice or the Swiss border, but it looked new and shining. The people of the hill towns were better served than he had imagined. Good, he thought: they must be tired of watching well-fed, well-dressed tourists who could afford to spend four weeks without working. And yet, as he opened the kitchen door and stepped into the cool shadows of the yard, he couldn't remember any signs of grudge or hostility or hidden jealousy from any of the people in the month he had spent among them. "Enjoy yourselves; smile: we only ask for politeness," they seemed to say to the visitors. "If we had your money, bless it, we'd do the same. And perhaps we shall, someday. Who knows? There's the lottery, there's my uncle in America, there's that job I may get if the typewriter factory opens near my home." They were a concentration of optimists—how else would they have survived so many centuries of invaders and looters?

Borrowing some of the Italians' perpetual hope, he crossed the shadows of the farmyard and entered the white blinding sunlight of the olive grove. Above, the sky was cobalt blue and cloudless; from the dry grass, came the cicadas' constant chorus. Round the gate, activity had died away. The meal of the day was approaching, and the women were in their kitchens. Only an old man stood there, a lonely sentinel leaning on a stick, squinting in the strong glare, supervising the plain below. "*Buon giorno!*" he said to the passing stranger, and looked back at the view. "*Buon giorno!*" Lammiter said, and stepped into the town.

The street ran straight up from the gate for no more than three hundred yards, and entered, at the top of its hill, into the beginning of a piazza. He glimpsed three or four tourists waiting for someone. They must have arrived with the bus. He dodged into the first small side street leading to the right, so narrow that one car would only scrape through at considerable risk to its paint work. He didn't imagine Pirotta would drive down here, with a bright smile and a wave of his hand to the children who played in the shade. Neither the children, nor the old men sitting at the doors, nor the women who had come out for a moment to make sure their street was still there, paid much attention to him after the first all-over glance. He noticed two girls, foreigners, taking photographs of an old doorway a little ahead of him. So he dodged again, into the first street on his right, and hoped it would bring him near the wall. His plan was to walk all round the town, following the inside of the wall wherever possible. He was curious to see not only the layout of the town, but how many entrances Montesecco had. When he found Eleanor again, a knowledge of this little town might mean the difference between entrapment and escape.

He had entered by the west gate. When he reached the south gate, he saw that it led nowadays only to a road that had degenerated into a rough track leading out to fields and trees. This couldn't have been the entrance Rosana and Joe had used: it would only have led them into the little street where he now stood. He walked on, toward the east. And then, suddenly, he saw he had reached a high-walled garden of some size, adjoining a three-storied house, dominating everything else on this street. A house? It was a small fifteenth-century palace, built to withstand an army. This wall of the house, rising blankly from the cobblestones, was formidable: there were few windows, and all of them covered in elaborate patterns with iron bars three inches thick.

He slowed his pace, for ahead of him was the gateway, which probably led into an interior courtyard. And then he saw that its massive doors were closed. They were enormous, these doors, of heavy timber studded with iron nailheads the size of a man's fist. Above them was a shield, carved out of stone, painted in red and gold and blue: a wolf's head and three beehives, telling him what he had already guessed. This was the Casa Grande. This was where Eleanor . . .

Careful, Lammiter, he told himself, and kept his steady pace. He had seen all he could bear to see, at this moment.

He swerved across the little piazza in front of the main gates (it was more of a respectful retreat by the other houses in the street than an architectural design) and took the first *calle* that would lead him away from the Casa Grande. Careful, he told himself again, for this street was taking him to the main piazza, to the heart of the little town. He swerved again, to his left, into an alley that twisted and turned between crowding houses. Direction was difficult without the town's wall to guide him. He would have a little trouble finding his way back to the south gate that led out to the fields and the wood. For somewhere beyond or near that wood must lie the back entrance to the princess's house.

He had more than a little trouble: this alley twisted like a snake. Suddenly it ended, right back on the main piazza itself. He halted, staring in surprise and anger at the open paved square before him, with its central fountain, a church on the opposite side, a town hall as big as the Casa Grande and as impregnable; and here, almost beside him, a sad little café-restaurant. A few people sat in the shade. It all looked peaceful enough, and safe. Then he noticed a bus drawn up against the wall of a museum, just round the corner from where he stood.

He had, after that one sweeping glance, been ready to retreat down the alley. But the bus—he looked at it again. Either it had forgotten its schedule, or it was not the local morning bus at all. As an answer, in the comic way that life so often presents its explanations, a small dust-covered bus came rattling and bouncing into the piazza. It stopped in front of the town hall. A woman with a large basket and a small boy got out. Three people, soberly dressed in their Sunday clothes, rose from their seats in the shade and climbed on board. That was the local bus, all right. Now it was swinging around the piazza to leave by the way it had entered, bugling its horn gaily at two young girls who had suddenly emerged from one of the side streets. Americans, he decided as he noted their clothes and cameras. He gave up all idea of taking a short cut along this side of the piazza to reach a south exit to the town wall.

Just as he was turning to retrace his steps down the alley he saw the two American girls stop as they looked across at the church, grasp each other's hands, and then run toward the nearest street. They were laughing. He glanced over at the church. Now he saw what had driven the girls away: a flutter of tourists, of all shapes and sizes, was coming slowly out of the church with the anesthetized look of those who had just swallowed a lecture, while their guide still talked as he shepherded them toward the little café-restaurant. He had his amusing moments, too, to judge from the sudden gust of laughter that blew across the piazza. He was a small man, thin, neatly dressed in a gray suit with a panama hat worn at a jaunty angle. Something in his movements, a quick grace, caught Lammiter's eye.

For a moment, Lammiter froze, staring at the man across the square. Then, instinctively, he turned on his heel and retreated down the alley, no longer cursing its curves and twists. Salvatore Sabatini . . . that had been Salvatore. Or have I just got him on the brain? he wondered. He wished now that he had waited to see the guide's face more clearly, or that the man had taken off his hat to mop his brow and show the color of his hair. But the guide had not been so obliging. He had only walked with a light step, made a dramatic gesture toward the town hall, raised a laugh with some merry quip, and then led his flock relentlessly toward the restaurant.

But I couldn't wait, Lammiter thought: once he was near enough to be identified, he could have seen me, too. Then Lammiter put aside all speculation and concentrated on his direction. His only aim now was to get back to the farmhouse. He hoped to heaven that Joe was there, waiting.

He had some more trouble, for he must not appear to be a man who was in a hurry. Or a man who was going anywhere. He tried to look like a tourist who was wandering around by himself. It took him ten minutes to fight his way out of the labyrinth of small streets and alleys, twice retracing his steps, once almost back on the piazza itself. But at last he came to the main street of the town, which would take him down to its entrance gate. Carefully, he made sure there were no tourists in sight. No, they must be back at the restaurant, settling down to plates of heaped spaghetti. And there, thank God, was the gateway itself.

He passed under its huge arch and a blast of heat engulfed him as he stepped onto the dusty road that led down the hill of olive trees to the plain beneath. The farmhouse dozed among its warm terraces. The cicadas were starting the ninety-fifth movement of their daily symphony.

"Mr. Lammiter!" The voice was young, surprised, and soprano. "Why, Mr. Lammiter!"

If only to silence a third "Mr. Lammiter!" ringing out over the countryside, he halted and looked around. The two American girls he had avoided in the town had been standing to one side of the gateway, studying the posters plastered up on the old wall. Now they ran toward him, bare feet sure in flat-heeled sandals, their wide skirts and crisp blouses looking cool and uncrushed even in this wilting heat. They had broad smiles on their pretty faces, flashing sets of very white and even teeth at him in delight. He didn't share it. Who the hell are they? he wondered.

The blonde one said, tossing back her horsetail of hair like a young colt, "Mr. Lammiter—don't you remember me?" Her voice, fortunately, had dropped back to normal.

"Sorry," he said, "I'm not Lammiter." He tried to walk on, but her child's blue eyes looked at him so accusingly that the moment of escape was lost.

"But you are, too," she said, hurt. Her friend with the Italian haircut was fixing the strap of her camera most tactfully. Then the blonde suddenly smiled again. "Oh—you're traveling *incognito!* I see—" She looked at the red-haired girl with relief. "He's traveling incognito, Julie. They always do that. I *told* you."

"Goodness," said the soft puzzled voice of Julie, "all my friends spend all their free time writing novels and things. But I don't think *any* of them know they'll have to travel incognito. I don't think any of them know *that.* Or they wouldn't be writing. I mean, why do you *get* famous if you don't want to be known?"

"Oh Julie!" the blonde said, taking charge. Then to Lammiter, "We saw you before. I *thought* it was you. I waved, but—"

"Was that in the piazza?" he asked quickly. He hadn't noticed any waving.

"No. In a little street, about half an hour ago. Just after the bus arrived."

"Did you point me out to the others from the bus?" He was smiling, playing it as easily as he could. But, again, his stomach muscles knotted and tightened.

"No!" the little blonde said most decidedly. Then she laughed. "We aren't speaking to *them!*"

"We're isolationists, temporarily," Julie said with a giggle.

"We've been abandoned," the blonde said, "abandoned on the doorstep of a little hill town. And it's *frustrating.* Because over there," she waved to the north section of the wall, "you can look out of a gate and *see* Perugia on a hill of its own."

"Look—this sun's pretty hot," Lammiter said. The approach to the town felt more open with every passing minute. His eyes searched for the nearest adequate cover. And it lay, unfortunately, in that row of trees at the edge of the road almost opposite the farmhouse. He looked in despair along the trail that circled the outside of the wall. At some distance, there was a patch of trees and another farmhouse. "What about walking along here?" he suggested. "There's shade among those trees." He pointed northward.

"Too far," the blonde said, shaking her head. "These trees here are much nearer," and she set off down the main road, Julie following her, handbags and cameras swinging blithely. Lammiter hesitated, debating whether it would be possible to steer them away from the direction of the farmhouse and onto the subject of the guide instead.

"Could you give us a lift to Perugia?" the blonde girl asked suddenly, turning around to wait for him.

"I haven't a car. Sorry."

"Then we really are stuck here until the five o'clock bus," she told Julie.

"Four hours!" Julie said in despair. "And we've photographed *everything* already. Except the white bulls. *Where* have they all gone? They *were* here. I saw two beauties just in front of the gates as we arrived—and a wooden yoke—and bells on the ends of their horns—and now there isn't even *one* in sight. It's *maddening!*" She stopped and opened her camera. "Just a moment! This might be something interesting."

Lammiter walked on quickly, veering toward the opposite side of the road from the farmhouse. "Why don't we sit here for a few minutes?" He stepped onto the grass, and then behind a tree. "Did your guide tell you what happened to the olives last winter? It seems that—"

"You *don't* remember me," the blonde said in a low voice, giving a quick look over her shoulder to make sure Julie was far enough away. "But it was only yesterday, and I sat on your suitcase and you wrote—"

"Of course I remember," he said quickly. He did, now. "Today you've got a green bow on your hair instead of blue. Very mixing."

"I'm Sally—Sally Maguire." She looked around again. But Julie was still on the road, her head bent over the camera's view finder.

"Burbank, California."

"Now I feel much better!" She smiled delightedly.

He wished he did. He'd have to wait at least three minutes before he mentioned the guide again. "Have a seat," he suggested.

She looked at the sparse dry grass doubtfully, but she sat down, gathering her wide skirts tightly and carefully around her legs. "Where are you stopping?"

"Oh, I just walked up here for exercise."

"You *walked?* From the valley?" She was horrified.

"I'm walking back for lunch, right now."

"Goodness!" she said. That prospect didn't rouse much enthusiasm. "Do you know Italian, Mr.—Mr.—?"

"A little," he admitted. "And Smith's the name at present. Original, isn't it?"

"If you could do some talking for us—I mean, could you come back to the town with us? I hate to ask you to do any extra walking, but—"

"I haven't very much time," he said awkwardly. "What's the trouble anyway?"

"Transportation," she said gloomily. "You see, this guide— Oh hello, Julie! Any luck?"

Julie came over to where they sat, closing her camera. "The light is wrong or something," she said ruefully. "All that scenery and nothing to take . . . The hills just flatten out like split peas. It's—"

"Maddening," Lammiter said abruptly. "Now, Sally—what about this guide?"

Julie didn't sit down. Perhaps she didn't like hearing herself quoted. She stood, looking around her. "I can see a farmhouse over there," she said, suddenly pointing across the road. "Haystacks . . . Why, there may be white bulls, too. And there's the farmer! Hi, there!" she called, and began to run toward Joe.

Lammiter rose quickly as Sally scrambled to her feet. She said, "So it is! Perhaps he will know!" And she began hurrying after Julie.

Joe had been crossing the yard when Julie called out, and he stood now, facing her, a jar of water in his hand, trapped. He made the decision to accept this complication, seemingly, for he set down the jar of water and came forward a few steps to intercept the girl and keep her away from the open kitchen door. From where he now stood, the Fiat could not be seen.

Lammiter lit a cigarette. Keep out of this, he told himself. But it was not so easy. "He can't speak English," Julie called back to Sally. "Hurry—you've got the phrase book!"

Sally had a better idea. She halted and looked back at Lammiter. "Mr. Smith— Please, would you help us?" She waved to him frantically, and then ran on. So he followed, crossing the road quickly, deciding, as Joe had decided, that the sooner this was over the better for everyone.

The girls' heads were bent over the phrase book as he joined the little group. Joe had somehow managed to edge them away from the open yard toward the shelter of a tree. For a moment, his eyes looked at Lammiter, half amused, half angry. Lammiter had only time to give one small helpless gesture before Sally looked up.

"Would you ask him if there are any other buses? *Before* five o'clock?"
Julie said, "Here it is! *Toro. Toro.* And *bianco*—that's white, isn't it?"
"I don't think the animal is a bull, exactly," Lammiter said. "Is that what you wanted to ask—permission to photograph his white oxen?"
"The bus," Sally said, "don't forget the bus."
Under Joe's critical eyes, Lammiter's Italian failed him. It degenerated into disjointed words and phrases.
"My!" said Sally, listening to Joe's flowing reply, "doesn't he make it sound so *easy!*" She looked at Lammiter. "Did you get all that?"
"Some of it. He says the oxen are mostly down in the fields with the men. You'll find them all dozing under the trees. It's siesta-time."
"*Siesta,*" Joe said, and nodded vigorously. "*Siesta.*" He looked as if he were about to leave.
"What about the bus?" Sally asked.
"It leaves at two," Lammiter said, definite about that. The afternoon bus left at two: the men who had forced Eleanor into the Lancia, their job over, were leaving then. It was the best news Joe had brought back that morning. Two o'clock, and two less to deal with at the Casa Grande.
Sally shook her head. "Two o'clock? But that's the bus that just *won't* take us any farther than here! It's a chartered bus, a tour, with a guide and all. Tell him that!"
"They put you off the bus?" Lammiter asked, in genuine amazement.
"Well, you see, we really weren't supposed to be on it. The guide was angry—"
"Oh, but he was nice afterward," Julie said.
"Not nice enough," Sally told her firmly. "We could have stood, couldn't we, to Perugia? Or sat on our suitcases in the aisle, or something? Couldn't we?"
"It's against the law, he said."
"Phooey!" said Sally. "If the peasants can stand in a bus, so can I. I've two legs like them, haven't I?" Then she turned to Lammiter. "Tell him *that* bus is all full. Two people are getting on here in—in—*what's* the name of this town?—Montesecco—and that's another thing, the bus wasn't even scheduled to come here. Assisi for lunch, we were told. And then Perugia. But we just rushed through the churches in Assisi, and here we are in Montesecco."
"He said this place was less crowded for lunch. I'll say it is!" Julie interposed.

"Tell him," Sally repeated, nodding toward Joe.

"Let me get it all straight first," Lammiter said. "You got onto this chartered bus in Rome—"

"Because there was no room, not a single seat, on any other of the buses. We hadn't any reservations—just decided last night we were going. So this morning we went along to the Esedra piazza, you know—the one with all the fountains and buses and things—and we couldn't get a seat *any*where. It was *frustrating!* Then this nice young man from the CIT offices—"

"*He* was very nice," Julie said.

"—tried to help us get to Perugia. He found these two seats on this bus, empty, no one in them. So he popped us and our luggage on board. The driver didn't say anything, just took our money. No one paid any attention—they were all too worried because the guide hadn't turned up. Then when we were almost out of Rome, the bus stopped at a little café, and this guide came on board, apologizing like mad. Then he saw us, and was absolutely furious. He wanted to put us off the bus right there. But we just sat and smiled. *No* one was using the old seats, anyway."

"But he was nice, afterward," Julie conceded. "And he could talk *five* languages: French, German, Swedish, Dutch, and English. That was for us—the English, I mean."

"And now," said Lammiter firmly, "the two seats on the bus are needed for two people boarding it at Montesecco. But why are you in such a hurry to get to Perugia?"

"Our friends are all there," Julie said with a smiling glance at Sally, "for the summer school. And by Saturday we'll have to leave Perugia to get to Genoa in time to catch our boat. It's maddening."

"It certainly is," Lammiter agreed gravely. "What is the guide's name, do you know? He could be reported."

"Oh, we wouldn't want to get him into trouble," Julie said. "He was an Italian. And the old ladies loved him, didn't they, Sally? It was Signore Samarini this and Signore Samarini that, all the way."

"Sabatini," Sally corrected. "Signore Sabatini."

Joe had been a very patient Italian, polite if not comprehending. But for one brief fraction of a second, his eyes looked very directly at Lammiter.

"Sabatini—you're sure?" Lammiter asked. And I was right, he thought in a quick moment of jubilation. That *was* Sabatini I saw.

She laughed. "I couldn't forget it. Once, my favorite novel was *Scaramouche.* I asked Signore Sabatini if he was any relation to the author, but he wasn't, and he didn't have time to read novels, either. Squelch!"

Julie said, "But I don't think you should report him. We don't want to get him into trouble. After all, it was a *chartered* bus."

"Where is it going?" Lammiter asked, casually. "Perugia, and then?" Beside him, Joe was standing very still.

"Florence tomorrow. Next day Venice," Sally said with the scorn of the tourist who has spent two months instead of two weeks on her travels.

Lammiter stared across at Joe. "They aren't having much of a stay in Perugia, are they?"

"Not much," Sally answered Lammiter. "They're leaving Perugia at the crack of dawn, practically. They'll just have this afternoon, that's all when you come to think of it. I bet they're in bed by nine o'clock."

"Wish I had the afternoon there," Julie said regretfully. She opened her camera and kneeled to look up at a haystack, symmetrically wound round a center pole that pointed into the sky. "Well, this will just have to do instead."

Sally said, "Ask the farmer if there is no one in Montesecco who could give us a ride to Perugia."

Lammiter translated. Joe, watching Julie carefully, was edging away. "Get them back to the road, for God's sake," he said, "and don't let them photograph you." He turned his back on Julie. "*Buon giorno!*" he said to Sally. Quickly, he lifted his water jar and carried it toward the farmhouse. Its doors closed firmly.

"No ride. No bus. What's happened to our luck?" Sally asked, finding a smile somehow.

"Well, he's got to catch up on his siesta." Lammiter began walking back to the road.

"If *only* he had waited," Julie said, "he'd have made *such* a good study. All those wrinkles and furrows—"

"The light's all wrong, too many shadows here," Lammiter said quickly. "Hey, don't waste your film on me, Julie."

She lowered her camera, frowning, calculating how much film she had left, and then sighed in agreement.

"Come on," he urged them, "there's another farm over there—along that trail under the wall." He pointed toward the north side of the town.

"They'll be having a siesta, too," Sally said gloomily. "I don't see it —this business of going to bed in the middle of the day."

"And there are some others who don't see it, either," he said thankfully. Three young boys were playing outside the gates: or, to be exact, they were having a wonderful time tearing large strips off all the posters. "There's a study for you, Julie. You can call it *And a little child shall lead them.*"

"Look, look, look!" cried Julie. Coming along the trail that Lammiter had pointed out was a farm cart drawn at a slow ceremonial pace by two stately white oxen. "And they've got hats on!" she added in delight as she ran past him, past Sally, racing over the rough ground without one thought of a sprained ankle.

"Perhaps," thought Sally out loud, new ideas popping into her bright blue eyes, "perhaps he's going down to the main road—and if he'd only wait until we got our suitcases—then we'll find a passing car in the valley —perhaps?"

"I don't think you'll need me as an interpreter this time," he said, as he listened to the mixture of broken English and one-word Italian that drifted over toward them. The driver was young, smiling, delighted with this break in boredom. "Good-by, Sally."

"Can't we give you a lift?"

"No, thanks. I'll cut down over the olive terraces and make good time."

"Thanks for *everything.* 'Bye."

"Thank *you,*" he said, as he watched her run toward Julie. The cameras were out. The children were gathering around. The driver beamed from his seat on the edge of the cart and straightened his hat. The oxen stood placidly. Everyone was happy.

For appearance's sake, although he didn't expect any further interest in him now, Lammiter climbed down through three terraces. It was harder work than it had looked, and the heat among the olive trees was blistering. So he veered to his left and circled cautiously back to the farmhouse.

The kitchen door was open. Joe was finishing a hasty meal. He looked up at Lammiter, shaking his head slowly.

"It's all right," said Lammiter. "They've met some friends up at the gate."

Joe pushed back his chair abruptly and went to the stairs.

"Where can I wash?—I'm filthy," Lammiter asked, helping himself to Chianti. Then he saw the water Joe had carried in, and a basin beside it. He ripped off his damp shirt. He was drying himself with it when Joe came downstairs. "Well, did you see them for yourself?"

"They're loading the suitcases onto the cart. But don't give me any more shocks like them." He sat down at the table. "Come on. Eat!" Then, as Lammiter helped himself to cheese and bread, Joe said, "Sabatini . . . There couldn't by any chance be another man using that name? Someone who was sent to take Sabatini's place?" Joe was arguing it out with himself. "He did not leave with the bus from the Piazza Esedra, remember. He got in much later, outside Rome. Why? To avoid all the guides and drivers who were gathered at the Esedra, perhaps?"

"Or the police," Lammiter said with a smile. "Stop kidding yourself, Joe." But it must be difficult for Joe to grant that someone had played the old confidence trick on him and on Brewster, and played it well: no one likes to admit he has bought the Brooklyn Bridge, or that someone he thought was a friend turns out to be a traitor. "No one has taken Sabatini's place to cover up his murder. He's alive. And in good spirits. I saw him."

"Where?" The word shot out like a bullet.

"In the piazza. He was taking his tourists to eat at the restaurant." He glanced at his watch. "Just three-quarters of an hour ago. They'll still be there."

Joe had risen to his feet. "But Sabatini won't eat with them. He didn't come to Montesecco to enjoy its cooking." He took a step toward the door, and then paused. "Sabatini—" he said, softly "—alive and walking around as if nothing had happened." His lips tightened.

Lammiter remembered last night in Joe's car. "At least," he said quietly, "we know the kind of man we have against us."

Joe nodded, grim-faced. Slowly, he said, still puzzling out the reason why Sabatini should have come to Montesecco, "He's making a check, making sure that everything is going well." Joe's eyes suddenly gleamed. "Or is there some change in plans, some last-minute instructions?"

"He doesn't trust Pirotta?"

"That kind of man trusts no one." Joe took some more steps toward the door. "*Mannaggia!* If only we had a telephone in this house!"

"You aren't thinking of walking into the town, now? My God—you are likely to run into Sabatini on the prowl. Wait until two o'clock comes, and the bus leaves."

"I want to see him with my own eyes."

"He's got eyes, too. And if he is making a last-minute check—" Lammiter stopped short. "Joe!"

"Some risks can't be avoided," Joe said angrily.

"Joe! Listen, will you? If this *is* a last-minute check, can the meeting be in Perugia today? He leaves tomorrow for Florence, remember?"

"He won't attend the meeting. That is not his job."

"What is his job? Security, isn't it?"

"If you are right and he isn't an Italian," Joe said, "he could be a member of the NKVD working in Italy."

Lammiter pushed aside his plate of bread and cheese. He tried not to think of Eleanor. He forced his mind back to Perugia. "Sabatini won't leave Perugia until Evans is safely out of there."

"You have only the word of two girls that Sabatini leaves Perugia tomorrow. He may not go with that bus. He may stay behind, rejoin the tour tomorrow night in Florence. What would be a safer way to travel to Venice?"

Venice—Lammiter thought. Why Venice?

Joe was saying, "You're putting more trust in your two maniacs than in Rosana."

"I'm putting more trust in them than in Pirotta. Rosana only repeated what he told the housekeeper. 'Tomorrow night—we'll be leaving then.' Very obliging of him to announce his departure so frankly." He rose. "The meeting is this afternoon. Pirotta takes Eleanor away with him tonight. Is that it?"

Joe looked at him. Slowly, he said, "Could be. Could be . . . I'll report it anyway. If you are wrong, Bill, then I'll come asking you for a job." He pulled a watch out of his pocket. "Half-past one."

"Half-past one it is." Lammiter timed his watch exactly.

Joe was calculating. He said, "I wait until ten minutes before the bus leaves. I make sure that Sabatini and his two men climb on board. Then I telephone. Then I see a couple of people. Then I come back here for you."

Lammiter shook his head. "I'll wait, too, until Sabatini leaves on that bus. But then I'm heading for the Casa Grande."

"No!"

"Yes! Don't worry. I'll keep out of Pirotta's sight. And as soon as he drives off for the meeting in Perugia, I'll bring Eleanor and Rosana out."

"No, Bill. There's too much risk. I don't want any alarms being telephoned to Perugia."

"But that mechanic—Giovanni—will be the only opposition left. He's harmless enough."

"Not as harmless as you think. He's already done a stretch in prison: assault and robbery. Now he's got a job to do that no honest man would take even for a million lire. And that's his price. We traced his girl this morning. She got scared and told us."

"A million lire?" That was less than seventeen hundred dollars, but it sounded better in lire. "What's the job?"

"She didn't know."

Lammiter said, "Joe—what are you trying to hide from me? Last night we talked about a lot of things. We gave ourselves a pretty clear view of the kind of man who had Brewster murdered. He is ruthless, cold-blooded, and as wily as they come. You told me he might think it wise to get rid of Eleanor, but he couldn't risk any publicity. Yet there's one kind of publicity he could risk. Eleanor could disappear with Pirotta, couldn't she? An elopement, Joe, an apparent elopement. Anyone would accept that story."

Joe was silent.

"Did the mechanic's girl tell the police where he is going? Didn't she know that?"

"Venice." Abruptly, Joe moved into the yard. He turned quickly to his left, toward the side of the house where the car lay.

Lammiter gripped the back of his wooden chair. Venice, he was thinking again, Venice . . . the place for lovers and elopements. But a gondola on the Grand Canal by moonlight was only one-half of Venice, the enchanted half. There was the workaday half, the quays where the ships of all nations lay and loaded and unloaded. Venice was an Adriatic port. You could take a ship there, in sight of the Grand Canal, and you could sail out through the lagoon to Greece, to Turkey, to the Black Sea.

He looked down at his hands, knuckles white through the deep tan. He swung round as a shadow fell on the oblique stream of sunlight now spreading over the threshold. It was Joe. Lammiter took a deep breath and relaxed his grip on the chair.

Joe said, "Ugly thoughts you were thinking. Here!" He held out a revolver. "That will keep them company." He looked at his watch. "Time to go. How do you plan to get into the Casa Grande?"

"By the gate down at the woods. There's a gamekeeper's cottage. His name is—Jacopone?"

Joe nodded. "I told him he might expect to see you." He half smiled. "I had a feeling you might get restless and do something damned stupid."

"Thanks," Lammiter said, "thanks, friend." He slipped the revolver into his pocket. "And here's something for you." He took out the folded handkerchief and passed it over to Joe. "It's the photograph Eleanor took of Evans, up at Tivoli. Perhaps you could send it to Perugia? It isn't very clear; but it's better than nothing."

Joe took the handkerchief, checked inside it but wasted no time in examining the photograph. "You took a long time to trust Joe," he said as he pocketed the handkerchief, and he smiled. "Oh well, now I can stop worrying about you."

"I forgot about that photograph." And that was true. He had forgotten, until he put his hand in his pocket.

"Sure, sure. Good luck!"

"Good luck to you. When do we meet?"

"Chi sa?"

Yes, Lammiter thought: who knows?

Suddenly Joe put his arms round Lammiter's shoulders, gave him a brief embrace and a thump on the back. Then he moved to the door, slipped quietly into the farmyard, and was gone.

Lammiter closed the door, ran upstairs, found his case and opened it. First thing needed was a shave. That cost three careful minutes in front of the fly-spotted glass. Quickly, he pulled on a clean shirt, a new tie, and a fresh jacket. He jammed the passport and wallet and checks into his pockets. If his plan failed, if he were to be discovered wandering around the princess's Casa Grande, he was going to look exactly like what he was: Bill Lammiter in search of his girl. That way, he wouldn't have to explain what he was doing in Montesecco. That way, Joe wouldn't be connected with him. He would make his story clear, and he would make his story hold.

When he was ready, the suitcase hidden once more, the bed smoothed down, nothing forgotten—he clamped a quick hand to each of his pockets and checked their various bulges—he crossed over to the window. He closed the shutters as he had found them when he first entered the room, leaving only a small crack of light which still would give him a glimpse of the entrance gate of the town. He glanced at his watch again. Two more minutes, and the bus would leave the piazza. He wished Joe luck, wherever he was.

As he waited, he perfected his story. The princess had told him Eleanor was at Montesecco. So he had come here. By bus—to Assisi—yes, that could be true: the buses stopped at Assisi for lunch, Sally—or was it Julie?—had said, bless both those inspired and amiable maniacs. And then, in Assisi, he had hired a taxi to the gates of Montesecco. His driver had pointed out the Casa Grande to him. He had got into the grounds by exploring along the outside of the wall and convincing the gamekeeper that the princess had sent him. Yes, that was the story. If he ever got time to explain it, he thought grimly.

Then he heard the heavy drone of the bus, lumbering cautiously down the street toward the gate. It came slowly out from under the heavy arch like an elephant testing its way cautiously at the edge of a water hole: and then its brakes were eased a little and it started to gather more speed down the road, leaving a large cloud of dust swirling around the torn posters. Signore Sabatini was no doubt pointing out and explaining the withered olive groves.

He closed the shutters and went downstairs. The table needed clearing. Then he decided to leave it littered. Two men had eaten there: that was all right—two men lived here, didn't they? Only, neither of them would have wasted any food. He dropped his unfinished piece of cheese back onto its platter, and pocketed the half-eaten crust of bread: the chickens in the yard would dispose of that evidence. Then he saw his damp and discarded shirt. He bundled it up and threw it under the bed. He smiled when he saw it was not alone. Someone else had the same idea about dirty clothes.

He opened the door, and looked back for a last reassurance. The sun streamed obliquely into the room. Still life, by Vermeer in rustic mood. He nodded, satisfied. He closed the door. Watchfully, he crossed the farmyard, and entered the olive grove.

This was sheltered ground. Even in the bad frost this year, these trees had had help from the winter sun. There were gray-green leaves on some of their branches, thriving on the warmth of the baking earth around their gnarled and twisted trunks. Then the grass of the field was under his feet, long and dry, but soft and yielding. Here the desultory breeze wandering aimlessly around the hills could stir the air gently with its warm breath, so that the rays of concentrated heat were broken and there was a feeling of almost coolness in comparison to the roasting oven around the olives. He reached the first green trees, the beginning of the wood. Bliss, bliss, this true coolness of dappled shade and softly stirring leaves. The wood was deep, a place for small game. He recalled now that of the dozen little shops he had passed that morning, scattered around the narrow streets, two had displayed good rifles, excellent shotguns. A lot of hunting took place among these little hill towns.

Under the cover of the trees, he could abandon his downward course. Abruptly, he turned to travel uphill toward the wall of the town. He began to worry that he might have gone beyond the gate in the wall that led to the gamekeeper's lodge. He reached the edge of the wood, and before him was the trail edging the vast encircling wall of Montesecco. Where now—to his left or to his right?

He turned to his right, his worry growing. Stupid, Joe had called him, and so, remembering that, he had been overcautious. Or had that been Joe's purpose? He increased his pace, angry with Joe, angry with himself.

And then, as the trail curved round with the wall, he saw the gate just ahead of him. It was not a giant, like the other gates. It was simply a good-sized opening, handsome enough, probably constructed to let the owner of the house inside the wall enjoy his hunting without having to ride through the town.

Even as Lammiter took a deep breath of relief, a man stepped out from the trees and faced him, a man with a gun under his arm. A shotgun or a rifle? A rifle, Lammiter decided. Could this be Jacopone? Yet a gamekeeper usually carried a shotgun.

For a moment, Lammiter hesitated. Then he walked on. The man was dressed as the farmer had been, except that his trousers were tucked into high laced boots. His felt hat was pulled down over his forehead to shade his eyes. They never left Lammiter.

"*Buon giorno,*" Lammiter said, smiled, looked at the rifle. He got no reply. The man was old, his brown face wrinkled, many creases around his keen gray eyes. His face was thin, hawk-nosed; his hair was white. And Lammiter noted, too, that he himself was being studied, slowly and carefully, not a detail missed, whether it was his shoelaces or his haircut.

"*Americano,*" the old man said at last. He smiled. He had few teeth, and those were dark in color; but Lammiter thought it the finest smile he had seen in years.

"Jacopone? Giuseppe told me—"

"*Sì, sì.*" Jacopone turned to the gate, beckoning Lammiter to follow. Quietly, without another word, he opened the gate and they entered. Carefully, the gate was locked behind them. Lammiter's eyes left the coat of arms—wolf's head, three beehives, this was the place all right—and turned to look at the garden. He was standing at the beginning of a short avenue of thick trees, their branches meeting overhead to form a green tunnel. At the other end of this short avenue, he could see a formal garden of shrubs and graveled walks, and then a terrace, and then a part of the house itself. But the tunnel of trees hid any windows.

Jacopone touched his arm and began walking toward a little cottage tucked well to one side of the gate. He walked without talking, but without much concern either. For there was a screen of shrubs and trees making sure that the gamekeeper's cottage would give no offense to any aesthetic eye looking out on the view from the Casa Grande.

They passed the cottage. There was a wooden chair at its door, and a large dog chained to a small tree beside it. The dog rose, faced Lammiter. But a word from Jacopone silenced the beginning of a suspicious growl, and the dog settled down again in its patch of cool shade. It even thumped a heavy tail by way of apology.

They followed a path that kept close to the high wall marking the boundary of the princess's land. But again they could walk normally without fear of being seen, for the path was hidden from the garden and the house by a continuous hedge of tall rhododendrons. This, Lammiter decided, must be the servants' entrance. It was probably as safe as old Jacopone seemed to think it was.

Quietly, Lammiter asked, "The American girl—is she safe?"

The old man frowned at him. He had difficulty in understanding Lammiter's Italian accent. Then he raised his shoulders for a brief moment: he didn't know, but he hoped for the best.

"And the Signorina Rosana?"

Jacopone smiled. "She is brave, that one. The courage of a man." Courage, he seemed to be saying, kept people safe. He nodded. He made a quick signal for silence.

The distance to the house had been short. Here they were, entering a neat square of hedged-in garden standing almost at the side of the house itself. It was the kitchen garden, Lammiter noted, with vegetables and peach trees, cutting flowers, vines, everything arranged in its own neat space so that not one yard of earth was wasted. He remembered how little room there was in this town: the grounds of the house were small, even if they were constructed in the grand manner.

"Wait!" Jacopone whispered, backing Lammiter determinedly behind the shelter of a peach tree. He pointed to himself, and then to the house. "*La signorina Rosana!*" he said, softly, hoarsely. "I tell her."

"I'll go with you." Lammiter took a step toward the house.

The gamekeeper shook his head with unexpected energy.

"But if there is any trouble—" Lammiter said.

The gamekeeper had understood that word, at least. "Trouble?" He smiled, raised his rifle to his shoulder, pointing its barrel into the sky. "I shoot."

"You'll give a warning shot if you need me?"

Jacopone frowned, and then gave up trying to understand. Again, he aimed a shot into the air, nodded, and turned away. He stepped through an opening in the hedge that lay nearest to this wing of the house, and vanished.

Patience, Lammiter told himself, patience: the old boy has saved you at least half an hour of prowling around, and you never could have climbed that wall in the first place. He resigned himself to waiting, forced down his rising anxiety, and studied the house.

From here, only the upper floors were visible, their windows tightly shuttered against the afternoon sun, but from the angles of the roofs he could make a guess at the size and shape of the place. It was larger than it had seemed from the street: that square of building could not be solid, it must have a central courtyard. It was strong, built in the days when the thickness of a wall was measured in feet, not in inches. No balconies, no loggias, only smooth walls of stone decorated with softly painted grotesques. The shuttered windows were large, spaced at wide intervals not only between each other, but between the floors themselves. Even a trained roof climber would find no help in that façade. Better put your trust in Jacopone, he thought, Jacopone and Rosana.

He glanced at his watch. Six minutes had passed since the old man had slipped through the hedge to find Rosana. Six minutes . . . seven . . .

He looked back at the house. Which was the room—what window? Or did the room, where Eleanor was left, face into the courtyard? Around him, the cicadas had become a permanent background of sound, no longer heard. The violence of brilliant light and black shadow, the contrast of scarlet flowers against blue sky, the heavy scent of sun-warmed fruit, the jagged rhythm of the yellow butterflies were no longer seen or felt. Nothing existed, nothing, except the silent house and the moving hand of his watch. Nine minutes now . . .

I'll give them one more, he thought, his anxiety shifting into foreboding. One more minute, an even ten altogether: no more. Then I'm going in.

Eleanor stood at the window of the room where she had slept out her drugged sleep. Here, Luigi had talked to her. Here, Rosana had made constant excuses to visit her all that dreary morning. A square, high-ceilinged room, a museum piece quickly made ready for her: a prison, with cupids on its painted ceiling and a rosy Venus, one leg trailing from a golden couch of clouds, waiting. But, she thought, as she looked down into the central courtyard round which the house was built, she had felt every emotion in this room except the one for which it was designed. Bewilderment and fear and despair: these had been her companions. And now, the hope that Rosana had kindled was fading away. Down there in the courtyard, both cars had been made ready. And there, beyond them, was the gateway leading to the street, strong wooden doors, enormous, heavy, locked. Why did she keep watching them? As if she could will them to open and let Bill Lammiter come walking into the courtyard.

But he wouldn't come. Not today, Rosana had said: tomorrow he would come. It was all planned. But would tomorrow be time enough? Eleanor looked at the two cars: both seemed so ready for flight.

I wish, she thought, I wish Rosana would come back. Where has she gone? So quickly, without explanation. Something is going wrong. I know it. I know it. I've known it ever since the bell at the gateway rang, and the red-haired man walked into the courtyard.

I was eating the bread that Rosana had smuggled up to my room: bread and San Pellegrino water, both safe. I hadn't touched the food on the lunch tray: doubtful, Rosana had warned me. But the bread was good, and I was hungry at last. And then, talking together, we heard the bell ringing at the gate. How long ago was that? Ten minutes? Less? There is no clock in this room: Venus resents clocks. It doesn't matter; time has lost all sense today, except that the red-haired man is still with Luigi, and Rosana hasn't come back.

When the bell rang, I ran to the window. "It can't be Bill," Rosana said, as if she had read my thoughts. And she was explaining again that once the meeting in Perugia had taken place, Bill would be here. But not until then. Nothing must alarm Luigi, nothing must happen to make him send any warning to his friends. The meeting had to take place. Couldn't I understand that?

"It's a man, someone from the city," I said in disappointment, watching the stranger, neat in his movements, dapper in his dress, who was now talking to Alberto. The man took off his hat, wiped his brow, and raised his voice to make himself better understood. "A man with red hair."

"No!" Rosana was beside me then. "Oh, no!" she said, and for the first time I heard despair in her voice. Her face was filled with fear, fear and hate. It frightened me. Into silence. We stood together at the window. I began to feel sick again. For it was all so innocent down in the courtyard, with only Rosana's grip on my arm to warn me that there was danger, too. The man was a guide: he only wanted permission to show the Signorelli fresco in the chapel to his tourists on his next visit here. That was all.

"It's an excuse," Rosana whispered, "an excuse to talk to Luigi."

"But Luigi won't talk to a guide."

"He will!" she said. "He will!"

She was right, for Luigi came hurrying out. He looked as if he had slept well. He had shaved and changed his clothes. He was brisk and smiling. I don't think he actually knew the man, for he stood there, hesitating a little. And the man repeated his request. "I am sorry," Luigi said. "I'm afraid that is impossible." But he did not turn away. He still waited.

The guide said he was sorry, too. Dottore Vannucci, the great expert in Florence, had assured him the Signorelli fresco was superb.

"Would you care to see it yourself?" Luigi asked quickly. "Let me show you it. Of course, you understand that my aunt would not approve of tourists coming here." He was talking pleasantly as he led the way into the house.

Behind me, the room door opened. Before I could turn round, it had closed. And Rosana had gone.

Outside in the corridor, the man on guard spoke to her. I heard Rosana say cheerfully, "Are you still here? Why—you'll miss your bus if you aren't careful!" Then I heard the key turn in the lock again. And Rosana laughed at something the man said. Her footsteps were less and less, until they became nothing. The man got up from his chair—it scraped as it was pushed back against the wall—he tested the door, and for a moment my heart missed a beat: all morning the fear had been that the man would come in, and catch my wrist, and drug me again. But the man walked away, down the corridor. It must be nearly two o'clock then. That was the time, Rosana had told me, when the guards would leave Montesecco. By two o'clock they weren't needed any more to guard me; and, perhaps, if I had eaten the drugged food the men had brought upstairs for me, if Rosana hadn't told me the truth, instead of Luigi's story, I would not have needed even a child of three to watch me.

So the guards were gone. The key was left in the lock. Surely Rosana would come back now. She could open the door and let me out.

But she didn't come back.

It was odd, the stupid things I tried on that lock: a tooth broken out of my comb (it was too slight); a lipstick case (too bulky); a nail file (too broad); and then a small pencil. That fitted, but the key wouldn't move. It had been twisted in the lock so that it could not be pushed out. And it would have been so easy to pull it into the room through the wide crack at the bottom of the door that I stood with the useless pencil in my hand and cried with disappointment.

Odd, too, how one's mind trusts and then distrusts. I walked back to the table in the center of the room and stood looking down at the lunch tray. I began to wonder if Rosana had drugged me, too, in her own way. Not with food. She had warned me to touch nothing from the trays. Yes, give her credit for that. Give her credit, too, that she got the guard with that stupid smile on his face out of the room—I was still half dressed. "I'll see she takes her lunch," she told him. But as soon as he had gone, she whispered, "Touch nothing on that tray. He wouldn't allow me to carry it upstairs. He sent me ahead of him so I couldn't see what he added to Anna-Maria's cooking." Then she stood very still. "But why do they want to start drugging you again? So soon?"

So soon . . . Perhaps, then, as my heart sank, I did know that something was going wrong for us. Tomorrow Luigi would take me away. Tomorrow was time enough to start drugging me.

But Rosana found her own answer. "Perhaps Luigi doesn't trust my powers of persuasion. Or perhaps he doesn't think you are too easily persuaded. So they drug the food, just a little, just enough to keep you calm, unworried." She was cheerful again. She was so sure that everything would come out right. "All we have to do is wait. Tomorrow, once the meeting in Perugia starts, we can act. When Luigi is at the meeting, we'll leave. It will be easy."

I shook my head.

"Bill will come for you. Nothing will stop him. I know. I saw him." Then she was watching me, almost studying me. "You're beautiful, yes," she said, "but no more beautiful than others." She stood in front of the looking glass. "Luigi had twenty women and never married one of them. And you came along—" She laughed. "I begin to believe what his friends said. The little American has a very special secret weapon."

I stood staring at her.

"I'm sorry," she said, and stepped away from the looking glass. "That was foolish of me to repeat the gossip. Of course, there is always gossip. . . . Jealousy makes tongues bitter." Suddenly, she threw her arms round me and kissed me. I never have liked people touching me, unless it was a man and I was in love with him. And there were only two men I had loved, and the second one—

Can you fall into hate as quickly as you can fall into love?

I shivered, and moved away from her, to pick up my dress. It had been taken away from me last night to be washed. "I'm cold," I said. I was wearing only a petticoat and brassière. "And thank Anna-Maria for laundering my dress so nicely."

"Yes," she said, looking at me strangely, "you seem cold. Yet you can't be." She laughed again, but this time she was honestly amused and the moment of bitterness was gone. "But don't put on your pretty dress yet. Keep it fresh. When Bill comes—"

"*Will* he come?" I had got too tangled up in all my emotions. I began to cry. And Rosana changed again, into someone gentle and kind. "I've done nothing but cry since yesterday," I said angrily. "I've done nothing but—"

"Why shouldn't you?" Rosana said comfortingly. "But don't let that barbarian outside the door hear you. You are supposed to be placid, my dear, a little drugged, and very much persuaded by clever Rosana. They are expecting no trouble at all, from either you or me—or from Bill."

Give Rosana all that credit: she comforted me with the only name I wanted to hear.

Yet now, as I stood beside the little table with its tray of cold congealed food, alone, Rosana gone, the key in the locked door tantalizingly secure, the feeling of being trapped came surging back. Has Rosana drugged me with the promise of tomorrow? Only pretend to be obedient, only play-act a little until tomorrow, and all will be well. Would it? Was Bill really here in this little town? Had she truly seen him?

Look, the other part of me told myself—and that's how Bill always started an explanation—look, Rosana *did* tell you the truth. She came to you this morning, after Luigi had left you. She helped you, didn't she? You were almost believing what he had said, for you had nothing else to believe, and you were still a little sick, dazed, frightened, bewildered.

And I'm still bewildered. All I know that is bad about Luigi came from Rosana. His story was so different. If I had still been in love with him, I might have believed him.

I wish I wouldn't have these waves of sickness.

The first one hit me as I got out of the car this morning, only half conscious, trying to fight my way to the surface of the hideous dream. Luigi's arms were around me, gentle as he always has been. I kept trying to push him away, to scream, "No, no!" But my voice was a whisper, and my hands were water. Two men were beside me. "Get away, get away!" Luigi said in anger.

Then quietly he said, "Take care of her," and two women came out of the shadows toward me.

His voice rose in a fury of bitter words. Not to me, not to the two women—one was young, the other old—who were trying to help me into the house. Luigi never spoke that way to women, not even when he was angry at Tivoli had he ever spoken like that. He was cursing the two men who had drugged me. I looked at the old woman who was helping me climb some stairs. I said, "But why did he let them do it?" My voice must have sounded like a child's, for the old wrinkled face pressed itself against my cheek and said something softly. In Italian. So she didn't understand what my question had been. But I kept repeating it to myself until the old woman and the girl brought me into a dark room. And then the second wave of sickness hit me.

I stood, twisted with nausea: long, long shuddering breaths of nausea. "Open the shutters," Luigi's voice said. "Get her undressed, into bed!"

I tried to tell them all, "Go away, go away, leave me alone!" But all I could do was to stand swaying like a drunken woman. I felt cold, ice-cold, as if winter had come, and the air from the unshuttered window were frost-edged.

"Rosana!" Luigi's voice said, "help Anna-Maria. Quick!" And the girl, who had kept away from me, began to help the old woman undress me. Someone pulled the sheets of the bed apart, someone lifted me in. So large, so tall was the bed, its posts soaring up into the ceiling, pink and white faces laughing down at me. And around me, the watching faces, the old and the young and Luigi's. I tried to pull the sheet over my shoulders. But all I could do was to close my eyes and blot out theirs.

"She'll be all right," Luigi was saying. Someone had brought a blanket and he folded it around me. "A little sleep . . ." He bent over me. I felt the roughness of his cheek on mine. "Darling, darling," he said softly in my ear, for me alone. His hand smoothed the hair back from my brow.

And that's how I fell asleep, Luigi's words soft in my ears, his hand gentle on my brow.

When I awoke, Luigi had come back. He was sitting on a chair, watching me, waiting for me to drift out of sleep. He sat quite still. He said nothing at all. And I lay still, not speaking. He hadn't changed his clothes, he couldn't have had any sleep as yet. He had just spent these first hours here, sitting beside me, watching. My anger left me; I felt only sad and miserable.

He rose and sat on the side of the bed and took my hand. He began talking to me. Gently. Everything he said and did was gentle, quieting my fears, calming my tense worry.

I think he believed what he said. His words were spoken so earnestly, so honestly. I think I would have believed him, too, except that I kept remembering last night. That shadow wouldn't go away, the shadow of all my unanswered questions, the shadow of a Luigi I had never known, of a world I had never imagined. And as I listened now to the Luigi I knew, my mind kept remembering the stranger. I lay quite silent, watching his face—a strong and noble face, proud, and yet, as at that moment, tender. I listened to his voice, filled with love and anxiety. And his words were right, too. Only remember all our weeks of happiness, he was saying: let them blot out the mistakes of the last three days, the stupid quarrels, the blunders. Forget, forget and forgive, and trust. Later, he could tell me the full story, but now it was enough to trust each other.

He would never question me again about Bill Lammiter. The man was an agent, in Rome on his own business, a man working with lies and hypocrisy, pulling me into suspicion and danger, thinking only of the information he could draw out of me. But forget all that now. Politics and love were two separate worlds. Luigi trusted me, and I must trust him. And now—today—I must rest and sleep and remember I was safe.

He bent down and kissed my cheek, as if I were a child who had wakened from a hideous dream and had to be comforted. I was safe, he told me again. He would place a guard outside my door and it would be locked. No one could harm me here. And he would send Rosana to keep me company. In a few days, we'd forget all this. Together, we'd forget. Meanwhile, I was safe. That was all that mattered.

But I felt only numbness in my heart, and my hand lay dead in his. "Sleep, darling," he said, "sleep some more." And then he left me.

I didn't sleep. I kept thinking of Luigi's words, last night, in Rome. I had listened then, and I had taken the first step into this trap. Or perhaps the first step had been my phone call to Bill. My two phone calls . . .

For they had brought Luigi to my apartment last night. His friends had been checking up at the hotel to make sure that Bill Lammiter was leaving Rome. And they had discovered I had been trying to get in touch with him. It was as simple as that.

I'll never forget the distraught look on Luigi's face as we stood together in the hall of my apartment. He gripped my arm and said, "Eleanor, *why* did you call him? *Why?*"

I stared blankly at him. "But what's *wrong* with a telephone call?"

Luigi was watching my eyes. His grip slackened on my arm. "It linked you with Lammiter."

"Is that any of your business now?" I walked into the living room. I had a moment of guilt as I looked at the little table where Bill and I had had supper together. Luigi was jealous; that was all I could think. What would he do if he heard that Bill had been here? Or did he know that, as he knew about the telephone calls?

"Yes," Luigi said. "It *is* my business. Lammiter is an agent."

"An agent? What kind of agent?" I began to laugh.

"Stop that! Don't you see I'm trying to help you? Where are the photographs? I'm burning them. Immediately."

I found them for him. He examined them carefully, and then set them on fire, one by one, over the large ashtray. Thank God, I thought, I had emptied it of Bill's cigarette end. And then I felt my sense of guilt, mean guilt, deepen. But I was also afraid. Without knowing what all this meant, I was afraid.

"Are there any more?" he asked suddenly.

"Some didn't come out. The light—" I felt stifled. It was true. But the truth also covered a lie. The longer I didn't explain about Bill, the more difficult it was to give the full truth.

He had caught the sound of strain in my voice. "I didn't tell anyone you had taken these photographs, Eleanor," he said very quietly. "I had to keep you safe. That's why I broke our engagement. You didn't think I was serious about that, did you? All I wanted was to get you out of Rome, safely away."

"Safe from what?"

He looked up suddenly from the last twisting black ashes. "Safe from Lammiter. When he goes back to the hotel for his raincoat, he will find your message. He will come here. Won't he?"

So he didn't know that Bill had already been here. I was too relieved to answer.

He said, "There are some people who wouldn't like that. They would think he was questioning you, finding out what he could about the people you saw at Tivoli. They might even think you had been recruited—to spy on me."

I stared at him. "You—you *can't* believe that!" I must have looked both so astonished and so horrified that his last doubt vanished.

He came over to where I stood, and took my hands. "I don't believe it but—" He hesitated.

"But some people do?"

"It's one of the oldest tricks. They've used it often enough themselves." He was smiling, as if it were a joke, now that he knew it was not being practiced against him.

I kept staring at him. "What kind of people are these? What have you got to do with them?"

"That's a story I'll tell you later. Now, you must leave."

"Leave?"

"Yes. I've come to get you away from here. Trust me, darling. I trust you. Remember?"

"Are these people your *friends?*" I was still groping for the truth. I knew too little, that was the trouble. Was Luigi an agent, working against them? He couldn't, surely he couldn't, be working with them. "It's all so mad, so completely crazy!" I said aloud.

"Not that. These people are realists. You've *got* to leave with me. Now. I'll take you to my aunt's villa. Then—" He laughed and didn't finish. He caught me in his arms and kissed me. "Don't worry about packing. I'll send someone to do that for you tomorrow. Leave a note for your maid. We don't want her running to the police and frightening everyone." His voice was soothing, unworried, confident. This is the only wise and reasonable thing to do, he seemed to believe. But I still hesitated. There was something wrong, something far wrong somewhere. I couldn't guess, I didn't know what to think. This secrecy, this haste, baffled me. I said, searching for a clue, "What if I don't go?"

"But you must! There's no other choice. Or else you'll prove that you *are* working with Lammiter."

"That's ridiculous!" I said impatiently. "You know that."

"Eleanor!" He pulled me round to face him. "I'm trying to keep you safe. Darling, believe me! These men have no time to waste. In a few days —nothing matters; but now—this is the moment of crisis. They cannot afford even a possible doubt. They will act—and act quickly."

His voice frightened me. Incredulously, I said, "Act? What do you mean?"

"They would have no remorse if you died."

"You mean, they'd kill me if necessary? Luigi, what *are* they?"

He didn't answer that directly. "They're fighting a war," he said. "Lammiter's friends are their enemies."

"If this is a kind of war," I said slowly, "then I'm on Bill's side."

"Because he's an American? You think that makes him right? But what makes you so sure that he is on the right side?"

I didn't quite follow. Was he saying that Bill was some kind of traitor? I couldn't believe that. "I know Bill—"

"Do you?" he asked bitterly. "Does one human being ever know another? Do you even know yourself?"

I looked at him. I shook my head. I knew Luigi least of all, I thought. And yet, watching him, I was sure of one thing: he did love me. And somehow I was also sure that, when he explained everything to me and I was no longer in ignorance, I would find honesty and courage in his story. It is difficult for a woman to admit that she could ever have fallen in love with a man who wasn't honest and courageous. These are the two qualities we value most, if any man wants to know.

Luigi was certainly honest then. "For God's sake, Eleanor, listen to me! You are in danger. So is Lammiter. Do you think these men will let either of you ruin months of careful planning?"

No, I had no doubt about that. "If I leave here, what will happen to Bill?"

"Nothing. He will be of no interest to anyone."

"Not even if he comes here?" For I knew he would come back.

"If he doesn't see you, how can he get the information he needs? He will be just another agent who failed in his mission." Then, sharply, "Why do you worry about him so much?"

"I don't want to be responsible for any man's death," I said, as easily as I could. "After all, I did make the telephone calls." Then I searched for a piece of paper and a pencil, and I wrote a message for the maid. There didn't seem to be much else I could do.

Later, I was thinking, we'll be able to talk at the villa. I'll learn the full truth then. (Yes, that's how stupid I was.)

At the villa, I learned nothing. I wasn't even allowed to talk to the princess alone. Poor old thing, she was as bewildered as I was. Her face enamel couldn't cover the misgivings in her eyes. Her clever-cruel tongue was silenced for once. She was kind to me, she had never been kinder, but she was just as helpless.

Then I knew I should never have come with Luigi to the villa. I knew too late what I ought to have done in the first place. Leave the apartment —yes, that had been right—and after that, I ought to have gone to the Embassy: I ought to have had them telephone the police, send out a warning to Bill, wherever he was. Only, would Luigi have allowed me to go to the Embassy?

I didn't know the answer to that question until a car came right up to the door of the villa. The two men, who had been standing outside the little sitting room where I was waiting for Luigi and the princess to come back, urged me to leave. "Leave? But I'm supposed to stay *here.* Leave for where?"

I went outside. I tried to run. I tried to scream to the princess, to anyone who might be passing along that quiet peaceful street. But the two men were beside me, holding my mouth, my waist, my wrists.

And there they are now—the two men, crossing the courtyard. Old Alberto is opening the gate. . . .

Eleanor stood at the window of her room, watching the two men walk out of her life as abruptly as they had entered it. Within a few minutes, the red-haired stranger had followed them. Old Alberto locked the gate, with Luigi standing beside him. The massive doors became a solid wall once more.

Luigi had not enjoyed the guide's visit. Eleanor could tell that by the way he stood down there in the courtyard, feet apart, hands on hips, face still turned to the locked gate as though his eyes could follow the red-haired man's progress along the road.

Then he swung round on his heel, caught sight of Alberto, who had been hovering uncertainly nearby, and said angrily, "Bring down my suitcases and put them in the Lancia."

The old man—he was very fond of Luigi, Rosana had said—didn't move.

"At once!" Luigi's voice rose.

Still Alberto didn't move. Instead, he began talking. All day, he had been morose and silent; whenever Eleanor had caught a glimpse of him from her window, he had been going about his tasks, his head bent, answering no one, paying no attention to anything. But now the words poured out of him. She couldn't understand much of them—they came too quickly, in an accent new to her ear. He was saying something about the principessa: the principessa had given orders, the principessa had commanded. . . . His recital goaded Luigi. "My aunt is a fool." And Luigi turned angrily on his heel and left. Alberto followed him, talking, talking, his voice rising in anger, too. Perhaps no one, not even Luigi, could call the princess a fool.

Behind Eleanor, the room door opened. It was Rosana at last. She brought the key inside with her and turned it in the lock.

"*Why* didn't you come back and let me out?" Eleanor asked. "The gate was open for a few moments; we could have—"

"We could have done nothing," Rosana said, coming slowly away from the door. "Not with Sabatini here." She sat down on the edge of a chair as if her strength had suddenly been drained away. "We've lost," she said dully. Her hands were trembling. She stared down at them and burst into tears. "Everything has gone wrong, everything. And everything will go more wrong." She brushed at her tears savagely with her knuckles. "And I couldn't wait to open your door. I *had* to get to the little gallery above the chapel before they entered. I *had* to find out why Sabatini came here. The man's a murderer. Don't you know that? And he is the man who is deciding about you—and me. He—" She caught hold of herself. The tears had gone but her hands still trembled.

Eleanor searched for a cigarette, lit it for her. She poured out the last of the water from the San Pellegrino bottle and handed the glass to Rosana. She said, not without respect, "You ran a terrible risk!"

"I got back, didn't I?" Rosana asked, almost fiercely. She took a deep shuddering breath. "Sabatini—he makes me feel sick, that man. Even to be in the same place as he is makes me feel—" Her whole body shuddered this time. "And Luigi—" she said contemptuously, "Luigi looking so noble, listening, never objecting. I kept thinking, he can't, he won't ever agree to that. But he did, he did!"

She's near breaking point, Eleanor thought. More calmly than she felt, she said, "All right, all right . . . What's the bad news? Just how lost are we?" She even managed a smile.

"The meeting is today. I told Joe it was tomorrow. But it is *today.* This afternoon. At three o'clock. Three! And it's almost two now. An hour, that's all we have . . . an hour!"

We'd better keep the exclamation marks out of our voices, Eleanor thought. She said, "So we'll find Joe and tell him."

"But *where* is he? I don't know. He was coming here this evening, to check up. This *evening!*" Rosana made a gesture of despair. "And that's not all my bad news," she said quickly. "Luigi's orders have been changed. He isn't to attend the meeting. Oh, he is going to Perugia, all right. But he isn't to attend the meeting. Sabatini says there has been too much trouble—Luigi may be followed."

"Why send him to Perugia at all?"

"Because Sabatini is *clever*—didn't I tell you?"

"Yes, yes. I'm sorry. Go on. About Luigi."

"Luigi will drive to Perugia without any luggage, in his own car. He is to leave it at the Piazza Italia, but on no account must he go near the Corso Vanucci. That's the main street, where people walk and sit at the cafés."

"Yes, yes," Eleanor said again, her impatience growing.

"Don't you see—the Corso Vanucci is the last place you'd expect a group of conspirators to gather? It's so open, so innocent. But that's where the meeting is going to be held. Luigi is to avoid it, to lead anyone following him *away* from it. Don't you see? He's a—a—"

"Decoy?"

Rosana nodded. "He is to walk down by the market, choose a little café there—any café, it doesn't matter—go inside, sit at the back, look as though he were waiting. After an hour, he can leave. Go back to his car, drive over one of the hill roads to Gubbio. There are so many small roads. He will lose anyone following him."

"What about the other car, the Lancia—and the suitcases?"

"These arrangements have not been changed," Rosana said, avoiding Eleanor's eyes. "The mechanic will take you in the Lancia, by the main route to Gubbio. And then Luigi will drive you across the Apennines, to—" She paused. "To Venice." She stared down at her hands.

Arrangements have not been changed. . . . Eleanor stared in amazement.

"You mean, Luigi knew all along that—" Eleanor's lips closed in anger, and she turned to the window. "And what are the 'arrangements' for you?" she asked.

"The *carabinieri* will be notified that I am here. The police in Rome want to question me." She added, almost hopelessly, "About Tony Brewster's death."

"But the police must know you were his friend."

"Murder is murder."

Eleanor took a deep breath. "We *have* to find Joe."

Rosana said nothing.

"He is known in Montesecco, isn't he? He's the princess's chauffeur. Surely he has friends you could telephone, send them looking—"

"I can't get near the telephone. The mechanic is guarding it now." She rested her brow on her hands. "I'll *have* to get out, that's all. Without being seen. If Luigi discovers I'm missing—" She paused. She was thinking aloud now. "Yes, I'll have to get out. But will Joe be at the farmhouse? And there is no telephone there. I may only waste time searching for him." And then a new fear spread over her face. "How do we even know he is still alive? Sabatini could have seen him, Sabatini—"

"Stop that, Rosana! Stop it. You outwitted Sabatini in the chapel. You'll do it again."

Rosana said slowly, "All day, you've been afraid. Now—" She shook her head in wonder.

"We can't afford to be afraid both at the same time," Eleanor said sharply.

"If you knew what I knew—" Rosana flashed back at her. Then she controlled her voice. "I'm sorry. I—I—" If only, she thought miserably, I didn't have to be responsible for both of us. The American is so helpless, so unaccustomed to danger.

"Rosana," said Eleanor, with a confidence that sounded real enough even to her own ears, "you *must* get to a telephone somewhere. Call Rome. Have your people there relay your message to Perugia. Isn't that possible?"

Rosana nodded. It was an idea to be considered. Only, she thought wearily, I wish I weren't alone. The American may give ideas, but no practical help. She means well, but— Rosana said, "I'll risk going out by the main gate. That will save fifteen minutes. I can telephone from the restaurant." She rose, frowning. "The post office is even nearer."

Eleanor looked down at the cars in the courtyard, and then back at the untouched luncheon tray on the little central table. "Telephone from here," she said, "that's quicker still." She walked over to the table. "I'll slash the tires. You give the mechanic the alarm. He'll leave that phone in a hurry." She picked up the knife and tested it. "Probably can't cut anything except spaghetti. Cooked spaghetti, at that. Still, woman with knife—always an alarming sight."

"You are mad," said Rosana, "quite mad." But there was interest in her eyes, and almost a smile on her lips.

Eleanor reached the door. She paused, her hand on the key. "Help me with my geography, in case I have to play hide-and-seek."

"Let me draw you a map."

"No time. The house is a square—four wings built around the courtyard. Where is the main staircase?"

"In the center of this wing."

"That's to my left as I go out of this door?"

"Yes. It leads down to the big hall, then into the courtyard. Then there are four other staircases, smaller ones—"

"Four?" I'll never remember them, Eleanor thought in alarm.

"It's quite simple—they lead out to the four corners of the courtyard."

"And where is the telephone?" Only one, of course. The princess no doubt thought telephones ruined her *décor,* all six centuries of it. But some might say that cupids playing around Venus were just as much of an anomaly to Signorelli's fresco.

"That's across the courtyard, in Alberto's office, beside the main gate. Alberto's quarters are over there, too."

"That's the east side," Eleanor said quickly, remembering the sun's rays that morning. "So we're in the west wing. What's in the north?"

Rosana looked at her. She has more brains than I guessed, Rosana thought: she has more courage, too. Her own confidence began to grow again. She said, "Kitchens, storerooms, stables, and garage."

"And Pirotta?"

She no longer called him Luigi, Rosana noticed again. "His rooms are in the south side of the house over the gun room and the chapel."

"Then, when the mechanic comes yelling into the courtyard, I run to the north," Eleanor said with a little smile. She unlocked the door and stepped into a shadowed corridor, with doors along one side, shuttered windows along the other. This was a good feeling, she thought, a good feeling to unlock a door and step out, of your own free will. Whatever happens now, I'm not going back into that room. Never, never . . .

"What's out there?" she whispered, pointing to the shuttered windows.

"The garden. The gamekeeper has his lodge down near the big wall. Jacopone. He's a friend."

Eleanor took a step to her left. "I'll go down the main staircase. And you?"

Rosana moved to her right. "North through the kitchen wing into the east one. Each wing is connected by corridors, upstairs and downstairs."

For a moment they stood looking at each other. Then they smiled.

"Remember," Eleanor said, "I escaped."

Rosana nodded. "You threatened me with that knife." Her smile deepened; she had to smother a laugh. Eleanor thought, at least she's out of the slump: she's all right. She's very much all right. Eleanor began walking toward the staircase.

The doors to the other rooms up here were all closed. Certainly it was comforting to know that Pirotta lived in another part of the house. But she was nervous, she might as well admit it. She could drop the pretense now that she wasn't afraid. Afraid? She was scared sick. She couldn't even laugh at the picture she must make, carrying this ridiculous knife in her hand. She could laugh later, if she were still free to laugh, at the comic relief. And then— Even thinking of comic relief made her feel a little better. She looked over her shoulder as she reached the staircase. The corridor behind her was empty. Rosana had been quick. There was no turning back now.

She started to descend the long flight of stairs. "Dear God," she was praying, "help us, help us." And then she added, praying fair, "If we are in the right. Dear God, just help those who are in the right."

The staircase running down the wall on her left had wide and shallow steps that stretched almost the full length of the hall. They were of stone, like the heavy balustrade, like the towering walls. This must be the oldest part of the house, perhaps the original building. No pink clouds and golden decorations here, no baroque twists and curves. The hall beneath seemed vast in its bareness. It was filled with shadows, dark and cold. At its large doorway, standing open, there was a stream of light slanting toward the foot of the staircase, at first strong, then weakening, then fading into the shadows. Outside, the heat blazed and shimmered.

She kept close to the wall of the staircase, sliding her left hand down its cool stone surface to steady her and keep her footsteps sure. A twisted ankle would be a foolish thing. I ought to take off my shoes, she thought, and paused for a moment to slip her feet out of them. She didn't stop to pick them up. She started to run lightly, noiselessly, down the broad steps. As she almost reached the pool of warm light, seeping up over the bottom steps, the oblique view through the doorway lengthened to show more of the courtyard. She could see part of the black shadow now cast by the south wing of the house, and the cars parked against the wall, carefully within the shade. And there, also, were two suitcases lying close to the Lancia's near wheel.

She stopped abruptly. From the opposite side of the hall came a little cry, quickly silenced. She looked over the balustrade. Anna-Maria and Alberto were down there, huddled together, standing quite still, undecided, waiting. It had been Anna-Maria who had almost cried out: her hand was still over her lips. Now they both stared up at her in amazement and wonder.

"It is all right," she said, and smiled. But they didn't smile back. Alberto pointed to the courtyard warningly. She heard a movement out there, and then a man's confident stride, crisp, unhurried. It could only be Pirotta.

She retreated back against the wall. Were its shadows deep enough to hide her? She could see him now, as he dropped a third suitcase beside the others. Then he turned toward the hall.

Swiftly, Eleanor moved away from the wall back to the balustrade again, and sank down on the step behind its waist-high pillars. Was this safer? At least, it felt less vulnerable than standing up. Thank God she didn't feel sick any longer; but her legs were trembling, and so were her hands.

"Well," he said at the doorway, "is the rebellion over?"

For a moment of shock, she stared down at him from between the banisters. Then she saw he wasn't looking at her. His eyes, frowning as they accustomed themselves from the blaze of sunlight to the dark shadows, were searching the hall. "There you are," he told Alberto and Anna-Maria, "just as I thought."

Alberto took a few steps forward, trying to pull his arm free from his wife's sudden grip. She cried out, "Alberto! No! No! You've done enough. He will strike you again, he will kill you this time! No! No!—"

"You're a very foolish old woman," Pirotta said coldly. "I don't kill people. And I did not strike Alberto."

"I saw you—" she began hysterically.

"You did not. You saw him try to stop me from taking the suitcases to the cars—a job he should have been doing. I pushed him aside: that was all. What did you expect, Anna-Maria? In my place, what would you have done? You would have struck him, and hard, wouldn't you?" The voice of quiet reason subdued the old woman. Now it changed to sharp authority. "Go back to your kitchen before I do lose my temper. Do you want me to report him to the princess? You'd both be out on the street, soon enough!"

"He—he was only doing what the princess told him to do." Anna-Maria made her last protest. She looked at her husband and began to cry.

Alberto said, "That is the truth. The princess gave her orders—"

"You've told me all that!"

"But you have not listened. You must wait here, until she comes," Alberto insisted, his words gathering strength. "The princess must talk to you—she has much to say—I have never heard her so angry—"

Pirotta said impatiently, "I shall talk to her when I get back here. Alberto, can't you understand that the American is *ill?* We must drive her to the hospital in Assisi—"

The old man shook his head. "You must not take the princess's car! That will make her angrier. She did not give permission—"

Running footsteps came across the courtyard, slipping and clattering on the cobbled stones.

Pirotta spun round on his heel. "Giovanni! What the devil are you doing out here?"

Giovanni reached the Lancia and walked around it anxiously, looking at the wheels. "No, the tires are all right. Perhaps she damaged the engine." He opened the car's hood.

"Who?"

"The American girl. She's escaped."

"Who told you that?"

"Signorina Di Feo. The American girl escaped and—"

"You locked the office? You didn't leave it unlocked?"

Giovanni stared at him. "But there was no one there! And the car was being—"

"Signorina Di Feo? Where is she?"

"She went away—to try to find the American."

"You fool, you idiot, you blundering— Don't you see it's a lie? The cars are all right. No one has escaped. Get back to that telephone. No—I'll go myself."

"It isn't a lie," Eleanor said, and rose to her feet. He turned and looked up at her. It was the first time she ever remembered seeing him completely and absolutely amazed. Keep talking, she told herself: anything, anything to silence questions about Rosana. "I did escape. I did mean to damage the car." She held out the knife, gripped firmly in her right hand, and Anna-Maria let out a piercing scream.

"You see," Pirotta told Alberto, "the *signorina Americana* is ill." Swiftly he crossed over to the foot of the staircase.

In Italian, she said, "I am not ill—I am not ill. I want to stay here. I do not want to go. I—"

"Eleanor—" he said worriedly. He shook his head. "You *are* ill, you know." He turned to Alberto and Anna-Maria. "See—she has even forgotten her shoes. Her feet are bare. Help me, will you? She must leave at once. Anna-Maria: find the signorina's shoes, her coat—" He began to mount the stairs, slowly.

"I am *not* leaving," Eleanor told him. "*You* are the one who's crazy. Alberto—"

"What nonsense you talk! What nonsense you've let yourself believe!" Suddenly his arm reached out to catch her wrist, and then pulled back as she slashed at it with the knife. "God in heaven!" He stared at her unbelievingly. He gave an incredulous laugh. "You little idiot . . ." he said gently. "Do you still not realize that if it hadn't been for me you would be dead?" His voice hardened. "I risked everything for you. I gave my word that you'd go with me, leave Italy until everything was forgotten, all interest ended."

"Ended? Forgotten?"

"People forget," he reminded her. "They like to forget. And sometimes, they find new—new interpretations, which help them to forget. Eleanor—you've been told so much nonsense, so many lies! Come with me. My plan will work. You'll see. We aren't monsters. We are reasonable men."

She stared at him. This was the first time he had identified himself openly. "And if I don't go, what will you do? Kill me—like Tony Brewster?"

His face tightened. "I am not a murderer. You know that. You know I would not even hurt you. But there are others who will." He took a deep breath. "Don't force me to telephone them, and admit that my plan has failed." He stepped back into the hall, waiting. "Do I telephone? Or do you go with me?"

Rosana, she thought worriedly, Rosana must surely have had the sense to lock herself securely inside the office, but she would need time. "Go—go where?" Anything to delay him, anything to let Rosana get that call through to Rome. How long did it take to get a call through, how long?

"Among friends. There is a freighter waiting now, ready to take us to them."

"Where?" she insisted.

He hesitated. Perhaps he was weighing the minimum truth he could tell her against a lie which would never be forgiven. Then, still evading a direct answer, "It will be a pleasant journey—through the Aegean, the Bosporus. . . ." He was watching her face. "It's only for a few months, darling. Then—we'll come back."

"You'll come back? To Italy?"

"I'll come back. Because I didn't leave in defeat." His confidence had returned. He had heard the worry, the uncertainty in her voice. He smiled, and held out his hand. Perhaps he never had any doubts about his power over a woman who had loved him, least of all when he loved her. Involuntarily, she flinched and took a step away from him. In that naked moment, he saw the contempt in her eyes. His smile faded as his hand dropped to his side. Grim-faced, he turned and moved to the door.

"Stop him, Alberto!" She ran down into the hall. She caught the old man's arm. "Rosana," she whispered, "Rosana," and she pointed across the courtyard. The old couple looked at each other: Anna-Maria, at least, began to understand something.

Pirotta had halted abruptly outside. He stood, puzzled, frowning, watching the solitary figure who had come out of the doorway near the gates in the east wing that led to the office and the servants' rooms.

"Jacopone!" Anna-Maria screamed. "Jacopone, we're here!"

The old man pulled his felt brim farther over his eyes to shield them from the glare, and he started across the courtyard, his heavy boots scraping on the cobblestones. He had a rifle under one arm.

Alberto shouted, pressing forward, "He's taking away the Americana—he's taking the car. He's—"

"Quiet!" Pirotta said angrily, pushing Alberto back into the hall. His eyes didn't leave Jacopone, or the rifle. "Come here, you!" he told him. "What were you doing over there at the office?"

The old man halted. "There was no one in the kitchen," he said slowly, his eyes fixed on the doorway as if he were trying to see into the shadows of the hall. "So I came looking. . . ." His voice drifted away uneasily.

"For what?" Pirotta's voice was alert.

"Anna-Maria . . . Alberto. I went to their room." He jerked a thumb back over his shoulder.

"Where's Giovanni?"

The old man shifted his feet. "Back there," he said, and he gave a small smile.

"Stop scraping your damned feet! And give me that rifle. You don't carry a rifle around this house. Give me it!"

"No!" Eleanor cried out, and tried to run into the courtyard. Pirotta reached out, caught her wrist, twisted it, and the knife fell from her hand. He kicked it aside.

Jacopone looked at her. Then, calmly, he aimed into the sky and pulled the trigger. The sharp crack of the rifle cut through the heavy warm air, a flock of startled pigeons rose and swept in a bewildered cloud over the courtyard.

Pirotta stared at the old man, and then at Eleanor. He tightened his grip on her wrist. There was suspicion in his eyes, suspicion growing. . . . Then he dropped her wrist and ran toward Jacopone.

The old man was slowly reloading. Pirotta dealt him a savage blow, which sent him staggering, and wrenched the rifle from his hand. Eleanor raced across the short stretch of burning cobblestones. Behind her, she heard Alberto's hoarse shout, Anna-Maria's high scream; but in the blinding glare, she only saw Jacopone lying where he had fallen, and Pirotta standing menacingly over him. He caught her arm as she sank to her knees beside the old man, and pulled her up again to face him. "Where's Rosana?" he asked harshly. "Where is she?" He dropped her arm.

"If you have betrayed me—" There was no need to finish his threat. She knew, then, that he would kill her. He began to run toward the office.

"Wrong direction, Pirotta," Bill Lammiter's voice called. "I'm over here."

Pirotta swung round to face the north end of the buildings. Lammiter left the shadow of the corner doorway, and stepped into the brilliant sunshine.

There was a long moment of silence, of complete surprise. No movement, no sound, except from Lammiter as he began to walk slowly across the courtyard. This long moment was in his favor. Nothing else. The sun was in his eyes. Joe's revolver was a .28, Belgian: he'd have to get at least twenty feet nearer. Against him, was a .22 one-shot rifle. He had heard that one shot fired as he stood in the deserted kitchen, but before he had been able to find a corridor that brought him out into the courtyard, there had been time for the rifle to be reloaded. Yes, it was loaded all right, judging by the way Pirotta faced him. One shot, then: he would drop flat on his face the moment Pirotta started raising that rifle above waist level, and fire from the ground. The books said it could be done. This was one time he hoped the books were right. At least, there was no one else within range.

Pirotta had recovered from his surprise. He watched the American walking slowly, steadily, toward him. "Isn't this unfair?" he asked with a smile. "You know so little about weapons, obviously. A man with a pistol never faces a man with a rifle." He raised the rifle a little. "Do you want me to complete your education?" He lowered the rifle. And then, quickly, he swung it to his shoulder and fired. Lammiter dropped flat on the ground. But there was no crack from a bullet.

It wasn't loaded, by God, it wasn't loaded, Lammiter thought, as the breath came painfully back into his body. And I was so damned busy hitting those cobblestones that I didn't even fire back. He rose. He began to laugh.

Pirotta looked with amazement at the rifle, and then at Jacopone. The old gamekeeper was rising to his feet, a broad grin on his wrinkled face. Pirotta flung the useless rifle at him, and turned to face Lammiter. The American began walking toward him again.

"You are close enough," Pirotta said contemptuously. "Or would you miss even at this distance?"

"I might at that," said Lammiter. Now he had time to glance at Eleanor. She was all right. She still had her hands clenched together at her lips in a kind of desperate prayer. Had that gesture been for him—or was it for Pirotta, even now? At that moment, she answered his thoughts: she dropped her hands, her eyes came to life again, and "Oh, Bill!" she said. That was all. But the way she said it was enough.

"Maybe," Lammiter told Pirotta, "I'd like to see you in a courtroom. Maybe I'd like to find out how many lies you can tell and still look noble." Odd, he was thinking: this morning he had said he would kill Pirotta. But now, he was finding it impossible to fire on someone just standing there, watching him. He ought to have shot at him the moment he dropped to the ground. Except, at that moment, every bone in his body had been jarred and he couldn't have hit an elephant.

Jacopone had picked up his rifle, examined it to make sure it had not been damaged. Now, with the bullet he had kept clenched in his right hand, he was reloading, expertly, definitely. He looked at Lammiter, his toothless grin widening, and nodded. Then with his deliberate pace he walked over to the cars and stood there, on guard, his eyes on Pirotta. Thank God for the Jacopones in this world, thought Lammiter.

Pirotta said derisively, "You can always shoot me in the back." He turned round. He looked at Jacopone. Then at Alberto. "Unlock the gates!" he told Alberto. But the old man made no move.

"You'll have to find a better solution than that for your problems," Lammiter said grimly. "But I'll tell you what I'll do for you—I'll shoot you in the leg if you start running for the gates. We'll just stay here until the *carabinieri* arrive. After all, I wasn't the only one who heard that rifle shot." He wasn't wholly bluffing: Joe must have heard the shot, and he would send someone.

"Rosana!" Eleanor called out, and everyone, even Pirotta, looked at the narrow doorway near the gate. Rosana was standing there, watching them all; and then, slowly, almost dejectedly, she stepped into the courtyard. "Rosana—" Eleanor began in alarm, "didn't you—"

"Yes," Rosana said quietly. "The warning went through. To Perugia." She looked away from Pirotta. She raised her voice. "I told them that the meeting was today at three o'clock. I told them to follow the two men who would arrive on the bus. I told them about Gubbio, about Venice. . . ." She looked at Pirotta, and her voice dropped. "I told them everything Sabatini told you, Luigi."

She began walking toward Lammiter.

Pirotta looked at his watch. His indecision ended. He ran swiftly toward the narrow door beside the gate.

"Rosana!" Lammiter yelled. "Get out of my way!" But she didn't. And before he could move to get a clear aim, Pirotta was safely inside. She caught Lammiter's arm as he started to follow.

"Are you crazy! He'll telephone his warning—" He pulled his arm free.

"No! No!" Rosana said. "His call won't go through." She caught his arm again. "Let him telephone. Let him give the number of the meeting place. That is all Joe needs to find its address." She turned to Eleanor, who had run over to join them. "Joe has had a man sitting beside the operator all day, waiting for every call from this house. I didn't have to telephone Rome after all." Suddenly she smiled and kissed Eleanor's cheek. "You and your funny old knife—you didn't do so badly, both of you, after all." Then the smile vanished, and she glanced across the courtyard at the door that led to the office. "Oh, I hate all this, I hate all this!" she burst out bitterly.

"Who started it all, anyway?" Lammiter said quietly. "Not you, not Joe, not Brewster."

She looked at him. "I keep forgetting that," she said. She drew away a little, her eyes once more on the door near the gate.

Lammiter asked, "What about that mechanic? Did he carry a gun?"

Rosana shook her head. "I told him if he didn't stop trying to force the door to the office, I'd name him to the police. And just as he was thinking about that, Jacopone came looking for Anna-Maria and Alberto. Their quarters are next door to the office. He locked the mechanic into Anna-Maria's bedroom."

"Joe heard the rifleshot, I hope."

"Yes. It was a signal he had prearranged."

"Damn it, I keep underestimating him."

"Who *is* he, Bill?"

"A Sicilian."

"Yes, yes, but . . ."

Eleanor looked at one and then at the other. There's so much I don't understand, she thought forlornly. There's so much I haven't been told. There's only one thing I do know: Bill never stopped loving me. Perhaps that's all I want to know, anyway. "The cobbles are hot," she said suddenly. "I'll find my shoes, I think." The excuse was real: now that the danger was over, she was aware, at last, of the pain in her burning feet. She tried to smile. Neither of them had heard her. They were listening for something else as they watched the door. I won't watch, she thought: I won't watch Pirotta come out. She turned toward the hall and ran. She heard Bill's voice, "Eleanor, wait—" And then, as she reached the dark silence of the hall, the stone floor, cold as the water of a mountain stream, under her burning feet, she heard the gate bell ring. That will be the police, she thought, the police or the *carabinieri*. . . . She didn't know why she should be crying.

She sank down on the bottom step of the staircase. She had suddenly no strength to climb toward her shoes. She sat, her head bowed, her hands covering her face. "If you have betrayed me—" he had said. Had she betrayed him? "You and your funny old knife," Rosana had said. Betrayed him? And then she remembered Bill's quiet voice back in the courtyard, "Who started it all, anyway?"

"Eleanor!" Lammiter tried to stop her, but she was already running toward the hall. That might be a safer place than the courtyard: he still had the worry that Pirotta would come out with a gun in his hand. Or with Giovanni. Or with both. He just didn't trust Pirotta. He started after Eleanor. "Wait for me!" He raised his voice. "Eleanor, wait for me in there!" And then he heard Pirotta's footsteps. He swung round again, cursing the moment.

Pirotta had come out from the doorway at the gate. He was alone and unarmed. For a brief moment, he had paused and looked at them all. Then it seemed as though they no longer existed; as though he had blotted out the whole picture of this courtyard from his mind. He began to walk toward the south wing of the house. The gate bell rang, but he paid no attention.

"What's over there?" Lammiter asked Rosana as he watched Pirotta's determined pace. Pirotta passed the cars. Jacopone made no attempt to stop him, and Pirotta went on. He entered a doorway.

"His own rooms," Rosana said, and put a hand on Lammiter's sleeve. "Don't follow him, Bill." She paused. She hesitated. And then, slowly, she said, "The gun room is over there, too."

"Locked?" he asked quickly. "Surely it's locked?"

"The princess told Alberto to unlock it. Those were the orders."

"*What?*" He stared at her. He started toward the south wing, but Rosana's hand tightened desperately on his arm.

"Do you *want* to stop him?" She shook her head. "What other solution is there?"

"But—" He hesitated. He didn't know what to do.

"What else?" she said fiercely. There were tears in her eyes. "What else? The princess is right. He has lived badly. Let him die well."

The gates were being opened. He pocketed Joe's revolver. "I just don't trust him," he said slowly.

Her tears changed to shocked anger. "Not even now? He's defeated. He knows it. He knew it when his telephone call didn't go through!" She looked at him almost accusingly. Then she pointed to the elderly captain and two boys in dark green uniforms who were coming through the gates. "They are in charge now, anyway."

"Suits me," he said. "I'll find Eleanor."

"And leave me to face the captain by myself?"

"Explain to him I'm a foreigner, can't speak the language." He turned toward the hall. This first meeting with Eleanor—it would be difficult. Odd, how easy it could have been five minutes ago, when she had called out "Oh, Bill!" and looked as if she would run straight into his arms. But Pirotta had been there, still undefeated, still dangerous. And now—how did you hold her and kiss her when you were listening for a shot from the gun room? Pirotta was still between them.

Rosana said, "Bill, what shall I tell him?" She was frightened. She made no move to go over to the captain and his two men.

Lammiter halted, and glanced at the little group moving away from the gate. Alberto and Anna-Maria had begun a long recital, no doubt making everything abundantly incomprehensible. Jacopone had added his stalwart silence to their story. "Tell him Jacopone was showing me how his rifle worked."

"And nothing else?"

"That's all he needs to know." And there I go, he thought savagely, starting to hush things up, just like the princess, just like Alberto.

"I suppose so." She wiped the tear marks from her cheeks. She added, pathetically, "It's so hard to remember what some know and others don't, and how much they can be told and can't be. Bill, I didn't say anything to Eleanor about Luigi's other—other organization. The narcotics one. I just told her about the politics. I thought that was—that was enough." She shivered and looked round the sunlit courtyard. "Strange that it should be here that everything was really decided. Not in Perugia. Here . . ."

Somehow, his worry grew as he watched the genial captain's stately progress slowed by that ancient mariner Alberto. Everyone was being so damned tactful and correct. Very serious were the two fresh-faced boys, and very impressed by the princess's Casa Grande. Yes, everyone was being so polite, so relieved that there was no ugly trouble to be found in this pleasant place after all. Decent, kindly people, trusting, ignorant. They had not one idea of the evil that had walked through this courtyard today. He looked at the south wing of the house. I still don't trust him, he thought.

Rosana, watching the captain approach her, said suddenly, "I—I don't think they've come to arrest me after all." She almost laughed in her relief. "That was the plan: Luigi was going to take Eleanor with him, but I was to be—"

"Rosana," Lammiter said urgently, "does this house all connect? Each wing leads into the other?"

She stared at him. "Bill!" she called out. But he was already racing across the short stretch of cobblestones toward the main door. He was pulling out the revolver again. He was running, she thought in amazement, not to the south wing, not toward the gun room, but straight for the hall. Eleanor, she suddenly remembered, he's worried about Eleanor. . . . Quickly she signaled the astounded captain, and they began to run, too.

"Eleanor!" It was Luigi Pirotta's voice, far away, calling her, calling her urgently.

Or was he near, and the voice was low? It came again. "Eleanor!"

She raised her head from her hands. She half rose, turned slowly round. Outside, in the sunlit courtyard, there were footsteps and voices.

Here, in the shadowed silence of the hall, was Pirotta. Somewhere in the hall, there was Pirotta.

She drew back, shrinking against the stone wall, and looked up the long flight of steps. He was standing there, at the head of the staircase, quite still. For a long moment, he stood looking at her. He raised the revolver he had held by his side.

From the door behind her, she heard a deafening explosion echoing around the high stone walls. She saw Pirotta's hand go to his right shoulder and hold it, his face twisted with pain. Then an arm swept round her waist and pulled her down into the hall behind the shelter of the balustrade. "It's all right, it's all right," Bill was saying, as she heard a second explosion, still louder, thunder through the hall.

There were people at the door.

"It's all right," Bill said again, his arms around her. And they stood there, together, her face pressed against his chest, his cheek against her hair, his arms around her, holding her, holding her, until their two bodies seemed to have been carved out of one piece of stone. She raised her head and their eyes met. Slowly, gently, he kissed her. "Never, never again—" he began; he couldn't go on. He kissed her hard, this time.

No one paid any attention to them. Everyone had started climbing the staircase. Someone began to speak. "Come away," Bill said, "come away from this place."

He led her toward the first room he could see. He wanted her away from the hall before Anna-Maria's cries became hysterics, before the captain would call out, "He's dead."

Perhaps twenty minutes later, certainly no more than that, the door opened and the captain of the *carabinieri* came into the room where Eleanor lay. Lammiter had ripped a sheet from a velvet couch, and propped her up with cushions. He sat beside her, talking quietly, holding her hands between his in a firm grasp. Afterward, he had no idea what he talked about: it didn't matter. All that mattered was to get the shadows out of her eyes, the frightened look away from her lips. She had listened, and yet at the same time she had been following her own troubled thoughts. For suddenly she asked, just as the captain came into the room, "He would have killed himself, even if I hadn't been here?" There was a question in her voice, the last remnant of fear.

"Yes." He was sure of that.

"He said a strange thing." Her soft voice hesitated.

"That's all right, darling. Forget it," he said gently. He looked at the captain, who was watching them somberly.

But she had to tell him. "He said that he could and would come back to Italy because he didn't leave in defeat. And then—"

And then defeat had come, and it had been complete. How could Pirotta have faced his political masters with such an overwhelming disaster behind him? They would add up the total loss—Sabatini arrested; Evans extradited; the meeting not only a failure but a permanent danger to all those who had taken part—and even call it treachery. They were capable of that. As Joe would say, it was in their pattern.

Eleanor said haltingly, watching him, "You don't blame me?" She closed her eyes and bit her lip. "He did."

"He made today's choice years ago. Long before he ever met you." He kissed her. Then he remembered the captain. He rose and faced the waiting man.

The captain had been remarkably patient. But he had found the little scene interesting. Each revelation, however small, was important. And he had got little help from Alberto or Anna-Maria: they were much too overwhelmed with grief. Jacopone, as usual, just stood around, saying and doing nothing. The Signorina Di Feo had told him a wild story of what she had seen as she entered the hall just ahead of him, and when he hadn't quite believed it, she had rushed to the telephone over in the office. And a stranger, a mechanic, had been found locked in Anna-Maria's room next door to the office. (Anna-Maria had had hysterics at that point.) The man had not complained about his imprisonment: he kept saying he knew nothing about anything, which might be true. Only one thing was certain: the count had died on the staircase, by his own hand. Accidentally? Or had it been deliberate? A crime of passion? Perhaps . . . The poor count had lost this young woman to the American, and so he blew out his brains. What a tragedy, what a terrible unhappiness for everyone, what a disaster. . . .

The captain studied the young woman. Yes, she was very beautiful. They always were. He had entered this room prepared to dislike these foreigners for the trouble they had caused. And yet—watching them—he wasn't so sure now that this was a heartless creature, or that the American was a ruthless Hollywood ruffian. There was something very —yes, very touching in the way they looked at each other, in the way the man now stood protectively over her. They were more like two people who had come through some frightful accident and could scarcely believe they were still alive. He had seen faces like these once, when a train had plunged over a bridge into a ravine and—but enough of disasters. Briskly, he held out a pair of high-heeled shoes. "These were found on the staircase," he said.

Thank God, he speaks English, Lammiter thought. "Thank you." He took the shoes and knelt to slip them on Eleanor's feet.

Now, the captain wondered, what is he thinking, what is he remembering? The American touched the girl's feet as if he had much to remember. (And indeed, Lammiter was remembering his first sight of Eleanor today, running across the burning cobblestones to reach Jacopone where the old man had fallen.) The girl was saying, "I was trying to escape. . . . I was afraid I'd twist my ankle—"

She glanced at Bill, wondering how foolish she must now seem. But he didn't look as if he thought she had been foolish. She gave her first smile, a small one but real. "I'm much better now," she told him. "When can we leave?"

"Soon," he said. But that was the problem. He rose and led the captain away from the couch toward the window. "She didn't actually see what happened," he said quietly. "Please don't question her. Not now."

"Later, later," the captain agreed quickly. "She is very tired. I see that." And so are you, he thought, studying the American's exhausted face. "But now, one thing. You have a gun?"

Lammiter drew out Joe's revolver and handed it over. "One bullet—"

"The bullet in the shoulder." The captain examined the revolver with interest. "Why?"

"He was going to shoot—" Lammiter glanced back at Eleanor. "I fired from the door, and hit his shoulder. He changed his revolver to his left hand. And then—well, you arrived then. You saw what happened."

"Yes, yes."

Lammiter took a deep breath of relief.

From the courtyard came the ringing of the bell at its gate. The captain's worried face, no longer bland, was etched with down-drawn lines. "He would have killed her. You are sure?"

"Yes."

And that was what the Signorina Di Feo had insisted: she had arrived just a few seconds behind Signore Lammiter; she had seen the gun pointed at the *Americana.* "It is so difficult to believe," he said. "Suicide, yes. That is understandable." He glanced at the girl. "But murder, no."

"Most truths are difficult to believe."

The captain was staring out of the window. He sighed unhappily. "What shall we tell the princess?" His hands stretched out, as if asking help, and then fell to his sides, acknowledging no help was possible.

Lammiter glanced out of the window. A cream-colored sports car was coming through the gate now. The princess had arrived.

The captain frowned down at his highly polished boots, as if willing them to start moving toward the courtyard. He took a reluctant step. He sighed. "It would be kinder not to mention attempted murder, yes?" He spoke the word with distaste.

Lammiter nodded.

"Then," the captain said more cheerfully, "the bullet in the shoulder, it is probably of little importance now." But he did not hand over Joe's revolver. He slipped it into his pocket. Under the warm cloak of politeness, business was still business. The princess could have her myth meanwhile, but reports had to be made, forms filled out, evidence noted. He looked out of the window again, and squared his shoulders. Then, with an impressive salute, he marched quickly out of the room.

"The princess is here," Lammiter told Eleanor. He stood for a moment, watching the courtyard. "With that Englishman," he added in some surprise as he noted the driver of the car. "You know—Whitelaw, Bertrand Whitelaw." And he didn't know which astounded him the more: Whitelaw's excellent if raffish taste in cars, or the princess's willingness to travel in what she would call a "contraption." She was sitting very erect and motionless, her head and neck wrapped in layers of chiffon, her face a complete mask. At first, she didn't seem to notice Whitelaw offering her his hand to descend. She didn't even look at Alberto. And then she stepped slowly, carefully, out of the car, and stood, almost unwilling to face the door of her house. "She's afraid," Lammiter told Eleanor. "She's afraid to enter." He left the window.

"She knows? But how?"

Lammiter was thinking of Whitelaw now. He, too, had been uncertain, but for quite another reason: he had been glancing at his watch, a man torn between politeness and impatience. "What is Whitelaw doing in Umbria, anyway?" he suddenly asked aloud. He halted, looking back at the window.

"Bill—I don't want to see the princess. I don't want to stay here." Eleanor had risen and come over to him. He put an arm around her waist. "I can't bear this place, I can't bear it."

"We'll leave," he told her reassuringly. From outside, he now heard the captain asking politely about the princess's journey.

"But can you leave?" She was watching him anxiously.

"Why not? The captain is in charge. As soon as he gives the signal, I'm taking you right out of here."

"Bill," she said very quietly, "tell me one thing. Are you a secret agent?"

He looked down at her in amazement. "Good God, no!" He tightened his arm around her. "Everything I did was—strictly personal." He smiled, a little embarrassed. "All for you, funny face."

"That was what I hoped," she said gravely.

He stared at her. "Surely you never believed—"

"Everyone else does."

"*What?* But that's all nonsense. Ellie—it's absolute nonsense. You know that, don't you?"

She nodded. She gave her second smile. "Then your job is all over. You can leave with me?"

"Nothing is going to stop me." He pushed the hair back from the nape of her neck and kissed it.

"Now I really do feel better," she said. She glanced toward the window. "The poor captain . . . He is having a little trouble." They could hear his rich baritone still hedging around the distasteful task of being the sad bearer of tragic news.

Whitelaw said, with an undiplomatic abruptness that was quite apart from his usual character, "What bad news? What are you trying to say?"

And at last the truth was jolted out. "Luigi, Count Pirotta, has shot himself."

There was a long moment of silence. Then the princess's clear voice said, "When did it happen? This morning?"

"No, Principessa. Half an hour ago."

There was another silence. Lammiter could imagine the cold, sad face paling even under its careful mask of rouge and powder. She had, he thought grimly, been almost too early in arriving, after all.

Eleanor had walked back to the couch. She looked up at the high ceiling with its carved and painted beams, at the tall wall covered with the treasure of centuries, at the rows of high-backed chairs waiting under their dust covers for the parties that never would take place here any more, at the long windows elaborately curtained which once had opened on a courtyard filled with the cheerful bustle of arriving guests, with the excitement of people who had come to enjoy themselves, elegants among elegance, an island of prerogative, of unreality, in a sea of constant struggle. Now the Casa Grande would become what it really was: a museum of beautiful things and evil memories.

Bill Lammiter, beside her, was watching her anxiously. "But perhaps," she said, letting him into her thoughts, "all that happened today was as much a part of this house as those pretty possessions." She pointed at random to a Cellini candelabrum on a Florentine mosaic table, and then to a Bronzino portrait of a handsome man, young, richly dressed, melancholy, who looked gravely down at her from his elaborately carved and gilded frame. Her eyes widened suddenly as she stared up at the Renaissance man. "He looks like—" She didn't finish. Lammiter, looking up at the portrait, saw the resemblance to Pirotta, too.

Instinctively, he took her hand. But she was in control of herself. She sat quite still, more curious than upset, as though she were trying to solve the puzzle that anyone who could bear a strong resemblance to such a noble face should have been driven by the forces that had controlled Pirotta. Was this, Lammiter wondered, the Pirotta she had fallen in love with? And it was your own God-damned fault, he cursed himself, remembering how he had let her go last spring, hadn't followed her until he realized he had lost her. She was watching him, holding his hand as if he were the one who needed comforting. "I was a swollen-headed fool," he said bitterly. "I was so busy giving away pieces of myself to everyone and everything that I'd soon have had nothing left to give to the only one who mattered." He paused. He gave a wry smile. "All a playwright has to do is to write good plays. All the rest is—sawing sawdust." He paused again. He had never found words so elusive and stupid. "I'm trying to say I am sorry," he said almost desperately.

"No—not you. It's I who should be saying—" She paused. The princess's voice came clearly from the hall. "Oh, Bill—is she coming in here?"

Too late to close the door. He could hardly shut it in the princess's face.

"It was an accident, of course," the princess told the captain. "He was cleaning his rifle in the gun room."

"Perhaps it was an accident," the captain said unhappily. "But it happened on the staircase."

There was a long pause. "I think I shall rest here for a little," the princess said in a low voice. She stopped abruptly at the threshold of the room as she saw Eleanor, sitting so still. Then she looked at Lammiter. A strange expression, not unkind, not even surprised, softened her carefully painted lips for a fleeting moment. She nodded. She walked on.

Lammiter knelt beside Eleanor. He kissed her hands. She looked at him, and then she touched his brow gently, and she laid her cheek against his.

Rosana brought Eleanor's coat and purse. She spoke quickly, tonelessly, with all life dredged out of her voice. Perhaps this was the only way she could keep her emotions under control: to be businesslike and almost aloof—even if that was, or perhaps indeed because it was, contrary to her nature—that was how she could build a wall around her emotions. If she let one part of that wall be displaced, the whole barrier would come falling down. "Joe is waiting," she told Bill Lammiter.

"Where?"

"Outside the gate."

"What brought him here?"

"I telephoned. I thought the captain was going to be—difficult."

"Thank you." Lammiter looked at the pale face, now coldly beautiful, a marble statue going through human motions of politeness. "Again," he added gently, "thank you."

"You must hurry."

"Before the captain changes his mind?" he asked with a smile.

"He's been told your address for the next few days. He knows where to find you—if he needs you."

"My address? I haven't got any address." But Rosana didn't explain.

Eleanor said impulsively, "Rosana—you don't want to stay here either. Come with us."

Rosana's face softened for a moment. Her lips began to tremble. "I must stay," she said, turning away. She walked back toward the door.

Lammiter took Eleanor's arm, and pressed her wrist gently. That warned her. She was still puzzled, but she said no more. She gave a last look round the white and green room, and then at the Bronzino portrait of the sad and proud young man. Rosana, waiting at the door for them, noticed that glance. She said, "Bronzino still enjoys his private joke. Every time someone stands in front of that portrait and exclaims 'What grace, what goodness! Ah—those were noble days!' then Bronzino's skeleton shakes with laughter. The Renaissance had its share of violence and evil. That young man was one of its monsters." She walked into the hall.

Quickly they followed her, quickly they passed over the stone-flagged floor. At the front door, Rosana halted. "Good-by," she said evenly. "I must go to the princess." She held out her hands to them both.

"Not good-by," he protested.

Rosana looked at him and then at Eleanor. She said, suddenly natural again, warm and vibrant, "You are my friends." She gave a smile that turned into a strangled sob as her guard went down. Then she turned abruptly, and retreated into the dark shadows of the vast hall. They began to walk, in silence, across the gold-lit courtyard.

It was a serene place, that courtyard. Under the five o'clock sun, warm and mellow, there was no movement except the flutter of a white pigeon over their heads, no sound except their footsteps on the stones. Near the gate, wide open now, showing the quiet little square outside, Lammiter suddenly said, "Where is Whitelaw?"

Eleanor looked at him in surprise. "I didn't hear him leave either." It was odd, she thought, that Whitelaw had left so immediately. He was a friend of the princess's, wasn't he? Strange that he should have left her at her doorstep. "Perhaps the princess sent him away."

"Perhaps."

"You're worried."

"I've reached the stage of worrying about everything," he told her. Then he thought, I never even noticed Whitelaw's car was gone until I had walked the breadth of this courtyard. What's gone wrong with your reactions, Lammiter? They are as slow as your feet at this moment.

He almost passed Jacopone. The gamekeeper was standing so motionless beside the gate that he might have been one of its carved decorations. He still carried his rifle under one arm. He looked at them both quite impassively. He nodded, and a smile entered those old watchful eyes. He seemed surprised and then pleased as Lammiter seized his free hand in a grasp that tightened as they stood in silence. "*Viva Garibaldi!*" Lammiter said suddenly.

A wide grin broke across the wrinkled face. "*Evviva!*" Jacopone said heartily. "*Viva Garibaldi!*" He pumped Lammiter's hand vigorously, clapped him on the shoulder with a hearty thump, smiled and nodded approvingly for Eleanor. "*Evviva!*" he said, and dropped Lammiter's hand. He turned and left them, clumping his way slowly toward the kitchen doorway.

"Now that you've stopped pinning medals on each other," Joe's voice said behind them, "shall we go and eat?"

Normal, that was Joe. That was the cue he was giving me, Lammiter thought as he helped Eleanor into the back seat of the small Fiat. He followed her stiffly. Physically, he was more exhausted than he wanted to admit. Mentally—well, that was another matter. Now that they were out of the Casa Grande, out into the free air of Montesecco, the intense pressure had lifted and left him feeling almost lightheaded. He had the impulse to make several wild jokes, mad suggestions, all irresponsible, all delightful. But he'd have to brake heavily on his emotions, control them, and keep his inner excitement something secret. "This is service," he said, looking at his suitcase in the front seat beside Joe. And now he noticed, too, that Joe had found time enough to shave, brush his hair, put on his tie again, and don his jacket.

"We'll get your possessions back to you, one by one," Joe told him. He looked at Eleanor, and nodded approvingly as he started the car. She returned his smile, leaned her head against Lammiter's shoulder, settled into his comforting grasp, and closed her eyes. And Lammiter fell silent, watching the little streets of the town: here was the main piazza, now stirring into life with the approach of evening. This was where he had seen Sabatini, that was the street down which he had retreated, here was the gate of the town, the olive trees where he had talked with his two amiable maniacs, the farmhouse. . . . And, as he remembered the desperate misery of those waiting hours, the happiness that now enveloped him seemed completely incredible. Or let's put it this way, he told himself: this is real, this is normal; and that—he turned his head to look at the walled town—that was the hideous dream, the trial. But he must take his cue from Joe: no postmortems. What was over was over, only to be remembered as a warning when life became too easy, too comfortable, for that was the funny thing about life: people always needed a warning every now and again, just to remind them of what might have been.

Down the hill, between the groves of olive trees, they traveled. Before them was the smiling placid valley, behind them the fortress walls.

"Not that way," Lammiter said sharply, as Joe swung the car to the right at the foot of Montesecco's hill. Joe slowed up. "You turn left for Rome."

"Rome's too far. Five minutes, and you'll be sitting down to a decent meal. Isn't that better?"

"And this decent meal is in Perugia?"

"It's the nearest place," Joe said cheerfully. "It's nice there. Good food, good hotels."

"We're staying there?" Lammiter was horrified.

"Why not? Rome's a long haul from here. Too much for Miss Halley."

That was true enough. "There's Assisi."

"Filled to the rafters with pilgrims. You'll be comfortable in Perugia."

"I'm not so sure," Lammiter said very quietly. "I don't want Eleanor to go near Perugia."

Joe halted the car and reached for a cigarette. He lit one for Lammiter. He said, watching a slow procession of farm carts coming back from work in the fields, "There is a small emergency."

"What?"

"About Evans," Joe said curtly. He was angry, but not at Lammiter. "Look, I didn't want this any more than you. My job's over: Sabatini was arrested, and none of his friends even know about it—yet. The meeting took place, and everyone attending it was observed and photographed: they will be watched when they get back to their own countries; all their contacts will be noted, and not one piece of advice or any reports from them will ever be accepted in good faith again. And, lastly, the big guy who organized a dope ring so efficiently that it could be taken over for political purposes by his Communist friends on the day they try to seize power—" he halted, looked at Lammiter, and was a little taken aback to find that the girl had opened her eyes and was watching him. He branched off. "You don't believe me? There's nothing Communism finds handier than a good tight organization with an efficient chain of command, all ready to be taken over. This one didn't even have to be infiltrated. It was created especially. It pulls in the money now. Later, it could supply the bully-boys, and whether they wear black, brown, or red shirts makes no difference." His mouth shut tightly. But he didn't finish his original sentence about the "big guy" who had organized a very efficient chain of command. Instead, he looked again at Eleanor. "My job's over. And so is yours. To hell with their emergencies. Let the English puzzle this one out. It's their headache. I'm only an underpaid Italian cop who hasn't had a night off in five weeks."

He must be pretty angry, Lammiter thought, to have broken his cover like that. He said, "What's this emergency?"

Joe gave a short laugh. "No one can identify Evans. A couple of fellows are being flown out from London right now. But there's no one here who knows him. Can you beat that?"

"But they saw him leave the meeting, didn't they? Don't tell me," Lammiter said in disgust, "that they let him slip between their fingers."

"No, no," Joe assured him. "They're keeping a close watch on the man. Tall, thin, fair hair—"

"Gray," Eleanor said.

He looked at her quickly. "Evans's description reads *fair hair*. And your photograph—"

"That was taken very late in the evening. The light was bad."

"So—" Joe said softly, "they have more reason for their doubts about Evans than they know."

Lammiter said, "What started the doubts?"

Joe shrugged his shoulders. "I wasn't there" was all he could say.

"And now," Lammiter said, his lips and voice tight, "they want Eleanor to make sure of the man they hope is Evans, but might not be. No, thanks. We are not taking Eleanor to Perugia."

"Then where? Back to Montesecco?"

"Stop being funny," Lammiter said sourly.

"But you don't find right places to eat and sleep in any little town. And your friend Camden has got a couple of good rooms for you in Perugia."

"Look, Joe—we don't need luxury. All we want is peace and quiet." He looked at Eleanor. "And safety."

There was a short silence.

Lammiter said testily, "I thought you said your job was over, you were glad it was over. Hell, what's this treatment, Joe? First you—"

Eleanor said, "Are there truly good restaurants in Perugia?" It's up to me, she thought wearily. Bill would go to Perugia if he were by himself and could identify the man Evans. And Joe, however much he doesn't feel like going, knows he must. The job is not over. It all began with Evans, and it must end with Evans.

Bill Lammiter said, "Eleanor—"

"I'm starving," she said. "Let's get all this business finished and then concentrate on us." She raised her voice, speaking to Joe now. "Let's go to Perugia."

Joe started the engine again. His furrowed face looked both pleased and unhappy. "Okay?" he asked Lammiter, his foot still on the brake.

Lammiter nodded. Two against one. He knew when he was in a minority. The car moved forward.

"How long were you in America, Joe?" Eleanor asked. A change of subject seemed advisable.

"Twelve years," said Joe. Then he gave her a startled look in the mirror. "Hey!" he said, "you know when to ask questions, don't you?" He grinned. Lammiter had to smile, too: he was willing to bet that Joe's true past was rarely jolted out of him.

"Only occasionally," Eleanor said. Too often, she thought, I've never asked any questions at all, just accepted everything on its surface value. But her inquiry had its effect: Joe was explaining those twelve years, Bill was interested, and blood pressure was falling back to normal all around her.

"Yes," Joe said. "Ten years as a kid; two years later on, as a college student in New York. I was brought up in Cleveland—I was only two when my father settled there. When he died, my mother brought the family back to Sicily. She had always kept talking about Sicily—the best place in the world, she said, the only place." Joe's smile broadened. "Funny thing, when she got to Sicily, she kept talking about America." He swerved round a pair of white oxen.

"Oh!" Eleanor sat up and looked at them.

"Want to take a photograph?" Joe asked, but he didn't slacken speed. "Or is the light not good enough? What color would their hair turn?"

She half smiled. She gave Bill's hand a little squeeze. See, she was telling him, I'm all right: I feel better every minute. And perhaps, she was thinking, I need this: I need to look out at the world, this heavenly scene of farmers and white oxen and rich fields and little hills and trees, all silhouetted so clearly against the western light. I need this sense of reality, as much as I need food or sleep. When Luigi and his two men brought me here, it was a nightmare journey through menacing shadows and grim black shapes. Now . . . She took a deep breath of the gentle air, with its first hint of coolness. Now, too, I begin to see the real reason behind everything Luigi did today. If this man Evans is so important, then now I see Luigi as clearly in perspective as these clear-cut hills. He lied, to the very end he lied to me. He wasn't taking me away to save me from danger. He was taking me away to make sure of saving Evans. And when he tried to kill me, it wasn't because he loved me so much, it wasn't any sweet romantic nonsense like that. He was simply protecting Evans. Luigi was the realist. It was not I who betrayed him. It was he who betrayed everyone who trusted him as a human being.

Bill was looking at her, worried again. She smiled for him. Some day, she thought, I'll talk to him about this. Not now. Some day . . . What makes a man into a machine? What kills conscience? Or did that die when self-criticism died? And did you stop criticizing yourself when you believed that anything you did was right? And if anyone else questioned you, there was always the Cause for an excuse? But how could you judge that a cause was good or bad unless you had enough feeling left in your veins for human beings? Not just "the people," a vague abstract mass, with as little real meaning as a linoleum pattern. But people like Rosana and Jacopone and Joe and old Alberto and Anna-Maria. People were not pawns, to be moved around and sacrificed, to be swept away if they did not fit into the grand design. People were this farmer here, riding slowly home with his daughter and son beside him; these two women walking with bundles of twigs on their backs; that boy on the bicycle; that man in the high-powered car; this bus load, Joe, Bill, me.

"Here we are," said Joe, swinging the car to his right.

They began to twist up the long arm of a hill between an avenue of trees. The town sprawled over the peak like a cap of snow on a Japanese mountain. Down here, the houses were new, neat modern shapes of plaster painted green or cream or pink, but above them the old buildings clustered together—perched, it seemed, on a precipice, an island of bleached stone and jutting shapes.

They had reached the end of the climb. They came into an open square with public buildings and a small park that overlooked the precipice. There, the main street began, the Corso Vanucci, running like a spine along the crest of the hill on which lay Perugia. There, too, the cars were parked, for the Corso itself was closed off to traffic. "It's usual," Joe told them as they got out. "At this hour, everyone strolls out to see the sunset."

"And one another," Lammiter added, looking at the groups of young girls walking arm in arm in their pretty dresses; of young men, tall and handsome, keeping together; of proud couples, with red-cheeked babies, all preened in starched frills. There was a strange hush over the street, broken only by the sound of light-soled shoes and the murmur of peaceful voices. The street was straight, wide, handsomely paved, and not very long. He could see the other end marked by a fountain, in front of a huge cathedral. Between the piazza, which they were leaving, and this stone giant, there was only a constant stream of gay clothes and well-brushed heads. Nothing could be more unlike Montesecco, he thought thankfully. He began to relax. And then, as they passed the last parked car and entered the wide stretch of street, he looked back swiftly.

"Yes?" asked Joe.

"That's Whitelaw's car. Bertrand Whitelaw. You know him?"

"I know about him."

"Where does he stand?"

"Does that matter?"

"He brought the princess from Rome. He knows Pirotta is dead."

Joe frowned. "Give me time. I'm slow. I have to think this one out."

Lammiter looked at Eleanor. *Pirotta is dead,* he had said, as cold-bloodedly as though he had been talking about Mussolini or Stalin. But all she noticed now was his concern over her. "How far do we walk?" she asked, keeping her voice light.

"Another fifty yards," Joe said. "That's all. We start slanting over to our left." He steered them expertly across the street, between the strolling groups, toward the broad sidewalk which was filled with café tables.

"The foreigners," said Eleanor, looking at the tables, "are here in force."

"Keep watching," Joe told her quietly. They walked slowly along the edge of the sidewalk. Joe had taken her other arm. He pressed it suddenly. "Don't stare, just look," he told her. "Anyone you know?"

"No one," she said, when she thought it was safe to speak. "No one at all."

"Did you see that fair-haired man in the gray flannel suit?"

"Yes."

"You've never seen him before?"

"No."

"Into this restaurant," Joe directed them suddenly. He led the way across the sidewalk. He seemed neither disappointed nor hurried.

The restaurant was empty, of course, and unlighted. No one ate until the promenade outside, the *passeggiata,* was over. Now Joe let his pace increase. He led them through the cool dark room into a tiled kitchen where a solitary cook under a spreading tree of pots and pans suspended from an overhead beam was busy with a bubbling pot. The cook, a bulky man who looked as though he enjoyed his own cooking, scarcely glanced around. "You're late. I was beginning to think you weren't coming." He pointed with a ladle to a closed door.

Joe nodded. As he opened the door leading them into a back room, he called to the cook, "Serve it up!"

"*Subito, subito!*" The ladle went back to stirring.

Through the doorway was a tiled room, ill lit from the single window near its ceiling, but cool. Its wooden table was ready for supper. There was a scraping of chairs on its stone floor as four men rose to their feet.

"Hello there!" said Bunny Camden, coming forward to welcome them. He looked at Eleanor, then at Lammiter. "Good," he said. "It's good to see you." Then he turned to introduce two of the men. "A couple of friends," he said, "MacLaren from Canada. Oglethorpe from England."

The Englishman's eyes had a suspicion of a smile for the name Bunny had invented for him. A Canadian and an Englishman, Lammiter remembered suddenly: last night, in that open-air movie house behind the Esedra, they had been mentioned. They must indeed have been as interested in Evans as Bunny had guessed. But the fourth man, an Italian, middle-aged, dark-haired, with a thin intelligent face and mournful eyes, did not come forward. He nodded pleasantly, but he seemed to prefer the most shadowed wall of the room. Or, Lammiter thought, watching the clever worried face, he is only an observer from some branch of Italian intelligence, and is tactfully being subsidiary, leaving the main problems to the others. Joe, too, had retreated into the background: in fact, at this moment, he was leaving, quietly, unobtrusively.

Eleanor sat down. So did Lammiter. The others stood.

"Did you see Evans sitting outside?" the Englishman asked.

Eleanor shook her head.

"He was wearing a gray flannel suit," Oglethorpe told her as he watched her face.

"That was not the man I met at Tivoli."

"You're quite sure, Miss Halley?"

"Yes. Quite sure."

The men exchanged glances. "That's just what I thought," MacLaren said in disgust. In this moment of sharp disappointment, his voice held a pugnacious note surprisingly in contrast with his expressionless face. Like Oglethorpe, he could easily be misplaced in a crowd, an unremarkable man, with nondescript features, unobtrusive clothes, nothing dramatic or eccentric in his gestures or manner. The eyes were alert, though. These men were nobody's fools, Lammiter decided. How, then, had they been deceived? Or perhaps it was not their fault. He glanced at the silent Italian. Another sharp character. Then how had the failure developed? A split in authority, divided responsibility, conflicting methods, all the headaches of international co-operation? Lammiter passed the basket of half-sliced bread to Eleanor. "Eat slowly," he told her.

"I've eaten bread all day," she said dejectedly. "Bread and water. Everything else was drugged." And all this trouble for nothing, she thought: Evans is free. He has been the cause of everything that has happened to Bill and to me. We could have been killed, both of us, and he would have brushed us off his memory like a couple of dead flies from a window sill.

The Italian spoke suddenly. "You are thinking we have been stupid?" He shook his head. "Even in the best plans, there is the moment of luck, of accident."

Lammiter said, "I could wish the moment of bad luck would strike Mr. Evans, too."

"It may. There are few roads out of a hill town such as this. We have them watched. Every car is being stopped, every foreign passport is being examined."

"Evans is probably leaving disguised as a white ox," Lammiter said abruptly. Anticlimax was one frustration that he didn't accept very gracefully. "Can't we get some soup or something?" he asked sharply. Camden nodded and left. "How did this situation develop, anyway?" He looked at them, trying to keep his temper from breaking loose. We deserve some kind of explanation, he thought angrily. Damn it, are we among friends, or aren't we?

Oglethorpe and MacLaren, moving to the door, halted. "Have you any special interest in Evans?" Oglethorpe asked, seemingly only politely curious.

"A personal matter."

"But you didn't know him."

"I have a little bill I'd like him to settle for the trouble he has caused several of my friends." Brewster, chiefly.

"Haven't we all?" said MacLaren. He was anxious to leave.

"But," Lammiter kept on doggedly, "I do have a special interest in that meeting. Don't tell me you slipped up on that, too!"

Oglethorpe's mouth tightened. "We don't always fail, Lammiter."

"Look," Lammiter said (and here, thank God, was Bunny himself, carrying in a tureen of soup), "this girl was nearly murdered in front of my eyes. Don't expect sweetness and light from me." Quickly he served Eleanor a plate of *minestrone.* That would put some color back in her cheeks. "Slowly, now," he told her again.

"Would one success make you feel any better?" There was a smile, now, in the Englishman's eyes.

"Much better." Even knowing that there had been success was as good as the smell of the soup from the plate before him.

"Seven men attended that meeting. All were secretly photographed as they left." Oglethorpe paused, and then decided to add an extra bonus. "Three of them were government officials from NATO countries, two were from the Middle East: none under the least previous suspicion of being Communists. So that is one success we have had."

Lammiter said, "And a big one."

Oglethorpe nodded. "Have you seen the newspapers today?"

"Too busy." He nodded his thanks to Camden, who now brought in a bottle of Orvieto.

"There's trouble simmering in the Middle East," Oglethorpe said. "The Communists will certainly try to make that pot boil over. So, you see, these five photographed men are the best news I can give you. Even better than Sabatini's arrest."

"And what about the two other men?—There were seven at the meeting, you said." Lammiter's voice had lost its edge: the soup was good. We'll live, he thought, watching Eleanor carefully.

"Oh yes, these other two . . ." Oglethorpe seemed just to have remembered them. "One answered Evans's description. The other was totally unknown. No one could place him. At best, he seemed to be Evans's bodyguard. He wore a loose American jacket, a bright tie, a beret pulled down over his head, dark glasses. And there was a cigar clamped in his mouth. Distorts the jaw line, you know."

"Very neat," Lammiter agreed. "So all he had to do was to dodge into the nearest men's room after he left the meeting, take off all his accessories—"

"He did better than that. After all, we are prepared for tricks in a men's room. He went into the cathedral. You've noticed it?"

"It would be hard to miss." It was an enormous place, that unfinished cathedral, six centuries old, so vast in conception that people had long ago given up any idea of completing it.

"Inside, it's practically pitch black. Gigantic pillars all over the floor. Chapels. Alcoves. Confessionals. Railings. Groups of groping tourists. Everything made to order. Including," Oglethorpe added gloomily, "two main doorways. So all he had to do was to dodge from pillar to pillar, quickly peel off that jacket, stuff the beret and glasses and cigar into a pocket, bundle the whole thing up, drop it behind an empty confessional, choose a collection of tourists, and straggle out with them into the street."

"Smart fellow." There was a slight movement at the door. He glanced quickly. But it was only Joe returning to slip quietly into place.

"Too smart for a bodyguard," MacLaren said.

And that, Lammiter thought, was where the first doubts started. "Talking of bodyguards," he said, "do you know a man called Whitelaw?"

They obviously did. "Where does he come in?" MacLaren asked quietly.

"He's on stage right now. I saw his car near the piazza. A cream-colored Ferrari. Joe—you tell them about last night in the garden and today at the Casa Grande." He concentrated on his soup. It was better than good. A warm glow spread through his belly and up over his body. For the first time in thirty-six hours he began to relax properly, not altogether, but just enough to make him feel more normal, less strained. He gave Eleanor a broad smile, poured a second glass of wine for them both, and said, "We leave it all to the experts now." He thought, Our job is really done. We can do no more. That was a good feeling, too.

She nodded. "Funny," she said, "I was so hungry. And now—I don't think I can eat anything more." She looked across the little room at Joe and at the men who listened to him so gravely.

"That's natural," he said. He studied her face, as if he were a doctor, carefully, unobtrusively. She looked all right, better than he could have hoped an hour ago. "To the prettiest girl in all Perugia," he said, lifting his glass. She smiled, as he always could make her smile, delighted and embarrassed in pleasing proportion. "You know what, Ellie? Apart from being in love with you, I like you. I like you very much. I like the way you smile, the way you tilt your head, that flutter of your eyelashes, the color coming and going in your cheeks, and your eyes—today they are blue, as blue as—" He paused. "Hell, what's the use of being a writer if I can't think of the right word?"

"You're falling asleep." She gave a little laugh. "And so am I. Oh, Bill! How do we get to the hotel?"

"We'll carry each other." He straightened his spine, stopped slouching comfortably. "The fresh air outside will wake us up enough. Too many people in here. Always too many people around." He looked across at the group of men. Even as he looked, they broke off their discussion. "It's one small chance," MacLaren, the Canadian, was saying as he began to move to the door, "but it isn't any more discouraging than searching a haystack for a needle."

"I've never understood," Lammiter told Eleanor, "why anyone should take her sewing out to a haystack in the first place, especially anyone who loses needles."

Oglethorpe, as he was leaving, called across to them, "Good-by. And thank you, Miss Halley, for coming here." His worried face relaxed for a moment. He had a singularly attractive smile. Or perhaps he liked to see two people holding hands so peaceably. MacLaren gave them a surprised look and a nod of farewell.

"A Scots Presbyterian, that one," said Lammiter. "Doesn't approve of mixing pleasure with business."

Bunny Camden looked down at them both. He grinned, shaking his head. "You're a couple of idiots," he said affectionately, and pulled up a chair. "Now eat! Both of you. Here's some chicken *cacciatore.*" The jovial cook had brought in a tray laden with food. "And let's light the candles."

"Where's Joe? And that other Italian?" Lammiter asked, suddenly aware that Camden was the only one left.

"He had some friends to see."

"That's Joe. A friend in every hill town. Useful man to know." But he was disappointed a little, even if good-bys were probably unnecessary in Joe's business. "Come on, Ellie, keep me company." He helped her to some food. "Just pretend you're hungry, to please me. Besides, I'm going to have what New York calls a full-course dinner. While you talk, Bunny."

"Me?"

"About Bertrand Whitelaw."

"You're like a terrier with a rat."

Lammiter looked up. "Is he one? I hoped not."

"I was speaking metaphorically."

"The Marine Corps uses all the big words nowadays," Lammiter told Eleanor. "That comes from carrying a copy of Homer in their pockets, to while away the hours between battles."

Camden said with a grin, "All right, all right. What do you want to know? He's a sort of journalist, political reporting—"

"Yes, yes. Sober thoughts, upper-level stuff. But did he ever *know* Evans?"

"Yes. He went to college with him, Oglethorpe says. Defended Evans when he disappeared from England, would not believe the worst; and then, when Evans turned up blithely in Russia, he insisted that Evans must have been kidnaped and was acting under duress. I gather that the whole Evans business was a very nasty shock to Whitelaw."

"So Whitelaw is not a Communist?"

"No."

"Well, there's the man to help Oglethorpe. . . ."

"Oglethorpe isn't so sure about that."

"Why not?"

"Whitelaw is now a 'neutralist.' "

"Oh? What type?" There were those who just wanted to be left alone. And those who airily said they saw no difference between Russia and America. And those who were scared. And those who used neutralism as a cover, an alibi, to conceal their secret adherence to Communism.

"That's hard to judge. By his own account, he is second to none in patriotism. And I think he is an honest British subject. But his judgment isn't always as good as he thinks it is. Evans was not the only hidden Communist who has used him as a transmission belt."

"He couldn't love England half so much, loved he not Whitelaw more?"

Camden smiled. "There's only one thing sure about Whitelaw. He will give no help to us. We are meddling in a matter that's strictly between two Englishmen: Whitelaw and Evans. Unjustifiable interference. Downright impertinence. Get it?"

"But Oglethorpe is as English as they come."

"To him, Oglethorpe is the contemptible instrument of a purely vindictive policy."

Suddenly, Eleanor spoke. "He just doesn't *know* enough. He just doesn't know what trouble Evans has caused . . . all of us. . . ." Her voice drifted away, unhappily.

"Or could cause," Camden added. "The sooner that man is extradited and taken out of circulation, the better for everyone. Today, his job here was obviously to receive last-minute reports, co-ordinate plans, give final instructions. A man like Evans is worth a whole armored division to the Russians."

"But what puzzles me—" Lammiter began.

"Yes?"

"How can he be extradited simply for having packed a bag and taken the first plane out of London?"

"He also packed a highly secret Cabinet report. Didn't have time to get it photographed, I expect." Camden frowned at the tablecloth and smoothed out the wrinkles that his hands had been busily folding into it.

"You're as troubled about Evans as Oglethorpe or MacLaren," Lammiter remarked. "Is he your business, too?"

"He is all our business. It isn't the first time an alliance has fallen apart because of a few carefully placed men whose secret instructions were sabotage. And if a small war starts, and the Western alliance crumbles, what will we have?—The big one."

"Tell that to Whitelaw."

Camden's eyes smiled. "You're recovering—started making your jokes again, have you?" Then, seriously, "In fact, Oglethorpe has gone searching for Whitelaw. Bevilacqua will help him, with phone calls to every hotel and lodginghouse."

"Oglethorpe really thinks that Whitelaw is in Perugia to meet Evans?"

"There are only two things possible: either Whitelaw is here for pleasure pure and simple or he is here on business."

"By business, you mean Evans?"

Camden nodded. "Oglethorpe thinks that Whitelaw may have heard Evans was in Italy. Or perhaps he saw Evans with Pirotta by accident, when they met in Rome. That could explain why he was so eager to see Pirotta: he was tracking Evans down."

"Why?" Lammiter asked bluntly.

"It's more than possible he still believes Evans is acting under duress. So if he could only talk to Evans, help him to escape from his bodyguards, help him to avoid us, then Evans would return of his own free will—always a most disarming gesture—and he would not be dragged back to England as a traitor. Evans could claim he had been kidnaped, and Whitelaw would feel happy that he had vindicated a friend. And, of course, his own judgment."

"I don't see why you're worrying about all that. Evans will never listen to Whitelaw."

"That's just the danger. Evans may pretend to listen. He may use Whitelaw as he used him before. In that case, he will take any help offered, use it to leave Perugia, and a month later turn up in Moscow and give a press conference. What do you bet?"

Lammiter's lips tightened. "Nothing!" He pushed his plate away from him.

"So you can see why Oglethorpe is so eager to find Whitelaw," Camden said equably.

"And when he does find him—what then?"

"Whitelaw will be followed. He will lead Oglethorpe to Evans. Oglethorpe doesn't want to waste a precious hour in trying to convince Whitelaw that two and two make five nor three, nor even four and a half."

Lammiter reached over for Eleanor's hand. She had only pretended to eat. "Come on, you old unjustified interferer, you! To bed, to bed . . . Let's catch some sleep and forget Whitelaw." But, he thought, poor old Oglethorpe, poor old MacLaren, men fighting an unseen war to defeat any chance of a real one, getting little help from people like Whitelaw, who would be the first to scream out when the bombs started falling. Whitelaw, living in comfort, with money and prestige and applause; Oglethorpe and MacLaren, unthanked, ill paid, with hardship and danger as their reward. "Come on, darling," he repeated, very gently. Either she was already half asleep or she was lost in a world of her own. He turned to Camden. "How far is this hotel?"

"I'll take you there. But have some coffee first."

"We'd better leave," Lammiter said, his eyes on Eleanor. He didn't like that world into which she had retreated: there was a drawn look on her face, a look of tension and sadness.

"Black and bitter," Camden insisted, pouring coffee for them both. "You'll have to walk to the hotel—it isn't far—the *passeggiata* is still going on outside. Until darkness falls, in fact."

Eleanor spoke, avoiding their eyes, looking down at her slender hands. "Luigi Pirotta's orders were to drive from Perugia to Gubbio. I was to be brought to meet him. Then we were driving to Venice. There's a freighter there, ready to sail. For the Black Sea." She glanced up at Camden's astonished face. "Is that how Evans will leave Italy? By car to Venice, then by that ship?"

There was pity and tenderness in Lammiter's startled face as he watched her speak, and something of alarm, too. He wished she had been spared that knowledge. Today, Joe and he had made their guesses about Venice, but it was still a shock to find that the guesses had been actual truth. It will be a long job to make her forget all these things, he was thinking: but it would be the best job he could ever do.

Camden had recovered his usual unperturbed expression. "Could be," he said very quietly. He frowned, as he always did when he was making some decision. He picked a bread stick out of its glass on the table, and began breaking it absent-mindedly. "Finish your coffee," he said, "and then I'll get you to your hotel." And then, he thought, I'll have to search for Oglethorpe and tell him that piece of information. It could be vital.

"I hope someone is keeping an eye on Whitelaw's car," Lammiter said. "Evans may be a man in need of a good fast car."

"Whitelaw wouldn't be such a damned fool—" Camden stopped abruptly. But Whitelaw might not have much choice in the matter. Once he made any contact with Evans, he would have no choice left. Camden's fingers snapped the bread stick into still smaller pieces. "Let's hope," he said, "that Oglethorpe finds Whitelaw in time. Are you ready to leave?"

"In time for what?"

Camden swept all the crumbs together and built them into a neat pyramid. "Let's get to the hotel," he suggested.

Lammiter rose, and went round to help Eleanor find her handbag. "You know," he said, keeping his voice as unperturbed as Bunny Camden's, "Whitelaw may have seen Evans with Pirotta in Rome, but how did he learn that Evans would be in Perugia today?"

Camden stared at him.

"It's been one of the best-arranged secrets of the year."

Camden nodded. True enough, Brewster had paid a heavy bill for uncovering it. Everyone who could have learned about Evans's visit had been living under a threat. But— He shook his head. "You think that Whitelaw was told, purposely? Do you mean that Evans telephoned him last night and—"

"No, this morning." Last night, Whitelaw had still been searching for information.

"All right—this morning, and laid on Whitelaw's visit here? Now, now, Bill—" He considered the idea from several angles. "I don't think Oglethorpe or MacLaren would buy that."

"Why not?"

"They'd say it would make a good plot for your next play," Camden replied with a smile as he rose. "All ready?" he asked Eleanor.

Lammiter, standing behind Eleanor's chair, her coat over his arm, faced Camden across the table. Doggedly, he said, "Look, Bunny—I *saw* Whitelaw in the courtyard at Montesecco. He could hardly wait, kept looking at his watch, didn't even stay long enough to help the princess face the first half hour in that house. He was a man with an urgent appointment. I tell you, Bunny, he was—"

"Then we're too late," Camden said. "If you are right, we're too late to prevent that appointment. Whitelaw and Evans could have met a couple of hours ago." He looked very directly at Lammiter. "If you are right," he repeated somberly.

"I know one thing for certain," Lammiter began, as he helped Eleanor to rise to her feet. He thought, I should never have let myself be persuaded to bring her here. "Damn it, I should never have let Eleanor come here," he exploded, his anger slipping to the surface in spite of his guard.

Eleanor's hand touched his arm gently. "It was my choice," she said. "Remember?" He mustn't blame himself so much. Bill looked down at her and knew her thoughts. He shook his head slowly. And I am to blame for all the danger she has known, he was thinking. If I had had more good sense back in New York, she would never have gone away without me.

Camden said, "If you would stop your interior conversations, we could start along the Corso. We'll keep arm in arm, and we'll talk about the weather, and look as though our only problem was where to find a dry Martini." He turned to Eleanor. "You can manage it?"

She nodded.

"Get him to smile," he told her with a grin, his eyes on Bill Lammiter.

"Will this do?" Lammiter asked sourly, and made a wide grimace.

"Diabolical," Camden pronounced. Eleanor began to laugh. Lammiter's face relaxed into a real smile.

"Hold it!" Camden said approvingly. They walked through the half-lit restaurant, still empty and still waiting for its customers, looking remarkably cheerful considering the giant worry that trod on their heels.

Outside, dusk was falling; the lights in the cafés and shops were being turned on. The tables were less crowded now, the strolling crowd had thinned out a little, too. But the three, Eleanor tightly gripped between Lammiter and Camden, looked a normal part of the scene as they walked westward along the smoothly paved Corso toward the piazza.

"Half-past seven," Camden said, glancing at his watch. "By eight it will be dark, this street will be almost empty, and the traffic will start moving out of the town. There will be a steady stream of cars and Vespas going down that hill." And, he added gloomily to himself, not only will the light be bad, but the policemen at the roadblocks will be overworked and harried. That was always the moment of mistake.

"I thought this peace was too good to last," Lammiter said lightly for Eleanor's benefit, as he listened to the soft fall of light footsteps around them. Benignly, the eighteenth-century houses over the cafés and shops looked down on their progress. "How far now?" He could feel Eleanor's weight beginning to sag on his arm.

"The hotel is at the end of this street, not far, just beyond the piazz—"

"Hello!" called a clear young voice, surprised, delighted, friendly. A girl's tanned arm waved to them from a table littered with orange-juice bottles round which a crowd of American students were gathered. "See—we got here!" the girl called. "And isn't it *fun?*"

"Great fun," said Lammiter, recovering quickly, smiling, waving back, walking on.

"I like the green bow on her hair," Camden said. His eyes were as quick as ever. "Who is she?"

"A maniac, bless her. Without whose help we might not be walking down the Corso right now."

"Oh?"

But Lammiter did not respond to that cue. He was looking, now, along the final stretch of the Corso, toward the piazza. That was where the row of cars lay tightly boxed, like cigars. Beyond, the street continued into a little park with trees and benches, and ended in a balustrade cutting across the green-tinged sky. The park lay right at the edge of the cliff he had noticed when Joe's car climbed up from the plain. Dusk was coming rapidly, bringing a sudden breeze, the last gasp of a dying sun. The far edges of sky were washed with dark blue light.

"It's still there," Lammiter said with relief. "Whitelaw's car. That cream-colored job. Do we have to pass it?"

"Yes," said Camden. "The hotel is just beyond it, facing the park. But don't look interested in the car. Ignore it!"

"Am I just a little too worried, or do there seem to be more innocent bystanders than necessary on this stretch of sidewalk?"

"Keep walking," Camden said abruptly.

"There's someone following us."

"That's one of Bevilacqua's men." At least, Camden thought, I hope it is. Bevilacqua had promised a constant guard on Eleanor for the next twenty-four hours. By that time, the trouble would be over. Evans would either have escaped or have been arrested, and Perugia could go back to entertaining its summer-school guests.

"I'd like to meet Bevilacqua," Lammiter was saying.

"You did," Camden said absent-mindedly, as his eyes now studied the little park, with its benches and trees and small groups of people.

"Where? When?" And then Lammiter guessed. "You mean that dark-haired Italian, back in the restaurant? The one who talked about the moment of luck, of accident?"

"I see our Canadian friend. He seems to be as interested in that car as we are," Camden said very quietly. MacLaren was slumped on a stone bench, giving an excellent imitation of an exhausted tourist who hadn't strength enough left even to invent a good way to spend his evening. "And I see Joe, too." Joe was in the park, arm in close arm with a yielding brunette. "We've got our point men out," Camden said, with forced cheerfulness. "The situation is well in hand. I hope." Then he added, "I've been thinking over your suggestion—that guess you made—"

"My plot for a play?" Lammiter couldn't resist a touch of sarcasm in his voice.

"That's right," Camden said equably. "You know, you may have something there."

"But no one will buy it. So you said."

"I was halfway to buying it," Camden admitted. "Not quite, but almost. Now—" he shook his head "—I've seen the car, and it's too noticeable. Our Mr. E. wouldn't set one foot inside it, right there on the main piazza. He's waiting quietly around some corner. He's the type who likes to fool people." And, thank God, here was the hotel. He ushered them both quickly through the wide-open mahogany and plate-glass doors.

Lammiter had noticed, too, how obvious the car looked. He relinquished part of his theory, but with regret. Not altogether, though: he was still quite sure that Whitelaw had come to Perugia to keep an appointment. He said, "You don't have to come any farther, Bunny." Camden must have his own plans for this evening.

"I'll see you into your rooms," Camden said determinedly. Convoy duty didn't end within sight of land. "You stay with Eleanor." He went over to the reception desk at one side of the small lobby, more like the entrance to a men's club than to a hotel.

And that last order, thought Lammiter with a touch of annoyance, was totally unnecessary. Then he decided, as he led Eleanor toward a big room opening out of the lobby, and found a massive chair at its entrance, that Bunny was perhaps more worried than he had allowed himself to appear as they walked along the Corso together. The unnecessary order was often a sign of worry. If Bunny Camden had had his own free choice, he would not have brought Eleanor to Perugia any more than Lammiter would have. Or Joe. Here we are, Lammiter thought, as he settled Eleanor into her chair and sat on its arm and pretended to look around him nonchalantly, all of us, caught up in a business that is none of our choosing. What day is it now—Friday? The beginning of a weekend, the time for relaxing . . . He gave an outright scowl at a potted palm beside him.

The hotel had been built for the convenience of the rich Englishman of seventy years ago who demanded all the amenities of home when he traveled abroad. Now, judging from the people who were making their way toward the dining room, the visitors were mostly scholars, interested in Etruscan remains or early Renaissance art, or tourists making a comfortable overnight stay in their journey through the Italian hill towns. But the atmosphere of solid Victorian respectability still hung placidly over the hotel. An Italian family, the only native sons among so many French, German, English, and Americans, completely subdued into silence, stared in horrified fascination from their circle of heavy armchairs and lace antimacassars, less at the foreigners marching at funeral pace to a ridiculously early dinner than at the surroundings: Knightsbridge Victorian was far removed from Milan Modern.

Camden came over to them. "All we need are the documents. Eleanor—have you your Embassy identity card? Good. We'll need it. And your passport, Bill. You do have your passport, don't you?" This moment of anxiety passed as Lammiter nodded.

"A foreigner wouldn't get very far without one," Lammiter said, and then, his hand still in his pocket, he looked quickly at Camden.

"What's wrong?"

Lammiter's face was taut. He kept his voice low. "What if our Mr. E. didn't telephone Whitelaw just because of a car?"

"No?" Camden was smiling a little. Here we go again, he seemed to be saying: another of old Bill's twists and double twists.

"No. That's what we were supposed to think, perhaps, if we were clever little boys who were trying to reason out Whitelaw's arrival in Perugia."

"And what weren't we supposed to think?"

Lammiter pulled out his passport. "Our Mr. E. may be more in need of a good authentic British passport with a name that is known. Whitelaw wouldn't be questioned at any roadblock, would he?"

Quickly, Camden said to Eleanor, "Did you notice any resemblance between those two men?"

"Well—not exactly, but they are something of the same type: well brushed, well shaven, gaunt cheekbones, bony forehead. And, of course, gray hair." She exchanged a little smile with Lammiter, at some private joke.

"Height?"

"Tall. And thin. Both of them."

"That's enough," Camden said dispiritedly. A passport carried height and weight: its photograph often was only half a resemblance. "It's a crazy idea of yours," he told Lammiter, "but I'll telephone Bevilacqua while you get your registration forms all filled up and signed." He turned back into the lobby, toward the porter's desk, where pigeon-holed keys and letters, sedate post cards and newspapers and telephones were to be found. Lammiter and Eleanor crossed over to the other desk, where the assistant manager, a man of thirty-five, neatly tailored, politely mannered, was waiting for them with an enormous ledger spread wide on a polished desk, a pen already dipped in ink, and a welcoming smile for the young lady.

She was pale: perhaps tired with her journey. He rushed round his desk to offer her a chair, while the American filled out the registration forms. "So tedious," he commiserated with her. "But soon it will be over." He made a sign over her shoulder to the policeman—a tourist policeman, but, *grazie a Dio,* in ordinary clothes, no scandal, no publicity—to be more alert. The young lady must be as important as she was beautiful to have been given such an escort. Film stars and cabinet ministers were always guarded like this. Who was she?

Bill Lammiter paused in filling out the registration details. "Eleanor, what date did you arrive in Italy?" He looked up with a smile to cover the embarrassment of his ignorance. And then he saw the strange look frozen on her face (a mixture of puzzled memory and hesitating doubt), and he turned to follow the direction of her eyes. They were fixed on the back of the man, a short and thickset man, fair-haired, wearing a broad-shouldered suit of extremely light gray, who was standing in front of the porter's desk. The man turned to leave—his expansive smile showed a mouthful of irregular teeth with lavish metal trim—and Eleanor's head was bent, her face hidden, as she searched in her bag for a handkerchief.

"Who's that square-shaped character?" Lammiter asked, as the man left the lobby.

"I—I've seen him—somewhere. Recently . . ."

The assistant manager said, "Signore Lammiter, if you would just finish writing . . ."

"*Subito, subito,*" Lammiter said impatiently, and turned back to Eleanor. "He must have been important," he suggested, "or you wouldn't have remembered you ought to remember him."

"That's just the trouble. He wasn't someone important, and yet—" She suddenly looked up at him. "I remember. Tivoli."

"Well—" Camden had returned and was looking at them worriedly. "What's the trouble?"

Quickly, quietly, Lammiter explained.

"You saw him out at Tivoli?" Camden insisted.

Eleanor nodded. "He served dinner. I'd never have paid any attention to him except that I felt he was watching all the time, watching and listening. Remember," she turned to Bill again, "I told you I was being inspected."

"By a servant?" Lammiter was a little incredulous. I was too eager to have her identify that man, he thought: I pushed her memory into being too helpful.

"Could be," Camden said. "That's the way they work. It's often the Soviet Embassy servant who—"

"I know, I know. Never look at the Ambassador, look at his chauffeur."

"The registration—" It was the assistant manager again.

"Shortly. But first—who was the man who just went out? A hotel guest?"

"No." The assistant manager was nervous. Could this be trouble, just after he had been congratulating himself on the peace of the evening? "I think he was leaving a message."

Camden said, "Let's go and find out." They moved in a close group to the porter's desk.

"I'm afraid—" the assistant manager began.

Camden said to the porter, a capable-looking Etruscan watching them as unemotionally as one of his ancestors from his funeral couch deep down in the underground tombs, "The *signore* who was just talking to you—did he leave a message?"

The porter nodded, and his cold blue eyes measured them in turn. "A message and a package." His English was excellent.

"Could you tell us—"

"I am sorry," the assistant manager said most unhappily, "it is impossible to tell anyone what messages are left. You understand, such things are private matters."

"Wait here," Camden told Lammiter. "I'll go and fetch someone who can be told." He almost ran out of the hotel's entrance.

Lammiter said to the porter, "For whom were the message and the package delivered?"

"For Professor Stark."

"English?"

"He is," the assistant manager inserted, "the famous archaeologist from the University of London. He arrived yesterday for the summer school for foreigners. You have heard of him? He is an expert on Etruscan tombs. He is spending the week here."

"Oh . . ." Lammiter's voice drifted. The moment of excitement drained out of him. He smiled for Eleanor. It was possible that Tivoli and its ill-omened dinner party had become a little confused in her mind: too much had happened since, too many emotions had been stirred, too many tensions and fears. "Let's sit down and wait for Bunny," he said, trying to lead her back to the chair, and failing.

"I didn't make a mistake," she told him, shaking her head. She was close to tears.

The porter—it was, of course, his normal routine, but Lammiter thought the man picked up the telephone very briskly—was now asking for room 67. "Professor Stark?" the porter asked. "Your taxi is waiting outside. And a package has been delivered for you. Shall we hold it here for you at the desk? Very good." And then to the assistant manager, "Professor Stark will collect the package on his way to the taxi." The porter's eyes, intelligent, sympathetic for all their coldness, swept over Eleanor's unhappy face as much to say, "There now, it wasn't very much to worry about, was it?" Then he scribbled a note on a pink slip and pushed it into pigeonhole 67 on the wall behind him.

Lammiter had automatically looked at pigeonhole No. 67. There was no package in it, only the pink slip, which possibly meant that a package too large for the pigeonhole was waiting to be collected. A passport, he thought, could surely have fitted into an envelope and be sitting in the pigeonhole right now. A passport?—He suddenly felt how ludicrous his suspicions had become. He had been trying to solve a puzzle simply by imagining himself the man Evans. It was the sure way to work the plot of a play, knowing his characters, being each of them in turn, letting the events form their decisions and their decisions shape events. But in real life, here in this hotel lobby, between his imagination and his belief in

Eleanor, he had almost created an Evans whose NKVD guard had murdered Whitelaw to obtain a passport to safety. Not that Evans's friends wouldn't hesitate at eliminating anything that stood in the way of their purpose, but still . . . Our apologies to the learned Professor Stark, he said to himself as he took Eleanor's arm and insisted on steering her back to the large armchair at the entrance to the sitting room.

"The registration forms—" the assistant manager reminded him in a relieved voice.

"In a minute." He looked at the quiet man, an Italian, who had left his post beside a potted palm to come forward to Eleanor. "Who is this?"

The assistant manager was rattled enough to say, "He is guarding the *signorina.* One of our tourist police. Very discreet, very capable."

"You can vouch for him? I mean, you know him?"

"But of course I know him. We went to school—"

"Then tell him to guard the *signorina* well." To Eleanor he said, "I'll be back in a moment. I just want to have one look at this taxi." He turned back to the lobby again.

The tourist policeman looked down at Eleanor, and then at the assistant manager. "There is some difficulty?" he asked.

"No," said the assistant manager and "Yes," said Eleanor, almost in unison. I'm so tired, she thought, I could scream. Instead, a few isolated tears forced their way to the surface.

"Ah," the policeman said, and looked protective. The assistant manager was visibly upset and apologetic. At least, Eleanor thought wearily, I could be in a country where men thought women were idiots and tears were ludicrous, but I am in Italy, where all women are beautiful and tears are a manifestation of charm. She gave them a little smile of thanks, and turned her eyes toward the door. Where was Bill? She waited, counting each second. There he was now, trying—as soon as he saw she was watching him—to look more cheerful. What was troubling him so much? Both he and Bunny Camden seemed to be sharing the same worry. And I never noticed anything, she thought; for the last half hour I've been in a kind of daze. I'm too tired, perhaps, just too tired. . . .

"The taxi was only a taxi," Bill told her. "No high-powered car." He sounded both relieved and disappointed. She looked at him, trying to follow his meaning, and failing. "Let's sign these registration forms, pick up the keys, and get upstairs." Gently, he helped her rise from the chair.

"This way—" The assistant manager was smiling now, and in his relief he became informative. "If you need a high-powered car, we could arrange to have that for you tomorrow. Usually, our guests only need the small Fiat to take them to the station."

"Station?" Then Lammiter added casually, "Professor Stark is leaving? Has he changed his mind about the summer school?" He smiled, turning his question into a little joke.

"No, no!" The assistant manager was very earnest. "He is simply going to meet his old friend, Dr. Benvenuto Corredi, who arrives tonight from Rome. Dr. Corredi is our Etruscan expert. He is quite famous. You have heard of him in America, no doubt?"

Lammiter thought, I wish that were the only kind of doubt that kept buzzing round my head like a mosquito. Then he had the unpleasant feeling that perhaps he had let an idea become an obsession. That was the kind of thing that happened when you were exhausted: your judgment warped.

"We have numbers of eminent scholars with us this week end," the assistant manager went on. "A great honor, a very great honor indeed." Scholars were peaceful men: no loud parties, no doubtful women. Virtue and culture combined. That compensated, almost, for their lack of spending power.

As Lammiter signed his name, he said, "I didn't realize Perugia had a station. You hide it well."

"We have always congratulated ourselves that we kept the railway where it belongs—down in the valley. A station is *not* a historical monument."

"Give it fifty more years," Lammiter predicted, and crossed over to the porter's desk for the keys. Forget everything, he told himself, except Eleanor: just get her upstairs and into bed—she's on the point of collapse. Behind him, he heard her being forgiven for the little contretemps she had initiated.

"Now," the assistant manager was saying to her with a playful smile, "you are sure all the statements in your registration card are true? It is a serious matter—" he laughed to make it quite clear that he was joking, and he looked at the policeman who was waiting beside her "—most serious, if you sign your name to statements that are not true. Eh, Giono?" But Giono, like Queen Victoria, was not amused. It *was* a most serious matter. He inclined his head as if he hadn't quite heard and upheld the dignity of the law. The joke dropped at his feet and crashed into silence.

Eleanor signed her name, and turned to look in Bill's direction. What was the delay? A boy was waiting, keys in hand, ready to conduct them both to their rooms. "Luggage?" the porter asked firmly. And Bill was saying that their luggage was outside, in a friend's car. Eleanor's heart sank. Bill's suitcase—that was all the luggage. More complications, more regulations; would she never reach that bedroom upstairs? She closed her eyes wearily; she would let Bill handle the problem of one suitcase between two people who had registered separately. Then she heard Bill say thankfully, "Bunny! Come and straighten this out, will you?" She opened her eyes. Camden had just entered, along with two neatly dressed, grave-faced Italians.

Behind Bill, one of the hotel guests was dropping his key on the porter's desk. He was a tall man, thin, with gray hair, dressed in a tweed jacket and unpressed flannel trousers. "Have you the package that was left for me?" he asked, annoyed with the porter's lack of attention.

"I'm sorry," the porter apologized. He had been watching the two grave-faced Italians with some apprehension: he knew a plain-clothes policeman when he saw one. And here were two. In *this* hotel? "I thought you would want me to keep it until you came back. It is only a magazine."

"I'll take it with me to read while I wait, thank you. One never knows how late the train may be, does one?" Professor Stark took the large, quarto-size envelope, and turned toward the door, unhurried and calm.

This, Eleanor thought, this is a dream. This, she almost cried out, cannot be real. But the man's voice took her back to Tivoli, to the garden beyond the shrubbery. . . . It was the same voice, cold, acid, superior. From here she could only see the back of his head—gray hair, yes, but now covered by the old felt hat he had pulled comfortably over his brow. This, she wanted to scream, is a nightmare—for there are Bill and Bunny Camden, talking together, turning back to the desk. And there is the man, passing behind them on his way to the door. No one knows, she thought, except me, and my feet won't move and my voice has gone. . . .

Then, suddenly, strength came back to her legs. She ran toward the door. You must be sure, she kept telling herself; you must see him as he faced you at Tivoli.

"Eleanor!" Bill cried, and started toward the doorway to intercept her.

At its threshold, she checked her mad flight and swung round to face the man who called himself Professor Stark. For a moment, their eyes met. For a moment, he halted. "Excuse me," he said coldly, trying to pass her. But Bill had reached her, had taken her arm. Together, they stood blocking the doorway.

Then strength returned to her voice, too. "Mr. Evans," she said. "How do you do, Mr. Evans. . . ."

The assistant manager surveyed the quiet lobby as he was about to go off duty at ten o'clock. "There was a little trouble here tonight," he told the night receptionist, who had just arrived, and then he fell silent: partly because the police (all kinds of policemen in plain clothes; *mamma mia,* had his hotel ever seen such a disaster as this?) had warned him against all discussion, partly because so many things had happened that he did not even know how to explain half of them, partly because it was superior wisdom to let the manager decide what should be announced.

"Oh?" said the night receptionist gloomily. Fortunately, he was rarely interested in anything except the Tombola. He had lost again today.

"Ah well," the assistant manager said, "good night." At least, he had been saved from the impulse to talk too much. But he wondered, as he left the silent lobby, its lights already half subdued, whether any other assistant managers had ever been faced with the discovery that a guest was a liar (everything that man had entered in his registration form was false), a cheat (he was no more a professor than his name was Stark), a receiver of stolen property (the envelope had contained someone else's passport). And had a guest *ever* been arrested right in the middle of the lobby?

Giono had done that. Of course, he had been helped by the two detectives who accompanied Mr. Camden. Two detectives—Thoughts failed the assistant manager for a full minute. Anyway, Giono would get his promotion. Lucky Giono . . . But perhaps, thought the assistant manager, I may be promoted, too. After all, everything was handled so quietly, so simply that none of the other hotel guests, not even these impossible Milanese in the adjoining room, working up an enormous appetite for dinner, had noticed anything particularly wrong. Yes, he thought, all things considered, we were lucky. For there had been worse trouble tonight outside of the hotel.

The stranger who had left the stolen passport for Professor Stark had been found in a car waiting at the station, down in the valley. So Professor Stark—no, the real name was Evans—so Evans must have planned to get out of his taxi and step into this car and drive away. . . .

Then there was the man, poor soul, who owned the stolen passport, an Englishman, they said. He had been found at the foot of the precipice near the church of San Angelo. These foreigners were so stupid, so incredibly stupid: whatever made them walk near the precipices, by themselves in fading light?

As he left the hotel, the assistant manager glanced up at the windows behind which most of his guests, thank God, were already safely in bed. Why, he asked himself angrily, why did that man Evans choose my hotel? Why couldn't he have found some miserable lodgings in one of the dark side streets? The American, Camden, had answered that question by saying that Evans chose the hotel for the simple reason that no one, *no one,* would ever suspect such effrontery, such temerity. And no one had, Signore Camden had said: Evans had not been discovered by suspicion; he had been discovered by the moment of accident, the moment of luck. Perhaps, the assistant manager thought as he walked through the soft night air of the little park to reach his motor bicycle, perhaps it is better if I do not try to understand too much about such things.

He halted and looked back at the hotel again. Now he could see the balconies of the Americans' rooms. (He had given them the best view he could provide, west and south, over the broad valley below, toward the further hills. It was a gesture of thanks on his part to the American girl, who had kept her voice so quiet. He could imagine his Maria facing such a man: all the guests would have been brought running from the dining room.) There was someone standing on the nearer balcony. That one belonged to the girl's room, but it was Signore Lammiter who was standing up there, facing this way, looking south. Ah well, the assistant manager thought, at least the trouble is over. And there will not even be any stories about it in the newspapers. The detectives had assured him of that.

He moved quickly away, to home and supper and Maria, who would count the minutes he was late. Out of sight of the hotel, he paused to light a cigarette, loosen his collar and tie, take off his carefully pressed jacket and fold it neatly over his arm. He unchained his Vespa, swung a leg over its seat, started the engine (it was splendidly unmuffled) and roared into the night. He was Colonel Eduardo Ricci, jet-propelled, breaking the sound barrier.

Bill Lammiter, standing on the balcony, watched the stars come out. Far beneath him—for this hotel wall seemed to rise out of one of Perugia's encircling precipices—came the roar of a Vespa as it joined the noisy stream of cars and motor bicycles sweeping down the steep twisting hill to the plain. But tonight, strangely enough, his nerves were better, or perhaps they were exhausted into numbness: loud belches from watered-down gas, unmuffled roars no longer irritated him. Noise was those people's innocent pleasure: they were alive and enjoying it. He wished them well. He wished everyone well. He had never felt more kindly to his fellow men, to the innocent and naïve and uncomplicated who had simple ambitions and honest loyalties.

He lit a cigarette and looked southward again. The bright lights of the little houses flanking Perugia's hill gave way to the mystery of sleeping countryside. Against the night sky, the far hills were black shadows. That's the way I traveled last night, he thought; a long, long way. Is it only two nights ago since I stood on another balcony, and wondered what lay north from Rome?

He heard a small movement from the room behind him. Quickly he stubbed out his cigarette, and left the balcony. Eleanor was still asleep. She had turned on her side, a light blanket over her legs had slithered to the floor. He picked it up, replacing it carefully, and stood watching her for a few minutes. Then he went back to the balcony again. Some people wanted to make speeches whenever they stood on a balcony. All he wanted to do was to give thanks. He gripped its iron railing. He felt strangely emotional, and then—as he overcame that unexpected and unusual onslaught—strangely at peace. A balcony was a very thanksgiving place.

"Bill," he heard her cry—a small, half-smothered cry of fear and bewilderment, "Bill—are you there?"

"Yes," he said, as he turned back into the room, "yes, I'm here."

The Double Image

To the men who don't get medals

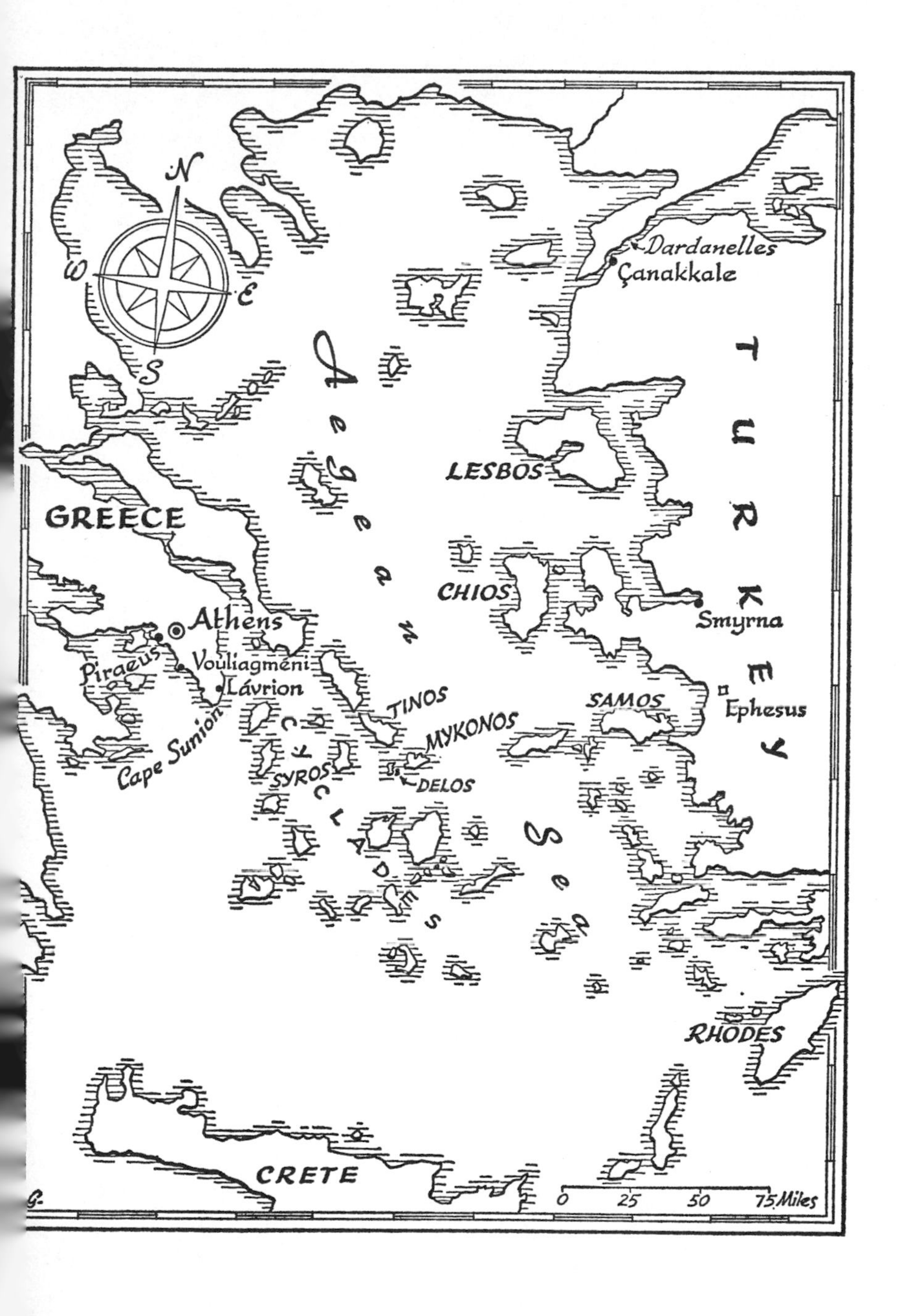
N
E
S
W
GREECE
Athens
Piraeus
Vouliagmeni
Lávrion
Cape Sunion
Aegean Sea
Cyclades
SYROS
TINOS
MYKONOS
DELOS
LESBOS
CHIOS
SAMOS
Dardanelles
Çanakkale
TURKEY
Smyrna
Ephesus
RHODES
CRETE
0
25
50
75 Miles

1

April in Paris, and a sprinkle of rain, a sudden whip of cool breeze, a graying sky to end the bright promise of the evening. John Craig decided that his saunter along the Boulevard Saint-Germain might come to a quick end any moment now, and began looking in earnest for a place of retreat.

He stretched his spine, bringing his height up to six feet, to let him look over the heads of the crowd and search for the café he wanted. His face, rugged in its features, was normally pleasant in expression, as if he were trying to soften the starker effect of a strong jaw and firm mouth. His eyes, under well-marked brows, were gray and alert; his neatly cut hair was dark and thick. He carried himself well, shoulders straight, waistline taut. He had the easy stride of an athlete; and yet, here again, he underplayed the effect by avoiding any flamboyance or overconfidence in his movements. An amiable young man, strangers thought when they met him, rather quiet on the whole. Later, they might change that opinion: he underplayed his real interests, too, as if he thought intellectual display was just another form of boasting, unnecessary if you were any good, embarrassing if you weren't. At this moment, the expression on his face was one of minor irritation. Damned fool, he told himself, to leave his raincoat back at the hotel.

The cafés were numerous along this stretch of the boulevard, some big and brassy, others dim and dreary, most of them with rows of little outside tables nudging the traffic on the broad sidewalk into a narrow stream. People hurried, either because of the time of day (half past five, a home to reach, friends to meet) or because of the threat of a soaking. Only one man, walking slowly toward Craig, seemed totally purposeless. He came to a halt, oblivious of the people behind, of their jostling and open annoyance as they maneuvered around him. Craig, his own path blocked by the bottleneck, drew aside to the curb and let three pretty girls regain their flouncing formation, then a stout woman pass with a bulging shopping bag and a bouquet of celery, then an old muttering man, then two young bearded men who had seized the chance to squeeze by, then—hey, enough of that! Craig stopped being polite and pushed on, glancing reprovingly at the daydreamer who had started it all. Dreamer? No. The man's face was pale, worried, frightened. His fine dark eyes, deep set, stared unseeingly at Craig. And at that instant, Craig recognized the high broad brow, the long narrowing face, the prominent nose and vanishing hairline. "Why," he said in complete astonishment, "it's Professor Sussman—" and broke off, embarrassed. Sussman, at the sound of his name, at the friendly voice, had left his own world of dark thought. His eyes stopped staring blindly; now they were alive again, but puzzled, half-recognition dawning.

Craig wished he had just walked on and left the eminent Professor of Art and Archaeology formulating some new idea about Etruscan tombs right on a busy Paris street. "I took one of your courses at Columbia," he said awkwardly, "just the year before you left for Berkeley." He made a quick grab for Sussman's arm as the man's small thin body was shouldered aside, almost off the sidewalk.

Sussman was smiling, the old warmth back in his eyes. "I remember, I remember. Carr, isn't it?"

"Craig. John Craig."

Sussman's quick, rushing voice said impatiently, "Carr or Craig, I am still sorry I did not convince you to become an archaeologist. You had the proper questioning mind. Modern history, weren't you? See, I do remember!" His hand was tight, his voice suddenly intense.

Craig's embarrassment deepened. There was too much emotion here for his taste. He tried, politely, to disengage his hand from Sussman's grip. A strange city, taken at its most blaring and bustling hour, might bewilder an elderly scholar, but surely not to this point of despair. "There's the second rain warning. I think I'd better—"

"Have a drink with me. You have time?" Again there was that pleading urgency in Sussman's voice.

Craig nodded. He is the drowning man and I am the life belt, he thought. "If you don't mind retracing your steps, we might just manage to reach the Deux Magots before the rain really sets in. Actually, I was heading there when I—"

Professor Sussman looked back along the boulevard, shook his head. "Too busy, too noisy. I know of another place."

You do? wondered Craig. So you aren't lost in Paris? But he said nothing, found he was retracing *his* steps with Professor Sussman's arm guiding his elbow.

"Around the corner," Sussman directed. "I used to come here when I lived in Paris. That was in the days of my exile. Just before the war. In fact, it was the favorite café of the young intellectuals in the thirties." He stopped in surprise, perhaps even in dismay, as they saw a narrow faded awning stretched over two miserable rows of small zinc tables. The tables were empty except for one couple, a young bearded man and a girl in a belted coat, sitting in gloomy silence. "Oh, well," said Professor Sussman philosophically, "everything changes, nothing stays the same. Shall we sit outside, until the rain drives us in?"

That shouldn't be long, Craig thought wryly: the narrow awning over the sidewalk of this dingy little side street wouldn't give much protection. Sussman, anyway, seemed improved in spirits; he was almost back to normal, a little lost in thought, but with no more blank fear staring nakedly out of his face. He had chosen a chair that let him watch the boulevard some fifty feet away, which left Craig with a view of the narrow street curving down toward some thin bare trees faintly touched with green. Its buildings were old and grimy with city air, too unimportant to be scrubbed and polished like the grand monuments of the New Paris. Across the street was a small night club which might be interesting six hours from now, a dingy printing shop, a battered-looking school resting from its labors. But there was also a clear view of the girl who sat five tables away, and even if she was sad and her lips drooping and her large eyes only aware of the knucklehead opposite her—what else could you call a man who'd make a girl like that look so unhappy and, judging by the angry tilt of his jaw, meant to keep her that way?—she was still a very pleasant view indeed.

Craig settled back in his chair, ordered Scotch, was surprised to hear Professor Sussman echo that. (Strange how you could attend a year of a man's lectures, admire his books, stand in awe of his international reputation as a scholar, be amused by his mannerisms, be delighted by his praise and stimulated by his ideas, and still not know one real thing about his personal tastes or his private life.) Craig lit a cigarette, listened to the soft fall of rain on the awning above him, studied the view. She was talking, now, in a voice too low to be identified. Was she French? English? There was no doubt about her companion: he had just raised his voice sharply, "For Christ's sake—" The rest of the sentence was lost as he dropped his voice again.

Craig shook his head, half-smiled, looked at Professor Sussman for an acid comment. But the professor had been watching his own view —the corner of the boulevard, less busy now with people although the cars and buses still charged along its broad length like a herd of elephants stampeding from a forest fire. Strain had come back into Sussman's face, but he was in control of his emotions. "No, don't look round," he warned quickly, as Craig shifted his chair a little to let him see the boulevard, too. "He has gone," Sussman said softly. "He didn't see us." He was speaking almost to himself.

"Are you being followed?" Craig was incredulous enough to be blunt.

"I don't know. Perhaps. It could be likely."

"But why—"

"No matter now. He didn't see us. Let's talk about something more civilized. What are you doing in Paris? Are you working here, or visiting?"

"I'm on my way to the Mediterranean—Italy and Greece. Perhaps to Turkey, if the money holds out. I'd like to see Troy."

"So! Perhaps I converted you a little?" Sussman was pleased. "Let me see—it is five years since you were coming to my lectures—the First World War, that was your field. Or have I forgotten?"

No, the professor was completely right. But he can't be interested in me, Craig thought; he is really only trying to forget something else. All right, let's take it from there. This may not be the way I planned to spend my first evening in Paris, but it seems I'm stuck with it, and I might as well make the most of it. What would Sussman think of my idea for a book?

Sussman was remembering hard. "Yes, that was it! Blockade as a weapon of war. Did you finish your thesis on that?"

Craig nodded. He smiled at himself a little. "Never could find a more appealing title."

"We leave that to the historical novelists. And now you are traveling, and you will write a book?"

"If all goes well." He felt pleased, flattered. Old Sussman really did remember him and some of his little ambitions.

"On more blockades? No, no—I am not laughing. It is an important subject. Anything that can help to decide the outcome of any war is something to be treated most seriously." Sussman was speaking rapidly, with real interest, his own problem seemingly forgotten.

"I'm thinking not so much about the endings of war, now, as its beginnings. I've been doing some work on trade routes as motives for war."

"Beginning with the Trojan War?" Sussman was even smiling broadly. "So you did believe some of my theories—"

"Couldn't forget them," Craig admitted with a grin. He hadn't accepted all of them, but Sussman had certainly opened the doors of history wide.

"Then ancient historians have some use, even to young economists? And where will you end your book? Trade routes and colonies and coaling stations have had their eras. Of course, you might say that today the new control points for the extension of power are newspapers, radio, televis— Something wrong?"

"Nothing." Craig hoped his voice was nonchalant enough. Better, he decided quickly, to appear inattentive and stupid than have Sussman turn his head to look down the little street. "Just watching the rain, and wondering if it will clear before I have to leave." Just watching the rain and the narrow curve of street, and the man who had come walking slowly into view, then stopped, looking at the café, and stepped back into a doorway. "If I can't get a taxi over to the Tuileries, is there any short cut I could take? You know Paris well, don't you? This little street—where does it lead?" His suspicion was idiotic, he told himself, but he waited anxiously for the answer to his apparently innocent question.

"Back to the Boulevard Saint-Germain. It wanders around like so many little Paris streets." Sussman shook his head, looking at Craig's flannel suit. "Americans always think Europe in spring means sunshine and warm evenings." He himself was wearing heavy tweeds under his raincoat, even rubbers over his shoes.

"How long did you live in Paris?" The man in the doorway was lighting a cigarette. And what was abnormal about that, or even the fact that he waited in a doorway on a rain-soaked street? Craig tried to concentrate on his drink, to ignore the fact that the man could have been the same one who had worried Sussman. Idiotic, he told himself again.

"I left Germany in 1934. I went to Rome, then Athens. In 1936, I came here. I taught, and wrote my first articles, and married a French girl, and had two children. And then, in 1940—" Sussman threw up his hands. "Friends sheltered my wife and children, got them false names, false papers, saved them. There wasn't much that could be done to disguise me." He tapped his nose, smiling, but watching Craig closely. "I almost reached the Swiss border. I ended in Auschwitz. And that is why, my friend, I am in Europe. To bear witness. I have been in Frankfurt—"

"The trials?" Good God, no wonder Sussman had looked as if he had been visiting a mortuary. "That must have been a painful experience."

"It had to be done. I am one of the survivors of Auschwitz who could testify against a certain group of Nazis."

"And they pleaded they were only taking orders?" Craig asked in derision.

Sussman nodded. "Their plea was true. That is one of the grim aspects of that trial. Because the man who directed their operations, or at least the man who seemed to be in charge when I saw him at Auschwitz—" He paused, his eyes staring at the table. "That man is buried in the British sector of Berlin. I went there to see that grave." He closed his eyes. "His name was Heinrich Berg."

"Well, that's all over now. You've only to finish your visit to Paris and go back to California. How do you like Berkeley?" The man in the doorway was still there. Waiting for a friend? The rain had almost stopped.

Sussman's instant look of delight, almost child-like in its wonder, transformed his face. "We live on top of a hill. We have a view of the Bay, of the sunset over the Pacific. And in the garden—did you know you can have an orange fruit and blossom both on the same tree at the same time?"

Craig had to smile, too.

"And tulips bloom at the same time as roses!"

"I didn't know you were a gardener." And when did tulips usually bloom anyway?

"Oh, Marie is the gardener. I watch from my study, and give advice. I'm leaving Paris tomorrow. I'll be home by Friday."

Home . . . So the exile had found his refuge.

"I wouldn't have come to Paris, except Marie wanted me to visit her people, bring back a firsthand report. I shall have to invent a lot of nice things about them. I never liked them, and now they are more stupid and selfish than ever. It was fortunate I had the good sense to stay at a hotel. Families!" He shook his head over them. Then he noticed that Craig's interest had been slipping away. He gazed over his shoulder to look, too, at the table where the couple sat. "I don't think their talk has been so friendly as ours," he said. "Shaw was right: youth is much too good to be wasted on the young. And she is quite beauti—" He did not finish the word. His eyes dilated; he turned back to face Craig. From the doorway down the street, the man had stepped out and was walking toward the café.

"Shall we leave? Can I take you back to your hotel?" Craig suggested. The man was still some distance away, walking slowly.

"No. That would be an admission. . . . Besides, I must make sure I was not wrong when I saw him the first time."

"An admission of what?" Craig's concern grew as he noticed the return of fear in Sussman's eyes.

"That I have recognized him. If it is he. Perhaps it isn't." There was more self-encouragement than real hope in that phrase.

Or perhaps Sussman had been thinking too much about Auschwitz. "When did you first see this character?"

"On the Boulevard Saint-Germain. I was buying a paper. Suddenly, he stood beside me. He waited for me to look at him."

"Waited?" This is crazy, thought Craig. He looked at Sussman's long, intent face, uncomfortably, nervously.

"I don't think he saw my panic. I think—I hope I kept my face frozen. I walked away. And then, only a few minutes later, the shock really struck me." Sussman's voice was almost in a whisper now.

"But why?"

"Because I had just seen a dead man walking the streets of Paris."

The slow footsteps stopped. A chair scraped as the man sat down. He took off his hat, shook it free of raindrops, turned down the collar of his black coat. He was fairly tall, well fed and well exercised, somewhere around fifty, with a slight wave in his dark hair touched with gray at the temples and a calm, almost benign look on a remarkably handsome face. He ordered a vermouth cassis in quick and authentic French, and paid no attention at all either to the young couple or to Sussman and Craig. He could have been a lawyer or a diplomat or a business executive or—as things went nowadays—a leader of a large trade union. Successful and tactfully prosperous and, certainly at this moment, no threat to anyone. A man who had been caught in a heavy shower of rain, taken shelter, stopped at the nearest café for a drink just like a dozen other people—for there were others appearing in the little street, now that the rain had ended, and several were even heading toward the awning.

Craig relaxed. Everything was beginning to look more normal, even to the cheerful voices of two women who had just entered the café with two joking escorts, a bitter look following them through the doorway from the unhappy young man who was still arguing with his girl. Next came two more men, talking earnestly. Then a man with fair hair and a tightly belted trench coat, soaking wet. All these entered the café, too. "Things are looking up," Craig said. "I guess we got here too early."

Sussman was recovering. He even made an effort at normal conversation. "I've been thinking about your book," he said as if to excuse his silence. "It is a good subject, rich enough for five books. Perhaps you will do that? Now, I think I could help you a little. I still have friends in Italy and Greece who are working on archaeological sites. Some are historians, others are art experts. Would you like me to give you their names? I shall write them to let them know you may call on them."

"That would be very useful indeed. Thank you—"

"I thank you," Sussman said very softly. "Besides, scholarship is not much different from business or politics—the right connections are always necessary, and usually rewarding." He pulled out several letters from his jacket pocket, selected an envelope, took out a pencil and glasses. "Give me your address in Paris."

"Hotel Saint-Honoré. Rue de Castiglione." Craig watched his name and address being carefully written on the back of a business envelope.

"I shall think of the people who would be most interesting for you to meet," Sussman said as he put letters and pencil and glasses carefully back into their proper places, "and I shall mail you the list tomorrow, before I leave. When do you expect to be in Greece?"

"In a couple of weeks. I had the idea—"

"Excuse me," a voice said in French. "My watch seems to have stopped. I wonder if you could tell me the right time?" The man in the black coat was standing at Sussman's elbow.

It was Sussman, surprisingly, who recovered first. While Craig was still startled by the abrupt interruption, Sussman was taking out a heavy silver watch from an inside pocket. He studied it, looked up at the smiling, polite face looking down at him. "It is exactly twenty-two minutes past six."

"Thank you." The man was on his way, pulling down his hat as he began the short walk toward the boulevard.

"I didn't even notice him leave his table," Craig said, glancing toward it with amazement. In the doorway of the café, he saw the fair-haired man in the wet raincoat watching them. Or perhaps the man had been only gauging the weather, or expecting a friend, for he lit a cigarette as he moved back into the room. Sussman, his eyes on the Boulevard Saint-Germain, was quite silent.

"So it was the wrong man. You didn't know him."

Sussman said slowly, "On the contrary. That was Heinrich Berg."

"You are sure?"

"Quite sure."

"But it's twenty years since you saw him at Auschwitz."

"And thirty years since we were students at Munich University. And fifty-two years since we were born in the little town of Grünwald, not far from Munich. As young boys, we used to play together. Did you notice the twist on his left eyebrow—just a small thin scar, not too noticeable except when he is under tension? He got that from a piece of broken glass when we were climbing over a wall into an orchard. Oh yes, I was quite acceptable then: my father had won a medal in the First World War; my mother had plenty of food on the dinner table for my friends to eat. What astonishes you? That we lived so well? Or that Berg and I are the same age? Or that I remember the expression of his eyes when he was calculating how far he could push me? Clever blue eyes, giving nothing away, hiding his real thoughts, looking so innocent. Yes, he has changed a lot. Once, he was very thin, very blond. But he has not changed in his eyes or in that little twist of the eyebrow where the hair never grew straight again. I know that man. The question is: did *he* learn that I know him?"

"You had me convinced that you didn't."

"Then I have to thank you again."

"For what?"

"For my recovery from shock." Sussman smiled in his relief. "Yes, I handled that quite well, I think. But it was typical. . . . The way he tried to force a recognition."

Craig felt a little uneasy. The incident had seemed insignificant, normal. He hadn't noticed any secret challenge in the stranger's face, or voice. "You are sure that he is Berg?"

"Positive."

"One of those who should be on trial?"

"Most definitely."

Craig, sensing the painful memories that the Frankfurt trials must have aroused in Sussman, said as tactfully as he knew how, "Couldn't it be possible that you might be—"

"Mistaken? No. He knew I was in Paris. He probably followed me from my hotel, chose the moment to confront me at the newspaper kiosk. He wasn't quite sure, he followed me again, and made me face him once more. You saw that part, at least."

"But how could he know you were in Paris or where—"

"It was no secret that I was coming to Paris," Sussman said angrily. "I was interviewed by a reporter in Frankfurt; I spoke of my plans quite naturally. Why not?"

Why not, indeed? "Well," said Craig slowly, uncertainly, "what are you going to do?" There might be a good deal of embarrassment for the professor if he couldn't bolster his assertions with some solid proof. Suspicions could become a neurosis, even a mania. They could destroy his work, all his career.

"I'm going back to my hotel and telephone the Embassy. If it is closed, I shall visit it tomorrow morning on my way to the airport. If I get no action there, I shall send a telegram to Frankfurt."

Craig was startled by all this unexpected efficiency. The old boy (not so old, if he was the same age as Berg—*if* that stranger had been Berg, *if* Berg were still alive and not six feet under Berlin soil) was not only aroused but determined.

"You are thinking it is all water under the bridge? That I am foolish to take action?"

"No, no. Not that, exactly. I just see you back at another trial in Frankfurt." Craig smiled to ease the small tension that had arisen between them.

"It would be worth it," Sussman said grimly. Then he smiled, too, rising to his feet, holding out his hand. "Water under the bridge flows on. There are other bridges, other people standing on them such as you and your generation, my friend. You think I should cling to the wreck of my bridge and not try to warn you of the hidden strength of that water?" He was shaking hands with great warmth. "Thank you again. Your moral support was all I needed, it seems."

"I'll walk part of the way with you. How far is your hotel?"

"Just a short block beyond the boulevard." He listened to the renewed patter of rain on the awning overhead, gestured to the splashing downpour on the street. "You stay here, I see."

"We'd better have another drink," Craig suggested. "It can't last long."

Sussman was buttoning his raincoat, pulling a small blue beret out from his pocket. "I'm prepared for it. Good luck, Craig. Write a fine book. Send me the proofs if you want an outside eye to read them." And he was off, stepping briskly up the street toward the bright boulevard.

As he stood watching Sussman's determined stride, Craig listened impatiently to the argument still coming from the bearded young man and his girl. Was this some new way of making love? Idiots, he thought, and turned away from the darkening street and the chill of the sidewalk to the warmly lit café. Another drink, even of that atrocious Scotch, would be welcome. He stepped quickly aside to avoid a collision with a man in a hurry—the fair-haired man in the damp raincoat, who was too busy looking up the street to notice Craig. Everyone's crazy except me, he thought in amusement, and I'm beginning to have some doubts about myself. For he was standing at the door, watching Sussman reach the boulevard, and behind him the man who had urgently remembered he had a train to catch. But the man's pace was more normal, now, and he started crossing the boulevard ahead of Sussman, who must have seen him and yet did not swerve or change direction. If Sussman paid no attention to this man, why should you? Craig asked himself: relax, fellow, relax.

He had his drink at the bar. The room was small, fairly clean, cosy enough, but sadly needing customers. It was just as well that Sussman hadn't come in here. The talk around the sparsely filled tables was uninspired, and even if French always gave an interesting flavor to the smallest remarks, they were still, when translated, just of the So-I-said-to-him and So-he-said-to-me variety. A large wooden Buddha was fixed up against one wall, smiling down at the tables through his coating of dust. Over the bar, above the bottles and new cheap chrome, hung a large yellowed lithograph of Socrates lifting his cup of hemlock in a farewell toast to his pupils. A little more of this cute irony, Craig thought, and it won't be this sickly tasting ice that makes me gag. He didn't finish his drink, but left in almost as great a hurry as the man in the wet raincoat.

The shower was tapering off. The awning dripped. Only the girl was sitting out there, now. She was sitting very still, hunched together, staring at the blackness of the night. How long has she been alone like this?

Craig hesitated under the awning's edge, glanced at her face. She was crying quite soundlessly. He looked away, but he didn't leave. His excuse could be that he was waiting for the last few splatters of rain to thin into nothing. But the silent crying troubled him. He hesitated, looked again. She seemed aware of nothing. She was trying to rise, stumbling against the corner of a chair. He caught her arm and steadied her. "Are you all right?"

She understood English, for she nodded. She drew her arm away, took a steadying breath, averted her face. The waiter, apologetic but insistent, called as he hurried out to them, "Mademoiselle, mademoiselle!"

Craig looked at the tab on her table, left under a saucer, completely forgotten in her man's Grand Exit. What does Sir Walter Raleigh do, he wondered now: pretend he has noticed nothing and stop embarrassing her? So Craig looked at the street, wet and shining, pulled up the collar of his jacket to protect his shirt from the last drops. She was fumbling with her purse. It dropped and scattered its contents. Sir Walter could at least bend his back and pick up the collection of small objects that bounced and rolled under the chairs. By the time she had paid the waiter, Craig had retrieved a compact, a lipstick, cigarette case and lighter.

"Anything else missing?"

First she shook her head, not looking at him. Then she said, in English, "Oh! My keys!" So he found them, too, after a little search. She was in control of herself by the time he had handed them over. She could face him for a moment, saying, "Thank you," before she stepped out into the street. Quite beautiful, Sussman had said, and the old boy had been right. Smooth black hair, pale fine skin, lips soft in color and in shape, dark eyes perhaps blue or gray. She drew the heavy collar of her sweater more closely around her neck, tightened the belt of her raincoat for warmth, shivered, and then started up toward the boulevard. Below the coat, her legs were slender, excellently shaped; her feet neat in high-heeled and very thin shoes.

He caught up with her near the corner. She hesitated there, as if the bright lights and the rush of traffic and the crowd of people, all purposeful, all knowing where they were going, had completely sapped the last remnants of decision. "If," he said as he stood beside her, "I'm lucky enough to get a cab, can I drop you somewhere?"

"No, thank you."

"If I'm lucky enough to get a cab, will you take it?"

She looked down at her purse, briefly, shook her head.

He remembered the bill she had given the waiter, not even bothering to wait for her change. Only a couple of francs, a few centimes left? As if to force the issue, he saw a taxi and signaled. Miraculously, it stopped.

"I'll give you a lift," he said firmly.

"No, thanks. I'll walk. Thank you." The quiet voice was less icy.

"On those wet streets, in these shoes? You're crazy." He held the door open. The driver looked round impatiently, firing off a staccato burst of short sharp syllables. "Get in," Craig told her. "I won't bite. I won't even bark." She stepped in.

"Now where?" he asked more gently. It would be just his luck if she lived out by the Champs-Elysées, or somewhere high on Montmartre. He would be late for Sue and George: a fine way for young brother to welcome them back from Moscow; a first meeting in almost four years and he wouldn't even have time to change his shirt and brush his hair. He glanced at his watch, but—he hoped—not too noticeably. "Where do I drop you?"

"Rue Bonaparte at the Quai Malaquais."

"That's no detour at all. Right on my way." And somehow, he was sorry about that.

She sat very still, head up, eyes front, her arms tightly folded as if to warm her body. He didn't press her for an exact address. He didn't ask her name, or where she lived in the United States. He kept his promise, and did not talk at all. He had a feeling she was very close to a second bout of tears. When he helped her out of the taxi, he only said, "I'd recommend two aspirin and a hot toddy."

She tried to smile, gave him her hand. "I hope I didn't make you late. I—" She turned away quickly, cutting her good-bye short. He watched her for a brief moment, and then got back into the cab.

Blue eyes. Of that, he was sure now. And a pity, a pity about everything. He hoped she'd have better luck with her next young man. Or perhaps tomorrow night she'd be sitting at another café table taking another emotional beating. Sussman, echoing Shaw, had been right: youth was far too good to be wasted on the young. Of course, Sussman probably included him among the oblivious; thirty-two would seem almost juvenile to Sussman. Good God, he thought suddenly, Sussman was just about my age when he was caught by the Gestapo. A cold finger touched his spine. If I had been he, would I have made as good a showing with my next twenty years? Some generations really got the sharp-toothed end of the stick.

He put these thoughts aside as they crossed the Seine. They were hardly good preparation for a family reunion. So he concentrated on the buildings rising around him, scrubbed back to the color they had been centuries ago. Calculated lights outlined their proportions, discovered their detail, added drama and grace to their solid strength. Trees along the winding river were covering bare arms with bright spring dresses. And above the rooftops, above the glow of a large city, high overhead in a clearing sky, there were the first stars shining into view. Paris in April. This was how it should be.

When a man was thirty minutes late for a party, he might as well take ten more and arrive in a clean shirt—especially when he was armed with a bottle of Piper-Heidsieck, 1955, to launch his apologies. The Farradays were at the Meurice, probably because that was the place most diplomats seemed to drift into. Fortunately, it was only a short distance from Craig's hotel, although a long way in price and style. But as his brother-in-law explained once the exuberant welcome eased off, he was celebrating hard, and Sue deserved a suite no less, and in any case it was only for one night, and even a press attaché who didn't rate this splendor could damned well dip into his own pocket for that length of time.

Craig had never heard so much rush of self-explanation from George. He was a lot thinner and looked more than his thirty-eight years. Sue, on the other hand, had put on some weight, cut her fair hair short and bushed it straight. Not pregnant, John Craig decided, glancing at her thickened hip line; just an excess of solid-silhouette food, and not enough exercise. That accounted also for the loss of color in her face. Her lipstick was much too dark and vivid, a remembrance of days past. It was the shadows under her eyes that really troubled him, along with the worry creases on her brow. But she was still as quick and sensitive as ever, still with her sense of humor. For she was laughing in the old way, pulling down the skirt of her dress from its wrinkles around the waist, guessing his thoughts correctly, saying, "George is the lucky one. When he worries, he loses weight. All I do is eat and eat. And sit brooding. Don't be so alarmed, John. I'll soon get rid of this." She smacked her waistline lightly, threw her arms wide. "I'm free, I'm free, I'm free! Oh, it's wonderful, wonderful. Wonderful to see you, wonderful to talk my head off, wonderful to go where I want when I want, wonderful—" She broke off, almost in tears. "John, you look exactly the same, and thank God for that." She gave him a very intense hug: he had always been her favorite brother.

Craig patted her shoulder, ruffled her hair, and looked over her head at George. "What was that you said about one night?" he asked, trying to get emotions calmed down. "I thought you were planning to be here for a week." And that's why I had planned two weeks in Paris, he thought ruefully: one week for family, one week to recover and see the town on my own.

"We're leaving tomorrow for Washington. Say, you got this champagne iced!"

"Four hours, courtesy of the barman at my hotel." And a nice-sized tip.

"Then it's just right for drinking. Sue, get some glasses—sure, these will do, over on the table."

Craig noticed that a little dining table, places for three, flowers, candles and all, had been set up near the window of the sitting room.

"We thought we'd have supper here, easier for talking, less waste of time," George said. "And we are having a few friends drop in here afterward. Just some men who have been stationed at one time or another in Moscow."

"They belong to the I-Was-There Club," Sue said cheerfully. She had quite recovered. She noticed the expression on her brother's face. "I'm sorry, John; we had to see them tonight—but you know how it is. There really is quite a bond between men who have lived through the same tensions—"

"A bond of curiosity," George said dryly. "They want to hear the latest inside gossip and informed guesses."

"Veterans of Foreign Peace?" Craig suggested.

"They'd never have forgiven us if we had slipped through Paris without seeing them," Sue went on. She had a habit of overexplaining out of sheer politeness.

"That doesn't surprise me," Craig assured her.

"But you look so astonished."

"Well, after all—one night in Paris!" And that really did amaze him. There must be some kind of emergency, he thought. "Why, you only got here a couple of hours ago."

"And we very nearly didn't," Sue burst out.

Craig stared.

George said quickly, "Now let's not exaggerate. We'd have got here eventually." He looked at the astounded Craig, gave a thin smile. "We were almost detained." His hand was steady as he poured the champagne and offered a glass to Craig.

Almost detained? Craig regained his breath. He raised the glass. "Then here's to your safe arrival!" He noticed that both drank to that without one smile. He tried to make a joke of it and lighten the heavy moment. "Don't tell me you were doing some cloak-and-daggering."

"Haven't the training, or the stamina. But that's the label Moscow wanted to pin on me."

"Don't you see," Sue said impatiently, "so many of their embassies are engaged in active espionage that every now and again they have to polish up their public image? So they tarnish ours."

"Now, Sue," Craig said, "we do have spies floating around. You know that."

"And that makes us just as bad as them? So there are no good ones and bad ones, and we are all equally to blame? Oh, John! Leave that kind of talk to the neutralists who want to justify their evasions!"

"Darling," George said quickly, "have some more champagne. We said we wouldn't talk about this, remember?"

"I think we'd better," Sue said determinedly, "or else we'll leave John thinking his sister is filled with prejudices instead of experiences. Dear John, I'm still me—just a lot older, a little wiser and much sadder. Come on, choose a Louis Fifteenth chair, and listen to George before you start judging me." She sat down, tried to relax, act normally. "George was arrested four days ago," she said.

"What?" Craig almost spilled his champagne over the blue-and-gold rug. He sat down, carefully, on a yellow satin sofa, placed his glass safely on a smoked-glass table top, lit a cigarette. "Ready and waiting," he said.

George Farraday chose to pace slowly around the room as he talked. He, too, had abandoned his glass for a cigarette. He tried to keep his voice light, as if to play down his memories. "Oh, it wasn't much. I was released in five hours. And I have to thank Sue for that."

"Wasn't much!" That was Sue, indignant. "Why, they hadn't even notified the Embassy that they had picked you up."

"That couldn't have been very pleasant," Craig said.

"No," Farraday admitted. "I kept thinking of Barghoorn, the Yale professor who got arrested last November. Not one of us knew about it for a couple of weeks. He wasn't guilty of a damned thing, either. That's one thing you've got to remember, John. When we detain a Russian or satellite citizen in the United States, we have an honest case against him. We have real evidence. The Russians invent evidence. So that is a big difference between them and us. Apart from all that good-ones and bad-ones talk, and God knows there are plenty of both groups in every country, there are some very big differences indeed between us and them." He looked at his brother-in-law, waiting.

There was no argument in Craig's eyes, simply curiosity.

"All right," Farraday went on, "then I can tell you what happened." He stopped at the mantelpiece to drain his glass and set it back on the marble top. "I had been having lunch with one of our visiting newsmen. I left him, and got onto a bus to get home. The bus was crowded. I was standing halfway down the aisle. A woman who had followed me onto the bus was standing beside me. Suddenly she whispered, in English, 'Mail this to my daughter in America for me. Please!' And she shoved an envelope into my hand. Now my arm was down by my side, just like this, and as she looked away I opened my hand and let the letter drop on the floor. No one noticed that. It was lost under the feet as I pushed toward the door, anywhere to get away from that letter. Almost at once, the bus stopped. And strange, strange—a black car was waiting just ahead of it. Two men got onto the bus, knew me at once, hustled me off. I made a bit of a protest. No one moved, no one did anything. The men strong-armed me into the car. I was taken to headquarters and charged with receiving secret information from one of my 'agents' who had already confessed. They were annoyed a little—" George paused to savor his understatement —"when they didn't find the envelope in any of my pockets. However, they found it in the bus, and then charged I had got rid of the 'evidence' when I saw I was about to be arrested. It could have been nasty. I kept demanding to get in touch with our Embassy but no one seemed to listen."

"Could they do that?" Craig was horrified.

"As long as the Embassy wasn't asking about me, they weren't worrying about protocol."

"Then how—"

"Sue. Your sister has brains; did you ever appreciate that?" George was smiling broadly, now, ready to tell the more pleasant part of his story. "She had been wary for the last few weeks, expected something to happen to someone at the Embassy—"

"I was only remembering their usual tit-for-tat diplomacy," Sue broke in, disclaiming any sixth sense. "After all, we had recently arrested some spies of theirs, and they would be looking for someone to hold as a future exchange if he hadn't diplomatic immunity—"

"But George *has* that," Craig interrupted.

"Let me finish, my bright young brother! Someone as an exchange if he hadn't diplomatic immunity, *or* someone with diplomatic immunity whom they could boot out of the country in disgrace. Get it now?"

"I get it. And were you booted out?"

Farraday said, "I just scraped through, there: no envelope on me, and the Embassy taking a very firm line. If you act fast enough, you can assert your rights."

"Well, congratulations to the Embassy!"

"The minute Sue told them I must be in trouble, they moved."

Sue? Craig looked at her in amazement. Old scatterbrained, happy-go-lucky, pink-bespectacled Sue?

"As I said, she had been expecting something. She had talked me into promising to telephone her every hour on the hour, no matter where I was. And a damned fool I felt keeping that promise. So, when three o'clock came that afternoon and no phone call, she got in touch with the Embassy, told them where I had lunched and with whom, told them she'd give me until four o'clock and if no call came from me by that time, she was pressing every panic button in sight. However, they took charge. We didn't even make the newspapers, thank God."

"She certainly deserves a suite at the Meurice," Craig conceded. He rose and went over to Sue, and kissed the tip of her nose. "That's for you, bright eyes. You can dine out for six months on that story."

"No, no. I keep my little lips tightly buttoned, even in Washington. There's always some goony bird who'll believe that if George was arrested, there must be a real reason and it's possible he was a spy; dear me, the Russians would never behave that way if he were not, now would they?"

"Let's finish the champagne," George said. "There will be more arriving with dinner any minute now."

"Cue to drop all interest in your story? But as family, George, and I hope not as a goony bird"—Craig shook his head over his sister's slang, as out-of-date as her lipstick—"why did the NKVD choose you? Or is it now the MVD? Or KGV? Never could keep those initials straight."

"Smart to change them," Sue said with one of her old light laughs. "Rouses hope way back in our minds that the secret police changes its nature along with its name. But security remains security, whether it's KGV or any other title. And one thing that's maintained is 'No ideological coexistence.' That's why they didn't like George."

George said briefly, "I just kept trying to persuade them to let a free flow of newspapers and magazines come in from the West. We can buy their newspapers in Times Square; why not our newspapers on sale in Moscow?"

"And they won't allow it?"

George shook his head. "Some of our representatives at that cultural-exchange meeting in Moscow, last January, pressed this point. All they got was a bang on the table and an angry 'There is no ideological coexistence possible!' I've had the same treatment twice. Really ends all conversation. As one of my British chums said, 'If that's final, what price peaceful coexistence?' Which, of course, is the sixty-four-dollar question." He fell silent, frowning. Then he forced a pretty good smile. "Where's that dinner, blast it? I'm hungry. What did you order, Sue?"

"What you used to like: oysters, *langoustes* and some Sancerre nicely chilled, *tournedos* with insertions of *pâté Strasbourg* and a Nuits-Saint-Georges, asparagus with drawn butter, followed by a little Brie just properly flowing, and brandied cherries straight from the flames."

"We'll be eating hamburger for the next three weeks." But his warning was decorated with a large and happy smile.

"We're celebrating," she said firmly, and laughed. She got up, and danced around the room. "Wonderful, wonderful night!" The waiter, whose well-trained knock had been lost in Sue's improvised singing, recovered his well-trained face after the initial shock of entry. Dinner was served.

And now there were only the pleasant things to be discussed: the comic things that had happened in Moscow, the kindly people, the family at home (Father Craig still being sought for advice by the old patients in his little town in Ohio; a country doctor never could retire, it seemed), and all the nephews and nieces scattered around the country (three brand new since Sue had last seen her four other brothers). Then there were John's plans to be talked over. Sue was relieved, tactfully, that her youngest brother had at last made up his mind what he wanted to do with his life. George was still enough of an old newspaperman to have some practical reservations.

"I suppose," he said, "this book will be read by five hundred people instead of five hundred thousand? In a way, that's a pity. You can write, John."

Sue said, "But they will be the most important five hundred."

"I guess so," George conceded. It had been an excellent dinner. "In fact, he'll probably end up in Washington as one of those whiz-bang economic historians telling all the rest of us what to do."

John Craig was amused, shook his head. There were some plans you couldn't formulate, not at this early stage of the game. It took a long time to build up any reputation, any standing in his world. He thought of Professor Sussman. There had been some pretty hideous and violent interruptions in Sussman's life, of course, but he was now becoming a "world authority" in his field. A heady phrase, world authority . . .

"A nice racket, anyway. You can choose where you want to travel," George said amiably. "Before you start writing a book, you say, 'Now let's see: what places do I want to visit?' And then you get hold of a map, and start planning your chapters. Back in my young days, there weren't so many foundations willing to give traveling fellowships for a tour through the Greek Islands. It's the splurge in culture."

"High time there was an explosion in that, too," Sue said. She was watching John. He had always had too many interests, spread his talents too widely, but now he was concentrating. She hoped it wasn't too narrowly. She remembered the slight family panic, some ten years ago, when a talent scout had offered John a test in Hollywood. "And to think you might have become one of those television stars with a long, lean look and a quizzical expression in your quiet gray eyes," she murmured. She studied him with approval. "You haven't altered, did I tell you? How nice that some people don't change much! Reassuring, somehow. But what are you thinking about, John?" It certainly wasn't about college dramatics, or weekend skiing parties, or all the girls he hadn't married.

"Actually, I was thinking of a professor I met today; bumped into him on the Boulevard Saint-Germain." He noticed the solemn polite silence settling on both their faces, and decided to startle them out of their incipient boredom. "He was on his way home to Berkeley from the Frankfurt trials. He had been giving evidence on Auschwitz. A strange mixed-up world, isn't it? He is an archaeologist."

"A cruel mixed-up world," Sue said softly. "That must have been a frightful experience, remembering all those hideous details."

"I'd like to have met him," George said, definitely interested. "A pity we aren't staying longer. What's his name?"

"Sussman. He's leaving tomorrow anyway. You might meet him on the plane. His flight leaves at noon."

"Must be hitchhiking, courtesy of army or air force," George decided. "We leave by regular flight in the evening. What was his impression of the trials? The Germans really do mean business?"

"He didn't talk so much about the trials—"

"Is archaeology as engrossing as all that?" George asked, astounded. "My God, those scholars—"

"He had his worries. He was sure he had just seen one of the important Nazis walking free on the streets of Paris."

"Well, that could be. There are several quiet ones who escaped in the general collapse."

"But this one is dead. At least, he has a grave, tombstone and all, in Berlin."

"Dead, and alive? Are you sure Professor Sussman hadn't been under too much strain?"

Craig didn't answer.

"That can happen, you know. When I got off the plane today I kept looking at every face, wondering who was friend or foe. Nerve ends rubbed just a little bit too raw. That's all."

Sue said, "If your professor really did see a war criminal, he'd better report it. Don't you think?"

"He was going to telephone the Embassy here."

"Poor old Embassy," George said. "It gets every traveling citizen's troubles."

"But where else can a citizen go? When we're up against something unexpected, what can we do? We don't know the proper channels."

George admitted that, with pursed lips and a shrug of his shoulders. "Oh, well, anyway, I think he'd have done better to get in touch with Frankfurt."

"He will do that if necessary."

"He really believes his story?"

"He's completely convinced."

"And you?"

Craig was saved by the ring of a telephone from the embarrassment of openly admitting his doubts. He had believed, and then he had retreated from that belief. All those details about being followed, tracked down from Frankfurt . . . Sussman had only been guessing; how could he have known? Yes, it had been the details that had stopped Craig believing. And yet, and yet . . . Why else would he have mentioned Sussman at all to George and Sue if he didn't deep down, somewhere inside his mind, believe part of the story?

George said from the telephone, "They are on their way. Let's get rid of that table, Sue. And where's the coffee? Perhaps we should order brandy, too."

"Scotch," Sue corrected. "They don't sip. They drink. Who's arriving first?"

"Bob and Ed. Val is on their heels, they say."

Sue, amid the flurry of waiters and table removal, of coffee tray brought in, of orders for extra ice and soda, briefed her brother. Bob Bradley was now with NATO; he had been with the State Department, for a short time; stationed in Moscow when they first arrived there. Ed Wilshot was a newsman, who also had been in Moscow then. Val Sutherland was another reporter, who had taken Wilshot's place after he had been asked to leave, and was now in transit to another post. Then there would be Tom O'Malley, an Australian journalist; and Joe Antonini, who had been one of the experts in tracking down all the hidden microphones that had recently been discovered in the U.S. Embassy in Moscow.

It was, thought John Craig, going to be a merry, merry evening for everyone except him. He had that stranger-at-the-reunion feeling even now as Farraday greeted the first arrivals. The Old Boys' Club, most definitely. Sue seemed to know what he was thinking. "You won't be the only one who hasn't been to Moscow," she told him gently. "Frank Rosenfeld is going to drop in. He's a businessman—refrigeration—used to be in charge of his firm's office in Saigon when George was a reporter there. Goodness, that's over ten years ago, when Viet Nam was still Indochina! Then Rosie was moved to the head office in Paris, and George was transferred to the Embassy here, so they got together again. He's not really very bright about the things that matter—"

"Snob," he told her.

"I mean, he's inclined to repeat this morning's editorial as his views on the world situation. But he's very sweet and helpful. About finding you an apartment, or a hotel at short notice. You know. . . ."

"He sounds as if he needed someone to be nice to him in this setup. Me?" He grinned widely, and pushed her off to welcome the rest of her guests. They were all here except the businessman. None of them looked as if they needed any help at all in feeling right at home. They were introduced to him, gave him a warm handshake and an appraising look, friendly enough; made a brief attempt at general remarks; and then grouped together talking their heads off. Once the questions they were firing at George Farraday were answered, or fended off (no mention, Craig noted, of the arrest), and the general talk of Moscow had simmered down, there might be some reasonable conversation.

Craig settled himself near the window, where Sue joined him tactfully. She wasn't much needed either, at this moment. She talked and he watched. It was interesting, in a way, to place character by voice, manner and face. It was dangerous, too, of course: the mildest-mannered man could turn out to be a roaring lion; the bellowing bull could be a braying donkey. And what do they think I am? he wondered with some amusement. A little frog puffed up in his own puddle of scholarship? Someone who was putting his brains and energies, such as they were, into tracking down facts that would never make tomorrow's headlines? And yet, the past was prologue.

The last guest arrived, and the tight group around the fireplace broke their close formation. He wasn't known to any of them, for

George was making careful introductions all around. He was a heavy-set, dark-haired man in a quiet dark gray suit, slightly formal in manner, almost solemn, although—as George made a few jokes—his grave politeness could ease into a beaming smile. They were talking as old friends do; no serious discussion about world-shaking problems there. The others drifted away, once the phrase ". . . sales conferences all week . . ." dropped like a dud bomb into the room's sudden silence. "Frank!" Sue called delightedly, and her sweet and helpful businessman started toward her with hands outstretched. His grip was strong, Craig noticed when his turn came to have his hand pumped. His smile divided his face into two camps: below, was a rounded jaw line, a full underlip, a chin with a marked cleft; above, was a sharp nose, clever brown eyes, a remarkable brow. He'd probably sell a lot of refrigerators, Craig decided. But what the hell do I talk to him about? The question was answered by Rosenfeld (after a warmly expressed welcome to Paris) wandering away toward Bradley and Antonini. Craig repressed a wry smile, caught Sue's worried eyes for a second, then looked around the blue-and-gold sitting room. There were more interesting prospects, tonight, than a slightly strayed scholar.

She went into action. "I'll get you another drink, John."

"No," he said quickly. "I'm all right." But his protest didn't stop her. He knew what would come next, and wished he was a couple of miles away, walking along the Boulevard Saint-Germain to have that drink at a crummy little bar. What was that girl with the blue eyes and smooth dark hair doing now?

Sue was saying, "Don't you men ever get tired standing around talking? It really is more comfortable to sit. We have plenty of chairs. George, help me." So the wide circle was formed, men sitting down around Craig in silence. Now what? he wondered. He thought he might try a question to start them off again; they were looking at him with polite expectancy. What about something wild like When will Stalin become an okay word again? Or, How many agents have the Russians infiltrated into NATO?

But Sue rushed on, most charmingly. "John was telling us about a very odd thing that happened to him today. He met one of his old professors who insisted that he had just seen a Nazi walking the streets of Paris. A supposedly *dead* Nazi—one who should have been on trial at Frankfurt!"

Oh no, thought Craig, not all that story to be told again to all those disbelieving faces!

"Did you get his name?" O'Malley, the tall Australian, asked. He had a thin face, a permanently tanned complexion which contrasted with his thick crown of white hair. He was the oldest man in this room; the others were in their thirties or forties, while he was at least around fifty. His manner was sharp, but his eyes were friendly.

"Berg," Craig said. "Heinrich Berg."

"What was his particular specialty?" Bradley, the representative from NATO, wanted to know in his calm quiet way. "Shoveling gassed corpses into ovens?"

"I have no idea."

"Your friend didn't tell you?" Bradley raised his eyebrows just a little. Everything he did would be just a little; he was much too well mannered to let emotion distort his handsome face. It wasn't just the neatly tailored tweed suit and the casual way it was worn that made Craig think Bradley was probably one of those intelligent civilians who had found a useful niche for their talents in NATO's vast organization. He had a diffident way, almost self-effacing, pleasantly modest, combined with the attentive eye of the natural diplomat. Even his indiscretions would be calculated.

"No, he didn't."

"But he can't go around pointing out someone on the streets of Paris, saying, 'There's a war criminal!' Now, can he?"

"No," Craig agreed with a smile.

Sue rushed in. "John, don't be so resistant. We're all interested. This professor—what's his name?"

"Sussman."

"He was a prisoner in Auschwitz, wasn't he? He had just been testifying at Frankfurt. So he could know what he was talking about, couldn't he?" She looked around the circle of polite faces.

"Perhaps. Perhaps not," O'Malley said slowly. "I covered some of the opening trials at Frankfurt last year. There were a lot of emotions aroused—horror, fear, bitterness, shame. And a lot of wild talk, including accusations."

"And denials," someone said.

"Fewer than you think," O'Malley asserted. "Give them credit for having the trials at all. That's more than the East Germans have done.

My God, when I think of the Nazis *they*'ve got as ministers of culture, agriculture, trade and supply. What about them, Val?"

"You're the expert on the Nazis," Sutherland said agreeably. "You tell me."

"Well, they've got Reichelet, and Merkel, and—" O'Malley stopped, noticing Sue's look of resignation. He turned back to Craig. "Look, Sussman's story is worth listening to. Where can I find him?"

"I don't know that, either. I just met him walking along the boulevard—"

"Accidentally?" Bradley asked. "I mean, you aren't an old friend of his?" Someone, his voice implied, you really know?

"Nothing like that. Haven't seen him since I took one of his classes at Columbia back in 1959. He's a remarkably sane and sensible man. Today, of course, he was upset. He was sure this Heinrich Berg—" He stopped. How could he explain Sussman's fears without making him seem ridiculous to a batch of strangers who had never known him? "Oh, well," he said, "I gave him a drink to cheer him up, and then he left. He's going back to Berkeley tomorrow."

"What does he teach?" This was Rosenfeld's only contribution to the conversation. But Craig was thankful for it.

"Art and archaeology."

That did it. Interest evaporated. Talk began about travel. O'Malley was trying to be sent to Rhodes; Sutherland was on his way to Viet Nam. (Rosenfeld didn't even bat an eyelash, far less talk about his experiences there, Craig noted, and George Farraday simply said, "I bet it isn't much changed since I was in Saigon. Rumor and suspicion and back-parlor plots. Just don't listen to too many Buddhists, Val. And make sure they really *are* Buddhists before you listen.") The morose Ed Wilshot poured himself another drink and mumbled something about taking three weeks off the chain and heading south for some sunshine. Joe Antonini, the hidden-microphone expert, was tight-lipped about his next assignment and turned that question neatly aside by saying to Bradley, "Hey, Bob, let me finish that story I was telling you. The day before I was leaving Moscow, I was hit by a car. Fortunately, I jumped in time. Just a scrape on my leg and a bruise on my shoulder. They took me to the hospital, very efficient, very polite, wanted to make sure there were no serious injuries. But once I was over the first shock, I felt fine. And I started using my head again. So I balked at the hospital door, made my good-byes, and struggled free from their help. It was like one of those old Keystone comedies—everyone gesticulating wildly, no one listening to anyone else. I ran for twenty yards, then turned and yelled, 'See, I'm all right! I just proved it. Thank you and good-bye.' "

"They slipped up there," Bradley said with a laugh.

"In more ways than one. If they wanted to inject truth serum into someone, and find out how many hidden microphones we had put out of commission, then I was the wrong man. I was only a very junior member of our team."

"I thought the number was published," O'Malley said. "Well over a hundred, weren't there? Or was that a careful underestimation?"

Craig was startled by the calm way they were talking about matters that would have roused loud headlines only a few years ago. He was still more startled when the full meaning of O'Malley's remark hit him. Was Soviet interest not so much in the number of microphones discovered in the Embassy's walls and ceilings, but in the few that had been discovered and left in position? Or in any which possibly had not yet been found? The difference between the answers to those two important questions would be vital for the assessment of any information gathered by the Soviet monitors.

"You look shocked," Bradley murmured. "Or is it difficult to swallow our little stories?"

It wasn't shock so much as surprise over Antonini's cool detachment. There he was now, telling of a light bulb discovered in a lady's bedroom that had transmitted everything from a sigh to a rustled nightgown, as if he had forgotten the threat of a forced stay in a Moscow hospital.

"Sue," Bradley went on, "I don't think your brother approves of our talk."

"Your brother," Craig assured her worried face, "hasn't a thought left in his head except that of bed, and sleep. It has been a long day." At least he had concealed his annoyance. Damn Bradley's eyes, did he think historians only studied the soft, sweet side of history? We don't shock so easily, he thought as he smiled all around and began shaking hands.

Bradley said, "Time for me, too. Can I give you a lift? You won't find a taxi at this hour."

"Oh, I'm close by, practically within running distance."

"Where are you staying?"

"The Saint-Honoré."

"I'll get in touch. We could have dinner some evening when I get into town. By the way, would you like me to take any steps about Professor Sussman's problem? I know some people in Frankfurt."

"That might do no harm."

"But not much good?"

Craig shrugged his shoulders. If he were Bradley, he'd take the necessary steps and risk looking foolish if Berg's body was found in Berg's grave. But that was for Bradley to decide.

"The trials always stir up a lot of ghosts from the past," Bradley said. "If I were Sussman, I suppose I'd suffer from delusions, too." So Bradley had decided. And he ought to know about such things, Craig thought as he hid his disappointment and made for the door. Sue and George were there. He found himself promising to come to breakfast next morning—they both had a very full day ahead of them before they left for New York. Breakfast, even with one eye open, was the only hour left for a family farewell.

"And," Sue added to her hug and kiss, "heaven knows when we'll see you again. We may be en route to Burma or Greenland by the time you get back to New York."

So breakfast it would be, promptly at nine. And after that, he thought more cheerfully, I'll be free; free to do what I want to do, to go where I want to go, and all in my own sweet time. Rosenfeld, standing behind him to make his own good-bye, was saying that it had been a wonderful party, a wonderful evening. A nice, simple-minded soul, Craig decided, and possibly a successful businessman, too.

Out in the cool, quiet street, there was only the sound of his footsteps ringing out rather more briskly than he actually felt. His sense of depression wouldn't leave him. He blamed it on the wasted evening. What else did you call a party where the men he had met would soon forget his face, even his name? Sue Farraday's young brother; that would be the fading memory, dimly recalled if he ever saw any of them again.

But he was wrong: in two places far removed from the Meurice, he was under serious discussion in Paris that night. One was a studio, high over a garage; the other, an unused dressing room behind the stage of a smart girl-show.

The garage was halfway down a most respectable street, part of an old building sandwiched between two new apartment houses. Soon the improvers would have their way; the old building would be torn down, replaced with a square block of unimaginative concrete and rows of mass-produced windows for decoration. It would be ten stories high to match its neighbors, and the last remnant of Toulouse-Lautrec in this district would be swept out with the plinth and plaster. Meanwhile, the garage was a useful place to have the car washed, a tire changed, a slow puncture repaired; something quiet and noiseless so as not to offend the status-conscious incomers.

Androuet, its owner, was an obliging fellow. He even sold gasoline by the can, the usual pumps being out of the question, and reserved some of his floor space, stretching far out behind the old building, for a few of his best customers. There they could park their cars overnight, or when they were away for weekends and didn't need them. There was even room for the light pickup truck which belonged to his only customer living in this building—the man who had rented the two old studios on the top floor for his antique furniture business. He was young, but he paid his rent regularly and didn't give any noisy parties to annoy the two old women, or the retired butcher and his wife, who rented the flats below him. Between them and the garage lay the overcrowded rooms of Androuet and his enormous family, and Androuet's only complaint about the top-floor tenant was that he had clients who would too often come blundering through the garage looking for the wooden stairway that led to the floors above. Others knew their way, didn't interrupt his work. And others, again, probably out-of-town dealers, stayed overnight. But without dealers and clients, there would be no regular rent: Androuet's complaints died away completely on the first day of each month.

He was waiting, now, one of the garage doors half open, for one of his customers to park his car. That would be the last tonight; he could close up and get to bed, and his oldest boy could take care of the early-morning business. It was past midnight, he noted, but he waited doggedly for Monsieur Rosenfeld to appear. And if M. Rosenfeld again protested that there was no need to have kept the garage open for him, that he could have left his car out in the street for one night, then Androuet must have a quick answer ready. He studied that problem as he stood at the door and looked down the street toward the well-lighted avenue—brakes were good, battery had been recharged last week, tires checked only yesterday, so what now? But there was M. Rosenfeld's gray Renault, making a left turn into the street. Androuet pushed the door wide, still debating his problem.

M. Rosenfeld wasn't in a talkative mood tonight. He drove the Renault into its own small parking place at the back of the garage, leaving the entrance clear for any other car in the morning. Not that he needed to bother. M. Rosenfeld was usually out first as well as last in. But Androuet admired neatness just as he liked earning some extra cash, so he was friendly and voluble in spite of his tired face and sore feet. "You must be missing the wife and kids, Monsieur Rosenfeld," he said, noting the time again on the big wall clock. Seven minutes past twelve, exact. "When do you expect them back from America?"

"In two or three weeks. Sorry I kept you up. Tomorrow, you'd better leave the door unlocked. I can push it aside myself."

"With all these crooks around nowadays? No, no, Monsieur Rosenfeld." Androuet's thin, earnest lips meant what they said. "We can't take chances like that. Besides, it was better to bring the car in here tonight. I've noticed the indicator for the last couple of days. It's not working properly. I'll get the boy to look it over in the morning. When do you want the car tomorrow?"

"Eight. Eight-thirty." Rosenfeld halted at the big door. "And you might get him to do a complete overhaul on the wiring. Something's wrong with the taillights. Good night, Androuet."

Androuet watched him go. It never ceased to cause him a little wonder, a little resentment, that an American could speak French just as accurately as he did. He forgot all that, however, as he locked the big door, then pulled a little book from his cash drawer and entered carefully under the date of Thursday, 16th April: *Arrived 12:07* A.M. *Unaccompanied.* He put his small record safely back in its locked compartment, switched off the one meager light, climbed the wooden stairs to his wife and twelve children. She would grumble at being disturbed so late, but five hundred new francs were good pay for a little overtime. As for the man who had made the bargain with him, two weeks ago—he was a detective hired by Madame Rosenfeld, to keep an eye on a lonely husband. It was an explanation Androuet easily accepted: his vision of life was always focused between two sheets of a bed.

Rosenfeld entered his apartment, switched on the lights in the living room. He threw aside his hat and raincoat, and walked slowly over to the window. Casually, he closed the long curtains, turned on some music, and settled down to wait for ten minutes. Then he entered his bedroom, switched on its lights, drew its heavy curtains as he unfastened his tie. After that, he moved quickly, turning off lights and music in the living room to show anyone who might be watching the windows that he was now going to bed. He put on a black raincoat, French in style and fabric, slipped his feet into black tight-fitting slippers, and checked his pockets for small flashlight and keys. Entering the bedroom again, he locked that door securely. From a drawer, he drew out a small tape recorder and, as he put it down at the side of his bed, started its play back. Gentle sounds of soporific music filled the rose-pink room. He left the small bed-table lamp glowing, but switched off the bright ceiling lights.

He paused at the bathroom door. Nice picture of a man reading in bed, he hoped. Soon, the music would end, and the sound of a man's deep breathing would be played; and then, as the table lamp on its automatic control blacked out, the sounds would change to a mixed variety of masculine snores. The boys who thought up that tape had a nice sense of humor as well as of timing. He gave a last glance at Milly's bed: yes, he missed her and the kids, all right. Tonight, though, he was glad they were safely out of this, three thousand miles away. He was suffering from an attack of premonitions, and that was something he had learned to take seriously. In his job, you had to develop a kind of built-in radar all your own.

With his hooded flashlight, and his two master keys ready, he began his journey. Quickly he passed through the bathroom, locked its door behind him. Quickly along the carpeted corridor, with the children's empty rooms staring blankly after him. Quickly through the small kitchen, out by its service door, into the back hall with its stone floor and garbage cans. Eight silent paces and he was at the service entrance of another apartment. He had every right to enter it. It was his.

He had leased it under another name, for a bachelor who only wanted a very small *pied-à-terre* in Paris. (The bachelor even made an appearance, now and again, whenever it seemed necessary.) The place was basically furnished and looked as heartless as that sounded. But even if it had no stretch of front windows, or no view of the rear courtyard, its position was good: it lay along the side wall of the apartment house, right up against the four-story building of Androuet's garage. And the chief asset was its bathroom window, standard in size, easily negotiated. It looked out over the flat crest of Androuet's roof.

Rosenfeld locked and bolted the bathroom door, swung open the bathroom window, stepped up on the toilet seat, climbed over the window sill, and was on the stretch of flat roof. A clutter of tipsy chimney pots, poking their ancient heads through the blue slate tiles, protected him from any watcher across the street. Eleven quiet paces toward the back of the building and he had reached the small attic door that had once let chimney sweeps and roof repairers get to work. He had a key for that, too. The inside ladder was short, thank God; that always seemed the worst part of this little journey. He lowered himself carefully.

He was now on the top landing of the old house, blocked off from the staircase by a very solid door so that this small area had become a private hall for the two studio doors. He stood in the darkness, by the ladder's bottom rung, and took out his flashlight again. The door that led into the front studio had an elegant sign in sixteenth-century cursive, no less, YVES DUCLOS, FURNITURE REPAIRS, ANTIQUES BOUGHT AND SOLD, BY APPOINTMENT ONLY. But it was to the other studio, at the back of the building, that Rosenfeld turned. He pressed the button beside the door. There was no sound of ringing. Instead, a small flashing light would now be signaling inside Duclos' living quarters. Duclos must have been waiting for it. The door opened at once. Rosenfeld stepped inside, glancing at his watch. Four and a half minutes, all told, since he had stood in his bedroom. Not bad, he thought, for a man in his forties. And five pounds overweight, too, he added, just to cut down his vanity.

Duclos said, "Don't worry about being late. I knew you were at the Farraday party." He spoke English fluently, without any trace of French accent. He was in his mid-thirties, of medium height and weight, with the dark hair, bright blue eyes and fresh complexion of a true Celt. He had brought some Breton touches into this large room, too, with a tier of heavy box beds blocking the fireplace completely (he distrusted chimneys), faded red linen covering every inch of the giant windows, heavy candlesticks on a long table (he also distrusted electric light bulbs in places where talk might be serious), a couple of carved wooden screens to give some tactful privacy as well as to break up the vast floor space. "How did it go?"

"Always good to see them." Rosenfeld was keeping his voice low as he took off his coat and threw it on the nearest chair. There were two men sitting behind the screen that lay farthest from the window. He could see their shapes through the latticework, but the candlelight wasn't strong enough to let them be identified. He nodded his head in their direction, cocked an eyebrow.

"Got in from Berlin today," Duclos murmured. "I told you this meeting was urgent."

Rosenfeld thought of Androuet. "When did they get here?" he asked, frowning.

"I picked them up this afternoon near Versailles, where I was buying a couple of chairs at an auction. They came here, inside the truck. No one saw them."

"What about Androuet?"

"Is he causing trouble?"

"No, but he's watching my times of arrival and departure. Someone is curious about me. You've had no signs?"

Duclos shook his head. "Androuet didn't see them, anyway. I drew him out of the garage by pretending to notice something interesting on the street, and then wandering out to have a look at it. He followed me like a lamb."

"I hope it was a good excuse, something that will stand up in Androuet's afterthoughts."

"It was a very handsome woman. Don't worry. My guests were out of the truck and upstairs before he stopped thinking of hips. I even got his help to carry the chairs upstairs to the landing."

It was possibly all right, Rosenfeld thought. Duclos had a lot of panache to disguise his essential caution. His chief, Bernard, over at the Sûreté, wouldn't have selected him to work on this special job of co-operation with the Americans if he wasn't one of his most careful, as well as diplomatic, operatives.

"Don't worry," Duclos repeated softly. "I'll watch Androuet from now on. How did they hook him? Women, or money?"

"I don't know if he is hooked yet. Probably just accepting a hefty bribe, and finding reasons to excuse himself."

"That's always the first step in being hooked," Duclos said, and he was right. It was one of the first steps, anyway, Rosenfeld thought, and—his warning about Androuet given and taken—he began walking toward the screen. Duclos caught his arm gently, and asked again, "How did the Farraday party go? I know who was there. Was Antonini questioned?"

Okay, okay, Rosenfeld thought: he co-operates with me and I cooperate with him. That's Bernard's bright idea, and it has been a good one so far. "Only in a general chitchat kind of way. He dodged giving any serious answers."

"Did no one show special interest in him?"

"No approaches that I saw, except normal friendly ones."

"Yet we had information that a Communist agent was going to be at that party tonight."

Rosenfeld halted completely. "Are you serious?"

"Never more serious."

"Any name?"

"No. But there was a photograph of the man. Our agent was bringing it to us yesterday morning. A truck smashed his small car to pieces."

Rosenfeld glanced over at the screen.

"Tell me. Quickly."

"He was following one of their couriers, saw him make a drop in the Bois de Boulogne at eight in the morning. He decided to stay around and see who would pick up the message. That's generally a long wait. So he took a chance, walked past the seat where the courier had sat and found an old pencil stub lying on the ground."

"Did he examine it?"

"Yes, he knew what to do. He pulled out the false lead to check if there was the usual roll of microfilm inside. Instead, there was a thin roll of paper with very small writing."

"What?" This was wrong, this was all wrong. . . .

"It read: *Get invitation for Farraday party tonight. Call us six o'clock further instructions.* He replaced it, sealed it with the lead, dropped it where he had found it. Then he waited almost two hours behind some trees, until a man stopped at the seat, picked up the pencil, and strolled off. He just had time to photograph the man—one shot caught him full face."

"How tall?" The French agent must have made some contact with the Sûreté before he was killed, Rosenfeld guessed, or else Duclos wouldn't know so much.

"Height was difficult to estimate accurately. Around average, perhaps a little over. He stooped, carried himself badly. Clever? Also, he wore a shapeless coat. So his weight and build were impossible to judge at that distance."

"Not six foot three, with white hair, deeply tanned complexion?"

"Nothing like that. Nothing particularly noticeable."

That eliminated Tom O'Malley, the Australian, from the Meurice gathering. "Then he was an American," Rosenfeld said. He sighed.

"Our agent got back to his car, and radiophoned us from there. He decided to bring in the photograph rather than try to follow the American. Ten minutes later, our man was dead."

"What about the camera?" A brutal question, but needed.

"Lifted from his pocket before we got to him."

They knew what they wanted, Rosenfeld thought. They must have seen him use it, probably were watching him ever since he picked up the pencil stub. Time enough, in those two hours, to sound an alert and be ready to act. It was the American they were protecting, not the simple little message. Yet it still baffled him, or, rather, the manner of delivery puzzled him. The Communists used such pencils, but only for some really important message, microfilmed, lengthy, usually filled with items about highly secret matters.

Duclos was saying, "The truck was stolen, of course. The driver and his helper vanished after they lifted the camera. There was a terrific uproar, complete traffic jam, shrieking women, crowds of people. If we hadn't received the radio report, we might have thought they were only two hijackers who panicked after an accident and ran. That is what we were supposed to think, I'm sure. And that's how we gave it out to the press."

Rosenfeld was still thinking about the pencil stub. "It's all wrong—using a valuable drop for a simple message like that. They could have telephoned him quite safely if that was all they had to say. D'you think—is it possible that they had no other way of contacting him that day, no way of instructing him to get an invitation to the Farraday party?"

"Just as we," suggested Duclos, "couldn't reach you before the party began to warn you who might be there?"

"Wednesday was my day off the chain this week," Rosenfeld said lightly. "I didn't expect business to pick up so—" He paused.

"Perhaps it was the American's day off, too?" Duclos asked thoughtfully. "We might begin from there."

Rosenfeld nodded. His lips tightened as he recalled the faces of the men he had met less than three hours ago. His eyes narrowed. He felt, as he always did when he found an American involved in such work, just a little sick.

Duclos probably suffered from French traitors in the same way, for he said tactfully, "Perhaps he didn't go to the party. The action today might have scared them off. His instructions could have been changed on that six o'clock call, you know."

That could be. Sue Farraday had mentioned three guests who had to beg off at the last minute. Poor Sue . . . she had been happy about reaching Paris, getting away from mystery and threat. And a man had died because of her little party, and what more would come of it? Rosenfeld decided he had better find out the names of the three missing guests. His feeling of sickness increased.

A cheerful voice said, "Haven't you chaps finished your local gossip? Hello, Rosie! Come in and join our little séance. We need help with an obstreperous ghost." The Englishman had risen and was standing at one side of the screen. He laughed with real pleasure as he saw the astonishment on Rosenfeld's face. "Rosie!" he said again, coming forward with his light step, his hand outstretched.

"Chris Holland!"

"Three years, isn't it? Well, well . . ."

"Two and a half."

"You've been taking it easy, I see. Putting on a little weight?"

"I can still buckle the same belt around my waist," Rosie protested. "With a struggle." As they shook hands, and kept shaking hands (Duclos was much impressed by this Anglo-American display of real affection), Rosenfeld was studying Holland's face. He was thinner, with a little more gray sprinkled through his neatly cut well-brushed hair. His skin, over the even, pleasant but unremarkable features, was now less tanned. Some lines had been added, too, around the grayish-brown eyes. But he still had that same amused look in them, that same quiet smile. "And how are the savage and licentious soldiery? Made you a colonel, yet?"

"Half-colonel," Holland murmured.

Not bad, not bad at all, thought Rosenfeld: British Intelligence didn't hand out promotions like *petits fours* with the ice cream. It must be some really big piece of news that had brought Holland to Paris, something that concerned the Americans and French as well as the British. And his feeling of urgency was increased as the other visitor from Berlin stepped forward and Holland introduced him, "Here is Partridge. We've been doing a little work together recently." Michael James Partridge, American, thirty-seven; Korea; then counterintelligence training at Fort Holabird in Maryland; became a civilian, moved to Berlin; past five years there spent in putting his education at the Army Intelligence School to very practical use. A good man, on his way up.

"I've heard of you," Rosenfeld said as he shook hands with the American. He looked at the light sandy hair, the gray eyes behind the thin-framed glasses, the lean face with its high brow, the shy smile, the casual clothes that increased the college-teacher look. So here, thought Rosenfeld, is my replacement. Once I get him squared away, show him the files, explain matters pending, instruct him in the local difficulties, this man will take over here when I go back to Washington. He smiled amiably. "Planning to stay long?" he asked casually.

"That depends." Partridge was equally casual. "Chris is going back to Berlin in a few days. We thought it better if we met you here, very quietly. After that Venetian affair—" He didn't end the sentence, just smiled pleasantly and led the way back to the four chairs grouped behind the screen around a small table.

Duclos looked enquiringly at Rosenfeld, who explained, "The last time Chris and I met was in Venice."

"September, 1961," Chris said smoothly. "That was a nice little job of co-operation."

Duclos caught on. "Ah—the plot to assassinate De Gaulle which you uncovered?" He relaxed and asked no more questions.

"And so," continued Chris, "Rosie and I must not even *seem* to meet again. We might alarm some more conspirators, and we don't want to warn them, do we? Really, by this time"—he was looking at Rosie, now—"I thought the cold war might actually have melted." He sighed. "They never give up, do they?"

"Some always keep trying. What is it now?"

"We have quite a story to tell you. Take place, as we say in Berlin." So they all sat down around the table. "This is highly classified information, old boy. Jim, have you got that damned gadget working?"

"It's working," Partridge said. Acquaintances making an effort to seem close to him would call him "Mike." His real friends knew better. Now, he pointed to the small box that lay beside his ash tray. "Present for you," he told Rosie. "Just something our engineers were fooling around with. It scrambles the sound waves within a twenty-foot radius."

"That's going to ease a lot of headaches. Sure it works? Okay, okay . . . And thanks." Rosenfeld was relaxing visibly. But he was still trying to guess what news from Berlin was so important that Holland had decided to bring it himself. "Don't you trust even a coded message any more?" he asked jokingly.

Chris Holland threw him a sharp look. Partridge's eyebrows went up for a split second. "Not at the moment," Chris said very evenly. "Because it happens to be a very special code that starts my story. A Russian code, only used since last November. A real puzzler." He smiled happily. "Fortunately, we had a warning about its importance along with information about its peculiar difficulties."

So, thought Rosie as he translated from Holland's understatement into more exact language, the British have a Soviet code clerk working for them, a defector in place. He knew better than to ask Holland the where or the how of the situation, far less the defector's name. But as he nodded approvingly and murmured "Congratulations," his mind went into high speed. A code as difficult and special as this one must have been would be used for high-priority messages from Moscow Central. And if it had come to Holland's attention, then the messages were being sent to Berlin; that was obvious. Possibly to the Soviet intelligence establishment there, the highly secret Rezidentura, with a senior intelligence agent in charge. "Sounds very high-level, indeed," Rosie said. But how, he wondered, did a Soviet code clerk manage to hear about such a special code? The master spy in charge of the Rezidentura would have memorized it, received all its messages himself. Unless, of course, the code had been so difficult that he had used the code clerk to help him break out the message—a violation of security regulations, certainly, but that had happened before.

Holland had been watching Rosie. The slight frown combined with the inflection in Rosie's voice when he had used the words "high level" were enough for Holland's own quick mind. "Our information was reliable," he said quietly. "So we found out."

"You managed to catch some of those coded messages coming into Berlin? That was a hell of a job. The directors of spy networks get three or four every week, don't they?"

"It was quite a job of work," Holland conceded. He glanced at Partridge. "We had some excellent co-operation, too. But even if it was difficult, it's still easier than catching the master spy with his little receiver. I wish, just once, that I could walk right in at the moment he was listening to Moscow."

Rosenfeld and Duclos both nodded. The director of a network, always a Russian, had several receiving sets in different parts of the foreign city in which he worked; he would even use a car for mobility, so that he couldn't be tracked down to one spot. And, because he had entered that foreign country illegally—on a false passport and with a carefully invented personal history—and then used various names and identities once he had established himself, he was difficult to uncover. Especially when none of the groups he organized ever knew who he was. To them, he was only one of his code names. Not even the leaders of those groups knew him, far less the exemplary citizens they had recruited as "sources" of information. He, and possibly the two other Russians who were his assistants (they had come into the country legally, as diplomats or trade representatives or newsmen for a Russian paper), knew the extent of the network that spread out from him. He alone knew all its members. And just as none knew him, so also none understood the real purpose of all the small bits and pieces of information they were instructed to collect, of the small actions they were called upon to perform. Theirs but to do, and protest their innocence when arrested. Or catch the public's tender emotions with a plea of blackmail or duress. It was, thought Rosenfeld, a sad, sad world.

Holland was saying, "At the very beginning of January, we noticed that this special code was being used in a strange way. It would appear, for one sentence, right in the middle of a message being sent in a quite different code."

"And these messages," Partridge explained quickly, "were on the steady three-a-week basis beamed at Berlin. They varied, naturally. But that one sentence, in its own special code, remained constant."

"A general directive to all areas of Berlin?" Duclos asked, frowning.

"We found it was going out to certain other areas in West Germany, too. So we checked quietly with our friends, and we pooled all our discoveries. But—" Partridge looked at Holland, becoming conscious of his silence—"that's your story. Sorry," he finished lamely. And don't let your excitement carry you away again, he told himself; you keep quiet, junior!

Holland resumed. "The sentence was very simple. It repeated the same warning and the same question, three times a week for three weeks running."

"It said?" Rosenfeld, about to light his cigarette, paused. This had to be really important.

"UTMOST CAUTION: IS THERE ANY TALK OF HEINRICH BERG?"

Rosenfeld took the unlit cigarette out of his mouth, staring at Holland.

Holland said quickly, "Oh no, Rosie, no! Blast you, man! Here I make this bloody journey to Paris, and you know all about Heinrich Berg." He threw up his hands, exchanged a wry smile with Partridge. Duclos was puzzled but gloomy; if Rosie knows, he was thinking, then he hasn't been co-operating fully with us. And I liked him, I really liked and trusted him. He looked reprovingly at Rosie.

Rosenfeld said quietly, "I don't. I only heard his name mentioned tonight at the Meurice party."

"By whom?" Duclos wanted to know. He was relieved, though.

"By a young American, John Craig. He didn't say much. And perhaps that was just as well. He's intelligent, I think—" Rosenfeld was frowning. He put the cigarette back between his lips and lit it. He decided to wait. "Go ahead, Chris. You have the real story. All I have is a small piece of conversation. It can be added later, as an interesting footnote."

Holland nodded, said briskly, "We all went to work to find out who Heinrich Berg was. You can imagine the files we examined, the search through old Nazi documents and newspapers, correspondence, everything. We put a silent team to work." A smile showed in his eyes, touched his lips briefly. "We, too, were using the utmost caution. There was no need to tip our hand and show we were intensely interested in Heinrich Berg. We found out, in short, that he had joined the Nazi party in 1934 after graduating from Munich University. He was a bright lad, took an advanced degree in psychology. He got into the brain-power group of the Nazis, and was attached in a seemingly minor capacity to the German Embassy in Moscow for four years. In 1941, he was back in Berlin, working unobtrusively under Himmler. Then he invented a special job for himself, in 1944, got Himmler's full approval, and—as a remarkably self-effacing officer in the Security Police—he made inspection tours of the concentration camps where political prisoners might be found and he would make a list of names of those whom he considered dangerous to the future of the Reich. That is, men who could be future leaders of anti-Nazi movements or regimes."

"1944 . . ." Rosenfeld said thoughtfully. "He was foreseeing a possible Nazi defeat, then?"

"Now, Rosie," Holland said with amusement, "you're jumping ahead of me and stealing some of Jim's thunder. He did a great deal of work on this. All I'm stating is that Heinrich Berg was removing all possible future opposition. The men he selected were sent to an extermination camp. But some, strangely enough, never arrived there at all. They seemingly managed to escape, and their escape was always expertly concealed, usually listed as 'dead in transit.' That is where Jim discovered something very interesting. But"—he looked at the younger man with a grin—"that's your story, isn't it?"

Partridge said, "The men who escaped turned out to be very much alive. After the war was over, they appeared in their own countries—

mostly Eastern European—where they helped establish Communist governments. That was what they were, Communists. And that was what Berg was really doing in 1944-45: getting rid of the democrats, keeping alive the Communists. Clever fellow?"

"A double agent," Rosenfeld said slowly.

"No. A Communist agent who had thoroughly infiltrated the Nazis. Another Richard Sorge, in fact. I began to get a glimmer of something like that when I puzzled over the lists of the politicals he had marked for extermination. So we began to dig deeply into his early life. We unearthed some secrets. He had become a member of the Communist party in 1931, recruited at Munich University. Spent three summers abroad, ostensibly to study psychology in Vienna, but I think he learned more Pavlov than Freud. He made at least two side trips into Russia—one to Moscow, one to Minsk. Ready to infiltrate by 1934, anyway."

Holland laughed softly. "A clever fellow, that's definite at least. He was registered as dead, April, 1945, and buried in Berlin. So we had a special squad dig up his grave one night and smuggle his coffin out where the experts could examine the remains of Heinrich Berg. The bone structure made the corpse some three inches taller than ever Berg had been. Also, Berg had a couple of molars missing—so his dentist's records said. The corpse had a full set, top and bottom. Careless? No. I'd imagine that in the holocaust raging around him when he was selecting a corpse for his coffin, he hadn't time to examine its teeth or measure it from tip of heel to crown of head. The remnants of an S.D. uniform, correct rank, had been thrown around the body. He was in a bit of a hurry."

"So where do you think he is now?" Rosenfeld asked too innocently.

Holland studied him. Partridge, who didn't know him so well, plunged right ahead. "Well, with that record, it was pretty obvious he slipped into the Russian lines and headed east. But we have uncovered surer proof than that. He had a wife and two children. They stayed behind, in the French zone—she got a job as a cleaning woman in a canteen. Then about three years later, in 1948, she suddenly packed up and left with the children. The French didn't quite like the way her departure was so secret, so well arranged. Cleaning women don't have that kind of influence. So they opened a file on her. It didn't collect much. Just one postcard to her mother from Minsk, saying she would write when her new address was settled, and then nothing for several years until one letter slipped through to the West, asking for warm clothing. The letter came from Yakutsk, in Siberia, and she asked that no German name be used, but gave a new one: Insarov."

"She said nothing about her husband?"

"Nothing. But we did find out that in 1956, among various people returning to Moscow from different parts of Siberia, there was an Igor Insarov, who was once more very much in favor. He has become important, no doubt of that. He is back with Intelligence again. Security, we think. We hear he heads a special unit on psychological control. That fits, all right. Insarov could be Berg."

"You got all that information in three and a half months? See what co-operation can do?" Rosenfeld smiled for Duclos.

"Three and a half months were one hundred and six days and one hundred and six nights," Partridge said wearily. "We knew we were working against time."

"Because," Holland explained, "in February, that special code was used in the same way, again. But this time the message was longer. IF FILES CONTAINING ANY IMPORTANT REFERENCE TO HEINRICH BERG STILL EXIST, REMOVE PERTINENT DATA AND DESTROY. REPORT ON FINDINGS AND ACTION TAKEN, BY REGULAR CHANNELS. Fortunately, we were in a position to make very quick copies of those references, and replace them in time. We didn't even arrest the agents who were suddenly interested in those files. Some of them had been totally unsuspected, but now—although they don't know it—they are helping us. That's quite a nice little bonus."

"So Berg was trying to blot out his identity?" Rosenfeld asked. In that case he could very well risk coming to Paris.

"Someone was. And why? I think the answer is in a report we had from one of our best sources in Moscow. At the beginning of this month, Igor Insarov left Moscow for Prague under the name of a Russian doctor. From Prague, we learned that a Soviet medical official had arrived and left the same day for Zürich, traveling now as an Austrian businessman. And from Zürich—well, we are still evaluating some of the reports that have come from there. One was much too definite, too quick. It came from a man we suspect is the kind of double agent who plays both sides for cash. He reported that the Austrian businessman had left for Rome. But we heard, two days ago, from one of our own men who has infiltrated a Soviet spy network in the Zürich area and works in its passport bureau. He says that the passport for an Austrian businessman had been turned in, and replaced by all the necessary papers for entry and residence in France." He smiled at Duclos. "You'll have your work cut out, I think."

"Very difficult," Duclos agreed worriedly. "If he has taken over the name and history and papers of a real French citizen—possibly of Alsatian origin, to account for any slight accent—then that is hard to trace. And if the French citizen has disappeared or died a long time ago, behind the Iron Curtain? Almost impossible to trace." He paused. "You really believe that Insarov is in France?"

"Frankly, we don't know. We only think he might be. We are checking in Rome, too. But one thing *is* certain. He is on the loose. And he wouldn't have come out so secretly if he wasn't up to something very big."

"What?"

"That's what all of us had better find out."

"And you really believe," Duclos insisted in his practical way, "that Berg and Insarov are the same man?"

"Again, we don't know. We only deduce from the facts we found that he could very well be."

"Did Berg's wife follow him to Moscow from Yakutsk?"

"No. She has vanished, and the two daughters as well. Insarov—as far as anyone knows—is unmarried."

"What about photographs?"

"None of Insarov. He is a most self-effacing and careful man. Perhaps his exile in Siberia taught him to be that. Of Heinrich Berg, we have two photographs: one when he attended a Nürnberg rally with Hitler, Goebbels and Himmler—but that black Security Police cap made Himmler's boys all look the same grim-faced type; the other was taken when he joined the Nazi party in 1934."

Rosenfeld waited. The silence continued. "Finished?" he asked Holland and Partridge. They nodded. "Then here is my footnote to your obstreperous ghost." And now it was making some real sense, Rosenfeld thought. "Heinrich Berg was seen yesterday in Paris. He was identified by a Professor Sussman, who had been a prisoner in Auschwitz. Sussman could have made a mistake, of course, but I'll check. I'll do that through John Craig. I think I can arrange to meet him tactfully. I'll start finding out what Sussman is doing here. If he is a French citizen, I'll get Yves to help me. You two"—he looked at Holland and Partridge, who were still staring at him in amazement—"can concentrate on Insarov. We'll concentrate on Berg."

"Fair enough," Holland agreed. "And we'll keep in close touch. Usual channels. I'll be leaving in a couple of days. Too bad we can't have a nice, relaxed dinner together."

"That's what comes from being a notorious character. You shouldn't have arrested a Communist agent right in the middle of the Piazza San Marco." Rosenfeld turned to Partridge. "You'll be around for some time?" I bet you will, he thought.

"He's unsullied, simon-pure," Holland said with a bright smile. "He has been just as self-effacing as Colonel Insarov."

"Then let's keep him that way. Don't contact me at my office." And then, as Partridge looked surprised—no doubt he had already worked out a nice role as a visiting salesman—Rosenfeld added, "Just a small premonition. Let's play this very carefully. Which reminds me—"

"Don't worry," Yves Duclos said, "I'll get them safely into the van by five-thirty, before young Androuet comes down into the garage at six and opens the doors."

Rosenfeld glanced at his watch, and got to his feet. "You have four hours for sleep. I'd better climb home. I've just invited myself to breakfast at the Meurice. I have to see the Farradays anyway." And now he looked grim and tired. "We think we may have an American on our hands who is devoted to Russian ideals," he said very quietly.

Holland looked at him with real sympathy. "Any clue?" So that was the reason that Rosie's usual jokes had been missing tonight.

Rosenfeld shook his head. "Well, good luck with everything."

Christopher Holland shook hands warmly. "Here's to our next meeting, Rosie." And let's hope it is one of those happy post-mortems, with all friends intact.

Perhaps Rosie had the same thoughts. He nodded, turned away without speaking. To Partridge, he said as he buttoned up his black raincoat, "I'll phone you tomorrow at noon. Where?"

Partridge gave him a number. He was certainly efficient, well prepared.

"Thanks, Jim," Rosenfeld said, and won a startled smile. Could he have been scared of me? Rosenfeld wondered in amazement. He looked almost natural, there. Scared of *me?* My God, I must be getting old.

Yves came out into the hall with him, turned on the light as he climbed toward the door in the roof. He paused as he unlocked it, signaled for the light to switch off before he opened the little panel of solid wood and stepped out on the roof. Now for all that locking, unlocking. Some months ago, when he had organized this route of arrival and departure, he had been inclined to laugh at his overcaution. Tonight, he blessed it. He blessed the soft clouds, too, that had covered the sky again with broken patterns of silvered fluff, casting vague shadows over the rooftops. The street was asleep, its windows shaded and quiet, strange contrast with the glow from the far-off boulevards, with the sound of traffic from the avenue.

It had all been a very cosy setup, a neat arrangement, he thought as he reached his own bedroom. Too bad he would have to stop visiting the studio for a while. He cursed Androuet's quick eye for a fast franc; and then laughed softly. Perhaps he ought to be thanking Androuet and his garage; they had supplied the first small warning signal. And for that, he was always grateful.

The smart girl-show had opened two months ago near the Rue d'Amsterdam. It was part of the new wave in small night clubs, rolling west and away from the clichés of Montmartre toward the unlikely surroundings of the Gare Saint-Lazare. Here, on a narrow, workaday street climbing the cobblestoned hill above the busy station, the club had taken over a cheap bar along with a neighboring cheese-and-sausage shop, converted them into one building, and used their rabbit-warren back premises for dressing rooms and offices.

Its patrons were a mixture of the restless rich and the pseudo avant-garde. It captured their trade with a room, subdued in décor and lighting, where the dance floor was twelve feet square and the music was both insistent and sour. Scotch was the correct drink at the crowded tables. Conversation was in French, Italian and English, with many references to the past season at Arosa, or the imminent trek to Sardinia and Elba (Saint-Moritz and Ischia were now definitely out), or *the* film festival (Venice was out, too), or the New York galleries, or the Dalmatian beaches. And occasionally, with correct unconcern, eyes would turn to watch the small stage, backed by black velvet, where the amusing revival of a real girl-show was now in progress. The girls were pale pink and white, no sun tan allowed, buttocks and bosoms thinned out into a streamlined contour so that the addition of surrealist items on the long lank bodies would have richest effect. Abruptly, unexpectedly, there would be a highly inventive interruption to their fertility-cult vibrations and rhythmical spasms: a moment of intellectual excitement combined with mental shock; an occurrence with content; a serious comment on the absurdity of life. It was to this interruption-moment-occurrence-comment that the club owed its newest name: Le Happening.

In the small entrance lobby, near the coatroom, a young woman was waiting for an escort who was ungallant enough to be late. (By arrangement. The number of late minutes was part of the recognition signal.) She was expensively dressed in simple black, a small green satin bag clutched in white-gloved hand, no jewels except for earrings. And they were very much in the atmosphere of the club. The right ear wore a ruby, the left ear an emerald, both encircled with pearls. Her face, pretty and cool, was deeply tanned; her eye shadow was green, her lips the palest pink. She slid her small watch back into the handbag. It was almost time: fifteen minutes after midnight. Quickly, she looked at the man who had just entered. Raincoat belted but *not* buttoned, thick-framed glasses, newspaper under one arm, new pigskin gloves, and a book with a red-and-white jacket. Yes, this must be he. Thank heavens he was presentable. He was eying her, too, looking at the red and green earrings, at her green bag and long white gloves.

"Sorry I'm late," he said, glancing at his watch. "Four minutes."

"Seven minutes, darling."

They both relaxed, smiling. "Then I'm *very* sorry." He jammed book and gloves into his coat pocket and handed it over, his face averted, to the elderly woman who looked after the coatroom. The folded newspaper, its Greek type clearly shown in the part of headline visible, was replaced under his left arm. "The train was late," he said. He was so sure that this was Erica that he had started leading her toward the curtained door even as she murmured correctly, "Next time, you must take a plane." Foolish but necessary, he supposed, like his car parked on the Rue Liége, where he had waited a full ten minutes for this entrance.

A table had been reserved for them near the door, but tucked protectingly against a wall. A "happening" was in progress, all eyes intent on the stage. Their entry, expertly guided by one of the owners of the place, who had glanced at the newspaper and the bright little green bag, then welcomed them with a nod, was unnoticed. They sat down in the semidarkness with some feeling of safety. Even when the muted blue illumination colored the room again, it was dim enough to keep their table nicely shadowed. Drinks came quietly. They didn't need to make a pretense of animated conversation. For no one seemed to be paying them the slightest attention. They looked, this well-dressed man and this elegant young woman, like many of the other couples who were watching the silvered square of dance floor with tolerant amusement.

So this was Alex, she thought, as he lit her cigarette. And can he be nervous, when he talks so little? Or is he trying to gauge me? After all, it is the first time we have made contact. But it won't be the last, so let's hope he loses some of this stiff manner. Would he have preferred to work with a man? Instinctively, she opened her bag, drew out her mirror, pretended to add some lipstick to her perfectly colored lips. She was reassured by what she saw. In the soft light, her face seemed luminous, as pretty as she remembered it: pale gold hair was perfect, slightly negligent, yet carefully in place; triangle of green shadow on each eyelid made the eyes look truly green. He was studying her profile. Now that was much better. She hoped he liked tiptilted noses and long lashes. One might as well enjoy one's work.

But, when he spoke, his voice was businesslike. His elbow was on the table, his chin resting in his cupped hand so that his lips were shielded. "Keep your bag open," he told her. "I have to leave soon."

"What a pity," she said. And I'm just a necessary nuisance, she thought angrily. She smiled brightly.

"That's better," he told her, glancing at his watch. "You were much too solemn."

She had to laugh. Alex was only anxious about his own private timetable. Where did he live? What did he do for a living? She would never know. He was an American, that was all she could guess; his French was fluent enough, but the accent was unmistakable. He knew how to dress, have his hair cut, hold himself. He was good-looking but in an inconspicuous way. For that, she was grateful. If one had to make a public appearance, perhaps run into friends, there would be no need to explain her companion. He would fit in perfectly. Even his age—the late thirties—was right; he would have money to spend. "When?" she asked, as the lights dimmed for another girl-show and the dancers started pushing their way through the tables to their own chairs. "Now?"

He nodded, relieved that he did not have to prompt her. He dropped his arm, straightened his sleeve, pulled his cuff into place. "Now."

Her lipstick fell from her fingers. He bent to pick it up, left it lying under the black shadow of the table, brought up his closed fist as if he held it safely retrieved. She showed only a fleeting astonishment as her hand felt the strange shape of the cuff link he had pressed into it. Quietly, she dropped it into the small zipper compartment in her bag, replaced her mirror, snapped everything secure. So, she thought, he had come prepared to meet Bruno, he was annoyed that he hadn't a lipstick to replace mine; idiot, did he imagine that I'd exclaim and open my hand and have a look at his cuff link? Does he think that a woman has to be plain, dowdy and intense before she can have brains? He was one of those very security-minded people, who liked things to go as planned. He would be frowning now, instead of smiling with relief, if he could know her guesses: he had got a message this evening, probably around six, when she had been given her emergency instructions, telling him to cancel Bruno and substitute her. She almost said, "Don't worry about how I get home. Someone is waiting for me in a car nearby. I'll see he gets your cuff link." But she resisted the impulse. She would only set him on edge again, at all this extra caution which spelled danger. Sources of information never liked the feeling of danger; couriers, like herself, were accustomed to it. She, for one, enjoyed it.

"Like to leave?" she asked, her hand lying lightly over her green bag. From now until she delivered the cuff link, that bag was part of her body. "I'll go first. That looks better. Shall I make my exit directly, or head for the ladies' room?"

"Directly." He wanted her out of this place before his visit backstage. That was another operation altogether, and it was its combination with this meeting with Erica that really had annoyed him. Much too dangerous, he felt, even if some crisis had caused it. But instructions were instructions, and you did not make a protest over a telephone.

"Then," she said with a pretty pout, "we are having a small quarrel. And I take my leave with a woman's last word." She tucked the bag under her arm, holding it securely with her hand. At least, he thought, she intends to keep it safe, but what if someone in French Counterintelligence arrested her on her way to deliver the gold cuff link? What if her purse was searched? Such an unlikely object would be at once examined; it wouldn't take long for trained men to find the way the heavy design lifted off, like a cap, and exposed the small flat square of microfilm. Blown up, it would make four full pages of concise information. He had found out all the answers to the questions in last week's pencil stub—a dangerous, worrying job. And now a woman, still in her twenties, enjoying every minute of her little play-acting, was holding his possible death warrant in her green satin purse. She was rising, saying clearly, "Thank you for a miserable evening. And don't call me tomorrow. Or the next day, either." She walked out as the lights dimmed completely, and all eyes turned to watch the stage.

He gave her five minutes to get her wrap and leave. Even if no one had been listening at all, she still would have played her exit lines perfectly. She was as exhibitionist as the girl-show. It wasn't difficult for him to look depressed as he paid and left the room, the folded newspaper in his hand. He had his handkerchief out as he entered the lobby, up at his face as if he were battling an attack of sneezing.

He collected his coat, for he wouldn't leave by the front entrance, and, as a seeming afterthought, made his way to the men's lavatory. With the show in progress, there was no one standing around the narrow corridors, and it was a simple matter to leave one and enter another that led behind the stage. A couple of men, watching the girls from the wings, paid him no attention—special friends dropped in to the dressing rooms frequently. A man fussed over lights, an elderly dresser argued quietly with the make-up artist, who practiced his technique too obviously on himself. He disliked this place the more he visited it; what had seemed intelligently amusing at first did not stand up to repetition, and was now preciously erotic and pretentiously boring. The nonsense world, he reflected, the supply and demand of decadence. It was comic, though, that the secret backers of this night club should find it so easy to stimulate the neurotic among their enemies and make them still more incompetent to deal with the real world.

The last corridor reached along the back of the night club. It contained four unused dressing rooms, two doors marked "Supplies, electrical," and the back entrance from the old delivery yard. It was poorly lit, its walls were peeling and cracked in the best Italian movie style, and it smelled faintly of cheese and sausage. A fair-haired young man in worn overalls and soiled undershirt was sitting on a crate near the entrance. He rose as he saw Alex, came toward him, his eyes checking the folded Greek newspaper, and knocked five times in rapid succession on a dressing-room door. It opened. A man's voice said quietly, "Come in!" It wasn't the voice that Alex had been expecting. Yet it held a familiar note as "Come in!" was repeated. Makarov—could it be Makarov?

And it was Konstantin Makarov who was sitting behind the door, keeping out of sight from the corridor. He closed the door swiftly, pointed to the chair that faced the looking glass on one wall, took the remaining chair (it was in the corner of the small empty room, beyond the stretch of light from the bulb that hung high over Alex's head), and lit another long cigarette. There were two stubs at his feet. Other stubs lay in the dust near Alex's feet. Whoever had been sitting here had retreated to the next dressing room through the connecting door that lay between Makarov's chair and the mirror.

Makarov glanced at his watch. "Well timed. Congratulations. You have been doing well in everything."

This was Makarov's old manner—cool, but pleasant, and completely professional. There was no reference to the fact that he had not seen Alex since he had recruited him in Moscow. Was he now stationed in Paris, perhaps as assistant to the director of the network which controlled Alex? The director, himself, might very well be the man watching this room from next door. The mirror was certainly a one-way arrangement, letting Alex be seen as clearly as through a window, while he stared blankly at its chipped frame and then let his eyes wander back to Makarov. He had no objection to being watched and studied. A director must have a definite curiosity about those who worked for him. He would be a Russian, of course, and, like Makarov, a highly trained intelligence agent. This meeting, thought Alex with rising excitement and pleasure, must be important if Makarov and his superior are taking a personal interest in it. But I can't even show that I'm honored he trusts me this much. He is merely the man I met in Moscow at many literary parties, under a name which was probably just as invented as the names he used in Washington and at the United Nations. Does he remember the night we got drunk together and he talked about his visits to America?

Makarov's cold gray eyes held a small smile, as if this meeting was a nice little joke to be shared between old friends. He was a short man, solid, square-faced, snub-nosed. Thinning red hair receded from a massive brow. He spoke English fluently, with a husky rasp in his voice—he always seemed to be on the point of clearing his throat—and his manner was that of a dependable and pleasant-tempered man. Suddenly, the joke was gone from his eyes. Briskly he said, "You will know me as Peter."

Alex nodded. That was definite: the past was wiped out; Makarov was dead, Peter lived.

"First," said Peter, "you made the delivery to Erica?"

"Yes."

"What did you think of her?"

"A pretty girl," Alex said coldly.

"And a clever one. Don't underestimate her, my friend. You did not like her? In one way, that has a big advantage. You will be able to keep your mind on business when you work with her. Oh, yes, you may have to see more of Erica. Bruno is out."

Alex asked, in quick alarm, "Something happened?"

"He was followed into the Bois, yesterday morning. The drop was intercepted—no, no, don't look so worried. We took quick action. Regrettable, of course. We would prefer not to be forced to defend ourselves in that way. But results justified our decision. Bruno has been saved from his carelessness and is now away from Paris, and you have been saved from discovery. You were in very great danger, my friend."

Alex was still too close to panic. He could say nothing.

"You will understand now why we advised you, on your six o'clock call to us, not to ask Antonini any direct questions at Farraday's party. We had hoped that by getting an invitation, you could talk closely with Antonini. But because of the interception of our orders to you, we decided that no suspicion must be aroused. We were forced to rely on what you could pick up in general conversation. Which leads me to our second point of business: what did Antonini say about the discovery of the microphones in the American Embassy in Moscow? Give me an exact report while the words are still fresh in your mind."

Alex told him, quickly, concisely.

"Was that all?" Peter hid his disappointment well.

"He said he was the wrong man to be asked any questions."

"Meaning that there was someone else who could tell more? Or was that just a feint, to save himself from further trouble, to pretend he is of less importance than he actually is?" The questions were rhetorical, for Peter was lost in thought. "Did the man Rosenfeld talk privately with Antonini? With any of the others? No?" Again there was only the hint of disappointment. "Well, then, anything else?"

"The usual stories about Moscow," Alex said. "And one story about a dead Nazi who may be alive." He smiled, allowing himself some credit for having waited, as a matter of tact and protocol, for the end of Peter's important questions before he presented his one small triumph. "The name was Heinrich Berg."

Peter said nothing. He did not move a muscle. He was watching and waiting.

Alex explained quickly, "I noted that name, late in February, when I was asked to check any files where Berg might be mentioned. I found nothing. I reported that back to headquarters, in March."

"Who was speaking of Berg?"

"Mrs. Farraday brought the subject up. Her brother, John Craig, had heard the story from one of his professors whom he met in Paris yesterday."

"And Craig believed this story?"

"No. But the professor—his name is Sussman—I think he should be questioned. If he did see Berg, then—"

"Berg is of no interest to us."

Isn't he? He certainly was last February. Alex remembered the chances he had taken to try to find out about Berg. And the extreme care to protect himself. Utmost caution, his instructions had read. Utmost danger of self-revelation, they should have been labeled.

"What kind of man is this John Craig?"

"Quiet, disinterested; perhaps stupid outside of his own subject; the type of intellectual who doesn't have much interest in what is going on. Politically immature. The talk, which was frank, seemed to shock him. Perhaps he did not want to believe what he heard. In that case, he might be useful to us. Physically, he is personable. Pleasant, easy manners. An economic historian, I believe."

"Why is he in Paris?"

"He is only passing through on his way to the Greek Islands—

Crete and Rhodes, places like that. So his sister told me. He is writing a book about trade routes. She told me that, too."

"Did he himself see this Heinrich Berg?"

Alex hid his surprise at the reintroduction of Berg, who was of no interest to anyone. "No. Craig only gave Sussman a drink to cheer him up—I'm quoting him—and then Sussman left. Craig was embarrassed at the story being spread around by his sister—he didn't believe it himself, as far as I could judge." And I don't make many mistakes, as Peter must well know if he has read any of my reports, and I think he has. "Craig is staying at the Saint-Honoré. Do you want me to see him soon?"

"No. Forget Berg. Forget this fantastic story. We have something more important to occupy your mind." Peter paused for emphasis. "Can you arrange for yourself to be assigned to Smyrna?"

"No."

"But there is a very large American installation near there! With their wives and children, the Americans have established—"

"I know. It is quite a civilian colony. Even so, I would need a very good excuse even to visit it. People would want to know why I was going to that part of Turkey."

"You have friends stationed there?"

You know I have, Alex thought; you've read my dossier. You've got all my possible sources of information around the world. He nodded.

"When do you go on vacation?"

"Actually, I've been planning to go to Spain for a few weeks."

"Have you talked about Spain?"

"Not yet . . ." Alex was embarrassed. "It's purely a private affair, not a business trip this time." It was a delicate reference to the fact that he hadn't had a real holiday in three years.

"Then you will cancel your idea of Spain. And you will spend your little holiday in visiting your friends around Smyrna. That is a good excuse, isn't it? Ephesus is near by, and many excursions you'll enjoy. You can also hire a boat in Smyrna and sail around some of the Greek Islands—even as far as the island of Mykonos. Yes, that would be a pleasant way to come back to Paris. On Mykonos, you could hand your information to Erica, herself. You wouldn't have to worry about meeting a stranger—no more tiresome identifications necessary.

Your work would be done, you would know you had delivered it into safe hands, you could forget about it and even have a few days of real vacation."

Alex had to smile at Peter's almost authentic enthusiasm. Smyrna should be pleasant at this time of year; the Greek Islands would be heaven. Too bad that he had business as well as pleasure on this vacation. Still, he could have been sent to Lille or Marseilles; that kind of "vacation" had happened before.

"And now you must leave," Peter said, rising to his feet, smiling regretfully. "You will hear from me. Then you will know the details of your assignment. Meanwhile, there will be no more visits to the Bois de Boulogne, no more meetings here. Not for you, my friend." He shook hands very formally. "We value you, comrade."

Alex flushed with pleasure. "I'll do my best."

"And that will be excellent."

Alex left quickly, ignoring the young man who let him out by the delivery entrance. I've been promoted, he was thinking: it is something big, and I've been picked for the job. He didn't even mind the devious journey back to his parked car, or the careful maneuverings before he could hit the right road. Even the dull drive back to his rooms, after this long day in Paris, didn't worry him tonight.

The man who now called himself Peter opened the connecting door between the dressing rooms. "What did you think of him?"

Insarov rose from his chair, switched off the translucent mirror. His usually calm face was frowning. He smoothed his dark hair, touched with gray at the temples, as he always did when he was making up his mind about a rather evasive problem. "Impression, favorable. He is intelligent. I could almost feel him making guesses about you, about me sitting in this room. But that is why you recruited him in the first place." Insarov's bright blue eyes looked very directly at Peter. "You say he is right for this job. I accept that." And I hold you responsible, the steady gaze said.

"He has never failed us yet. When something is impossible, he says so frankly. His judgment is good. He is cautious. He is punctual. He does not do this for the money. He is dedicated, completely."

"Yes, yes, I know that. Pity, though, that we haven't something to hold him—if necessary. Weren't there photographs?"

"We have some, taken at a Moscow party," Peter said nervously. "But we have never needed to use them." And we never will, he hoped. His own contributions to that party still made him sweat cold. He repressed a shiver, and smiled.

"Then good." Insarov stopped smoothing his hair; the frown vanished. "We needed an American with the right connections for this job. We have one." He pulled on his coat. "Make sure the corridor is safe."

Peter moved to the door, then, with his hand on the key, paused to ask, "That other American—Craig—I think we should keep an eye on him."

"Just normal surveillance until you are satisfied." Insarov did not seem too worried by that problem.

"But does Craig really disbelieve Sussman's story?" Peter asked, frowning. "Berg is important to us, isn't he?"

Insarov's handsome face was bland. "I really don't know," he said, and shrugged. "Now I'll say good night. Or is it good morning? I shall be in touch," he promised. As he signed to Peter to open the door, he smiled at his understatement. In the next ten days, he would keep Peter very busy indeed. But had he been noncommittal enough about Berg? Uninterested enough in Craig so as not to stress any personal connection with Berg? As for Craig—he would be watched, his background checked, more thoroughly than Peter was planning to do. Fate took care of those who take care of themselves, and Insarov was one who took most excellent care. Even his wildest risks were calculated. Methodical Peter would shudder at them, but that was why he would always stay second in command. Without risk, there was no victory. "Good night, Comrade Makarov," he murmured as he stepped into the silent corridor.

Peter stared after him. So he knows about that, too? Peter's rising terror needed all of the ten minutes of waiting, while Insarov walked through the dark streets, before it was repressed. He might think he had mastered it, but it would never leave him. It would ensure complete obedience, a nicely conditioned devotion. He would be praised for his loyalty to Insarov, and he would be flattered by such a public image, even come to believe it himself and maintain it wholeheartedly.

A strenuous day, thought Insarov as he entered the waiting car. He said nothing to the driver, who knew his business. In silence, they headed south toward the Seine, crossed it, and turned east to the labyrinth of the Left Bank. A successful day, he thought, as they reached the Saint-Germain district once more. At the intersection of two small, scarcely lighted streets, he got out, waited in a doorway for the car to speed away, and then strolled back to his rented apartment.

John Craig had slept too well, but that left him with such a feeling of energy and general cheerfulness that he had no qualms over the small margin he had given himself to reach the Meurice. He shaved, showered and dressed in twelve minutes. He was putting the last things into his pockets, searching for a small map of Paris to make sure he wandered in the right directions once he had said good-bye to Sue and George, congratulating himself on having made it as he picked up his key, when the telephone rang. There were two gentlemen downstairs who wanted to see him most urgently. "Sorry," he told the desk clerk, it would have to be some other time; he was leaving for breakfast. "They are already on their way, monsieur," the clerk said and hung up. Like hell they are, Craig thought, and locked his door.

They came out of the elevator just as he was starting along the corridor. They were mild-looking men, who appraised him with sad thoughtful eyes. "I'm sorry," he said, "I have an engagement at nine o'clock."

"We shall not detain you long, Monsieur Craig," the younger one said in good English. He gestured to his friend. "This is Detective Galland of the *Sixième Arrondissement*—the Sixth District, you would say? I am Tillier, also of that *arrondissement*. Perhaps we should go to the shelter of your room? Just a few questions, only formalities. We visited your hotel last evening, about ten o'clock, but we were told you were out for the evening." Carrying a bottle of champagne, he remembered. Who said the police of Paris were tactless? "We thought you might not be returning until very, very late. And so we must catch you at this hour. Because we should like to have your opinion of Professor Sussman."

Craig, who hadn't budged an inch toward his door, looked at them sharply, then moved back toward his room. So Sussman went to the police, he thought; he must really be desperate. "Come in," he said. "I know that Professor Sussman's problem isn't actually in your line, but I hope you'll help him and perhaps even get in touch with the right people who could—"

"Monsieur Craig," Tillier said gently, "the professor is dead."

Craig stared at Tillier, then at Galland. "What?"

"A suicide. Yesterday evening."

Craig sat down on his bed. Galland talked in quick French to Tillier, who nodded. The American's shock was very real, he decided. No need to waste too much time here. "If you could just explain this?" He pointed to the envelope that Galland drew out of his pocket. It was the one on which Sussman had written down Craig's address.

"He was going to send me some names of his friends in Rome and Athens—I'll be traveling in that direction soon—and I gave him that address when we had a drink together yesterday."

"When and where?"

Craig answered the questions briefly. Tillier was making notes.

"Was he depressed when you saw him?"

"At first, yes."

"He stopped being depressed?"

"Not exactly. He was—" Grim, determined, shocked; but also confident, hopeful, looking forward to his return to California and his family. "Suicide?" asked Craig angrily. "I don't believe it. He wasn't the type—"

"But he was depressed. You said so. And that verifies what his wife's relatives in Paris have told us. He was very morose, gloomy."

"He disliked them. No wonder he felt morose when he had to visit them."

Tillier nodded, but hesitated in entering that in his notebook. "Have you met them? Are they disagreeable?"

"Never seen them. Look, I'm not a close friend of Sussman. I only met him by accident yesterday. But I do know—at least I feel sure—that he didn't commit—"

"It would have been impossible for his death to be caused by an accident, Monsieur Craig."

"How did he die?"

The two policemen exchanged glances. "He fell from his window," Tillier said. "And it was of such a nature, I assure you, that he could not have overbalanced and fallen. There is a railing, as high as my waist, outside of his window, and I am taller than he was. And much heavier. No, even if he stumbled at his window, he would not have fallen over into the courtyard of his hotel. Have you visited him there? Then perhaps you remember—"

"I don't even know the name of his hotel."

"You did not expect to meet him again?"

Craig shook his head. "He was leaving today for America."

The telephone rang. "That's my breakfast engagement," Craig said, and picked up the telephone before Galland could reach it. It was Sue. He wasn't forgetting; no, far from it, he reassured her: it was just that two policemen were here asking him about Sussman, yes, Sussman; they said he had committed suicide and he was telling them that he couldn't believe it. Then he stopped as he heard some mumbling, an exclamation, at the other end of the line. Galland was looking at him with tight lips. "Sue . . . Sue—are you there?" he asked.

A man's voice took over. "Look, Craig, I want to make sure that these two guys are policemen. Put one of them on the line."

"They say they're from the sixth *arrondissement.*" And what's the additional fuss about? he wondered.

"Put one of them on the line."

Craig gave the receiver to Galland, who was standing at his elbow. He took it, answered curtly, speaking in French. Yes, of the Sixth District . . . the Twenty-fourth Precinct, Saint-Germain-des-Prés . . . Fourteen Rue de l'Abbaye . . . Yes, of course . . . He quite understood. . . . But yes, certainly . . . And he was politely at ease again as he handed the receiver back to Craig.

The man's voice—was it Rosenfeld's?—told Craig briskly, "Just say good-bye and get over here. Don't argue the toss with them. Or else you'll spend the next eight weeks hanging round Paris while they investigate. Got it?"

Not quite. But I'll catch on, Craig thought. He said, "I'll be over in five minutes."

Galland had been talking quickly to Tillier. "Just one thing," Tillier suggested, as Craig turned away from the telephone, "if it was not suicide, if it could not be an accident, then what? Murder?"

Craig began to catch on, all right. "I just don't know," he said. And that was true enough. He had no proof of anything, just a lot of vague suspicions running wild; it would take more than eight weeks to check them out, if they could be checked. The police would end by thinking he was crazy, just as he had thought Sussman was a little crazy. "If it is, I hope you catch him," he added grimly.

"Well, that's about all." Tillier closed his notebook quickly, and followed Galland to the door. "We regret we made you late for the farewell breakfast party with your sister."

Rosenfeld really had pulled sentiment, Craig thought. "That couldn't be helped."

"Your brother-in-law has our address. If we have any more questions, he assures us that you will be delighted to pay us a visit."

Craig nodded. Brother-in-law, he was thinking. "Yes, of course," he said.

In the blue-and-gold sitting room, Sue was pouring coffee at the table near the opened window, George was busy looking through a newspaper with a quick and practiced eye, Rosenfeld was finishing his third croissant as he listened. "I tell you," Craig said, ending his brief recital of the detectives' visit, "I don't believe that Sussman committed suicide."

George folded the newspaper quickly, pointed to a small corner tucked away on the back page. "Just a moment! Here it is: Professor Jacob Sussman, et cetera, et cetera, suicide, by throwing himself from his hotel-room window. Estimated time of death, between seven and eight-thirty, when the body was discovered. Had been suffering from severe depression. Hotel owner says he behaved oddly when he returned to his room about seven. American Consulate is taking charge of arrangements, et cetera, et cetera." He handed the paper over to Rosenfeld's outstretched hand, then glanced at his watch and shook his head. "I'll have to run. Got meetings of one sort or another till late this afternoon. Rosie, you take charge here. Tell John to relax and leave police business to policemen. Especially when he's a foreigner."

But Rosenfeld was getting to his feet. "I'd better move out, too."

And again avoid the front lobby, he thought. No use having Sue and George identified with this visit of his to the Meurice. Keep them out of trouble; they've had enough of their own in the last few weeks. He had managed to pick up the information he had come here to find; it solved nothing. Still, it did narrow the field, and that was always a small step in the right direction. The three guests who had called off from last night's party were no longer interesting. Two were French reporters who had been sent to Marseilles yesterday morning in order to cover the heroin-factory story. The third man was a Canadian, but he had eliminated himself by falling in his bathtub a couple of days ago and was in the hospital at the time the stranger in the Bois de Boulogne had been collecting that chewed-up pencil stub. As for the guest who had practically invited himself to the party, there were two candidates for that distinction, one of them slightly more emphatic than the other. Wilshot had telephoned to say he was coming to welcome the Farradays that evening. Bradley was more diplomatic: he had called to ask when he'd have a chance of seeing them, and been invited. And their height? Around average, no more than a couple of inches' difference between them. They both could qualify. So did every other man at that party, last night, except Craig and the Australian. Rosenfeld looked at Craig's set face, now, and hesitated. Better spend a few more minutes here, he thought, and keep Craig out of trouble, too. He's in a dangerous mood. George's advice has riled him. Rosenfeld said gently, "George is right, you know. But so are you, possibly."

Craig looked at him with renewed interest.

"Judging by that newspaper report," Rosenfeld went on, "I shouldn't wonder if the police agree with you. Why else should they let that item be published and still go on checking every lead?"

"You mean the report is a smoke screen?"

Rosenfeld waited until George and Sue, comparing their timetables for today, had drawn out of earshot. "It could be. They never would have bothered visiting you this morning if they were quite sure it was suicide. So you just leave it to them. They are very good. Don't worry about that."

But Craig's worry was about something else. "I ought to have stayed and talked. If they are thinking about murder—perhaps they would have listened to me after all."

"Talk about what?" Rosenfeld was instantly alert. "About Berg being seen? About Sussman's suspicion?"

"About the man I saw leaving the café in such a damned hurry. He was right on Sussman's heels. At the time—well, I thought I was starting to imagine things, like Sussman."

"How old was this man?"

"He was young. Fair hair, wet raincoat . . ." Craig paused, looked at Rosenfeld speculatively. "Berg was much older, about fifty, I'd guess."

Rosenfeld's face went completely blank with the shock. His voice dropped. "You *saw* Berg? Craig—" He gestured to two chairs in a quiet corner of the room.

But George Farraday, his last-minute instructions to Sue now ended, came over to join them for a hearty but hurried good-bye to Craig. "Aren't you coming?" he asked Rosenfeld.

"Shortly."

"That's too late for me. I'm already ten minutes behind schedule. What about meeting me for lunch, along with Sutherland and three fellows from the—"

"No. In fact, George, you haven't met me today at all."

George Farraday half smiled. "I haven't? Okay. Anything else I haven't done?"

"You haven't heard that your brother-in-law was visited by the police this morning. And you haven't heard him say Sussman wasn't a suicide. You only know what he told you last night. And that goes for Sue, too. Right?"

Farraday said, "There dies another good story. Surprising how many of them, nowadays, have got to be smothered." He seemed to be joking, but his eyes were thoughtful.

"That keeps it a lot safer for everyone." Rosie looked pointedly at Craig. "Good-bye, George. And take off the pack. I'll handle this."

That reassured George. A last kiss for Sue, a wave to Craig, a nod to Rosie, and he was out of the room. She wasn't so easily persuaded. Perhaps she didn't know Rosie as well as she thought she did. "You mean there could be danger for John in all this business? Good heavens, Rosie, he only gave the poor man a drink!"

"Oh, not any real danger. Just publicity in newspapers, delays in getting away from Paris, complications . . . *You* know, Sue. Now, I want to hear from John everything he can tell me about Sussman's career. So why don't you start changing into street clothes, and pack your overnight things, and make a list of all that shopping you want to get done?"

Sue went toward the bedroom, even if a little reluctantly. She had a busy day ahead of her, that was true. "I had some things to discuss with John," she protested faintly. "Don't be too long, Rosie. I have a hairdresser's appointment at half past ten. And don't tell me my hair looks fine as it is!" She closed the bedroom door with a firm little bang.

"Craig—" Rosenfeld was beginning exactly where he had been interrupted. "Let's sit over here. Tell me what happened yesterday when you met Sussman, from the very first minute you saw him until the last. Anything could be important, even a seemingly stupid detail. It's all fresh in your memory, isn't it?" For Craig still hesitated, as if he were weighing him up. "Why am I so damned curious, is that what you're thinking? Well, it's obvious that this could have been a political murder, an assassination. Right? In that case, I wouldn't advise you to take your story to the sixth *arrondissement*. It isn't in their line of business. You need something like the Sûreté for this. I have made some friends in Paris who have certain contacts, even some influence, there. They are the kind of people you should be getting in touch with. You give me the facts and I'll see they get them. Today."

Craig was watching him, with amusement showing in his cool gray eyes.

"Well, what?"

"I was just wondering how many refrigerators you do sell."

"Refrigeration. Not refrigerators." Rosenfeld grinned, inclined his head. "I like your caution, anyway." He lit a cigarette, sat back, did no more persuading. A man like Craig made up his own mind. It would be easy to enlist Craig's help by explaining a number of facts about Heinrich Berg; it was also impossible. He thought, perhaps—if he won't talk now—I'll have to get Bernard at the Sûreté to send a couple of men and pick Craig up at his hotel. He wouldn't like that. Nor would I. It could put him in danger, bring his name into the open. And much might be lost: time, surprise, Berg himself. Rosenfeld drew a deep, silent breath.

And Craig was thinking, I'll have to trust him. George does, that's evident. And who else is there, anyway? "Sussman's death is more than a French problem. Is that it, Rosie?" he asked quietly.

Rosie looked at him in amazement. "That's it, exactly." By God, he thought, this man is no fool.

"All right," said Craig, and began his story. "I met him by accident. . . ."

The story ended. Rosie, his face expressionless, was silent. Craig rose, poured himself a glass of water. It was a relief to get rid of all those facts; it was strange, too, when he had been forced to produce them in sequence, how they began to explain each other. "One thing I do know about you, Rosie," he said with a smile. "You're a good listener."

Rosie had looked up quickly, and then relaxed. "I was just giving thanks," he said and rose, too. "It is really a pleasure to watch an accurate memory at work. Is that what they teach you in history?"

And what does that small joke mean? That he doesn't really believe Sussman's story? He is letting me down lightly? "Isn't it possible," Craig tried, "that Berg stopped at our table to point out Sussman to the man in the raincoat? The more I think of the sequence of events—the way Berg waited across the street until his man arrived, as if he had sent for him or—"

"Don't," said Rosie gently, "don't think about them any more." Pretty good, he thought of Craig's remarks, pretty good at that.

"You didn't believe—" Craig began sharply.

"I believe everything you said. I am asking you to forget it. Let me do the remembering. I will." Rosie was thinking, Berg and Insarov. . . . Yes, that seemed more and more likely. Better get in touch with Partridge and Duclos, as soon as possible. Let them contact Holland and Bernard at the Sûreté.

"Forget it? That's a steep order."

"It's just practical advice. Berg isn't alone. I can see the mark of an organization, a well-disciplined and powerful group."

"An organization?" Craig didn't like the sound of that word in the way Rosie had spoken it: it carried a threat. Was Rosie trying to warn him, without giving too much away? "He could have been acting alone, you know—with a friend or paid thug to help him."

"If he were alone and wanted to escape arrest as a Nazi war criminal, he only had to pick up and run, hide somewhere else, adopt a new name, a new life. There's plenty of space in this world for clever fugitives. But he wanted to stay here, unmolested. Why? A mission to perform, perhaps? Then he isn't alone. He didn't kill Sussman, but he ordered the killing. If he has done that once, he can do it again. And for the same reason: protection of his mission. Dedicated men, you know, have a brutal logic. To them, people like Sussman are just specks of dust in the machinery—to be wiped off, and forgotten."

"I get the message," Craig said abruptly. "I don't talk about Berg."

"And you follow your own routine exactly, as if yesterday had never happened."

"You think they'll be interested in me even if I keep my mouth shut?"

"Very interested—until they are convinced they don't have to reckon with you. So play it safe, Craig. Play it very safe."

Craig took a deep breath. He walked over to the window and looked out over the busy street. Beyond it were the Tuileries Gardens, neat paths and flower beds and carefully arranged trees. Children playing, people walking, sitting, talking, thinking. About what? Families and illness and holidays; bills to be paid, a dress to be bought, a new car, a television set; marriages and love affairs, business and pleasure . . . Nice, normal world, whose worries and alarms now seemed very simple. "And only yesterday morning," he said with a wry smile, "I was a reasonably happy man."

"So was I," said Rosie.

Craig looked back at him. I ought to be thanking him for his warning, he thought, instead of feeling sorry for myself. "When will I see you again? And where? I'd like to know how the action goes. I'll breathe a little easier when I hear that Berg is arrested." Now did I say something simple-minded, there? he wondered, as he noticed the amusement showing briefly in Rosie's eyes.

Rosie came over to stand beside him. "I'll miss this city when I have to leave it," he said, looking across the Tuileries to the Seine. "Possibly the next time we'll meet will be in New York in the fall."

"I'd like to know sooner than that."

"I'll telephone you, keep you posted. But no meetings here. No visible contact."

"Are you sure they won't tap my phone at the hotel?" Craig asked, half joking, half annoyed.

"They might at that. If I can't risk telephoning, then I'll have to send someone with a message."

Disguises are coming off, thought Craig: Rosie trusts me a little, at least. And that restored something of his good humor. Distrust, when it wasn't earned, had a savage bite.

"He will know you," Rosie went on. "He'll make contact quite easily."

"You disappoint me, Rosie. No high-signs?"

"Oh, he will shake hands, and leave a nickel in your palm."

"I'll end up rich if you send me enough contacts."

Rosie laughed, clapped his shoulder. "See you in New York, Craig, and you can tell me all about Troy. That's one place I really want to visit. I'd like to stand on the walls, look out over the plain down to the sea where the Argive fleet—" He laughed at the expression on the younger man's face. "Do you know what I once thought I was going to be? An archaeologist." He moved, still shaking his head, to the bedroom door. "All clear, Sue. Do I rate a farewell kiss, or aren't you talking to me any more?" His good-bye was easy and affectionate, and remarkably quick. Craig, watching it from the window, had to admire the tact with which Rosie could fend off questions and yet give acceptable answers. In two minutes, Sue, who thought she was being considerably enlightened, had learned exactly nothing.

"But how nice," she said as the door to the sitting room closed, and they were left alone, "how nice that Rosie knows someone at the police station who can really keep your name out of the papers. I want to see Sussman's murderer caught, but I don't want to see you mixed up in it. These Nazis can be so vindictive, you know."

"Suicide. *Not* murder. And I'll be careful," he promised. "Now what about your hair appointment? I'll walk you there, and we can talk about Father. I'm more anxious about him than I admitted last night."

"What?" she said, her worries flowing into new channels.

And how's that for a brief imitation of Rosie? he asked himself as they set out together. It worked, too. It was family, family, all the way, until the last kiss and parting hug.

"Follow your own routine," Rosie had told him, and that was exactly what John Craig did for the next five days.

He admired some of the pictures at the Louvre and most of the sculpture, preferred Sainte-Chapelle to Notre-Dame, took refuge from Sacré-Cœur in Saint-Pierre-de-Montmartre, spent an afternoon in Versailles, a day at Chartres, wandered through Les Halles (and ate one of the best luncheons he had in Paris in the packed company of solid merchants and stall-holders testing the meat and cheese they had sold that morning), explored the various little *quartiers,* looked at Paris from all sides of the Eiffel Tower, loitered at the bookstalls when he meant to be walking through more museums, got some almost-exercise in the parks, took in a couple of night clubs and three movies, tried several restaurants with stars before their names (he balanced this expenditure with *bistros* and Left Bank *brasseries*), and blessed the prevalence of the French café as pleasant easement for tired feet.

And no one followed him. Or perhaps he was trying not to notice, and succeeding remarkably well. There was, he decided, no use worrying over something beyond his control. He was a traveler on his first voyage of discovery to Europe, something he had begun to plan as far back as his Korean days, when his one ambition was to get as far away from the Pacific as possible and leave the mysterious East to newcomers who didn't remember foxholes. And the plans had lain at the back of his mind during the years at college, during the postgraduate grind, and the extra jobs, and the teaching, and all the damned budgeting for pleasures and weekends that disrupted his time but were a hell of a lot of fun, too, and the articles and reviews that had led gradually, slowly but surely, to this visit to Europe. It was more than a bit of travel: it was the cumulation of hopes and despairs, of dreams and decisions, twelve years in the making and now actually his.

Or was it?

He might not have noticed anyone trailing behind him trying to play the invisible man, but strange encounters were not so easily ignored. There had been several of them, most of them either definitely or possibly innocent; but two were more serious (although if Rosie hadn't planted a warning in his mind, he might have just classified them under odd coincidence, the kind of thing that added a little spice to life), and one took his breath away. Fortunately, no one was testing his pulse at that moment.

Under definitely innocent came the old lady who had lost the right Métro; the young Dutch couple who wanted their photograph taken against the gargoyles of Notre-Dame (they had set the focus; all he was asked to do was to push the button of their camera); an American who was looking for a restaurant where prices were reasonable and the waiter might say thank you for his tip.

Under possibly innocent came the two English girls who attached themselves to him as a useful translator and then proceeded to give him a history lesson through the corridors of Versailles, ending with a shy invitation to a nice spot of tea somewhere in the little town before they all caught the bus back to Paris; and the Algerian student, of an age that indicated he was one of the chronics—the perpetual undergraduates who followed a policy of drift and never took a degree in anything. He shared Craig's lunch table in an overcrowded *brasserie,* talked volubly about universities and politics, expressed the wish to visit the United States and, in between scathing denunciations of imperialism in Cuba and Viet Nam, wondered what American scholarships or grants he could get to keep him at a college there. He ended with a handsome invitation for the evening: he would act as Craig's guide to the more recherché night clubs in Montmartre. He seemed disconsolate over Craig's smiling but definite refusal, the end of a most promising friendship as well as a free night out on the town.

But two encounters were more serious, definitely disturbing. Their skill and effrontery might have been amusing if they hadn't left Craig with the feeling that he was skirting disaster. The first was with a man possibly in his late twenties, nice clean-cut American-boy type, who bumped into him in the lobby of his own hotel, late Saturday afternoon.

"Pardon me," the stranger said, and then grinned widely as he caught Craig's arm. "Hi! Remember me? I'm Willis Jordan, Columbia 'fifty-nine. Now let me see, you're—yes, you're Craig. How's that for memory?"

It was pretty good, Craig thought. He hadn't the smallest recollection of Jordan. Not that that proved anything. Columbia University was a big place. He shook hands, half expecting to feel a nickel crushed into his palm, but there was nothing. "Frankly, I don't remember you at all," he said, keeping his voice friendly. After all, he had just shaken hands.

"Why should you? I was just one of the College boys trying to crash an advanced course on ancient history. You were one of the regulars, a graduate student no less. You didn't think much of us, did you? Quite right. We didn't last more than three lectures. Way beyond me, that stuff. But it made us feel good at the time. Big deal. Between you and me, did you ever learn much from old Sussman? He was the worst lecturer I ever heard, couldn't make out what he was saying most of the time. Or was that just because I was stupid? Could be." He laughed very generously at himself. "Come on and have a drink, just one, and give me all the news on Columbia. Haven't seen it in years."

And how do you know that I have? Craig wondered, and let that slip pass. The rest was so very good; simple and friendly, a little overconfident, like the undergraduate who had crashed Professor Sussman's course. He resisted the impulse to say good-bye and clear out, but that would look as if the name of Sussman had scared him off. "Fine," he said, and led the way into the hotel bar. It was small, square in shape, discreetly lit from the shaded brackets on its walls, a pleasant little place whose nineteenth-century elegance was fading into something cosy and comfortable. There were a few tables, thoughtfully spaced, and green velvet armchairs to match the antique green walls. Everything was old, a little worn, but clean and welcoming. Rather like the solitary bartender, behind his small mahogany counter with its three stools, stirring a dry Martini for a quietly dressed American with light sandy hair, a high forehead and thin-framed glasses. Craig had seen him around on other evenings, so he was a guest here, too. He could have been a young college professor, only his interests—judging from the magazines he always seemed to be reading—lay in auctions and antiques. "No luck at all, today," he was answering the barman, as Craig and his hail-fellow came to stand beside him. "Nothing but junk, Jules, nothing but trash held together by some glue."

Jules shook his head over the temerity of the furniture market, poured the Martini carefully, said, "You should try the Loire Valley, Monsieur Partreege. There are fine things to be discovered there."

"Perhaps I shall. Thank you, Jules." The American took his glass, tasted the Martini, nodded his approval, and left the bar for the one table still free, where he could study his catalogue in peace.

Mr. Jordan seemed relieved that the other American had gone. "Now we'll have room for our elbows," he said, grinning widely. "What's yours, Craig? Scotch? I'll try one of Jules' Martinis." Jules hardly flickered an eyebrow even if his first name was reserved for guests who came steadily. Jordan was too busy to notice. He was studying Craig, his smile still in place, trying to get back onto the subject of Sussman. "And what are you doing here?"

"Seeing Paris."

"For how long?"

"Another few days."

"Thinking of going skiing?"

Craig stared. "It's a bit late in the year for that."

"You know, funny thing, that's how I remembered your face. I'll never forget you hobbling on crutches around the campus—broke a leg, didn't you? Made a big impression on me. Here's someone who goes skiing and can understand Sussman, too!"

And here's someone who has been reading through the old class yearbooks, thought Craig. Then he had a stab of guilt. Perhaps he was being too unkind to Mr. Jordan, perhaps the man had really been around Columbia from 1955 to 1959. "It's easy enough to go skiing if you do tutoring on the weekends and your pupil has an uncle who owns a ski lodge."

But Jordan twisted back to the real subject. "And how is old Sussman? Still teaching away?"

Craig looked at the smiling face and took a deep breath. Then he said, very quietly, "He's dead."

"When?" The smile faded perfectly.

"Three days ago. In Paris. It was in all the papers. Suicide." And that, thought Craig grimly, will save unnecessary questions.

"Now what could have caused it, d'you suppose?" Jordan's sympathy was even harder to take than his genial curiosity. Craig shrugged. "Tough," said Jordan. "You always liked him. When did you last see him?"

"We had a drink together on the day he died."

"How was he then? I mean—it's a really terrible thing, suicide. Didn't you feel something was wrong?"

"No. Or I wouldn't have said good-bye to him and let him walk away."

"You mean, he was quite normal—just sat talking about nothing, passing the time of day?"

"I hope not. He asked me about my work, gave me some advice, a lot of encouragement."

"I can see why you feel so bad, talking about yourself and all the time he must have been worrying about something else."

"Now, look here, Jordan—" Craig began in real anger, and stopped. Don't be goaded, he reminded himself. "How the hell do I know what *you*'re thinking? You might be planning suicide right now. How does a man read another's thoughts? Sussman was depressed, yes: he had just been giving testimony at Frankfurt. I thought some talk about his own subject would get his mind off those trials, make him forget. I was wrong. So—"

"Hold on, hold on, I didn't mean it that way. Of course you couldn't guess. But something must have been troubling him badly. Now you'd think, wouldn't you, that he had a fine chance to tell you his problems when he met you, and get rid of them? You knew him well—"

"I guess I didn't know him well enough," Craig said sadly, honestly. He frowned at his drink. I used to laugh at movies where one guy at a bar hit out at another guy, but I swear if Jordan doesn't take that sympathetic voice out of my hearing in the next three minutes, he isn't going to have much voice left. One sharp blow across his throat with the back of my hand—yes, just the way I used to practice it in Korea for night-patrol work. *Karate in Saint-Honoré bar*. A nice headline.

"Now that's an interesting thought, whatever it is," Jordan said, watching his face.

"Who knows anyone well enough?" Craig finished his drink. "What about another? You haven't told me yet what you're doing in Europe. Business or pleasure?"

Jordan looked at his watch. "It's past six. Got to get going. I have to meet a lawyer tonight; I'm publicity man for Eurasia Films, and we're running into trouble over distribution of a movie about the French Army."

"Business on a Saturday night? That's working you hard."

"Has to be, has to be . . . I'm back in Brussels tomorrow. That's the way it goes. Well, good to see you again. Here, Jules, keep the change." He pushed some ready francs across the counter, patted Craig's shoulder, and left.

"Another Scotch, Mr. Craig?"

Craig nodded. If ever a man needed grog it was John Craig, standing in a quiet and pleasant little bar, with the gentle hum of innocent voices rising from the tables behind him.

"And what about you, Mr. Partreege?" Jules asked of the thin-faced American, who had come back to the bar.

"No, thanks. Just put the rest on the bill." He dropped an extra tip near Jules, glanced at Craig, almost spoke, hesitated, then said, "Sorry, I thought I had met you before. My mistake." He looked enquiringly at Jules with a touch of perplexity mixed with amusement over his small error.

Jules said quickly, "This is Mr. Craig, who is a guest here, too."

Partridge, pausing as he was about to turn away, said, "You really look very much like a man I knew in Japan about ten years ago."

"I've been there, but I don't think we ever met." Is this another try? They're keeping me busy, Craig thought.

"My name's Jim Partridge." The stranger put out his hand. Craig took it. Pressed into his palm, he felt a small round object. "Perhaps we can have a drink together some evening?"

"No reason why we shouldn't."

Partridge said very quietly, "You handled him well. No slips." And turned away definitely, this time.

Craig finished his drink slowly. The tension was gone. So was that very unpleasant feeling of actual fear, when the man who called himself Jordan had patted his shoulder and left. He had stood there, waiting for the second drink, wondering what mistakes he had made.

Thank God for Jim Partridge. "No slips," he had said. But how had he known? Had he been able to listen to the conversation? It was a fantastic thought. Possible? Gadgets, nowadays, were ingenious. Perhaps I'll learn when we do have that drink together. At least one thing I do know now: I'm not alone.

That was a good feeling. He could even look back on the encounter with Jordan and study it with cool amusement.

Then there was, two days later, the second encounter. It began, in contrast to the Jordan incident, very quietly indeed. And ended with no amusement at all.

It was late on Monday afternoon. Craig had been searching for old maps of ancient Greece and the eastern Mediterranean, the kind of thing that he might possibly discover in the secondhand bookshops around the Beaux-Arts district. That was also the district where the girl lived, the girl with the dark hair and blue eyes who had walked away from his taxi five nights ago, name unknown, address unknown, swallowed up in the maze of streets, vanishing into the shadows. And although he produced a reasonable excuse each day to get him over to the Left Bank and keep an eye open for that smooth dark head, he had no luck at all. He had the fanciful idea that if he only kept thinking hard enough about her, she might walk out of that baker's shop, or down the street, or be standing in this bookstore like the hundred other students who did much of their pleasure reading there. But like all fanciful ideas, it was high in expectations and low in results. He never saw her. Perhaps she had left Paris, perhaps she wasn't a student. And probably she had forgotten all about him by this time. Why, he wondered with considerable irritation, why the hell didn't he forget her?

His search for maps and ancient charts had led him along the Rue de Seine toward the Boulevard Saint-Germain. He saw a possible bookshop, entered it, and found so much to interest him that he was there for half an hour or more. There were a dozen people around, picking up books, flipping over pages, putting the books down, choosing others, reading. The shelves were crowded to the ceiling, the stacks were so close together that the alleys between them allowed only one-way passage. Craig was in such an alley when a polite French voice said, "Pardon, monsieur." Craig looked up and saw a middle-aged man with kindly eyes in a likable face. Craig closed the book he had been reading and stuffed it back quickly on its shelf. "Sorry," he said, "I'm in your way."

The stranger broke into English. "Not at all. I don't think I'm going to find what I'm looking for, either." Then he laughed. "Are you following me? We are becoming good acquaintances, this afternoon. Didn't I hear you asking for maps down on the Rue Bonaparte? No luck? I, too, have had no success." His English was very passable, and saved Craig groping around for a few polite phrases in return.

"I'm giving up the search," Craig said, coming out of the book-lined passage. "It's all yours." He stood aside to let the Frenchman enter. The man's eyes were studying the shelves. He shook his head. "Not here," he said resignedly. "Just let me ask the owner. Perhaps he can tell us of another bookshop that might have your maps and my Leonardo da Vinci illustrations. One moment, monsieur!" He pressed his way through the groups of students and elderly men, reached the owner behind his table stacked high with dusty books. There was a quick outflow of fine French phrases. Craig made his way to the door, hesitated, started slowly toward the Boulevard Saint-Germain. Helpful people were pleasant, but generally useless. And yet he didn't want to be rude in return for some politeness (heaven knew it was scarce enough in Paris, nowadays, where foreigners were considered a necessary nuisance), and so he halted to wait for the stranger and at least say thank you.

"You are going in the right direction," his mentor told him cheerfully. "There is a shop, very big, very new, you might not think it of any help; but there is a back room, I am told, with all kinds of amazing curiosities. Let me show you. It is on the boulevard itself." He fell into step beside Craig, mentioning his name (Ardouin), his profession ("an engineer for aeroplanes"), his hobby (collecting illustrations of old inventions for warfare such as da Vinci's designs). There was such a bookstore, but the back room had been cleared for new stock.

Ardouin, in his own words, was desolated. This extra journey for nothing! Craig must have a drink with him, and they could finish their talk about ancient cartographers who guessed so much and were sometimes almost right.

Craig, ready to call it the end of an acquaintanceship yet still unwilling to cut it short rudely, walked along with the little Frenchman, trying to think of a chance for disengagement. And suddenly, against the friendly chatter at his elbow, against the background of cheerful street noise and bustle, there was a grim and warning note. They were walking along the same part of the boulevard where he had met Sussman. They were passing two cafés where they could have had that drink. "No, no," said his new friend, "not here! There is a much more interesting place quite near. When I was a student in Paris, it was where the amusing people met. Just down here, around this corner!"

Craig kept his steady pace, didn't let himself hesitate. He even managed to hold back the quick flash of anger that surged through his body. You'll have to go through with it, he told himself, go through with it to the end. "But of course," he heard himself say in a natural voice, answering a question about New York. "There are fashions in cafés everywhere, I guess." He looked at the faded little awning they were now reaching, the few tables on the narrow sidewalk. "Why," he said, "I know this place! I was here only a few nights ago. There's a Buddha inside, and a picture of Socrates. Right?"

Again Ardouin was desolated. "And I thought I would show you something new, something different," he said. "Shall we sit outside?" And he was choosing the table where Craig had sat before, selecting Sussman's chair for himself. He fell very silent.

"Yes," said Craig, "this is even the same table. I hope you aren't superstitious."

Ardouin blinked a little. "Engineers are not usually superstitious," he said with a smile.

"You've taken the same chair where my friend sat. And he is now dead."

"But I am sorry! Does that worry you?"

"I don't find it exactly cheerful."

"A drink is what we need," Ardouin said quickly, and signaled the waiter—he was new but he looked just as sad and slow as the other one, five nights ago. "All Americans drink Scotch, no?"

"It isn't very good Scotch, here. I'll try Cinzano. I must say—" he looked around, noticing a car parked nearby with its driver reading a newspaper—"this café is really on the losing end of this street." It was almost as woebegone in sunshine as it had been in the rain. Few people walked here, and those were in a hurry, as if they were using it only as a short cut to some place more important.

"Then we shall talk about pleasant things. Last time, perhaps you were listening to depressing talk?"

From the doorway farther down the curving street, on its opposite side, a man in a black overcoat stepped out and came walking slowly toward the café. For a moment, Craig had no answer. He looked away from the walking man, found a cigarette and his lighter, was relieved to see that his hands were steadier than he felt. "I spent more time looking than listening," he said. Good God, he was thinking, is Heinrich Berg going to walk up *here?*

"Looking?" The Frenchman was alert. "And what was so interesting on this street?"

"A girl. She was sitting over there, behind your chair. And having a very bad time." Quickly, he gave a brief description of the quarrel.

"How extraordinary," Ardouin said with complete indifference.

"It was. I mean, what could have caused such a long quarrel as that? I keep thinking about it." Yes, Heinrich Berg was sitting down at the very same table he had occupied last Wednesday. "Or, rather, I keep wondering what her man would have thought if he could have sat here, where I am, and watched his own performance. Or would he have needed a stranger's eyes, too, to see what he was throwing away?"

"I don't understand why you should be so concerned," began Ardouin impatiently, and then corrected his tone of voice to something more natural. "Unless, of course, she was very pretty."

"But naturally! That is what was so extraordinary." Craig looked in astonishment at Ardouin. "Haven't you noticed a considerable decline in pretty girls in the last few years? What's gone wrong? A cult of ugliness? Or it might be that this is a base form of democracy—let everyone look equally unappetizing, destroy the beauties, turn all girls into the same type with the same hair styles, the same grotesque eyes, the same vapid lips? Now I'm assuming that as a Frenchman you have certain standards for the chic and the beautiful, but—looking around Paris—I'd like to ask you what has been happening." Craig rattled on, listening to himself with a mild disbelief and a touch of rising laughter. For Ardouin was taking him seriously. Ardouin was looking at him nervously, and then with annoyance, and then with complete irritation; the once kindly eyes were showing both contempt and impatience. He finished his drink quickly, glanced at his watch.

"You must go?" Craig asked. Now it's my turn to be desolated. "I think I'll wait here for a while."

"Still hoping that you will see the girl again?" Ardouin asked, shaking his head. These Americans . . .

"Why not? This place seems to have its regulars." He glanced at some new arrivals, recognizing them faintly from his last visit. "She may be one of them. Good luck with the war machines!"

That produced a startled look, and then a very quick *"Merci. Au revoir."* A nice formal bow, and Ardouin was in retreat toward the boulevard. Leaving me to pay for the drinks, thought Craig. But it had been worth it.

He did wait for a while. He let Berg pass him with only a cursory, natural glance. Just another regular, that was Craig's attitude. He noticed that the car, parked not far away, had started to leave, too. He wondered whether he might not have ended inside it if he had started to tell Ardouin to phone for the police, for anyone, to catch a man who was possibly connected with a murder. Even if that was a bit of imaginative exaggeration about the car, he was thinking how he might have behaved if Rosie hadn't given him fair warning. Rosie had only been wrong in one thing so far: he hadn't given him any telephone number to call in an emergency like this. With the right number, he could have said, "If you want Berg, then he is sitting at a table only twenty feet or so away from me." And then, annoyance fading, he knew Rosie had been right. One step toward a telephone, either before or after Berg had left, and Craig might have found out whether his crude guess about the waiting car was fantastic or not.

I suppose, he thought heavily, I'm being watched even now. So he paid and left. If he looked depressed, the enemy could assume that he had become tired of waiting for a girl. And who was the enemy? That was one question he was going to ask Rosie. He would like to know who was turning his visit to Paris into a nightmare. That was a score that needed a little settling, quite apart from the bill that had mounted high with Sussman's death.

He went back to the Saint-Honoré, with the hope that Jim Partridge would be reading quietly in the bar—the news about Berg must be passed on as quickly as possible. But Partridge was entertaining two French friends tonight, a dark-haired young man with blue eyes and ruddy cheeks, and a charming red-haired Frenchwoman. They were talking of furniture, of designs in fabrics, with occasional laughter over Partridge's brave attempts at French and their equally comic efforts in English to help him out. It was a merry little business meeting, and Craig, just two tables away, found himself believing it authentic. Partridge had only given a polite nod of recognition and a bare "Good evening" as he had entered and found a seat. It was a frustrating feeling to sit there, in possession of some real news, and to have to keep it clamped to himself. Eventually, as Partridge and his friends left, he got the silent message: we'll contact you when we are good and ready, so sit tight and keep your mouth shut. What the flaming hell, he thought; don't they want to catch Berg?

He went out searching for dinner, which he didn't enjoy and which cost far too much anyway. And that was another thing, he told himself as he went angrily to bed after a disappointing movie: you'd better clear out to the Mediterranean; another week of Paris and your budget will be so wrecked that you'll have only a few weeks left in Europe. Get back to your own world, Craig, and stay where you belong. But can there be any separate worlds? he wondered as he thought of Sussman.

7

"It was tempting," Rosie said softly. "It was very tempting to have that man followed."

"You think he might have been Berg?" Partridge asked.

"The waiter's description of him was almost a duplicate of what Craig told me at the Meurice last Thursday morning. He wore the same kind of coat, walked from the same doorway, sat down at the exact table."

"No wonder Craig was so tight-faced this evening. He came into the Saint-Honoré bar about seven when I was there with Yves Duclos and Mimi. He looked as if he had just about had it." Partridge watched Rosie prowling around the small room restlessly, checking the locked window, pulling the torn shade closer to the sill, dragging the narrow strips of curtain more together. Fortunately, the light was too dim to throw any shadows in the direction of the run-down street outside. "Not very elegant," Partridge agreed as Rosie stared at the brash cubist design on the curtains, "but this is the kind of place where everyone finds it pays to mind his own business. Balances my room over at the Saint-Honoré very nicely." Both hotels had been Partridge's own idea. He had moved into them last Thursday soon after he had arrived in Paris; a cheap bag for this room, a leather suitcase respectably labeled for the Saint-Honoré, and he was nicely set up. "Easy commuting, too."

"Very neat," agreed Rosie, and gave his full approval. He sat down once more on the only chair, and faced Partridge, who was lounging on the narrow bed.

"So Berg walked away from that café," Partridge said thoughtfully, wondering what agent had slipped up there.

"If that was a mistake, then it's mine. Berg has not only brains but intuition. Better give him no warning signals of any kind. Better wait, try to find out what his mission in Paris is. Then we can pick him up, get Insarov-Berg in one neat package. That's the way I see it anyway. I may be wrong. I've been arguing with Bernard over at the Sûreté about this. He is, naturally enough, interested in any spy networks that are working in Paris. I feel that there may be more than a network involved. If Berg *is* Insarov, that is . . ." His voice trailed away with his thoughts.

"You're beginning to believe it, too?" Partridge asked quickly, and he couldn't be more delighted.

"Yes, but not for a very satisfactory reason—that is, not satisfactory to anyone except myself. I read through the dossiers you collected on both Berg and Insarov. And it was by remembering some of the Insarov details that I—well, let's say that Berg's actions today didn't astonish me too much."

"You studied Insarov and came up with Berg?"

"That's about it. But it doesn't prove a thing. I could be wrong."

Yet he had believed it enough, himself, to persuade Bernard to have a waiter installed for the last four days in the café, Partridge thought. "No photographs possible?"

He doesn't miss much, thought Rosie, and smiled. "No. The waiter had a microfilm lighter all ready to use, but Berg didn't take out a cigarette. And he kept his back turned to the restaurant. And he waved away any attempt to take an order; managed to avert his face, too. So the waiter followed his basic orders, which were to note any middle-aged man who wasn't known as a regular customer and to report to the Sûreté at once. He did this, but Berg was already leaving. He staged his exit right past Craig's table, and then was picked up by a car that had been waiting near by." Rosie thought that over. "I didn't have anyone ready to follow him, but you know something? I feel relieved about that. If it was a mistake, I think it was a mistake in the right direction. One suspicion aroused, and the whole Berg-Insarov operation would plunge underground. When, and where, it would emerge wouldn't even be worth a guess." He made a good attempt at a smile. "Yes, you could say that I had almost as bad a day as Craig, poor devil."

Partridge nodded understandingly. They could easily lose the fingertip hold they had on this case. Then all the work Chris Holland and he had done in those intense four months would be made useless. "I think the French might be pretty riled, too, if we lost Insarov just at this time. Duclos was pretty excited about some new developments."

"Oh?"

"He gave me a few background details over dinner, asked me to pass them on to you tonight. He's missing your visits to his studio."

"Better to get his news this way," Rosie said tersely.

"Someone still interested in you?"

"Infatuated with me, damn them. But let's disappoint them, shall we?" His smile became blandly innocent. "And what's exciting the French?"

"A night club called Le Happening. And guess who gave them the break on this? Interpol."

"Interpol? What were they expecting at Le Happening—heroin or white-slave traffic?"

"Either. One of the part-owners was almost convicted twelve years ago of smuggling drugs and shipping stranded chorus girls into the slave states. So when this new club was started a few months ago with no visible backers, Interpol took a quiet interest. The Paris police cooperated and placed three of its agents as a waiter, a stagehand, and the coatroom biddy. She reported that last Wednesday night, or, rather, in the small hours of Thursday morning, a blonde girl waited for an American in the lobby. He wore dark glasses. He carried a book in a bright jacket, and displayed a pair of new gloves quite prominently. He also had a folded newspaper under his arm in a distinctive alphabet—she thought Greek. He just dumped his coat on the counter, keeping his face turned to the girl. They did not call each other by any name when they met. They only stayed a brief time. The girl left first. The American collected his coat—he had a handkerchief up at his face, blast him—and then made for the men's room. But he didn't go in. He kept on going, past the back of the stage, to the rear of the building. He never came back. Must have left by one of the old entrances to the delivery yard."

"Good for the hat-check chick!" Rosie was always delighted by efficiency.

"She's reaching sixty. One of the best operatives in the Narcotics branch. She knows a recognition signal when she sees one. Oh, yes—the girl wore odd earrings: one emerald, one ruby. Sounds charming, don't you think?"

"And what did the Narcotics Squad find next morning—I suppose they searched the back premises?"

"They certainly did. In the hours when the place is closed except for cleaners, they got one of their men to slip into the back corridor. Storage and unused dressing rooms. Nothing there in the way of cartons or containers. No sign of heroin in the dust on the floor. But there was a mirror on the wall between two rooms. A see-through mirror."

"Well, now—the clever little rascals."

"That was when Interpol and the French police decided it might be espionage, and not drug-smuggling. They handed the problem over to the Sûreté. Bernard has been working on it."

"He has, has he?"

"I think he was waiting to get some results before he told us about it," Partridge said tactfully.

"Very thoughtful of him." Rosie took a long breath. "Co-operation! Oh well, it's his country. But dammit, you'd think—" He caught hold of himself. "Perhaps I've lived too long here. I'm beginning to assume this is partly my country, too. All right, all right . . . He's working on the problem?"

"He had some of his experts install a listening device in the rooms with the connecting mirror. It wasn't too easy—no furniture worth mentioning, no lamp shades, and the electric bulbs are doubtless changed regularly." Partridge's amusement boiled over into a fit of laughter. "So they wired the mirror for sound—used its frame."

Very funny, very funny, thought Rosie, but where does this lead us?

"And it worked!" Partridge said, recovering himself. "At two a.m. on Saturday morning, there was a brief conversation between a Russian and a man who was to use the name of Jordan. Instructions were given to Jordan about meeting Craig that afternoon or evening in the Saint-Honoré lobby. Also, he learned certain information about Craig based on a telephoned report from New York about a Columbia College yearbook. Also, a photograph taken of Craig at the Eiffel Tower was examined and discussed."

Rosie relaxed. "We're in business," he said very softly. He studied the arm of his chair. It was a violent purplish red, a cheap imitation velvet worn into mauve patches. He picked at a loose thread. "You'll call me as soon as Duclos passes on any more news?" It was Rosie's way of giving an order. He rose from the abominable chair, caught sight of the giant yellow roses on the blue wallpaper, and groaned. "I hope you don't ever have to sleep here."

Partridge was picking up the soiled raincoat which had lain near him on the bed. He pulled it on, and it transformed his gray flannel suit into something less affluent and more suitable for his departure through the neglected lobby downstairs. "I'll follow you out—I want to get back to the Saint-Honoré tonight."

So Jim Partridge was worried about Craig, too. And with every reason. Rosie said regretfully, "It would be easier on him if we could explain things more."

"You'd trust him as far as that?"

"If we were forced to, I'd trust him. But let's hope it never comes to that."

"Amateurs worry me. They're too big a responsibility."

Rosie inclined his head in half-agreement. Sometimes, though, they produced the most astounding results. He thought of Venice, almost three years ago. "Bless their little hearts," he said.

"Of course, Craig seems to have the right impulses. I mean, if you trusted him with the truth, he'd probably accept it. He wouldn't start trying to prove you're an idiot or a liar just so he could dodge the real issue and still keep his conscience happy."

"You seem to know him well," Rosie murmured.

"I've been listening to you. I think you like the guy. By the way, what happened to the man who took Craig to the café?"

"Photographed and followed. He may lead us to interesting people."

"And Jordan? The same treatment?"

"Yes."

"Well, that's progress of sorts. You know, I think Berg must be staying some place very close to that café. How else could he have appeared so quickly once his man had delivered Craig to the right table? And there's the problem, too, of how that man knew that Craig was going to be wandering through bookshops."

"My guess is that he didn't know, that he was told to go to work on

Craig whenever Craig was visiting the Left Bank. And that has been quite often. He seemingly likes the place."

"The curious thing," Partridge said thoughtfully, "is the difference between the two sets of instructions. Those given Jordan were precise. Those given the second man, if you are right, were much more—imaginative. What's your hunch, Rosie? That there are two different bosses giving their own type of instructions? Or is there a split in command?"

"Jim, you know I'm always battling against hunches. They seem so damned idiotic when they don't pay off." Rosie's amused eyes studied the younger man's face. He relented. "But I wouldn't discard that guess of yours. Every small idea counts in this game. And that was a good one." Rosie paused at the door. "When you call me, add ninety minutes to the time you fix for the meeting. Where shall it be?"

"Duclos suggested Mimi's shop. Rue La Fay—"

"I've heard of it. Hand-blocked linens and upholstery satin, all for the Cadillac trade. You'd never believe it, but the last time I saw Mimi she had the Lido all tied up with her bikini." Rosie was still grinning broadly as he left. For such a solidly constructed man, his movements were surprisingly light. Partridge, standing at the door, couldn't even hear the usual creak of the faulty floor boards.

He gave Rosie six minutes before he buckled the belt of his coat, turned up its collar to hide his clean shirt, pulled on a battered hat with a dipping brim, slipped off his glasses and put them into his pocket. He only needed them for reading, but they had become a habit; made him look more responsible, he had thought, a little more serious, older, more eligible for promotion. A bad habit, he decided, breeding the type of mind that was afraid of hunches. For he was still puzzling out Insarov, the man with the imaginative instructions, the man who played it by ear as well as relying on a machine-like mind. Insarov's specialty was psychological warfare, wasn't it? So that's how Rosie guessed he would stage a confrontation scene. Damn it all, he said to himself, I made out all those reports; Rosie only read them. So why couldn't I have risked a guess at Insarov's behavior patterns? Re-enactment, disclosure through shock? Yes, it was easy to see it all now, once it had happened. A nice case of hindsight. Not good enough; not good enough, when you dealt with a man like Insarov.

Then, as he left the room, he knew one of the answers to the puzzle.

He had kept thinking of Insarov as some fantastic brain, some inexorable planner, a powerful force gathering strength to destroy his enemy. But Rosie had met that type before; Rosie knew he was human. And one thing all human beings shared in common, apart from the need to eat and drink and sleep and function as a body: each had his Achilles' heel. What was Insarov's? And what's yours, Jim? He reached the desolate lobby, pushed open the finger-smeared door, and stepped into the dark street.

Partridge's call came sooner than expected. It caught Rosie in his office, just before noon on Tuesday, the very next day. *"Ici* Basdevant," began Partridge crisply, and then continued in heavily accented English. "About the question of the new refrigeration unit for the Caen Sausage and Tripe Distributors' processing plant—when can you have it installed?"

"Any time. Just sign the order and we can start work on it at once."

"Good. Then I shall sign the contract at four o'clock this afternoon, if that is suitable for you."

"Most suitable," said Rosie. "We shall have everything drawn up and ready. At your convenience, Monsieur Basdevant." He could not resist adding, "The first name is Alphonse, is it not?"

"Correct. There will be no delay in installation?"

"I assure you, we have the unit available. I realize the urgency of your problem."

"With the approach of a warm spring," the Sausage and Tripe distributor said, "we must insist—"

"Have no fear, monsieur, your products will be safe with us."

Monsieur Alphonse Basdevant bade a pleasant good day.

So, Rosie thought, we meet at half past two, and don't be late. Something has developed, has it? Something big? In addition to that encouraging piece of news, he was beginning to have high hopes for Partridge. The over-serious calculating machine was showing a touch of humor. Or perhaps he had had it all along, and Rosie had smothered it. Some light relief was welcome, anyway; there was no better safety valve. It counteracted Rosie's depressing discovery of that morning. His telephone had been tapped.

He became businesslike, instructed his secretary to fill out a standard contract for a refrigeration unit, to be signed this afternoon on behalf of Caen Sausage and Tripe Distributors by their agent Alphonse Basdevant. Time and place of delivery to be added on Basdevant's instructions. She could leave it on his desk. He was now going to lunch and then to a fitting at his tailor's. About time, too, didn't she think?

Rosie approved of Mimi's shop. It was close to a Métro, a bus stop, and a taxi rank. It lay on a busy street. And it shared the same entrance with five other specialized places—a little dressmaker, a little hat designer, a little travel agency, a little boutique for Florentine handbags and Perugian sweaters, and a little man for big parties. (The adjective "little" showed how talented and expensive they all were.) There were constant comings and goings, a perpetual drift of people so intent on their highly important business that the more ordinary mortals such as Rosie were not even worth one glance.

Mimi, in person, was far from little. She was the only girl that Rosie could remember who had made a bikini look as if it had been designed for a Caryatid solemnly gazing over the Acropolis, one thigh forward ready to march in sacred procession to Athena's high altar. Her hair was now a rich ripe auburn, piled loosely over a white face and dark eyebrows. But the smoke-gray eyes still had the pure intent gaze of the Caryatid, seemingly blank, aware of everything. She opened the door, with its CLOSED ON TUESDAY sign already displayed, and locked it securely behind him. "*Cher* Rosee!" she said, giving him a soft cheek to kiss and an enveloping hug from her beautiful strong arms. Then she retired with her long slow stride to her own corner, settled before her drawing board, continued her work on a current design, and left the three men to themselves.

Duclos' eyes were a bright blue today, a sign that excitement was running through his veins. Partridge had been anxious, even tense, but with Rosie's safe arrival he relaxed. Now he was watching Duclos, impatient and curious. Rosie looked at them both, pushed aside a bolt of antique satin from the one comfortable chair over which it had been draped to entice a customer, and sat down. My news will keep, he thought, looking at the expectant faces. He put aside the memory of a hurried and horrible lunch, of the long, long journey to cover the equivalent of ten blocks between the restaurant and Mimi's. "Sorry I'm late. I'm ready, Yves. Don't disappoint me."

"Jim told you about Le Happening and the mirror we wired for sound?" Duclos began. "It works. There was a long session in the unused dressing rooms last night. We picked it up, all of it. And taped it. You can hear it in detail when you visit Bernard. Part of it is in Russian, of course. We've had that translated. Part of it is in French, when a woman was getting her instructions from someone who gave his code name as Peter. Her name is Erica. She's the same woman, the coatroom attendant assures us, who met the American in the lobby last week. His name came into Erica's conversation with Peter. It is Alex. Her instructions were to travel to Greece and take up residence on the island of Mykonos. Alex would visit her there, briefly, on his way back to Paris. He would pass her some information of the highest importance. She would deliver it within a few hours to someone on the island. She would receive further instructions about that later. In the meantime, she is to concentrate on making her journey to Mykonos seem plausible. She is borrowing a house, rented by her uncle, so that she can enjoy a summer of painting. She will invite another girl to accompany her, someone who also is an artist. Then the two of them can have many parties, meet many people. In this way, the couriers or agents who make contact with her during the summer will seem to be a natural part of the general picture. Alex will be her first visitor. She is to expect him in the early part of May."

Duclos paused to take a map out of his pocket, unfold it, stretch it flat on a small table.

"Mykonos." Rosie glanced over at Partridge, who only smiled quietly. Mykonos had appeared in Partridge's report on Heinrich Berg, a small item dealing with Berg's closest friends in Nazi Germany who were still known to be alive and free. There were only two of them left in that category: one was a woman, Berg's mistress, who had shared his politics as well as his bed, and was now rumored to be in Milan;

the other was Gerhard Ludwig, who had never been a member of the Nazi party but had left Germany in 1950. It was known that he had been living in Greece and writing travel books. Three years ago, he had left Athens for the Greek Islands. He was reported living in Mykonos.

"Yes, Mykonos!" Duclos answered. "It's the most perfect place for their purpose. It has a constant stream of visitors—writers, painters, scholars, ordinary tourists who are cruising through the Aegean. It has an art colony—quite a number of French intellectuals have rented houses. There is a harbor for small yachts, sailing boats, fishing boats. The cruise ships call there; and so do the inter-island mail boats. And then Delos—"

"Yes, it's perfect," agreed Rosie. Unlikely in its innocence; and therefore all the more perfect. He rose and went over to look at the map. Mykonos had a central position among the scattered groups of islands in the Aegean.

"But where," asked Partridge, "is Alex arriving from? Mykonos gives us no indication where he has been gathering information: it's just about halfway between Greece and Turkey." He came over to join the others at the map. "It was a simpler problem for us two years ago, when we had some worry about the islands of Lesbos and Chios which lie very close to Turkey—Chios is only a few miles, practically swimming distance, from the Turkish coast, and the quickest way to get from Greece to Smyrna."

Duclos was startled. "Just one second!" he said sharply. He looked annoyed, almost deflated. "Will you please wait until we finish with questions about Mykonos before you start talking of Smyrna, or Izmir, as the Turks call it?" Having established control, he added with a friendly smile, "You Americans—you are always blasting off in every direction."

"Okay," said Partridge with a grin. "I was heading right back to Mykonos anyway, because what worried us in Lesbos particularly was an attempt to form a base of Communist espionage operations which would gather information about the Turkish coast all the way south from Çanakkale on the Dardanelles to the American base near Smyrna using Chios as either a cutout or a handy transit station but if you look at these islands' position on the map you'll agree the project was a bit too obvious even if daring and so it failed and I'm only blasting off because Rosie says they always keep trying bless the clever little rascals and that lands me right smack on Mykonos." He paused for breath, his grin broadening. If you talked fast enough, you could still make your point at the right and proper time. "All right; over to you, Yves. Questions about Mykonos."

"I have a couple," Rosie said, repressing his own smile. "But let me ask them sitting down. I had a lot of exercise today." He led the return to their chairs, settled himself once more, avoided Partridge's quick, enquiring eyes. "First, who is the girl that Erica will invite to Mykonos? Any indications?" She could be another member of Erica's Communist group; or a sympathizer, eager to help and obey; or some innocent who hadn't the faintest idea for what purpose she was being used.

"There were two definite specifications," Duclos said. "The girl must be politically immature and emotionally unattached. There were also suggestions that she must be charming enough to attract friends on Mykonos, trusting enough so that she would not be suspicious. Perfect cover for Erica, isn't it?"

"So the girl will go in good faith. She will hear and see no political evil because she doesn't believe that people like Erica can be part of her world." Rosie shook his head; how often he had seen that pattern repeated. It never amused him.

"Exactly. Erica will choose her, herself. In fact, she had two possibilities in mind, right away, and gave their names to Peter so that he could have a check made on them for security. Her favorite candidate was—" and here Duclos cleared his throat lightly—"an American student in Paris. Erica and she have attended the same art classes, seemingly. Name: Veronica Clark. Age: twenty-five. She lives in a small hotel in the Beaux-Arts district: Hotel Beauharnais."

"Poor Veronica," Partridge said. "What art student would refuse a visit to Mykonos?"

Rosie looked at him thoughtfully. "What intelligence agent, for that matter? You seem to be the expert on the Aegean, Jim. If it isn't a rude question, how did you manage that, sitting at a desk in Germany?"

"The nucleus of the Lesbos organization was recruited from a Communist network in West Berlin. We seem to be facing the same kind of thing now, but this time they're working out of Paris. And—

this time, too—the boss-man has appeared, himself, to make sure that there will be no more failures. Could be?"

"Insarov?" Rosie nodded. That could be.

Duclos threw up his hands. "Let us finish with Erica, first," he insisted. "You had two questions about her, Rosie. You've only asked one."

"Had she anything to say about the American called Alex? Anything that could give us a lead on him?"

"She remarked that her meeting with Alex last week had troubled her; he was cautious to an extreme. But perhaps he would feel easier when he did not have to carry new gloves and a travel book on tours to Scandinavia. She was reproved for her flippancy. She was told that he had every reason to be cautious in Paris."

"Meaning he is well known? Of some importance?" Rosie asked quickly.

"He has an important job, certainly. That we learned from the Russian conversation that followed next. Shall I go on with it, now?"

"One last question about dear Erica," Partridge said, glancing at Rosie. "Did you have her followed, photographed?"

Duclos looked at Rosie, too. "We tried to play it your way," he told him. "We only followed a little. After she changed cars twice, we decided that any more following would only lead to discovery."

"We'll get her on Mykonos, anyway," Rosie said impatiently.

"If you play it carefully."

"You mean Mykonos is of no interest to you?"

"Personally, I am interested. But Bernard sees his first duty in putting the spy network in Paris quite out of business. Understandably. After all, the American base in Turkey is your affair, not ours." He was watching Partridge's astonished eyes with some amusement. "Yes, at Smyrna. It is nice to know you may be very near the truth," he agreed.

"Any proof?" Partridge asked intently.

"Only what we heard in the conversation between two Russians as soon as Erica had departed. One was Peter—his voice is deep, hoarse, identifiable. The other we could not place, but he is most certainly Peter's superior. Now, let me remember. . . ." Yves was putting his facts into the neat and logical order that he found agreeable: the free-floating ideas, the quick jumps in thinking practiced by his American friends were something that irked his sense of balance and proportion. Small details, perhaps of greatest importance, could be lost in the excitement of discovery. This report was his to give, and he was determined to give it in his way.

"Alex is going to Smyrna. Purpose not disclosed. He has important contacts there. Names not disclosed—but from Peter's remarks, we judge that these contacts do not know that Alex is a Communist agent. After that, he proceeds to Mykonos. His mission accomplished, he returns to Paris. So much for Alex, except that reference was made by Peter to the Farraday party, *which Alex attended.* So he is the American you are looking for, Rosie."

Rosie, grimly silent, nodded.

"Next, there was talk of John Craig. They are no longer interested in him. They know, now, his purpose for traveling abroad; they checked thoroughly on his credentials as a historian. Peter had some reservations. What if Craig were to extend his visit to Troy down as far as Ephesus, which is close to Smyrna? What if he were to meet Alex by chance? There, the other Russian was much more casual and confident. Overcaution, he said, was another name for timidity. Alex would meet several people who knew him, no doubt. That was why he would use his real name in Smyrna and have an innocent excuse for his travels. No one would question him unless he seemed evasive. If he was not good enough to stand up to a meeting with Craig or anyone else who knew him, he was of no use for this mission. Peter made a hasty retraction. Alex, it seems, had been his choice."

"So Craig is off their list," Partridge said reflectively, and caught Rosie's speculative eye on him, and shrugged apologetically. Still, he thought, that wasn't a bad idea of mine; Craig's a natural for this job.

"It was just then," Duclos continued, his voice quickening, rising, "at the point where Peter was flustered, and as annoyed as he dared to be, that he made a slip. He said, 'In spite of what you think, I did not select Alex because of any personal interest. You will find, Comrade Insarov, that he *is* the man for this mission.' There followed a very definite silence. As now." Duclos smiled at Partridge. "That guess of yours was certainly right. Insarov must be Berg—why else would he be interested in Craig, whose only claim to notice is that he has seen Berg?"

"There was more than guessing involved," said Rosie, giving Partridge his full due.

"And more than one man involved, too," Partridge reminded them. How many agents had been alerted, each producing a small fraction of information, and some of it useless, all risking their lives? How many analysts breaking down those fractions? How many evaluators fitting them together in different ways? "You know, when I started work in Intelligence, I had a vision of Partridge, out there all by himself, keeping the peace with his little pistol and brilliant action, a life of fast cars and beautiful women and expense accounts that didn't have to be rendered." He allowed himself a laugh then, covering his own elation with a touch of self-ridicule.

"And lastly"—Duclos insisted on giving the report in full, in logical order—"they may be closing down Le Happening. Its uses are over, I suppose."

"Or have they noticed your interest in the club? These things do get around," Rosie said. That had been one of his chief problems, all along.

"Fortunately," Duclos assured him, "I think our interest in Le Happening will be blamed on Interpol. Bernard is adding a little proof of that: he is getting the police to raid the club for narcotics tonight. I thought I might drop around—" He looked at Rosie, who had glanced up sharply and raised an eyebrow. But Rosie made no other comment. And that, thought Duclos, saves a useless argument. He went on, "As for Insarov, he is leaving Paris this afternoon. He mentioned business in Milan next week. If everything goes well, Peter is to set their plan in motion. From Paris? We couldn't fathom that. Our experts are working over that part of the transcript, phrase by phrase."

"Poor old bloody experts," Partridge said cheerfully, "and they never get a trip to Mykonos, either." He choked back some of his jubilation. "I hope you're planning to send me along, Rosie. Are you going, Yves?"

Duclos grinned widely. "I'm doing my best on that, right now. Erica is possibly a French national, and she is certainly part of a Paris network. She would be a good catch for us. And she knows Peter, who is obviously the director, or one of the aides to the director, of that network. So—" Duclos spread his hands, and beamed. "It seems as if you'll get one of your old dreams, Jim: she's very pretty, this Erica, and with style. Bernard had a good picture of her made for his files, drawn from a precise description by the coatroom attendant. Blond, nose retroussé, green eyes, excellent figure, good clothes. But naturally—she must fit the circles in which she seems to move."

Rosie was not listening. He didn't even respond with the joke that Yves had expected. He said, "Jim, I'm turning this operation over to you. From today. The best thing I can do is to retire into the background."

Partridge and Duclos stared at him, at each other. "But—" Partridge began.

"Let them think I haven't one suspicion that something big is shaping up. Relax their nerves for them, shall we? Yes, Jim, that's the way it has to be. They don't know you at all. But apparently they know me."

"So you *were* followed today," Partridge said. He wished his guess about Rosie's delay in arriving here hadn't been so right.

"Very intently. I shook them off, I think. They'll only allow me one success like that. Just one more, and they'll know I'm on guard, expecting something. Which is proof I know something." He studied his hands. "Damn their eyes and ears, they've even tapped my telephone," he said in rising anger.

"They've really drawn a bead on you," Partridge said slowly.

Duclos was perturbed. "But Rosie, how could that be? You're careful, you're—"

"They are only testing me, so far. But I'd like to know who gave them the clue that I was the man to watch," Rosie said softly, dangerously. "It's someone in security, that's for sure. Or someone who is in contact with him."

"I don't think the leak came from us," Duclos said quickly. "After all, there is only Bernard and I who know—"

"It didn't come from you, Yves," Rosie said heavily. "It came from someone who has connections or trusting friends in a branch of our own security. And that's one thing I'm going to find out, even if I'm sitting on the side lines. By God, I'll find that out." He glared around the room. Then he relaxed, forcing a smile. "Now I had better make an involved exit from this place. Said I would be back at the office by four. Which reminds me, Jim, there's a contract waiting on my desk for you to sign." And how will he handle that? Rosie wondered.

Partridge rose and went over to the telephone beside Mimi. He was the Caen Distributor once more, telling Rosie's secretary that he wanted to speak with Monsieur Rosenfeld. Not yet returned? Then let him be most kindly informed that it was unfortunately impossible to sign the agreement today; another offer at a much better price was under consideration. With regrets and distinguished salutations . . .

He'll do all right, Rosie admitted to himself. He knows as much as you do about this project, perhaps even more in some of the details he gathered during the last four months. He knows the support we can give him, and where to get it. He can cope with Greek and Turkish Intelligence—he must have worked closely with them on the Lesbos-Izmir affair. He's the eventual replacement for you, anyway, so shut up. But all these admissions didn't comfort Rosie. This was one operation that he would have liked to see through, all the way to the very end. Oh, well, there was no use in delaying his exit. He shook hands with Yves. "That was an excellent report you made, a good piece of work by everyone concerned. My congratulations to Bernard. Tell him I'll be at the golf club on Sunday. I'll thank him, then, myself."

"And just when the overhead route to my studio was working so perfectly," Duclos said with real regret. "Never mind, Rosie. You'll be using it again by August. Want to bet?"

To Partridge, Rosie said, "Don't let the blue skies of Mykonos deceive you. This will be no picnic."

"I could use your advice—"

"You don't need it." He knows the ropes, he knows where to get help and how to use it. "Except," Rosie added lightly, "I think you'd better pack that little pistol, too."

Partridge grinned. "I still need your advice. Can I contact you?"

"Not in person. Through channels. I'll always be available even if I'm in the background. And I'll send you all new information I turn up on Wilshot and Bradley." His voice had been kept low. Then, more naturally, "Oh, and Jim—"

"Yes?"

"Go easy on Craig."

Partridge's grin widened. "He's a natural."

"I know. That's our big temptation, isn't it?" Rosie clapped Partridge's shoulder as he turned away to cross the room to Mimi. She was working happily at her desk, and had turned on her radio to keep her company; perhaps also to show she was much too busy listening to *Les Sylphides* to have heard any of their long discussion. She was a woman of infinite tact. Rosie slipped his arm around the strong waist as they walked in close step to the door. "Take care of yourself, Mimi."

"But I always do, Rosee!" She gave him a generous hug, a kiss on both cheeks. He left without looking back at the watching faces. "Was that good-bye?" she asked as she locked the door and was startled by an afterthought.

"A temporary one," Jim Partridge said. He actually meant that, which startled him, too. His promotion was exhilarating, he might as well admit it. But he hadn't wanted it, not quite this way. He wondered if he'd have the good sense and the guts to step aside like that, let a younger man who could be a competitor take over? Then the weight of the new responsibility hit him, full force. He walked over to the small table, pulled a stool beside it, and sat down to look at the map.

Duclos was still thinking about Rosie. "Perhaps he was too quick, there. He knows enough dodges to cover up his moves. He didn't need to—"

"Didn't he? I'll quote you, Yves: 'If everything goes well, Peter is to set their plan in motion.' But if they think that we are interested in them, then everything is not going well and Peter will set quite a different plan in motion." Insarov hadn't prepared so thoroughly without having some alternative to fall back on. Not Insarov. "You know what that could mean for us."

"They win; we lose," Duclos said soberly. "Are you planning to go to Mykonos yourself or are you sending someone else?"

Partridge thought of three men who could be sent. And yet, time was short. There would have to be a long briefing, a thorough preparation. "There are so many small pieces to be remembered in this damned jigsaw puzzle," he said, "and if they are not placed correctly, then—" He searched for a cigarette and lit it.

"Then," Duclos finished for him, "the main pieces won't drop naturally into place?"

Partridge nodded.

Duclos placed his finger on Smyrna. "What's their plan? To make sure of Cyprus, once the U.N. troops leave it? To play the same game on Rhodes, setting Turk against Greek, and both against the Americans? They tried that before. And when they fail, they wait a little, learn from their mistakes, try another way. Get rid of American bases, isn't that their purpose?"

Partridge looked at Duclos' finger, now tapping Smyrna impatiently. The American base there was NATO's chief installation in the eastern Mediterranean. "I didn't think you worried so much about NATO," he teased gently.

"I've criticized it," the Frenchman admitted, "and, from our point of view, with justification. But as of this moment, I prefer not to see it castrated." He relaxed into a smile. "Friends are the only people who can agree to disagree, no? Besides, Jim, it is one thing to give up a base by your own decision; quite another to be forced out of it by your enemy's skill in psychological warfare. That would only prove to the world that we are very, very stupid. It is not an agreeable label to have hung around our necks."

Partridge stubbed out his half-finished cigarette. "Self-defeating," he admitted. Duclos and I can work together, he thought, and gave thanks. "I wonder if you could handle Milan for us, try to discover where Insarov goes from there?"

"I'll talk with Bernard about that."

"That would be helpful. It's just possible that Insarov would discount any co-operation between you and us. Under present conditions," he added tactfully, not mentioning De Gaulle. "By the way, I think you'd be interested to know that we've sent Antonini to the Smyrna base. There is quite a job for him to do there, I hear."

"More listening devices—just like those he found in your Moscow Embassy?" Duclos was shocked.

"Also," Partridge went on, "Val Sutherland is following him."

Duclos stared. He inclined his head, pursed his lips. "Then he is not a journalist? And his Saigon assignment was only a cover story?"

"It still is. He is supposed to be in Viet Nam, right now, but he will make a long tour of news-gathering in and out of the front lines, which will explain any absence from Saigon. It was thought best to keep his visit to Smyrna quite incognito. You agree?"

Duclos did agree, emphatically, and with considerable relief. What he had been told was a demonstration of trust. Rosie's going would not make so much difference after all. "So Sutherland is the man the Communists ought to have tried to question, and not Antonini?" The idea amused him. That had been one small victory, at least.

"Sutherland is the head of our tear-out-the-walls-and-ceilings experts. He has quite a sense of humor in fixing the Russians' gadgets so that they don't know which to trust—or distrust. That can really foul up their calculations. They don't like to move unless they are really sure—they learned that lesson from Khrushchev's rockets in Cuba, remember? A big mistake."

"A mistake only because it failed," Duclos said. "We have information that the military will never forgive Khrushchev for that. Another excuse will be found to be used against him in the history books, of course—something more peace-like than charging him with the Cuban failure. It would never do to emphasize how important those rockets in Cuba really were."

Partridge looked at Duclos thoughtfully. Rockets in Cuba . . . rockets in Cyprus? "Do you suppose," he asked slowly, "that Alex is being sent to Smyrna to learn who Sutherland is and what he has discovered? As I said, one of Sutherland's jokes is to leave a few of their listening devices working so that we can feed bits and pieces of false information through them. He does this because we can never be sure that we've discovered all the gadgets they've installed. Yet, if they don't know what information they can trust, their next big operation may be turned into another fiasco. So they need Sutherland. They have got to have him."

"Abduction?" Duclos was startled.

"And questioning. They tried that on Antonini in Moscow, remember? How else could they get the completely full information they want? They've got to have it before they start setting any plan into operation."

"Then you'd do well to guard Sutherland. Completely. Every way." A new idea gleamed brightly in Duclos' eyes. "Insarov . . . Isn't he interested in psychology, in the art of questioning a prisoner? Would he deal with Sutherland himself, if they managed to get him?"

"Sutherland might be considered too important for subordinates to deal with," Partridge agreed. His worry grew.

"Perhaps they'll still aim for Antonini. Even I assumed he was your chief expert until you told me the facts."

"I think they may now be looking around for another man. Antonini let one small remark slip at the Farradays' party. Something about not being the guy the Russians were looking for. He said it half-jokingly, among friends. But Alex was there. He would pick it up and report it. So the question is now: does Insarov believe it was a joke or the truth? I don't think we can risk anything on his answer. We'd better make sure that we have someone else in Smyrna along with Antonini and Sutherland. Someone who was in Moscow at the time they were there. Someone who was one of Antonini's friends." Partridge's voice quickened as if he already could see the man. "And now he turns up in Smyrna, is seen again with Antonini. Not constantly. Just enough. As if they were together but trying to conceal the fact. How's that for a nice red herring?"

"Thank God I don't fit the rôle," Duclos said. "Who is he? George Farraday?"

"No amateurs on this job. We want a professional who knows what he is letting himself in for. Thomas O'Malley."

"The Australian? Who is he working for—you?" And I never guessed it, Duclos thought with annoyance. He liked O'Malley, had known him for a couple of years.

"For British Intelligence. And if you don't know that, Yves, then I don't think Insarov will."

"But he might not believe, either, that an Australian could be on your team of experts."

"Except that O'Malley was born in the United States and lived there until his people took him back to Australia when he was twelve years old. Insarov will soon find that out, once he starts digging into O'Malley's history."

"But will he believe that 'Australian journalist' could be a cover for working with Americans?"

"Why not? He has been conditioned by his own experience to believe such a pattern of espionage exists—it's employed constantly by his own side. Think of the Polish journalists and the Czech diplomats who have been working for the Russians."

Duclos nodded. Yes, he had to admit, even chauffeurs attached to the Eastern European missions abroad had turned out to be radio experts or fully qualified engineers, often of far more importance in rank than the diplomats they drove around. All of them had been trained by the Russians; all of them acted on Moscow's instructions. Their own countries, Communist as they were, came second.

"Yes, O'Malley's the man for this job. He is as tough as they come," Partridge was saying. "He has such a sense of humor that he might even enjoy it."

"That depends on how far Insarov will go with his questioning, doesn't it?" Duclos asked grimly.

"We make sure," Partridge said equally grimly, "that Insarov never reaches that distance."

"It is still a cold-blooded idea—using O'Malley as a decoy."

"You inspired it. You said Insarov might deal with the questioning himself. If he thought O'Malley was the man they wanted, he would be on hand when they tried to take him. It's easier to question a man near the abduction point than to smuggle him through hostile territory, like Turkey, into Russia. If you were Insarov, where would you have your prisoner taken out from Smyrna?" Partridge pointed toward the map.

Duclos didn't even need to look at it. "Into the Aegean," he said. "But that doesn't necessarily mean Mykonos."

"No," Partridge agreed. But, he thought, it does mean some place where Insarov feels he has established a margin of safety.

"The examination of a prisoner could even be done on a boat, a small yacht," Duclos said unhappily.

"Yes," Partridge agreed again. But, he thought, that depends on the weather and Insarov's seamanship. The Aegean could make more people helpless in shorter time than any other body of water. Even the best of sailors ran for the shelter of an island when the north wind suddenly rose. "Anyway," he said, closing the topic, "it will be entirely up to O'Malley whether he wants to help us in this. I'll contact him through Chris Holland, of course."

"That should make everything quite regular," Duclos said acidly.

"We are not asking O'Malley to do anything we wouldn't be prepared to do ourselves."

"You mean you'd let yourself be abducted by Insarov to help the British?"

"If it would catch Insarov—yes. And so would you."

"I'd have to think about that. To help my own country—I'd agree. But, for the sake of the British—" He shrugged his shoulders. "I don't know," he said honestly.

"Against men like Insarov," Partridge said, "there are no French or British or Americans. Let's leave that kind of stupidity to our politicians."

Duclos was smiling. Partridge had offered him one of his own favorite arguments. *"Touché,"* he said quietly.

Partridge relaxed. "Why argue, anyway? As Rosie would say, we could all be wrong. Insarov may now be en route back to Moscow by way of Milan."

Duclos laughed briefly at some thought of his own. "Sorry. I was thinking of that innocent little party at the Meurice. Apart from the Farradays and John Craig, everyone else was Intelligence of some kind, except for Wilshot and Bradley."

"And which of those two is Alex?"

"The one who is planning to go to Smyrna."

Partridge smiled. "They are both going to Greece. Separately. Seemingly quite ignorant of each other's vacation plans. Bradley has leave coming up from his job with NATO; Wilshot has been talking of finding some sun and a story about Grivas in Athens. Take your pick, Yves. Which?"

"Then we'll have to wait and see which one travels farther east than Athens," said Duclos amiably.

"That's about it," Partridge agreed. Unless, of course, Rosie turned up some extra information: Alex seen without horn-rimmed glasses or his face averted or his handkerchief covering his nose and mouth. Too cautious, Erica had called him. But *she* was the one whose picture was filed in Bernard's office. "Erica's choice—the American girl over at the Hotel Beauharnais—what do you think we should do about her?"

"Nothing."

"Let her be played for an idiot?"

"Just that," Duclos said. "It's better than having her dead, isn't it?"

Put that way, it was. "Well, I'd better get back to the Saint-Honoré," Partridge said, glancing at his watch.

"Are you going to talk with Craig?"

"If he hasn't already packed and left Paris in disgust." Partridge could guess Craig's view of the situation: we do nothing, while Berg walks around unarrested.

"That would be a pity. As you said, he's a natural."

He is more than that now, thought Partridge. Craig is a necessity. He has met both Wilshot and Bradley; he can identify Berg at one glance. And who else have we got who can make that claim? "We'll keep in touch. By telephone. I don't think we should meet again in Paris."

"You won't drop in at Le Happening tonight? We needn't meet. But you never know who may be drifting around there. Alex, for instance? And there are a couple of other men who have been making weekly visits behind stage. They're due to turn up this evening. So the coatroom attendant tells me."

"Have you talked much with her?" Partridge asked quickly.

"No, no. Just a word in passing. Don't worry. She thinks I'm another policeman, one of her own crowd."

"You know," Partridge began, and then stopped short. He wasn't only taking over Rosie's job, it seemed; he was taking over Rosie's supercaution. Anyway, Duclos had his own job to do for Bernard, and the night club had become part of their action. "Can I plan on your help in Mykonos, or will Bernard need you here?" he asked.

"Plan on it," Duclos said with a wide grin. "I've always wanted to paint. Mimi, will you come as my model?" He caught up some opalescent silk from a display stand and draped its transparency around her shoulders. Partridge closed the door on their laughter. No picnic, Rosie had said. But Partridge was smiling as he straightened the CLOSED ON TUESDAY notice. From what he had heard, Mimi at a picnic could be as dangerous as a sidewinder.

Then he put thoughts, ideas, guesses, worries out of his mind, and concentrated on his careful journey to the Saint-Honoré.

Partridge had been right about John Craig. That afternoon he decided to leave Paris and head for Rome and points east. Possibly tomorrow, Wednesday, marking a week exactly since he had arrived here and gone strolling along the Boulevard Saint-Germain. Almost a week since Sussman had died; almost a week for Heinrich Berg to walk around the streets of Paris, a completely free man enjoying his victory. What was Rosie doing, Partridge, Messieurs Galland and Tillier of the *Sixième Arrondissement?* What the hell was anyone doing?

After an angry lunch, he tried to walk some of his bad temper away by marching at a good pace along the left bank of the Seine. He didn't stop at the bookstalls today. He didn't even slow up for the corner of the Rue Bonaparte as he usually did when he passed this way. The girl was never in sight. Around this district he had passed hundreds of pretty girls, hundreds of students, singly, in groups, but she was never one of them. By half past three his temper was less ragged. He took a bus back across the Seine toward the Avenue de l'Opéra, and walked on to the American Express office. There was sunshine above, trees were now a brighter green. Spring clothes were venturing out, faces looked happy to be breathing gentler air. April was a resurgence, a welling of plans and hopes. And all he could feel was annoyance and disappointment mixed with incredible loneliness. Why, he thought suddenly, no one has stopped to speak to me or strike up an acquaintance in the last twenty-four hours. And at that, he had to smile at himself.

He felt still better when he reached his destination and collected a nice assortment of travel folders. Rome, Brindisi, Corfu, Athens, Crete, Rhodes, Istanbul . . . Domes and towers, blue skies and minarets, sunshine and rippling water; delightful exaggeration and a highly colored come-on? Even so, this was more like it. Now for some airline details, an enjoyable hour of decision, and then back to the hotel to pack.

But, standing in the downstairs hall, studying a flight schedule for Rome, a crowd of young Americans around him opening letters they had just collected, he glanced up at a couple of long-haired jubilants pulling out their expected checks, and beyond them, now visible, now half-hidden, now visible again, he saw the girl. Or was it? Quickly he pushed his way through the various small groups, some triumphant, some downcast, clustering together as if they were afraid of being alone, and almost reached the smooth dark head, the profile that he remembered. Then he halted, amazed at his speedy reaction; embarrassed, too. It was the girl, all right, a slender outline in gray suit and white silk shirt among the sloppy Joes and straggle-headed Janes flapping around in their uniform of beatnik conformity—dirty blue jeans and drooping sweaters, straight from the Rue de la Huchette. From her thin-heeled pumps to her softly brushed hair, she was quite remarkable. Simplicity. A distinction of taste, of quiet manners, of independence.

He stood, hesitating. He could hardly go up and say, "Remember me?" He was the man who had witnessed her hurt. Watching her now, he could realize how her tears, shed in public, would be an agonizing memory. He had been the invading stranger, someone she never wanted to see again.

She was studying a list which she held in her hand, her facc grave as she calculated and then relaxing a little as she came to some decision. As she slipped the piece of paper into her handbag, she glanced up as if she had actually felt him look at her. For a moment, her eyes widened. She had recognized him. Then, just as abruptly, she averted her head and turned toward the door. He let her go. And I'll never get a second chance, he thought; luck doesn't run that way. He followed slowly, giving her plenty of time to escape from an unwelcome encounter.

But as he came through the doorway into the gentle warm sunshine, she was standing there. Waiting. Looking toward him. Slightly uncertain, she took a step forward; then thought better of it. Does she think *I* don't want to meet her again? he wondered in amazement. This time, as she moved away with her head high, he caught up with her. "Hello, there!" he said, and stopped her completely. "Sorry for staring. I didn't think you'd recognize me."

"And I wasn't sure that you remembered me." She smiled. "I wanted to—I wanted to thank you."

"Then come and have a drink with me." He glanced at his watch. "Or tea, or coffee, or something." My God, he thought, where has all my conversation gone to?

"I'm meeting some people at half past four." She frowned at her own watch. "It isn't far, fortunately."

"That gives us exactly ten minutes to get to know each other. Couldn't you be late? Or send despairing messages?"

"Such as?" Her eyes were actually smiling.

"Oh, that you're coming down with measles."

She laughed, shook her head. "This is too important for me. You see, I'm running away." The laughter had vanished; her voice and eyes became expressionless.

He stared at her. "Where are you meeting your friends?"

"The Café de la Paix."

"I'll walk you there. If I may."

"Of course." She started walking slowly, and he fell into pace. She glanced at the folders in his hand. "Are you leaving Paris, too?"

"Tomorrow. At least, that was the plan."

She took the folders and looked through them. "All these places? But how wonderful!"

"I'm traveling until September. Getting material for a book."

"On what?" She was genuinely interested.

"Trade routes," he said, and waited for her comments. They weren't stupid. She didn't gush "How fascinating!" She didn't take refuge in a blank "Oh!" She said, "I think we'd need more than ten minutes to hear about that. Are you an economist?"

"Partly that, partly a historian."

"Ancient history?"

"Trying to learn something about it," he said with an attempt at diffidence.

"Rhodes," she said softly. "I've always wanted to visit it. Do you know, in June, there's a valley filled with butterflies? They rise in a cloud—" She smiled, handing him back the folders, checking her enthusiasm. "Of course, if the cloud was so thick that it blotted out everything, it might be more frightening than beautiful."

"So you're leaving Paris, too," he said, wondering where she was going. Back to America?

"For a little while." She added with painful frankness, "I think that's the best cure, don't you?"

He thought of last Wednesday evening, of that long and unhappy quarrel. So she was still vulnerable, was she? "It usually works," he said briefly.

"I'd have thought you would never run away from your emotions." She looked at him with new interest.

"I guess we all do, at times." He stopped thinking of his own defeats. "And where are you bound for?"

"Mykonos."

"That isn't so far from Rhodes. Perhaps you'll see your cloud of butterflies yet."

She shook her head. "The budget won't stretch as far as that. I can just manage the fare to Mykonos and back. I don't have to worry about hotel bills. I'm staying with a friend—a girl I know at art school here. Her uncle has lent her his house for the summer. It must be nice to have uncles like that."

"Provided they stay in the background and don't arrange your days for you."

"Oh, Maritta's uncle isn't going to be around much, if at all."

"Then it sounds perfect. How long will you actually stay with your Greek friend? I might be passing Mykonos in July—"

"Greek? Maritta is French. Her father was Flemish, I think. Her second name is Maas. Anyway, she was born in Paris. But lots of French artists and writers go to Mykonos, you know."

"You're going to paint?"

"And relax."

And forget, he thought. "How long—" he began again.

"Three weeks. I have to be back in Paris to finish my classes."

"You take them very seriously. More than your friend does."

"Maritta doesn't have to take anything very seriously," she said with a smile.

"Ah, those rich uncles again."

"There's only one, as far as I know. And not so rich, really. He just knows *how* to spend the money he has. That's an art in itself, isn't it?"

"Wish I could afford it," he said with a grin. He saw the Café de la Paix just ahead of them. He had passed this corner several times in the last few days, and it always reminded him of a bend in a river with several currents all jostling in perpetual motion. People rose from tables, people sat down at tables, people walked past on the narrow strip of sidewalk left to them, buses and cars poured in and out of seven tributaries to sweep around the Place de l'Opéra and gouge their way through the persistent streams of pedestrians. "This may hardly be the place," he said, raising his voice to be heard above the grinding gears and screeching brakes, "but don't you think it's time we introduced ourselves? I'm John Craig."

"And I'm Veronica Clark."

"What's your address, by the way?"

"The Hotel Beauharnais."

"Would you have—" A sad-faced woman, with a basket of posies for sale, stepped backward from a table and separated them. "Would you—"

"I see them," she said in a low voice. "Uncle Peter looks very solemn. Do you think he is wondering if I'll be a good influence on Maritta after all? How late are we?"

"Thirty-five seconds." Craig looked over the tables, caught sight of a blonde girl with her hand upraised as a welcoming sign. "Are you afraid of him?" he asked, looking now at the square-faced, blunt-nosed man who sat, Spanish grandee fashion, beside her. He was middle-aged, heavily constructed, and very well dressed. Not that that meant a thing: the first three hundred dollars that any fly-by-night operator made seemed to go on a suit nowadays. I'm doing him an injustice, Craig thought; he looks a very solid citizen, indeed.

"I don't know him. Maritta is a little nervous about him, though. He's very old-fashioned, she says." Veronica waved back to her friend.

"Let me come and apologize for you." Thirty-five seconds' worth of apology. He led her toward the table where the blonde and her tight-faced uncle waited. Maritta might be quite a handful at that, Craig decided, admiring the tiptilted nose, marking the expensively casual hair and the little black dress with its mink jacket. Green eyes, he noted, and a warmly welcoming smile. "I'm sorry," he said, ignoring introductions to prove he wasn't staying. "It's my fault. We met by accident. No, thank you"—this to Maritta, who was pointing to the chair beside her—"I'm on my way. Miss Clark and I didn't quite finish our conversation." He pulled out a chair for Veronica, said to her quietly, "Would you have dinner with me tonight?"

"I'd love to."

"Oh, dear," Maritta said, "I'm leaving tomorrow, Ronnie. I thought we'd go over—" She paused, looking at Craig with a dazzling smile of sweet apology. "I'm really so sorry."

"Then we'll lunch tomorrow, instead," he told Veronica. "I'll call you in the morning?" He shook her hand. "Good-bye," with a bow for Green Eyes. "Good-bye, sir. Sorry to intrude." And that should hold the old bastard, he thought, turning to make a quick and efficient exit, bumping into the sad-faced flower girl again. Well, he thought now, as he left the tight rows of tables and waited for the traffic to stop so that he could cross the street, it's always the way; you wander around Paris for a week and never see her, and when you do meet her you are granted ten minutes and thirty-five seconds. But even two minutes and twenty-seven seconds would have been worth it.

Perhaps he wouldn't leave tomorrow. A few more days would be pleasant. The week of tensions and loneliness dropped away from him, and he strode down the avenue with as much zest and interest as if he were setting out for his first walk through Paris.

When he came down to the hotel bar at six, showered, changed, and very much in his right mind, he found the small green room empty except for an Indian drinking orange juice and an Egyptian sipping lemonade. Jules' welcome was astoundingly warm. He rushed to mix a Scotch and soda, and his voice almost trembled as he confided that, today, two English ladies had come in demanding tea. With cake. Yesterday, there had been three American children wanting something called Cokes. Cokes, cakes and fruit drinks, Craig reflected, would convert Jules to tolerating heretics like himself who drank Scotch with ice and soda. It was not, Jules went on, that he disliked tea or those other drinks, except this room was *not* the place; it was an invasion of sacred rights, and he was not a cow to dispense milk.

Besides, it drove away the real customers. And there's the rub, thought Craig, and drank his Scotch and seemed to listen. She was a quite remarkable girl. In the middle of that tourist and expatriate crowd in the American Express building, she had been unique among beehive hair styles and haystack heads. At the Café de la Paix, she had made mink look negligible. He had known a lot of girls in the last fourteen years, some rather more than well. Two he had almost married. In every case, he had drifted into love before he had headed out, sometimes with regrets to remember, more often with frank relief. But drifted was the word; it had been a gradual thing of weeks, getting pleasanter and pleasanter until is seemed inevitable. That was love, he had thought. Love at first sight? He had never believed in it. He still didn't. . . . Impossible. At his age? It was worse than impossible; it was silly.

"Good evening, Jules," Jim Partridge said, sliding onto the stool next to Craig. "Hello, there! And how are you?"

"Feeling my age. How are you?" He looks exhausted, Craig thought. Business must have been hard today.

Partridge was studying the younger man with amusement. "Is that what's making you so happy and scared?"

"What?" Damn it all, I'm not so transparent as that. Or has Partridge got a gadget for thought-reading as well as one for listening to conversations across a room? Craig shook his head and laughed.

"Glad to see you in a better mood than I expected," Partridge said softly. "Make it a double Martini, tonight," he told Jules in a cheerful voice. "Found a couple of good chairs today, authentic Louis Fifteenth, with some of the original tapestry still on them. A little careful cleaning and cautious repairs and we've really got something."

"Better mood?" Craig echoed, suddenly remembering the recriminations he had worked up over lunch today. "I've a few complaints—"

"That's right," Partridge said smoothly. "Let's get the dust out of my throat, first, shall we? And what about resting our backs in a comfortable chair?" He took a sip of his drink, gave Jules his approval, and led the way to a table against a wall. He sat down with visible relief, took off his glasses, looked ten years younger and gave a grin to match. "Are you doing anything this evening? I'm at a loose end myself. What about dinner together, in some nice quiet little place not too far away? That will save time."

"Suits me. I've a lot to say. And the quicker, the better."

"How soon do you feel like eating?"

"Any time. I didn't have much lunch, today."

And I had none at all, thought Partridge. "Fine. We'll shock the French but we'll get a dining room to ourselves. Just let me finish this drink gratefully. Have another, won't you?"

Craig shook his head. All he wanted was a subdued corner in that quiet dining room. Still, he was going to be given at least some time with Partridge, so he might as well look cheerful meanwhile and talk politely.

Partridge didn't hurry. He smoked a cigarette as he finished his drink at normal speed, and listened to Craig. I'll have to remember, Partridge told himself, how little he knows. I'll have to try to put myself in his place, forget everything I've discussed with Rosie and Bernard and Duclos and Chris Holland in these last six days; forget everything I've read in those last months, every clue, guess, inference, deduction, fact. All he knows is that Heinrich Berg is a Nazi, the kind who would be none the worse of a hanging. All he knows is that Berg has friends who've given him a hard time this week. All he knows is that Berg walks free, and Sussman's murder is being called suicide. That is all he knows. Good God, where do I begin to talk with him? And how much could he stand? How much is safe—for him, for us?

"You've really been very patient," Partridge said, finishing his drink at last. "Look, can I borrow ten more minutes from you? I need to wash up. Came straight from the street. I'll admit I was anxious in case you had left Paris. And I wouldn't have blamed you, either." He drew out his wallet, riffled through some business cards and a snapshot of a girl in a bathing suit, found a small photograph and handed it over to Craig. "Recognize your friend?"

Craig, completely disarmed by this time, took it with the same easy smile with which it had been presented to him. It was a small study in truculence, unflattering enough to be a police photograph. The man staring back at him under the sharp lighting was young, fair-haired. He wore a belted raincoat. In the picture, the raincoat was dry. Apart from that, it was the man who had rushed from the café to follow Sussman.

"Thought that would keep you happy, meanwhile," Partridge murmured, taking the photograph back as he rose.

"Who got him?"

"Galland and Tillier, of course. Strictly police business. See you in ten minutes? I'll meet you at the corner of the street." Partridge made his way leisurely out of the bar, which was now beginning to have a few more customers. To his practiced eye, they all seemed reasonable people. No more Jordans swooping down on Craig, anyway. Once out into the lobby and past the observant porter, he increased his speed. Ten minutes weren't so long, considering he had to make his usual evening phone check with Bernard's office. Not that Bernard's man could have had many worries trailing Craig today: suspicion was off him, thank heavens. But it was wise to keep a finger on the pulse; in this line of business anything could happen.

The restaurant was about two blocks' walking distance from the Rue Saint-Honoré. It lay at the junction of several small streets lined with newly built butcher shops. Nearby was a giant, smoothly surfaced square almost filled with the solid bulk of a huge garage. As they skirted it, Partridge had looked at it without much enthusiasm. "You'd never believe it," he said, breaking his long silence, "but only four years ago this was one of the old Paris markets. Open stalls, cobblestones, sixteenth-century houses as background. It used to amuse me to find all that tucked away behind bright avenues and smart shops. Let's hope progress hasn't dolled up our restaurant with chrome and steam tables." But the restaurant had insisted on keeping its own character. And it was good. Not expensive. Just good. Craig relaxed completely.

The room, almost empty at this early hour, was pleasant and placid. The waiters, old as the furniture, knew how to retire into the background as soon as they had served the food. The corner which Partridge had chosen was lit just enough to let one see what one was eating. The leather backs on the chairs, padded and buttoned, were comfortable. This, decided Craig, was the kind of place people could talk. He waited expectantly, but Partridge again was in no hurry. He seemed contented with lighthearted quips through the main course, but Craig had the feeling that he was paying as little attention to the general gossip as he was to the excellent lamb chops and asparagus on his plate. Behind his easy words was a thoughtfulness. He had been like this ever since he had come down from his room at the Saint-Honoré and joined Craig with a nod and a searching glance. Those ten minutes upstairs had produced something more than a clean shirt, a fresh tie, and neatly brushed hair. And what's wrong now? Craig wondered. "You know," he said as the coffee was served, "I hope that route we took along the Rue Saint-Honoré to get here wasn't symbolic. In the days of the Terror, it was the main drag for the tumbrils on their way to the guillotine." He dropped his light tone, let some of his rising annoyance show. "Whose neck is going to get chopped this time?" he demanded. What had happened to that trust Partridge had seemed to feel in him earlier this evening? If any reproof is in order here, thought Craig, it's mine to give, not to take.

"You can begin with my neck," Partridge said evenly. "You've got a few cutting remarks to make, I bet."

"And you'd win it. Sure, the murderer has been caught, but what about the man who gave him orders to murder? Yes, Berg. I saw him yesterday. He walked right past me. And I had no number to phone, nobody to warn. I got back to the Saint-Honoré, practically exploding with the news, and I couldn't even talk to you."

"That was just as well," Partridge said very quietly. "There was one of Berg's agents watching you, at that very minute. They've been tailing you ever since last Thursday morning. But so have we. Now, go on: you've got every right to complain. You've had it rough, and we didn't seem to be doing much, did we? It was a difficult situation, and you handled it well. I'll say that for you."

Craig could only stare. Grouches were not so easily registered when you were told they were thoroughly justified, even expected. Compliments added, too. "What's this about having me followed?"

"Protection. Just in case a car knocked you down and its passengers wanted to take you to the hospital. Or in case a man grasped your wrist, told you he had instructions to bring you to see Detectives Galland and Tillier and, when the needle in your wrist made you black out, helped you most kindly into a waiting car. Little things like that. Troublesome. So some self-effacing Frenchmen have been keeping an eye on you, ready to rush to the rescue. Now, now, don't look so startled. We think that phase is all over. In fact, this afternoon we were quite sure that Berg had no more interest in you. But one thing does puzzle me—"

"I haven't finished," Craig cut in. "You mean you knew about my second meeting with Berg?"

"We had reports on it."

"And you didn't follow him?"

"Let's say we weren't geared for that."

"Tell me one thing." Craig leaned forward on his elbows. His eyes were cold and skeptical. "Do you want to catch Berg?"

Partridge looked at the tightly pressed lips, the hard-set jaw. Craig could be a tough customer if he chose. "Yes. We'll catch him, and a lot more besides."

"Well what's being done about it? Don't you think you owe me a holding explanation at least? In return for handling certain difficult situations? I'd like a little more than some sugar-coated approval! Sweet suffering—"

"Take it easy, pal. We are allowed to have some serious after-dinner conversation in a public restaurant, but not to frighten the waiters out of their shirt fronts."

"Sorry." But there was no retreat in the quieted voice.

"You know, I agree with every word you say. Only, I do see things from a different angle, from a different set of facts."

"Of course," said Craig, coldly.

"I was prepared to give you one or two of them. I'd want to know them, if I were you. But—"

"That's right. There's always a but."

"You could clear it away."

"I?"

Partridge's light tone changed to sudden attack. "This afternoon you talked with a man at the Café de la Paix. Why?"

"Why? For Christ's sake—I just went to—" Craig stopped short. "How did you know about that? Oh, I see. One of those self-effacing Frenchmen, again?"

Partridge relaxed a little. Craig hadn't denied it, and that at least was a good start on this difficult topic. "You really had us all puzzled, and in our job it isn't really pleasant to be puzzled about friends. You see, one of our agents snapped a picture of that table just as a flower vendor ran some interference for him. It made a nice diversion."

"He took a photograph?" Craig hadn't seen even a Minox camera around. "How?"

"He lit a cigarette."

"I didn't even notice anyone doing that," Craig admitted ruefully.

"Good. You weren't meant to."

"Have you been photographing me all over Paris?" Craig was sharp-voiced again.

"Only when you met someone. You don't know how useful it has been to a friend of mine at the Sûreté who collects photographs and drawings for his file on subversives. In fact, he has the best file on Communists, French or otherwise, who have been active in France. You've added two to his collection in the last few days. And perhaps you could even help with some added information about a third—the man at the table. Yes, he's on file, too. He worked in Paris four years ago, then went back to Moscow. Now, judging from the photograph, he's returned to France. What's the name he is using, nowadays?"

Craig could only sit staring at the quiet face opposite him. "Communists . . . I begin to see why you're so damned slow to take an interest in Berg. A Nazi isn't worth bothering about when a Communist can be caught," he said bitterly. "Is that it?"

Partridge only shook his head.

"What are you trying to tell me?" Craig demanded.

"I've already told you. I said we would catch Berg—*and a lot more besides.*"

There was a pause. "A Nazi working with Communists?" Craig's disbelief was clear.

"You're getting close. I knew you would, once you started using your brain instead of your emotions. Actually, Berg never was a Nazi, except for show. And he did it very well, according to reports. He was said to be such a virulent Nazi that he embarrassed some neutralists, 1943 brand—Pétainists—who met him in Berlin; and they did not embarrass easily."

"I'm so damned stupid," Craig said softly. Berg's agents had been following him, accosting him, hadn't they? Berg's agents were being photographed for the Communist file at the Sûreté. Therefore Berg had to be a Communist or else the Sûreté was completely crazy. His face tightened. "Is the man at the Café de la Paix another of Berg's?"

"We don't know that. We only know that he is a trained GRU agent, holding the rank of colonel. That's big stuff, let me tell you. What is he pretending to be?"

"What's Veronica getting into?" Craig asked, lost in his own worries. "Good God, what's she getting into?"

"Veronica?" Partridge was remarkably still.

"Yes, the girl I was with—Veronica Clark. The dark-haired one—"

"I haven't seen the photograph, just heard about it," Partridge told him. "There was a fair-haired girl at the table, too. Who was she?"

"Maritta Maas, a friend of Veronica's. They're art students. Look, Jim—" Craig discovered he was almost desperate—"Veronica's in the clear. She can't be—"

"Who was the man?" Partridge's quiet voice insisted.

"Uncle Peter. Maritta's Uncle Peter. I didn't wait for an introduction. The only reason I was at that table, frankly, was to finish my invitation to dinner. I was asking Veronica—"

"Peter . . ." Partridge took a deep breath. "So he was looking her over," he said softly.

Craig's face hardened. "You know, I believe you *are* crazy. You and your friend at the Sûreté with his little catalogue of faces. He thinks a man at a table looks something like a man in his files! Is he positive? Why, he didn't even know the name of the man at the table, did he? Just a likeness, that's all. You're pouring an awful lot of heavy concrete on top of clay. I saw Maritta—a pretty little nitwit, gay, charming. The man *was* her uncle, too. I tell you—"

"Which uncle? The one who has the house on Mykonos?"

Craig froze.

"And let me be still crazier. Maritta has invited Veronica Clark to visit her on Mykonos?"

Craig could only stare, and nod.

"Then here's the craziest news of all. Dear, gay and charming Maritta knows very well what her uncle is. She doesn't know his real name, of course, she doesn't know who he is; but she knows what he is."

"Veronica?" Craig asked slowly.

"She knows nothing at all."

"Why did they invite her?"

"Not out of the kindness of their hearts," Partridge told him. "How well do you know the girl? And that's not a casual question. Tell me the details."

Craig, unwilling but troubled enough to take a hint, did just that.

"So you know her only casually," Partridge said when Craig had ended the brief story of their two meetings. "At least," he corrected himself, "that's how it would appear to most people." If I hadn't been watching Craig's face for the last ten minutes, I'd have called it casual, myself. "You know that they must have questioned her about you. I wish I could have seen Peter's face when she told him your name."

"How would he recognize it?" asked Craig, and brought Partridge up sharply.

"You called yourself stupid," Partridge said, covering up his mistake, "but I think you're too damned quick. Let's call it a crazy guess."

"I'm getting a little leery of that adjective," Craig admitted with a wry grin. But he wasn't going to be sidetracked. He came back to his question about Uncle Peter. "How would he—"

"Now the problem is this," Partridge ran on. "Will they believe you are just a casual acquaintance of Veronica's? Or will they think you're possibly a dangerous character after all—one of our agents, perhaps, using Veronica to trap them? No, I don't think they will. . . . You didn't exactly force yourself on them; you paid little attention to them. Good. They'll possibly still want her out there on Mykonos—she's perfect for them, from what you tell me. Why, even you accepted Maritta because Veronica was her friend. Yes, perfect. So—"

"You aren't letting Veronica go to Mykonos?" Craig interrupted. "You can't."

"I can. And must. What else?"

"Warn her."

"How?"

Craig finished his last glass of wine. It tasted as bitter as his thoughts. "I can see no way," he admitted. Expect a girl to listen to a stranger, like Partridge, telling her he was saving her from Maritta? Or to listen to me? "She'd think we were—" he half smiled, in spite of his worry—"crazy."

"You just can't warn people by telling them a little," Partridge agreed. As I've found out, he thought. What would Rosie have done? he wondered. Told Craig as much? Yet compared to what Rosie and he knew, Craig had been told very little.

"I'll go to Mykonos," Craig decided. "I'll be there, at least."

"To keep an eye on her or for your own peace of mind?"

"A little of each."

Partridge laughed. Then shook his head, and fell silent.

"What's the joke?"

"Me, you, and me again."

"Don't you want me to go to Mykonos?"

Partridge took a very long and deep breath. This evening, on his roundabout journey back from Mimi's shop, he had racked his brains for a reasonable approach to Craig on the subject of Mykonos; he had thought of every possible objection that might be made—this isn't my business, I've a book to write, I've got just so much time and money, I hadn't planned on Mykonos, why the hell do you have to drag me into this, why the hell can't you take peaceful coexistence at its face value and stop rocking the boat, a plague on both your houses, there's not much difference between You and Them, so why expect me to get excited? (It wasn't that the amateurs were so much a responsibility, as he had said to Rosie, but that they were such damned wearisome arguers with prejudgments popping up all over the place like the dragon's teeth in Colchis.) And suddenly, determinedly, no argument brooked, Craig had said, "I'll go to Mykonos." Partridge studied the tablecloth.

"Because," finished Craig, "I'm going in any case."

"Well—" Partridge hesitated, made a good effort at being uncertain.

"I have a perfectly good excuse. Old trade-routes Craig. You see, the island of Delos can only be reached from Mykonos, unless you have a private yacht and can cruise around in your own good time. Delos is a collection of ruins now; no one lives there. But once it was pretty important in the struggle for power between Persians and Greeks, Asia Minor and Rome. It was a control point for a lot of trade, believe me. So, I've added Delos to my list. And I'll have to stay in Mykonos. Simple."

"There's only one way you could do this with safety."

"How's that?"

"Let us supply some people to keep a close eye on you. There will be several Americans, perhaps a couple of French, and—of course—Greeks. It's their country, after all."

"Are you recruiting me?" And into what branch of Intelligence? Craig wondered. The FBI have liaison agents abroad, co-operating with foreign police and security departments. But this operation sounds more to me like something involving either G2 or the CIA. Or perhaps there is some new outfit I haven't even heard of. Still, Partridge is Rosie's man—there is no doubt about that. And there is no doubt, too, that Rosie is completely authentic and reliable or else I wouldn't have been commended to his charge by my most discreet and knowledgeable brother-in-law. "Are you?" Craig repeated, restraining his amusement as he watched Partridge's blank face.

"Good heavens, no. Although, of course, as well as keeping an eye on Veronica, and giving yourself some peace of mind, and studying trade routes, you perhaps possibly just could—do something for Uncle Sam? In the odd free moments, of course."

"Is that irony, sarcasm, or just smooth operation? All right. What can I do for you?"

"You are one of the few people in this world who could recognize Heinrich Berg."

Craig's joking stopped. "Will he be there?" he asked, his eyes narrowing.

"Perhaps. You'd know, anyway, wouldn't you? Certainly, his associates will be there. Maritta, for one."

"So," Craig said slowly, the light dawning at last at the end of the long dark tunnel, "Uncle Peter knows Berg, and that's how he heard my name before Veronica ever mentioned it to him. You could have told me. Why didn't you?"

"Everything in its place and proper time," Partridge said gently.

Craig smiled and wondered how much else he might have to learn in its proper place and time. "You'll keep me informed, won't you?" he asked, his smile broadening into a grin. "When it is suitable, of course."

"Of course," Partridge assured him, wide-eyed, innocent. "When do you leave Paris?"

"Any day. I thought I'd go to Italy first."

"Then avoid Milan. In fact, you could postpone Italy altogether—meanwhile. Try Athens. Stay at the Grande Bretagne; then we know where to reach you easily. By the beginning of May, be in Mykonos. Plan on two weeks there. We'll book your hotels, and leave the reservations in your name at the American Express in Athens. We'll pay for them."

"No need," Craig interjected sharply. When had Partridge thought out all this flow of instructions?

I bet there is, too, decided Partridge. "We'll book, anyway. Have to know where all our friends and helpers are in place, you know. There's some planning to do, so we'll call this a day, shall we? I'll see you tomorrow evening. In the bar, as usual. And you can tell me how Veronica couldn't lunch with you." He smiled briefly at Craig's disbelief. "Just another of those crazy notions, of course, but don't count on being allowed to meet her. That is, if her invitation to Mykonos is still valid."

"And if they have canceled her invitation—then what?"

"Then you can't go, either."

"I still could use the Delos excuse."

Partridge studied Craig: a reliable face, bright intelligence in the eyes and brow, strength in the mouth, a firm jaw line; a body kept in good condition, no flabbiness there, either. Partridge shook his head regretfully. "If they are so suspicious of you that they cancel her visit, then you're not going."

"If I'm willing to risk it—"

Partridge shook his head again. It was quite final. "Sorry," he said. And he meant it. His hand went up to summon the waiter and pay the bill. "Okay?" he asked as he prepared to rise. He had a hard evening ahead of him.

"Think I've got it all straight. And if Veronica doesn't go, then I forget everything."

"Exactly." As Partridge led the way to the door, he turned his head to say very quietly, a smile in his usually serious eyes, "And I hope you don't talk in your sleep."

10

Craig returned to the hotel alone. Partridge had pointed him in the direction of the Avenue de l'Opéra, from where he could easily strike toward home by well-known, well-lighted routes. Partridge, himself, had vanished into a dark street of closed butcher shops. It was scarcely nine o'clock. Early for Craig to go up to his room, but he was tired of the cosy little bar downstairs, of the same old faces and the same light chitchat around him. Besides, he had quite a number of thoughts to set in order. The place for that was upstairs in his dull bedroom, with no one else's clinking glass or braying laughter to catch his attention. He was far from antisocial—his life was one long struggle to get his work done in spite of friends and the new Italian movie around the corner—but there were times when people blotted out thought. Perhaps that was what was so beguiling about them: a kind of sweet forgetting about the realities, a reassurance of freedom from anxiety as long as they all gathered together and joked their troubles away.

He picked up his key and a letter from Sue at the porter's desk. There was also a verbal message from the punctilious porter, himself, delivered with his usual lugubriousness. There had been a telephone call for Craig, a lady's voice, no name. That was all. "When?" asked Craig. "Five minutes ago," the porter said and, his duty done, turned to sorting out keys for the pigeonholes behind his desk.

It couldn't have been Veronica, Craig decided, as he crossed the worn carpet and entered the gilded cage of the elevator. He hadn't had time to give her his address. So who was it? It didn't matter much, if no name had been left. He forgot about it as soon as he opened Sue's letter and was caught up in her effervescent style. Cheerful as usual, of course, hiding disquiet behind natural optimism. George was going to be in Washington for some time. News of his arrest in Moscow had been leaked, somehow, and had even reached a newspaper column, which made a new post abroad difficult—what foreign government wanted someone who had been publicly labeled as a spy to be stationed in its capital? Once a charge like that appeared in print, it became awkward to handle and difficult to ignore. It didn't matter if—in George's words—it was a god-damned lie. The lie was read, while the denial was ignored. "So," wrote Sue, "that's how a careless journalist can ruin the entire career of someone who has done more for his country than ever *he* has done with his little typewriter." However (the word was heavily underlined, as if to cheer herself up), this otherwise quiet stay in Washington might be the chance to start raising a family. She had had two miscarriages in Moscow, but the doctor now said she was absolutely fine, and so wasn't that wonderful? There had been some talk of poor Professor Sussman's suicide, too, even on the flight over the Atlantic. Such a small world, wasn't it, with so many unexpected people knowing everyone else? Father seemed much better and would visit them in June, when they hoped to have some air conditioning installed in their new Georgetown apartment. Take care and good luck. . . .

I'll need both, he thought, as he dropped the letter on top of his dresser. As he took off his jacket and tie, and undid the top button of his shirt, he was wondering how, exactly, George's story had "been leaked." Purposely, of course. Sue's phrase told him that. But by whom? He could guess the reason behind the planted rumor; George's career was being spiked. How many other Georges were there, anyway, saying nothing, swallowing their disappointments, covering up the wounds they had received in the hidden war? And Sue—strange how people could keep silent about their personal tragedies. Two miscarriages . . . Good God, he thought, and I used to tease her about the time she was taking to produce a nephew for Christmas. Yes, people were surprising in the way they could disguise their feelings; or their thoughts; or even their actions. Never, in fact, underestimate anybody. A historian shouldn't need to be reminded of that. He had three thousand years of human examples, taking his choice from any century, which could amaze—or shock. Nothing that actually happened could be called unbelievable nonsense, no matter how fantastic it appeared. I ought to have remembered that, he told himself, when I listened to Sussman.

And if Sussman had not died, would he have listened to Rosie, to Partridge?

Craig pulled the one chair closer to a small table, sat down, propped up his legs, began to go over in his mind all the facts, the hints, the suggestions that Partridge had given him. Heinrich Berg was not so astonishing once you thought about him in cold blood: a hidden Communist who openly joined the Nazi party. There had been at least one other man like Berg; now let's see, what was that guy's name—Richard Sorge? Sorge; the German-born Soviet spy who had been a trusted Nazi in the German Embassy in Tokyo during the Second World War. He had let Moscow know about Pearl Harbor in advance, too. Yes, that was something that needed remembering. . . .

There had been other men like Berg in those recent years, all shaping history in their own way. History wasn't just a record of wars and peace conferences; history was a long and bitter story of intrigue and grab, of hidden movements and determined leaders, of men who knew what they wanted manipulating men who hadn't one idea that anything was at stake: the innocent and the ignorant being used according to someone else's plan. But every now and again, the plan would fail. Because people could be surprising, too, in their resistance—once they knew what was actually happening. Once they knew. But before they knew? Then we have men like Partridge, he thought, or else we could lose.

And why did Partridge trust me? After all, I could be another Sorge, another Berg, waiting for my chance to infiltrate. How is he sure that I'm not a Soviet agent? We have our share of them in America. The British and Swedish and French varieties have been grabbing the headlines recently, but we've got them, too. And I could be one of them. A sleeper, they'd call me in the trade. Partridge isn't trusting me for my honest gray eyes; or the books I'm planning to write; or the friends I have chosen. He isn't judging me on these things, not by a long, long mile. They could be part of the myth I was busy creating for myself. Then why?

It could be—yes, it could be that he knows a little of my life, enough of it to give him a measuring gauge. The army must have done some work on putting my history together when I was cleared for codes in Korea. But there was college after that, graduate work, teaching. . . . Yet there haven't been any unexplained gaps in that span of my life which could have been used for indoctrination or training. No unaccountable visits to strange places, no disappearances from public view for a few weeks each year. No peculiar hiatus there, or a jump here; no special introductions into sensitive jobs, no help from outside sources. Whatever I've attempted, I've done on my own steam; there have been a few almost-successes, a lot of failures, but they are all my own.

Now a man like Berg cannot function alone. He gets a lot of assistance on his way up: the right recommendation to slip him into certain jobs, the right changes and promotions made with quiet help, always moving him closer to the center of power or—just as important for his purposes—to the centers of influence. And those who help the Bergs in this world to infiltrate have helped others like him, too. That's their purpose, their justification for existing. Yes, if I were in Partridge's field, I'd be interested in recommendations. Because anyone can make a mistake in recommending a man for a job, but no one can go on making recommendations that somehow always turn out to be against his own country's interests. Unless he is, of course, just that—against his own country's interests. If challenged, he will give that self-justification routine—who is to judge his country's interests? Meaning himself and his friends, no doubt. There are some who just can't resist playing God. And if you argue back that a country is a collection of people, not just him and his group, you'd be told that things weren't quite so simple as that. Simple? It's the majority that still counts *if* a country is free to decide its own interests. It may be a bad decider at times, slow and uncertain and blundering, but it does the deciding. It is in control. And *that* is the first of all its interests. None higher . . . Attack that, and you attack all of us. Including me. Simple? So are bread and water, rain and sun. The basics come first, then the elaborations. Anyway, there's the reason that I met Jim Partridge halfway tonight. And perhaps his reason for trusting me is just as simple and basic: he has to.

Of course, Partridge's trust wasn't excessive. I already knew about

Berg—as the Nazi, at least; I knew there was an organization behind him, and a hell of a time some of them gave me. I knew Veronica was going to Mykonos before he did—correction: before he told me about it. And I might as well admit that the idea of drifting into Mykonos, one pleasant morning in May, was already circling around the back of my mind. (It's no farther away from Athens than East Hampton or Stonington from New York—perhaps less; weekend distance, easily. I've even traveled more than that for a weekend of skiing.) So Partridge only entrusted me with a little more than I already knew, perhaps to keep me from guessing wildly and blundering into the kind of situation where even professionals fear to tread. Certainly there's a lot more to this picture than I am allowed to see. I may be told more when I reach Athens, more again on Mykonos. That depends on how I perform, I expect. Or, more likely, on what Jim Partridge needs of me. I have few illusions about Partridge, just as he has none about me.

Craig rose, found his map of Greece and the Aegean, spread it out on the table. In spite of his determination to look at this assignment coldly, as a student of history-in-the-making, his mind was alert and excited, his blood pressure rising. By God, he thought, I could enjoy this line of work. Then he laughed at himself.

There was a gentle rap on his door. Craig glanced at his watch; it was almost midnight. "What is it?" he called, but there was no answer, just another gentle rap. So he pushed aside the table, crossed the room in five steps, wondering why the porter's desk hadn't telephoned the message instead of sending it upstairs at this hour. He had the tip ready in his hand as he opened the door. Maritta Maas smiled at him.

"May I?" she asked, already inside the room, leaving a drift of perfume as she passed by. "Hotel corridors are so depressing. Don't you agree?" She turned to look at him, her head tilted just a little, her green eyes dancing with amusement.

He closed the door, smiling back. "I'm sure I'd agree with anything you said."

"That's very gallant."

"I can do better when I'm less surprised."

"I love to give surprises."

"Just like Santa Claus," he said, helping her off with her white silk coat. That was what she wanted, seemingly. The black dress was short, slender, sleeveless, low-necked.

"Oh?" She was puzzled for an instant. Then she laughed. "I hope I'm prettier than he is."

"I think you have the edge."

Again she frowned. "You know, if you speak that way you will have to translate for me. Why don't Americans speak English?"

"Because they aren't English, I suppose. But they usually speak American fairly well. Have this chair. It's more comfortable than it looks. Cigarette?" He was recovering himself. "Or would you like to go down to the bar and have a drink there?"

"It is much too crowded. I want to talk to you. Seriously."

"That's going to be difficult."

She had looked around the room before she sat down, noticing the half-packed suitcase, the travel folders scattered over the bed, the guidebook to Greece and the map on the small table. Her glance swept back to him. "Why?"

"Look at you," he suggested. She might start by pulling the tight skirt down over her knees, unpointing her slender shoes, uncrossing the elegantly posed legs, if she wanted any serious talk.

"Do you say such things to Ronnie, too?"

"No," he said frankly. And how cosy we are with Veronica's name, so natural and easy and amiable! Just a sweet old dependable, that was friend Maritta.

"Then am I being flattered or insulted?" She laughed to take any offense away from her words.

Playful, he thought. That's the word for Maritta. As playful as a green-eyed panther. He stared at her—the passing thought was so exactly right.

"No, no, no," she said, misreading the stare. "I am flattered. I cannot imagine you insulting anybody."

"Then let's begin all over again."

"And we should introduce ourselves properly. Maritta Geneviève Maas."

"John Craig."

"That's all?"

"All."

"You disappeared so quickly today, without waiting for any introductions—" Her voice trailed away, her hands gestured in regret.

"I only came to apologize for keeping Veronica late, and after that—well, I didn't want to intrude."

"You are so polite!"

"Americans have occasional attacks of politeness," he admitted, and had her laughing again. Did she really think that was funny, or was she trying some flattery, too?

Suddenly she was serious. "I'm a little—troubled. What did you think of Ronnie, today?"

"A charming girl."

"No, no—I mean, did you see much difference in her?"

"Difference from what?"

"From the time you used to know her. In America."

"I didn't know her in America. I don't really know her at all."

"But you asked her to dinner—like an old friend."

"On the contrary. I asked her to dinner to get to know her better."

Maritta was completely and delightfully embarrassed. "Oh, I am sorry! Ronnie spoke so much of you this evening that I thought you were old, old friends."

Somehow he was reminded of the question-and-answer game played by Jordan last Saturday. He might as well hurry the process along, give her all the information she was looking for. Veronica must have talked very little, if at all, about him; that was clear. "I wish we were. Actually, that's been one of the disappointments in Paris—no friends of any description. Funny, isn't it? I'm on the point of leaving, and so I meet someone I like. Two people, in fact: both girls, both pretty." He looked at Maritta with frank admiration, and won what could have been a real smile. "That's the way it goes, I suppose," he added regretfully.

"But how awful—to have walked around Paris all alone! No one to talk to . . . That couldn't have been very enjoyable."

"No. But very educational. Oh, there was an old lady who was looking for the right Métro, and a student who wanted a scholarship, and an American who spoke to me at the bar downstairs, and Jules the bartender, and a man in a bookshop, and a—"

"Next time you visit Paris, you must let us know when you are coming. Will you?"

"Will I?" he asked, and laughed.

She was very amused about something. "My uncle—I suppose Ronnie told you all about him?"

"No. We had scarcely time to talk about families. She just mentioned that an uncle had lent you a house for the summer, and she was going to spend a few weeks with you. Nice deal, if you can get it." Then he looked as if a new idea had just dawned. "Didn't she like your uncle? Is that what's bothering you about Veronica?"

"No, no, no," she said quickly, "I was only thinking that my uncle would be very shocked if he heard that Ronnie had—what do you say?—picked you up. It really is a joke, you know. She is supposed to chaperone me on Mykonos."

"I couldn't imagine you needing that," he said with a wide grin. "And anyway, it wasn't so much a matter of anyone being picked up. It was a very wet night, about a week ago. I had a taxi, she hadn't. It was a case either of giving her first rights on the cab, or of keeping my suit dry. I did both: I gave her a lift for the few blocks she had to go. Thank you and good night. That was all."

"And you didn't ask her to dinner? What were you thinking of, John?" Her eyes were wide, teasing.

"Yes," he admitted, "I slipped up there. I might have found Paris less educational. Do you know how many museums you have? Forty-nine. And how many—"

"Are you never serious?"

"As rarely as possible. But I'll make an effort. You were troubled, you said?"

"I suppose you intend to see her again?" Maritta's eyes flickered toward the map of the Aegean and then met his.

"I hope I'll see both of you. I have to visit Delos, so I'll be dropping in at Mykonos some time or other." He let her eyes hold his. And he could sense that it had been the right thing to say. Not just to speak casually of Mykonos, but to include Maritta in his hopes. She liked to play, this girl, and she would never play second lead to any other girl. In some ways, she reminded him of a few he had known back in New York.

"Then I should warn you. Be careful with Ronnie. I mean—she takes things so seriously, so intensely. She is just coming out of a very bad time as it is. I think she is still in love with him. An American. Did she tell you?"

He shook his head.

"He is one of those expatriate poets. They've been living together for almost a year. He exists on the small checks he gets from home each month. He believes in his genius. Ronnie believes in him. But he left her—just like that! He walked out of their studio one day. She hasn't seen him since. That was two weeks ago. Ronnie took a room at the Beauharnais, gave up her studio, couldn't bear it any longer. You see? Any other girl would have known this would happen. Any other girl would have left him months ago. But Ronnie—" She sighed. "I think she shouldn't take life so seriously, not for a long, long time. Do you see?"

He saw very clearly. Half-truth, half-fiction, beautifully blended. Veronica, if he came to Mykonos, was to be untouchable. Why? Making sure that she would be isolated from someone who might ask questions? Making sure that she could be properly controlled by Maritta—a very skillful, gentle surveillance? They were taking no chances with him, even if he seemed innocent enough. "Yes," he said at last, "I see."

"And you agree?"

He hadn't much other choice. "You could be right."

"I *am* right!"

"Just an Americanism," he said with a smile.

"You've no idea how upset she has been."

"It was a nice idea to ask her to Mykonos. That should help to take her mind off Paris. But are you going to warn off all the men who look at Veronica? You'll be kept busy."

"Of course not. I shan't have to warn them, unless they are very attractive and unmarried—like you. There are not so many of them." She was amused at the expression on his face. "I've embarrassed you?"

"I'd imagine that there would be quite a crowd of—"

"Oh yes, there will be men on Mykonos, but only the kind one takes lightly. They come, they go. Ships passing in the night. You are that, too, in a sense. Except Ronnie likes you. And she is *so* vulnerable at present. You know. . . ."

"I don't."

"It is a matter of—rebound. Isn't that what you call it?"

"She isn't in any danger of falling in love with me," he said, his embarrassment growing. "She doesn't know me, to begin with."

"Do you think that matters to a woman?" She watched him, half smiling, her lips softening. "It wouldn't matter to me." There was a little silence. "Of course, if you were really serious about her, I shouldn't worry."

"Didn't I tell you I was serious as rarely as possible?" he asked jokingly. That passed her scrutiny. He could feel her relax. The softness in her lips spread to her eyes. "Do I see you at all on Mykonos?"

That pleased her. She rose, laughing. "Why not? We can't have you wandering around all alone again."

"Oh, I'll have several friends there," he said easily.

"Really?"

"Of course. It isn't only painters and poets who visit Mykonos."

"Oh—historians?"

She really had done her homework, he thought. "I'll be spending most of my time on Delos, anyway."

"But there's no village, no hotel, on Delos. Just a small tourist pavilion with a few beds for—well, emergencies. You'll have to sleep on Mykonos."

He nodded, watching her. "That's right. I'll sleep on Mykonos," he said softly. He had actually managed to embarrass her, but she enjoyed it too.

She laughed again, turned away, walked slowly over to the dresser. She straightened his comb and brushes, fiddled with a pair of cuff links, picked up a small plastic jar of hair cream. "Men are so businesslike," she said. "So simple, the way they travel." She opened the jar and pretended to smell the cream. "Nice and uncomplicated," she told him. She replaced the jar neatly, examined a small leather box in which he kept studs and collar-stays. "This is from Florence, isn't it?" she asked casually, opening it, too.

"By way of Madison Avenue." He came forward. What the devil was she doing, pretending to play like this with all these small possessions? Or was it the letter from Sue, lying openly beside his hairbrush, that interested her?

She put down the leather box, seemed to notice the time on his small traveling clock. She turned to him, held out both her hands in farewell. "I must go. Yes, I must. I leave tomorrow. That's why I came to see you now, even if it is late. What else could I do? The dinner party went on and on and on."

He kept hold of her hands. "How was it? Plenty of advice?"

"A complete bore. My uncle had two of his friends from Mykonos to meet me—they have a house there, too. And they want to entertain Ronnie and me, introduce us around. You know. . . ."

"That might not be so bad."

"But they are so dull! I prefer to choose my own friends, don't you?"

"Much more satisfactory."

"Of course, an uncle who is one's only remaining relative must worry, I suppose," she said with a sigh.

Craig said with a broad smile as he looked at the clock, "How could he ever worry about you, Maritta?"

But irony was lost on her. Or she had finished with the topic of uncle. She said, "You are telephoning Ronnie tomorrow morning, aren't you?"

"I said I would."

"She won't be able to lunch with you." Maritta's voice was low, hesitant, and just the right amount sad. "Blame me. I asked her to attend to some business I hadn't time to finish."

"Well, I suppose it's kinder to let her do the refusing."

"But she will be free for dinner," Maritta said, watching him now with eyes wide and hesitant, as if she were letting him make the decision.

He couldn't feel one tremble in her cool hands, couldn't see one flickering evasion in her pleading green eyes. He waited for a few seconds, just to keep her impatience simmering behind that beautifully controlled face. "You don't want me to ask her to dinner?"

Her hands had tightened, her eyes blinked. "I thought we agreed—"

"I'll probably be on my way to Greece by dinnertime," he told her. He released her hands and turned to pick up her coat from the bed.

"You are annoyed with me, and I didn't want that. Please, John—I would never have asked you except that I didn't want to see Ronnie have her hopes all built up again and then find them come crashing down; you know what I mean."

"I know." And if he hadn't known so much, he would have believed the soft, anxious, urgent voice, and that pathetic look of the good friend who was doing everything for the best.

"I've embarrassed you again."

"Because I couldn't care less." Not about what you think or you want, my sweet-faced liar, he thought. Get her out of here, he told himself, or you might describe her in a five-letter word to her face. He held out her coat, and she slipped her soft white arms into the sleeves, turning her head to look up at him. "I'll see you on Mykonos," he said, "unless your uncle flays me alive for having you up in my room at one in the morning. How did you find me, anyway?"

"Oh, Ronnie told us," she said most innocently. "She even telephoned you just before dinner to see if you would join us. Didn't you get the message?"

"Someone called, I heard. No name left, though."

"How typical!" She shook her head. "But you know, it was Ronnie's call that decided me she really was rushing much too quickly— Sorry. I promise never to mention the subject again."

He opened the door, glanced into the deserted corridor with only its lonely pairs of dusty shoes waiting patiently outside each bedroom.

"Expecting anyone?" she asked.

"Your uncle and his posse of vigilantes."

"I beg your pardon?" Then she shrugged her shoulders, looked amused. "Oh, really! You Americans! . . . And where are *you* going?"

"To see you into the elevator."

This startled her into a laugh. Perhaps the well-dressed spy was not accustomed to being shown out at such an hour by her unsuspecting quarry. "But there is no need—" she began, and jumped as a sudden, sleepy protest came from the room they were passing: "Knock it off! Go to bed!" A tired groan followed, then a resigned sigh.

"Another American," she said in a stage whisper, and clamped her hands to her lips to stifle an outburst of real laughter. For a moment, Craig had a glimpse of a different Maritta, someone she could have been if she hadn't chosen another rôle for herself, someone younghearted and merry, trying to smother a second attack of giggles as the signal for the elevator sounded with extra loudness through the silence of the hotel. Then, as the creaking cage began its slow and dignified ascent, she became the Maritta he knew. "Go back to your room. Please!" she whispered quickly, and gestured with her hand. He nodded understandingly, retreated obligingly. Who was he to compromise the good name of such a charming lady? He wondered whom she was supposed to be visiting. Someone who belonged to the elderly female shoes he had almost stepped upon?

He was at his door, waving a good early morning to her, as the elevator reached his floor. She stepped inside quickly, not looking back, doing nothing to attract the attendant's notice to Craig's closing door. What, he thought, not even a blown kiss? I bet she would do that really elegantly.

He closed the door, waited until the last whirr of the elevator had ground into silence, then opened his door one small crack. The voice that had advised them to knock it off and go to bed was Jim Partridge's. Craig was sure of that. But Partridge's door remained closed. All right, Craig thought, I can take a hint. He shut his door carefully, soundlessly, but left it unlocked. Why else would Partridge let him know he was on the same floor unless he planned to pay a visit?

By two o'clock, Craig decided that he had been too bright in his quick ideas. There was no sign of Partridge. So he went to bed. Not to sleep. This was not a night for the quiet, untroubled mind that would allow him to slip over the edge of consciousness and fall into soft oblivion. He lay staring at the darkened ceiling, the reading light at his bedside still turned on, the book in his hand dropped at his side. He was going over and over in his restless mind the myth that Maritta Maas had created. My God, he thought, if Jim Partridge hadn't warned me about her, I might have believed—I would probably have believed her. Yes, I could have believed it. I would scarcely have noticed the lie that undermined everything she said: Veronica could not have telephoned me or mentioned my hotel to anyone, for she did not know my address. I would scarcely have noticed that unobtrusive lie, simply because I wasn't being given much time for any real thought—just emotions. And I would have cut off the small warning signal at the back of my brain, the way we all do when we don't expect, far less suspect. That's how the confidence game was worked, was it? To the outside observer, removed and uncommitted, blessed with hindsight, he would have seemed more than naïve if he had believed Maritta's story. But involved as he had been, with all the little hints and honest-eyed explanations and the seemingly logical sequiturs—oh no, that was another proposition. Without Partridge, he would have been properly taken. Let's face it, men were flattered even if embarrassed by the idea that a girl like Veronica might be falling hard for them. Vanity, vanity, and all is flattery. Then he stopped thinking of himself, and began worrying about Veronica. He felt a surge of both pity and fear. Veronica was headed for tragedy. "I'll be damned," he said softly, "if I let that happen."

At four o'clock, his door opened and Partridge came in. Craig, almost asleep, stared at him dizzily, then raised himself quickly. Partridge gestured for silence, cutting off Craig's "Thank God you came" before it was uttered. He seemed normal, unconcerned, in spite of all the caution he was using. He had a quick nod of approval for the tightly drawn curtains and the meager light, perhaps, too, for the unlocked door which had let him enter so quietly. He pocketed a key which he hadn't needed to use as he bolted the door carefully behind him. Then, from the other pocket of his dressing gown, he pulled out a small box of some kind, set it carefully on the small table, and touched a switch. Nothing happened as far as Craig could hear or see, but Partridge was obviously pleased with it. Only then did he come forward to join Craig, who was sitting on the edge of the bed. "Who was she?" he asked, his voice held as low as possible.

"Maritta Maas."

"I nearly walked in, you know. I wanted to see you when I came back to the hotel, and got as far as your door. I heard voices. So I retreated. But boy oh boy, that was nearly a blooper."

"Would she have known you?"

Partridge shook his head. "It's better if she doesn't see me until Mykonos." If at all, he thought.

"So you'll be there." And thank heaven for that.

"Eventually." The visit to Rhodes and a talk with O'Malley came first. Some quiet, if reluctant, permission had come from Washington, but it was obvious that this was the type of operation which might need emergency, on-the-spot decisions; regular channels would only delay critical action, conventional controls could mean defeat. Christopher Holland, who considered red tape as only something to be cut, had thought Partridge's idea good. The rest would be up to O'Malley.

He's looking haggard, Craig thought. "When will—"

"What did she want?" Partridge asked crisply.

Craig poured it out. One thing about a sleepless night—it let him have the sequences of Maritta's talk quite clear in his mind. He included her movements over by his dresser, her tender curiosity about his small possessions. (That had struck him as odd. If he had wanted to learn about a man, he would have looked at the books propped up against the mirror.)

Partridge heard him without interruption, and then sat in silence when he had ended.

Craig said, "The only bit of real truth in all that was the fact that Veronica was in love and got ditched. The rest is invention or manipulation of the facts." He paused, but Partridge still frowned down at the rug as if its faded arabesques fascinated him. Craig tried again. "Can't we give Veronica some protection?"

Partridge nodded. "We can try. There's a girl I know who might strike up a friendship with her on Mykonos. That would be the best angle, I think. We mustn't lose contact with her. But we can't warn her, either; we've already discussed all that. It still stands."

"I'm keeping an eye on her," Craig said grimly.

"Don't stir up Maritta's jealousy," Partridge warned him. "There's something personal there, too, not just her job—"

"She'd be that way with any man. She may not want him, but no one near her is going to get him."

Partridge rose and crossed over to the dresser. He examined everything there, quickly, methodically, even running his fingers around the protruding edge of the wooden top. "Just seeing if she left any presents for you such as some gadget to bug this room. Did you express your opinion about her, for instance, when you came back in here?" The question was offhand, slightly joking, but Partridge was waiting for the answer.

"By transference. I needed a drink and got my flask and dropped a tumbler—it broke over there by the bathroom door. So I cursed it heavily for the full minute it took me to get the pieces gathered together." Craig's voice was still grim, as if he couldn't relax even over a comic incident.

Partridge glanced at Sue's letter as he turned away. Whatever he had been able to read, as Maritta must have seen it, gave him no cause for alarm. He studied Craig's tense face. This won't do, he thought. Nonchalantly, he said, "I guess she was really making a little test to see if you were a courier of some kind. Her friends go in for false lids on jars and boxes, hollow cuff links, all that stuff. They're like the inquisitive carpenter who unscrewed his navel and his bottom fell off." He searched in his breast pocket and said, "In fact, here's one example I brought along for you tonight. The police found it on the man charged with Sussman's murder. It proves he had more connection with Soviet espionage than a criminal usually has." He held out a tie clip. "Go on, open it. I filled it to let you see the kind of thing you might expect to find inside."

Craig took the tie clip. It was thicker than most, but of the usual length and decoration. He examined it, felt he was now wrestling with a Chinese puzzle, pressed and pulled and cajoled the small strip of imitation gold without any effect. He could see no join, no seam in the heavy bar of the clip.

"This way," Partridge said, taking it from him, sliding the top apart. In the lower section, there nestled a small strip of microfilm protected by an equally small strip of tissue paper. "When that's developed, you could fill twenty full-sized sheets of typing paper—perhaps even more—with the information it holds. Some of their couriers, the smart dressers, object to wearing a clip as bulky as this. They prefer cuff links. Their women use the lids of compacts, metal frames of handbags, lipsticks, watches with the works removed. . . . And then there are the flashlight batteries, hollowed out; and the special spaces inside tubes of artists' colors; toothpaste ditto. Et cetera, et cetera . . . You name them, we've found them. So have the British, the French, the Italians, and all the rest of our allies. You think I'm exaggerating? Inventing? Next time you visit Washington, I'll ask my friend at FBI headquarters to show you some of the Soviet gadgets they've discovered right in the old U.S.A. It's quite a collection, believe me. And then we meet some jovial type at dinner who tells us that we have a fixation about Soviet espionage, and couldn't we just forget the whole thing, relax the way he does, live and let live?" Partridge's quiet voice broke into a brief but genuine laugh.

Craig said nothing. But he really concentrated on the tie clip this time, his lips tight. He succeeded in opening it. He grinned as he handed the two pieces back to Partridge.

"You fix it," Partridge told him. "Their cuff links work on the same idea. Ingenious bastards, aren't they?"

"One thing's certain," Craig said, completing the small operation successfully. "They don't trust the mail, these boys."

That's better, thought Partridge, watching Craig's face, listening to the tone of his voice. "Another thing's certain," he said as he pocketed the tie clip. "They've given you just about enough basic training for my taste. I want you to pack and leave. Oh yes, telephone Veronica, but be damned casual. Play it Maritta's way and keep the Clark girl safe. Yes, safe." He paused to let that sink in. "And a lot more will stay safe, too. We are in too good a position to throw the game away now. I don't think they have any real suspicions about what we actually know. Sure they were suspicious of you, but they're suspicious of everyone, including each other. They don't know, for instance, that we have been playing along with them to give them confidence, or that we have been reacting to every move they are taking. Oh, well—perhaps not every move; that's a counterespionage dream, too good to be true. Still, we are in there guessing, with some very solid facts to back up the possibilities. So when you get to Mykonos, play it very cool with Veronica. You are bound to see her—it's a small place. But let us do the worrying about her. Okay?"

"Will you have time?" Craig asked wryly.

"We'll have to make the time." Then Partridge's voice became brisk. "In Athens, we are going to play it very loose indeed. We won't make any effort to get in touch with you unless there is some real emergency."

"Meaning I'm back on their danger list again?" Craig was grinning.

"But," said Partridge as if he hadn't heard that suggestion, "if a Frenchman makes friends with you, don't resist. His name is Yves Duclos. He will keep you in touch with me. It's safer that way. Maritta's bosses don't expect the French to be co-operating with us. Let's surprise them about that, shall we?"

"It's good to hear we can surprise them sometimes."

Partridge smiled, at that. "You saw Duclos with me last Monday evening, in the bar downstairs."

"I remember. That's when I came in, raging quietly. There was a redhead with you, too, wasn't there?"

"Can you describe Duclos for me?"

"Black hair, bright blue eyes, good healthy color in his cheeks. I couldn't see his height, of course. He looked tall, sitting down."

"Just medium height when he stands—five feet eight. Around one hundred and sixty-five pounds. Think you can recognize him easily?"

"I think so. Of course, I didn't really look at him too hard."

"He's a Breton. And he always wears a gold signet ring with an odd twisted design. If you ask him, he will tell you it's fourteenth century from Rennes. Got that?"

Craig nodded.

Partridge was frowning at the rug again, hesitating. "Yes," he said at last, "I'd better pass on the warning. One of the men you met at your sister's party is working with Maritta. He collects information; she passes it on. We expect him to appear on Mykonos."

"What?" Craig asked sharply. He lost his breath, regained it. *"What?"*

Partridge nodded. That was as far as he would go. He was tempted, just a little, to add that the man could be one of two. But what was the point? Craig wouldn't have been made any the wiser by an exact name. No use loading him with extra information that would only be dangerous for him to carry around. Two men . . . Is one being used, like Veronica Clark, to cover up the man we want? Partridge suddenly wondered. They are both traveling in the same direction—the Aegean area. Both have good contacts, friends in sensitive jobs who'd trust them; both would make useful enemy agents. Both, again, have spent some time in Russia; both could have been recruited there; both have been living normal lives since they came to Paris.

Craig was still recovering from the shock. He asked slowly, "But you don't know his name?"

"Not yet," Partridge said. Robert Maybrick Bradley, with a security job, no less, in NATO . . . Edward Maclennan Wilshot, who has written many articles on NATO and its problems . . . Wilshot gets a free-lance assignment from a French magazine, not always friendly to NATO, to cover the eastern Mediterranean on the day that Bradley claims the leave that is due him. That's the latest report from Rosie on the subject. But who is being used to cover for whom? That's a new angle. Better get Rosie on to it right away. Unless he has thought about it, of course . . . No, this is possibly my own idea, thanks to Veronica Clark. It could, it just could solve the problem of two men with similar journeys at the same time near the same target area. "It's been a bit of a puzzle," he admitted. "Sorry I'm so vague. But after Maritta's performance tonight, I think you needed the warning, such as it is. It would be easy to assume that everyone at your sister's party was just as trustworthy as old Rosie."

"How is he?"

"Still worrying about his weight. Played bowls, last night. Golfing on Saturday." Partridge picked up the small box from the table, went over to the door, gave an easy salute and—after a careful look into the corridor—slipped outside.

See you on Mykonos, Craig thought, and went to bed. Strangely enough, this time he slept.

He awoke at ten on a bright cool morning, and before he shaved or ordered breakfast he called Veronica.

"There's this matter of lunch," he began. "When can I pick you up?"

She seemed rather taken aback by this brusque approach. "I'm terribly sorry. I can't manage lunch today. I've got some business to—"

"That's too bad."

"I should be free by four o'clock," she said shyly, "but I suppose you have plans of your own for the afternoon."

"As a matter of fact, I have. I'm just about to leave Paris."

"I'm really awfully sorry that I disappointed—"

"Don't give it a thought. That's the way things go. . . . Well, I suppose this is good-bye."

"Oh!" Then she rallied. "Have a very good trip."

"The same to you."

"Good-bye," she said, quietly and gently and—he hoped—a little sadly.

He replaced the receiver, sat staring at it for a full minute. Then he rose, thinking now of Maritta, and his eyes weren't so pleasant to see.

11

Yves Duclos arrived at the Athens airport early on Sunday afternoon. He had taken his journey from Paris in easy stages: Thursday had seen him in Milan for a quiet talk with Italian Intelligence; Friday, he had been in Florence to meet some furniture designers; Saturday, he had spent in Rome purely for pleasure. . . . Altogether, it had been an excellent trip without any alarms or tensions. And the four days ahead of him in Athens should be fairly easy, too. It was always the same—after a week of work and urgency, of meetings and plans and problems and decisions, he was now in the waiting period. But it was not often that the waiting could be done in a place as beautiful as Athens.

The flight had brought him right over the city, with the Acropolis in full view beneath him. Like most of his fellow passengers, he was still vibrating from that spectacular approach: a precipice rising out of city roofs, golden-white columns growing out of rocky crags, and—within seconds—a landing by a bay of blue rippling water. Not so far out there, south and eastward, lay Mykonos. . . . But that, he thought as he walked briskly into the low-roofed hall where the Customs officers waited, would come later. He had four days, meanwhile, to enjoy Athens. He might manage a visit to Delphi, too; it was the French archaeologists, after all, who had dug the place out of its rubble and put the pieces together. His first visit to Greece certainly ought to include Delphi. "Nothing to declare," he told the Greek who had checked his two cases. Nothing except good intentions and high expectations.

Duclos picked up his luggage and started toward the wall of glass windows which lay at the end of the small Customs Hall, separating it from a corridor packed with waiting people. Across the corridor, he could see more windows and wide-open doors with the bright sunshine pouring in from a wide square or plaza. No doubt the buses and taxis were out there. In half an hour, he would be reaching Athens itself.

From the crowd of people pressed close to the corridor's glass windows, a pleasant voice said, "Monsieur Duclos?" It was a small, light-boned man in a pale gray suit, his hat in his hand, a smile on his face, his dark eyes questioning politely. He was middle-aged, sallow in complexion, dark in hair and mustache. Greek, decided Duclos, as he listened to the halting French, bravely tried. "Monsieur Duclos! At your service. I am from the office of Colonel Zafiris." He showed a small identification card, tactfully, briefly. "There is one of your countrymen who has been waiting to meet you. He came yesterday from Paris, from Inspector Galland. There is some new development about a prisoner of the inspector's which could be of importance—but here he is, himself." He pointed to a younger man, about the same height and weight as Duclos, fair-haired, blue-eyed, who waited with hands plunged in the pockets of his light coat, a cigarette between his lips, a bored expression on his handsome face. "I am Tillier," the Frenchman said, coming to life as he looked at Duclos. "I did not have the pleasure of meeting you on your visit to Galland last Tuesday morning. I only saw you very briefly as you left. Yes, the murderer of Professor Sussman has talked a little since you interviewed him. But we shall leave that to discuss in your hotel. We could not find where you are staying, so we had to meet you here. Let me help you." He made a gesture toward one of Duclos' suitcases.

"I can manage, thank you," Duclos said. He went through the nearest door and found himself on the crowded sidewalk filled with noise and bustle and bright sunshine. Tillier was the detective who had been assisting Galland in the Sussman case, that he knew. And this man—possibly a Norman by coloring and accent—was definitely French. What was more, if Sussman's murderer had given any information at all, then that could be of great importance. It might mean a change, perhaps subtle, perhaps bold, in the plan that Duclos and Partridge had agreed upon for Mykonos. Colonel Zafiris was Greek Counterintelligence, that Duclos also knew. Yet why this tie-in between Greek Intelligence and Paris police? Unless the Sûreté itself had telescoped action, decided that the Greeks should learn along with Duclos whatever Galland had discovered. Certainly there wasn't much time now for last-minute conferences. And yet, and yet— Duclos looked around at the family groups, at the mixture of rich and poor, of nationalities, happy faces, worried faces, no one giving one good English goddamn about anyone else except his own problems. He looked at Tillier, who was standing beside him, and tried to measure him. The face was vaguely familiar: he could have seen it last Tuesday as he left Galland's office. Yes, he had seen it. Last Tuesday? He said, "There's too much crowd here. Better if we separate. I'll go by bus. You can follow me in your car. You'll find me at the King George Hotel. I'll expect you at five o'clock. Does that suit you?" By then, he thought, I'll have checked with Zafiris as well as Paris.

"Of course. My only worry is that I must return to Paris this evening."

The little Greek said, "But Colonel Zafiris has sent his car to save time! It is over there!" He pointed to a space filled with cars and waiting taxis. A small car, dark brownish-green in color, was already making a wide turn to reach them. Its driver was in khaki uniform.

This may be the way things are done in Greece, thought Duclos, but I don't want any part of it. It is too official. He smiled genially as he moved off. "See you at the hotel," he said quietly.

"Fine," Tillier said. "If you prefer it that way—" He shrugged, walking beside Duclos. "Just one thing," he added, "have you got a room definitely at the King George? That's where I am and it's crowded. If you can't get it there, where can we meet you?" He halted as he stepped in front of Duclos, blocking his way. "Or perhaps you'd leave word at the desk for me where you've found a room? I must make tonight's flight back to Paris. I'm a day late as it is."

It was reasonable. It was time-consuming, just enough moments spent to let the official-looking car drive right up to the curb where they stood. "Oh, why not take this and save all trouble?" Tillier asked now, as the Greek opened the car door. He reached for the nearer suitcase most helpfully.

"No need," began Duclos, ready to crash through the crowd pressing around them—there was a terrace, a restaurant, just beyond the thick stream of people. But Tillier's hand switched from the suitcase to the wrist that held it. Duclos felt a sharp and painful bite as a needle pressed deep into his flesh. His voice came in a desperate gasp. "Help me, help, in the name of God, help—" But the foreigners' faces only stared blankly, briefly, as his words trailed into a drunken blur. His eyes, turned toward two children and their grandmother who had halted near him, closed. His legs buckled as his head dropped on his breast and Tillier's arms pushed him into the car.

Tillier propped up Duclos against the seat, held his weight in position with his own body. "Quick!" he told the Greek, who was handing in the suitcases.

"Not too quickly," the Greek said softly, slipping into the seat, closing the door.

The small boy tugged at the black skirt of his grandmother. "Was that man sick?" he asked.

"What man?" She pulled the skirt free from his hand, took a larger grip on the paper parcel she carried. "Stop looking at strangers," she said, her voice harsh with her own worries, "and watch out for your mother. She said she would meet us here. Where is she? Keep hold of your sister, now!"

The small boy did as he was told. He only let his eyes wander once back to the car but it was already moving away. It went so quietly, so smoothly. Not like his uncle's truck on the farm.

The car left the low cluster of airport buildings, continued its steady pace down toward the highway. It swept slowly past flower beds and fluttering flags, past tourist police and flocks of airline hostesses; past people arriving, departing, enjoying a Sunday outing; past parked cars and waiting buses, until it reached the main road that skirted the bay of blue water. It turned left and gathered speed at last. It was traveling away from Athens.

The man who had called himself Tillier took a deep breath, pushed Duclos farther into the corner. "Soon now—just past the fish restaurant and the filling station. We'll change cars there," he told the driver, "and you can get rid of that uniform." He removed his revolver from his pocket as he pulled his coat off and dropped it at his feet. "Don't forget the suitcases," he warned the Greek. "I need them."

The Greek nodded, glanced at his watch. "Four and a half minutes from here to there, all told," he said with considerable satisfaction. He looked at Duclos. "How long will he sleep?"

"Until we reach Cape Sunion."

"I would not advise taking the new shore road—too crowded on Sunday. Better strike inland a little—come round by Lávrion—"

"I know, I know," the Frenchman said impatiently. He sat forward, watching the stream of cars on the road ahead, all out on their Sunday picnics. "There's the restaurant! Get ready—" He tapped the driver on the shoulder. "Now!"

Duclos came out of his stupor as they skirted the mining town of Lávrion. He had enough returning sense to keep slumped in his corner, changing neither balance nor position. He listened to the Greek and Frenchman arguing, a faint jangle of phrases at first, then words becoming clearer as his own mind began working. All he could see through the carefully opened slits of his eyes was a desolate hillside, a few rows of workmen's houses, low and strung out over grassless earth. Where was this? Greece? The hideous smell, constant, persistent, made him think of Hades. But it wasn't sulphur—was it manganese, lead?

"Those filthy slag heaps!" the Frenchman said, and reached angrily past Duclos to shut the window. Duclos jolted forward, but was caught and held, and propped back into his corner. He had had time, though, to see the hilltops on his right where chimney stacks were perched.

"You should smell them during the week," the Greek was saying, "when the smoke belches out. That's why they're built up there, to keep people from being poisoned. They say they get lead and silver out of that slag. It's a French company that started working the mines —they take the profits and leave us with the stink."

"You know everything. Could you stop that yapping just for the last ten minutes?" the Frenchman asked sharply.

The driver laughed softly, taking no sides. He was a man who enjoyed other people's bickering.

A happy trio, thought Duclos, and wondered if there could be any dividend for him in that. He felt sick and tired, perhaps with the drug that had been pumped into him, perhaps with his own stupidity; he had expected nothing and that was the greatest of all stupidities. Now, he lay seemingly helpless in his corner while he let his brain start functioning again.

The rows of houses were gone, replaced by moorland. No sign of people here. The ground was too open to risk anything. Ahead of him he saw the beginning of trees. Perhaps there he could quickly get the door unlocked and jump and run for shelter. But the hope was too optimistic. He still felt weak; the Frenchman was holding a revolver on his lap; and when they reached the trees they were thin, giving way to more moorland. Then more trees, thicker trees, came into sight. Snatch the revolver first, he told himself, before you open the door.

The Greek was pointing to a large villa, boarded and shuttered, explaining that it was the first of many country places along this road where the rich from Athens came for the summer and shot doves in August. "He should have been a schoolmaster, this one," the Frenchman was telling the driver when Duclos reached for the revolver. But his body was slower than he had thought. It was only a vague, uncoordinated movement that came from his arm. The Frenchman cursed and hit him a crashing blow over the head with the revolver butt.

"You've killed him!" the Greek said in alarm.

"Not him. Bretons' heads are made of teak."

"The orders were not to injure him, to keep him well until—"

"He'll be well enough to answer our questions."

"He may take a little persuasion," the Greek said, with a spreading smile. "I remember in 'forty-five—"

"Keep your eyes open!" the Frenchman told the driver. "Just as you catch first sight of the pillars at Cape Sunion, there's a big house and two cottages on your left toward the sea. Stop at the second cottage. Got it?" He looked at the Greek beside him, wondering why he had to have this kind of guy along. Always talking of the civil war, he must have been only a kid of eighteen when he left villages in flames and snatched the children and carved up the men with his knife. You'd have thought he might have forgotten those things in those years in Bulgaria, but no, here he was back, looking like a bank clerk but still nursing his dreams of glory. "Keep your mouth shut when the boss arrives. We've changed our methods, didn't you know?"

"We nearly won," the Greek protested angrily. "We were closer to winning than you ever were."

"And what happened to your leaders? Heads cut off by the peasants and displayed in the market place! Signs still painted on the barns all over Thessaly calling us murderers! You 'nearly won' brilliantly." And that will shut up this know-all for the next hour at least, the

Frenchman thought. I'm in charge here and he'd better understand that. If it had not been for me, who could have identified Duclos at the airport so quickly, so quietly?

"There's the sea," the driver said. And far off, there was a glimpse of a ruined Greek temple on its high headland in stark silhouette against the western sun. Mission accomplished, the Frenchman thought with considerable satisfaction. We got him here, and there's no escape for him now.

It was dusk when Duclos regained consciousness. The room was square and small, half filled by the low wooden platform on which he had been thrown. The walls were of rough stone, once whitewashed, now gray-streaked in the fading light. There was a small window high above his head, unglassed, barred. The one low, narrow door looked solid and heavy. He put his feet on the hard-packed earth floor, carefully, testing his balance. He could stand. And walk. He made his way slowly across to the door. Yes, it was as strong as it had looked. And he could hear nothing through it.

Yet the room was not quiet. Through the window came the distant fall and surge of the sea. The air smelled clean, and it felt cool, almost cold. He crossed the room again and stood on the low platform—a communal bed, he guessed, there would be space for four rough mattresses on it—and reached for the bars. He could grasp their lower edge. Painfully, he pulled himself up to let his chin reach the stone sill, held on with his arm muscles tearing, and looked out. A bare, rocky field sloping downward to cliffs, beyond that a flat stretch of dark gray water reaching to a dark gray sky. No houses, no lights; nothing except the steady beat of waves. He dropped back onto the wooden bed, his arms trembling with the strain. He was still weak, much weaker than he had thought.

He sat on the bed, his back propped up against the heavy stone wall, and considered his position. They had taken away his tie, his belt, his shoes. They had taken his jacket and emptied his trouser pockets. They had taken his watch and his ring. From the papers in his passport-wallet, they would know that he had reservations for the Grande Bretagne. What would they do—have someone placed there to watch for any person asking about Yves Duclos, for anyone leaving a message for him? They wouldn't get much, that way. Mimi was staying at the Hilton and wasn't even going to get in touch with him until they sailed on the same boat for Mykonos on Thursday. Four days away. . . . Then he froze: his tickets for the steamer, his cabin reservation, would be left for him at his hotel. It had been necessary to book ahead to get a cabin and have Mimi in the one next door.

But how in the first place had they known where to pick him up? An informant? Or had they followed him to Rome, and, learning his destination there, jumped ahead of him to Athens? But why wait until then? They could have made an attempt on him in Milan or Florence or Rome itself. Perhaps they wanted to make sure he was heading for Greece before they moved. Yes, that could be it. Greece was the danger signal to them. But that could also show, perhaps, that they did not know too much about his mission or else they would never have waited to act until today. And so they want me for information, he thought somberly. That's why I'm still alive. Information to fill in the gaps in their suspicions. And I could give them a lot. . . . He had no illusions about human capacity to withstand physical persuasion. In the last extreme they'd use torture, that unpleasant word which so many pleasant people discarded as fantastic nonsense.

I'll have to play this carefully, he thought. When they question me reasonably, I'll have to be ready with answers that will give them no lead to Mykonos and the rest of us there. But when that type of questioning is over, then— He felt inside the waistband of his trousers, and pulled off one of the suspender buttons. He cracked it open with his fingers, and took out a small flat pellet wrapped in its thin saliva-proof coating. He clicked the two pieces of button together again, and threw it under the bed. The pellet, he placed in the breast pocket of his shirt. At the first sound of the door opening, he'd transfer it to his mouth. It could lie quite unobtrusively, he had heard, against his cheek. He would have to trust the waterproof coating—better that than finding his arms held or his hands tied when he needed that capsule. *If* he needed it, he added with a determined attempt at optimism.

It was dark now, and the wind must have risen, for the surge of sea had a heavier rhythm. Cold, too, in here. And he was thirsty. Not hungry—some of the awakening nausea still clung to his throat. He tried to forget his thirst by thinking about the Frenchman who had used the name of Tillier. That was the man who had placed him, he was convinced. What could the Frenchman know, and how much? He had seen that face, briefly, and only once. Where? Not on his visit to police headquarters, of that he was sure now. Not on Tuesday morning, then, but very close to that time. Tuesday afternoon had been the meeting at Mimi's, with Rosie and Jim Partridge. No, later than that, but still around Tuesday. . . . The evening, the late evening—at the club called Le Happening? Stagehands, waiters, doorman . . . and the man who had come from the rear of the building, when the narcotics raid started—a janitor of some kind, fair-haired, wearing torn overalls over a dirty undershirt. Yes, that was the man. He had mixed into the crowd of employees being gathered together backstage. I was just leaving, Duclos remembered. If he had quick-enough eyes to note my face and a good-enough memory to report it once the raid was over and he was freed, then one thing is sure—he was no ordinary janitor.

My God, he thought, how could one small thing like that trip me up? There must have been something else to add to it. Where did I make another mistake? Or was it chance?

He had plenty of time to try to think his way through that puzzle. For most of the night in the cold black room, he sat hunched over his thoughts. Now and again he would break away from them, rise, walk around, bend and stretch to get the chill out of his bones. Twice he lifted himself up to window level, but there was nothing to see; no lights, not even a night animal. He couldn't even guess where he was.

He must have dozed off. He awoke in bright daylight to find that a hunk of brown bread and a paper cup of coffee had been left on the floor just inside the door. It was the closing of the door that had wakened him. He ate some of the bread—it tasted sour—and drank the lukewarm coffee, heavy with its fine grounds. Still, it was liquid of a kind. His thirst was half quenched. But in five minutes he slumped into sleep. The drug lasted twenty-four hours. When he awoke, he saw the same bright sunshine coming through the small barred window. At first, he thought he had been asleep for an hour or so, perhaps less, and that it was still Monday morning. Then he had his doubts; he had slept too deeply. He felt too exhausted.

Outside, there was nothing but the lonely field, a few sea gulls wheeling with their harsh cries over the edge of the land, and far offshore two ships and a fishing boat. They disappeared out of his view as he clung to the strong bars, and then there was nothing on the shimmering blue water. Greece could be as lonely as Brittany, he thought, as he lowered himself back onto the wooden bed. Lonelier, he added grimly. There was no escape from this room. His one chance might come when they took him out for questioning, or when that door was opened again. He sat down facing it, to wait and get some strength back into his body.

In the late afternoon, when the sun had left the room but still struck sidewise across the field and the sea, the door opened just enough to let food and drink be set on the floor. Duclos jumped for the handle, tried to force the door farther open but it was chained from the outside. He heard the Greek call out a warning, "André! André!" The Frenchman answered angrily as he rushed to help pull the door shut. So they were both on guard, still bickering with each other, and the Frenchman was called André. That was all he had achieved, Duclos thought, that and the spilling of the coffee.

The dark liquid lay thick and puddled at his feet. He knelt, dipped a finger in the mudlike grounds and tasted gingerly. Yes, something had been added to the coffee, something to scatter his brains still more. There was a lump of goat cheese on the bread, this time. It smelled so sour that it could disguise anything, so he threw it out the window. The bread—was it also doctored? They might leave one thing uncontaminated, just to entice him to trust everything. But hungry as he was, he didn't risk it. He threw the bread out, too, and ended all temptation. The only weapon he had was his brains. He had better keep them working.

He had guessed right about the prepared supper, for when the sun had set and the dusk was darkening into night they came to get him. As the door was unlocked and the chain rattled, he had time to slip the pellet carefully into the side of his mouth between the cheek and the lower gum. It was comfortable enough, hardly noticeable even to him. The Greek came into the room, nodded as if he had expected to find Duclos inert and helpless, pulled the Frenchman to his feet. This is how I will play it, Duclos thought. He staggered, let himself be supported unresisting to the door.

He entered another room only slightly bigger than his own. It was lit by candles on the table; shadows were deep in its corners, its two small windows were covered with heavy sacks, its massive front door was probably locked and certainly bolted. The Greek thrust him into the one chair at the table and then went to wait under a window.

André was standing just behind the chair. A third man was seated in the darkest corner, not the man who had driven the car, someone more important, someone before whom both the Greek and André kept silent.

The voice from the corner was speaking French, quite accurately, almost fluently. The underlying accent hinted at German, with a strange overtone of Russian. He wasn't a Frenchman, certainly. Or English. Or Italian or Spanish or Scandinavian. German mostly; Russian inflections added. Duclos felt his pulse quicken, but he stared dully at the table in front of him as if he were half drugged, wholly stupefied. "Monsieur Duclos," the voice was saying, "let us not waste time. We know a great deal. We only want a small explanation from you. Why are you in Greece?"

"I am on holiday," Duclos said slowly, thickly.

"You can do better than that. Why are you in Greece?"

"On holiday. Some business, too." He was pausing between the phrases, just enough to give the impression of exhaustion, of scattered wits.

"What business?"

"Designs—I am interested in design. Greek revival—nineteenth century."

"Why did you visit Galland?"

"Burglary, burglary in my studio."

"Nonsense! Why did you visit Galland? We know you interviewed a man, accused of murder, in Galland's private office. Why?"

"Burglar. No murder, just burglary." Stick with that, Duclos told himself. You were called to the police station to identify a possible thief, arrested on another charge. You don't know the other charge. You only know there was a burglary in your studio. You had wakened to see the man escape; not the man at the police station; no identification made. Stick with that . . .

"Why did you visit that man?" the voice went on. And on. Duclos gave the same answers, again, and again, and again.

Suddenly a power flashlight switched on. The Greek directed its strong flood into Duclos' face. He closed his eyes. "Open them!" André said at his elbow, and struck him smartly on the side of the head. Just as quickly, he coiled a rope around Duclos, tying his arms to his sides and his back against the wooden chair, and knotted it securely.

"Why were you at Le Happening?" the voice asked now.

Duclos blinked in the strong light. "I go often."

"You were there when it was raided."

"I didn't know—"

"You spoke to the coatroom attendant. You spoke with her twice. You asked her about two men, didn't you? Didn't you?"

Duclos shook his head, tried to get his eyes out of the light, as he thought around this question.

"You are saying no?"

"The light—it hurts my eyes." He shook his head again.

"Closer!" André told the Greek. The beam came nearer.

"What two men?" the quiet voice went on.

"Friends—I was looking for my friends."

"Stop lying! We have a record of everything the attendant said over her counter that night. We were suspicious of her, with good reason. We know what you said. Tell us, now, in your own words."

Duclos thought, nothing I said could have identified those two men as having any connection with Comrade Peter. Nothing I said to the attendant gave that away. Only two men, two men, that was all I asked about. . . . "I hoped to meet them at the club. They never came. I asked if they had come earlier, and left."

"Your studio lies next to the building where Frank Rosenfeld lives. Does he visit you each week?"

Duclos looked stupidly at the dark corner. "Closer!" André said to the Greek. He twisted Duclos' face to meet the savage beam of light. The power lamp now rested on the table.

"Frank Rosenfeld," the voice said. "We know he is an American agent. We know that. We know everything. Give up and save yourself. He has saved himself. He isn't here. You are. Why should you suffer for an American? Give up." The light was switched off, and Duclos almost groaned with the relief of darkness. "It would be pleasant to give up, wouldn't it? Tell me how he came to see you over the roof, down the ladder into your studio. That's how he came. There is a ladder, there. The door to the roof opens easily. That's how he came. Tell us about him."

Duclos said, "The burglar came that way. He used the ladder. He came over the roof."

The light switched on, came still nearer, burning.

"It is Rosenfeld who sends you to Mykonos. Why?"

Duclos shook his head. "Rosenfeld? I have no client called Rosenfeld. Rosenblum, yes. Rosenblum . . . But he didn't send me to Greece."

"Why are you going to Mykonos?"

Duclos was sagging under the heat of the lamp. "To Mykonos, and Rhodes, and the islands—Syros and Tinos, and Lindos on Rhodes and Delos near Mykonos, and—" He let his voice trail away.

"I could make him talk," the Greek said. "I could—"

"No," the voice said, "not yet. He is stubborn, but he will be more helpful when he knows how hopeless it all is. It amuses me to ask him questions and to hear his quick lies."

And that, thought Duclos, is a lie in itself. They have only been trying to connect my visit at the club, the police station, the ladder, the roof, Rosie next door, the reservation for Mykonos. They sense something, know nothing. Stay stupid and ignorant, Duclos; it may be hopeless for you but not for your friends. They don't even know your connection with the Sûreté, or they would not try to make you confess you were an American agent. He said, "You're crazy men, all crazy. Why are you doing this to me? Why? I step off a plane and you—"

"Why did you visit Milan?"

So there was that, too, was there? Duclos sighed. "Business there. And business in Florence."

"Business in Milan with Italian Intelligence?"

Duclos stared, groaned as his eyeballs seemed to be singed with fire. "With an art dealer."

"In Milan you met an Italian agent."

"An art dealer," Duclos repeated.

"An agent of the Italian government," the quiet voice insisted. "Rosenfeld sent you."

Duclos shook his head. "An art dealer," he kept on. "He comes to Paris—he sees me. I go to Milan—I see him. A friend. Art dealer." He closed his eyes. André opened them with a dash of hot wax from the candle he had shaken over Duclos' face.

"You can't be so tired as that," the voice said from the corner. "I have only begun my questions. They will last until dawn, until noon, until tomorrow evening if necessary." There was a pause. The light was switched off. "Why not tell me what you know, in your own words? It would be so easy to talk with me. I know a great deal about you. I know too much about you. Tell me about your friends. Why should you face this unpleasantness for them? You are alone. They did not protect you. They left you. You are alone. Helpless. And hopeless. That need not be. Isn't it silly to argue with me like this? There is so little difference between us—no difference at all. We both want the same things in life, don't we? Peace. Peace, and pleasures, and peace. But the Americans have not let you see that. They would have you destroy me, wouldn't they? They have betrayed you and attacked us. Why don't we make friends? We could work together. And have peace. There is no difference to divide us, except the lies that the Americans have told you. Listen to me. And talk with me. Meet me halfway. Talk. That's all. And I shall tell André to loosen the rope and make Demetrios remove the lamp. I don't want to use such things. Believe me. . . ."

Again there was silence. The rope was loosened a little, not enough to free him, just enough to relieve the pain in his arms. By the soft candlelight, he saw the gleam of a revolver in André's hand. Someone forgot to tell him there was no difference between us, Duclos thought and half smiled in spite of his real exhaustion. He was faking nothing now, except stupefied ignorance.

"Begin at the beginning, tell me everything. You will be glad you did this, tomorrow."

Tomorrow, even if I talked, I would be dead, thought Duclos as he looked at the knife that the Greek had whipped out when the rope had been slackened. Demetrios might be the type of barbarian who enjoyed using a knife. He would be efficient with an ax, too. Cold metal, that was Demetrios.

"Tell me about your friends. First, the ones in Paris. When did you meet Rosenfeld?"

I have said all I dare say, Duclos thought now. Any more talk, any elaborations, and I will be tripped up. He knows no more than he did when he started his persuasion. Perhaps less. I have given him explanations that he had not expected, and he is stuck with them. He cannot move forward, find firmer footing, unless I provide the steps. So I stay silent, now. I'm weak with lack of food and water, weak with the drugs they managed to put into my body, weaker perhaps than I realize. By dawn, or noon tomorrow, I would even begin to forget the things I did tell them, change them a little, become confused. So now I don't talk at all, not at all. There is no choice really, between life and death; he would never have spoken the names of André and Demetrios if he meant to let me leave here alive. Duclos looked at André's revolver, at the Greek knife. I'll choose André, he thought. And above all, I must choose the right moment.

"When did you meet him first?" the casual voice asked as if this were a harmless conversation about a common friend.

Duclos was thinking, I must choose carefully and well. They must not learn that death comes from a small pellet broken between my teeth. How could a man on holiday, a man interested in antique design, possess such a thing as the pellet? If they learn about that, they learn that their suspicions are right. It would be stupid to give them that consolation. But how do I choose the right moment? Even make it a last attempt to escape? Would there be any chance of success? With luck, wild luck? He knew better. Only in the storybooks and adventure films did you have Duclos, with one bound, going free.

"Do I amuse you?" the voice asked quickly.

Duclos allowed himself one last sentence. "You have kidnapped the wrong man—I have no money for any ransom."

"Duclos, we know who you are. Stop this! We know. Now, in your own words—"

Duclos shook his head slowly. The rope would soon be tightened again, the squat power lamp with its beam directed at his eyes would be turned on. Questions and questions, hour after hour. No food, no drink, no rest, no sleep. I am to fear André and Demetrios, the hidden threats of violence. I am to trust the quiet voice of the unseen man, his offers of help, his touches of sympathy, his suggestions which will seem more reasonable as I grow weaker, tireder. And after that, if I haven't broken, then the real work on me will start. But I will not die as a whimpering animal, he told himself in rising anger. I am a man.

He lunged forward at the table, the rope around his body running loose, and managed to tilt it. The two candles toppled and rolled, the lamp slid onto the floor with a crash. Behind him, André caught a loop of the rope, pulled him back, raised the butt of the revolver. Duclos bit down hard on the pellet between his teeth as André struck. He let himself fall sideways, taking the chair with him. The guttering candles dripped their smoking wax on the floor beside him, flickered faintly. The room darkened. The shouts, commands, confusion were moving farther and farther away, a blur of sound fading softly into nothing. Nothing.

The Greek found the lamp and switched it on. André picked up the candles, placed them back on the table, tried to light them. But the wicks were smothered in wax. "Get fresh candles," he told Demetrios, "then give me a hand with him." He looked at Duclos lying half tied to the chair on the dark floor.

"Is he faking?" the voice from the corner asked.

"No. He's out all right." André pulled the loosened rope as tight as it would go and tied the ends into a firm knot at the back of the chair. "He's out for a good ten minutes." He stood back, waiting for Demetrios, and lit a cigarette.

Insarov rose, came out of the black shadows. "He's secure?"

"Like a trussed chicken."

"Then we'll get some air." And talk. A little talk is certainly needed. I begin to think that the alarm flashed through Peter in Paris brought me here on a futile mission. Unnecessary exposure is always disastrous. "Tell the Greek to call out if Duclos makes one sound, one small move. We'll be near at hand." He lit a cigarette as André unlocked and unbolted the heavy door, then stepped out into the cold darkness. The man on guard by the stone wall swung round with his shotgun held at the ready. "Check with my driver," Insarov told him, and sent the man stumbling along the rough path toward the road, past the second of the two small stone houses tightly shuttered, closed, empty. He disappeared into the mass of wild bushes and scrub trees near the sheltered spot, off the road, where Insarov had left his car. Insarov shook his head at the man's clumsiness. Too eager. Fortunately, this whole area was deserted during the week at this time of year. Still— He half turned to look at André, who had approached silently enough to please him. "Keep that cigarette shaded," he said sharply. "Did it take so long to make the Greek understand my orders?"

"Oh, well—you know the Greeks." André was always a little nervous with Insarov. In Paris he had only seen him vaguely, fleetingly, either when he passed through the back corridor of Le Happening or when André had been called in to the dressing room for instructions from Peter. He had never expected to see him here, hadn't even known he was in Athens. Athens? No. The car had been driven only an hour, so the driver had let slip to Demetrios—those Greeks, always imagining that you couldn't understand their language!

"You don't like them?"

"They think they are the only people with brains and courage."

Insarov smiled acidly. "And do you think your Frenchman has brains and courage? Or is he just stupid and innocent?"

André stared in surprise. "But he listened to me at the airport—he went along with me, then. That's some kind of proof, isn't it? He can't be what he pretends he is." And I saw him at the club, André thought indignantly, I saw him wandering round the back of the stage, talking with the coatroom woman, and we know now what she was. Comrade Peter took me seriously enough, trusted me. . . .

"Did he really go along with you at the airport? He might only have been humoring you to gain time to call a policeman. He directed you to a wrong hotel, didn't he? That proves he wasn't believing what you said. Did he make any reference to Zafiris?"

"No."

"He made no remark we could use against him?"

André thought back to the airport meeting. Apart from refusals to be helped with his luggage, and an attempt to leave, Duclos had made only one blunder. "He said it would be better to travel separately to Athens, better to meet at the King George. That implied something, didn't it?"

"That implies he was trying to get rid of you."

"Then who is he?"

"Perhaps working for Interpol—narcotics."

"But the connection with Rosenfeld—"

"There is no actual connection we have been able to discover. I was only trying to see if there might be one."

"And I believed—" André began in amazement, and then laughed softly.

Insarov wasn't even flattered. He looked at the Frenchman contemptuously. Did he really think this was a proper interrogation? "If you had questioned the coatroom attendant thoroughly, for several days, we might have had one piece of information to rely on. Or if you had fully investigated the report you had from your Paris sources about Duclos' visit to the police station, you could have given me more facts about any supposed burglary. We've been working only on coincidences."

"There was so little time. We gathered what we could." And it had been gathered well. Until this minute he had thought of it as a triumph that would leave even a Russian speechless. The risks had been incredible. Nervously, he smoothed his well-brushed hair; and as he felt its new coarse texture, he saw himself on Sunday night, walking into the Grande Bretagne with Duclos' luggage and passport, hair dyed dark brown, cheeks pinked up like a damned woman, wearing Duclos' jacket and hat and his watch and his ring, scrawling a signature at the reservation desk, asking for his mail, going up to the right room, staying there thirty-six hours, keeping out of sight, waiting for telephone calls. "Well, we did pick up his tickets for Mykonos," André said, still angry.

"That boat also stops at Syros and Tinos. And goes on to Rhodes. You heard him."

"You don't think he is important to us?"

"I would need two weeks of preparation, at least; another two weeks for questioning; perhaps four weeks of letting him wait in solitary confinement; more questioning. And only after all that, we might begin to know, not guess, his importance."

"Why go on, now? Why not turn him over to Demetrios?"

"Torture can be a great stupidity. If used too early, it is a self-defeating process. A weak man will agree to any story to please the torturer. I do not want agreement. I want the truth. Who *is* Duclos? Where is he going? Why? Once we learn all that, we can see what further questions must be asked. Then, and only then, has Demetrios something to work on."

"But do you expect him to answer your questions—"

"I never expect. I listen. And in his evasions, he will answer more than my questions." Insarov smiled, watching André, who was another type who thought that only he had brains and courage. "Clever men can never resist talking even to show they can outwit you. In another hour of questioning he will begin to think he has beaten me. The hour after that, all I do is to pick his story to pieces. He will be goaded to talk more, change his story, forget what he said hours before. And then, we have him."

"So you do think he is important?" André insisted, and some of his pride surged back. He had caught Duclos. Of course there were others, too, who had helped. But he had started the chase, he had followed it through.

"I hear our heavy-footed friend returning," Insarov answered, as the man came plodding back through the dark bushes. "Better tell him that silence can be of more importance than speed," he said acidly. "Better still, send him back to Bulgaria. He won't always find a place as desolate as this." He turned away before the man started reporting that all was well, no one was on the road, there had been no traffic for the last three hours.

André caught up with Insarov at the door. Insarov was looking down toward the sea, a molten mass of metal under the night sky. His mood had changed again. "It should be an interesting week," he said softly, his eyes still watching the Aegean. Then, as André swung the door open for him, he strode into the room, smiling and confident, and made for his corner. "Get him up!" He pointed to Duclos, tied to the fallen chair.

Demetrios had been sitting on the corner of the table. He reported, with his thin smile, "Never made one sound. He's still out."

"Then throw a bucket of water over him."

André had secured the door. He looked puzzled, and crossed so quickly to the fallen chair that Insarov came forward, too. "I didn't hit him as hard as all that," André said. "He ought to be—"

Insarov pushed both men aside and knelt by the chair. "He's dead," he said very quietly. And stood up, looking at André.

"But I didn't—" André protested. He turned on Demetrios. "What did you do to him?"

"Nothing. Nothing! You hit him once too often. I told you you'd kill him."

Insarov walked to the door. "You know what to do about the body. Follow my instructions exactly. No deviations from my orders. Not this time." He looked at André. "When you finish here, drive back to the Grande Bretagne, stay in your room, collect all mail and messages for Duclos. That's important. On Thursday morning, pay the bill, take his luggage, and get on board the ship for Mykonos. You will get off before you reach Mykonos, at Syros, wearing your own clothes, leaving his luggage and passport in his cabin. Hire a fishing boat, make your way to Athens. Then to Paris. Report to Peter, there."

Back to Paris? André stared in disbelief. He doesn't trust me to go on with the job. He's disciplining me. Even those detailed instructions are a proof of distrust, of censure.

"Have you got that?"

"Yes. I understand, Comrade Colonel."

"Your trouble is," Insarov said coldly, "that you have been seeing too many American movies. In future, use your brains; not your gun." He left.

André avoided the Greek's mocking smile. He looked down at the white face of Duclos, the fixed stare of the blue eyes. Even in death, losing their brightness, they seemed to be laughing at him.

"Too bad," Demetrios said, and sheathed his knife regretfully. His smile broadened. "So our methods have changed? You think you can hit a man and as long as he doesn't die, you are his kind friend? You treat this kind of vermin as if he were a naughty child. The Russian uses drugs and lies, you use your fists, and you both think you're subtle." Demetrios laughed openly and patted the knife inside his jacket with his long slender fingers. "Here is subtlety. Here is something that can ask questions all night long, and get the answers." Demetrios pushed at the body with his foot. "He knew that. And you will know it, too, Frenchman, if ever *you* are tied to a chair."

Duclos had known that? André stared at the Greek's mocking eyes, bent down beside the body, looked at its lips, sniffed like a dog. Demetrios watched him, and went into a fit of laughter. Those simple-minded foreigners, thinking they knew everything . . . Instead of treating him like a servant, talking together where he couldn't hear them, they ought to have tested the dead man's mouth. In the first few minutes they might have smelled the truth. But now the slight, bitter scent was gone.

"There's nothing there," André said angrily, getting to his feet. All he had done was to make a fool of himself for the Greek.

"How could there be? It was you who insisted on searching him when we brought him here. You wouldn't let anything slip past you. Of course not—"

"He was of no importance anyway," André said, tight-faced.

"That's what I thought all along," Demetrios said softly. So why report his suspicion and take Comrade André off the hook? "What was at stake?"

"Nothing."

"Nothing? A wasted weekend for nothing?"

"Nothing for you to worry about," André said coldly.

Then I worry about nothing, thought Demetrios, and smiled again.

"Untie the body, get the Bulgarian in here to help you carry it to the fishing boat before daylight, drop it well out to sea near Syros—"

"And not before Thursday," Demetrios cut in. "I know, I know." He took out his knife, slashed the ropes lightly and deftly. "See how fast and easy it would have been," he said, looking up at André for some small tribute to his dexterity. But the Frenchman had left. "Come on, come on," he told the Bulgarian, who was hesitating at the door. "We haven't much time."

"They left in a hurry. Anything wrong?"

"Everything according to plan," Demetrios assured him, and laughed contemptuously. He was beginning to feel very, very good, indeed. Quickly—and it was a pleasure to speak in Greek again—he rattled off the orders for the disposal of the body.

"But aren't you coming?"

"You can manage it. The fishermen will help you. I'm no sailor." No garbage remover, either.

"They've had their instructions?"

"And their money. Remember one thing—not before Thursday."

The Bulgarian hoisted Duclos over his broad back. "I'll remember," he promised. "So their scythe struck a stone?" he asked with a grin as he shifted the body's weight more evenly. "I wondered why they went off so quickly."

Yes, thought Demetrios, leaving us to clean up here. Now if the Russian had been really comradely, he could have taken the body in his fast car back to Vouliagmeni, from where he could easily reach the yacht his driver had mentioned—there were several anchorages all along that coast. But no. Swift in, swift out, that was the Russian. Dropping a body from his yacht at sea would be too much of a danger for him. Too much for Comrade André, too. Couldn't he have waited, at least, until Demetrios was ready to leave and give him a lift back to Athens? Oh no, no, no . . . "If you don't move off quickly," he told the Bulgarian, "you'll have more problems than a body over your shoulder."

"See you in Athens, comrade," the Bulgarian said cheerfully and left.

It may be back to Sofia for both of us, Demetrios thought as he picked up the lamp to take with him. The rest of the mess could stay as it was. If the rich had so many houses that they didn't need them except for a couple of months each summer, they deserved thieves to break in and leave a place filthy. He wasn't going to risk staying here any longer than he had to. He looked around the desolate room, remembering the voices. A wasted effort.

He pinched out the candles. Blue eyes brought a curse, the old wives said. He spat solemnly on the threshold, and closed the door.

12

Thursday was going to be a pleasant day, early-morning sun and blue sky promising good sailing to Mykonos. It was also a pleasant end to a very pleasant week in Athens. John Craig had his last cup of coffee out on his small balcony, watching the white-skirted Evzones on guard at the Parliament sentry boxes across the square. He was packed, ready to leave. He felt healthy and rested. There had been enough exercise in the constant walking through the Plaka or over the Acropolis or up to the American School to keep him happy. His one dislike of most cities was the way they forced you to take a bus or a subway, feel heavy with food and soft with unused muscles. But here, over the low-storied houses, the sun could bathe a street and fill it with light and entice you to walk. He had developed his first tan of the season, even if he had worked each morning in the School's library on the days he had actually spent in Athens. His own private conscience was at rest; no guilt about lazing around, or about the nights off with his friends from the School. As for his public conscience—play it loose, Partridge had said. There had been no alarms, no threats, no tensions. He had had a very pleasant week, indeed.

Time to go. If Paul and Pam Mortimer were coming to see him off—though he doubted it—they might be waiting downstairs even now. He had his last look at the streets surrounding the square—people, people, exploding everywhere. If we all keep crowding to the cities, he thought as he remembered the long stretches of lonely empty country, the villages left to sleep away the twentieth century that he had seen in the Peloponnese, perhaps that will be the real time bomb we ought to be worried about. Everyone wants the bright lights and running water, hot and cold. Everyone wants the theaters and cafés and the girls in high heels, the museums and concerts, the newspapers fresh off the press. That is one thing that Athens shares with New York (and Moscow, Rome, Paris and London, too); just name the big cities of the world and you see the same wenlike growth—the more and, if not the merrier, certainly the busier. It makes politicians' eyes bulge in delight as they count heads and think of next election's votes. It keeps a businessman beaming as he hears the music of ringing cash registers. Bigger and better . . . But what does a historian think of? Or, rather, what does he try not to think of? One of the main reasons for the fall of the Roman Empire. People. Just people, bless their happy hearts and their congregating feet.

Indeed time to go. A balcony does funny things to a man. Either he wants to make speeches, have every face upturned, shouts from every throat to prove how right, how gloriously right, he is; or he looks down over the black dots of heads carried along on the two little matchstick legs, and he thinks where do all the people come from? Where are they going? How many more can crowd onto a city sidewalk before the imbalance sets off the population bomb?

I've been too deep in history for this last week, he thought with a smile at himself as he telephoned the desk to get his bill ready. (Yes, he was checking out. On his way, right now.) I've been seeing too many remains of past glories; I can't even look at a row of overpowering columns in a ruined temple without thinking of the men who built them and walked there. And of their great-great and not so great grandsons who let them be destroyed. Let them be destroyed? What else, when you counted the years of acquiescence and drift before the actual destruction began? Yes, you looked at the temples, at the nobility of man's taste, and you remembered the art and the law and the philosophy and the knowledge that had gone with them; and then you thought, unhappily, angrily, why did those men let all that pass out of their hands into alien control? They had something worth keeping and they let it slip away. At what point could they have saved it? The point just before they started to be afraid of dying? Better barbarians than death—had that been their comfort? And the beginning of their end?

Not such pleasing thoughts on a pleasant morning . . . But as he stepped out of the elevator into the enormous lobby with its bustle of people intent on enjoying themselves, he slipped into a cheerier mood. He couldn't see any sign of the Mortimers, but the international circus was in full swing in ten different languages with ten different ways of dressing, from tight trousers to flowing robes. There were loose groups of straying Americans (pity their poor guides), tight families of French, pairs of English, solitary Arabs, explorers from Africa, Hindu saris in flocks, quiet clusters of thin diplomats, a solidity of foreign generals with high-peaked caps over brown faces and pigeon chests weighed down by medals (could one man's lifetime win so many victories?); and of course the ordinary men like Craig, in tweed jackets bulging with passports and tickets, who were wondering whether they'd make that boat or plane if the three lines at the accountants' desk didn't move along more quickly.

The Frenchman in front of Craig finished checking his bill, item by item, paid in hard cash, and waited impatiently for his change. His hands were outstretched on the counter, squarely keeping his place. His fingers tapped, as if each second of waiting was added annoyance. He wore a very handsome signet ring of gold with a strange design. Craig noticed that first. Then he noticed the man's black hair. And his height was about five feet eight, his weight not far from one hundred and sixty-five pounds. Duclos.

So he has been staying here, thought Craig, and is now checking out. Strange that I haven't seen him around, in the restaurant or lobby or bar. Still, the Grande Bretagne in its recently expanded state was a lot of space, and people had to search for each other at the crowded hours. Duclos was counting his change—he must have a rigorous expense account, to be so exact—as he turned away from the desk. The first move comes from him, Craig reminded himself, tactfully avoided looking at Duclos, and stepped forward to say to the hotel clerk, "John Craig, Room 308. *To logariasmo, parakalo.*" That always raised a smile on both sides: the clerk's, because he liked the compliment of a foreigner trying to speak his language; Craig's, because he enjoyed having to ask for his logarithm—it would have to be the Greeks who'd call your bill just that. Anyway, he had spoken his name clearly enough, and if Duclos ignored this chance meeting then Craig could stop worrying about what might have been going on during this last week of sheer enjoyment. In the early mornings after the late nights on the town, Craig had even begun to wonder, as he went to bed, if all the tensions and hidden dangers of his week in Paris hadn't been—well, not exactly unreal; Sussman was dead, wasn't he? —perhaps, just a little, exaggerated. Yet Partridge was not exactly an exaggerating type. He wasn't the kind of man who scratched his hand and yelled that his arm was wounded. He didn't ham things up. Neither did Rosie. Offhand jokers, that was what they seemed in retrospect. Craig waited now for Duclos to drop some money on the floor so that he could help pick it up, pass the time of day as a kind of introduction to a further meeting on the boat to Mykonos. It certainly looked as if Duclos must be taking the same little inter-island ship that Craig was booked for.

But either Craig's idea about how to make a subtle contact in a big hotel lobby was too corny or Duclos had no need to speak to him. For the Frenchman moved away from the line at the accountants' desk, not even glancing in Craig's direction. Everything must be normal, Craig thought as he paid his logarithm; no alarms or special messages, no advice or counsel to be heeded. So relax, Craig, and laugh at yourself a little. You'd have thought you were a prize retriever, the way your instincts pointed at that ring the minute you saw it.

As he turned away from the desk, he saw Duclos' trim figure walking briskly toward the entrance. He followed leisurely, saying goodbye with the right tips for the pecking order in their brass-buttoned jackets, and left the indirect lighting of the lobby for the brilliant, cutting light of Athens' skies. He stood on the steps, waiting, getting his eyesight back into focus after the sun's bright glare. His suitcases were in charge of a bellhop, one of several with many suitcases. Adonis, the porter-in-charge, was gesturing up taxis as firmly as any New York cop directing traffic. But there was a small crowd of travelers down there on the sidewalk, so he might as well enjoy the scene until his turn came. Duclos was less patient, which surprised him—the Frenchman was even trying to thwart Adonis and take the nearest cab as his. And now, too, he could see Duclos' face. It was about twenty feet away, as against ten feet in the Saint-Honoré bar, but it added to his surprise. Hair and coloring were the same; but surely the jaw line had retreated. Or was he seeing it from another perspective, looking down the slope of sidewalk instead of from across a level room? He lit a cigarette as Duclos, politely but definitely put in place, cabless, paced up and down, drifting nearer.

Craig glanced casually back at the man. It was either the same gray tweed jacket that Duclos had worn that Monday evening or something very close to its color and cut. But the profile wasn't quite the same. Near enough, but not exact. Damn it all, thought Craig, if there's one small pride I enjoy, it's my memory for faces; I remember them better than I do names. At that moment, Duclos, halting by the steps, looked in his direction, and he could see the man's eyes. They were blue, certainly; but even under the bright sky that intensified all blue eyes, they hadn't the remarkably clear color that Craig recalled. Duclos turned at the steps and paced downhill toward the diminishing queue.

Craig drew a deep slow breath, his first in the last ten seconds. His cigarette was out. He threw it away. And what do we do now? He looked quickly at the people standing near him outside the entrance to the hotel, and wondered if they had noted his brief confusion. He thought not. He felt a mask settle over his face automatically, a kind of instinctive self-protection. Then a vintage Chrysler came moving slowly up the street and, as it approached him, an arm waved wildly and he heard Pam Mortimer's voice calling. Paul was driving. And was that Clothilde and Bannerman in the back seat? So these crazy characters actually have come to see me off, he thought, and ran down the steps toward them.

"Hi!" Pam said, talking across her husband, "where's your luggage, we've come to take you to the pier, didn't you expect us?"

"Any promise given at one in the morning in a *bouzoukia* joint is not meant to be held against you," Craig said, but he was delighted.

"Tim roused us out of bed. Said you ought to have *someone* to wave at!"

"Let me get my luggage away from Adonis, and I'll be with you."

"And in a hurry," said Paul. "I'll have to keep the car running." He was holding it expertly with the clutch on the incline of the street. "The traffic cops around here would have New Yorkers screaming."

"I'll get out," said Clothilde, and she did, "and I'll put one foot on the sidewalk and another in the car and that should establish our claim to this patch of pavement for at least two minutes." She was also pleased, thought Craig smiling, to show her early-tanned legs and her black patent sandals. She noticed his glance, for she laughed and told him, "All dressed up to wave good-bye. Hurree, hurree . . ."

He turned and headed down the street for the luggage. Duclos was getting into a cab now, suitcases and all. Duclos? Very close, but not Duclos, Craig decided. And what do I do? Just travel with my amiable maniacs down to the Piraeus and get onto the boat there as if nothing had happened? He felt the same frustrated anger that had attacked him in Paris, on the evening he had seen Heinrich Berg for the second time without being able to do anything about it. Unless, of course, he thought hopefully as he tipped everyone in sight (it always felt like that, anyway), there was someone around keeping an eye on thee and me, someone who really knew Duclos and could spot the difference. One of the bellhops was now hurrying up to the car with his two bags. Craig, still stumbling over his problem, followed more slowly. He found it was hard to smile and make the necessary jokes as he climbed in beside Clothilde and Bannerman.

Clothilde said, "Don't look so worried, John, you really were very quick. Besides, Paul enjoys holding a car on a hill—it reminds him of San Francisco."

"And that reminds me of something else again," Paul said, now quite serious. "Did you hear that Sussman was dead?"

"Yes. The Paris papers said suicide." There had been no public mention, as far as Craig had seen, of the arrest for murder.

"That's too bad. They tried to entice him to Stanford, but Berkeley got him first. Wonder who'll succeed him there?" Paul talked on for a bit about university gossip, about visiting archaeologists, about the new discoveries in Crete.

"Oh, Paul," said his wife, flinching nervously as they skimmed past lumbering cement trucks on the Piraeus highway, "please don't talk while you drive—it always makes you forget to look at the speedometer."

Mortimer laughed and slackened speed slightly. The old car handled well, could pass anything on the road, and that was all he cared about.

"Put him in Crete," Pam went on, her tone kept light to show she intended no public snub, "and he's the most cautious archaeologist, everything dug up with a teaspoon. Put him behind a wheel, and he's a fiend."

"Have I ever had one accident?" Paul asked.

"Let's not break that record on the day you're shipping John out to Mykonos." The car slowed still more, and everyone stopped sitting so tensely. Wives, thought Craig, were really useful at times.

Clothilde said, "We're all going to come and visit you for a weekend, John. At least, I'm trying to round up a group of us. We'll hire a caïque and come sailing in like a bird on the wing." There was still much of the wandering minstrel in Clothilde, even if she had been spending the last five years of her life putting fragments of ancient vases together. She was the kind of woman, Craig thought, who'd always be split right down the middle between her intellect and her emotions. A pretty girl with brains had a hard life, almost as hard as a historian being caught up in power politics. But a girl could always solve that split by getting married and forgetting that her brains and training were the equal of any man's. Of course, only a man would think of that. It was his world, all right, and it was a neat solution for him, too, to see the pretty invader repulsed from serious competition and invited to join his bed and board instead. Yes, thought Craig, men had it every which way. He smiled and shook his head.

Clothilde said quickly, "You don't like a caïque, John? But it's wonderful, so—so—"

"Watch out, Craig," said Bannerman, speaking at last, "or she'll have you bobbing around the Mediterranean in one of those walnut shells following the course of Odysseus or some damn Homeric hero."

"Now you enjoyed it," Clothilde told Bannerman, "you know you did. Look at the photographs you took, and the article you wrote for *Horizon*—"

"Which got turned down. I guess it made them as seasick as I was."

"Then you can use it for a chapter in your new book." And thinking of books in progress, she looked at Craig, was about to say something and then didn't. Everyone who was writing a book had his hours of gloom, she thought.

"Yes?" he asked her.

"Don't fret," she said understandingly. "On Mykonos, you'll have the most *wonderful* sense of peace. You'll be able to write there—I couldn't imagine anything more soothing."

Craig gave her soft brown eyes a special smile of thanks, patted her knee, and then looked quickly at Bannerman in case he had overstepped. It was possibly Clothilde who kept Tim Bannerman hovering around Athens. He was one of those humorous types, dark-haired, dark-eyed, fairly tall, with good shoulders and a well-disciplined waist, that seemed to get along with women and men for very different reasons. He fitted into a variety of circles, too, American and Greek, everything from scholars and journalists to poets and peasants. Bannerman didn't lift an eyebrow, one of his favorite comments; he was looking at Craig blankly, as if his mind were very far away from the back seat of this car. "As long as the sea stays nice and flat, I won't worry about anything," Craig told Clothilde. "Hey, Pam, what do you think the prospects are today?"

That set the women talking, with interjections from Paul to keep them right: anyone who lived in Greece always seemed to become a specialist on winds and weather. So in a general sweep of conversation, with Craig's relapse into silence nicely covered, they arrived in the busy streets of Piraeus. Paul threaded his way through them skillfully to reach the broad confusion of the water front. Everyone was now giving directions, except Craig. The inter-island boats were that way, not over here, this was where the liners docked and there the freighters; aim left now, go beyond the wharves, those ones—see?

"I know the way," said Paul and made a wrong turning. "I swear they keep moving these crazy wharves around," he said, as he got back onto the right route.

It would have been easier on the nerves, Craig thought as they avoided loaded carts rushing in all directions, to have taken a taxi, but not so good for the liver. They bumped their way over the rough pavement, skidded on some inset rail lines, swerved around a pyramid of baskets almost twenty feet high, and saw three small ships in various stages of loading at a long quay. "I knew they were around here somewhere," Paul said, chose the ship where the most frenetic efforts were being made, and eased the car as near as possible to the mixture of objects and people spread around the dock in utmost confusion. There were wardrobes and bedsteads, sacks of sugar, crates of oranges, goats and chickens, ancient trunks roped round, battered cases and brown-paper packages, women in shapeless cotton dresses and draggled cardigans, women in smart suits with high heels and swollen hair styles, men in rough caps and wide-lapeled jackets that never matched the trousers, pale students with bulging rucksacks and thin beards, red-faced young soldiers on leave, men in snap-brims and natty double-breasters, children bundled tightly in heavy clothing for the big ocean journey.

"Oh dear," Pam said as she stepped out and looked at the smallest of the ships, "I hope you have an outside cabin, John. Here, better take these Dramamine. I brought them just in case." And wouldn't you know it, she thought, the new boat for the Mykonos-Rhodes run had to be laid off today. Poor John . . .

Craig burst out laughing in spite of his worry.

Bannerman grinned. "I'd take them if I were you." He added quietly, "And that's the first laugh you've given today. Feeling okay?"

"Sure. Just wondering how we're all going to get packed in. We're sailing in ten minutes."

"The farther east from Gibraltar, the longer the minute," Paul said, and became very businesslike. "First thing is to find a steward and get him to take your cases down to your cabin. That makes sure of your space, too. Then you can wander around and join the fun. Like some help with the language?"

"You take charge," Craig said with relief. The only English being spoken around him was by two American middle-aged women with sensible shoes and guidebooks. Everything else was in a torrent of Greek, except for a trickle here and there of French. Even the laughter, harsh and strong, sounded foreign.

"You couldn't have pleased Paul more," Pam said, watching her husband walking over to the gangway. "He adores being demotic in Greek. Come on, let's investigate the baskets. Whoever piled them so high and so neatly?" Clothilde was already halfway to the pyramid. That kind of mystery delighted her. It was obviously done by a nimble-handed gnome in a state of weightlessness, she called back over her shoulder.

"I'll see about the luggage, first," said Craig, and began hauling his bags out of the trunk. Bannerman helped, politely, not too energetically. He was looking at Craig with some deepening speculation all his own. Just then, a taxi drew up and the imitation Duclos stepped out. Craig saw him, froze for a moment, reached back into the car for his raincoat. "That's everything, I think." His words felt as tight as his face. He avoided glancing in the man's direction.

Bannerman said, "Hey, you dropped something!" He bent quickly and picked it up, pressed it securely into Craig's hand. "I've been wondering how to get it there for the last five minutes," he admitted with a short laugh. Craig glanced at the coin in his palm: it was a nickel, all right. Bannerman was saying quietly, "I know, I know. Contact only in an emergency. My feeling is you've got one on your hands. What's been troubling you?"

"Duclos." The Frenchman was now carrying his suitcases on board. His head was bent, eyes on the steep gangway. He looked to neither right nor left. He was a man who didn't want to be noticed.

"Didn't he make contact with you at the Grande Bretagne?"

Craig shook his head. "Do you know him?"

"By description and photograph. He is just getting on board, now."

"Not Duclos. That's someone else."

Bannerman actually stared. "Are you sure?"

"Almost sure. Enough to worry about it."

"Look—why don't you join Paul? Stick close to him. I have a couple of Greek friends I'd better talk with. Yes, they're going to Mykonos, too. Perhaps—" he paused again, and smiled—"yes, we'll let the Greeks handle this little business. They're very resourceful." He stepped away, seemingly to avoid a cart being pushed along, piled high with mattresses.

Craig lit a cigarette, threw his coat over his shoulder, picked up his two bags, and set out for Paul and the steward he had collected. "Now," said Paul, once the formalities of documents and tip were over, "we can stroll around and watch what's going on. Wouldn't miss this for anything. It's a slice of real life."

"How long do we have?" Craig's eyes were looking around the dock. Bannerman had disappeared. Or was hidden by the crowd. There was no sign of the man who was pretending to be Duclos—he must have settled in his cabin. He certainly wasn't among those who hung over the ship's rail and yelled last messages down to the people on the dock. No transatlantic sailing had more enthusiasm.

"Oh, about fifteen minutes—yes, when they are really good and ready to sail, they'll whisk all this stuff off the dock. You'll be amazed how quickly they'll do it. Now, where are Pam and Clothilde? And where's Bannerman?"

Fifteen minutes turned to twenty. "Where's Bannerman?" Paul was still asking.

"He met that architect friend of his—" Pam said. "What's his name? Elias something or other. Look, there they are!"

Bannerman was coming forward with a small dark-haired man, dressed neatly in gray, who carried a suitcase. They were talking casually, cheerfully, in English. "Elias is also going to Mykonos," Bannerman announced as he completed the introductions. "He's studying the ground for a new hotel."

Craig shook hands and felt he was being quietly studied, too. But pleasantly. Elias had an easy smile, brightly intelligent brown eyes, a thin dark mustache stretched over sensuous red lips, and gleaming white teeth. Shirt, suit and tie were restrained and elegant. A successful young man, you'd say, and a happy one. No worries, no strain on that thin, handsome face. "I think we go on the boat," Elias said. "It is time."

"Wish I were coming with you," Bannerman said, enthusiasm for travel apparently breaking loose. "What do you say, Clothilde, shall we go?"

Clothilde looked willing. She always was. But Pam said quickly, "Timmy, don't be silly. She hasn't even a coat to keep her warm."

"Well, don't be surprised if you see me tomorrow or the next day," Bannerman told Elias and Craig, still keeping a joke in his voice. "Better get on board, now."

"Can't imagine why they are so late," said Paul. The cargo, both things and people, was mostly loaded. He looked up at the crowded railings of the ship and saw a redhead. "Now isn't that something? Was that what caught your eye, Bannerman?"

Craig looked up, too, and recognized the girl. He was sure of her: she had sat at the same table in the Saint-Honoré bar with Partridge and Duclos. She wasn't laughing, today. She was grave-faced as her eyes searched the dock. Pam was saying, "French. You always can tell." And Clothilde, studying the simple gray wool dress and the high-brushed hair, said nothing at all.

"On board!" Bannerman said briskly, ending Craig's good-byes and thanks, pushing him firmly toward the gangway. Elias was already stepping onto the deck. What's the big hurry? Craig wondered, but he smiled all around and waved as he followed the Greek. And just as he reached the deck and was searching for a free space at the rails, he began to understand. Two olive-green cars, neat and businesslike, were drawing up quietly on the dock. Three men, neat and businesslike, too, moved with precision and speed toward the ship. They boarded her easily, with no questions. The purser was there to welcome them, as serious and silent as they were. They disappeared down the narrow staircase into the section where the first-class cabins lay. Few people noticed; most were still concentrating on calling last-minute messages to their friends on the pier. The crew were standing by the lines, ready to cast off. The narrow planks aft were already being removed. Only the first-class gangway still waited.

Four minutes passed by Craig's count. It was now twelve-fifteen. On shore, Bannerman was pointing out something interesting at the ship's stern to Clothilde and Pam Mortimer while Paul stayed by his car, looking at his watch, no doubt wondering about that one o'clock lunch party he was scheduled to give for two visiting scholars. Beside Craig, two men who had been talking quietly together in an incomprehensible language—they were northerners, definitely, judging from their heavy blunt features, white faces, fairish hair: Balts or Poles, perhaps Czechs?—fell totally silent. The bogus Duclos and the three imperturbable Greeks were leaving the ship in close formation, complete with his luggage.

Before their tight group had even reached the dock, one of the men near Craig went into action. He headed for the gangway, got one foot on it, began explaining in a mixture of inadequate Greek and useless French that he had left a suitcase behind—he must get it—it was impossible to sail without it. He ended the argument abruptly by pulling free from a restraining hand, made a dangerous dash down the half-free gangway, jumped onto firm ground. He stood there only for a few seconds as he recovered breath and dignity, then stalked off in high dudgeon. To the nearest telephone? His report would be a shocker, Craig thought, watching the dwindling figure of the hurrying man, watching the two official cars speed away with their prisoner. Now there's a slice of real life for Paul to observe. . . . But Paul had barely noticed, if at all. And the others? They were gathered around Paul, laughing at one of Bannerman's quips as he pointed to the ship, arms circling high, Clothilde's long green scarf fluttering.

That reminded Craig to start waving, too. Paul, still glancing at his watch, was ready to drive off. Bannerman gave one last salute as he stepped into the car. Craig returned it, with a broad grin. Bannerman certainly had the most resourceful of Greek friends.

As they sailed out of the enormous port, siren-blasting their way between fishing boats, freighters flying every imaginable flag, two destroyers making for the naval dockyards on the opposite shore, an Italian liner, a Greek cruise ship, launches, more fishing boats, Elias halted nonchalantly beside Craig. "It's going to be quite a pleasant trip," he said, smiling brightly.

"Slow in starting. What was all that commotion on the dock?"

"The purser tells me there was a smuggler on board. Narcotics."

"Really?"

"Yes. A Frenchman named Duclos, the purser said. One of the detectives told him the man had been chased all across Europe." Elias shook his head over such an extraordinary world. "I think I will make a constitutional before lunch. Would you care to join me?"

"I had better get below and check on my suitcases. See you later."

They went their separate ways. At the railing, the light-haired man gripped the rails and stared straight ahead. Strange, thought Craig in amusement, to show so little concern for the traveling companion who was left behind, to stand so tensely when Duclos was named as a wanted man. His amusement ended when he thought of Duclos—surely that was really taking a lot of liberty with a name, to tie it up with narcotics, even in rumor. Why? And where was the real Duclos, anyway?

He went down the narrow companionway to the next deck. Here were about twenty cabins along a narrow passage. The first one was empty, its door swinging to the rhythm of the boat. They were coming into more open sea, now. The next one had its door open, too. There was a woman inside—the French girl with the superlative figure in the simple gray dress. She was standing, holding onto the narrow bunk, her head bent. She raised her face as she heard his footsteps halt. She had been crying.

"Can I help?" he asked awkwardly.

She shook her head, picked up her coat and bag from the bunk, brushed past him, her face now calm, determined. Head erect, she climbed the steps, vanished out of sight.

13

They came to Mykonos in a blaze of pink and vermilion sky, with feathered sweeps of cirrus clouds so high that they had already shaded into gray, leaving the last golden glow to the threatening mass of cumulus on the north horizon. The island was a spreading slope of hard rock molded into small hills, barely green, its contours carved so near the bone that the occasional farm scattered over the rising land must have its richest harvest in stones. Down below was a curve of bay, with the little town at one side—flat-roofed houses of brilliant white, their square outlines broken by blue- or red-domed churches, clustering in a tight mass at the water's edge—and there the long jetty formed a breakwater to harbor small craft, fishing boats, masted caïques. Across the bay, at the other tip of its crescent, there was a mooring quay in the shelter of a rocky headland for a few yachts. Anything larger had to anchor outside.

Craig stood on thc rising and falling ship with the rcst of thc passengers who were going ashore, looking over the rail at the motorboats and light launches coming out from the shelter of the breakwater, dipping and rolling as they met the heavy waves of the rising sea. There was a marked silence around him, ship friendships forgotten, the rough squalls that had sent them all retreating to their cabins or huddling in joint misery in the bar now merely minor interludes. A loose gangway had been rigged against the side of the ship. "You just grip hard, and don't look down," one of the American women began telling her companion. "I remember arriving here from Rhodes at one in the morning during a *real* storm—" Yes, thought Craig, that kind of traveler was always remembering, and bringing less comfort than she intended. He waved down to the upturned brown faces, far below, of the thin agile Greeks who were maneuvering their small boats near the bottom step of the gangway, calculating pitch and toss with expectant grins. Now, *there* are people who are really enjoying themselves. If that fat lady falls into the water, they'll have the best laugh of the week.

The French redhead was a practical woman, Craig noted. She had tied her head securely in a large scarf, bundled herself against wind and spray in a tightly belted coat, put her high-heeled shoes into her pockets, and was leading the way down the swaying stairs in her nylons as if she had been doing this every morning for setting-up exercises. He followed her, carrying the fat lady's handbag, with Elias steadily coaxing them onward from the rear. The operation, from something a little tricky and outside of most experience, turned into a comedy routine. Craig, safe in the steadily swaying launch, waited for it to be filled—to the gunwales, naturally; Greeks never did things by half—and found he was watching the slow procession downward with a relaxed smile. It was all a matter of perspective. From here, the gangway looked solid, the ship enormous, and only the hesitant feet were dangerous. The Greeks laughed, pushed, pulled, and yelled encouragements. The confusion was complete and yet under control.

"I think," said the French girl, as she put on her shoes and stood up beside him, "that the worst is yet to come." She looked at the darkening stretch of open sea between them and the breakwater. "You are John Craig? Yes, Jim told me. . . . I am Marie Aubernon. Mimi for short. I am staying at the Leto, around the bay. And you?"

"At the Triton—it's in the town itself." Could she hear that, he wondered, with all those shouts around us?

She nodded, looked away, studied the little boat alongside that was being loaded with luggage. "Yves Duclos was to have introduced us," she said very quietly. "But—" She shrugged her shoulders, her face impassive, only her eyes troubled. "What happened to him?"

"I don't know."

She bent her head, tightened the belt of her coat. "We'll meet on shore," she said, moving away to the shelter of the small cabin.

The boat was packed, at last, and started its homeward voyage.

Mimi had been right about the stretch of rough sea, but once they were inside the breakwater the violence of wave and wind abruptly ended. Dusk had fallen and the lights of the front-street cafés welcomed the passengers as they began their long walk up the jetty. "Tomorrow night," Elias said cheerfully at Craig's elbow, "we'll be sitting at one of those tables, watching the new arrivals. We'll meet, of course. Everyone meets in Mykonos."

"Any sign of the man whose friend left him in such a hurry?" Craig asked quietly.

"Got off the boat at Syros, more than three hours ago."

"Good. That's one less to worry about."

Elias only smiled. He increased his pace, drew well ahead, and was lost among the straggle of arrivals.

Craig followed the porter who had picked up his bags and taken the lead. As they reached the front street, he pulled off his raincoat—it was now too warm, away from the sea wind—and began to relax completely. Everyone meets on Mykonos, Elias had said. At this hour, certainly, it looked as if the entire population of three thousand-odd had flocked to the water front for the main event of the day. The broad street ran level with the shore, was in fact part of it. On one side were beached rowboats and fishing nets, on the other arcades and café tables. Brown faces everywhere, bare arms, bare legs, sun-bleached hair, and curious eyes. Ahead of him, Craig saw Mimi with her coat and scarf over her arm. Judging from the prolonged, swivel-headed stares that followed her slow, even stride, Mimi was going to be quite a success on Mykonos.

Purposely, he had avoided returning the cool appraisal from the café tables. This was a night to slip into Mykonos quietly, not a time to be noticeably curious. Besides, he preferred watching Mimi and her triumphal progress: her skirt was just tight enough to give it full advantage. Then he heard his name clearly called, and was forced to look to his right. It was Maritta Maas, waving gaily. Beside her was Veronica Clark. He ignored the two handsome long-haired types in mock fishermen's jerseys and tight red pants who sat with them. Nor did he stop. He called back laughingly, pointed to the porter waiting now at the corner of a small street, waved, and went on his way. He was glad to get out of sight, worrying now whether he had sounded natural enough, whether he had hurried too much, whether he had succeeded in seeming just a casual kind of character; and he couldn't even remember what he had called to them, not exactly—but thank heavens they had found it funny. At least, he had left Veronica laughing.

You'll have to get used to this, he told himself as he followed the porter along the narrow twisting street, so narrow that he could touch the whitewashed walls of the houses on either side. And all the little wandering streets were the same, their paving stones whitewashed to match the houses with their balconies and narrow stone staircases that led to the upper floors. You'll have to get used to coming around a corner and meeting Veronica face to face. You won't even see her until she's twenty feet away from you. And the hell of it is, your heart will leap every time you catch sight of her, just as it did back there.

In a few minutes, they had walked through five of those quiet crisscrossing streets, the porter always a little ahead, for there was no room for two to walk abreast in comfort unless closely arm in arm. A town with possibilities, thought Craig. No worry about getting lost, either. You only had to head toward the sea breeze and you'd be back at the bay. The street-lighting system was simple, too: single bulbs in brackets attached to house walls; not too many, just enough to show the way through the white maze. By moonlight, street lights wouldn't even be necessary.

The porter halted and looked back, a sign perhaps that they had reached the hotel. It was at the end of this fifth small street, on the edge of what seemed to be a wider stretch of flagstones. In fact it was a square, a miniature one, with a very small church and a couple of dark spiky trees—cypress? cedar? something like that—and two other narrow streets leading out of it.

"The Triton?" Craig asked. The place looked like any of the larger houses around the square.

His guide nodded, spread a white smile over his wrinkled brown face, and pointed to the stone staircase that hugged the side wall. Craig climbed up its steps, narrow and high, avoiding the pots of flowers on each tread, and stood on the entrance balcony under a pergola of vine leaves. From here, he could see part of the street along which he had come, half of the ghostlike square, and about ten yards into the streets on its other side. Where was everyone? Down at the bay, or eating supper, or already in bed? Suddenly, he heard footsteps; two men walking into the square, crossing it. One was speaking in German, a quiet continuous stream of words. He was small and fat, wearing shorts and a bulky sweater. The other, tall and powerfully built, dressed in white trousers and dark blue blazer with a scarf folded at his neck, looked up instinctively at the open belfry of the church as if something there had caught his eye—a gentle swing of the bell's tongue, perhaps, or the stirring of a bird. It was Heinrich Berg.

Craig moved against the wall, out of the lighted threshold, stood motionless. But Berg had heard Craig's brief, careful step. Quickly, his eyes glanced up at the hotel balcony and saw the Greek porter standing in the doorway. His friend was pointing at the vine on the pergola—it seemed, for a moment, to Craig that the finger was aimed straight at him—and then burst into explanation. In the autumn, that vine was covered with huge clusters of grapes, unbelievable, most useful as well as decorative, the wine in Mykonos was quite passable. . . . The footsteps passed on, the voice died into a murmur, a door somewhere around the corner—in the square, perhaps, or in one of the small streets leading off from that corner—closed heavily, and there was silence again.

The porter was gesticulating politely. Enter, he was saying, and welcome, and there are the bags which I have carried with the greatest care and brought safely to your destination. Craig couldn't understand a word of the dialect, but he offered the man his choice of money from a handful of coins in his hand. It was a system that worked well. The man clattered down the steps happily, with more good wishes for a long and healthful stay, and Craig stepped into the small low-ceilinged room that had been turned into a reception lobby. There was a gray-haired woman, brisk and formidable, waiting behind a desk; a smiling but silent young man in a very correct dark suit, who came hurrying at the clang of Madame's bell; two young maids, with shining cheeks and nervous giggles, to seize the luggage and bear it away down a small dark corridor. Reservation, passport . . . It was the usual routine. Madame made it protocol. He floundered through a Greek phrase, trying to ease the extreme formality, and was corrected firmly. So he fell silent.

She studied him as he signed the register. "You admired our view," she told him severely in halting but determined English, which might be another way of reminding him that he had kept her waiting for at least five minutes before deigning to put a foot across her threshold. Or was she curious about what he had seen out there? She was frowning heavily, gathering strength for another attack on the English language. "It is beautiful?"

"Beautiful," he assured her. "The flowers are beautiful also," he added most politely. Now can I leave? he wondered.

She bowed in agreement rather than dismissal. Her voice became less harsh, although it would never be called mellifluous. "Herr Ludwig admires the vine. He always admires the vine."

Craig decided not to leave, not quite so hurriedly at least. "Herr Ludwig?"

"You hear his words tonight? He admires very much."

"Perhaps Herr Ludwig would like to have a few bottles of its wine." But he had gone too quickly for her, there, so he slowed down and said, "Herr Ludwig also admires the wine."

There was a bright gleam of laughter in her sharp brown eyes. "For three years, he admires. He does not get."

"Poor Herr Ludwig," he said, and friend of Heinrich Berg at that. But this wasn't the time for any direct questions; better to follow the silent man who was waiting for him at the door. Ludwig was a three-year-old institution here, at least; and Heinrich Berg was visiting him, judging by the guided tour he had been given through the square.

"Dinner is nine o'clock," Madame called after him. He bowed again, smiled amiably, but his thoughts on Berg were now passing into light shock. Berg—here, on Mykonos? It was Berg, all right. The black hair was the same, although the gray at the temples hadn't been noticeable—either it was a trick of the lighting in the square or it had been darkened. And the handsome face was Berg's, too. So was its calm, almost benign look. Even when he had glanced upward, alert, watchful, Berg had not dropped that expression. By God, thought Craig, I'd like to be around when he loses that mask.

When did he get here anyway?

The yacht *Stefanie* had arrived with the sunset at Mykonos and moored under the headland on the quiet end of the bay. She was one of the newer craft that were being built to capture the tourist trade, a hundred and fifty tons of compact pleasure for five passengers and three crew—one to steer and chart, one to fuss around, one to cook and clean up. She had two 120 h.p. diesels capable of driving her along at twelve knots, and two masts mostly for decoration or romantic moods, although—when necessary—they could be rigged for silent approaches and departures. They were rigged now, as if the *Stefanie* was just a pleasure schooner with no real power within her neat white hull.

The *Stefanie* was slightly different in other ways from the usual yachts hired to sail through the Aegean. The crew had been replaced by three excellent sailors who were not Greek. This had happened when the yacht had begun its present charter, in Corfu, an Ionian island just a short haul from the Albanian coast. There was rather an original turn in the chartering, too. An attractive woman of fifty, no less, with a French passport in the name of Jeanne Saverne, a slight hint of German in her accent, residence in Milan, had paid a handsome fee to have the *Stefanie* delivered to her at Corfu. Not to her, exactly. To some friends who would use the yacht until she was able, later in May, to enjoy the Greek Islands herself. (Bless all insurance companies, Jim Partridge had thought, when he came across this piece of information in the careful records of the agent who was responsible for the *Stefanie*'s safe handling. The insurance agent had only made one mistake: he had assumed, since the yacht had been sent especially to Corfu, that the "Greek Islands" would be those in the Ionian Sea. But after a quick call at Brindisi, the *Stefanie* had quietly abandoned the Ionian and headed for the waters around Athens. Which was, after all, halfway to the Aegean.)

It was such a neat operation, beautifully calculated, simple and innocent in appearance and yet—once questions started being asked—as complicated and peculiar as an artichoke being peeled leaf by leaf, that Partridge and his friends would have felt considerable satisfaction if they had seen the small red boat that drifted gently over the bay when the *Stefanie* sailed into the harbor. And they deserved some congratulations. Partridge had raised the first questions. (If Insarov is renting a house on Mykonos, what will he need for transportation—something safe, discreet, nonremarkable? The usual Greek yacht? What yachts have been chartered this season? Where? By whom?) His friends went out searching for the answers. Within one week they had peeled the artichoke nicely. The four previous months helped, too, of course. Four months of facts dredged up, examined, correlated, remembered—even such small details as the various names used by Heinrich Berg's mistress of twenty-five years ago. Jeanne Saverne, there it was, the name she adopted along with a new identity when she had slipped into France after the war; the name she was still using in Milan, where she had been living for the last few months, quietly, discreetly, with no overt political connections whatsoever but enough spending money to charter a yacht. So Partridge had hired a fishing boat. Or, rather, he had suggested his idea to Elias (in charge of the Greek end of this counteroperation), who had the right contacts on Mykonos. And there, floating around so innocently, were the small red boat and a couple of thin-faced Greeks with dark eyes and black mustaches, caps tilted over their tanned foreheads, patched trousers and work-stained jerseys. It had been very simple, indeed, once the *Stefanie* had been noted in Phaleron Bay last Tuesday, to track her by each port of call, arrival and departure, as she sailed nearer and nearer Mykonos.

"Here she comes," said one of the fishermen, and rearranged the fish they hadn't caught in the bottom of their boat. "She made good time from Paros. I can count three passengers." Taking it easy, they were, lounging on deck chairs, looking back at the sunset.

"Three," agreed the man at the oars. He dipped them slowly, gently. "Shall we draw closer?"

"We're near enough. They are using binoculars."

"Admiring the town across the bay?" The rower had that Greek sardonic smile on his intelligent face.

"But of course. Just normal tourists . . ." The fish-arranger looked over the side of the small boat and studied the water. "Better ease us in toward the shore, near the Leto. That's a good halfway point between the town and them." And the road to town passed that way, too, if anyone should set off from the *Stefanie* on foot. Most people would use the dinghies from their yachts to ferry them across the bay; but these strangers might plan the opposite—the road at this time of day was deserted. "They've timed their arrival well. There's the mail boat from Athens, standing in." Everyone would be gathering on the front street to watch the new arrivals. Dusk would soon be here, too. "Start rowing. Stand up and face the way you're going. I'll keep watch on the yacht now." He began playing around with the folded net coiled in the prow of the boat, his back to the land, as if he were trying to straighten some tangle. The yacht was moored by one rope only. She had dropped anchor, too, to prevent swinging. She was secure, yet not so tied up that departure would be complicated.

"There's a storm coming up." Even inside the bay, there was a difference in the bobbing waves, still small but now sharply chopped, with even a few miniature whitecaps beginning to show. "I'm going closer to the shore."

"Don't get me out of sight of the yacht, that's all. Take it easy, easy. Not too fast. That's fine. You look like a real Mykoniot."

I wish I felt like one, the other thought, as the strain on his thighs and shoulders increased. This wasn't as easy as it looked. Next time, he told himself, I'll let someone else do the rowing. I can't even look around and see what's happening. "What's going on?"

"Nothing."

That was always the way . . . nothing, and waiting, and nothing, watching and waiting, nothing.

"Two men leaving the yacht, taking the path to the road."

"Then what?"

"They've turned right. They're walking briskly. Very clever. It's dusk, but the street lights aren't yet switched on. They could reach town before that happens." There was a long pause. "Yes, they are coming around the bay. Get to the shore."

They were pulling their boat up over the narrow stretch of beach when the two yachtsmen came walking past, only separated from the fishermen by the low stone wall that edged the deserted road. In the fading light, the two strangers looked very similar, both in clothes and in height. They walked straight on, in silence, barely glancing at one fisherman now unloading his catch while the other balanced the oars over his shoulders, and didn't slacken pace until they reached the part of the road where it turned away from the shore as it reached the outskirts of the town, to swing around some buildings at the water's edge. And there an odd thing happened. A third man had been waiting for them near the buildings, a small, fat man in shorts with a bulky sweater pulled over a flowered shirt. He shook hands solemnly with one of the men and fell into step beside him, while the other simply turned on his heel and retraced his steps at the same brisk pace. He passed the two fishermen on their way into town and gave them a sharp glance. But they were too busy discussing the possible price they could ask for their catch at the Triton to pay him any attention.

They had other reasons, too: the man hurrying back to the yacht anchorage was obviously of less importance; he had only been escorting his companion safely to the meeting place. "Protection?" murmured one of the fishermen. "Or is it to confuse anyone who might be watching the *Stefanie?* And who is the fat friend who is now doing convoy duty?"

The other fisherman shook his head. "We're in trouble," he said worriedly, looking for a place to ditch the oars and the fish. For the two men ahead of them had disappeared down the narrow lane, just beyond the group of buildings, which would lead them into the big main square which lay at this end of the town. "They're not going to parade along the front street, you may be sure of that. They'll use the square to branch off on a road right around the back of the town."

He increased his pace as he spoke, but even so, when they reached the wide, deserted square, all they saw of the stranger from the yacht and his solid guide was their backs as they vanished up one of the small streets on its other side. "You follow, if you can. Don't let them get suspicious, though. A safe distance, these were the instructions." He took the fish from his companion's hand and watched him hurry across the square. Here's a town, he thought angrily as he looked down the full stretch of the front street with its café lights welcoming the procession of travelers from the Athens boat, here's a town where you can walk its length or breadth in five minutes, and where you lose a man in three seconds flat. The dusk was deepening, more lights were coming on, here by the water front. He watched a red-haired beauty, following her porter and luggage, strolling toward him; French, he guessed by her clothes, and probably going to the Leto—she was entering the dark lane now to reach the shore road around the bay. That's right, he told himself bitterly, you know everything except where that man from the yacht was going.

There were several small pieces of comfort, though. The man had been seen. The man had been followed into town, and not to one of the houses scattered on the hills around the town. The man would never have put a foot off his yacht, never even have anchored, if he had any suspicion at all. The man's friend could be identified with a little work and care; he was either a tourist or a foreign resident—certainly not a self-respecting Mykoniot in that ridiculous clothing. So these were the crumbs of comfort. Now we shall wait on that road around the bay, and wait, and wait, until the man returns to the *Stefanie*. A clever man, certainly. Who is he?

The lights went on in the little streets and lanes. Perhaps in time to let us catch up with him after all? Always keeping, of course, at a safe distance; these were the American instructions. The fisherman laughed silently. Whoever gave these directions had never seen Mykonos.

14

Dinner at nine meant nine-thirty. It ended almost at eleven. This was due partly to the amount of food divided into many courses, and partly to the valiant attempts of the young smiling fishergirls, decked up in spotless aprons, to serve from the left and pour from the right and remember all the funny ways of foreigners. It was a generous and comic meal, actually the best of combinations. Nor did Craig have to do much talking. The other guests were either French or English, and both groups showed something of the new nationalism in Europe by disliking to speak in anything but their own language.

When he stood once more in his small, low-ceilinged room that overlooked the little square, his plans for the rest of the evening—to wander around the town for an hour, find his bearings—were now quite discouraged. Everyone here was already in bed, it seemed; Mykonos had closed down for the night. There wasn't a movement or sound from the lanes around the church square; windows were shuttered, lights were out. This was a place of sea air and heavy slumber, and probably of early rising. He might as well call it a day, catch up on his own sleep (twenty-four hours short after his week of *tavernas* in Athens) and face Mykonos tomorrow. There were also two immediate problems: how to be able to avoid Veronica Clark nonchalantly; how to avoid Heinrich Berg completely. He could solve them for tonight, at least, by going to bed.

He had been right about sea air and heavy sleep, but he didn't get down to breakfast until almost ten. The rest of the guests in this rambling hotel (three houses joined together by Madame's will power and run on her indomitable energy, with scurrying maids dropping spoons or unrestrained giggles as light relief to complete obedience) had already left for bathing beaches or high-minded excursions to Delos. He had the small enclosed garden all to himself. It was really only an alcove formed by the jut of the hotel's second house into the church square, shut off from the two sides of public view by a thick high wall, whitewashed like the flagstones and every other stretch of stone in sight. It contained three tables, seven pots of flowers (the softer side of Madame the Terrible), vines growing around the second-floor windows overhead (they might even bloom as hibiscus once summer was here), and three oleander bushes to break the hard line of the eight-foot wall. Everything, except the rampant vines, was miniature in scale. It was therefore also excessively private. It was a corner of complete peace—the good-natured shrieks from the kitchen were a long way off—and, what seemed even more important, of reasonable security. No one from the outside, not even the houses around the square, could look into this patch of garden. Comrade Berg, if he were studying his neighbors this fine blue-skied morning, would need something stronger than binoculars to pierce the Triton's high, thick wall.

Madame came to supervise for a few minutes. He admired everything, he assured her. Yes, he was most comfortable, the coffee was excellent. He would sit a little longer, look at some guidebooks, study some maps, and might he have another cup of coffee?

And after that? he wondered. Out. Out to meet Veronica with Maritta smiling in the background? As for Berg—well, it was more than possible that he would not do much walking through Mykonos by this excessively clear and bright daylight. Yes, morning, and breakfast, changed one's perspective on problems, thought Craig.

"May I have some coffee, too, Madame Iphigenia?" an American voice asked from the dining room's doorway, and Jim Partridge stepped out onto the terrace. He was tanned and smiling, a little leaner, a little more gaunt under the cheekbones. He was dressed, like Craig, in a dark cotton shirt and gray slacks. He was adding a few phrases in atrocious Greek to please Madame and send her beaming toward the kitchen; perhaps to help Craig, too. For there had been a moment of blank astonishment, and then—as Madame's attention was diverted—time for recovery. "Do you mind if I join you?" Partridge asked in a normal tone of voice. He glanced around the enclosed terrace. "It would be difficult to sit in lonely state in a place this size."

"There are some guests at this hotel who could manage it very well," Craig said with a grin, remembering last night's deep freeze. "Delighted. Sit down. My name's Craig."

"I'm Partridge."

They shook hands solemnly and sat down, and looked at each other. "Thank God you're here," Craig said in a low voice. He glanced briefly at the hotel's two second-floor windows that overlooked the terrace.

"Anyone up there?"

"Just a couple of maids. And the silent young man."

"Then we'll talk about the weather and skin-diving until coffee arrives." Partridge tilted his chair comfortably, lit a cigarette, stretched his shoulders. "That was quite a storm last night. I was on one of those cruise ships—five glorious days on five famous islands; you know the routine—and bucked a north wind all the way from Crete to here. So when I stepped on land this morning, I decided I'd stay awhile and let the cruise do without me."

Now, come on, thought Craig as he listened with a broadening smile. Partridge on a cruise—that would be the day! Still, it all sounded authentic, and just the usual routine of new arrivals: my storm was bigger than yours. He will end by persuading me he has done nothing but pleasure-hop all around these islands since I last saw him in Paris.

The coffee arrived with one of Madame's laughing handmaidens, and they could drop the light chitchat. Upstairs, the beds had been made, the rooms tidied, and there was no more rustling at the windows, no more whispered comments on the two men sitting so lazily in the garden. The silent young man had left for some errands in town; Madame's instructions to him floated out in all their detail, and would keep him busy for a full hour. "A grand old girl," Partridge said softly.

"Carved in granite. The Mount Rushmore type."

"And a heart of—well, let's say solid silver. You can trust her."

"She knows what?"

"Nothing at all. But Elias—you came over on the boat with him yesterday, didn't you?—well, he's the nephew of her sister's husband. That makes him family."

"Very special?"

"Special enough on these islands. His friends are her friends. He brought me here, this morning."

"Didn't she expect him to stay, too?"

"And occupy a room that earns five dollars a day? Elias has tact. That is why she thinks so highly of him."

"Well, that's nice to know. What about the silent young man? Last night he stared too much, for my comfort."

"Probably he was just admiring the cut of your jacket. I bet he intends to have his next suit built exactly like that." As Craig relaxed and laughed, Partridge added, "Tourists are just like lions in cages—a kind of zoo for the local inhabitants. Don't let a few stares worry you. If a Greek looks at you at all he is paying you a compliment. How about the windows upstairs? Are we still being complimented?"

"They're empty."

"All right, then. Let's talk. But keep your voice down as low as possible. Tell me all about the Duclos incident. Where did you first spot him?"

Craig gave the brief account as crisply as he could. "Have they found the real Duclos?" he asked. Partridge shook his head. "What happened to him?"

"He arrived at the Athens airport last Sunday. That, we do know. Later, a stolen car was found abandoned a few miles away, along with a stolen uniform." He paused. Then he added grimly, "The man who impersonated Duclos may have been one of the kidnappers. The Greek police will get more out of him yet. They know how to handle that type, but it takes time. So far, he is saying nothing at all, not even with Duclos' ring and passport confronting him. Once a man starts inventing a story, it's easy enough to let his own quick wits trap him. It's a kind of mental jujitsu. You lead him on, let him think he is superior mentally to you. And then he outwits himself." Partridge had lost his taste for coffee; he pushed his cup away, stubbed out his cigarette. "So if ever you find yourself questioned, throw away your pride and play stupid. Name, rank and serial number—the last two being as misleading as possible. That's the safe way, perhaps not for you, but certainly for your friends."

"Did Duclos play it safe, like that?" Not for himself, but for Mimi and Partridge and all the rest. For me, too, Craig suddenly realized.

"If he had a chance to give a false rank and serial number, he'd keep them simple. And stay with them."

If he had a chance . . . "I suppose everyone breaks under torture."

Partridge nodded. "Either that," he said at last, "or he killed himself to prevent it. He would size up his captors, know how far they'd go. He was a very levelheaded man, and a brave one."

"You think he is dead?"

"I think so." There was emphasis on the pronoun.

"The others don't?"

"Division of opinion. The usual flap. Suggestions that we even get the Greek police to move in on Maritta Maas right now, while the French pick up Uncle Peter back in Paris. Better those two than nothing at all, that's the feeling. And that's why I'm here, actually. I wanted to see for myself if there were any storm signals around you. If there are, then I'm wrong about Duclos and he did talk. In which case, I'd better get you out of here as quickly as possible."

"I think you are right about Duclos," Craig said very quietly. "For two reasons. The first one is the minor one—me. Remember what I told you about the man with the high cheekbones and blunt nose who left the boat hurriedly at the Piraeus dock? Well, he had a friend with him on board. At first I thought the two of them might have been tailing me. But the one who sailed didn't come to Mykonos. He got off at Syros. Now, if Duclos had given my name to his—his examiners, would that man have got off at Syros? Paid no attention to me? He didn't even know who I was. He was on that boat, I now think, simply to keep an eye on the fake Duclos. They knew it was a tricky business, that impersonation, and if anything went wrong they wanted to learn who had recognized the fake. That could be the reason why they were sailing with him." He paused. Partridge was looking at him with an odd expression in his light gray eyes. "Could be?" Craig asked, wondering if he had been too blatantly stupid.

"Could very well be," Partridge murmured. "And if that's your minor reason, I'd like to hear what you think is more important."

"Heinrich Berg is here."

Partridge was really startled, and didn't even hide it. "Here—on Mykonos?"

"I saw him last night," Craig began, and gave a quick account of the whole incident, from his view of the square to Herr Ludwig's taste for wine. "Do you think Berg would have appeared on Mykonos if Duclos had told him we were all gathering here?" he ended. "So that's the second reason why I think you're right. Duclos didn't talk."

Partridge sat very still. "Then," he said, "we now have three people who can actually identify Insar—can identify Berg, right on this very island. You, and two of Elias' agents who were pretending to be fishermen yesterday when a yacht came into the harbor. They saw one of its passengers being met by a small stout man in shorts, a flowered shirt, and a large sweater." Wouldn't you know it, he thought, two rather minor agents and a complete amateur? "Three who can identify," he repeated, a smile beginning to break. "We're really getting ahead in this game, aren't we?" His smile faded and he was back to some anxious thinking again.

"I can manage to dodge Berg," Craig said, misreading the frown on Partridge's face. "He won't risk walking about in daylight; you notice he came into town in the dusk, when the streets were mostly empty. So if I avoid the small square, show no interest in the Ludwig house, arouse no suspicion that I know he is here, I can wander around the rest of Mykonos quite normally. Of course, there is just one thing. He may not be in Ludwig's house. He may be right back on the yacht. In that case, I'll keep away from that side of the bay. Okay?"

"The yacht sailed at six this morning. But he wasn't on board."

"And that worries you?" Craig asked, watching Partridge's tense eyes.

"Now that I know that it's Berg himself who is in Mykonos—yes." Partridge hesitated, then added, "I'll have to leave, right away. As soon as I can get transportation out."

And here I'm stuck again, just guessing, just wondering what the whole thing is the hell about. Craig said, "I wish I didn't feel I were punching my way into a sack of cotton wool." He tried his coffee, but it was cold. Madame would be shocked at such waste, such casual treatment of her time and coffee beans. He picked up both their cups, rose, and emptied them into a pot of flowers.

Partridge had been studying him as if he were deciding something. Suddenly, he made up his mind. "What worries me is simply this. Everything is moving far too quickly. I've miscalculated. I thought from the information we had that there was a week ahead of us, at least a few more days, to get everything set up here, and wait. But if Insarov has already arrived—yes, Insarov is the name that Berg has used for nineteen years—then he must expect the information from our base near Smyrna to be delivered very, very soon."

Craig stared at him. "So that's your real problem," he said slowly. Heinrich Berg and Sussman's murder had led all the way to Smyrna. . . . "How soon?" he asked bluntly. "Perhaps even now—by radio transmission?"

Partridge shook his head. "He'll use the *Stefanie*—the yacht that brought him here. It has twin diesels. Say around twelve knots. We're about eighty miles at most from that part of the Turkish coast. The *Stefanie* could make it in six to eight hours of straight sailing."

"Then she could be back here tonight."

"No, she'll wait for darkness off the Turkish coast before she can risk her pickup. And she will need darkness here, again, to deliver it. If she can't reach Mykonos before dawn, and I doubt that, then she'll have to wait and sail in at sunset tomorrow. Yes, sunset tomorrow is the more likely hour."

"That seems a pretty complicated maneuver for a Soviet agent to deliver a strip of microfilm."

"Not just microfilm. It has to be something more than that. Two houses and a yacht are hardly necessary for passing information, disguised in a lipstick or cuff link, over a café table on the water front. No, this information is more important than any microfilmed report could be. That's how we reason it."

Craig thought that over. What would be the most important kind of information that could be discovered? It would have to be as full as possible, quantity as well as quality, rich in details, completely authentic. And that, he thought with a shake of his head and a wry smile, would be any foreign agent's dream. To get all that and get it quickly—not just in one stolen document here, a report there, and weeks of fitting all the fragments of information together . . . "So they are going to abduct an expert, are they?" he asked quietly. He had startled Partridge, but it wasn't such a brash assumption. It had happened before, or almost. The American expert on electronics whom he had met at the Meurice party—Antonini, wasn't it?—had nearly been kidnapped right into a hospital bed in Moscow.

"That's what they think," Partridge said, recovering.

"Then you'd better guard your expert."

"We have. For the last ten days we have been doing our best to steer their attention onto the wrong man. Let's hope we have succeeded."

"And all this is going on at the base near Smyrna?"

Partridge nodded.

Craig whistled softly. "Not something to do with electronics again?" He had meant it as light relief, but Partridge's narrowed eyes looked at him sharply. "I did meet Antonini," Craig reminded him.

Partridge relaxed. "You're too damn quick," he said. And you're forcing my hand, he thought. One could tell a stupid man very little, and not worry about his safety. But one couldn't stop an intelligent man from thinking his way through a puzzle. The trouble was, even a man with bright brains could go off on a tangent if he weren't given some basic facts. Tangents could be dangerous. "You were right," he said, weighing his words. "It's that old devil electronics again. The Communists never give up, do they? It's obvious that our real expert would be invaluable to them. As well as the recent alterations he has been making in their wiring system at our H.Q., he also remembers the alterations he made in our Moscow Embassy. You see—" he was about to explain carefully.

"Yes, I remember thinking in Paris—on my first night there, at my sister's party—just how important it would be for the Russians to know which of their listening gadgets were still functioning reliably." He looked at Partridge's blank face. Possibly he wasn't accustomed to being interrupted. "Sorry," Craig said. "Perhaps I'm jumping off on the wrong foot."

A smile flickered at the back of Partridge's eyes. "You've saved me a lot of time," he said blandly. "Any further ideas?"

"Just one question. Back in Paris, you told me an American was bringing information to Maritta. Is he involved in *this?"* Craig's voice was a mixture of distaste and doubt. The man was a traitor, but would he aid and abet a political abduction that could only mean torture and eventual murder?

"He could very well be."

"You aren't sure?"

"You can't be sure of anything, not at this stage. But I do know one thing. He couldn't refuse, or else he'd be ditched. He's ambitious as well as dedicated. That type can persuade himself into accepting any order. He may not enjoy this extension of his duties. But he is being tested by this additional assignment, and he knows that."

"You mean they chose him just to test him?"

"If you work for men like Insarov, there's always a test of complete obedience. But also—he happens to be one man who could entice our expert, or his stand-in, on board the *Stefanie*. You see, he is a friend of both of them."

Craig drew a deep, slow breath. His lips tightened. "Who is he?"

"If we knew that, it would simplify everything. We still only know him as Alex." Partridge hesitated briefly. Better warn him, he decided. Something may go wrong. Alex may slip through our fingers, turn up here. "We do know one thing about him. Alex is one of two men. He could be either Bradley or Wilshot."

"Then both Bradley and Wilshot are in the Smyrna area?"

Partridge nodded. "One of them is being used, obviously, to cover the other. A very clever and cautious man is Alex. He will go far, if he succeeds in this assignment."

If he succeeds . . . "You are putting your substitute expert in a pretty nasty position," Craig said frankly, and didn't disguise his aversion. He didn't like the idea one bit. Was Partridge only one of those damned calculating machines after all?

"Not if he follows instructions. We don't intend to have him abducted. We only want him to discover who Alex is. Whoever invites him for a quick and pleasant trip on the *Stefanie*—that's the American we're looking for. We'll have Alex quietly arrested, right then and there, in Smyrna. And we'll pick up the rest of his friends, simultaneously, here and in Athens and in Milan and in Paris. That's how we've planned it."

"And if it doesn't work that way?"

"We'll board the *Stefanie* the minute she docks in Mykonos," Partridge said grimly. His worry was deep and real.

"Why not before then?"

"At sea, they might have time to send a radio warning to Insarov when they saw us approaching. They could even kill our agent, and dump him overboard. But—" Partridge took a deep breath—"we won't have any of those problems if he follows instructions."

That's the second time Partridge had said that. He's worried about it, really worried, thought Craig. "Is your man one of these heroic types who thinks he can solve everything by himself?"

Partridge shook his head.

"Perhaps you haven't told him enough."

Partridge raised an eyebrow.

"Then, he might not realize how important your instructions were. Knowledge is sobering. A kind of restraint on bright impulses."

"You make me relieved that I've told you too much," Partridge said dryly.

"Much safer," Craig assured him. Although, he thought with amusement, he didn't go as far as telling me the name of either the real or substitute expert. There's a lot he hasn't told me, probably never will. All he has done, really, is to give me full warning on what's at stake. "Much safer for everyone. I'll keep my head down, well down."

"And if they were to start questioning you?"

"You thought about that before you even started talking with me. When they are on the point of hooking the really big fish, you know they aren't going to waste time or run any unnecessary risks with a minnow."

"I wouldn't rate you quite as small as a minnow," Partridge said with a smile.

"It's how *they* rate me that's important. And to them I'm just an annoying coincidence, perhaps not even that." Craig paused. "What do you want me to do?"

"As little as possible."

"I ought to make some contact with Maritta, find out quietly when she is expecting new guests. That's what you brought me here for, wasn't it? To identify this Alex if he slips through to Mykonos in spite of your plan. You know—I have a feeling that he has become just as important to you as Berg."

"He is as important, now, as Berg was twenty years ago."

"You think he could become another Insarov?"

Partridge nodded. "And for that reason, he *is* one of our main targets in this counteroperation. Because, in terms of the future, we're responsible. When we deal with men like Alex, we are really like doctors practicing preventive medicine. In twenty years, even less, Alex could become the most dangerous man in America." Alex, tested by this assignment, adopted by Insarov as his bright young man, trained and guided, pushed and helped . . . "He is trusted now, by a lot of reliable people. He has their confidence. He could infiltrate higher and higher. He could go very far, indeed."

Craig said nothing.

Partridge, looking at his watch, had his own grim thoughts. How did he get back to Smyrna? There was no ship arriving here until the evening, and it was traveling in the wrong direction. So, now that he had given Craig an over-all warning, he had better start sending a message to Smyrna. Relay it through Athens, utmost urgency. Tell them to double the watch on O'Malley. Even more important, make sure he follows his instructions to the very last letter—and no more.

For that was the real joker in the pack, thought Partridge. O'Malley and Duclos were friends. At least, they met in Berlin two years ago, and liked each other. And O'Malley has heard about Duclos by this time. He might just have one of those wild attacks of stubborn Australian courage, decide to go all the way with Alex in order to make sure of leading us to Insarov. Because he doesn't know we've found Insarov, that we've got him if only we keep our heads and don't spread that piece of news around. But how do I get this information through to O'Malley without warning Insarov? For he has his ear close to the ground, that's certain. How else could he have heard, except through some leak in security, that our chief expert's part of the job in Smyrna was just about ending? He must have several agents around; Alex, alone, couldn't find that out. Let's hope to God that Insarov hasn't discovered the real expert is Val Sutherland. Let's hope Insarov isn't having a very big laugh right now, over O'Malley.

"You look," said Craig, "like a man on a high wire working without safety nets."

"That's how I feel," agreed Partridge, and tried to smile. No, he couldn't risk getting news through to Smyrna that Insarov was actually here. All he could do was to warn O'Malley to stick with his instructions, to do no more than that on any account. If only he could have seen O'Malley, spoken with him— He looked at his watch again. "Involved, isn't it, getting in and out of this island?"

"Hire a submarine," said Craig with a wide smile.

"Damned if I wouldn't—if there wasn't so much daylight around. That sea out there seems lonely until you start counting the fishing boats or the caïques. And there's one thing about sailors, they have long eyesight. No, I think I had best start sending messages to Aunt Matilda in Athens." He rose, and then stopped as if a new idea had struck him. He considered it for a full half-minute. "Look, if Madame Iphigenia wonders why I don't turn up for dinner this evening, tell her I went over to Delos this afternoon and probably am staying at the tourist pavilion over there for the night. Will you?"

Craig nodded. Had Partridge really thought of a way to get back to Smyrna? But why the rush? "Half a second!" he said, reaching for the map in his guidebook. "Just where," he asked very quietly, "is Maritta's house?"

Partridge hesitated.

"I'll do nothing rash," Craig said irritably.

"It stands by itself on the hillside above the bay. Here, in this direction." Partridge pointed to the map. "Don't mark it. Memorize. But that's not much of a map, is it? I can get you a better one. I'll leave it in one of your suitcases. Or are they locked?"

"No."

Partridge seemed amused by that. He was about to add something more, but decided footsteps were marching through the dining room. He only said, "Give me five minutes. Then look. *And* lock." He signaled good-bye, and left, almost bumping into Madame at the dining-room door. "Just leaving," he told her cheerfully. "Your nephew is going to take me out to Megali Ammos for a swim."

"Such a nice man," Madame Iphigenia told Craig, looking at Partridge's retreating back. "So gentle. So well behaved." She looked now, severely, at the tray of dirty breakfast dishes.

Craig repressed a smile, gathered his map and books as Madame picked up the tray to remove such an eyesore from her garden. He rose to open the dining-room door still more for Madame's widespread elbows.

"You swim also?" she asked. "Our visitors admire our beaches."

"I think I'll walk around the town and admire the windmills."

That mollified her slightly. He wasn't just someone who sat around a garden all day, dirtying dishes. "There is much to do in Mykonos," she assured him, and hurried on.

"Let me help," he suggested, but she resisted. So he crossed the dining room and opened that door for her, too. It led into a winding corridor which made communication with the kitchen, a full-throated shout away, a fine example of modern labor-saving ingenuity.

"You admire this house?" she asked.

"Very much." Sharp eyes, had Madame Iphigenia. He had been looking for any outside doors—surely a wandering place like this must have more than one entrance. "I'm interested in architecture," he added to excuse his curiosity. That was true enough, anyway.

"Americans admire old houses?" she asked now, in obvious unbelief.

"Why, yes." Where had Madame got her ideas about Americans?

Madame stared, shouted toward the kitchen, brought a maid running along the corridor, delivered over the tray with a burst of instructions, and then looked at Craig. "Come!" she told him, and led the way.

It was a quick and complete tour through corridors, under arches that supported ceilings, up and down narrow staircases, past corners of rooms jutting at odd angles. It left Craig a little dazed, almost breathless. But he did discover he had been right in his guess. There were three separate exits to the hotel, one of them on the church square. That was the one to be avoided.

Before he set out for his stroll through the town, he went up to his room. Partridge had already been there. In the smaller bag, under his camera, there was a neat pistol. Loaded. There was also the promised map, binoculars, and a pocketknife which, startlingly, turned into a switchblade. He decided to carry it. And the map. He put the binoculars into his camera case and decided to carry that, too. He buried the pistol inside a pair of socks, replaced them in the bag. He locked it securely, shoved it on the top shelf of the wardrobe.

Two weeks ago, he thought, I'd have been laughing fit to crack my ribs, making bright remarks about what the best-dressed agent is wearing this season; yesterday, I might have produced a grin, felt a touch of embarrassment when I next met Partridge. But today? Well, I've learned about Duclos; about a lot of things. The more you know, the less you scoff. . . . If I came to Europe to fill in some gaps in my education, I've certainly succeeded.

He picked up his sunglasses—he'd need them for that strong light and those brilliant walls—combed his hair roughly to give him the right tourist look. From a distance, he wouldn't appear much like the man in the neatly tailored jacket, correct collar and tie, who had stepped on shore last night. He slung the camera case over his shoulder, checked map and knife in his pocket, and left. Much to do on Mykonos, Madame had said. She could be right, but not in the way she meant it.

15

In half an hour, Craig had walked through and around the town. It was a place of patterns, imposed, interposed. Cubes, arches, horizontals of steps, vertical balustrades, curves of domed churches, cylindrical windmills each with twelve triangular sails in clocklike precision. Bright sunlight cast black sharp-edged shadow. Houses, stairways, pavement were a blazing white. Color was left to the domes, to the fishing boats drawn up along the front street, to the potted flowers on the stone staircases, to the twisted dark green trees with their sculptural trunks, to the carved doors, to the inside shutters of the windows that stared out in bare rectangles from their whitewashed walls. People had their patterns, too: slender girls, stout women, headcloths and cotton dresses gathered around the wells; thin boys on small mules; men in caps, with creased brown faces and dark mustaches, some working in bare feet with trousers rolled up modestly only to mid-leg, others already gathered around their own tables at their special cafés; and the tourists—those who kept themselves covered like the Mykoniots, those who bared thigh and arm as much as possible—wandering aimlessly.

But among all those faces, all those walkers and talkers, there was no one he recognized. And then, just as he was looking at some of the arts and crafts in a shop window on one of the narrow streets, Mimi came strolling along in green trousers and a white silk shirt patterned to match.

"I followed you for three streets," she said in triumph. Her face was pale, there were deep shadows under her dark gray eyes as she lifted her sunglasses to look at him more clearly, but her voice sounded normal and she was even producing a small smile. A girl who hadn't slept much, he decided, but who was determined to face the day.

"I never even saw you," he admitted, annoyed with himself.

"You weren't meant to."

"Not even in those tight pants?"

"That makes it a greater triumph." She looked down at her thighs. "Too tight?"

"Not on you, Mimi."

"Now look at that darling little horrible skirt in the window, and we shall pretend to be discussing its hideous stripes."

"A skirt? I thought it was a tent."

"Keep looking at the window as we talk. Your friend is in that little shop just three houses away. She is alone."

Veronica? "Thank you for the warning."

"But it isn't a warning. I want to meet her. Shall we go and look at its window?"

"Look, Mimi—I don't think this is a good idea."

"It is. I want to make friends with her as quickly as possible." She smiled again. "I bumped into her once, this morning, but she did not stay to talk. Is she shy or proud? Or frightened?"

"Is something wrong?" he asked sharply. Mimi started walking toward the other shop. He had to follow her, even if he didn't want to go near the place, to get her answer. "Look, I don't think we should go in there."

"Why not? The sooner I meet her the better."

"Don't girls ever talk to each other quite naturally?" he asked in exasperation.

"If she sees we are friends, she will trust me much more."

"You know, Mimi, this is not an easy situation."

"I know. Jim told me all about it."

"He did, did he?"

"He also told me to take care of Veronica."

Craig halted at the shop window, looked at a death mask of Agamemnon, several models of windmills, fishermen's striped shirts that owed more to the Riviera than the Mykonos harbor, guidebooks, glossy oils of storm-lashed rocks, replicas of the Parthenon, hand-loomed cloth that was at least authentic. Was Mimi's interest in Veronica only a short cut to Maritta Maas? The French were chiefly interested in her, he remembered.

Mimi was watching him with a small sad smile, as if she guessed his doubts. "I won't draw her into danger, John," she said very softly. "Let me worry about her. Meanwhile. You can't."

"All right," he said, and stood aside to let her enter.

Mimi was saying over her shoulder, her voice now bright and clear, "You know, these materials are really beautiful. Magnificent texture —and look at this design!" She pointed to the hand-loomed cloth displayed against the walls of the small room and took off her sunglasses to study its patterns and colors.

But he was looking at Veronica, barely six feet away from him. She glanced up from some notes she had been making at a table where the shopkeeper had cleared a space for her. Beside her was a slightly battered book, almost like a ledger, with handwritten paragraphs in Greek and French and English. As he came up to her, he caught a glimpse of one heading: Room for rent. She closed the ledger quickly, dropped her pencil and notebook into a large straw bag, and faced him—confused and startled and yet, he felt, delighted. She wore a simple dress of blue linen, the color of the sky over Mykonos. Her arms and legs were bare and tanned; her dark hair was brushed smooth, falling to one side of her forehead; her lips, parted in that wonderfully real and spontaneous smile, were colored a soft but glowing pink. Then, as he stood there, looking at her, saying nothing, the welcome in her face died away, first in the blue eyes, then in the lips. The smile became a formality, her face guarded.

"Hello," he said casually, "I thought you'd have been swimming this morning. Or painting. How's the work going?"

"Too many distractions, I'm afraid." She gathered up her bag from the table, seemed to be leaving. Yet she hesitated. Something *is* wrong, he thought; Mimi was right. Something is troubling Veronica. But what?

Craig looked at Mimi, who had wandered back to him. "Here's someone else from Paris. Mam'selle Marie Aubernon—Miss Veronica Clark."

"From Monterey, actually," Veronica said as she shook hands with

Mimi. Large blue eyes met large gray eyes. They seemed to like what they saw, or felt. "I'm only on a prolonged visit to Paris. I'm studying art there."

"But so did I! And then I stayed on. I came from the Auvergne originally. Do you know it?"

"No, but I've always wanted to visit it."

"Mountains and mists. And rain."

"And folk songs."

"You like music, too? But of course—" Mimi addressed Craig, "Now, don't laugh at me—I often do my best work with a stack of records playing beside me."

"Perhaps that's what you need," he told Veronica, "to get inspiration started." Well, he thought thankfully, the two of them seem to have hit it off. Mimi's warmth was real enough when she let it rise above that cool, detached exterior. It was time for him to move on. The small room was becoming crowded with the three new customers who were strolling in. Two were English, a quiet couple. The third was by himself, middle-aged, broad in face and shoulders, dressed in shorts and a striped shirt hanging loosely over his solid waistline, still wearing his sunglasses so that Craig couldn't be sure of the direction of his eyes. I saw that man, Craig remembered, strolling up and down outside this shop, as if he were waiting for someone. And as that thought struck him, Craig noticed how still Veronica was standing, her eyes on the man's back. Automatically, he asked, "Where is Maritta?"

"Somewhere in town, seeing friends. I—I had some shopping to do." Veronica glanced again at the stranger, who was interested now in model windmills.

"So have I," Mimi said quickly. "But I'm completely bewildered. The shops are so—so separated. Some don't even *look* like shops! I need sun-tan lotion, film for my camera. And can you tell me where these materials are woven? You see, that's my business now—I'm a decorator, and fabrics are my special thing. Do you know where the looms are? On this island itself?"

"Right in town."

"You know the street? Would you show me?"

"Of course. When would you like to—"

"Now. Why not? Or have you some engagement for lunch?"

Veronica shook her head.

"Then will you lunch with me? Unless, of course, Mr. Craig—"

Craig smiled for Mimi. I could wring your pretty little neck, most lovingly, right here and now. "I've had enough shopping for one day," he told them. "See you around." He paid the smiling woman, who kept shop with such hopeful patience, for the half-dozen postcards he had picked up; someone ought to buy something, he had thought, as the English couple left without finding anything they wanted and the man in the striped shirt still poked and touched and handled and wasted time. Craig moved to the door. Then we'll see whether that man is interested in me, he thought; or is this Maritta's idea of how to keep watch on Veronica when she strays alone into town? He stepped into the narrow street, put on his sunglasses, began walking slowly toward the bay. But he hadn't drawn off the man in the striped shirt. The man was still staying near Veronica.

It was just after noon. At once, the streets were deserted, all work stopped, everyone indoors. Only a few bemused visitors still wandered around, trying for camera angles in the white silence. Now's the time, thought Craig, and left the big square at the end of the front street, choosing the steep road which would lead him up onto the hillside. Above the town there were groupings of houses and dovecotes, small white cubes set down on harsh gray earth, with long walls of rough gray stones forming terraces to hold whatever soil there was from slipping into the bay. He sat down with his back to one of those walls in order to get off the sky line—the hillside was as bare as that. There must be other ways to Maritta's house. Certainly, he couldn't dare approach it in daylight. Still, this was the time to get his bearings. And admire the view. It was magnificent: deep blue sea, other islands, high blue sky, white clouds.

He had only walked for ten minutes, but he was far enough up on the hill to see all the houses, sparsely scattered, that stretched along its wide flank. Some of the houses followed the curve of Mykonos' small bay; others climbed high above it. He got out Partridge's map and compared it with his own. Just there, Partridge had pointed. That was the area high above the north end of the bay where the yachts sheltered. He could see five or six houses in that direction, spread over the steep slopes of barren ground. But which house? Partridge had been deliberately vague, just to keep him out of trouble, no doubt.

Partridge's map was good, well detailed. But houses were only indicated by dots, and the house which Maritta's dear kind Uncle Peter had rented could be one of five, at least.

He took out the binoculars and brought them all up amazingly close. Too close. What he could be doing to someone, someone could be doing to him. So he swung around in the other direction, facing southward—more bare hills and the road leading to the beaches; and then he looked directly ahead of him, over the town, westward. But he was still keeping the pattern of the view to the north end of the bay in his mind. There were two houses, well separated from each and any other, that had paths leading down to the road around the bay. For that reason alone they were his likeliest candidates. One of them had some kind of small building on its far side—perhaps a cottage or one of the ubiquitous dovecotes. Otherwise, from this distance, they were much the same. They even had brave attempts at gardens—he had seen rounded tops of trees inside their white walls. By contrast, the rest of the houses above the bay stood bare, open. If I were someone like dear Uncle Peter, he thought, what would I rent? Protecting walls, shading trees, and a road however rough and rugged right down toward the yacht anchorage. He put away the glasses and his maps; lit a cigarette, lounged against the gray buttress at his back, and watched the drifting clouds sending their shadows chasing over sea and islands. Then he rose, dusted off his trousers and shirt, walked down to the town. The small excursion had taken only half an hour altogether. A wasted half hour? No, he decided. He hadn't found what he wanted, but he had learned that by night he could easily find his way on those ribbon paths that followed the stone terraces right across the length of hillside. And he had seen a view.

He found a quiet *taverna* on the shady side of the big square where a few of the local men, regulars obviously, were grouped around a couple of tables. They looked at him gravely, accepted him with a nod when he made his good day with *"Kali mera sas,"* and returned to their discussion. The talk was always in a low steady murmur, he noticed, just as the drink before them was always a glass of water with an occasional small cup of coffee. There were a couple of fishermen, some men from the harbor, a carpenter, a few old men, and possibly the driver of the taxi that stood on the other side of the square beside three small carriages with bonneted horses. Or mules. The ears twitching through the holes in their straw hats looked very pronounced, even from this distance. It was a peaceful scene: sunlight viewed from shadow, men's voices harshly droning, horses dozing, a taxi waiting for an afternoon hire to the beach; and dominating it all, from the center of the deserted square, was the bust of a strong-faced woman who stared defiantly out to sea, much in the way she must have rallied the fishermen of Mykonos, back in 1822, to sail out and fight the Turks. Craig settled in his corner, behind the screen of talking men, and looked out to sea, too. From here, he had a view not only of the front street right down to the breakwater, but of the several exits from this square. Opposite him, toward the shore, was the beginning of the road that led away from the town around the rest of the bay. That was the way that Veronica must take to meet the path up to the house on the hill. That was the way that Mimi would follow to reach her hotel.

He ordered lunch from a small boy in a large apron—rice and chopped veal wrapped inside vine leaves, served cold—and ate it slowly, studied his map, kept an eye ready for any movement along the front street or into the square, and finished a glass of resinated wine, amber in color, revolting at first but at least liquid and cool. If you drank it long enough, he thought, you'd probably begin to think this was the way wine should taste. Like those inland ranchers in Argentina who imported fish for Fridays from the coast, and before refrigeration was in use came to believe that bad fish was a delicacy. Like the grouse-eaters, too, in London, who had accustomed themselves to high game because once there was no other way to eat it.

There was still no sign of Mimi.

He made his half-cup of coffee last almost as long as the natives could. They were drifting away now. Only four men still sat around. And no sign of Mimi. I've guessed wrong, he thought. She must have cut lunch in town and gone back to her hotel. But if that had happened in the thirty minutes he had taken to explore the hillside up above the square, then it looked as if Veronica and she hadn't got on so well together after all. Which meant, in turn, that Veronica was still more isolated than ever. Damn it, he thought, his worry now churning into anger, I'll have to think of some plan of my own. If Mimi has failed, I'll have to take some action. And what is Partridge going to say to that? *Do as little as possible*, that was his firm advice this morning. But since then, there has been a slight change in the situation here. If Veronica is searching for a room in town, what's the reason behind it?

Calm down, calm down, he told himself irritably. Give Mimi another half hour. Once you've talked with her, you'll have something to go on. Then you can start thinking about some plan of action—if that's necessary. You know the dangers; you know what's at stake. . . . He reached for a cigarette, lit it slowly, stared gloomily at the empty square.

Suddenly, he was aware of someone standing in the shadowed doorway beside him. He turned his head sharply, saw Elias. And how long has he been there? Craig wondered, both startled and annoyed.

Elias was surveying the peaceful harbor, as if he had just enjoyed a lengthy meal indoors and was speculating on how to spend the rest of a sleepy afternoon. But unless he had been sitting behind the stone arch that held up the small dining room's ceiling, or had been in the kitchen itself, Craig was positive that Elias had not been there when he had taken this outside table. Elias was speaking to the four men—friendly, desultory talk that lasted a few minutes. This politeness over, Elias looked at Craig, nodded. "Did you have a pleasant walk?" He pulled a chair up to Craig's table, sat down and accepted a cigarette. "Very quiet," he went on, glancing around the square.

"Too quiet," Craig said, recovering his breath. Who told him I went for a walk, this morning? The same person who told him I was here?

Elias was now studying Craig. "Was it wise to climb up the hillside?" he asked gently, but there was sharp reproof in his eyes.

"Just normal tourist behavior," Craig tried. "Wanted to photograph the dovecotes and windmills."

"You were not using a camera," Elias said, looking pointedly at its case. He added magnanimously, if coldly, "You were very careful, that I must say."

"Keeping an eye on me?" Craig asked with a grin.

"I'm in charge of you. For the time being." Elias was not smiling.

"Oh?" Craig glanced across at the other men.

"They don't understand English. Besides, they saw us arriving from Athens last night on the same ship. It is natural that we talk for a little."

"Were you telling me that Partridge has left?" Craig asked very quietly. So he did find a way off the island, and more quickly than I expected.

"Almost," Elias said. Even if his friends at the other table did not speak English, he seemed a little shocked by the direct question. "And you—how do you like Mykonos?"

"I'd like to be able to rent a house here some day." If he doesn't like it straight, I'll give it to him sideways, thought Craig. And I'm not going to waste time either. Once he finishes that cigarette, he'll rise, talk to the others and then drift off. "I saw two, with a fine view, up above the north end of the bay. They had trees, looked cool." He watched the small smile spreading under Elias' dark mustache. "Are they ever offered for rent?"

"One was rented this summer."

"Oh?"

"But very expensive, I hear."

"Well, you always have to pay for privacy."

Elias was studying him, head slightly held to one side, fine dark eyes gleaming in amusement. He only nodded.

"Which one?" Craig insisted. "Oh, of course I shan't do anything about it, this year. But some time in the future—"

"I wouldn't recommend it unless you like the sound of doves."

So, thought Craig, the house had a dovecote. "Noisy?"

"In the early morning—impossible. Unless you like to be wakened with the dawn, of course." He turned his head to see what had so quickly caught the American's attention. Down along the water front there was a group of visitors easily remarked by their fancy dress. The two young men—the bearded one was an English novelist, he had heard; the other, with the long shock of hair, was a French painter—wore yellow and red linen shorts, respectively. The three young women wore blue, green, and flaming pink: the American girl, Mimi, and Maritta Maas, in that order. At least the American girl had the taste to wear a dress in public. Oh, well, bright colors made one's job easier. Elias rose, paused with a frown as he noticed the baffled look on Craig's face. Trust Maritta, Craig was thinking as he stared at the blonde girl in the pink trousers, trust her to complicate his simple plan. How did he manage to talk to Mimi, now? How long, in any case, had she managed to be alone with Veronica before Maritta had joined them? Long enough to get any information about what was going on, up in that house on the hill? Something was wrong, somewhere. He usually could shake off his premonitions, but this one had stuck with him ever since the meeting with Veronica. It was raising its nagging little voice again, even as he watched the group sauntering nearer and nearer, listened to the talk and laughter beginning to invade the square.

Elias shrugged, sat down beside the other men, and observed as they did, with a mixture of amusement and irritation, the strange behavior patterns of those foreigners: the women wore trousers, the men wore little-boy clothes. If they came here saying that life was absurd, it was because they made it so. The only one he would worry about was the woman called Maas, but at present she seemed positively harmless in her gaiety and charm. She was giving the little boys some last-minute instructions as they halted to say good-bye. "Not a minute later than five o'clock," she called over her shoulder as she walked on toward the taxi. "We mustn't miss the sunset!" She halted to wait for the American girl in the blue dress whose hand was still held by the bearded Englishman. Ah, thought Elias, I can guess what is troubling Craig. He glanced at Craig's table, and was confounded.

For Craig had seized the chance when Maritta's back was turned to rise and wave to Mimi. The quick movement caught her eye. She stared across the wide square at the *taverna,* then walked slowly on. Craig stepped into the safety of the room behind him, called for his bill.

Most unorthodox, Elias thought, but even if crude it had produced the required result. Maritta Maas was now on her way to the taxi, looking over at the *taverna,* only seeing the group of five men around a table. The taxi driver was on his feet, pulling on his jacket, shouting that he was coming. Mimi was searching her handbag, exclaiming in dismay. She had left something—her sun-tan lotion—where? Had it fallen out in the café, or in a shop? The American girl was trying to remember.

Maritta Maas cut the discussion short. There was no time to go back to search, she was late, she had so much to do, there was only one taxi left, she couldn't risk losing it, and where was the other taxi anyway? (Ah, thought Elias, she would notice that; she would ask that question.) But the driver's answer was accepted. It had taken a sick man over to the monastery at Tourliani. It wouldn't be back for another hour, perhaps two. Mimi was insisting she had to have that lotion; she was starting to burn with the sun and sea air. There was no female argument against that, it seemed. Mimi set off toward a small street, Maritta calling directions to the nearest shop. And the American girl, who had been watching the battle of wills in silence, said very sharply, "Oh, stop being such an idiot, Maritta; she won't get lost. Why are you bossing everyone around nowadays?" That subdued Maritta completely. She got into the waiting car with only a small laugh of protest. They drove off.

Yes, thought Elias as he glanced with unexpected approval at Craig standing within the shadows of the doorway, the unorthodox maneuver had been very effective. But that was the way. . . . Sometimes you planned carefully, found nothing. Sometimes you acted on impulse, discovered much. The small scene in the square had revealed enough to rouse his curiosity. The Maas woman wanted everyone under her eye, her control. The Maas woman was in a very great hurry. The Maas woman was under considerable tension. Now, why? On a placid day like this, with no action yet expected, with only patient waiting ahead of them all, why should a well-trained agent like Maritta Maas have such seemingly small and stupid anxieties?

Quickly Elias spoke to one of the fishermen sitting beside him and sent him walking after Mimi. Then he rose, too, and joined Craig. "There's a lavatory near the kitchen, beside the back entrance. I'll meet you on the lane outside. In two minutes." He smiled and added, "That was interesting, wasn't it?" His good humor was completely restored.

Most interesting, Craig thought. Veronica is on the point of complete revolt. But why? He nodded and moved to the upholding arch which framed, inside the alcove it formed at the back of the room, shelves of bottles in neat rows. There was a counter, with glasses, in front of them; and the small boy watching water boil on a small stove to one side. This was the kitchen, Craig decided and pointed to the only door he saw. *"To meros?"* he asked and headed through. He found himself on a narrow street, an outhouse door built under the usual flight of stone stairs to the second floor. He slowed his pace, put on his sunglasses against the white glare, lit a cigarette, consulted his guidebook, stepped aside for a girl riding sidesaddle on a small mule, nodded to two old men holding up the side of a house, and put in the required two minutes without much trouble. "Just across the next street," Elias said behind him, and fell into step.

"Mimi?"

"I have arranged it."

That was all. But the tone was amicable, a return to yesterday's pleasant interchanges on the journey here. He has decided to forget my climb onto the hillside, Craig thought, and smiled. Greeks, he was discovering, might tolerate fools, but not gladly. And yet who had been foolish? he couldn't help wondering. Elias probably knew every inch of that hillside for a three-mile stretch on either side of the town. But had he forgotten how it might feel to be a stranger, dumped down in the middle of strange terrain, strange voices? Or does he think my job is over, now that I've placed Berg right here on Mykonos? In that case, he'll have to do some rethinking. I am in, for the duration. Whatever is going to happen, I'm staying in.

16

Mimi was sitting with her back to the window in the barely furnished room, watching the door as if she weren't quite sure whom to expect. The fisherman was standing near her, studying her with interest, from her slenderly tapered trouser legs to the hand she kept hidden inside her large bag. When she saw Elias and Craig, she relaxed. The hand slipped out of the bag, and she laughed for the fisherman, who was just about to leave. He grinned back, saluted her, and, with a few remarks for Elias, left.

"The language difficulty was extreme," Mimi said. "I was beginning to wonder if I had made a mistake."

"But surely he gave the password," Elias said.

Mimi nodded. "I was beginning to wonder if I had mistaken that, too. Pear tree. That is a very strange password."

"All the better," Elias said.

"Who chose it?" Craig asked, beginning to smile. "Partridge?"

Mimi shook her head. "He doesn't like it, either. No, he said some—joker in Paris chose it. Operation Pear Tree."

"An American joker, at that." I can hear Rosie's voice, thought Craig, and smiled widely.

"A password may seem foolish," Elias said severely, "but in this operation with so many foreigners working together, there are times when we must know quickly who is to be trusted. Such as that moment," he added for Mimi's benefit, "after you left the square." He went over to the window, stood carefully at its side, looked out. "Begin!" his back seemed to say to Craig.

Craig glanced at the view outside as he pulled a chair over to Mimi. He could see clear across the small bay to the yacht anchorage under its sheltering headland. This room—or, rather, this office, for there was nothing here but a couple of chairs, a wooden table and a telephone—must lie right over one of the arcades along the front street. At least he knew where he was. In his quick journey here, Elias had really bewildered him. A very cautious man, Elias. Craig sat down, and asked bluntly, "What's worrying Veronica?"

Elias stirred restlessly, frowned at the harbor. Surely it wasn't some personal matter that had brought Craig hurrying here? Sometimes Americans were really—then he was listening intently as Mimi began to talk. For her voice was urgent, serious.

"For the first few days after Veronica and Maritta got here, everything was normal. Very pleasant. Just the two girls alone in the house, and two servants."

Elias broke in, still watching the harbor. "They were brought especially from Paris, two weeks ago, well in advance. Does Miss Clark realize that?"

"No. She said they were the disagreeable type—nothing but glum silence. She was astonished that there were any servants at all just for Maritta and herself. But extra guests have appeared. Two men. One came three nights ago. The other came the following night. Friends of Uncle Peter. Maritta said it was most annoying, but what could she do—tell them to go away? Everyone wants a free bed on Mykonos. That is the trouble with renting a house."

"Plausible," agreed Craig. "But haven't they started arriving a little early?" He looked over at Elias.

Elias' lips tightened. Yes, it was early; too early. But something else annoyed him. "We have had expert observation on that house for almost a week. Two days ago, when extra food was ordered for this weekend, we checked. We had reports that friends of Miss Clark were expected for a short vacation."

"Friends of Veronica?" Craig exchanged a glance with Mimi.

"That is what the delivery men were told. So far, these visitors have not been seen. No one knows that they have arrived." He looked at Mimi almost angrily.

Mimi shrugged her shoulders as much as to say, "Well, it isn't my fault." Then she smiled gently. "They don't come into town. They seem to stay around the garden, in the shade of the trees or on the porch, which is well covered. And there is a wall around that garden. I know. I've tried to see inside, too, from a back window of my hotel. Quite useless."

Elias was still brooding bitterly about the unseen arrival of the two men. "They must have come from the north, from another part of the island. They did not arrive by Mykonos itself."

Craig nodded. Silent sympathy, not criticism, was what was needed at this point. Besides, remembering the map he had been studying, there were plenty of coves and inlets around the island's broken coast line. The small bay that formed the harbor of the town itself was really only part of a large desolate bay that stretched north far beyond the headland sheltering the yacht anchorage. That's one route, he thought, noticing Elias' face, that will be watched with extra care from here in.

Elias' anger was suppressed. But his voice was still acid with annoyance. "Miss Clark does not seem to be so stupid as the Maas woman judged. Yet did she not find it very strange that the two visitors made no effort to go out?"

"Yes. But Maritta said one had been ill, and the other did not care for too much sun."

"What do they talk about? What language do they use?"

"French, mostly, although they speak it with a foreign accent. But Veronica does not meet them much. Maritta has been taking her to lunch and dinner in town. In fact, Maritta always seemed to be with her in those last two days. This has irritated Veronica. Then last night, she was awakened by the doves. Something had disturbed them. She could see no one from her window, but she was sure she heard voices from the direction of the dovecote. She tried to warn Maritta, only—she could not leave her room. Its door was locked. And that made her angry, my friends."

"And that was why she decided to find a place in town," Craig said thoughtfully. He was pleased, too; Veronica was not the simple little fool that Maritta had taken her for. Thank God for that. The perpetual innocent was a compulsive loser. "Well, good for her! If she can get away with it," he added more soberly.

"She will never be allowed to leave," Elias cut in, "not at this critical stage of their plans."

"Did she tell Maritta at breakfast that she was going to look for a room?" Craig asked quickly.

"Yes. Maritta just laughed, rushed off to an appointment in town, said they could talk about that later. Veronica went for a walk in the garden to try to think what she should do: wait to discuss it with Maritta or go straight into town herself? And then, as she passed the dovecote, she noticed a great silence. And no movement. The doves had been taken away. She tried to go in, but one of the servants stopped her, said the doves were diseased and had to be removed." Mimi paused, watching Craig's face. Even Elias had turned around to stare at her. "Somehow, that troubled her." And I've troubled you, too, she thought, looking with surprise at the men's faces.

Craig was remembering the usual shape of a Mykonos dovecote: a square, squat tower with decorative ventilations on top and solid blank walls beneath. "Are they preparing to house a prisoner?" he asked softly. Elias only shrugged, pursed his lips. He turned back, grave-faced, to look out of the window. Craig said to Mimi, "So Veronica came right into town? And found that she wasn't alone, even then. That man in the striped shirt was keeping an eye on her, wasn't he?"

"Yes. She became really frightened then. But he did it so openly and seemed so ordinary that by the time we went to the café on the *quai* for lunch, she could even laugh at him. He didn't stay. He went to report, no doubt." Mimi was smiling. "Because, before we had finished lunch, Maritta arrived with Tony and Michel."

"The Beard and Flowing Locks?"

Mimi didn't quite follow, but she caught Craig's sharp tone. "But they are such nice boys," she murmured. "Really very sweet."

Boys . . . "They are older than you are, baby."

"They are children," she said gently. "Maritta is using them—as she has used Veronica. That is all."

"Have you anything on them?" he called over to Elias.

Elias shook his head. He stood very still, and then pointed to the sky. "There it goes!" he said softly.

Both Mimi and Craig rose to look. There were shouts from the street below. The fishermen, spreading russet nets to dry in the sun, were watching, too. "That's a very small plane," Craig began, and then stopped. Where could any aircraft land on this rocky island? "It's a helicopter!" he said, watching the nose-tipping black dot as it circled widely toward the northwest as if it were headed for Athens. "When did it get here? I heard nothing."

"It came in by the south," Elias said smoothly. "It landed about fifteen minutes ago near the monastery of Tourliani in the center of the island to pick up a man who is very sick—he needs an immediate operation. It took off for Athens at once. As you see." He turned away from the window. He said to Mimi, "I had some questions about the Maas woman, but I think you have already answered them. Except one: why was she in such haste to get back to her house? Why couldn't she wait five minutes, ten minutes, and give you a lift to your hotel? It is on her way."

"That," Mimi said firmly, "is my last piece of news. Are there any other questions before it? John—" For Craig was still watching the vanishing dot. He came away from the window, sat down again. Plenty of questions, he was thinking as he looked at Elias. Why Tourliani? He remembered his guidebook's photograph; a very small village, a few houses around a long, wide, and open square—good landing ground, certainly, and ten miles from nowhere. And once that helicopter is out of any telescope's sight, will it stop heading northwest and swing east? "You boys really amuse me," he told Elias with a wide grin. So Partridge was on his way to Smyrna.

"Boys?" picked up Mimi. "I thought you didn't like—"

"Boys in red and yellow shorts with shirts open to their navels. Okay, okay. They're sweet, bare feet and all." Then he relented: Mimi's English was almost perfect, but her sense of joshing was still undeveloped. He became serious again. "Did Veronica read her declaration of independence to Maritta over your lunch table? Did she say she was absolutely decided about finding a room of her own?"

"She tried. But Maritta's technique was brilliant. She was full of understanding. She started telling me, and Tony and Michel, what a miserable place her uncle's house had become with his friends—they were so dull and stupid. She said no wonder poor Veronica wanted to leave. She wanted to move out, too. Why, she couldn't give any more amusing parties, couldn't feel free to enjoy herself! She had become a housekeeper, worrying about their food and drinks and what they liked and did not like. She was going to ask them to leave. She had been cabling her Uncle Peter that morning, begging him to stop giving out invitations, she hadn't come to Mykonos as a housekeeper."

"You used that word twice. Did she?"

"She used it several times. She was implanting her reason, you see, for being in such a hurry to return to the house." Mimi smiled for

Elias. "There is your answer," she told him. "She was rushing home to arrange a very special dinner for them, tonight, in order to put them in a good mood when she asked them to leave tomorrow."

"Po, po, po!" Elias said. "Did she expect anyone to believe that? She will have to find a better excuse to cover her real business. She spent much time, this morning, in the house of Mr. Gerhard Ludwig."

"It was only half of her excuse," Mimi said. "The other half made it very plausible, indeed."

"And what was the rest of her excuse?"

"She is giving a party—on the island of Delos. Yes, she has already reserved the rooms at the tourist pavilion there—it is a simple place, so she will take food and extra blankets, and she is hiring a boat to take us across. All *we* have to worry about is our coats and toothbrushes. She is arranging everything. We sail at five o'clock." Mimi laughed softly. "And it is a heavenly idea. She made it so—so—inspired. She woke this morning, remembered it was May Day—a time for parties—saw the sea was calm, thought of Delos, imagined how peaceful it would be at night when all the tourists had gone, how wonderful the ruined temples would look under moonlight." Mimi looked at Elias with amused eyes. "Oh no, everyone believed she had much to arrange for us before five o'clock, except me, and I had to pretend to believe her more than anyone."

"Surely Veronica didn't forget all her fears so—" Craig began.

"I accepted for us both, before she could make any objections," said Mimi calmly. *"And* kicked her leg gently under the table."

"Is this wise?"

"I think it is very wise to follow Maritta's wishes."

Elias nodded. "So there are five of you going."

"Eight—that fills the little pavilion, doesn't it? There will be two of Tony's friends, whom Veronica likes. And you."

"Me?" Craig was incredulous. "That's the last thing that Maritta wants. She has done everything to keep me from talking to Veronica. No, Mimi, she isn't going to risk any confidences between Veronica and me."

"She is going to call your hotel and invite you herself."

"She doesn't know my hotel."

"How many are there in Mykonos? Five, six at the most. She can try them all in a few minutes."

Craig looked quickly at Elias. "She will, too," he said grimly. "Better give Madame Iphigenia instructions how to deal with that call."

"You are not going?" Elias asked as he moved slowly to the telephone on the table. He stood frowning at it, not touching it.

Mimi had risen and was on her way to the door. She had given all her news; it was time to leave. She halted, looking at Craig in wonder. "John—surely you can't refuse a night on Delos! Think—"

"I've thought of it," he said bitterly. Marble shimmering in the moonlight, a mile of ancient columns and temples, a silver sea around them. "An island all to ourselves. I can even set it to music."

Mimi shrugged. "I think it's wise to follow Maritta's wishes," she said again. "She does nothing without a purpose. Well—make up your mind. I'm leaving. The same way as I came in?" she asked Elias.

"Do you remember it?"

"I hope so. I spent a lot of energy memorizing it."

"And my congratulations," Elias said unexpectedly. "You have been most helpful."

"My thanks, too," Craig said, and gave her a warm smile. "You'd terrify Maritta if she knew how much you learned from Veronica in a couple of hours. That was one thing she never intended to happen."

Mimi laughed, delighted with both their words and that idea. "Oh, I knew how to steer the conversation, that was all. And Veronica needed to talk. But I would have learned much less, I think, if it had not been for you." Her dark gray eyes looked at Craig, and turned most serious. "I did tell one fib. I said I had known your sister when she lived in Paris, was devoted to her, so I felt I knew you well, too. And I thought you were someone Veronica could trust, quite apart from being two Americans in a foreign land. Then she said that she had wanted to speak to you, this morning, but—just couldn't; you might be embarrassed, you weren't really interested in her or her troubles. 'Tell me what they are,' I said. 'I'll talk with John Craig. He is a very casual type. But he will listen, I'm sure.' And that decided her. You had helped her once before, she said." Mimi's eyes were studying him thoughtfully. "Whatever you did, then, certainly had results this morning." She opened the door carefully, glanced out into the empty corridor. "All peaceful," she said softly. "How very nice . . ." She closed the door soundlessly behind her.

Elias was looking at the telephone again. "Do I call my aunt and tell her that you were only staying at the Triton for one night until you found a room to rent? That is quite usual, you know. Most people rent rooms; much cheaper. And there are so many hundreds of them, here on Mykonos, that even Maas might take a week to find you." He paused, then added casually, as if he had only just thought of it, "Of course, you could accept her invitation—meanwhile."

"Is that what you want me to do?" Craig asked bluntly.

"I am not in charge of you." Elias was slightly amused. "Certainly not for the last ten minutes or so." He glanced at his watch.

"But who else? Partridge is halfway to Smyrna." Craig was unexpectedly depressed about that fact. It left him feeling isolated, uncertain. "Who is the new man in charge here?"

"In charge of the Americans?" Elias' emphasis was polite but decided. "Why not Bannerman? I think our friend is now walking toward the Triton Hotel. He should have arrived in the taxi that returned from Tourliani some ten minutes ago."

"He stepped out of the helicopter as Partridge stepped on?" Craig found the vision amused him, even lightened part of his depression.

Elias nodded. His fingers touched the telephone. "Do I call the Triton and block that invitation?"

"I'll take your advice and keep Maritta happy."

"That is always the clever thing to do."

"Meanwhile," added Craig.

He had left Elias and taken a circuitous route back to the hotel. He needed the walk, he needed a fifteen-minute delay before he met Tim Bannerman. There were a number of things he had to sort out in his mind. Craig always found that his brain worked best if he brought himself right up against his problems, examined their variables, and then established the precedence of their importance. Nice comforting procrastinations, a general wait-and-see feeling, were not for him. On the one hand but on the other hand—no thank you. He liked to catch the facts by the scruff of their necks, pull them face up and have a good look at them, however unpleasant. And if he couldn't catch them all—for he was the amateur wading in very deep waters—he could at least see their shape if he thought hard enough about what he had actually glimpsed.

So . . .

The Smyrna area was Partridge's first concern. He had only visited

Mykonos to make sure that the situation had not been endangered by any information that might have been tortured out of Duclos. Even Insarov's arrival here had not shifted Partridge's concern. Rather, it had intensified it. It was clear warning that the climax was approaching. Hence the haste in which Partridge had returned to Smyrna. For that was where he intended this whole counteroperation to be completed successfully. It was in Smyrna that the dangerous rôle, played by one of his agents, could be safely ended along with the career of an American called Alex. From Smyrna, too, would come the instructions to pick up Insarov and all his friends.

The Mykonos area was therefore of secondary importance, so far. It was only a kind of safety net, carefully rigged to save Partridge's agent and catch Alex if the plans at Smyrna swung out of control.

But that was all from Partridge's point of view, thought Craig. From Insarov's? In his calculations, Mykonos was to be the successful climax of all this operation. He had geared everything to that. Therefore, any instructions followed by Maritta Maas were geared to that, too. Therefore, even such a small thing as this invitation to Delos was to be examined from every side. Nothing that Maritta was told to do could be considered as whim or charming fancy.

Maritta and this bright idea for a party . . . What had she said back in his hotel room in Paris about Delos? Yes, in Paris Maritta had already known about the small tourist pavilion on Delos. For emergencies, she had said. Emergencies. Were the emergencies on Delos tonight—or here on Mykonos? Certainly, Maritta had made sure her uncle's friends would have the house on the hillside, emptied dovecote and all, very much to themselves. She had also made sure that Veronica and the people she liked, the people to whom she might have talked, were all safely off this island. Tonight. And if these inferences seemed a little farfetched, he had only to remind himself that nothing Maritta did could be considered whim or fancy.

Yet, one thing puzzled him. He was remembering Paris again; this time Partridge talking to him about the man at his sister's party—the man called Alex—who was coming to Mykonos, where he would hand over to Maritta the information he had collected. (But now it seemed that the information to be delivered was the source itself—an abducted expert.) Maritta and Alex had worked together before. Therefore they could identify each other quickly, and Alex's delivery would be safely made with neither doubt nor delay. But that meant

Maritta had to be here when Alex arrived. She, alone, was Alex's contact. In that case, she would never have arranged to go to Delos if the *Stefanie* were expected tonight. Craig, he told himself sadly, you just got carried away in your deductions: a hell of a historian you'll make.

And then his thoughts leaped. If Alex was sailing on the *Stefanie,* why should he need anyone to identify him? Or why should he have to come here, at all, if the *Stefanie* brought in its prize? His job was over in Smyrna when he enticed that man aboard. Or wasn't it?

Craig smothered his rising excitement. Once more, he went over the facts he knew about Alex, few as they were. Yes, Alex was a courier, passing on information to a safe contact whom he definitely knew. Now what was it Partridge had said in the Triton's little garden? Something—oh dammit, it was a phrase, a simple but revealing phrase. About Alex and his duties. No, it had slipped to the back of Craig's mind, was hovering there, tantalizing, elusive. Relax; don't strain it, he told himself. If the phrase was important, it would turn up in its own good time.

He headed for the little street where the Triton stood. There were a lot of people around now. Shops had opened again. Trade was brisk. Life was normal. "I tell you," one white-haired Englishwoman was saying to her exhausted friend, as Craig stood aside to let them pass, "there *are* three hundred and sixty-five churches, and we've only found two hundred and ninety-three."

Madame Iphigenia was at her post in the Triton's small lobby. "There was a telephone call," she announced. "A woman's voice."

"Did she leave any number?"

"She refused to give it," Madame Iphigenia said with annoyance.

Then that was Maritta. "She will call again. I'll be in my room."

"We change your room." Madame had dropped her voice to a conspiratorial whisper. "My nephew Elias advises that. It has not such a pleasant view, but no one knows you are now there except myself and one maid. My nephew also advises you leave most of your luggage in your old room. Come. I show you."

"Just let me get my toothbrush."

"It is already provided."

"Well, just let me get my camera. Right?"

So they made the quick and familiar journey, and he managed to get

Partridge's automatic safely into his pocket in a matter of seconds while Madame Iphigenia played watchdog at the door. He changed into a fresh shirt, picked up his raincoat and a sweater for tonight's journey. It would be a cool trip across the strait to Delos. He almost forgot razor and toothbrush. A man spending a night on Delos would certainly take these. Now let anyone check on this place, he thought, as he slipped them into his coat pocket.

"You remember this way?" Madame whispered as she led him along a twisting corridor. Indeed, he did. That morning, it had been part of their tour of inspection. The rooms were unused in this wing of the house, under change and construction for the summer season. "I am sorry," she said with real anguish as she showed him into his new quarters, still smelling of paint. "The workmen will not be back until Monday. No one comes up here. It is all right?"

"It's very much all right. Thank you for helping me. What did Elias expect?" A secret search, or some unexpected visit?

She hesitated. "I do not know what this trouble is. I do know my nephew." And with that, she left him. As she disappeared around a corner, he heard a distant voice calling her back to the front desk. He dumped his coat, camera and sweater, and after a last glance at the makeshift arrangements he made his way down by the back stairs to the enclosed garden. It would be better that he be found easily when that telephone call came for him. There was also the matter of Bannerman.

The telephone call came first. "I thought I wasn't going to find you," Maritta began.

"And I've been looking for you all day."

"Have you heard about my party on Delos?"

"Are you turning archaeologist?"

"No, no. It's a moonlight party. Tonight. Will you come?"

"Yes. But how? Do we swim?"

"Five o'clock at the harbor. Bring a coat. And a bright smile."

"When do we get back?"

"Oh, we'll stay overnight. There are eight of us. Veronica included. I'm glad you accepted before you heard she was coming."

"There's only one thing. I'm expecting some of my friends from Athens to arrive tomorrow evening."

"Oh, we'll be back before that. I've arranged for our boat to pick us up at three tomorrow. It's only an hour's journey from Delos."

"Weather permitting."

"We are in luck, I think. The water has scarcely one ripple. At five o'clock, then?"

"At five. Coat, smile and camera."

"Tomorrow morning you can take some heavenly pictures by the dawn's early light." She laughed, rang off.

He replaced the receiver, stood frowning down at it. He had managed that all right, but he felt no sense of achievement. Without Partridge's warnings, he thought, where would I have been with a girl like that? Neatly wrapped up in a package labeled *Fool.* I wouldn't have been the first, and certainly not the last. And she could fool me yet, he thought somberly.

Madame Iphigenia cleared her throat tactfully. He swung out of his thoughts, looked up and saw Bannerman, as natty a tourist as ever dawdled along the cafés on the water front. Faded red shorts and a pink linen shirt, no less. Behind him, the silent young assistant manager was absolutely slain with admiration.

"Hello, John!" Bannerman said. "Told you I'd join you for some *bouzoukia.* Found any places, yet, where they haven't heard of 'Never on Sunday'?"

So we continue Athens, thought Craig, and gave a smile of relief. "How's Clothilde? And the Mortimers? Still in Athens?"

"They'll be here this weekend. Clothilde really means to arrive in a caïque. She always seems to find one that hauls coal. So I backed out of that. What about a drink?"

"Fine. I'm on my way to Delos at five, so we'll have one for the road."

"Any room for me on that trip?" Bannerman asked with a grin as he clattered downstairs to the dining room and bar.

"Not unless you like sleeping on the cold hard ground."

The silent young man was on their heels, ready to see that they were served, no doubt. He took their order, relayed it to the kitchen, busied himself in the dining room as they went into the small garden. "Hell," Bannerman said softly. But he didn't have to worry long about continuing their light conversation, for Madame's stern voice sent her assistant back upstairs to take charge of the desk, and they were free to talk.

"Partridge thought he was just curious," Craig said quietly as the young man left the dining room with a last backward glance.

"Well, people are innocent until they give cause for suspicion. Can't go around thinking everyone is part of a nasty plot," Bannerman said lightly. "But that little guy isn't local. Elias has been checking. He came in as a replacement only three days ago—from Athens. Highly recommended. Madame Iphigenia is about to blow a fuse. She's kept him so busy running errands all day that he's worn out. Didn't even have the energy, or time, to check on your luggage." Bannerman's broad smile was reassuring. "They've planted an eye in every hotel, of course, just in case someone recognizable—like Rosie—suddenly turned up as Mr. Smith." He studied Craig's face. "Nothing to worry about. Elias has good eyes of his own."

Madame Iphigenia was making sure of that. She had installed herself in the dining room and was checking linen and silver.

"Both houses are being watched?" Craig was still uneasy. There had been a slip-up three nights ago, when Maritta's guests began arriving. But that, of course, had been before Elias had appeared.

"Closely. He has men on the square next door as well as up on the hillside, too. Believe me—"

"I do." Craig had to smile. Now he could see why Elias had taken such a dim view of his own stroll up there today.

"He has a man up on the headland above the yacht anchorage, just to see what's sailing in from the north. He has a man in touch with the harbor master who checks every vessel in and out. He has even made sure that the launch taking you to Delos is manned by the usual local men. You can leave all the details dealing with geography to Elias. He knows how."

"And what's your job?" Craig asked, some of his anxiety leaving him. "Looking after me?"

"And myself, and a couple of other Americans who are wandering around looking like poet and painter. Also, we are keeping our own lines of communication open. Co-operation doesn't go as far as letting the other fellow handle your own particular business." Bannerman grinned cheerfully. "The English have sent at least one man here, too. They have a certain interest." He sounded vague about that. "Then the French—well, they'll be breathing hard on Elias' neck."

"I take it, when you didn't mention him, that there is no word of Duclos?"

"None." Bannerman watched Craig's face. Quietly, he added,

"That's the second good man the French have lost in this operation. The first was in Paris on the morning you arrived there—they killed him to protect Alex, we think. Yes, you could say that the French are hopping mad. They won't let one escape, you can be sure of that. So ease up."

"Alex—" began Craig, and stopped. Suddenly the lost phrase had decided to stop playing coy and came right to the front of Craig's mind. "Extension of his duties," Partridge had said, talking of Alex and the attempt at abduction. Yes, an extension of his duties . . . And there was something else too: Alex's special mission had been an "additional assignment."

"Come on now. Share that one," Bannerman said with amusement.

"Haven't thought it out yet," Craig admitted. "It may mean nothing. He's a careful, supercautious man, isn't he?"

"Alex? As cagey as they come."

In that case, would he arrive here on the *Stefanie?* Craig's mind was racing now. "Suppose he had his usual job to do, as well. Wouldn't that explain why he had to come to Mykonos at all? Otherwise—why should he endanger himself by appearing here? The additional assignment—" Craig paused to make sure that Bannerman had caught his meaning—"was completed when he trapped our expert. Or a reasonable facsimile thereof."

"Go on."

"He would probably balk at traveling in the same yacht as the man he helped to capture, wouldn't he? He might be the type who would complete his special assignment, and then want to forget he had anything to do with it. The supercautious wash their hands of everything as quickly as possible."

"They do." A small smile glimmered at the back of Bannerman's intelligent eyes. "And I'm not stealing any of your thunder if I tell you we had some similar thoughts. Why else did we want you on Mykonos? But there's one thing—we don't intend to let that son of a bitch get out of Turkey. That's why Partridge is there." He looked at his watch. "He's there, all right."

Craig was silent.

"Now what?" Bannerman asked sharply. "Do you agree with Elias?"

"Elias? I wouldn't know. I keep trying to guess what Elias is thinking and come up with the wrong answers."

"You froze when I mentioned Partridge and Smyrna. Why?" As Craig still hesitated, Bannerman added with one of his old friendly smiles, "I really want to hear what you think, John. Come on, give!"

"Well—" He decided to risk it. "I feel that the kidnapping may be completed. Partridge could have reached Smyrna too late to prevent it." He hesitated, but Bannerman was listening seriously, waiting for Craig's reasons, face and eyes now intent. Craig said, "There has been too much happening under the surface today, too many preparations right here on Mykonos. That house on the hill is ready and waiting. Maritta spent the morning at the Gerhard Ludwig place in town—so Elias' men reported. She wouldn't go there except under orders, and they wouldn't be given her unless something important had developed. So important that it was time to give her final and detailed instructions? They're so confident of success that they may actually know they have succeeded." He hesitated, decided he had said more than enough. "And that—for what it's worth—is how I see it. I hope I'm wrong."

"Elias didn't discuss this with you?"

"No."

"Two separate opinions," Bannerman said slowly, thoughtfully. And from two very different points of view. Both added up to the same thing. Mimi's report on the Clark girl had turned out to be a depth charge. "If Elias and you are right, we have real trouble ahead." But he did not sound overpessimistic at the prospect. Perhaps he enjoyed the idea that, instead of being assigned to a place of secondary importance, he had stepped right into the critical area. He tried to check his rising excitement. "*If* you are right," he repeated. "Poor old Partridge," he added with some real sympathy, "he will be even madder than the French." Strange how things break, he thought; Partridge has worked for four solid months, day and night, on the Berg-Insarov puzzle. "This is really his show, you know. We wouldn't be here, any of us, if he hadn't seen one small glimmer of light in a purposely thick fog."

"Operation Pear Tree," Craig said. He was feeling slightly better now that Elias was expecting anything to happen, any time. At least, he thought, we won't come in for a landing with the wheels up.

"Did he tell you?" Bannerman asked in surprise.

"No. Mimi dropped the word. It's puzzling our allies, I think."

"Then it should puzzle the opposition still more. I don't expect many of them know 'The Twelve Days of Christmas.' Do you remember the tune? Good. When you've got something to tell me, or vice versa, and there's a crowd around or something, whistle a few bars, will you? Keep it just for emergencies." He rose, clapped Craig on the shoulder. "I may come to wave you off to Delos. We'll see. . . ." He raised his voice to normal as he reached the dining room. "I'll wire Clothilde in Athens and tell her that the Triton is keeping a couple of rooms for her and the Mortimers."

"When do they get here?" Craig called back. "I was thinking they'd arrive tomorrow evening."

"Sunday. Perhaps even Monday. They may find themselves unloading coal or sugar all around the Aegean. Clothilde has a special knack of picking the slowest caïque." Bannerman, taking the steps two at a time, clattered his way up into the lobby. Madame Iphigenia had reached it just ahead of him: she knew when to take her cue. The very correct and silent young man was at the desk. He was a little flustered, as if he had just made it there before Madame had started up the staircase. "I have a wire to send to Athens," Bannerman confided earnestly. "How do I go about it?" There wasn't even a small smile showing on his face.

"Markos will translate it for you and send it," Madame said, staring fixedly at her assistant. She looked exactly like that statue on the main square, as if she were facing the Turkish fleet, her chin out, jaw set, eyes steeled, and a two-thousand-year-old Greek curse right there on her lips.

17

It was almost five o'clock, and the strong western sun shone straight into the harbor of Mykonos. Even as Craig walked along the water front, raincoat over his shoulder, sweater and camera case in one hand, he could easily distinguish the launch Maritta had hired from the other boats moored all along the wharf. It was the one with the crowd of people around it. Either the party had grown or the send-off was to be an event. Strange how the news had spread—there must be at least thirty of Mykonos' younger set grouped together on the breakwater. Or quay. Or jetty. Or mole. Or wharf. He never could make up his mind what to call it. It served all these purposes. It was a bulwark of heavy stones rising less than five feet above sea level, with a flat top of cement, twelve feet or so wide, on which crates and sacks and men and mules could all find space. On its left was the open sea, if not wine-colored in the evening glow then certainly dark blue tinged with copper, and a protecting waist-high wall to discourage the spray. On its right was the still water of the harbor, and an array of small craft roped to their moorings on the wharf.

He passed two caïques still unloading crates of fruit and boxes of soft drinks, several fishing boats now being scoured clean, rowing boats, another caïque, and reached the crowd—a merry one, as he had guessed by the drift of voices over the calm water. French, English, American. No wonder the German, Swedish and Dutch tourists had looked a little sourly at the breakwater from their café tables under the arcades. It was a fine evening for a sail across a few miles of rippling sea to Delos. And this *was* a wonderful idea for a party, he thought as his eyes looked over the bronzed faces and bright clothes for someone he could recognize; if only, he added to that, Maritta had not been instructed to invent it. For a moment he envied all these innocents, hooting and hollering around, who took it at face value.

And there was Veronica. With Tony and Michel in attendance. They were grouped in front of the launch. He hoped she wasn't looking so relaxed and happy because of them. They couldn't be as witty as all that, dammit, he thought as he heard her laugh.

"Yes, she's beautiful," Mimi's voice said at his elbow. She pulled him gently over to the sea wall, with a smile of apology to three girls with swinging hair and pink-white lips who were just about to surround him. "They want to go, too," she murmured. "You looked a very pleasing prospect." She leaned against the wall, stared out to the open sea, and pointed to a far-off island. "Maritta is not coming," she said softly.

He studied the island.

"The blankets and food arrived with one of the servants in charge. Don't look around, John! He's standing over at the other side of the mole. The caïque is just behind him."

"Checking us on board?" He forced a smile, tried to look as if they were talking about something pleasant. He swung himself up to sit on the wall, which let him have a quick glance at the man standing by the edge of the quay. Thin expressionless face, watchful eyes. From where he stood, he could keep easy count of everyone who stepped on board the launch. "What excuse did Maritta send? I bet it was a beauty."

Mimi nodded. "Better get the details from Veronica. We've been talking long enough together. I'll start making the rounds—just the girl who wants to meet everyone. One thing: I told her I had let you know about her problems. I said you would help her. I had to, John! Why else did I listen to her this morning if I was not going to tell you? That was my story, remember!" She looked toward the north and pointed again. "Look! Fishing boats! Where did *they* come from?" She was including two young Frenchmen in her question. Craig jumped down and left them speculating about their cameras. The tantalizations of photography (it sounded all right in French) were the perfect pictures always presented when the light was too yellow, the sun too glaring and direct.

Craig moved through the crowd, and then halted, avoiding the interested glance of one of the girls with the pink-white lips so very pale against her tanned skin. He stood for an agonizing minute, looking toward the north headland, staring at the three red fishing boats and the cabin cruiser that was following them in to the smooth waters of the harbor. Then his mind began to work. He calculated quickly and waited. His timing must be exact. The cruiser was drawing toward the yacht anchorage. The three boats were gliding around to find a space somewhere along the quay, their sails now flapping idly. Okay, he told himself, okay. He walked straight over to Veronica.

"Hello!" he said with a wide smile. "And when do we shove off?" He gave Tony and Michel a friendly nod.

"Five o'clock always means five-thirty in this part of the world," Michel announced. "That is one of its charms."

"We seem to have some extra company," Craig said, looking at two men with sleeping bags and a girl carrying a blanket.

"Why, it's Josie!" Michel exclaimed, and turned to welcome her.

Craig looked at Veronica. "What's this I hear about Maritta?"

Tony said, "One of those impossible guests fell down some stairs and broke his leg. Maritta is staying with him until the doctor arrives. Really bad luck."

"Yes. Pity he didn't break his neck."

Tony laughed before he looked shocked. Then laughed again.

"Don't you think someone should start loading people onto the boat? It would be a pity to miss the sunset on Delos."

"But they all want to come," Tony said in mock despair.

"Then let them. They can sail over there and back, anyway. The launch will hold about thirty, tightly packed. In this sea there's no danger." The launch was an odd contraption, definitely one of those mad Greek inventions, with a flat-topped hatch rising out of the deck and taking up most of it. On either side of this protuberance there were long shelves, acting as benches, facing out to sea, backed by ropes for the seated to grasp. The railing in front of their legs was another lightly strung rope. The captain and his mate were aft, along with a high smell of kerosene. Their smiles were cheerful.

"It can take forty, even in a storm," Tony told him, in the tone of an old-timer. "Never lost a passenger yet. It bobs like a cork, even up the highest wave."

"That must be fun," Craig observed and half turned from Tony, edging him out. "And when did the broken leg take place?"

Veronica's smile widened as Tony drifted away to start organizing. "He will never manage it under twenty minutes," she warned Craig.

"That's a pity. I was counting on ten." He was watching the three fishing boats. Soon they would be very close, blotting this part of the quay from any watcher on the hillside. If Maritta or her friends had a telescope trained on the launch, their view was about to be ruined. Perhaps permanently. The three boats, barely fifteen feet long, had stopped moving. It looked as if they were waiting for the launch to leave and give them space to tie up. There was a good deal of raucous shouting, anyway, between its captain and the fishermen.

Veronica studied his face. She said, "It really was an accident. I saw it. But his leg isn't broken. Only a twisted ankle, I think. He complained a lot, though."

"And it happened just before you left?"

"Why, yes."

"Veronica," he asked quickly, "will you help me?" He looked deep into her blue eyes. "I mean that. Will you?"

"Of course," she said slowly, trying to hide her growing astonishment. But I thought I was the one who needed help. Is he in some kind of trouble, too? "What's wrong?"

"Trust me. Please! And cover up for me, will you? I'm not going to Delos."

The soft smile was wiped off her face.

"No, no," he said urgently, "keep smiling as we talk. Please. The monster is watching us."

Her eyes flickered over toward the man Maritta had sent. He was staring at her, in that grim and sullen way which she disliked so much. She forced a smile as she looked back at Craig. "I won't notice your absence until we reach Delos. And then I'll laugh it off. Is that what you want?"

"Yes. Say that I probably stayed behind to keep Maritta company, cheer her up."

She dropped her eyes. She was half believing that herself. Her smile vanished.

He grasped her hands. "Please!" he said again.

She nodded.

His grip on her hands tightened. "That's my girl," he said softly as he released her. She looked at him, wide-eyed. If the monster hadn't been watching them, he would have kissed her, right there and then.

Instead, he backed away, seemingly still continuing their conversation. "I'll give Tony a hand," he called to her. "It's time we were leaving. Save a seat for me!" He kept on backing to the edge of the quay, then turned very quickly as he reached the haggard-faced man, bumping heavily into him, saying "Sorry!" as his hands went out as if to save the man from toppling back into the water. He seemed to lose his own balance. His shoulder crashed against the swaying figure. The man fell, too astonished to shout, and landed with a splash between the launch's stern and the high prow of the caïque.

There were screams, yells, and a rush of excitement. "Throw a life preserver!" Craig told Tony. "I'll get a small boat to pick him up." He left, making his way through the jam of people. The shouts had given way to laughter, loud advice, raucous comment. There was a mixed stream of Mykoniots and visitors beginning to run up the quay. Craig bundled his coat tightly around the camera case, looked for the likeliest small boy. He found one, trying to edge his way into the steadily growing crowd.

Craig caught his arm gently, smiled, bent down to reach the right eye level, held out thirty drachmas (a round dollar in any man's money) and offered the bundle. "Triton," he said, pointing to the bundle, then back over his shoulder in the direction of the town. "Triton?" The boy nodded. He was about eleven or twelve years old, large brown eyes in a thin intelligent face. Craig tapped the bundle again. "Triton. Madame Iphigenia." No, that was the wrong word. "Kiria Iphigenia. Triton."

I know, I know, the boy's eyes seemed to say impatiently. He took the thirty drachmas, tucked the bundle under his arm, looked in the direction of the excitement around the launch. A cheer was being raised.

"It's all over," Craig said. "Get going, buster!" He gestured down the jetty, quietly, urgently. The boy folded the bill safely into his pocket. He tapped his narrow chest. "Petros," he told Craig solemnly. Craig shook hands formally. That seemed to seal the bargain.

"Triton. Kiria Iphigenia," the boy assured him, as if he were addressing a very small child.

Craig nodded, put a finger briefly up to his lips. Let's hope, he thought, that the gesture translates itself properly into Greek.

It must have. The boy's eyes opened wide, bright with a new excitement. He grinned widely, tapped the side of his nose, pushed his way through the fringes of the crowd, headed for town.

Craig straightened his legs, pulling on his sweater. It was too hot for this time of evening, but its dark blue color disguised the striped shirt he had worn for the trip to Delos. Now all he had to do was to find a straggle of tourists. He chose a clump of people, fishermen and visitors combined, and filtered into its center. The trek along the breakwater became short and simple. Alone, he would have felt every step under sharp-eyed scrutiny from either the front-street arcades or the house on the hillside. He kept his head down, his hands in his pockets, and stayed with the crowd.

Far behind him, now, he heard the launch let off a high tenor blast. He didn't look around, kept on walking, and was still in the shelter of the group as he reached real land. He passed three fishermen leaning against the wall of a chapel as he made the sharp left turn into the front street. He was almost certain that the youngest was the man Elias had sent chasing after Mimi, today, but he had only time for one quick glance and one returned stare. He walked on nonchalantly, chose the first café he saw, and slipped out of the cluster of tourists to find a small table at the very back of its deep awning. The trouble was that those Greeks, to foreign eyes, seemed very much alike, with their grave faces and dark hair and heavy mustaches. The fishermen had noticed him certainly. If he was Elias' man, then all Craig had to do was to sit here and get some thoughts back into order. Also, he'd like to watch a little.

He edged his chair around just enough to let him have clear sight past the screen of men at the front-row tables. Now he had a good but protected view of the long breakwater. To his surprise and pleasure, the launch had already moved away from its moorings. Quick work after all, he thought gratefully. Tony must have got them all on board in record time once the man was pulled out of the harbor. There was a small close group on the deck of the caïque, as if that was where he had been deposited. No doubt they were getting him to cough up a surfeit of water, and telling him never to stand again at the edge of a wharf crowded with young maniacs. Certainly there was no sight of the man on the jetty itself. It was rapidly emptying, returning to its usual placid routine.

Craig watched the launch move into the harbor, sweep around

widely to port, pass the end of the breakwater and out to sea. It gave three short and cheerful blasts of farewell. In a similar mood, he ordered ouzo and coffee. Well, there I go, he thought, bound for Delos. Not even the waterlogged man in the dark suit, now climbing onto the jetty from the deck of the caïque, would guess otherwise.

It was forty minutes later, almost six o'clock, before Bannerman strolled in. He looked around the few tables that were occupied—this was a fisherman's haunt; later in the evening it would be crowded with them—and said, "You've got good taste in cafés." He sat down facing Craig, his back turned to the street.

"It was the first place I could duck into and stay out of sight."

"Sorry I missed the fun on the dock. But there was an emergency. I came here as soon as possible."

Judging from Bannerman's face, his news was bad. Craig said, "Well I'm glad our communications system is working, anyway. That was Elias' man I saw?"

Bannerman nodded. "What made you bug out?"

"Because Maritta did."

"Oh!" said Bannerman, a new light dawning. Quickly he asked, "And they think you've left?"

"I tried raising a little fuss, enough to cover my retreat back into town, I hope."

"I heard about that." Bannerman almost smiled. "Veronica Clark was a great help, too. Got them on board and the launch moving before anyone could count who was sailing. What did you tell her?"

Craig was still staring. Veronica had done that?

"What did you tell her to get her co-operation?"

"Nothing. Just that I wasn't going. Just that I needed her to cover for me. That's all."

"She certainly did." Bannerman sounded relieved. "Didn't waste a second. Good girl. If I felt in a better mood, I'd be laughing out loud." He leaned both elbows on the table, cupped his chin in his hands so that his lips were guarded. "Bad news from Smyrna. You and Elias guessed right."

Craig bent his head over his cup of coffee, studying the heavy mass of thick muddy grounds. "They got our man?"

"This morning."

This morning, thought Craig in dismay. If only I had known where to report, last night, that Heinrich Berg was walking through Mykonos—if only I had tried to get hold of Elias—if only I had telephoned Bannerman in Athens. There would have been time to warn Smyrna, to have all precautions doubled. But I didn't think, I didn't know what was at stake. There I was, imagining that I was becoming ridiculous, taking too many precautions, having too many suspicions. And the truth was I didn't have enough. He remembered Rosie telling him that the smallest things could be of the greatest importance. . . . Do we always have to remember, too late? he wondered. "If only," he said, "I had got in touch with you last night."

"You didn't know—" began Bannerman.

"I didn't have to know. I ought to have reported one small fact, and let others do the evaluating."

"Look—it's over. Over, and nothing can change it. Stop those 'if only's.' Don't you think we each carry a pack of them around on our breaking backs?"

"Okay." Craig drew a deep breath. "So they got him this morning."

"And the news wasn't known until late this afternoon. They used timing as part of their plan. It's always a winner."

"Who was he?"

"A volunteer. Only three people know his name, and I'm not one of them. There was a fourth, but he's dead." Bannerman's lips tightened as he thought of Duclos. Yes, only three now: Rosie, the Englishman Christopher Holland, and Partridge. "The fewer the better, of course. Or else Insarov might have learned he was abducting someone who didn't know one thing about microphones and similar gadgets."

"Then he won't get much out of your man."

"Nothing that is of any use to him. I suppose we could say that's one success we had," Bannerman said gloomily.

And a grim one, thought Craig. "What now?"

Bannerman dropped his hands, looked casually over his shoulder, glanced at the breakwater, surveyed the water front. "I'd like you to keep out of sight, until it's worth while showing yourself. Never spoil a surprise." Only the front-row tables had their groups of men so far, all friends, all knowing each other. That was a safeguard in itself. No unaccountable fisherman, no inquisitive tourist. "We're out of the main drag here. We might as well relax and have some coffee."

"We could move inside—it's empty. Or is that more noticeable than sitting here like two normal people?"

Bannerman nodded. "Besides, I want you to keep your eyes on the breakwater. I'll watch the street. I don't think pretty little Maritta stayed home from Delos just to play pinochle with her abominable house guests. What excuse did she give?" He signed to the waiter for coffee and angled his chair to look along the water front.

Craig told him and raised the first smile of the evening. "Maritta as Florence Nightingale," Bannerman said. "So far, there have been no reports that any doctor was sent for. But you didn't expect that, did you?" He shook his head. "What *will* she think up next?"

"That's what I'm waiting to see. If she weren't so dangerous, she'd be my choice for Comedy Queen."

The coffee came, and Bannerman began giving the rest of his news. "The yacht *Stefanie* never entered Turkish waters," he said quietly, his left hand holding a cigarette close to his lips. "Nor did she visit Chios, which is the Greek island nearest Smyrna—there's even a small ferryboat that runs between Chios and Smyrna. So Chios seemed the logical place, but it wasn't planned that way. Instead, she docked at the island of Samos, farther to the south."

"That's the closest Greek island to the Turkish coast. It's less than two miles across the strait, there."

"You know your geography."

Craig smiled. "Blame it on history. The ruins of Ephesus are near that strait."

"Yes," said Bannerman very softly, "and Ephesus is just about fifty miles south from Smyrna. . . . Get it?"

So that was the route of operation: Smyrna, to Ephesus, to the coast, to Samos. And the *Stefanie*. "Alex made up a party for Ephesus," Craig said thoughtfully. Clever bastard . . . It was a popular trip; anyone visiting Smyrna usually made it. He had been warned, back in New York, that if he ever went there he could expect busloads of tourists from the cruise ships docking at Smyrna. A man could easily go unnoticed in a polyglot crowd surrounded by miles of ruins. Ephesus was big. And yet— "Surely," Craig added irritably, "our man was being guarded?"

Bannerman nodded. "There was one of our agents with him constantly—pretended he was some kind of assistant and close friend.

We couldn't have a phalanx of guards around the pseudo expert; that would have looked too obvious, as if we were expecting trouble. We had plenty of checks on his movements around Smyrna, though. He had his instructions to stay there. He should never have accepted the idea for a jaunt to Ephesus—I don't know what got into him." Bannerman sighed deeply, frowning. "Seven people made up that party. Two cars. That was the way the kidnapping was worked."

"How?" pressed Craig. He could scarcely believe that two trained and experienced men could have been so easily trapped.

"The group scattered, spent a couple of hours wandering around Ephesus. They planned to meet at the cars at a fixed time—they were returning to Smyrna for lunch. But one of the cars drove off just ahead of the other. Those who gathered at the second car found they were two short—the 'expert' and his assistant—but assumed they had got tired waiting and taken the first car."

"And those in the first car took it for granted that the two men were returning in the second car?"

"So they say."

"But if they reached Smyrna by one o'clock or so, why didn't Partridge get the news here before he left? Someone must have been dragging his feet."

Bannerman shook his head. "The first car decided to make a detour, visit a nomad encampment." He looked at Craig. "Ever seen one? The Turks keep them well outside their towns. Black leather tents, beehive shape. Camels. Slit-eyed people. Straight Genghis Khan. Sounds good, doesn't it? Good enough to keep that first car from returning to Smyrna until almost five o'clock this afternoon. Some detour."

And only then would the disappearance have been discovered. Clever Alex. "By that time, the *Stefanie* had left Samos?"

"She left at three."

"Which means she could arrive here any time tonight," Craig said softly.

Bannerman said nothing. He was a worried man.

"At least," Craig added, "you've got Alex. He's stuck in Smyrna until everyone is questioned, and he won't have much choice in his answers, either. Which car was he in? The first, I bet."

There was a strange expression on Bannerman's face.

"Don't tell me that both Wilshot and Bradley went on that trip to Ephesus!"

Bannerman glanced up quickly. "Who gave you the names?" he asked sharply. "Partridge?"

"As a kind of afterthought this morning."

"Just as well," Bannerman said, alarm giving way to relief. Now he could talk more freely. If Craig knew as much as this, he could help. Every ounce of assistance was needed. "The situation is becoming high emergency," he admitted.

"Alex—"

"He backed out of the trip to Ephesus early this morning."

"Both Bradley and Wilshot backed out?"

"Both. They had a chance of a free ride on a plane to Rhodes today. They took it. Begged off Ephesus."

"They seem to be pretty close friends."

"They've become quite good friends in this last week. They reached Rhodes around nine this morning. We checked. They left before ten o'clock, hitching another ride—this time on one of those twin-diesel yachts that would give them a cruise through the Aegean en route to Athens. Bradley's leave is just about up; he is heading back to Paris. We know that. Wilshot's articles on the Turks' new attitude toward America, because of this damned Cyprus trouble, are completed. Everyone knows that, too. So everything seems perfectly regular. Even the hitchhiking. Anyone who visits this part of the world is always on the lookout for a free ride so he can see as much as possible. Just tell him he can sail with you here, or there, and his eyes start glinting. Have you noticed?"

Craig nodded. He was still thinking of Alex. Careful and cautious, Partridge had called him. "Who actually arranged that trip to Ephesus?"

"It was dreamed up, yesterday evening, at a cocktail party in Smyrna given by Bradley and Wilshot. It seemed one of those spontaneous-combustion ideas that come with the fourth Martini."

"Who first suggested it?"

"That's being investigated right now, you can bet all your traveler's checks. But does anyone remember exactly who said what and how and when at a cocktail party?" Bannerman smiled sourly. "Yes, even that was calculated."

They were silent for a full minute. Then Craig said, still puzzled, "That agent of yours—the one who was keeping an eye on your expert—did he sell out, you think?"

"No. Not he. I've worked with him."

"But how—"

"They'd deal with him first. Probably he is lying behind some ruined temple, his skull smashed in with a chunk of marble." He fell silent again, his face cold and expressionless. "Three men dead, one captured for interrogation. The cost comes high." He looked at Craig. "It may come higher. You could bow out now and no one would blame you."

"There's a matter of identifying Alex."

"Yes, I admit I'd like your help with that. I know both Wilshot and Bradley from their photographs. Never met them. And there's two of them."

"They'll come ashore together?"

"That's my guess. Alex will make sure of a cover to the very end. They'll separate, of course, when Alex is really getting down to business."

"I'll take one, you take the other. How's that?"

There was a broad smile on Bannerman's face. "Perfect."

"When do you expect them?"

"Any time, frankly."

"And meanwhile, I just keep looking across the harbor?" Craig asked, and did. "So far, no twin-diesel job is anywhere on the horizon. There's that cabin cruiser over at the anchorage, of course. It's scarcely powerful enough, though, to get from Rhodes to here by five o'clock."

"The harbor master reports it came from Delos. Before that, Tinos. Wrong direction for Rhodes, anyway. It plans to spend the weekend at Mykonos. Two men and a woman. That's the crew."

"Two men?" Craig was still hanging on to his doubts.

"Look—" Bannerman raised an eyebrow. "Elias phoned Delos, and that cabin cruiser *was* there."

And did a more powerful boat, arriving from Rhodes, touch in at Delos just before the cabin cruiser left? Craig looked at Bannerman, one of the nicest guys he had met in a long, long time, and wished Partridge were here. "I believe you. It was there all right. But damned if I wouldn't find some excuse for a visit over to that anchorage except that—" He shrugged in a good imitation of Elias.

Bannerman noticed, and smiled. "Except what?" he asked.

"Both Bradley and Wilshot would spot me and wonder why I was snooping around."

Bannerman's amusement doubled. That was the way with those amateurs, he thought, all bright-eyed and bushy-tailed. Let them have one or two small triumphs and they start teaching everyone his business. "I have a very good reason for not snooping around, too. I've got to stay here. Period. A matter of keeping in touch with the big outside world. We don't work that through the Greeks or anyone else. Stop raising your blood pressure." And then he relented. "Elias made an excuse to have their passports checked: not one name we knew."

"And their faces matched the photographs?"

"Exactly. Elias' man even went into the cabin and glanced at one of the men, who was taking a nap. Okay bud? And yes," Bannerman added emphatically, "it was all handled tactfully, sort of offhand style, to raise no suspicions that they were being checked. Does that answer all objections?"

"Meanwhile," said Craig with a grin.

At least he can take a reprimand well enough, Bannerman thought. "Now this is what we do. When that twin-diesel job arrives from Rhodes, I'm going to be heading around to that anchorage. Alex has never seen me. I'll make sure—without going through the passport routine—who is on board. That gives us the warning, right? After that, we wait until they move ashore. I don't think Alex will go up to the house on the hill to see Maritta, not right away."

Not ever, thought Craig. Alex, cautious and careful, wouldn't be seen near that house. "Do you really think he might go there?" he asked very carefully. No criticism, Tim; no criticism implied at all.

"When it's dark, perhaps. Maritta has got rid of Veronica for the night. The house will be safe enough, even for Alex."

Now that's what Bannerman would do, or I would do, if we were in Alex's shoes. But will Alex? . . . Craig frowned, looked at the placid harbor. Outside the breakwater, the sunset was starting. And not a sign of a ship coming from any direction. "Maritta may have been making the house safe for the *Stefanie*'s arrival."

"It needs darkness to unload its cargo," Bannerman said abruptly.

"And it isn't taking the direct route to Mykonos from Samos. That, we do know. They'll make very sure that all is well before they touch land."

Craig agreed with that. In the art of caution, Insarov could give Alex some twenty years.

"And it won't arrive while Alex is here. *He* will make sure of that."

Craig could agree with that, too.

"He is due first. He has to be. If he is Bradley, he has got to be back at his desk in Paris by Monday morning. If he is Wilshot, he has a final interview with Grivas near Athens on Sunday. Neither can hang around here too long."

Craig nodded again.

"We can only make some educated guesses about what Alex will do once he sails in here. We just have to be ready for anything. You stay and watch the town while I'm around near the anchorage. Any suggestions?"

"I'd like to know how the hell I get in touch with you if necessary when you're on the other side of the harbor. It's a damned loud whistle from here to there."

"Relax, relax . . . That's all set up. Why do you think I've been waiting here?" Bannerman glanced at his watch. "They should be passing any minute now."

"I hope they speak English. I know about four phrases in Greek: good day, thank you, please, where is the toilet?"

Bannerman grinned. "They know more Greek than that. I'll leave one of them with you and take the other with me. Adam is the name of the guy who will keep fairly close to you. Only get in touch—" He broke off. "See those two characters ambling down the street. The fair-haired guy with the sunburn is Adam: green sweater, medium height, round face—got him? The stocky dark-haired chap is Bill. Okay?"

The two Americans, hands in pockets, strolled slowly past the café.

"Consider yourselves introduced," said Bannerman. "Now I can leave you. Only get in touch with Adam if you really need a contact."

"Whistle a bar or two?"

"Yes. Our little theme song." Bannerman was in good humor again. He rose. "I'll be with Elias for the next half hour or so—just checking." He sighed, but not too deeply. "This is the stage that kills me. All these damned decisions . . ."

"And I stay here?"

"Why not? You can admire the sunset and keep your eye on that street." He gave an easy wave, and left.

In spite of the low, carefree voice, there had been an edge of urgency in that last instruction. Keep your eye on the street. . . . Whom did Bannerman expect to come walking down there—Maritta?

If so, Alex won't be far behind. Maritta's actions are tied to his arrival. Of that, I'm convinced. Or at least, that's what I think. Think? Or feel? Or am I wandering in outer space? I could be wrong, there's always that doubt. He looked across the harbor at the anchorage—two placid boats lying close together, painted ships on a painted bay—all peace, all innocence. I could be wrong, he thought again, the doubt growing. All right, all right, he told himself irritably, let's watch this blasted street.

18

The street was busy now, so busy that it was baffling. Faces and voices and footsteps; and no one recognizable. The cafés, too, were filling up with people who had come out to admire the sunset. Even this one, where Craig sat patiently (obedient but bored, he thought wryly), was showing life. Some of the more artistic visitors were wandering in with their girls. "This is really authentic!" one said in delight as her friends pulled two tables together and corralled every available chair. The fishermen paid little notice, but their talk paused heavily and philosophic gloom masked their faces as they stared out at the calm harbor, only seeing another refuge invaded and about to be permanently occupied. Craig's lifeline, Adam, arrived, too, bringing three friends to sit only a couple of tables away. Craig felt cheerier, ordered coffee and another ouzo to keep the waiter happy, and returned his full attention to the street.

Then he heard the steady grumble of an outboard motor, and looked quickly at the quiet waters of the harbor. A small boat was halfway across from the yacht anchorage, moving smoothly in toward the breakwater. Where had it come from? The sloop or the cabin cruiser? It was edging its way past the fishing boats and caïques, coming as far inshore as possible. There was a man and some luggage in the prow; a woman at the tiller. Craig looked quickly around the tables, but the men there didn't seem to find it strange. They were more concerned with watching to see if the woman would make a mistake in steering, for, once she had nosed the boat into an opening between two fishing boats and brought it neatly against the jetty, they lost interest and found something else to talk about.

Craig looked along the street. No one was hurrying to meet the man on the jetty, now standing there with his two suitcases at his feet, watching the boat reverse safely. The woman waved; the engine roared for the first minute and then settled into its steady beat. The boat headed right back to the yacht anchorage.

Craig glanced at Adam's table. The conversation there was hilarious, but Adam had noticed, too, in between laughs. The man was picking up his suitcases, walking smartly to the head of the quay. He stopped to speak with a group of fishermen beside the small chapel there, but seemingly found no helpful answers. Next, he spoke to an old man, was directed on to another group. Someone gave him the information he was seeking. It was, apparently, a place to leave his two suitcases: a cart, standing by itself at the end of the quay with a few bundles already waiting for shipment out on the next boat. It was a slightly offhand baggage room, but the stranger accepted it after a little hesitation. Then, with his suitcases deposited neatly, the man headed for the front street. He was walking at a medium pace, obviously interested in everything he saw, someone who was putting in time before he caught the evening boat. No one was paying him the least attention. His actions explained themselves. He had arrived too early, which—in any Mykoniot's opinion—was wiser than appearing at the last minute and expecting miracles. Such things happened constantly; foreigners neither understood boat schedules nor made allowances for weather.

The stranger had plenty of time. He stopped to look at the painted fishing boats drawn up on the beach, at the nets spread over the short stretch of sand and pebbles. An Englishman, Craig guessed. He was wearing a faded blue blazer, loosely cut dark gray flannels bagging a little from travel. He took out a pipe and pouch, began the ritual of filling and lighting as he crossed the street toward the first café. Now Craig could see a thin tanned face above a nonchalant collar and tightly knotted tie. Striped, of course. He was almost a professional Englishman, from well-brushed hair down to solid shoes. As he reached the front-row tables, he glanced at his watch, decided to have a drink. He entered casually, eyes searching for an agreeable spot.

Craig's spine stiffened. He sat staring. My God, he thought, I didn't find Bradley; he found me! For at the moment of sure recognition, Bradley's eyes had swept along the back row of tables and seen Craig. He stopped, looked again, hesitated. Then, hand outstretched, he came forward. "Craig, isn't it? Why, this is a delightful surprise!"

"Bradley!" Craig's voice was astounded enough to carry across several tables. "Sorry. I didn't recognize you at first." Which was true.

"I didn't know you were here," said Bradley, completely at ease again. "And how is your charming sister?"

"Sue and George are both fine. They're in Washington now. Sit down, why not? Have a drink."

"If there is anything drinkable." Bradley smiled, hesitated again, then sat down. He looked around, adjusted the knot of his tie, pulled at his cuffs. "I feel rather overdressed. But I'm in transit. Returning to the big city tonight—catching the boat for Athens when it does come in. Thought I'd come over and have a look at Mykonos and something to eat before we sail. That's around ten, isn't it?"

"Give or take an hour. But I expect it will be fairly punctual tonight. The weather is good. You're in luck. What will you have?"

"Nothing at present, thank you. I have to meet a friend for a last drink together. Remember Wilshot?"

Craig reflected a little. "Wasn't he at the Meurice party, too? Yes, I remember him vaguely. We didn't talk."

"We came up from Rhodes, today. One of his friends offered us a lift—if that's the right word. Nautical terms are out of my line. Anyway, it gave us a last chance to see some of the islands. Otherwise, I think it was a mistake. Wilshot was seasick from start to finish. He is looking for a room now, at a hotel. Says he is going to spend tonight on terra firma, and look up some old friends. Extraordinary chap. He seems to have friends everywhere."

"Too bad you can't stay longer, yourself."

"Yes, it looks a quaint little place. Definitely informal." He looked around again, studying the people at the tables. "And how's your book coming along?"

"By fits and starts—the way most work gets done out here. I'll be spending some time on Delos. And then I'll push on."

"You know, I was thinking of you last week. When I was in Troy."

"How was it?" Craig asked with real interest.

Bradley plunged into a quick account, mostly on the peculiarities of getting there, of traveling through the naval and military zones that fringed both sides of the Dardanelles. "Then I drove on down to Smyrna. Fantastic journey on incredible roads, camels around every corner. Don't miss Bursa, by the way, when you go to Troy. It's the old Turkish capital—before they took Constantinople. The Green Mosque there is quite remarkable. Well—" he looked around again—"it seems as if I'll have to search elsewhere for Wilshot. Say, why don't we all have dinner later tonight?"

"I'd like that. But I'm waiting for a girl."

Bradley looked at the three coffee cups and two ouzo glasses. "You've had quite a wait, I see."

"No one is very punctual around here. And it's just possible that I'm at the wrong café. I haven't really got accustomed to Mykonos yet—only arrived here last night." He glanced at his watch. "After seven," he said in amazement.

Bradley rose. "If you see Wilshot, tell him I'm around, will you? I'll have a quick look at the town and then find a likely place to eat along here somewhere." He looked vaguely at the water front. He smiled and added, "I was told that the best way to catch the boat is to sit at a café until you see it approach."

"That saves a lot of fussing and fuming," Craig agreed. "Well—I won't say good-bye. We'll probably keep bumping into each other for the rest of the evening. Everyone does in Mykonos." Adam had already risen, along with two of his friends (Greek, they were), and was leading the way out into the street, talking over his shoulder to them about Kazantzakis. The third (a Frenchman, Craig had decided) still sat at their littered table, looking at the English girls across the café with a lazy interest which might win him a very successful evening indeed.

"If your girl doesn't appear, join us for dinner," Bradley said. He nodded pleasantly and walked off.

Magnificent sunset, thought Craig, and studied it for the next two minutes. Anything to keep him from his impulse to look after Bradley. Or after the two Greeks who were tagging along at a respectable distance. Adam had left in the other direction. Do I wait for Bannerman, wondered Craig, or do I follow my own impulses and leave this damned table and go looking for Maritta? For the truth is that we'll never know who Alex is until we see him with her. Bradley or Wilshot? . . . He had thought Partridge and all his boys a little slow at deciding. And yet, he found he wouldn't make up his mind, either. You couldn't pin treason lightly on any man. And this double play, carefully calculated, was as baffling as Alex had intended it. Friendly innocent or confidence trickster, which was Bradley? No, Craig thought, the only sure way of knowing will be when Maritta makes contact with Alex.

Bannerman arrived to find Craig paying the bill. "Going some place?" he asked with a grin.

"You know damned well where I'm going."

Bannerman looked around, checked on the nearest tables, seemed reassured, sat down beside Craig, and dropped his voice to a low murmur. "Take it easy. Maritta only left the house on the hill five minutes ago. She is walking in. That means we have at least fifteen minutes more before she reaches town. What did you make of Bradley?"

Craig shook his head. "He says Wilshot is in town."

"I know. He's at the Triton now, trying to get a room."

At the Triton. "Right next door to Herr Gerhard Ludwig?" The odds were increasing on Wilshot.

"He says he was advised to go there."

"Advised or instructed?"

"You really are getting the hang of this," Bannerman said in great good humor.

"I'm getting holes in the seat of my pants from so much damned sitting."

"And what had you in mind? Take a stroll and walk right up to Erika and her dear Alex?"

"Erika?"

"Her play name."

"I'll stick with Maritta." He still couldn't get accustomed to Insarov, still called him Berg as often as not. And the man *was* Berg. Maritta *was* Maritta. The rest was smoke screen.

"Safer for you," Bannerman agreed. Names had a habit of slipping out sometimes, as he had just proven to himself. "*If* you insist on talking with her. But why? And have you a real excuse? You'll need it, or you'll be blown sky-high. And perhaps us along with you."

Craig shook his head. "Let's leave here, and I'll tell you what I have in mind. It could work." Dusk was just about to cast its first thin veil over the sky. Soon the gray hour would come, the café lights would go on. He rose and made his way out. Bannerman had to rise and follow. Craig turned to his left, avoiding the front street, talking casually about Fellini and De Sica, as if Italian films had been their discussion. Bannerman noted all that and approved. They took the first whitewashed lane away from the water front, then cut along to their left again on the next narrow street, circling around to reach its other end. The crisscrossing streets had their evening quota of women standing at their doorways, of old men here and there watching with interest. Everyone else had left for a stroll along the water front.

Craig had begun speaking very quietly from the minute they had branched up into the alley, walking closely in between its tight walls. "I won't press my luck. I'll disengage if I see it's near breaking point. Contact *has* to be made between Maritta and Alex if there is any exchange of information between them at all. Right? This isn't the kind of place where you can drop something for another agent to pick up casually—too many people, too many kids around who could pick it up first. How much chance would one of those trick pencil stubs have, for instance, if a small boy saw it? Mykoniots don't waste one inch of string. Right?"

Bannerman nodded.

"So it has to be direct contact for safety. From one hand to another, or at least within sight of each other. Could be?"

Bannerman nodded. It was an odd feeling to hear Craig arguing everything out for himself, reaching conclusions that had been made days ago in Athens.

"So you need someone to get as close to them as possible. And that's me."

"Is it?"

"Have you got anyone who could walk right up to them and join them? With a perfectly good excuse? If Alex is Wilshot, I'll tell him that Bradley has been looking for him all over the place. If Alex is Bradley, I'll take him up on his dinner invitation. How's that?"

"Tempting."

"You'll have your men all around, anyway. If I get the deep-freeze treatment and have to bow out, nothing is lost. What d'you think?"

"I like it. Especially the bit where you make them break their rules. They'll learn each other's real names from you." He laughed softly.

"They don't know—" began Craig in astonishment.

"Neither name, nor occupation. Safeguard." Bannerman laughed again. "These are real conspirators, you know. Not counterespionage agents. There's a difference; in purpose and methods. They are the masters of the double image." Then Bannerman shook his head regretfully as he came back to Craig's idea. "I like it, but I'm not going to let you do it. You've forgotten two things: yourself, and what could come afterward."

"But I'm leaving that to you," Craig said with a smile. "You've got your alternative plans all made for dealing with Alex, haven't you? How many?" he asked jokingly. "A, B, C and D?"

Bannerman looked at him impassively.

"But how are you going to deal with Maritta? If you have Elias pick her up, take her out of circulation—well, that could cause a five-alarm fire. And yet, you'd like to keep her from handing that information from Alex over to—well, who's your guess?"

Bannerman's eyebrow lifted. "Is this what I get for leaving you alone with a sunset?"

"Inspiring," Craig admitted with a grin. "Come on, you old *bouzoukia* expert, what's there to lose if I play it very, very cool?"

"And where do you propose to start this operation? You can't be in two places at once—and there are two men."

"I'll compromise. I'll stay near Maritta. And leave the hard work to all you boys."

"There aren't so many of us now," Bannerman said very quietly indeed. "Elias is putting every man available, once darkness sets in, up on the hills as lookouts around the nearest bays and coves. We figure the *Stefanie* will drop off her cargo in a quiet spot and cruise peacefully at sea until morning. Then she makes a nice innocent approach to Mykonos."

"So that leaves—"

"Adam and myself. Bill has gone with the Greeks into the hills—liaison between them and us." Bannerman barely paused as he gave a passing thought to two other Americans, cosily installed this morning with complete transmitting and receiving facilities. He wondered briefly if any further news had come in from Smyrna, or—just as important now—if the wave length for local communication between here and the hills was working out all right. "Then there is an Englishman, but he is over on Delos, tonight." Craig looked swiftly at Bannerman, who didn't elaborate but went on smoothly, "And there's Mimi, at Delos; which leaves one Frenchman here. He's a good man. But the French are so damned eager to get Maritta that they may act if they think she is slipping away from them. From their point of view, they are within their rights. But from ours—well, all we'd get out of it would be Alex."

"And another man dead," said Craig, thinking of the *Stefanie*'s prisoner. And Heinrich Berg free. "Then you need me, whether you like it or not. So let's get moving." He halted at the next corner. "This street takes me back to the water front. I know, because this is the way I arrived yesterday evening." The dusk was thickening now. The white houses were luminous ghosts. Soon the lights, here too, would be switched on. "I think I even know her favorite café—I saw her there, last night, just around this time." He started down toward the front street.

Bannerman came with him. "Why not?" Bannerman said to Craig's unasked question. "We were seen constantly in Athens together." And then, as they were almost at the water front, he asked, "What makes you think she'll meet Alex at a café? Why not in one of those quiet streets we've just been passing?" He had his own answer but he was curious to find out if Craig did have a reason. That was important—no adequate reply, or a wrong one, and he'd stop Craig even now.

"He's a complete stranger to Mykonos. So was I last night. And I couldn't have been sure of meeting anyone in the dusk, at the right time, on the right street. The water front was the only place I could have reached with any certainty."

"Good enough," Bannerman said quietly, and walked on.

"What's more, this isn't the place of big hotels and public lobbies. Strangers are noticed here if they are in places where they don't belong. And any walk up to a lonely mill, or onto the hillside, could be noted, too: this is the time of day when women have stopped work to look out of their doorways. So the safest place is the most normal place—the water front, where all visitors congregate. That raises no speculations. Right? Or wrong?"

It was right as far as Mykonos went. Bannerman nodded, glanced at his watch, increased his pace. "Let's cross the front street, walk on the beach, look at a fishing boat or two. Adam is waiting at the square; he will follow her in once she passes through it. If you are right, she should be swinging along in a few—" He did not even have to finish his sentence. He grasped Craig's arm, pulled him behind a stone staircase as Maritta Maas strolled along the water front barely thirty feet away.

"Quick reflexes," Craig said, looking with respect at Bannerman.

"And damned poor timing." Bannerman drew a deep breath, and gestured to Craig to resume walking. "We could have run smack into her. She must be pretty confident to come so quickly into town. All the better," he added with a broad smile. "She'll really be set back a mile when she sees you. Now, look, I agree to your plan, with one addition. Me."

"We're going in together?" I might have guessed that was why he listened, Craig thought wryly. He's using me to get close to Alex. "I introduce you all around?"

"That's the idea. I'll stick with Alex. You hold onto Maritta. Spend the evening with her if necessary. Keep her from delivering that information anywhere, until Adam and his French friend think up a way of getting it from her. Of course, there is another way—" He looked at Craig, reflectively.

"No thanks," Craig said sharply. "I don't tangle with any girl unless I like her. Just keep my love life out of this, will you?"

"Only a mild suggestion." They had reached the front street. Bannerman grasped Craig's arm again. "Gently does it." Adam was walking past the entrance of their lane. He noticed them, all right, but didn't stop. Something more interesting seemed to lie ahead of him. "Give him a minute," Bannerman said, and paused to light a cigarette. "Let them all get into place. Then we walk in."

"I don't think it will be as easy as that."

"Nothing ever is. But I'm counting on you to startle Maritta. Set her off balance. That's when mistakes are made."

"Alex will keep his head—"

"Let him. We've got him, whatever happens. False passport, the use of, however temporary. Elias will hold him on that."

They turned the corner carefully. Maritta had halted in front of her usual café. She was standing, her back turned to them, looking out to sea. The small launch she had hired for her party was returning from Delos, easing its way around the breakwater to come into the shelter of the harbor.

Again, Bannerman had to light his cigarette. They stood for another full minute behind a pillar of the nearest colonnade. There was no sign of Adam; he made good use of every available shadow, seemingly. Craig wondered if Maritta had not her own watchers posted along this water front. And inside the café?

"Take it easy," said Bannerman softly, and kept talking. "You know, that was a clever dodge with the fake passports." He passed over his own mistake in letting it work; he ought to have gone over to the anchorage himself, just to make sure who had arrived. "Hindsight is easy," was all he said. "It's clear now that the man sleeping below was the non-Alex. The real Alex handled the passport identification on deck while his stupefied friend didn't even know what was going on."

"Which makes his record just about perfect for the whole trip."

"They slipped something into his cocktail. Elias' man thought he was drunk." Bannerman grinned cheerfully. "So keep your glass in your hand, tonight. Useful tip when drinking with Alex."

At this moment, Craig was wondering if he would even meet Alex. Maritta might be merely taking an evening stroll. That's the way she looked from here. Casual, untroubled, innocent. Abruptly, she swung around toward the café. Hair slightly ruffled from the sea breeze, hands deep in the pockets of her belted fleece coat—a pale green that came to life as she stepped into the circle of light—she walked slowly through the rows of outside tables. She smiled to one group of acquaintances, waved to another, managed somehow to be drawn into neither. She paused at the wide entrance to the room, hesitated whether she'd go inside or sit under the colonnades at her usual table. She decided that it was perhaps turning chillier than she had expected and stepped over the threshold.

"Damn," said Bannerman softly. "It would have been so easy to watch her if she had sat outside."

"Too easy. Come on, let's go." She could be meeting Alex, right now, thought Craig worriedly.

"There's Adam," Bannerman said as they approached the café. Adam had decided on an inside table, too, tonight. The Frenchman with the bedroom eyes was drifting in, looking around with his usual lazy appraisal even if he had managed to bring along two of the English girls with him. "Technique," Bannerman said with admiration.

"If he has to leave them quickly, two are company and they won't feel so lonely." He raised his voice as they reached the first row of tables. "The trouble about these Karagöz plays is that you never can find them. You hear plenty about them—"

Craig had paused, almost imperceptibly, as he noticed the lonely American seated at one table, a man in his thirties, well-dressed in a light tweed jacket, who was watching the people stroll by. He glanced at Craig but didn't recognize him in the broken light. It was Ed Wilshot.

Craig walked on, saying, "They are pure folk art, of course, as raw as it can come. You may be able to find them in the smaller places—perhaps they'd have to be toned down for Athens."

"Until the avant-garde discovers them," Bannerman said, looking at Ed Wilshot as he passed. His face was impassive. "And that will really muck them up." Better keep Maritta in view, he decided.

They halted at the doorway, accustoming their eyes to the bright lights inside. Craig was saying, "What do you think, Tim? Outside or in here?"

"Chilly out there. It looks as if there's going to be a change in weather. Let's find a table inside." They entered casually.

It was a square room, with the usual massive arch framing the shelves of bottles on its back wall. The twenty tables, plastic-topped, had clusters of rush-bottomed chairs. It was simple, clean and fairly crowded. Adam was seated near the door, talking with two local men. The Frenchman and his two excellent excuses were at a table against one wall. And Maritta was there. By herself. She was staring at Craig unbelievingly.

He pretended to catch sight of her then, and waved as he started toward her. His hand almost froze in mid-air. At the next table to Maritta's, tucked into a corner behind the arch, reading a paper while he enjoyed a lonely *apéritif,* was Robert Bradley.

"Hey!" Craig said to Bannerman, who seemed to be heading for the opposite wall, "I'm going in this direction." He nodded with a grin toward Maritta. She had recovered enough to smile back. She was even primping, getting ready to welcome him; she had taken out her compact and lipstick from her deep pocket, and was studying the need for repairs in a small mirror.

Bannerman was looking at her, too, a bright smile spreading over his handsome dark face. "That's an idea!"

"I didn't ask you," Craig said, leading the way.

"I'm still accepting," Bannerman told him, following him with a laugh.

It sounded natural enough. As natural as the sudden falling of the lipstick, which landed with a light clatter near Robert Bradley's feet.

He bent to pick it up, rose to return it into Maritta's cupped hand, smiled politely at her thanks, and sat down again, adjusting his tie as he picked up his newspaper.

Bannerman's trained eye was admiring. That was one of the neatest exchanges he had seen in a long time—a double exchange. First, Bradley had substituted a fake lipstick for Maritta's; secondly, as he had placed it in her palm, he had found something there to pick up. Bradley hadn't enjoyed receiving in addition to giving. For a moment, his face was tight, the nostrils slightly dilated. The hand that had made the exchange was now slipping casually into his pocket. Then he was adjusting his tie again. Bradley really was a cool—Bradley? Alex. We've got Alex, Bannerman thought, and gave Maritta his very best smile.

She was a cool operator, too. She had taken off the cap of the lipstick she had received from Bradley, to show it was apparently authentic. Quickly, she colored her lips, closed the lipstick, and dropped both it and her compact back into her coat's deep pocket. She tilted her head and looked at Craig.

Craig was concentrating on Maritta, not even noticing Bradley. That lipstick is a stronger pink than she usually wears, he noted as he grinned like a happy idiot. "I've been searching for you everywhere, just about giving up hope. What took you so long to get into town?"

This approach startled her again. "Why—" She looked at him blankly, recovered. "And how did you get here from Delos? Swim?" There was challenge in her voice and eyes.

"But I didn't go! You didn't expect me to, did you, when you never turned up?" Craig looked incredulous. "Didn't you know I'd get your message?"

The brilliant green eyes flickered nervously at Bradley's back. "But I didn't send any—"

"Maritta," Craig said gently, "don't tell me you didn't want to see me. Without benefit of the usual rabble." He looked with a grin at Bannerman.

Bannerman said, putting out his hand, "This oaf doesn't seem to want to introduce me. So I'll do it myself. Tim Bannerman."

She shook hands, smiled, but only said, "Why don't you sit down, Mr. Bannerman?"

No name given, Craig noted. And just what had been exchanged between Maritta and Bradley? The lipstick, probably; and anything else? It had been too quick for him. But Bannerman was in such good spirits that he must have noticed something important. Craig looked at Bradley's back, and decided to make this a really merry party. "Hello, Bradley!" he said. "I thought I saw Ed Wilshot hanging around outside. But come and meet the prettiest girl on Mykonos."

Bradley had turned around, resigned. He mustered a correct smile. He rose again, the always perfect gentleman.

"Mr. Robert Bradley, Miss Maritta Maas—" Craig clapped Bannerman's back—"and Mr. Timothy Bannerman the Fourth." Craig pulled around an extra chair. Just the life of the party, he told himself; but he was, in fact, enjoying himself immensely. "Join us, Bradley. It must be gloomy waiting for a boat all by yourself. Have you had dinner, yet? Well, join us again. I wish you'd take Bannerman off my hands, though. Maritta and I were planning to—"

"We were not!" Maritta said sharply, and looked at Bradley.

"Sorry, sorry," Craig said very quietly, "I didn't know we had to keep it a secret." Then he smiled brightly all around and signaled to the waiter. The mention of Wilshot's name, he noticed, was keeping Bradley nicely in place: it might be difficult to explain to Wilshot why he had been given wrong directions where to sit. At any rate, Bradley wasn't leaving to meet his friend outside. Or perhaps he was more interested in Maritta's connection with Craig. The more she protested, the more coldly he looked at her. Do these people have to make reports on each other? Craig wondered. Maritta was certainly ill at ease. She had even forgotten to challenge him with shouldering her servant off the dock.

But once the drinks arrived, and Bradley's attention was held by Bannerman's easy flow of talk, she made an effort and recovered herself. And she didn't disappoint Craig. "What was that story I heard," she asked coldly, "about a man falling into the water?"

"He did. It was some idiot who was standing on the edge of the quay. There was a jam of people. What did he expect, anyway?"

"And you stumbled against him?"

"Look, Maritta, he tried to pull me in," Craig said with a hint of protest in his voice. "I nearly took a high dive, myself."

She studied him. "So you didn't go to Delos. . . . Veronica will be quite upset."

"No one is going to miss me one bit. There was a mob scene on that jetty. Everything just got out of hand. Not my idea of a romantic picnic. Besides, I told you I had lost interest. Can't you get it through your pretty blond head that I only accepted the invitation because of you?"

"I thought your chief interest was in old ruins."

"In daylight. By myself. When I can keep my mind on my work." He glanced at the other two men. Bannerman was at his best in this kind of confrontation; he was talking amusingly, constantly, holding Bradley's attention in spite of his wary coldness. It was thawing a little, as if Bradley had completed the job of sizing Bannerman up and had decided that he would prefer to talk with him rather than seem to have any contact with Maritta. He ignored her completely, a man who had no interest in her whatsoever. And for once Maritta did not seem to mind such neglect. Craig said very quietly, "Maritta—what about having dinner with me?"

"I'm sorry. I have to get back to the house. I only slipped away for an hour to—to get some medicine in town. I had nothing stronger than aspirin."

"Oh, yes, I forgot. Tony or Veronica, or someone, told me your guest broke his leg. Is it serious?"

She hadn't been listening. A new idea had entered that quick little mind. She smiled brightly. "You know, John, I might stay and have dinner with you. The house is really so unbearable—like a hospital. Why do men with a small hurt always think they are dying? It's nothing serious, really. And I couldn't find anything stronger than aspirin in town, anyway."

"Then that's fine. Let's start moving out."

"Where shall we have dinner? The best food is at either the Leto or the Triton. The Triton is nearer. Why don't we go there?"

And since when did a slender figure think about the importance of good food? The Triton—with three exits, one of them right next door to the Ludwig house. It would be a simple way, with a few more excuses like washing her hands, tidying up, to make sure of delivering that lipstick. Craig smiled. "That's an idea." He glanced at Bannerman, wondering if he had heard. Craig did some quick calculations of his own. He rose, helping her pull the coat around her shoulders—she had kept it with her, all this time, instead of throwing it over a spare chair. "Good-bye," he said to Bradley. "Have a good trip."

"Give my best to Sue and George."

Craig's eyes noticed the small addition to Bradley's dress: the striped tie was now held by a clip of gold. He wasn't wearing any tie clip when I first met him today, Craig thought, I'm sure he wasn't, I'm positive. "I'll do that," he said, shaking hands.

Bradley's bow to Maritta was no more than politeness demanded. That might even be relief in his eyes, as if he were glad to be rid of her. She was equally distant. Her smile for Bannerman was enchanting.

Craig caught her arm and started leading her toward the bar at the back of the room.

"Why—" she asked, halting, looking at him.

"I've got to call the Triton and arrange for a table for two. And why don't you call home and tell them you won't be back until—" he smiled down at her—"well, let's say midnight. Then they won't start worrying about you."

"Midnight?"

"Unless you could manage to spend the night in town." He held her eyes with his.

"Just a minute, my friend, not so fast!" Bannerman was beside them, his voice clear and carrying. "Where do I join you later in the evening?"

"You don't," Craig said with a grin, "you old—" he dropped his voice as if his description of Bannerman wasn't for any lady's ears—"tie clip."

Bannerman heard it, barely, but enough. He laughed. "Okay, okay." To Maritta he said, "What about going swimming tomorrow? I'll meet you at the taxi stand at eleven."

"We'll see about that," Craig said, took Maritta's arm and led her to the telephone that sat proudly at the end of the bar.

"What did you call him?" she wanted to know, smiling.

"Oh, just a term of endearment among sailors."

She didn't know her Dr. Johnson, but she got the idea. "I think he's charming," she said. She was so much back to normal, so much enjoying herself, that she did not even notice Adam was strolling to the door or that the Frenchman was leaving his two pretty girls. Bannerman had rejoined Bradley with a joking remark, while Bradley ordered something to eat with a look of distaste for the limited menu. Maritta glanced back at their table. "And I think that other man is horrid. He never even spoke to me. I don't think he really likes women, do you? Perhaps you ought to warn your nice friend. How long have you known Mr. Bannerman?"

"Long enough not to trust him near you. He has been visiting Athens for several months—he's a writer. Now, ladies first." He handed her the telephone. "Make it nice and vague. I don't want your friends chasing into the Triton with a shotgun. Tell them they haven't a thing to worry about. You are spending the night with a friend. Right?"

She smiled. "Perhaps," she said. And then as she waited for an answer to her call, she laughed softly and said, "Perhaps that would be wise."

She did keep it vague. She did not mention the Triton. She did not even mention John Craig. No worry, she told them, everything was splendid; everything was well. They asked her one question. Her answer was a decided "Yes!" A touch of triumph was in it, too. She ended quickly, "I'll manage. Don't worry. I won't be late."

She replaced the receiver. "I have to be back by ten tomorrow," she said, not blinking one eyelash, to explain that last quick sentence. "Now it's your turn—" She followed the direction of his eyes. Sauntering into the café were Tony and Mimi. "What—" She hurried toward them. "What on earth happened?"

"We came back with the launch," Mimi said. "Oh, how nice and *warm* it is in here!"

Tony was looking around in his vague English way, nodding to various groups, noticing Bannerman and Bradley. "Everything went wrong," he told Maritta. "They swarmed ashore on Delos, all having the time of their little lives. We kept the launch waiting, tried to coax them back on board. They wouldn't go. It was, I suppose, absolutely hilarious. I'll see the joke tomorrow."

"How many stayed?"

"Hundreds."

Mimi laughed and said, "I counted eighteen. They'll freeze to death."

"Unless they bundle," Craig said with a grin. No one got the joke.

"There would have been no beds left for us," Mimi said, shaking her head. "They ran faster than we did."

"Yes," said Tony to Craig, "we were properly up a pear tree. So Veronica and Mimi and I decided we'd—"

"Veronica?" Maritta's voice was sharp. "Where is she?"

"Oh, we left her looking for the man who drives the taxi. I told her it was no use. Either he's in bed or he is at the fishermen's pub down the street dancing a mad *bouzoukia.*"

"Is she going to the house?" Maritta was tense.

"I should think that was the idea. She said she was going to pack."

But Maritta was already halfway to the door.

"I couldn't stop Veronica from coming back," Mimi said very quietly as she and Craig followed. "I did not want to, of course. Tony and I were glad of the excuse. I think we are needed here tonight."

"When did she decide?"

"Just as we reached Delos. She did not speak all the way across. All at once, she made up her mind—like that!" Mimi snapped her fingers. "And then Tony managed to start everyone landing. He would make a very good *agent provocateur.*" She laughed for Tony, slid her arm through Craig's. "Now it is our turn, I think," she said as they all came out into the colonnade.

Maritta was standing in the middle of the street, looking toward the main square where the two taxis were parked during the day. "I can't see her," she called over her shoulder to Craig. She was frightened, really frightened. "And there is no taxi."

"Then she is walking," Craig said more calmly then he felt. "Forget it, Maritta. Let's have dinner."

"But she can't go—" Maritta bit the phrase short. She was close to complete panic.

"We can easily catch up with her, if that is what you want."

Maritta made an effort and tried to look normal. "It makes everything so awkward. Don't you see, I can't possibly stay in town if she is alone at the house? It wouldn't be—*convenable.*" She looked up at him so disappointedly. "It just ruins everything, doesn't it?" She set off at a very brisk pace.

Craig called after her, "Mimi says she is packing and coming back into town—so why bother?"

Maritta pretended she hadn't heard. Her pace increased. Just ahead of her, Adam and the Frenchman were sitting on the low wall that edged the beach near the square.

"Maritta! Wait for me!" Craig shouted. But she hurried on. Adam and his friend now saw her direction. They slipped off the wall, began walking ahead of her. It looked as if she were following them.

"Oh, let her be!" Tony said loudly. He had a tight grip on Craig's arm. "Remarkable thing!" he said very quietly. "Why doesn't she want anyone near that house at such an early hour?"

Mimi was watching the two men walking ahead of Maritta. They were reaching the narrow lane that disappeared around some buildings at the water's edge. They entered it, vanished from sight. Maritta would have to take that way, too. It was the quick route to the bay road. "Time for me to leave," she said quietly. "I'll be needed, I think." There was a strange small smile on her lips. "Where did she put the information she received? In her pocket?" Then she looked at Craig's face. "Don't worry," she said. "She will be luckier than Duclos." She left them, walking swiftly, her graceful stride surviving even the broken paving stones. She waved back. "See you tomorrow," she called over her shoulder.

"I wonder if Tim needs any help," Tony said, and looked toward the café. He saw Elias and another Greek sitting quietly in the shadows outside. "No, I think not."

Craig was still watching Maritta as she reached that dark lane. She was almost running, now. Running right into it, he thought.

"She'll be all right," Tony murmured. "Just an informal arrest. A quiet detention, until it's safe to make it known." His grip on Craig's arm slackened as he drew him casually toward the deeply shadowed beach.

"I'm not worrying about her," Craig said grimly. Maritta and Alex—the hell with them. "It's Veronica."

"Yes," the Englishman agreed. "I think I'll pass the word. You'd better wait here for Bannerman." He glanced at the American's face, and then looked back at the colonnade. "Do nothing rash."

"Nothing you wouldn't do."

"I don't like the sound of that one bit," Tony said with a smile. "Meanwhile, there's a chap over at the darkest table—by the edge of the colonnade. He's the one who was trailing Veronica this morning."

"Striped shirt?" Craig resisted glancing around.

Tony nodded. "He has been trying to make up his mind whether he ought to keep an eye on Maritta, or whether he should phone in his report. I know the feeling well. . . . The telephone wins, I hope. . . . Good. He doesn't think Maritta is in any trouble. She probably gave him no signal of distress. So a report is sufficient unto the evil thereof. I don't imagine we want even that, do we? Shall I deal with him? Or you?"

"I think your touch is more inspired."

"Thank you," Tony said gravely, and moved with unconcerned nonchalance toward the man who had left his table and was heading, cautiously but definitely, for the café entrance. The man halted, stood aside. Bradley and Bannerman were coming out. Bannerman was still talking his head off; Bradley was looking peeved, as if he had just about reached saturation point. But he kept his polite mask in place.

"No trouble at all," Bannerman was saying. "You'll need an extra hand with your luggage, and we may have to hurry. I think I see her lights now!" He pointed out beyond the breakwater. "These mail boats slip in so quickly. And they don't always wait. She's early tonight. Must have been good weather all the way. Come on, let's run. No one will hold it against us."

Bradley and Bannerman started at a very quick pace down the water front. Elias and his man rose and followed at a half-run, passed them, drew ahead. They, too, were apparently worried about catching that boat. Other prospective passengers were rising from their café tables; some even began to run. The power of suggestion, thought Craig, lighting a cigarette to give him time to think. Think of a plan of his own . . . No use waiting for Bannerman. Once Tony could pass on the news about the house on the hill, Bannerman's hands would be even fuller than they were now. Craig watched the distant figure of his friend running close beside Bradley. And suddenly, an extraordinary thing happened.

Perhaps it was one of the paving stones with its raised edge that had caused it, perhaps the patched shadows on the street were to blame. Bradley stumbled, pitched forward. Bannerman was helping him up, dusting him off. Then they were hurrying again down the street.

From the colonnade, came Tony's voice calling out loudly for help. "I say—someone—quick! This man seems ill!"

Craig's eyes glanced over at the café. Tony was looking in bewilderment at the stout figure he had propped into the nearest chair. Three people went forward. "Is he drunk?" someone asked.

"I don't know. He collapsed practically on top of me," Tony said. "Most peculiar, really." He stepped back, let the waiter and some fishermen take over. There was a good deal of growing excitement, various suggestions, and then a simple solution arrived at. The inert body was carried indoors and the problem deposited on the poor woman who ran the place.

Tony came back to where Craig was standing at the edge of the beach. "He will live," he said. "But he won't wake up for another six hours. Just in time to be arrested along with the rest of his friends. He was, you might say, a standing duck."

"You play rough."

"Only when I'm *very* hard pressed," Tony said in his gentlest voice. "And we don't have much time, you know." He looked across the dark waters of the harbor to the breakwater. Under its meager lights, the small crowd of travelers were carrying their luggage up to the motorboats that would take them to the ship waiting out at sea. "Good-bye Alex," he murmured.

"They'll let him get on board?"

"Of course; he must be seen to be leaving safely. But on board—well, I suppose Elias has some way of having him detained in a cabin."

A matter of false passport, thought Craig. "Look, when Bannerman gets back, tell him I'm—"

"You wait and tell him yourself. Why did he go down to the pier, anyway? Elias and his man were there."

"They didn't know about a tie clip."

"Oh?" Then Tony laughed. "So that's why old Tim clicked his heels together? That stumble, you know."

Yes, thought Craig, understanding it now, a fall and a brush-down from helping hands was a very quiet way of losing a tie clip. "Once Alex stopped being hurried, he would notice it."

"Too late, too late." Tony started to stroll down the street. "I had better meet Bannerman. Coming?"

"No, I'm going."

"I think you should wait," Tony said. He halted, frowning slightly.

"Tell him not to worry. I'm using the direct method." Craig moved off. Time to go. Maritta would have made her quiet exit. Alex had made his. Nothing would be endangered at this moment. "I'll be there in fifteen minutes," he said as Tony came after him. "I'll have Veronica back here in another twenty."

"Things are moving very rapidly," Tony said, his voice no longer vague and drifting. "You heard Maritta."

"I know. That's why we can't wait." Craig walked off rapidly toward the square. Tony watched him go. As soon as he was out of sight he'd probably start running. I would, thought Tony. And if I hadn't to stay here and pass the word that the volcano is about to go up, I'd be on his heels.

He waited patiently, smoking, wandering around the fishing boats on the dark beach, until he saw first Bannerman and then Elias returning in the very best of spirits. He crossed the street slowly, hands in pockets. "Now hear this," Tony said, very quietly, as he joined them.

Craig followed the shore road, curving around the semicircle of the small bay, until it almost reached the yacht anchorage. Just before that point, marked by a sparse grouping of meager trees, there was a rough track branching to his right up the hilly fields. This should bring him fairly close to the house he had marked on his walk that morning: the one with the dovecote, Elias had said. The track, trail, or fourth-class road should lead to the house itself.

He glanced back as he started the winding climb. All was peace. The town clustering at the other end of the bay was a spreading galaxy of lights surrounded by darkness: a string of naked bulbs along the breakwater; another on the road he had traveled around the bay; a bright glimmer from the hotel and houses spaced along the shore; riding lights on the cabin cruiser and sloop, seemingly asleep at their anchorage; and, far out beyond the breakwater, the brilliance of the inter-island boat, lit from stem to stern, like a beacon of welcome on the black water. Above him was the vast stretch of ink-blue sky over sea, some stars appearing gradually, the waning moon now five nights into its last quarter, softly silvered clouds blowing gently in from the north.

The breeze touched his cheek, cooled his brow. Down on the road, he had run as lightly, as silently as possible whenever the patches of shadows had been deep enough. Now, on the open hillside, he climbed at a steady pace. If he was being watched, he wanted to give no impression of abnormal haste.

Normal. That was to be his password.

And he was being watched. From behind him, down at the small cluster of stunted trees that marked the cutoff, came the soft cooing of a dove. It was so natural that he almost believed it, except that another dove sounded immediately, plaintively, from one of the long retaining walls that stretched along the dark hillside back toward Mykonos. He didn't alter his pace or turn his head. But the careful warnings changed the house just above him, sheltering quietly behind its high white walls, from a place of comfortable innocence to something more formidable. The downstairs windows were shuttered, giving only a few streaks of light. Upstairs, everything was in darkness except for one window that lay at the extreme end of the house. Verónica's, possibly. Certainly it overlooked the opposite side of the rough garden from where the dovecote stood.

The front gate was unlocked. The garden was a mass of shadows. He slowed his pace, marking the path that branched left to the dovecote, the clusters of bushes, the grouping of small trees, as he followed the paved walk to the house. There was a porch in front, covered with climbing vines, and then the door.

His mouth went dry. Name, rank and serial number. Or name, purpose of visit, reason for making it. And that's all, he reminded himself as he reached the three steps to the porch. Keep it simple: that's what Partridge advised you. And check your arsenal. The automatic was deep in his right-hand pocket; the knife in his left. He knocked on the door. Come on, come on, he thought irritably: you know someone is here; don't tell me you haven't radio contact between your man on the hillside and this house. The door opened.

"Is Miss Clark ready?" Craig asked, clearly but pleasantly.

The man who had opened the door, a dark silhouette against the light from the hall behind him, stood in stolid silence, unmoving. Then, "Come in," he said, drawing aside.

"That's all right. I don't want to trouble you. I can wait for Miss Clark out here on the porch."

"No trouble," the man insisted. He spoke English well. His first hesitation had not been caused by any language difficulties; perhaps he had been puzzled by Craig's direct approach or by his total lack of interest in gaining entry to the house. He had had his orders, for he now led the way directly toward a well-lighted room on the left side of the high-ceilinged hall. There was another room, opposite, and the clatter of plates being cleared. Dinner was already over. Early for Mykonos, thought Craig, glancing at the narrow staircase that began outside the dining-room door and mounted steeply to a wooden gallery under a curved arch. Veronica, he was asking her silently, didn't you hear my voice? I spoke loudly enough.

"Go in," said the man, who was dressed like a servant in a black alpaca jacket and narrow bow tie and yet seemed very much his own master. He nodded to the arched doorway of the sitting room, and Craig walked in. He halted, looking around, ready for anything; and tried to hide his sudden sense of foolishness. He had interrupted a bridge game. No more than that. The whole setup couldn't have been more suburban. Three men and a woman at a green card table in a large and handsome room, shutters cosily closed, a coffee tray in front of a large fireplace, couches covered with roses, pink silk shades on a dozen fussy lamps, too many pictures, too much bric-à-brac.

The woman rose and came forward to welcome him. She was a faded beauty but still strong and graceful in body. She had a charming smile, as soft as the low-necked lace blouse she wore with her long silk skirt. "Do come in," she said in pleasantly accented English. She was, possibly, French.

"I don't want to disturb you." Craig was keeping near the door, hanging on to his smile, which he hoped didn't seem as unnatural as it felt. "I've come to help Veronica back to town with her overnight case. Has she finished packing?"

"How very thoughtful of you, Mr.—?"

"Craig. John Craig."

"You are not disturbing us in the slightest. We were only cutting for deal."

The three men murmured their agreement but did not rise. Two were quiet-faced unknowns; but the third man, who now turned to look over his shoulder and nod across the room in greeting, froze Craig's spine. He was Heinrich Berg. Insarov.

"Do sit down, Mr. Craig," the woman was saying in her best hostess style. She had a delicately studied way of pointing, with her palm held upward, fingers relaxed.

"No, thank you. I can't stay long. The party is just about to begin in town. Would you tell Veronica I'm here?"

"A party?" asked Berg, rising, drifting slowly over to where Craig stood. His voice was politely interested, quiet and even to match the look in his eyes.

Craig was forced to look back at him. "It's to replace the one that fell flat on Delos."

"And Maritta?"

"She is staying in town overnight, too."

"Why didn't she come here for Miss Clark?" The blue eyes were disingenuous.

He is measuring me, Craig thought. He is wondering if my smile is as stupid as I hope it looks: he is like a wrestler, circling around, arms lax, muscles loose. All right, I'll be the fatuous American. "No taxis," he replied, and laughed.

They all smiled, as if they knew Maritta.

"Jeanne," said Berg, "why don't you go upstairs and tell Miss Clark that her friend is here?"

She nodded and went into the hall. If, thought Craig, I were to see her in a heavy sweater, yachting style, I might even identify her as the woman who brought Bradley so expertly across the harbor this evening.

Berg was saying, "Miss Clark is a charming girl. But she worries us. Why does she want to leave this house? We think it is rather comfortable." He smiled sadly back at his friends around the table, who nodded and agreed with an equally desolated smile. "In fact, Mr. Craig—Craig?"

"Craig."

"We were a little hurt. After all, Maritta has been very kind, everyone has tried to make Miss Clark feel at home. Now why should she want to leave? Do you know?"

Craig shook his head. "But I'd make one guess."

"Oh?" The blue eyes were blandly innocent, but the scarred eyebrow was more noticeable.

"Transportation."

"I beg your pardon?"

"If you were twenty-five, and a girl, and with all your friends living right in Mykonos, would you enjoy walking back and forth three times a day?"

Berg stared at him. And then was amused. His silent friends were amused, too. "I suppose this house might seem inconvenient if one did not enjoy walking," he agreed. "And Americans do not walk very much, do they?" He turned toward a servant who was carrying in a silver tray with bottle, snifters, and cigars. "Ah, here is the brandy. Will you join us, Mr. Craig? You know, I keep feeling we have met. Some place. Where?"

Craig looked thoughtful, polite. Then he smiled and shook his head. "I think," he said, moving toward the hall, "I hear Veronica now." He ignored the servant with the tray, although it was hard to be oblivious of someone he had shouldered off the jetty into the harbor only four hours ago. The man's cold look pierced his shoulders. And I bet that quick whisper to Berg has nothing to do with the selection of a cigar, Craig thought. Now what happens? We were so close to leaving, so damned close. He smiled up the staircase and said, "Hello, there! Everyone is gathering at Tony's place. The fun starts any minute. Come on, Veronica, we'll have to hurry." He took her small night case. Her face was too pale, he noted; her eyes were frightened, her smile taut. She took his outstretched hand. Her fingers were ice cold, their clutch desperate. "We'll get the rest of your things tomorrow, when we find a taxi. There wasn't one in sight tonight. We'll have to walk. Sorry." He looked down at her shoes and saw with relief that they were flat-heeled. "But there's some moonlight, so a walk has its compensations," he went on, still speaking rapidly, still trying to get her back to normal. Thank God she hadn't blurted out some innocent question about what was he doing here or how had he known she was leaving. "Maritta is sorry the Delos picnic turned into such a rabble. We'll have a better party right in town. You know, you should wear blue more often; it suits you."

She laughed at that. And the tight grip of his hand as he steadied her down the last few stairs was reassuring. "My trouble is I can't resist wearing it," she could joke back, and faced the men in the room with growing confidence. "Good-bye," she said, still trying to keep her voice normal, walking on to the front door. "Good-bye," she repeated to the woman, who followed them across the hall.

Will we really be allowed to leave? Craig wondered. His back was turned to the two servants, now; his hands were fully occupied with Veronica and her small case. But the door was opened and he was thanking the faded glamour girl and calling good night in general over his shoulder. The door closed behind them. We made it, he thought, we made it.

He took a deep breath as they left the porch. He kept their pace normal, although his first inclination was to run. "Talk normally," he whispered. "About anything. Laugh, too, if you can." He shifted his grip from her hand to her arm, drawing her closer to him. We made it, he thought again, as they reached the gate. But why? His story had just managed to pass, but then that blasted servant appeared to have a close look at him; and there had been some trouble with Veronica, too. She had been both scared and angry, almost reaching the fine Celtic pitch of being fighting mad. Yes, there had been bad trouble upstairs. So why had they been allowed to walk out like this, as if nothing was at stake?

The answer came to him as he closed the gate behind them. A dove cooed twice, and then twice more, from the hillside shadows; a dove answered gently from the road below. So we didn't make it, he thought. They only wanted us clear of the house, far enough away to cause it no trouble. He pulled Veronica quickly in front of him, his own back against the wall near the gate. "Just for a minute," he told her. "Put your arms around my waist. Make it look good. Someone is watching us from the trees down by the road. That's the way. Just give me a chance to see where we'll move next."

"Then there *is* danger," she said softly. She put her hands lightly around him, leaned her cheek against his breast.

"Yes." He looked over her head, down the rough track to the main road. His eyes picked out the scraps of possible cover: an outcrop of rock, a few bushes, another of those long retaining walls that terraced the hillside, the thin group of trees at the sharp turn into the road. Not much. Not much at all.

"In a way, I'm glad," Veronica was saying. "I thought I was going just a little crazy. They locked my door, you know. If you hadn't come, I'd have been kept there all night. The woman pretended it had only stuck when she came to tell me you were downstairs. But it was locked all right." But why? But why? . . . She said nothing more, waited, feeling the strong steady heartbeat against her cheek.

He said at last, "They expect us to head for town. So we take the opposite direction. We'll go halfway down this trail, walking normally. We reach the bushes, dump your case, keep low, and run like hell along the shelter of the stone wall that leads north beyond the headland. There's another bay there, a big one—" He tried to remember the details of his map. "There's a road edging it, too, part of the way at least—"

"I know the bay—it's just a continuation of this small one—or is it the other way around? I went exploring for a place to swim there."

"What's it like?" he asked quickly.

"Cliffs, caves, coves with little beaches. Stony hillside, a few scattered houses mostly closed until summer. Lonely."

"Good. Let's head that way. Find a nice comfortable wall. And sit it out until dawn comes up." He felt the fleece of her blue coat, warm and soft to his touch; she wouldn't freeze, thank heaven for that.

"Won't they still be searching for us then?" And why, she wondered again, why? . . .

"I don't think so." We may not even have to wait until dawn, he was thinking. If Maritta's panic had any meaning, the end of all waiting should be nearer than that. He remembered, too, the feeling of calm expectancy in the house on the hill: dinner over, everything cleared for action, nothing to do but play bridge until the *Stefanie* unloaded her cargo; and the dovecote, empty, ready for its prisoner. "Zero hour is too close." He turned her head gently to look downhill. "See where we are going. The bushes—the wall—and then straight north. Got it?"

"Yes."

"Once we leave this trail, move quietly. Keep your head well down. If I drop on my face, you fall flat, too. All right—here goes!" They left the garden wall and started down the rough path. He walked slowly, his arm around her waist. He looked at her. She had lost her fear; her eyes were wide, her face alert, but the strain had gone. "No questions?" he asked softly.

"Later," she said, and smiled.

She really believes I can get her out of this, he thought, and felt strangely more confident. Later . . . A very encouraging word, tonight. It implied a future.

From behind the shelter of the thin trees at the fork in the road, a man in rough clothes, as dark as the shadows around him, watched the couple leave the wall. They had stopped their love-making at last, and were now walking slowly down toward the main road. "They'll be here in five minutes at this rate," he told the man who had slipped down through the fields to join him. "What instructions? Hit and hold?"

"Eliminate. Both could be dangerous. They are on their way back to town."

"Dangerous?" They look harmless enough to me, he thought. Still, that wasn't for him to decide.

"We can take no chances with them—not at this hour. Now, let's see—the path is too open. We'll wait for them as they turn this corner to reach the harbor road." For a brief instant, he looked up the hillside. The couple, arms linked, were almost halfway down the trail. "Get in position. Let's see how the shadows lie." He led the way, carefully from tree to tree, over the rough ground. There was not much cover to work on. But he had begun their retreat just in time: the couple were still far enough away not to be warned by any movement. "We'll have to stand down there," he decided as the trees ended and the ground fell away steeply in a bank of bare rock to reach the road. "As near the corner as possible. Then they won't notice us until they come around the turn."

"They won't notice anything. They didn't even see you come down off the hill."

"I didn't intend them to see me," the other answered curtly. He slipped down onto the road. "Quiet!" he warned, as his companion's heel scraped against the rock. "No firing, remember! A shot from here could be heard clear across the harbor."

"I know, I know. Hit hard. And then?" There was no shelter here at all. The first man looked worriedly along the road to town that stretched around the harbor. No one there, *Gott sei Dank;* everyone indoors, eating.

"Hit very hard. Then we carry them. To the cliff over there. And drop them. A romantic walk—dangerous by night. What better?"

"It's a fifteen-minute haul up that headland."

"And five minutes back. That leaves us plenty of time to get into position again."

"It won't be so easy," said the man in the rough clothes. He disliked wearing them as much as taking orders from this jumped-up Czech colonel.

"You take the girl, then." The other was contemptuous. "These were the orders from the house. No suspicions of any kind to be directed toward it."

And that was that. *"Zu Befehl."*

"Quiet! They should soon be here."

"Pity that we had to lose sight of them."

"If we could see them, they could see us. Keep silent! Listen!"

A minute passed. Almost two. The man who had been giving the orders cursed under his breath. He moved back from the corner—he dared not risk looking around it—and scrambled quietly up the rock face of the bank, his big and powerful body moving lightly, cautiously. He advanced carefully through the trees, stood very still. He cursed aloud. The other came after him. "But where are they?" he asked, his eyes searching the empty trail up to the house.

"They have taken a short cut over the fields back to town. But it's too rough for the girl. They'll have to get down to the main road by the path behind that large hotel. Come!"

"But we can't get them there—"

"We can get them before they reach it." Quickly, he turned and jumped down the bank, started running lightly along the road in the direction of town. In two minutes, even less, he could branch up one of those straggling mule paths before he was near the hotel. He could intercept them there, near the little graveyard's wall. "We'll get them," he told the other, who was loping swiftly by his side. He believed it.

"Someone," Craig had said softly to Veronica as they came down the rough path from the house, "has just snaked down that hillside on our left. Keep looking at me. That's the way." So there would be two men down by the corner of the road, two sweet-cooing doves. "You're doing fine," he told her, and shifted his arm from her waist to let him clasp her hand. They were halfway to the road, almost at the clump of bushes he had chosen for their turnoff point. He could feel Veronica's hand tighten in his, making sure of her grip as she prepared to run. They kept the same steady pace, slow, nonchalant, for those last twenty yards.

Abruptly he pulled her off the path, dropping her case among the bushes, raced for the long stone wall and its dark band of heavy shadow. Shoulders bent, heads down, they kept on going. The earth under their feet was soft and loose, easier than he had judged. Then the field ended, and the rougher ground began. He pulled her down into the shadow of the wall. He put a finger gently to her lips. Together, unmoving, they sat with legs pulled up under them, well within the sheltering band of blackness.

Now it was the time to wait. They had only been running for a full minute, not much more. They were still too near the path for safety, yet the ground had become too difficult, too deceiving, to take at such a speed. Better to stake everything on remaining hidden from eyes that start scanning the open hillside, he thought, than on placing distance between the waiting men and us. So we wait; and we'll soon know if we managed to baffle them. They had to take cover from us down on the road. I saw a movement in the trees, and then nothing. How much time will they give us to appear around that corner? And when we don't? Well, we'll wait. And see.

He placed an arm around Veronica's shoulder and drew her close to him. They sat very still, keeping their silence. His eyes were fixed on the little group of trees down by the main road. Strange thing, this rising moonlight. It both hid and revealed unexpectedly. From a distance, roughness and smoothness could hardly be accurately judged; a dark shadow could be a hole or a sharp-edged rock. But there was one real piece of luck for them: the bay of Mykonos faced westward. So these long, retaining walls over the hillside all faced west, too. At this time of night, with the moon coming up behind them, the shadows were just right; a few hours later, the moon would be overhead, and these shadows would be gone. Luck? Heinrich Berg would share the same luck, but he would be contemptuous of that word. Why else had he chosen such and such a time, and such and such a place, if he did not make use of all the help both time and place could give him? Berg, or Insarov—there he sits peacefully in his quiet house, thought Craig, a man who likes his comfort and a game of cards with amiable friends. He has planned every move his agents make, every action. He has planned for months. And when someone unforeseen, like Sussman or Duclos, threatens the perfection of those plans, he is dealt with quickly, summarily, without benefit of hesitation.

Craig glanced at Veronica. She was watching him. Her blue eyes would be large with questions, if he could only see them clearly. He tightened his grip on her shoulders reassuringly, and looked back at the trees. Were we about to be dealt with in just that way? he wondered. As Sussman was? And Duclos? He wouldn't like to put that question to the test. Evasive action along this hillside seemed a more comfortable answer, even if the earth was cold and the stone wall hard. His back stiffened as he heard a distant voice. From the trees. A short phrase. Perhaps some kind of oath? He hadn't caught the language—perhaps it was one he couldn't understand. He thought he heard a scramble of feet over rocks. But he could see nothing. He took a deep breath. Waited. And then signed to Veronica that they were moving on, over the rough flank of hill stretching northward. Let's get as far away from that house as possible, he was thinking; as far away from that road into town, too.

He helped her rise, pushed her head down with a grin to remind her to keep as low as possible, and took the lead. They moved with caution. The need was for quietness, not haste.

Following the wall, the terraced fields falling away on their left, they passed the small headland and could see the beginning curve of the large bay. A deserted coast it seemed, with neither village nor hamlet in sight; rough and dangerous, perhaps, with cloud shadows chasing over a gun-metal sea and the far-off islands. Bare, bleak, empty.

"We've come far enough," he said, looking back. The house on the hill was no longer visible. Carefully, he selected an outcrop of rock just ahead of them that looked as if it might give better protection than any wall. "Down there," he told her, pointing. It would give them a good view of the narrow road (his map had been right) that followed the shore. At least, he thought thankfully, when the time comes to get back to Mykonos we can walk on a strip of hard-packed earth instead of scrambling over a hillside from shadow to shadow. As they drew nearer the outcrop of rock, it looked better and better. Its bulge and jut would shelter them completely from the house they had left behind them and from the rising moon.

He led her, quietly, around the prow of weathered rock, steadying her over the rough fragments underfoot. Then, suddenly, he heard a rustle. He turned to see two black shadows break off from the darkness of the wall of stone, reached for his knife, snapped it open. A strong hand gripped his wrist, a hard body turned his weight and threw him. He tried to twist free, to strike out. A knee pressed firmly down on his chest, a tight grasp was on his throat. He looked up and saw Partridge.

21

Blankly, Craig and Partridge stared at each other.

"Well," said Partridge softly, rising and letting Craig breathe again, "you do get around, don't you?"

"And where the hell did *you* come from?" Craig asked angrily, picking up the knife that had been smashed out of his grip. He rubbed his wrist, easing its numbness, and looked for Veronica. She had stopped struggling in the firm hold of a small, lean character who had caught her from behind, around waist and shoulders. Like Partridge, he was dressed in black, an invisible shadow once he drew back against the sheltering strata of rock. There was a third man, also dark-clothed, crouching over a radio set. He was now canceling the alarm he had sent out about the two prowlers who had come down the hill-side.

At least, thought Craig, his anger beginning to subside into annoyance with himself at the way he had been so neatly ambushed, at least we seem to have got organized around here. And he felt better. "Are you all right?" he asked Veronica as they followed Partridge into the shelter of the outcropping rock. She took a deep breath and nodded.

"I took your advice," Partridge was saying, "and hired a submarine." He grinned and pointed to the bay beneath them. "Landed half an hour ago by way of a small rubber boat. Chris knows all about such gadgets." He nodded to the man who had held Veronica so effectively. "Colonel Holland, to be precise."

"Takes me back twenty years," Chris said, sucking the heel of his hand. "Used to pop in and out of Crete like that, right under the Nazis' guns." He spoke nostalgically, with a definite English accent. "No strain." He looked at his hand, still slightly bleeding, and then at Veronica. "And what on earth is a girl doing here?" he asked very quietly.

"I haven't the faintest idea," Veronica said with a touch of sharpness. "I just go where John pulls me."

Craig said quickly, "Veronica was being held at the house. I had to get her out before the balloon went up. They're expecting the *Stefanie* any minute now. So—well, I got her out. Our road back to town was blocked by two men. I thought it wiser to get as far away as possible from them. This seemed the safest direction."

Partridge and Holland had exchanged a long glance. Partridge asked, "And how did you get her out of that house?"

"No trouble, there. We walked out. Politely."

"Explain."

Craig explained. "Okay?" he asked worriedly as he ended.

Partridge looked at him blankly, checked a laugh. Okay? It could have been very far from that. Amateurs walked in where professionals would hesitate; and walked out, too. Politely. This one had also produced useful verification of a puzzled report: it had actually been Insarov himself who walked quite openly over the hillside to that house at dusk this evening. But if Craig had been held and questioned, if there had been time for Insarov to go to work on him? Partridge repressed his anger. "Okay," he said quietly. He looked at Veronica. "How much does she know about all this?"

"Nothing."

Holland looked disbelieving. He cleared his throat. His comment was quite clear.

"Nothing," Veronica said sharply. "I warn you I have a lot of questions. But I'll ask them when I feel sure I'll get some honest answers. In this last week, I've become very tired of lies." She drew the collar of her coat more closely around her neck, chose the flattest stone, and sat down.

Chris Holland watched her thoughtfully. This was not the time for light relief and pretty females. She was a complete nuisance on this hillside, but she knew it. He relaxed visibly. "Discreet," he admitted in frank surprise. She stared out at the dark fields falling away beneath them. He added, "You bite very nicely, too." She had to smile, then, and he could turn back to Partridge and Craig.

Partridge had been doing some very quick explaining: Elias had left Mykonos and circled widely over the hillside to join some of his men stationed along this bay, while Bannerman had been instructed to stay in Mykonos in charge of radio contacts. (Partridge did not specify, but Craig made his own guesses. There had to be direct links with the various groups on the hill as well as lines of communication with Athens, Smyrna, if not Paris.) But when it came to a report on the enemy operations, Partridge was more expansive. The *Stefanie,* lights out, had anchored briefly off a lonely stretch of shore farther north. She had unloaded two men and a large sack into a small boat, and then slipped out to sea under sail, lights beginning to show as land was left behind, a pretty picture of happy innocence. The small boat had brought its cargo safely into a cove where a man, a boy and a mule were waiting. "They have loaded the mule and left the cove. They're coming down that road," Partridge said, pointing toward the shoreline. "The boy and man are with the mule; the two men from the ship are following close behind. According to our reports, we'll sight them in ten minutes or so."

"There's the *Stefanie,*" Chris murmured, looking at the lights of a yacht some distance out at sea. "She has made a little detour, bless her sweet heart. I suppose she'll dock at Mykonos just as O'Malley is being brought to the house. Nice diversion." He noticed Craig's head turn at the mention of O'Malley. "That's why I'm here, if you wondered. O'Malley happens to be a special—friend of mine."

"I had been wondering," Craig admitted frankly. It had been easy to place the Greeks' interest in this operation, easy to understand the French participation. So O'Malley was a British agent, was he? "I've also been wondering why the hell you don't have that mule train intercepted right now. Unless, of course, you fellows like to do things the hard way."

"We would also like to catch the man behind it all," Partridge said dryly. "Before we make one move to find out what's in that sack, we had better be sure that we've picked up any of Insarov's men who may be stationed around this bay. Otherwise, there could be some warning signal, and Insarov would be gone. He's an expert in flight and concealment. He has had nineteen years of practice."

Craig looked down over the bleak flank of hillside, its shadows darkening as the clouds rolled in from the sea. "Who is picking up Insarov's men? The Greeks?" And one hell of a job that would be.

Partridge nodded, keeping his eyes on the road. He was no longer interested in the *Stefanie*. "They watched them take position an hour ago. It won't be too difficult."

"Not if Elias' men can move in as you did." Craig was still smarting from the way Partridge had pinned him down so easily. Dammit, he thought, I was supposed to know something about hand-to-hand combat at one time in my life.

"They're the experts," was all that Partridge said. "Chris, what about getting closer to the road?" He looked up at the sky. "Now's the time. In ten minutes, that cloud patch will have passed over."

"The nearer we get, the better I'll like it," Chris said grimly. Partridge moved quietly toward the man who was concentrating on the radio. There was a low mumble of voices—no doubt, thought Craig, the change in position was being given out, perhaps some new reports from Elias added to complete the picture—and then Partridge slid back to him.

"All set," Partridge said, trying to hide his growing excitement. "Elias is giving Insarov's men time to report that all is well as the mule enters the homestretch. Then he closes in. From their flank and rear. We intercept, down by that biggest group of rocks near the road. There's a mule path that branches up this hill from there, Elias tells me. That's the quickest way to the house. It's his bet that they'll take it. Ready?"

Chris nodded. He signed to the radioman to come along. "Always make sure of your communications," he told Craig. "Coming?" he added in his offhand way. "We could use you, if you felt like it."

That was obvious, thought Craig; there were a man and a boy with the mule, as well as the two men who had brought O'Malley ashore. He looked at Veronica.

She had read his thoughts. "I'm all right," she said miserably, and tried to smile. "I'd only get in the way down there." And it's no use trying to explain that I grew up fighting and wrestling with five brothers, she thought unhappily. "If I need you, I'll pretend I'm a dove." She smothered a small laugh.

"Come on," Partridge said to Craig, deciding for him. "She's well hidden here." The deep blue of her coat melted into the night. "Just stay exactly where you are," he told her.

"I won't even breathe," she assured him, and huddled still more against the rock.

"God in heaven!" Chris said softly, staring down at the white ribbon of road. Craig looked, too. The mule and a cluster of dark shadows had just appeared in view. They were still about two hundred yards away, he calculated, little black shapes slowly moving, steadily drawing nearer. Over the mule's back was a shapeless burden. It was one thing to talk of "cargo" and a sack being brought ashore; it was quite another to see it. Could O'Malley be alive? Craig looked at Chris, but the Englishman had already left, taking the most direct route to the road. Partridge had slipped away, too; so had the radio expert. Craig glanced around at Veronica.

She was watching the road. "What's the mule carrying?"

"A man."

She drew a sharp, quick breath. "Go! Please go," she told him. He moved off swiftly, making for the nearest stone wall, taking cover in every patch of available shadow. He is as good as they are at this, she thought with a touch of defensive pride; and they were very good indeed. She couldn't actually be sure that she was seeing them, now: movements here and there, yes; but what or who was moving, no. She thought she saw one black shadow reach the cluster of rocks by the road, and possibly a second. She stopped searching for them, and looked along the road, watching the mule and its sagging load.

I asked my first question, she thought, and perhaps I shan't need to ask any more. That answer was enough. She felt chilled to her spine, and it wasn't the night air that made her shudder.

Craig reached the boulders by the road. From above, they had looked fairly protective; down here, they seemed dangerously few, none higher than a man's shoulder. Still, this was the only real cover for a silent ambush. The drifting clouds had swept over and away, just as Partridge had predicted, and the moon was beginning to swim clear of their last seaweed-like strands. Soon, the road would be brightly lit until the next cluster of clouds came blowing across the land. But if the strengthening light made Craig uneasy, how much more would the men on the road feel exposed? They were about a hundred yards away from where Partridge and Chris waited beside him—the radioman had chosen a niche between two boulders, where he was already in contact with Elias and pleased with what he heard for his thin dark face split into a reassuring grin as Craig glanced at him curiously. And they were hurrying. Or trying to hurry. A mule took its own good time. Obviously, they were hoping to reach the path that Elias had mentioned before the moon was cleared of cloud and the road became too uncomfortable. It was possible, thought Craig, that their nerves were in a worse state than his.

How was Veronica? He looked over his shoulder, up toward where he had left her. He could see nothing except the deep band of heavy shadow under the long ledge of rock. He could stop worrying about her. It was the safest spot on all that bleak slope of hillside.

And where was Elias? Partridge had been talking in a whisper with the Greek at the radio. Now he edged back to Craig, noticed his eyes searching the hillside to the east of the road—to the west there was only a strip of land edging the restless sea—and nodded reassuringly. "They're out there," he whispered, just as Craig saw some shadows moving down the terraced fields from the north. "They've got their end well under control." He was silent for a long moment, perhaps thinking that his end had better be under control, too. One mistake, and the whole effort could be ruined. "The idea is this: as the mule reaches the boulders, Chris and I slip around them to get the two men at the rear. You step out in front of the mule and stop the other man. The Greek will deal with the boy. He says Americans are too trusting, that you might hesitate, think he is only a kid of sixteen, and then we'd be in trouble. That boy could make a quick run for it. Any warning at this stage could cripple the whole operation."

"I get it. No firing. How do I stop the man? Wave this around?" Craig drew the automatic from his pocket. It was a neat little weapon, more for close defense than any real attack. If his visit to Insarov had gone wrong, he could have found it very useful. Here, with open ground around and a chance to dodge and run, he doubted if any man was going to find it intimidating.

Partridge pulled a revolver and a silencer from a pocket, fitted them together, handed the complete weapon over, and took the automatic in exchange. "They'll be heavily armed. Our best plan is complete surprise. Don't let them have a chance to reach for a knife or a gun. All set? Remember—fast and silent, don't give him time to yell a warning. A shout could carry back to the headland." And there were two men near there, Craig remembered, guarding the approach to the house itself. Were they still searching for Veronica and him, or had they reported failure?

"All set," he told Partridge quietly, listening now to the plodding hoofs of the mule, the shuffle of quiet footsteps. Partridge and the grimly silent Chris moved past him, slowly, step by step around the boulders. Craig edged the other way, joining the Greek almost at the side of the road.

They crouched low, shoulders pressed against a curve of rock. Five seconds to wait, perhaps less . . . Craig counted them off. At two seconds to go, he heard the crack of a stick against the flank of the mule, saw its head jerking sharply, its pace quickened for an instant. Then it slowed back to its own rhythm, almost stopped. The boy was at its side, tightening a loosened rope around the shapeless sack. The man had his stick raised for another encouraging blow. Suddenly they stood still, looked back as they heard the sound of scuffling. The boy was reaching for his knife as Craig and the Greek moved in.

The man was quick, quicker than the boy. He whirled around on Craig, his stick aiming for the wrist that held the revolver, and then—as Craig side-stepped that blow—hit backhand at Craig's throat. Craig dodged, came in to strike down the stick with the butt of his revolver, struck again at the man's mouth opening in a shout. The man staggered, turned, tried to run. Craig struck for the third time, at the base of his neck. The man fell, lay motionless.

Partridge, a little out of breath, came to stand beside Craig, made a quick check. "Well," he said with cold satisfaction, "you didn't do him one bit of good, did you?" Then he went over to the mule, where Chris and the Greek were already starting to unknot the ropes.

Craig was still looking down at the man near his feet. I got mad, he thought, I got really mad there. He looked at the other two men and the boy, who were also stretched out on the road, and then at the obscene sack now being lowered gently from the mule's back. He took a deep breath. I guess we all did, he thought as he went over to help.

They carried the sack to the shelter of the boulders. In the moonlight, O'Malley's face looked like death itself.

"Alive?" Partridge asked.

Chris, listening for a heartbeat, didn't answer. Then he nodded. "Barely. Heavily drugged." He searched in one of his pockets, found small wire cutters, started snipping the cruel strands that bound O'Malley's wrists and ankles. He took off his jacket, covered O'Malley's thin shirt. "Where's Elias?" he asked irritably. "We'll need help."

"The vanguard's arriving," Partridge reassured him. Craig counted four men, then a fifth, coming down to the road. They were coming fast, caution discarded for the present in the mounting sense of triumph. But everyone seemed to know what to do. They worked quickly and silently. The unconscious men were dragged to the side of the road, their jackets and rough sweaters removed, their mouths gagged with tape, their hands and feet tied. Two of the Greeks were improvising a sling to carry O'Malley down to the beach. "A boat will pick him up there," Partridge told Craig. "Don't worry, we've got it all planned out. We hope. So far, it has worked." He pointed to the mule, then to the sack, now being partly filled with stones and spare clothing. "That's how we get close to Insarov."

"You are going to walk in?" The idea was so simple that it staggered Craig.

"Right into the dovecote. Four men, a mule, and a sack. That's how we get Insarov to open that big front door. Like to make one of the four? I'm serious. You know the way. You've seen the layout."

Craig glanced up the hill.

"She'll be all right," Partridge said, following his glance. "Elias is sending a couple of men to get her back into town. They'll soon be joining her. Sorry I can't spare any from here."

"Do they speak English?"

"That's the problem," Partridge admitted.

"Then I'll cut up the hill and tell her to expect friends. I'll join you on the mule path. Just point it out, will you?"

Partridge didn't look too pleased, but he pointed it out. "That's the one. And take care. We've a long way to go yet." He handed Craig a cap and a jacket. "You'll need these to make you look authentic."

The cap was too big, the jacket too small, but possibly that was very authentic. Craig stuck the revolver securely in his belt, and started looking for patches of shadow on the hillside again. Thank God, the clouds were thickening once more. Behind him, the constant surge of sea seemed louder, more insistent. The wind from the north had freshened. There was a salt smell to the air. He hoped that the boat picking up O'Malley would get him safe to harbor before any squall started. Poor bastard, Craig thought, he didn't even know he was with friends again.

Halfway up the hill, with only about fifty yards to go before he reached the rock strata where Veronica sheltered, he stopped in the shadow of a rough stone wall. And looked back. If he hadn't known about the activity and bustle down on the road behind those boulders, he would never have guessed just what was going on. He would have sensed something was happening, certainly. But what, exactly? It was difficult to judge. What had Veronica made of all this? She couldn't have had as clear a view as he had expected. He could imagine the questions piling up inside that beautifully shaped head with its smooth dark hair. Blue eyes and a perfect profile. Would he ever be given a chance to sit down opposite her at a harmless café table, and admire? Like a normal human being?

He had his breath back now after that wild crouching sprint up the hillside. He pulled himself up over the edge of the retaining wall, rolled over onto the next terraced field. He was thinking that some farmer was going to explode tomorrow when he saw his spring planting of barley. And at that moment, he heard a dove. It sounded again. It's one of them, he thought at first, flattening himself on the green shoots, motionless. Then he remembered. It's Veronica warning us. Veronica . . .

Veronica had been watching the road so intensely that she had not even noticed the man who had come over the hillside from the direction of the house. It was when he stopped abruptly, his feet scraping over a rough fragment of stone, that she knew he was there. And very near. She could hear his heavy breathing, as if he had been hurrying, before she caught sight of the crouching man. He was trying to find a place where he could see what was actually happening down on the road. He still wasn't sure. He half rose from his kneeling position, staring down at the boulders.

So he has just got here, she thought thankfully, once her first attack of fright and panic subsided; and there isn't so much to see down there at all, now. Five minutes earlier, and he would really have known what to worry about. He is so busy watching the road that he hasn't noticed John—I know it must be John who started up the hill toward me. But he will see him as soon as John leaves that wall. Oh stay there, stay there, forget about me, don't come! But he will come—oh, let me think, let me think. . . .

The stranger's breathing was normal now. He moved a step forward, and she could mark his profile quite clearly. He hadn't noticed her, possibly couldn't see her as long as she kept quite still within the rock's deep shadows. That was all she had to do. Keep still, stay safe. But solutions were never as simple as that. There was John, just about to come over that wall any time now. There were the men, three of them, following a loaded mule as it started forward. There were other figures, too, down there, melting away like silent ghosts. They had only been visible briefly, but that instant had been enough. She knew it, even before she glanced quickly back at the man.

He stood absolutely still, completely astonished, unbelieving, staring down at the road. Then he swung the strap of his radio free from his shoulder with savage haste, and, as he pulled out its aerial, stepped toward the shelter of the rock.

She came out of her feeling of helplessness. She called; called again.

John had heard her at least. She saw him drop to the ground as her hand searched for one of the heavier stones at her feet. She turned to face the man.

He couldn't see her clearly, even at this short distance. But he hadn't yet made his radio warning. "Boris?" he asked, took a step forward, then halted abruptly. His free hand reached into his jacket. Veronica rose and threw the stone.

It caught him sharply on his forehead, and he stumbled onto his knees, head sagging. His hand was still inside his jacket but the other arm had let the radio slip from its grasp. It lay beside him, its strap loose over his wrist. She reached for it, wrenched it free, hurled it aside. It didn't go far enough, not as far as she had hoped. "Oh!" she said in despair, and started toward it.

The man staggered erect, pulled his hand from his jacket and aimed. And in that split second between taking aim and pulling the trigger, a quick movement downhill caught his eye. He glanced instinctively to his left even as he fired. Veronica felt the breeze of the bullet kiss her cheek, heard the soft sigh of the revolver. She did not risk his aim being spoiled a second time, but dropped flat on her face. She heard another shot fired, again with that gentle sigh. This time it was the man who fell, and moaned quietly, and then lay still.

"Veronica!" It was John kneeling beside her, touching her gently, almost fearfully.

She tried to rise, to be practical, to be nonchalant, and only half succeeded. "He didn't have time to send out a warning." Her voice broke; she bit her lip.

"Veronica—"

"I'm all right. You spoiled his aim." She tried to laugh and failed in that, completely.

Craig lifted her and carried her out of the deep shadow to a softer patch of earth where he could see her more clearly. Again he knelt beside her. No, she hadn't been wounded. Bruised and shaken; but no bullet graze, no rock splinters. She was all right.

She lay back, looking at the sky. It had never looked so beautiful. I'm alive, she was thinking, I'm alive. . . . His arms went around her, drawing her up to him. She met his kiss with hers.

The ambush at the road had taken seven minutes by Partridge's watch. Seven minutes of delay; that was how Insarov would see it. He must have checked with each of his outposts as the mule had come on its hour-long journey, making sure of the time for each stage. And now there were seven minutes to be accounted for. "Keep your eyes open," Partridge told Chris Holland needlessly. "We may expect one of Insarov's men appearing on that hillside above us, just to make sure everything is all right."

Holland's high spirits had returned: his fears were over; O'Malley was alive and safe. "Ease up, old boy. All he will see is one mule, gaunt and revolting; three men prodding the poor beast along, giving a convincing imitation of real fishermen; and a very silent package being brought safely to the house. A little late, it's true, but you know what mules are. The worst part of this whole operation was getting that bloody animal to start up again. Thank God we had our Greek friend with us." He grinned widely. "A Greek-speaking mule. That's all I needed to send me to bed laughing."

"What did you expect it to speak?" Partridge was trying to take Holland's advice, but he was still on edge. Sure, everything was going well, but it was just at a time like this that something went wrong. It always did.

"You're a real worrier," Chris Holland told him cheerfully. "Craig knows how to handle himself. He will dodge any of Insarov's scouts and join us exactly where you told him to meet us. Where was it, anyway?"

"Before the path branches down to the main road again. I thought we'd better start up the trail to the house in full strength."

"Nice clusters of clouds." Chris looked approvingly at the veiled moon, and then at the rising terraces of bleak land, ridged with walls. "Sure we didn't land on the dark side of the moon?" But for all his light talk, he had his gun out first as the Greek spoke a low warning and nodded to the path just ahead of them.

"It's Craig," Partridge said with a surge of relief. Perhaps I do worry too much, he conceded to himself. Or perhaps when I've put in another ten years on operations like this one, I'll be as cool as Holland. Or perhaps I'll worry even more. Anyway, he thought, looking at Craig, so far so good. So far . . .

Craig had left the shelter of the low wall where he had been lying, and was taking his place in the procession. "Thought I had missed you. I had to wait until the two Greeks arrived."

"Didn't they arrive just when we got the mule going?" Partridge asked sharply. There had been movement up there by the rock strata. Too much damned movement, he had thought at the time.

"No. That was one of Insarov's men. He tried to send a message, but Veronica delayed him. And I got close enough to have a shot at him. Cancel that one."

"Pretty good shooting," Chris said.

"Not so good. I aimed for his knees and caught his chest." He paused. "He shot at Veronica."

"She's all right?" Partridge asked.

"Fine."

"But how did she delay—"

"Post-mortems later," Chris said, dropping his voice from its low tone into a whisper. "From now on, let our Greek friend do the talking." They had passed the small neck of headland and were almost back on the main road to Mykonos. In a few minutes they'd reach the sparse group of trees and the track that branched up to the house.

Partridge nodded, looked curiously at Craig, and wondered.

At the trees, the Greek urged the mule uphill with a couple of shoves and a flow of demotic oaths. Craig, the collar of his borrowed jacket turned up, the cap well down on his head, his face tilted as if he were watching the sack on the mule's back, must have passed unrecognized. He breathed more easily as he heard the cooing of a dove behind him, and then the answering call from the same old wall on the hillside. The rest of Elias' men, now surrounding the house, would find these two easy to pick up. The same thought must have struck the Greek, for he slowly nodded in solemn agreement as he made way for Craig to take the lead.

They came to the small clump of bushes where Veronica's case had been dropped, and then—as the mule decided to snatch a bite of spring leaves—were halted, milling around (the Greek cursing the mule's ancestry, blessing its lack of progeny, in a sibilant whisper), pulling and pushing and hauling.

Okay, okay, thought Partridge, anyone watching would think he now understood the delay of seven minutes.

Look out for that damned sack, thought Holland, and lunged at the rope as it began to slip.

That lousy mule, thought Craig, he'll nose right into Veronica's case and come up with it between those long yellow teeth.

The Greek's thoughts were totally unprintable even in the twentieth century. He vented them all in a kick where it would do the most good. The mule set off at a run uphill, one wisp of branch dangling from its mouth.

"Come on, Carmen," Craig said between his teeth as he caught up with it and grasped its rope halter. It quieted unexpectedly. The entry through the gate in the white wall was sedate, circumspect. Sweat could now break out on four brows.

Firmly, Craig turned the mule's head toward the path on his left. It was quite dark here, with bushes and shrubs growing wild. He didn't look toward the placid house, shuttered and quiet, not even when the front door swung open and a stream of light fell across the porch. A tempting target, he thought, but he did as he had been told and kept on going at the same steady pace toward the dovecote. The mule was amiable enough now, as it drew the dangling branch into its mouth inch by inch, chewing noisily. The Greek brushed lightly past him in the shadows, heading for the dovecote's door, a knife in his hand. Craig felt for his revolver. So did Partridge and Holland, close on his heels. The door of the dovecote was open. A small light burned inside.

The Greek stopped at the side of the door, motioned to the mule to hurry. Which it did not. He followed it into the stone-walled room. Someone spoke. The Greek replied. Then he must have struck, for something fell. The Greek was back at the door, beckoning them in.

"You know this character?" Partridge whispered.

Craig looked at the man on the floor beside a rough wooden table. He nodded. It was the man he had shouldered into the harbor. "One of the servants."

Holland had lifted the candle from the table and was also studying him, eyes narrowed, recalling a photograph in a secret file. Servant? Assistant chief of the secret police in Khrushchev's brutal cleanup of the Ukraine in 'forty-eight; promoted to full charge in the Hungarian investigations, possibly responsible for the betrayal and disappearance of General Maleter. The Hungarian Freedom Fighters would say a clean knifing had been too good for him. A nice little nest we've uncovered here, thought Holland, and exchanged glances with Partridge as he replaced the candle.

The Greek whispered a warning from the door. Partridge and Craig hauled the body to the side of the room, while Holland pulled the sack free from the mule's back and threw it on top of the dead man. That, he thought grim-faced, could have been O'Malley lying there.

Craig stood by one side of the mule, drawn against a wall, and kept his back turned to the doorway. Recognition was his chief danger, meanwhile. Partridge sat on the edge of the table, Chris stood in front of the sack; each had one hand nonchalantly on his hip, the other behind his back. The Greek loitered near the door, shoulders slumped, hands in the pockets of his ragged trousers.

Two men entered. Craig glanced briefly from under the peak of his cloth cap, saw one of the house guests and the other servant. Insarov was still taking his time, was he? Craig bent to rub the flank of the mule, and it kicked out gratefully.

The servant spoke sharply to him in a language he didn't understand. He nodded, keeping his head turned away, and tightened his hold on the mule. "Get it out of here!" the man repeated, now in German, then in French. He looked more closely at Craig, took a step forward. His back was turned to Partridge, giving a perfect target for the revolver butt that smashed down on his skull. Holland and the Greek moved simultaneously on the other man. The surprise was complete and effective. He went down like a wall of loose bricks.

"Never," said Chris Holland softly, as they used the ropes from the sack, along with belts and ties, to truss the two men as helpless as chickens for roasting, "did I think I'd bless that mule." He removed their weapons: an automatic and a revolver apiece, large caliber, fully loaded. Pessimists, he thought.

"We were obviously supposed to get it out of here," Partridge said, back to worrying. "But where?" We'll keep this element of surprise, he thought, if we don't step away from the pattern of their arrangements. "Did you notice any stable?"

Craig shook his head. "Let it chew its head off in the garden," he suggested, crossing quickly to the door as lookout. The Greek was more expert than he was at tying the unloosenable knot.

"And have Elias, when he arrives, think someone is waiting in ambush for him?" Partridge asked testily. No, it was too tricky having a mule blundering around the strange shapes and shadows of this garden. Dangerous, too, to keep it in here. It was restless, perhaps it had smelled the blood on the floor; if it started kicking, in one of its sudden frenzies, all hell would sound broken loose. It's always the way, he thought bitterly: at a time like this, we've got a mule on our hands.

Craig could see the upper side windows of the house, shuttered and dark. No gleam of light, either, from the direction of the porch. "They've closed the front door again," he reported. Dismay gave way to irritation, to real anxiety. It would have been better after all, he was thinking, if we had rushed the house when the door was first opened. A very solid door, he remembered; it would take a battering ram to force it open once it was locked and bolted.

"The problem is not insoluble," said the Greek quietly in excellent English and a highly educated voice. "We'll get the door open when we want it." He came over to stand beside Craig, smiled enigmatically, and looked not at the house but in the direction of the hillside to the north. He made a polite gesture for silence and settled to wait.

Wait for what? Craig wondered. He had his answer when a small blue flare, a safe distance away, shot up over the fields.

Partridge took a deep breath of relief: Elias was in position, Insarov's men had been neutralized, time to move in. At last, he thought, at last. . . . He beckoned to Chris, who had been spending those three last agonizing minutes in examining the contents of a large wooden box in the far corner of the dovecote.

Chris came forward, saying, "All their usual paraphernalia. Thorough questioners, those boys. They'd make the Inquisition look like a

Sunday-school picnic. Come on." He took Craig's arm and led him out onto the path. The Greek was ahead of them, dropping from his normal walk into a shambling slouch.

Craig looked around for Partridge.

"He's tying that damned mule to a tree," Chris whispered, and shook his head. Insarov would simply have put a silenced bullet into it.

The Greek was almost at the beginning of the path to the front door. He halted, drawing close to a tree, looking back. Chris halted, too, kept Craig with him. Partridge joined them, running silently. Partridge whispered to Craig, "You lead. Get us to the porch under the best cover you can. Okay?"

Craig nodded and started quickly up through the garden, desperately remembering the trees and clumps of bushes he had noted earlier tonight. The Greek was hurrying up the longer path to the house, quite openly, a messenger with urgent news.

Craig reached the side of the porch, hoisted himself over its wooden railing. Partridge and Holland followed silently. The Greek was almost at the steps. Someone had been watching the front path, for the door of the house opened. At the first gleam of light over the threshold, Partridge and Holland flattened themselves against the house wall. Craig was not quick enough. He stood motionless against one of the wooden uprights on the porch, and hoped its mass of encircling vine disguised his outline. He need not have worried. The Greek's wild string of sentences was holding all attention.

"What is he saying?" the woman's voice asked inside the hall.

The Greek came up the steps, speaking more slowly. "Dead," he kept repeating, "the man is dead." He gestured back in the direction of the dovecote.

"Dead?" a man's voice asked. The door opened more widely. He shouted back over his shoulder, "The American agent is dead!"

"Achtung—" That was Insarov's voice, clear, decisive, quick.

But the warning was too late. Partridge and the Greek lunged together, caught the man as he reached into his pocket, knocked him senseless. Holland had blocked the door, kept the woman from closing it. The front gate burst open; Elias and two men came running at full speed toward the house. The woman screamed. Holland and Partridge stepped into the hall.

As simple as that? thought Craig, and followed them. The woman had stopped screaming. She had backed away to the staircase but someone grasped her wrist and pulled her into the main room. Insarov was in there.

As simple as that, thought Craig. If he had had his way, he would have forced the house some fifteen minutes ago; and he would have failed. There would have been five men facing them, and no help from Elias possible. A little waiting was a necessary thing, it seemed. He glanced at his watch as he nodded to Elias. Fifteen minutes, all told, since they had first turned inside that front gate with a temperamental mule. Barely two hours since he had stood on this very spot and looked up that staircase, worrying about Veronica. The life and education of John Craig, he told himself wryly, and moved toward the room. At the door he hesitated, and let Elias join Partridge and Holland inside. He stood with some other men, a tight group of watchful faces, but made sure he could see Insarov. This was the moment he had promised himself: the dropping of the mask, the abandonment of that bland, benign look on the face of Heinrich Berg.

But the mask was still in place. If there had been alarm, or fear, it was under control. Berg—or Insarov—was standing at the fireplace, facing Partridge and Holland and Elias as the master of this house. Not even as he watched the handcuffs, which a Greek detective was clamping around the woman's wrists, did his expression change. Nor did Partridge's words make any impact as he pointed to the woman and said, "The French want her. Jeanne Saverne. Take her down to the house where they are holding Maritta Maas. Also the man at the front door. He is using a French passport."

"And I think," said Holland, watching the unemotional face staring so calmly at him, "you could put out the message to Athens for relay to Paris: Pear Tree is in full harvest. Then," he was smiling at the certain embarrassment on Partridge's face, but still watching Insarov, "Uncle Peter can be picked up."

"And we'll let Smyrna know," Partridge took over, watching Insarov, "that O'Malley is well, and in good hands. He is regaining consciousness in a nice soft bed. Also, we have caught Alex. His name is Robert Maybrick Bradley. We'll pass that news to Paris, too. Our agent there would be very interested in tracing his contacts at NATO."

"And I shall advise Athens," Elias said, joining in, watching Insarov, "to inform the Communist agent whom we arrested yesterday morning as he attempted to take a ship from the Piraeus that he might as well tell everything about the kidnapping and murder of Yves Duclos. Because the man responsible for Duclos' death has now been arrested." He nodded to one of his men. "Take him," he said, pointing to Insarov.

Insarov's cold glance lingered on them one by one: Elias, Holland, Partridge. I shall remember you, he seemed to be saying. He did not bother to glance at the four other men crowded near the door. They were the subordinates, only worth thinking about if he were to try to break out of this room. The time was not right for that. They were all too excited, too ready to fire their revolvers. It would be madness to reach for his. There was a suspicion of a smile on his lips, but the scarred eyebrow was markedly noticeable. "A mistake," he said ominously, watching Partridge. "Put away those silly pistols. What a ridiculous figure you cut!" Then he looked at Holland. "A man of your age, and of some experience no doubt, ought to know better than to come in here like an American gangster." And now it was Elias on whom the sharp blue eyes rested. "There will be repercussions. Very grave repercussions, indeed. You will be reduced to peddling fruit on the streets of Athens." He waved a hand, dismissing them all, and turned his back to look at the picture over the fireplace.

Elias said, "You are under arrest, Igor Insarov." He nodded to two of his men. "Search him."

Insarov tried to pull his arms away from their grip, then—as they swung him around to face Elias again—dropped all resistance. He even smiled. "Another mistake. Insarov left half an hour ago. You will find him on the *Stefanie,* now out at sea. If you can find the *Stefanie.*"

"Dear dear dear me," Holland murmured. "We did make a mistake. We forgot to tell him that the *Stefanie* and the cabin cruiser, and even that harmless sloop, were all boarded with little resistance, just ten minutes ago."

"Search him," repeated Elias.

"Take your hands off me! Diplomatic immunity!" Quickly, he repeated it in Greek.

The two detectives froze, looked at Elias.

Partridge shook his head. "Ah, that old story. Is it the best you can do, Insarov?"

"Search him," said Elias.

"My name is Pavel Ulinov, I am a citizen of the U.S.S.R. I am a special adviser to our Economic Trade Mission visiting Milan in connection with a projected contract for the sale of petroleum. I have the standing of assistant to the third secretary at our Embassy in Rome. I have full diplomatic immunity."

"He sounds almost convincing." Partridge was more interested in the revolver, the flat silver case with two bogus cork-tipped cigarettes inserted among the regular ones, the metal lighter, the heavy fountain pen, which were being taken from Insarov's well-cut blue blazer and crisply pressed gray trousers.

"He's a bloody arsenal," Holland was saying, examining the cyanide-gas pen very gingerly, and then the one-bullet lighter, and the poison cork-tips, before he laid them all out in a neat row on the card table. "I'd give this chap a body search. He's a really comic character. If he thought our pistols were stupid, God knows what he has taped under his armpit. You amuse me, Insarov."

There was the first sign of anger on Insarov's face. "My name is Pavel Ulinov. I have diplomatic immunity," he repeated, his voice harsh with controlled rage. "You will regret—"

"And now you are beginning to disappoint me," Partridge said. "You should know better than to try that gag on us. Diplomatic immunity does not extend to officials who operate outside the jurisdiction which grants that immunity. So cut out the double talk."

"I demand—"

"You demand nothing. Since when did the Soviet Union give diplomatic protection to a Nazi war criminal?"

There was complete silence.

"If you insist on claiming the protection of the Soviet Union," Partridge went on, "we shall give the full details of your Nazi career to the newspapers. In fact, there is a journalist on Mykonos, right now, who might think this was the biggest story of his career. Ed Wilshot."

"I believe you know his name at least," Holland said. His voice was becoming more and more gentle. He had been examining Insarov's revolver with respect. "Special job," he told Elias, "no expense spared." He laid it back in place on the card table to take the cuff links from one of Elias' men. "Really, my dear fellow, you fascinate me," he said to Insarov, as he found a hinge in one of the cuff links and sniffed at the powder inside. "You have a Borgia complex a mile wide."

"And once the Wilshot story was spread all over the front pages of the world," Partridge said with a grin, "what government, however much it has owed you, would even admit it knew you? No, you would be branded traitor at once, Insarov. Or should I say, Heinrich Berg?"

"I have never been a traitor. Heinrich Berg means nothing. To me, to anyone." The voice was tight, clipped; the words were spoken with dignity.

"Heinrich Berg is of no importance?" Holland asked too gently.

"None." The clever eyes were measuring the watching faces again, trying to gauge what they actually knew.

"Not even to the Israeli Vengeance Squad?" asked Holland, leaving the card table, sitting on the arm of a chair. "You know," he said almost conversationally to Partridge and Elias, "we might possibly make a telephone call right now to their man in Athens. That could be the quickest solution. It would spare the courts at Frankfurt a lot of trouble and expense."

The clever eyes flickered. The lips tightened. "I have been a trusted Communist agent for twenty-seven years. I saved many lives in the concentration camps—"

"Communists' lives. What about the others you sent to their deaths? Or don't they count?"

"There is no proof, no evidence, that such things happened. I did not look at a man's politics—"

"You didn't?" Partridge asked softly. "Professor Sussman thought otherwise. That was why you had him murdered, wasn't it?"

Berg looked at Partridge in bland astonishment. "Sussman? And who is he? I never knew anyone called Sussman. Your charges are a mockery, based on completely false assumptions. You have turned your opinions into facts. No court of law would listen to them, not even a Western court ready to believe any lies—"

Partridge signaled to Craig. "Would you step over here for a minute?" To the others beside Craig, he said, "Wait outside on the porch." Elias made certain of that by adding a quick phrase in Greek.

"Sure," said Craig, and left the doorway and came forward. "That's

Heinrich Berg. Sussman knew him. And he knew Sussman." He looked at Berg. "That is not an opinion," he told him. "That's solid fact."

Berg stared at Craig. The mask of confidence slipped. For at least ten seconds, he stared at Craig, desperately searching for an evasion, another plausible defense, a subterfuge. His lips tightened, his eyes narrowed, his voice rose. "And you are prepared to stand in court and swear to it? You are prepared to face the retribution of my comrades? You think I am the only one who pretended to serve the Nazis for the sake of a greater—" He had revealed too much. He caught his breath, forced back his anger. His voice almost returned to normal. "I say Sussman was lying. You say he is dead. I know nothing of that, either." His eyes looked vaguely around the room, noticed that the hall had indeed been cleared. The policemen beside him, now that they had searched him, were no longer holding him by force. They were waiting for further instructions, trying not to look baffled—as they must be—by the flood of foreign words they didn't understand. The older American was consulting quietly with the Greek; the Englishman was studying the ceiling with folded arms and bored insolence. Berg looked at Craig, the one man who was still watching him intently, and measured the distance to the card table as he pulled down the disarranged sleeve of his jacket. "My one mistake," he said, half to himself. The mask was back in place. "Is that how you like to imagine yourself?" He smiled tolerantly. Craig was empty-handed, his revolver stuck back in his belt.

"You made several," Craig said, trying to control his temper.

"Indeed? Name them." Berg took a few nonchalant steps away from the fireplace, clearing his path to the card table, and halted to face his accuser. The policemen had followed, but his arms were still free. "Name them," he repeated, almost conversationally, and could feel the policemen's suspicion subsiding at his quiet voice.

"Duclos."

"Duclos? And who was he?"

A man to whom I owe my life, thought Craig. He said nothing.

"Do go on, Mr. Craig. You interest me." The voice was friendly, the eyes aloof. He was thinking in quick complete jumps: the revolver, first—it's at the edge of the table; then Craig as a shield; then out of this room, into the hall; a farewell bullet for my one mistake; the door under the staircase—they haven't found it, there has been no alarm, Jeanne did not have time to use it—yes, surprise is the most powerful weapon of all. He glanced again at the Englishman's folded arms. Too casual . . . So not that way, Insarov told himself, and checked his move to the card table.

"Disappointing?" he asked the Englishman, and turned his back on the table. "You can remove that tempting revolver. I am not one of your wild Americans who shoots his way free. Why should I? I am innocent of all your charges." He addressed himself to Elias. "If you persist in this folly of having me arrested, I demand you take me at once to Athens where I can meet representatives of my government and prove my innocence. I am not, I repeat I am *not* Insarov. I am only here in this house as a guest. My real mistake, Mr. Craig—" he studied the younger American with cold eyes—"was to trust Insarov when I accepted his invitation to dinner and a game of cards. And—" he turned on Partridge now—"if I lied to protect my host—a foolish story about his escape on the *Stefanie,* I admit—it was only because he went to the dovecote and I thought I could give him a chance to escape. Or did you kill him? No doubt. Washington won't care for that, will they? They have this strange idea that a captured man will talk, give them information in exchange for a cigarette and a few kind words. I do know one thing about Insarov. He would not have been what you call a—a singing canary."

"So Insarov is dead, is he?" Holland asked softly. "And you only carry that little arsenal around with you for fun?"

"My life has been threatened twice in the last ten days. I am only protecting myself."

"Of course."

"Judging from your performance tonight, my precautions were thoroughly justified," Insarov flashed back. There, he thought, I've silenced the Englishman's sneering laugh. In better humor, he added calmly, "I know nothing of Sussman or Duclos. The men you have already arrested for their murders will not involve me in any confession you force out of them. You have no evidence against me at all."

"I have a list," Partridge said very quietly, "of three hundred and four men condemned to torture and death in a Nazi extermination camp. They were selected by Heinrich Berg."

"Fascists. Who weeps for them?"

"Fascists?" Partridge's anger came to the surface. "They never were fascists. Never! They were future leaders of a democratic Europe, men who'd oppose any totalitarian—"

"Berg was acting under orders, risking his life to defeat the Nazis. He will take his chances in a fair trial. World opinion will not judge him as you have done."

"World opinion? Or do you mean arranged demonstrations, carefully rigged picketing?"

Holland said, "I can see the placards right now. SAVE HEINRICH BERG! BERG WAS OUR ALLY, HAVE WE FORGOTTEN? BERG, SI; YANKEE, NO." He paused, added, "You know, Insarov, you have almost talked me into a telephone call to my Israeli friends."

"And tell them—if they abduct or kill me—they will lose *three* of their leaders! Two can play at their game!"

"Get him out of here," Partridge said tensely.

Insarov started walking slowly to the door of his own accord. "I know," he sympathized, "you must feel completely frustrated. Such a brilliant operation to end with the capture of the wrong man. What *will* Washington say?" He turned to the two Greeks, who were taking their place on either side of him. "Coming?" he asked genially. He was passing Craig now, ignoring him completely. "Are these really necessary?" he was saying to one of the Greeks, who had produced handcuffs. "I assure you I am more eager to get safely to Athens than even you are." He halted as if to let the handcuffs be snapped over his freely extended wrists. He brought his hands up in a violent blow against one Greek's throat and the other's jaw, lunged for Craig, caught him from behind with a tightly hooked left arm, reached with his right hand to pull Craig's revolver free from his belt, jabbed it against Craig's spine. "Don't shoot!" he warned. "Or Mr. Craig will regret it." He moved the revolver to the nape of Craig's neck. He felt Craig's resistance ebb. "That's wise. Now we back out. Into the hall. Steady pace." He unlocked his arm, gripped Craig's left shoulder, began his retreat to the door with Craig shielding him perfectly.

Craig took the first few steps backward, forced his body to relax. Desperately, he looked at Holland's watching eyes. One more step . . . He swung fast to the left, pivoting on the ball of his foot, dropping his weight to the floor. Christopher Holland fired from under the cover of his folded arm.

"My one worry was that I'd get you, too," Holland said to Craig as he walked over to look down at Heinrich Berg. He helped Craig to his feet. He waved aside Craig's word of thanks. "Just concentrate on getting your breath back again."

Craig looked down, too, and regretted the movement. He must have jerked his neck when he had made that quick lunge away from Berg. Partridge was saying nothing as he joined them.

Craig rubbed the nape of his neck, had three questions at least on the tip of his tongue, decided this wasn't the time. Then Elias asked one of them. "But *where* was he going?" He crossed quickly to the door, staring into the hall as if he could find his answer there. He waved impatiently to the two other Greeks to follow—one was still nursing his jaw as they clattered after him to the rear of the house.

Partridge came out of his thoughts, glanced quickly at the door. Bill and two of his friends had run in from the garden and were standing there, revolvers ready. "All over," he told them. "Bill, give Bannerman the signal to start sending. He knows what. And you can add the news: the big boy is dead. Details will follow." Once Bill and the Greeks had left, he added quietly, "I suggest that we keep Craig's name out of our reports about tonight. Much safer for him. No one heard him identify Berg, except us and the two detectives. Elias assures me they don't understand English."

"Much safer," Holland agreed.

Craig looked at them both. That answered another of his questions. "He actually has friends who'd—"

"You heard him, John," Partridge said. "That threat against you wasn't part of his bluster."

"Ex-Nazis who are Communis—" Craig began.

"Take our word for it," Holland said grimly. "They exist." He glanced at Partridge, lightened his voice. "Stop worrying about Washington. Tell them that if a dead man gives no information, he also commits no more murders. Frankly, I wouldn't have laid one shilling on his staying in jail. He would have weaseled his way out, or his friends would have pried him loose—probably just as well he forced the solution. He was a—"

Elias entered alone. "Yes, he could have managed it! He could have escaped." His face was tight with anger. "There was a door under the staircase; it has been blocked for four years, but no longer. It was made ready for use."

"Leading where?" Partridge asked sharply.

"Into a clump of bushes, planted there when the door was sealed up. The garden wall is only a few yards away at that point."

"It's still a ten-foot wall." Surely any ladder must have been discovered when the grounds were searched just after entry; not every man had crowded into the hall.

"There was a gardener's barrow filled with hard-packed earth against the wall."

"That would give him one step. He'd need at least two others."

"He had them. There were two wooden pegs, painted white, driven into the wall, one above the other. All he had to do was reach the top, roll over, drop down onto the hillside." Elias looked bitterly down at the body of Berg-Insarov. "This was the only solution, my friends." He glanced up at Craig, added somberly, "You were almost a dead man."

Which answers my third question, Craig thought.

Partridge rested his hand on Craig's shoulder. "The Greeks always have a phrase ready. All I do is tell you to get back to your hotel. There's no need for you to hang around here." He grinned and added, "Look out for the traffic, will you?"

"I'll do that." Craig glanced at Berg for the last time and left.

He came slowly out onto the porch. There were several men there, two of them bandaged, talking quietly, keeping guard over three firmly tied prisoners and a body in a sack. The woman called Saverne had already been taken away. The moon was high now, and in the cool night air there was the faint fragrance of a flowering vine. Craig took off his cap and tossed it away. There was a sympathetic laugh from the men around him; they were tired, they were hungry, they were filthy, but soon they, too, would be throwing off their rough clothes. He dropped his borrowed jacket over the mule's back, down by the gate. Someone had set it free, shooed it home, but it had just remained standing there, dozing in the moonlight.

That was the last picture he had of the house on the hill; a mule nosing in to a white wall, a torn gray jacket warming its sprung back, its ears twitching spasmodically as it dreamed of a life where there were bushes in abundance and no more burdens to be carried. Which reminded him. He stopped at the bushes and found Veronica's case.

The doves had been silenced, he noted grimly as he rounded the corner with its sparse trees and took the main road for Mykonos. The little bay seemed placid, sheltered from the rough sea by the long breakwater. The lights around the harbor were bright and welcoming. It was twenty-five minutes to twelve. In the big hotel, people had just finished dinner.

24

Craig was exhausted, but he never walked a quicker mile than the one that brought him around the bay into town. He came down the narrow ill-lit lane almost at a run, into the wide empty square with its Heroine of the Turkish Repulsion gazing out to sea from her central pedestal. Tony was lounging against her, hands in pockets, still dressed for the aborted picnic on Delos.

"Welcome back," he said, drifting over the square to join Craig. "Did you have enough exercise for one night?"

"Just about."

"We've heard the news. Don't rupture yourself trying to tell me all about it." He grinned widely. "If I sound slightly miffed, I am. And Tim Bannerman, in his own phrase, is fit to be tied. We missed out on this show completely."

"You had your share," Craig said. "You were promoted, I guess."

"Kicked upstairs to communications. I did get a little breath of salt air for a while—brought O'Malley back in a howling squall, and frankly, I was sicker than he was."

"Where is Bannerman now?"

"Still talking with Paris and points west. He's on the upper floor of that windmill just above the breakwater with a couple of other hard-working types. Don't tell him I know." He stopped, listening, his head cocked to one side. From a café along the water front came the music of a mandolin, a guitar and a zither. They were playing, in the strange half-tone scale of Greek folk songs, a brave attempt at "The Twelve Days of Christmas."

Craig halted, making sure; and mustered a smile.

"Much too good a tune to let die away unsung." Tony addressed the distant café impatiently in his low voice, "Come on, boys, come on. You finished the introduction six bars ago. Must do better than that for the party tomorrow night. That's the way!" Men's voices had begun to sing. In Greek. "I've only had time to get them as far as the sixth night," Tony said, "but we'll manage the rest tomorrow. Catchy little thing, isn't it?" He smiled delightedly as Craig began to laugh.

"Old Partridge is going to be fit to be tied, too," Craig predicted, recovering himself. But he felt better, much better, for that fit of laughter.

"See you tomorrow," Tony said vaguely, leaving Craig to cut up the little streets toward the Triton. He wandered down the front street toward the music, joining with the hoarse Greek voices in his flat tenor.

"The sixth day of Christmas
My true love sent to me
Six geese a-laying,
Five gold rings,
Four colly birds,
Three French hens,
Two turtledoves, and
A partridge in a pear tree."

Craig's pace quickened. He was still relaxed, still humming in rhythm to the flowing, ebbing tune drifting over the town from the water front. Tomorrow everyone would be singing it; by next week everyone would be dancing to it. Old Rosie, back in Paris, would never guess the influence of his brain child on the cultural patterns of an Aegean island. Craig began to laugh again, and then sobered up. He had come into the little square with its church and ghostlike houses. Other ghosts were wandering around there, too. He could see Berg stopping beside the church, looking at its small belfry; suddenly swinging around to look up at the hotel's high entrance under the heavy vine. Even now, thought Craig, I can feel the chill in my blood as I drew back, stood motionless, against that wall. The man is dead, lying in a room of rose-patterned chintz and pink lamp shades. If he were alive? I wouldn't climb these steps so confidently.

He reached the entrance under the vine. Madame Iphigenia, a

shawl around her shoulders, was there to greet him. "She is well," she whispered. "She would not eat until you came. I have kept food in the kitchen for you both. Hot food. You wash and change. In your old room. They entered. They searched. What a mess! We have cleaned it all. It is comfortable again." She fell silent, looking at him, taking the small suitcase from his hand, shook her head. "But it is good, now?"

"Very good." Then he smiled, and said, "Madame Iphigenia, I admire you very much."

He ducked under the low lintel of the door and entered the small lobby. One light burned there, casting a soft shadow. Veronica was sitting in a high-backed armchair. She had bathed, and washed her hair—it fell loose and clean over her face. She was asleep, huddled into a thick dressing gown that was twice her size.

He put his hands on the arms of the chair, bent down, kissed her gently.

She was awake at once, looking up at him with those wonderful eyes.

"I didn't mean to do that," he said softly. He kissed her gently again.

"All right?" she asked, still anxious. "Everything is—"

"All right," he told her quietly.

She looked at him. She smiled. "That will be my only question," she promised him.

"We'll have plenty of other things to talk about." He kissed her once more. "Plenty."